PRAISE FOR THE INSPECTOR DAVID GRAHAM MYSTERY SERIES

"The characters feel like old friends."
"Phenomenal!"
"Alison Golden has done it again."
"Powerful stuff!"
"Inspector Graham is my favorite."
"I'm in love with him and his colleagues."
"A terrific mystery."
"This newest is like seeing old friends again and catching up on the latest news."
"These books certainly have the potential to become a PBS series with the likeable character of Inspector Graham and his fellow officers."
"Delightful writing that keeps moving, never a dull moment."
"I know I have a winner of a book when I toss and turn at night worrying about how the characters are doing."
"Love it and love the author."
"Refreshingly unique and so well written."
"Solid proof that a book can rely on good storytelling and good writing without needing blood or sex."

"This series just gets better and better."
"DI Graham is wonderful and his old school way of doing things, charming."
"Great character development."
"Kept me entertained all day."
"I didn't want the story to end."
"Please write more!"

THE INSPECTOR GRAHAM MYSTERIES

ALSO BY ALISON GOLDEN

THE INSPECTOR GRAHAM MYSTERIES

BOOKS 5-7

ALISON GOLDEN

GRACE DAGNALL

Cover Illustration: Richard Eijkenbroek

Published by Mesa Verde Publishing
P.O. Box 1002
San Carlos, CA 94070

ISBN-13: 978-0-9887955-9-4

Edited by
Marjorie Kramer

No entertainment is so cheap as reading, nor any pleasure so lasting.
~Lady Mary Wortley Montagu

To get free books, updates about new releases, promotions, and other Insider exclusives, please sign up for Alison's mailing list at:

https://www.alisongolden.com/graham

THE CASE OF THE
MISSING
LETTER

ALISON GOLDEN   Grace Dagnall

THE CASE OF THE MISSING LETTER

BOOK FIVE

Published by Mesa Verde Publishing
P.O. Box 1002
San Carlos, CA 94070

Edited by
Marjorie Kramer

MAP OF GOREY LIBRARY

To see a larger version of this map, go to
https://www.alisongolden.com/missing-letter-map

CHAPTER ONE

D AVID GRAHAM TROTTED downstairs. The dining room was becoming busier by the week, but at least his favorite table by the window was still available on this bright Saturday morning. The White House Inn staff were busier than they had been since Christmas, welcoming and looking after new arrivals who had chosen to exchange the snow of Scotland or the dreary rain of Manchester for a few sunny days in Jersey. He took his seat and opened the morning paper, part of a reassuring and established routine he had enjoyably been following for the last six months.

As he settled into life on Jersey, Graham had followed the changing of the seasons as the island's surprisingly mild winter gave way to an even warmer and quite invigorating early spring. By mid-March, the island was once again beginning to look its splendid and colorful best. The spring blooms were out. Swathes of bright yellow daffodils and the unmistakable, bell-shaped blue hyacinth dotted the island. Economically, Jersey had also started to blossom. Most of Gorey's small fishing fleet had completed a month of refit and repair. Shortly, they would be heading out among the Channel Islands to catch lobster and oysters, or further into the Atlantic for cod.

"Good morning, Detective Inspector," Polly offered carefully. Before his first cup of tea, Graham could be sleepy and even uncharacteristically sour. Guesthouse owner, the redoubtable Mrs. Taylor, occasionally reminded staff not to engage him in anything beyond perfunctory morning pleasantries before he was at least partially caffeinated. "What will it be today? Or are you going to make me guess again?"

Graham peered over his newspaper at the freckled twenty-something redhead who had become perhaps his favorite of the staff. "I have to say, Polly," Graham told her, folding the paper and setting it on the table, "that you're becoming something of a psychic. What is it now, four correct guesses in a row?"

"Five," Polly said proudly. "But on three of those days, it was that new Assam you were so excited about."

"True, true," Graham noted. "And I hope you'll agree it was worth getting excited over."

Polly shrugged. "I'm not really a tea drinker," she confessed. "But today I'm going to guess you're in... what do you call it some-times... a 'traditional mood'?"

"I might be," Graham grinned. "Or I might be feeling spon-taneous."

"Lady Grey," Polly guessed. "Large pot, two bags, sugar to be decided on a cup-by-cup basis."

Impressed, Graham raised his eyebrows and gave her a warm smile. "Precisely. I don't know how you do it."

Polly tapped her forehead cryptically and sashayed off to the kitchen to place Graham's order. Since arriving at the White House Inn, and with the enthusiastic support of the staff and Mrs. Taylor, Graham had taken sole "curatorial control" over the dining room's tea selection. He took this role exceptionally seriously. The kitchen's shelves were now stocked with an impressive array of Asian teas, from the sweet and fruity to the fragranced and flowery, with much else in between.

Lady Grey, though, was becoming Graham's favorite "first pot." It was often given the responsibility of awakening the Detective Inspector's mental faculties first thing in the morning. It was in the moments after the first life-giving infusion of caffeine, antioxidants, and other herbal empowerments that Graham's mind came alive.

One useful byproduct of his daily tea ritual was the ability to memorize almost everything he read. His knowledge of local events was becoming peerless. With the aid of the local newspaper, Graham stored away the information that Easter was two weekends away, and the town's churches were inviting volunteers to bake, sing, decorate the church, and organize the Easter egg hunts.

Also stashed away for future retrieval was the nugget that Gorey Castle's much anticipated "Treason and Torture" exhibit was about to open. The gruesome displays were only part of the attraction, however. Two recently opened chambers had, until their inadvertent discovery a few months earlier, contained an unlikely and entirely unsuspected trove of artistic treasures. The discovered paintings had mostly been returned to their owners or loaned to museums that were better equipped to display pieces of such importance. But, interest in the find was still high, and ticket sales had been, to quote the Castle's events director, the ever-upbeat Stephen Jeffries, "brisk beyond belief."

"Lady Grey," Polly announced, delivering the tray with Graham's customary digital timer which was just passing the three-minute mark.

"First class, Polly. And it'll be bacon, two eggs, and toast today, please."

"Right, you are," she nodded.

Graham put the paper aside and focused on this most pleasing of ceremonies. First came the tea, promisingly dark and full-bodied, tumbling into the china cup. Then came the enchanting aroma, an endless complexity from such a surprisingly simple source. Next would come the careful decision-making process regarding the addition of milk; too much would bring down the temperature, and as Graham liked to think of it, risked muddling what the tea was attempting to express.

Finally, he would add just the right amount of sugar. Graham had taken pains to instruct the wait staff to ensure that it was available in loose, as well as cubed form, so that he might more carefully adjudicate its addition. He tipped an eighth of a teaspoonful into the cup and stirred nine times, counter-clockwise. Some things, as he was so fond of reminding his fellow police officers, are worth doing well. He chose to ignore their barely suppressed eye-rolls.

He took a sip and savored the fragrance of the black tea blend mixed with orange and lemon peel and enhanced with bergamot oil. But then, contrary to his usual practice, Graham set down the cup. An article on page six of the newspaper was demanding his attention. The headline was *Our Cops are Tops*, and he read on with a quiet flush of pride.

After their successes in recent months, it goes without saying that Gorey has the most capable police officers on the island. Led by the indefatigable Detective Inspector Graham, the Gorey Constabulary has successfully raised the rate at which it solves reported crimes from twenty-six percent, one year ago, to forty-nine percent, today.

"For once," Graham muttered contentedly into his paper, "the media have got their numbers spot-on." It meant, he had observed proudly to his team the previous day, that anyone planning a crime in their small field of jurisdiction would know that they had a one in two chance of getting caught. "Splendid."

Moreover, the actual crime rate has dropped by sixteen percent in the last twelve months. This is surely cause to congratulate DI Graham and his team, but Sergeant Janice Harding was modest when asked for a comment. "The Gorey public have been enormously supportive," she pointed out. "We rely on their vigilance and common sense, and they've stood by us through some complex and challenging cases." The popular sergeant, who has lived on Jersey for nearly seven years, was referring to the conviction of former teacher Andrew Lyon, who began a seven-year sentence at Wormwood Scrubs in January. Gorey Constabulary also met with success after murder investigations at the Castle and the White House Inn. It seems our "top cops" are equal to any challenge. Gorey is fortunate to have such a dedicated and dependable crime-fighting team.

"'Top cops.' Sounds like one of those ghastly TV reality shows," Graham grumbled. "But I'll take it."

CHAPTER TWO

MRS. TAYLOR WAS striding through the dining room in her trademark flowery blouse when she spotted Graham looking just a little smug. "Someone's been reading about himself in the paper, I see," she concluded with a smile.

"The whole team was mentioned, I was glad to see," Graham said. His pride was hard to miss.

"Enjoy your moment in the sun," Mrs. Taylor said warmly. "You deserve it." She patted Graham on the shoulder and continued toward the check-in desk where a tall, blond woman was quietly waiting, a single slender suitcase by her side.

Graham returned to the article. His two constables, Roach and Barnwell, were mentioned by name, including a brief recounting of Barnwell's heroics in the Channel some four months before and his subsequent trip to Buckingham Palace to receive the Queen's Gallantry Medal. The article even contained the customary photograph of Barnwell showing off his award in the palace courtyard. He was accompanied by his mother who shared a remarkable resemblance with her son, but who looked like she couldn't quite believe where she was, who she was with, or why she was there. For his part, Graham couldn't have been more proud of his small team, who were admittedly proving very effective after a somewhat shaky start.

He quickly took another sip of tea before it got cooler than he liked. It was just occurring to him that Polly was a few minutes later than usual with his breakfast when Mrs. Taylor returned. This time she was not alone.

"Detective Inspector Graham, I thought you might like to meet our newest resident, Miss Laura Beecham." Graham stood automatically, setting down his teacup once more. He found himself being introduced to the woman who had been standing at the reception desk earlier. She had the bluest possible eyes and was even taller up close, within an inch of Graham himself. "Just arrived from... Where was it you said, Miss Beecham?" Mrs. Taylor asked.

"Down from London," Laura said, extending a hand. She had a city dweller's pale complexion, but her direct gaze, wide cheekbones, and petite upturned nose gave her an honest, girlish look. "Just fancied a change of scenery. Nice to meet you." She wore a small fish pendant on a simple gold chain and was dressed for travel in a comfortable maroon t-shirt and black stretch pants.

"Welcome," Graham said, a little surprised by his own shyness. It was some time since he had met anyone quite so striking or indeed, his own age. "You'll be staying here at the Inn?" he asked.

Laura nodded. "At least for a while. I haven't really decided yet. I'm fresh off the boat, quite literally," she smiled.

"Our beloved Detective Inspector Graham runs the local police station," Mrs. Taylor said, as though boasting of her son's recent acceptance into medical school. "You simply *must* read the article about our local boys in blue." She caught Graham's eye, "Oh, and girl, of course." She tapped the morning paper that lay next to Graham's cup and saucer.

"*Sergeant* Janice Harding is one of our most highly respected officers," Graham told Laura. He stood up a little straighter, "The article was very flattering, but we were just doing our jobs."

"I'm told Gorey is a very safe place," Laura commented. "Quiet."

Mrs. Taylor opened her mouth but closed it again. Although Laura was technically correct, and Gorey boasted an enviable safety record, one of the very few recent murders in the town had befallen a White House Inn *resident*. Mrs. Taylor had been about to mention it until she remembered it wasn't something she should draw attention to.

"I'm sure you'll be very happy here," DI Graham said.

"Are you looking for work?" Mrs. Taylor interjected, "or will you be relaxing during your stay, Miss Beecham?"

"Actually, I was lucky enough to find a job at the library," Laura said, still clearly surprised at her own good fortune. "I start there tomorrow. Can't wait," she added brightly.

"Splendid," Graham said. "It's a small place, but very popular. Their local history section is especially strong," he added. "I'll say hello if I see you there."

Mrs. Taylor had taken a step back to observe the effect of her well-intentioned intervention in DI Graham's social life. Her soft spot for the Detective Inspector was well known. As a professional, he was enormously respected, but Mrs. Taylor just plain liked him too. She found him wonderfully thoughtful and courteous in an endearingly old-fashioned way that reminded her, more often than anyone else, of her late husband. It troubled her that such a fine man, still in his thirties and with no wedding ring to deter would-be admirers, was still living the bachelor life. She liked having him around, but she had been keeping an eye out for ladies who seemed to fit the bill: youthful, intelligent, well-read. And, of course, single.

Stepping forward again, she said to Laura, "Will you be with us long?"

"Just as long as it takes me to find somewhere more permanent, Mrs. Taylor," she replied.

"Ah, well now, I hear rumors that DI Graham is looking for an apartment in Gorey. Perhaps the two of you could share the flat-hunting burden?"

Graham turned toward Laura and confided, "Mrs. Taylor is only moonlighting as a hotelier. She's actually a top-notch government spy."

His little quip achieved the desired effect, and Graham's suspicion that Laura had a beautiful smile was entirely borne out. "I'll remember to sweep for bugs when I get to my room," she whispered back.

"Now, there's no need to poke fun," Mrs. Taylor chided gently. "I'm sure everyone here would understand if you left us, Detective Inspector, but I hope you know that we'd miss you terribly."

Mrs. Taylor deserved plaudits for her persistence, Graham thought. "I'll be curating your tea selection for a few months yet, Mrs. Taylor. Still looking for just the right place." He turned to Laura. "Have you any idea what you're looking for?"

"Oh, no," Laura explained. "That's way down my list of things to do. Besides, I haven't even properly checked in yet." Graham saw that Laura's suitcase remained with Otto at the reception desk. It seemed that Mrs. Taylor, never one to miss an opportunity, had prioritized matchmaking over showing the new guest to her room.

"Well, it's been nice to meet you, Detective Inspector. I'm sure we'll meet again." Laura turned to Mrs. Taylor and an almost imperceptible flash of her eyes told the guesthouse proprietor that she'd been rumbled. This impromptu speed-dating interview was over.

Mrs. Taylor shepherded Laura back to reception and then

upstairs, but not before throwing a self-satisfied smile over her shoulder at Graham.

"For crying out loud," he muttered as he sat once more and refreshed his tea cup. But he found himself smiling, and not purely, if he were honest, because of the glowing newspaper article.

CHAPTER THREE

DON ENGLISH WOKE to the sound of his mother softly singing along with the radio. The room's blinds were open, and bright afternoon sunshine gave a warm luster to the yellow tulips by Susannah's bed. Don shifted in the armchair and rubbed his eyes. He watched for a moment as his mother sang quietly, mumbling most of the words, her eyes closed, and a happy little smile on her face. It was something by the Beatles, but he didn't know the name.

"How are you feeling, Mum?" he asked. He pushed his heavy, soft bulk out of the chair with a groan and stood by her bed, flexing his left foot that had gone to sleep during his half-hour nap. "You've always liked this song, haven't you?"

Susannah was smiling contentedly to herself. Her eyes opened. She seemed not to take in her surroundings for a long moment, and when she finally turned to Don, there was a visible struggle in her eyes. Finally, she asked, "Play it again?"

Don sat on the bed and took her hand in his. He was finding it remarkably slight and cool these days, her skin mottled with age and soft like an old parchment. "It's on the radio, Mum," he reminded her. "What's the name of the song?" he prompted hoping to focus her thought.

But it was too late, Susannah was focused on the tulips. "Who brought those?" she asked, gazing at them. "They're lovely."

"I did, Mum," Don replied. It could not have been anyone else.

"Oh, thank you, sweetheart," she said, just as she had an hour ago and twice yesterday. "You're always so good to me." Another song came on, something from the sixties that Susannah recognized, and she had her eyes closed again, humming to the chorus.

Don held her hand, feeling the tiny tapping of her fingers on his palm as she followed the beat. As the song ended, Susannah's eyes stayed closed, and her hand was still once more. He listened closely and found that her breathing was regular and slow. "You have another little nap, Mum," he said, kissing her forehead. "Going to find some coffee. I'll be right back."

St. Cuthbert's was a bright, airy place with the most thoughtful and attentive staff anyone could hope for, and certainly a huge improvement upon his mother's dreary existence at Kerry Hill. He had come to know two or three of the nurses who were competent and kind. The most senior of them, Nurse Watkins, was responsible for implementing day-to-day medical decisions regarding his mother's "palliative care." After three weeks here, Susannah Hughes-English was reaching the end. Don caught the nurse as she left the reception area.

"Oh, hello Don, m'love. How's your mother today?"

"Comfortable," Don replied. "She's been singing along with songs from the sixties again."

"That's nice," she said. "Does she need anything?" Her caring blue eyes and that wonderfully lilting Welsh accent always made Don feel better about this whole sad ordeal.

"I don't think so, but thanks. I'm just going to get some coffee, and I'll stay until eight."

"Right you are, m'love," the veteran nurse said, and gave Don's burly forearm a comforting squeeze before setting off on her rounds.

The atmosphere at St. Cuthbert's was pleasant and carefully maintained. Most of the conversations were hushed and private. Doors were closed quietly, and sometimes it felt as much like a small town public library as a hospice. Don reminded himself that this was not the emergency room or even a conventional hospital. No one would be rushed in for treatment and few resuscitation attempts would ever be made. This place, he knew full well, would be the final stop on his mother's long journey.

He took a sip from his cup. The machine in reception produced a highly caffeinated, dark-brown liquid that brazenly masqueraded as coffee. It would keep him awake, at least. Don sat in the reception area for a few minutes. A woman about his own age sat opposite him, her fingers quietly drumming on the leather handbag in her lap. She wore sunglasses and was dressed expensively enough to stand out.

"Waiting for someone?" Don asked, pleasantly. "A ride?"

She nodded. "My husband. We've been here all day." It had not, quite clearly, been an easy one.

"You'll be ready to get home, I imagine," he said.

"As soon as he's finished the paperwork." She glanced around, but there was still no sign of her spouse. "It's mad that they don't allow smoking in here," she said, her fingers continuing their drumming. "I mean, it's not as if..." She left the thought unsaid. "I'm sorry."

Don was always wary of asking personal questions, but he wanted to think about something other than his own impending loss. "Is it one of your parents?" he asked. "I mean, who you're visiting?"

"My father-in-law. He passed this morning." She stated it as a fact, with little obvious emotion.

"I'm sorry," Don said. There was an awkward silence. He

sipped from the brown plastic cup of coffee and asked, "Had he been ill for long?"

"Alzheimer's," the woman said, the single word summing up a decade of struggle and sadness. "A blessing, in the end. You know?"

Don nodded. "My mother is here. Bone cancer," he said, the words feeling harsh and unwelcome as always, "but her dementia has become a lot more advanced recently. Doesn't remember anything from the last few years."

"But her memories from fifty years ago are clear as a bell, right?" the woman speculated.

"Right," Don said. "She can still sing all the old song lyrics, but she forgets where she is.

Don couldn't make out the woman's eyes behind the sunglasses, but her body language seemed vaguely sympathetic. A moment later, her husband arrived, looking red-eyed and pale. "Okay, dear. We've done everything we need to," he said, his tired whisper only adding to the subdued atmosphere. The woman stood and graciously shook Don's hand before leaving.

He finished the dreadful coffee before it could cool any further and returned to his mother's room. She was snoozing, but the armchair squeaked as he sat, and she woke. She looked at him, blinking over and over. "Don!" she grinned. "My sweet boy. Where did you come from?"

He was learning to let these comments go. "How was your nap, Mum?" he asked, taking her hand again.

"You know," she said, "I wish your father could be here. He's so busy." Susannah shook her head slightly. "Busy, busy, busy."

Again, Don held his tongue. He could have reminded his mother that his real father had walked out on them over forty-five years before, but he knew she meant that self-serving old crook, Sir Thomas Hughes, her second husband, the man she had insisted he call "Father."

"He was such a good sailor," Susannah said, out of nowhere.

"Yes, Mum," Don said. He was used to these *non sequiturs*, part of a fragmented commentary on the home movies playing in his mother's ailing mind. Three weeks ago, she was still remembering recent events, but now, the only memories that surfaced were those from her earlier life, the seventies and before. It would not be much longer before she would forget who Don was completely. The thought made him shiver.

"The *Gypsy Dancer*," Susannah recalled. "Thirty-six feet long. Our home for two wonderful weeks."

"Where did you go, Mum?" Don asked. The nurses said that it was good to keep her talking during these more lucid moments.

"All over," she said with a gleeful little laugh. "Mexico and Jamaica, lots of little reefs and inlets. Two weeks and then back to San Marcos." She sighed and her eyes grew misty. "We were inseparable back then. Before everything."

CHAPTER FOUR

D ON FROWNED. HIS mother seldom mentioned her relationship with Sir Thomas Hughes. Their marriage had deteriorated badly enough to prompt a serious nervous breakdown in Susannah back when Don was a teenager. He had barely spoken to the industrialist again after Thomas's decision to commit his wife to an "in-patient care facility." Don had known immediately what the place truly was: somewhere for the broken-minded to be kept safe and for a small minority of fortunate patients, nursed back to health. In his mother's case, the bumbling of the doctors and the grim, hopeless atmosphere had made her mental state worse. Susannah had attempted two disastrous spates of "care in the community," and after that, made her home at Kerry Hill for nearly forty years, right up until her final transfer to St. Cuthbert's.

"What was it like before everything, Mum?" Don asked.

"He was always busy, busy, busy," she said again. "Meetings and traveling and managing his factories. You know," she continued, "he built four factories from *nothing*." She held up four pale, slender fingers. "Just like that!" she marveled. "*Thousands* of people. All depending on him. Busy, busy, busy."

Don decided that silence was the most prudent option. He had never felt anything but hatred for Thomas Hughes. Not only had the man condemned his mother to an asylum, but he'd also wrecked Don's life. As an angry, sidelined stepson, he was banished to the care of his elderly, uneducated maternal grandparents when his mother was hospitalized. They could barely read. Life with them had been tedious and limited. He had felt like a burden.

Hughes had granted Don a stipend, but it dwindled to a pittance that ensured that he would have no college degree, nor any of the world adventures that were Susannah's dearest wish for her son. Instead, his adolescence unfurled in a fug of cigarette smoke, beer fumes, and betting slips.

Now, Don held his mother's hand and let her carry on, her hoarse little whisper almost painful to hear, but it was far better than what would come later. Don dreaded even the idea of that final silence and pushed the thought away every time.

"Sometimes he wouldn't get up from his desk until two or three in the morning," Susannah was saying. She tapped Don's hand with deliberate fingertips. "Writing and thinking and planning. Hardly ever had time for me. Busy, busy, busy. I wish he'd come to see me," she said again.

Don didn't remind his mother that Sir Thomas had succumbed to a heart attack seven years before. Instead, he reached for something positive to say. "You were good to him, Mum. A good wife." Hughes had had a busy, complex life, and Don knew that his mother had tried her best to be a good partner through the eight difficult years they were together.

She had been a gentle, sweet, kind person, and Don, while he didn't know for sure, always believed that Sir Thomas had done something to anger her, some transgression or lie that served to corrode her already fragile mind to the point where it snapped.

On his darkest days, Don imagined Sir Thomas tormenting her, berating her, forcing her closer to the edge, and then calling for the "men in the white coats" once he'd finally tired of her despairing, tearful complaints.

"I used to watch him, you know," Susannah said after a pause. Her blue eyes twinkled a little now, framed by neatly combed, soft white locks.

"Watch him?" Don asked, at a loss once more.

"At his desk. That lovely antique desk he bought himself when his third factory opened. He used to sit there," she told Don, "until two or three in the morning."

"Yes, Mum," Don sighed. "You said."

"He loved reading that letter." She paused and turned to her son with an earnest expression. "You know, don't you? Thomas read it over and over," Susannah recalled, "but always in secret. He made me promise."

"Promise what, Mum?" Don said. "What did the letter say?"

"It was beautifully written," she continued, as if she hadn't heard the question. "Thomas was so proud to receive it. He never cared about all the terrible things people said. There was a photo of the three of us on the beach. Summer of seventy-two, it was. I wanted to put it up on the mantel, but Thomas said I couldn't. Oh, the color of the water." Her eyes glazed over once more. "I *adored* that shimmering blue. Always so warm." She sighed. "So *warm*."

Don was racing to catch up, fearful that this moment of lucidity and revelation would pass all too quickly. "Where were you, Mum?" he asked.

But his mother was hazy-eyed, dwelling in her own memories. "Long, lazy days," she recalled with a sigh. "Just the three of us and his servants. They caught big, tropical fish off the stern and grilled them for us on the deck."

Servants? "Who was the third person in the photo, Mum? Where were you?"

Susannah shook off the daydream and frowned at Don as though he'd forgotten his own name. "*San Marcos*, silly!" she said. "He was so charming. And so very handsome in his uniform. 'A strong and wise man,' your father used to say. Thomas always hid that letter in its own little box inside his desk. Secret, secret, secret." She trailed off, her eyes beginning to close again.

Don was desperate to know more. Who was the wealthy, uniformed individual she was talking about? And what was so very *secret*?

"Mum, listen to me. Tell me about the letter."

Her eyes opened just a fraction. "Hmm?" she said, her voice tiny and plaintive.

"The *letter*, Mum," he said, more loudly. "Tell me about the letter. Who was it from?" But Susannah was sinking back into sleep.

Don stared at his mother for a long moment, hoping she might jolt back to wakefulness. He knew she would have no memory of this fragmented conversation when she woke up. He took out his cellphone and quickly wrote himself a note, including the details he could remember. It all seemed important, although he couldn't put his finger on exactly why.

Nurse Watkins appeared at the door just as he was returning the phone to his pocket. She looked kindly at Susannah and moved to pull the covers up over the frail woman's shoulders a little more. "Has she been talking much?" the nurse asked quietly.

"Yes, a little," Don said. "But just fragments. Bits and pieces. I've been trying to make sense of it, but..."

The nurse nodded. "It's nearly eight, m'love, and you've been here all day. Why not get some rest? She's in good hands."

Don rubbed his eyes and gave the nurse a grateful smile. "She is," he agreed. "The best." He kissed his mother's forehead once more, and then he turned down the bedside lights before leaving her room.

As he walked across the rain-soaked parking lot to his battered old VW, as he drove home down the quiet A282, and for the rest of the evening, Don English thought about Sir Thomas Hughes and his writing desk. "Who was that other person, Mum?" he asked the walls of his basement apartment. There was no reply, but still he asked the most pressing of questions: "Why did this letter have to remain so secret?" Unable to sleep, Don went for a walk just after midnight, his scuffed brown shoes splashing slightly in the puddles. "Secret, secret, secret."

Back at home, he set his alarm for the next morning but then sat in his old armchair in the living room, sipping a glass of cheap whisky. He finally went to bed sometime after two o'clock, drained by events and bothered by his mother's cryptic reminiscences.

His phone woke him just after four. "Mr. English? It's Nurse Watkins."

He was bolt upright in seconds. "What's happened?" he asked, but he knew the answer, even before the nurse's kindly, Welsh voice confirmed it.

"I'm so sorry, m'love. It was just ten minutes ago. She slipped away in her sleep."

CHAPTER FIVE

THE WALK FROM the White House Inn to the library was a good deal further than Laura anticipated. As she passed along the cobbled streets, she mused over the idea of purchasing a small car. Arriving with minutes to spare, she took a deep breath and walked inside. She found herself in a spacious building that seemed larger on the inside than she had expected. The distribution desk was in front of her, to her left. She readied a pleasant smile and approached.

"Erm, hello," she said to the librarian, a petite woman with dark hair whose name badge read "Nat." She was slightly older than Laura. "I'm Laura Beecham."

"Oh, hi!" Nat replied. "Welcome to Gorey. Hang on a sec." Nat set down the pile of books she was holding and lifted the counter so Laura could walk through. "I'm Nguyen Ling Phuong, head librarian," she said, shaking hands.

"It's very nice to meet you, Miss... um, sorry, what was your...?"

"Please don't worry. Everyone calls me 'Nat.' Much easier. I'm from Vietnam originally."

"Nice to meet you, Nat," Laura smiled, a little relieved.

"Have you just arrived on the island?"

Laura nodded. "Just yesterday. All a bit of a rush, but I love what I've seen of the place so far."

"It's beautiful, isn't it? The weather's pretty good, by British standards anyway, and there's always something to do," Nat enthused. "I've been here for six years, and I wouldn't live anywhere else."

"That's great to hear. It's certainly a big change from London," Laura said.

"London? Oooh, London's too big! I grew up in a village. Two hundred people. Gorey is perfect for me. Come on, I'll show you around."

The library was a single large room with thick, old beams supporting its sloping roof. The rectangular distribution desk was nearest the door, with racks of CDs on the wall to the right and the interlibrary loans to the left. Past the distribution desk were four computer stations, and behind those, six reading desks sat at the center of the room between rows of very tall wooden shelves full of books. Half a dozen readers were sitting at the tables, while others browsed the neatly arranged collection; sections labeled "New Acquisitions" and "Nat's Recommendations" stood against the left and right walls. DI Graham was right. It was a solid, fit-for-purpose library, one that any town the size of Gorey could be proud of.

"It's a nice space, isn't it?" Nat asked. "It was a church hall for a long time, until the council decided Gorey needed a library, back in the fifties," she explained. "Before that, the Germans used it as a garrison. When we dug the new garden out back a couple of years ago, we found all kinds of army buttons and pins, even the odd bullet, but no bombs, thankfully."

"It's very nice," Laura agreed. "You must like working here."

Nat shepherded Laura along the shelves, showing her the Dewey Decimal System and where the stepladder was stored.

"One thing I really like," Nat confided, "is that there are very few *hassles*. The people here don't need much help. We get some questions about loans from other libraries, but mostly people just read the paper or a magazine, or check out some books. They keep themselves to themselves mostly. During the daytime, it's sometimes just me here, keeping things neat and tidy, while three silent, possibly sleeping, old men read the *Racing Post*."

"Sounds idyllic," Laura said. "I've been looking forward to a quieter life."

Back at the distribution desk, Nat gave Laura a quick demonstration of the library's book catalog software. It seemed simple enough, as did the interlibrary loan system and new library card and renewal procedures. "The only time," Nat warned, "that it gets a bit rowdy is right after the schools get out, between half past three and four."

"Rowdy?" Laura asked. She visualized hordes of uniformed teenagers rampaging among Nat's neatly arranged shelves.

"Well, we had to change our Internet policy. I'll spare you the details. Just kids being kids, I suppose."

"I can imagine," Laura said. Nat printed Laura's new credentials and a plastic ID badge that would be pinned to her top.

A patron approached the distribution desk with two novels, and Nat efficiently checked the books out. "New librarian?" the elderly man asked.

"First day," Nat explained. "I was just telling her how the place gets crazy when the school kids are here."

The man gave a gentle laugh. "It's the boys, mostly," he explained. "A pretty lady is always going to get those teenage hormones racing." Nat threw a paperclip at him, and the old man left with his books, chuckling.

"Bad boy," she said jokingly after him. "It isn't just the teenagers. You'll be finding that out for yourself. But don't worry," Nat smiled. "They know not to go too far. Good people here. Kind."

Laura spent a few minutes trying "dummy runs" to learn the library's distribution software. Then, a pair of eyes framed with wire-rimmed glasses appeared just above the counter top. "Hi," he said.

Laura blinked. "Oh, hello. How can I help you?"

"Got another loan request," the boy said. He couldn't have been older than nine.

"Sure," Laura said. "You'll be my first, so it might take a moment."

Nat appeared at her shoulder. "I'll help. Hey, Billy!"

"Hey, Miss Nat," the young man replied. He had straight-as-a-rod brown hair and a sprinkling of freckles across his snub nose. His eyes were hazel and framed by unusually fair, almost white eyelashes. "I think I'm onto something," he said seriously.

"Oh, really? Making progress with your moon project?" Nat asked, tapping briskly through the loan form; she knew Billy's details by heart.

"Yeah," he said. "I can prove there's still a prototype Russian moon lander orbiting the Earth!" he enthused. "Above our heads, right now!"

Nat showed Laura how to complete the form, and they typed in Billy's request for a book with a lengthy title available only from London. "Billy is passionate about space," Nat explained. "He's trying to figure out what happened to the secret Russian moon-landing project in the sixties."

Laura regarded the young man, whose eyes shone at the mention of his favorite topic. "Secret, huh? Didn't know they'd had a project like that." Billy gave her a quick look that was hard to read. Disbelief? Disapproval?

He launched, with the gusto known only to nine year olds, into an explanation of how the Soviet Union had almost bankrupted itself trying to race NASA to the moon. Four minutes in, Laura felt sure that Billy could easily give an hour's lecture on the subject, without notes, to an expert audience.

"Okay, Space Commander-in-Chief," Nat said, curtailing his spirited performance. "Laura has a lot of learning to do. Your book will be here in..."

"Ten to fourteen days," Billy finished for her.

"Indeed. And we'll notify you, as usual," Nat said. "Anything else?"

"Nope," Billy said, and headed off back to the Science shelves in search of more clues.

"Quite a character," Laura said.

"Billy? He's the smartest person in Gorey, in his own way," Nat said. "Unfortunately, his mother thinks books are a waste of time. I watched her chase him out of here once. You'd have thought we were offering him drugs or something, rather than a little knowledge and a safe place to hang out."

Laura watched Billy scouring the shelves, mouthing a Dewey Decimal number over and over to himself so he wouldn't forget. He found the book he was looking for and grinned merrily to himself. He scuttled over to a desk to begin reading. "That's sad," Laura said. "But at least he seems happy here."

"He's our best customer. I stopped charging him for inter-library loans six months ago."

"That's kind of you." Clearly the small library was, for many people, a storehouse of information, a community hub, and a place of refuge.

And that reassured her. After all Laura had been through, it was exactly what she needed.

CHAPTER SIX

FIVE DAYS LATER...

DON STUMBLED DOWN the last two steps. He found his slippers at the bottom of the stairs, and frowned at the sorry state of his living room. Glancing at the clock, he saw it was lunchtime. Hungover or not, action was urgently needed.

He poured a large glass of cold water and swallowed four extra-strength painkillers. Stumbling slightly, he made the decision to fling aside the living room curtains and push open the windows. The daylight made him squint uncomfortably for the next few moments, but the fresh air revived him a little and helped cleanse the living room of its dismal, smoky aroma. As he waited for the kettle to boil for a pot of tea, he bustled about, cleaning off ash and bottle tops from the cracked glass surface of his old coffee table and setting out his blue plastic folder of notes.

"DESK," was the heading of one sheet. On this page, he had written out everything he knew about Sir Thomas Hughes' famous writing desk. There wasn't much. Digging through his brain, he'd managed to remember the desk's maker and roughly when Sir Thomas had acquired it, but his notes were absent a clue as to the most important detail: its location.

The next sheet of paper related to "MYSTERY PERSON." Don had little to go on except his mother's mention of San Marcos. He'd found the tiny nation on a map, nestled between larger neighbors in Central America, but he knew no more than that. His notes were largely speculative: *Rich? Playboy? Business associate?*

The third page was neatly entitled, "LETTER." He had already transcribed the notes he'd hurriedly tapped out on his cellphone at the hospice as his mother slept that night. They remained the only record of her cryptic, confusing narrative.

Underneath each page of notes were some pictures and related articles photocopied from the library or printed from the Internet. For now, the "Letter" pile was less substantial, but also less important. His top priority remained learning about the elusive piece of furniture that had been known in the Hughes family as the "Satterthwaite Desk" after its illustrious maker, Ezekiel Satterthwaite.

The furniture maker had been born to a cobbler and his wife in 1761, one of nine children. He had looked destined to follow in his poverty-stricken father's footsteps, but defying his working class roots, Satterthwaite built a reputation for designing fine furniture in rococo and neoclassical styles. His work had become highly sought after by the wealthiest people in Britain and Europe in the latter part of the eighteenth and early nineteenth centuries, and Satterthwaite's work now regularly exchanged hands for over a million pounds each.

In addition to having creative flair, Don learned that Satterthwaite had a strong engineering bent. His furniture was robust as well as beautiful. He was a well-loved and kindly man who had a childish fondness for secrets. A signature whimsy was to occasionally, but not always, place compartments inside his pieces. He never announced their existence. As his reputation grew, it became a source of pride and excitement among those who owned his work to learn that theirs contained one of Satterthwaite's secret additions. Many others spent hours examining their commissions only to be disappointed. Many more were never sure either way.

An idea formed in Don's mind. He wanted to locate the desk, but he had no earthly idea even where to start. Or at least he hadn't until eleven-thirty the previous night.

It had been the bitter end of the toughest and most despairing day Don had ever lived through. Susannah's funeral had been held at the tiny St. Mark's Church, a few miles from where she'd grown up. The small volunteer choir had outnumbered the congregation.

The priest made some heartwarming references during the service. There was no way of knowing if he said them at every funeral, but he seemed to have known Susannah a little. He had called Don the previous Wednesday, inviting him to speak at the funeral, but on reflection, Don had decided not to.

Someone from Kerry Hill was there, a man in a dark suit who spoke briefly with Don after the service and then left. There was Angela, an old school friend of Susannah's, who claimed to have visited her regularly at Kerry Hill, though Don couldn't ever remember meeting her. And there was Miss Pardew, who had been running the corner shop for decades. She told Don an endearing story about how a young Susannah had helped look after the store when old Mr. Pardew was losing his battle with heart failure. In all, they'd managed to say goodbye to his mother with dignity and sincerity, even if the loneliness she often felt in life was mirrored in death.

The silence in Don's living room in the hours after the funeral was utterly intolerable, so he'd laid out the complete contents of his liquor cabinet and methodically steered himself toward a state of oblivion. As midnight approached, there was a brief moment of clarity amid the crushing depression and loss.

Still able to hold a pen at that point, Don had roughly scribbled a word at the bottom of the "DESK" sheet. Now, in the light of the following morning, it took a little deciphering. The first letter was certainly a "P," but recognizing the other letters was a struggle. Eventually, Don recognized the name. And it was one which, if he were lucky, could really open some doors.

He drank the tea he had made and rummaged in a couple of drawers looking for his address book. It hadn't been used since the days before cellphones. Finally armed with the number, he tried to think back to when they had last spoken. Was it ten years? Twelve, probably. Don decided it didn't matter. The awkwardness of a Friday afternoon call following years of silence was trifling compared to the importance of his task.

The phone rang at length. Don looked out onto his dejected garden, finding that the weeds had truly taken over following a year of neglect. After eight rings, to Don's great relief, there was a voice.

"Prendergast."

Thank God. "Carl? Hey... It's Don English."

"Don?" There was a pause. "Ah, Don! Yes. Sorry," the man chuckled. Carl Prendergast was the Hughes family lawyer, a slight, wiry man with rimless round spectacles, and a spectacularly creased face. "How are you?" Prendergast asked, politely enough.

Hurting, lonely as hell, and probably still drunk. "I've seen better times, Carl. Did anyone give you the news about my mother?" Nobody had, of course, and so Don was obliged to recount her story once more: the steady decline in Susannah's memory during those last few months at Kerry Hill, the lazy, negligent staff, and then the peaceful three weeks at St. Cuthbert's when the nurses had made her comfortable so she could die with dignity.

"I'll be sure to tell the rest of the family," Prendergast said, after offering his condolences. "I'm sure they'd wish to keep your mother in their thoughts." *Yeah, right.* "While we're talking, I should ask, is everything alright with the stipend?" There was a rustling of papers, evidence that Carl liked to keep things old-school. "No change in the account numbers, or anything?

"The money's fine," Don lied. It hadn't covered half of his bills even ten years ago, and the forty-year-old agreement didn't even provide for an inflation-based increase. These days, a month of Sir Thomas' generosity wouldn't have bought a bottle of whisky. Even the cheap stuff. "Actually, I'm calling about something else. I've got a question about one of Sir Thomas' possessions."

Carl clicked a pen. "Oh?" he asked warily.

"There was a desk. A rare collectors' piece." Don picked up the best picture he'd found, printed from a website on antique furniture. "I'm probably going to say this wrong, and I can barely spell it, but the designer's name was..."

"Ezekiel Satterthwaite," Carl announced. "I know, it's a mouthful, isn't it? Beautiful piece, though. One-of-a-kind, hand-crafted, a stunning example of his work. What do you want to know about it?"

Don leveled with the lawyer. "What happened to it, Carl?"

"The desk?"

Don knew that this was not the kind of question the lawyer would be expecting from the estranged stepson of a wealthy, dead client.

"That's right. Was it sold, or does someone in the family have it?"

More papers shuffled. "Don, would you mind holding the line for a moment? I've been the Hughes' family lawyer for thirty years, but I'm afraid I haven't memorized every last detail of the estate."

"Take your time," Don said, and took two more painkillers.

"Right," Prendergast said, moments later. "I've got the will, and the desk is near the top of the list, as you might imagine."

"Okay," Don said. He managed to keep his tone even, but he was trembling with impatience. His fingers rattled quietly on the scratched wooden surface of his coffee table.

"I'm just tracing the disbursement of assets," Carl explained. "Desk....desk.... where are you, desk?" he muttered, flipping pages. "Ah-hah! Right, yes. I remember now."

Don waited, his nerves jangling.

"It's on Jersey."

Don blinked hard. "Eh?"

"Yes, I remember now. Sir Thomas left strict instructions," Carl explained. "On his death, the Satterthwaite Desk was to be bequeathed in perpetuity and without further family discussion to the Jersey Heritage Museum, where it was to be displayed in honor of the craftsman's connection with the Bailiwick of Jersey."

"Hang on," Don said, pinching the bridge of his nose. "Are you talking about *New* Jersey, in America?"

"No, no. The island near France," Prendergast clarified. "Satterthwaite's father was born on Jersey, and though the great man kept his workshop in London – logically enough, I suppose – he retired to the island and died there. Some time in the 1820s, I believe."

This was hardly the worst case scenario, but it wasn't a straightforward outcome, either. "So, it's on display at a museum? On Jersey?" Don asked.

"Indeed. Damned difficult to get it there, as I recall now. Your father," he began, "Sir Thomas, that is, felt strongly that the museum should have an important Satterthwaite piece. I haven't been to the museum, but one can guess that such an elegant, seminal work now has pride of place in their collection. Um, may I ask as to the nature of your inquiry?"

"Oh, you know, I was just wondering. I've been reminiscing and was curious as to what had happened to it."

A museum. Don would have given it odds of twenty-to-one. It was a real surprise to him that Sir Thomas hadn't kept the valuable desk in his family. Selling it for a quick profit would not have been out of character for his stepsiblings. This was an interesting outcome and also his first lucky break in a long time. "Okay, Carl. That's very helpful," Don said, scribbling notes.

"No trouble at all," Carl said. "Anything else I can help you with?"

"Actually, yes," Don said. "It's about the stipend..."

"Well, I'm afraid my hands are tied there," Prendergast explained. "You see, the agreement is binding, so any alteration has to be co-signed by..."

"Carl?"

"Er... yes?"

"Stop sending it."

"I'm sorry?" Carl said.

"I want you to stop paying it into my account. Send it to a dementia charity."

Carl was shuffling papers again. "Really? You're quite sure?"

Don considered for one more moment, but then couldn't resist. "Absolutely sure. Thomas Hughes was a liar, a cheat, and an all-round nasty piece of work. I don't want any more of his dirty money. Understand? Good." *Click*.

CHAPTER SEVEN

J ANICE PUSHED open the double doors with her hip, holding one of them ajar with her elbow as she maneuvered her way through. She held two coffees in front of her. They sat precariously in a cardboard tray. She hadn't shoved them far enough into their slots, and they were threatening to tip over. Adding to the threat of disaster, the strap of her shoulder bag was slipping down her arm. It was about to make the quick slide to the crook of her elbow, at which point she knew her efforts to keep the coffees upright would be in vain. She awkwardly sidled over to the reception desk as fast as she dare, scuttling like a crab, and lay the coffee tray down on its flat, solid surface. She heaved a sigh of relief.

"'Morning, Janice. To what do I owe this pleasure?" Constable Jim Roach asked, looking up at her from behind the desk, slipping his phone onto his lap and from there into the desk drawer. It had been a slow morning, and he'd taken advantage of the peace and quiet to catch up on yesterday's soccer results.

"Just thought I'd pop in, Jim. See how things are going. Anything interesting?"

"Nah, nothing really. I'm just catching up on paperwork. Bazza's out and about. He'll be back soon." Jim sipped greedily at the coffee Janice offered him.

"How was your Saturday night? How's things going with that nurse you were telling me about?" Janice grinned.

Roach opened a file on top of a pile in front of him and shrugged. "She's alright."

"She's more than 'alright' from what you told me," Janice pressed. "I didn't even know you liked blonds."

Roach looked up and smirked at her. "There's quite enough romance going on around here at the moment, wouldn't you say? How's things going with Jack?"

Jack Wentworth was a computer engineer. He provided digital forensic support to the constabulary when they needed it. He was also Janice's boyfriend.

Try as she might, Janice couldn't keep the flush from her cheeks. After a period of being single so long that it threatened to become permanent, Janice was beyond delighted to be regularly going out to restaurants, movies, and, most recently, the farmer's market with the handsome and thoughtful Jack Wentworth. The young man was proving to be cultured, well-read, and a gifted cook.

"Fine, just fine," she said. "He's a nice guy."

Roach chuckled and hummed the first measures of *Here Comes the Bride.*

"Wind your neck in, Sherlock," she said, regretting she'd ever brought up the subject of romantic entanglements. "I'm going to check in with Viv Foster while I'm here."

"Ah yes. Gorey's Mother of the Year," Roach muttered.

"I hope Billy's alright. He's hanging around the library more these days. Viv left a message yesterday, but I didn't have time to call her back."

"Welp," Roach said, continuing to leaf through a report, "Let's hope she's doing better."

THE CASE OF THE MISSING LETTER 45

"Yes, let's," Janice said, heading to her office. It was seldom that she received good news from the Fosters, whose paths had crossed hers several times over the six years she had been on Jersey. Ever since she'd found a three-year-old Billy snuggled up to his unresponsive mother, Janice had kept a concerned and proprietary eye on him. The image of the tiny boy patting his mother's face as he tried to wake her had never left her mind. Recently, Billy had complained of being bullied at school, but he was doing a little better according to his teachers. He was unbelievably smart but not very socially adept, and it was easy to imagine him falling afoul of those with more muscle than brains.

She dialed Viv Foster's number. "Hello?" It was Billy's voice on the end of the line.

"Oh, hello Billy. It's Sergeant Harding from the station. How are you doing?"

A big sigh came down the line. "Mum's not very well."

Janice knew that meant Viv was either drunk or high. At eleven-thirty on a Sunday morning, it could be either. "Okay, Billy. Is she asleep right now?"

"I can't tell. But she's breathing. She hasn't said anything for an hour or two."

High, then. "Alright, son. You want to come here for a while?" Along with the library, the police station was a sanctuary for Billy. Although he felt a little uncomfortable "running to the police" when his mother relinquished her duties, it was a safe place. Even at the library, he'd occasionally run into groups of older kids, and they just loved to tease him about his glasses, his mother, his penchant for reading and memorizing facts, and his ungainly, uncoordinated movements. One tried nicknaming him "Puppet Boy" but it hadn't yet stuck.

"Er, no thanks. I'll stay with her for a bit longer."

"Okay, Billy. I'll call in an hour and see how you're doing, alright?"

"Yeah, okay," he replied. Then he whispered, "Should I take

it away from her again?"

"No, lad. I think that'll cause more harm than good, don't you?"

"Yeah, you're probably right," Billy agreed. "I don't want her chasing me around again. And I've run out of places to hide the stuff."

Janice gave him some more words of encouragement. She bit down the urge to say much more, and hung up. There had been perhaps four of these calls over the past eighteen months, and each one left her feeling angry and despairing. As a police officer, Janice's instinct was to arrest Viv for possession of a banned substance and arrange for Billy to be taken into care, but she believed in keeping families together wherever possible. Billy's mother was an addict and utterly unreliable. Her own child parented her and yet he loved her. So while Billy's was a far from ideal situation, Janice couldn't see that moving him to a foster home, most likely on the mainland, would be much better. Keeping him close, in a small place like Gorey, meant she and the local community could keep an eye on him.

As she put the phone down, Janice heard a lot of banging and clattering, accompanied by a significant degree of colorful language. She recognized the voice. "Oi, you. Watch your language," she called out. Janice stood and walked out into the reception area. Constable Barry Barnwell was wheeling his regulation police bicycle into the back where they stored everything they wanted to keep out of sight from the public.

The area needed a good cleaning out. Tins containing an assortment of teas, biscuits, and coffee lay atop reams of paper. Next to that sat a toolbox that couldn't be closed due to the claw hammer and screwdriver haphazardly thrown into it. The floor space was largely taken up by a discarded desk and a file cabinet between which the Gorey police team had resorted to storing a couple of riot shields. Barnwell propped his bike up against the desk.

"There has to be a better way. It's like Piccadilly Circus in there," he grumbled. "Couldn't I just leave it out front when I'm off duty? Or take it home? Trying to get a bike through those doors at the end of a shift is a nightmare."

"Had a good morning, Bazza?" Janice asked cheerily.

"Not especially, no," he replied. There was a mulish look on his face. Janice raised her eyebrows. Barnwell took it as a sign to air his grievances. "First, we lost at the rugby yesterday. Second, that new couple in the flat upstairs didn't invite me to their housewarming party. And third, they kept me up all night with the noise!"

"Why didn't you tell them to keep it down? You are the police," Jim asked reasonably. Barnwell merely grunted before carrying on.

"And then this mornin', old Mr. Golightly at number seven bent my ear off for a good fifteen minutes about his neighbor's trees blocking his view *again*."

"Neighbor disputes are the worst," Janice said sympathetically.

"You're telling me. Been going at each other for *five* years, they have."

"Won't stop until one of them's in their grave, mark my words," Jim said sagely.

"Well, I'm off down the pub." Barnwell started to unbutton his reflective jacket. "A pint and a Sunday roast will do me right."

"And a snooze, I reckon," Jim said.

"Yeah, that too. Ha, I'm cheering up already." Barnwell went to hang up his jacket and replace it with a beat-up leather jacket.

"Anything else to report before you go?" Janice inquired.

"Nope, all's quiet on the Western front. Everyone seems to be enjoying the good weather. A few tourists are around, but everything's pretty sleepy and uneventful. No trouble other than those bloomin' trees."

CHAPTER EIGHT

DON FELT LIKE a new man. In contrast to Shropshire's weather, which apparently, hadn't yet received the springtime memo, Jersey was a riot of color. Yellow, blue, pink, and white flowers lined the roadside and beamed from the window boxes and front gardens of the neat houses near the B&B he had chosen.

Although the denizens of BedAdvisor.com had insisted that the White House Inn was *the* place to stay in Gorey, their rates had been a little beyond Don's modest budget, and he'd already spent a small fortune hiring a car for a few days. Instead, he opted to stay at a townhouse owned by an elderly widow just off the main thoroughfare through Gorey. His landlady was obviously supplementing her meager pension by letting out a spare room, but his accommodation was pleasant and the breakfast tasty and plentiful.

Don closed the wrought iron gate to the townhouse's postage-stamp-sized front garden and walked the few steps to his rental car. He settled himself behind the steering wheel and let out a deep sigh, pausing for a second to consider his plan. Leaning forward, he turned the key in the ignition. The car's engine started with a quick shake and a low purr.

He easily pulled away from the curb, the hour being early and the streets of Gorey less than busy. Don spun the steering wheel calmly as he made his way through the town's mostly empty streets. The drive to the museum was peaceful as he took the small roads out of town at a deliberately steady speed.

At around ten o'clock the previous night, Don had found to his surprise that he was further from home than he'd ever been in his life. Although his mother traveled extensively after meeting Sir Thomas, Don had never been invited on their luxurious Caribbean cruises or their romantic weeks hiking their beloved Rockies. Don's departure from the mainland had involved six tiring hours of train journey and a nerve-wracking change in London. Don had rushed headlong across town from Paddington to Waterloo, only to find that he still had another hour to wait for his train to Poole.

The ferry ride across the Channel, however, was a real joy. Leaving behind the smog and chaos of the capital, and the drab, nondescript port town from which he'd left the mainland, Don reveled in the fresh sea air and spent most of the journey enjoyably wandering around on the deck. There was nothing like crossing a body of water to remind a traveler that they were arriving somewhere brand new.

In truth, Don was more than ready for a change of scenery. Everything in his life and everything about it reminded him of his mother, so the decision to head to Jersey had been an unusually decisive one. Within an hour of his call to Carl Prendergast, he found himself staring at a half-empty whisky bottle on one hand, and his growing pile of research notes on the other. "Bugger," he said to the forlorn living room. "I'm off." It had likely been the only time in his life that he had possessed enough mettle to make a snap decision and carry it through.

Don parked the tiny hire car at the museum. He was early. It didn't open until midday on a Sunday. He took a walk around the area while he waited. The museum building was a large, ostentatious house with a plaque inset into the sandstone façade. The plaque announced that the building had been built in 1613 and was the original home of John Cateshull. Don presumed he was a local wealthy man of note, but in whom he wasn't sufficiently interested to delve further. The house was located on a quiet, expansive, and verdant part of the island, about a mile from Gorey itself. He could see the Gorey Grammar School playing field beyond the house's grounds on one side, and there was a large park on the other, complete with a bandstand and duck pond.

His plan, so far as he actually *had* one, was to merely lay eyes on the desk and try to judge what might be required for him to closely examine it. He meant the masterpiece no harm whatsoever, but his suspicion, fanciful as he told himself it might be, was that it may just contain something very meaningful indeed.

Don dearly wanted to fill in the gaps of his mother's mysterious story. Who was this wealthy individual she had holidayed with? Who wrote the letter she had talked about, and what did its contents contain that were so secret? Don felt sure the Satterthwaite Desk was the key to answering these questions and besides, traveling down here to Jersey and working on this mystery were all a *lot* more fun than sitting on his couch at home, trying to ignore the ceaseless allure of the scotch bottle.

When it opened, Don found the entrance to the museum exceptionally grand. Converted to its new function after a lengthy funding drive, the house now acted as a display space for artifacts related to Jersey's history. A large chandelier sparkled above a hallway lined with paintings of Jersey luminaries and leaders, none of whom Don recognized. He paid the entrance fee and walked into the main display space, which was the former ballroom. Don's shoes tapped crisply on the highly polished wooden floor. More portraits and works by local painters adorned the walls, and in one corner sat a beautiful, jet-black grand piano, a storied possession of the house's former owners, according to a sign mounted on a music stand in front of it.

There was another musical instrument, a *clavichord*, and several sculptures crafted from local stone. But, Don noted, there was no desk.

The ballroom led out into a three-room suite that occupied the back of the house. There were mannequins wearing ball gowns and wedding dresses, displays of military medals and ceremonial swords, signed first editions of classic books Don had never read or even heard of, and a large, framed, nautical chart of the waters to the east of Jersey.

Frustrated, Don quietly muttered, "Come on, come on, where the hell is..."

And then he saw it, sitting on its own, surrounded by red rope under the back window. It stopped Don dead in his tracks.

CHAPTER NINE

SIR THOMAS HAD firmly prohibited all of his children from entering his private study, so Don was seeing the Satterthwaite Desk for the first time. He had never suspected that it might be so *beautiful*. It wasn't just the wood tone, which struck a balance between formal and playful, between depth and sheen. And it wasn't merely the inlaid mother of pearl, which gave this singular piece of furniture a crystalline glimmer as the dark and light swept alongside each other in sumptuous, elegant curves. It was also the *shape*, the very proportions of the desk. It was a geometric perfection, conceived perhaps by a master mathematician but then realized in wood and leather and semi-precious stone by a consummate professional at the very height of his powers.

Don stared, slack-jawed. This was, he tried to remind himself, a *desk*.

Four sinuous, delicately feminine legs, so slender as to be unlikely, supported a broad, glass-smooth surface made, quite obviously, from a single length of the highest quality timber. There was a large, central drawer, flanked by two others, all with glinting, filigreed handles in solid brass. The sides were adorned with carvings so detailed and careful that they could almost have been etchings. The symmetrical blossoms, captivatingly three-dimensional, spoke of many dedicated, painstaking hours of work.

The accompanying booklet described the Satterthwaite Desk as, "perhaps the perfect synergy of form and function," a description that Don found somewhat overripe, but admittedly, only a little. The museum was proud of its most spectacular acquisition, and with good reason. It was, without exception, the most remarkable piece of furniture Don had ever seen. There was just one problem. After ten minutes of careful reconnaissance, he concluded that there was absolutely no way *whatsoever* he would be getting anywhere near it.

The red rope was not simply an ornate deterrent to keep visitors from touching the desk. Discreetly taped to the floor underneath it was a thin, black wire that would assuredly trigger a noisy alarm if anyone crossed it. And there were *four* cameras in the room, as well as a permanently stationed security guard whose solidly muscular build would deter most would-be transgressors.

Don asked for and received permission to take some photographs. He took just enough, he hoped, to avoid arousing suspicion. There were no switches, catches or buttons on the exterior, and he obviously couldn't crawl on his knees to view the desk's underside without attracting unwanted attention. Whatever Sir Thomas Hughes' secrets might be, they would remain hidden for the time being. With frustration threatening to bleed into his behavior, Don hurriedly took his leave.

Outside, spring was flooding the park and the school field next door to the museum with brilliant sunshine. Don breathed in the air, so different from back home, so much more *nourishing*, and then sat in his car with the windows open to digest what he had seen. The desk was a marvel, an absolute treasure. But security was tight. Accessing the closely guarded desk and searching for a secret compartment was, undoubtedly, going to be a three-pint problem.

He started the car and drove around the island for a couple of hours, partly to clear his head, and also to enjoy the peaceful scenery in Jersey's spring sunshine. With each passing mile traveled, he felt the stress and depression of the past few days leave him like a fog lifting on a spring morning. He found his thought patterns shifting as his mood improved.

He took a back road through a quiet village with a bright, glistening green. In the middle of the grass stood a memorial to the village's war dead. He thought carefully. The search for the letter was providing him with something to *do* in the quiet, sullen days after his mother's funeral.

As he continued down the country lanes, tall grasses serenading the car from both sides of the road, he realized that there was a dark side to his motivation for finding the letter. Certainly, it would be satisfying to come to a greater understanding of his mother's life with Sir Thomas, their trips abroad, and their associations, but there was a suspicion in Don's mind that the letter may reveal some information, some dirt on Sir Thomas Hughes. Don considered his mother's treatment at the hands of her husband to have been cruel and inhumane while the rest of the family had stood aside. They had been complicit. If they were embarrassed or even scandalized in some way, it wouldn't bother him a bit. Whatever secrets the letter may expose, he wasn't above gaining some measure of revenge for his mother's and his own unhappiness at their hands.

Don slowed before turning into the parking lot of a quiet country pub. Another thought occurred to him. It was something his mother had stated – about the "terrible things" people had said about the author of the letter. "What was all that about?" he asked the interior of his hire car as he killed the engine.

Don ducked as he passed through the doorway of the pub

into the deep, dark interior. Outside, the quaintly named *Frog and Bottle,* with its whitewashed frontage and tiny windows, had offered the prospect of a wonderfully varied selection of beers. Don found the promise kept as he perused the chalkboard on the bar. But before ordering a pint to go with his sandwich, he stopped himself short. He would drink no booze, no whisky, no wine, and none of the dozen items on the beer menu he was anxious to try, until he finally had the letter in his possession. That would be reason for real celebration.

CHAPTER TEN

CONSTABLE JIM ROACH jogged into the reception area carrying his football boots in one hand and his gym bag in the other. "Thanks so much for this, sir," he said. "It's the last but one game of the indoor season, and we're playing the Civil Servants again. One more win and we'll be confirmed Division champions."

DI Graham cut a slightly incongruous figure behind the reception desk, dressed in his white shirt and brown blazer instead of the customary desk officer's police blue. "Go ahead and grab yourself a hat trick. I only hope you don't get spotted by some talent scout and offered a contract by AC Milan. I don't know what we'd do without you."

Roach acknowledged the compliment with a nod. "Old Mrs. Hollingsworth has called in again. A suspicious character, she says. I'll drop by on my way. Check it out. I'm sure it's nothing. It never is." Roach said.

"Okay, let me know if anything changes."

Roach grinned and headed to his recently acquired, third-hand car. If he were lucky, he'd arrive in time to warm up before the game. He was the team's first choice midfielder, but he was useful on the wing and even played up front when pressed. Roach was looking forward to giving their pen-pushing opponents a good thrashing. First though, he'd attend to Mrs. Hollingsworth's call. It shouldn't take too long.

The man observed the library through a side window. He could see the woman he was looking for. For a library as small as this, it was taking Laura a long time to tidy it up. She had put away newspapers and stacked some other things that he couldn't see on the shelves. Then she busied herself around the distribution desk and moved some more piles of books from place to place, checking items off a list on her clipboard. She turned off the library's lights, section by section, until only those above the distribution desk remained lit. She would be out soon. He was ready for her.

Tires crunched on the gravel of the library's short driveway. A car was approaching. The man swore colorfully under his breath and headed along the side of the building and into the park where he sprinted a short distance. He was lost in the shadows within moments.

He turned and looked back. The car had stopped, and a young man had got out. He recognized him as one of the coppers he'd familiarized himself with when he arrived on the island. The policeman nosed around for a moment, shining his flashlight into the bushes and around the back of the building, but he didn't come close to illuminating him before returning to his car and driving off. The man turned his attention back to the library.

Laura appeared to have seen and heard nothing, finishing her tasks just as the clock struck seven. All was quiet and dark. She came outside with an armful of books and made her way over to her car. When the library door slammed shut behind her, she stopped suddenly and raised her face to the sky, but after hesitating for a few seconds, she continued over to her hatchback and deposited the books in the back. She climbed into her car and drove away.

The man edged back toward the library parking lot and watched her leave. He cursed again. Foiled and frustrated, he sat on a bench in the park, listening to an owl hooting in the distance. He cursed his luck. He made sure that his silenced pistol had its safety on, deep in his jacket pocket, and then sent a brief text: *Found her, getting closer, all under control. Will update tomorrow.*

The man sighed and headed back to his digs, a simple B&B in the town.

It hadn't been a difficult decision for Graham to head to the station after his Sunday dinner. His evening options basically boiled down to sitting around in the dining room or on the terrace of the White House Inn, where there was every chance Mrs. Taylor would bring over at least one likely female companion to entertain him. To escape that, he occasionally took himself down the pub, but that was something, with his history, he was keen to avoid. This evening, he'd determined that if he were going to be sitting, he may as well catch up on some paperwork at the office.

Graham was leafing through a file when a figure appeared at the lobby doors. "Er, hello?" she said tentatively, as though uncertain anyone would be there.

Of all the gin joints in all the world...

Graham gave her a welcoming wave. "Good evening, Miss Beecham."

"Laura, please," she said, huffing a little as she calmed herself down.

"What can I do for you, Laura? Is everything alright?"

"I'm very relieved you're here. I'm afraid I've gone and done something rather silly."

Graham put down the file. "How do you mean?"

Laura's shoulders sank. "Well... But... It's just that... Well..."

"Miss Beecham, Laura," Graham began, "if I told you the top five most embarrassing things that have happened while I've been working here, you wouldn't believe three of them."

Laura couldn't help but laugh at that. She looked a little chilly, dressed only in a blouse and a long wrap skirt. "Well, alright then, I've locked myself out of the library."

Graham couldn't repress a chuckle. "I wondered if that might be it," he said. "Well, at least it's an easy fix." He tapped out a number from memory, spoke briefly with someone called Jock, and replaced the receiver. "Help is on its way. Now, if you don't mind me asking," Graham said, "how did you manage it?"

Laura began to relax a little. "I was putting some books in my car and the door shut behind me just after I'd set it to lock. The library keys are inside."

"You didn't call the other librarian for help?"

After an embarrassed glance down toward the lobby's linoleum floor, Laura admitted, "I left my phone on the distribution desk. And, did you know, the police station is actually closer to the library than the nearest phone box?"

"I'm a bit surprised we still have any," Graham said. "But I'm pleased you came here first. The ever-helpful Jock will be along presently."

Laura raised an eyebrow. "Does he work for you?"

"No," Graham laughed. "Jock is a very fine locksmith. He used to work for the wrong team, but these days, I put a little work his way when I can. Please, take a seat."

They waited together, sitting in the reception area's blue plastic chairs. "I haven't seen you around the White House Inn for a few days," Graham offered.

"My shifts at the library mean that I grab a late breakfast and

I miss dinner. Mrs. Taylor leaves a plate out for me. She said you'd been here about six months," Laura added, crossing her legs and rubbing her shoulders with both hands to warm up. "Down from London too, I hear?"

Graham grabbed his own jacket from the coat stand and offered it to Laura. "Ah, the formidable intelligence-gathering apparatus that is Mrs. Taylor," he marveled. "Yes, I was in the Metropolitan police, but I fancied a new start. Sounds like you're a little bit the same."

"Something like that," Laura said, gratefully sliding the jacket over her chilly shoulders. "London was getting a little too... how shall I say... *intense* for me. Too crowded, too big."

"Lots of people down here would agree," Graham said. "Jersey's a great escape from city life. It's quiet."

"So," Laura asked, "you haven't been up to your ears in big cases?"

Graham gave an equivocating shrug. "Not up to my ears exactly, but there's been more action than I expected."

"Really?" Laura frowned.

"But most of it's small, everyday stuff that you see in police stations the world over. The odd drunk, theft, locked-out person..." His eyes twinkled as he looked over at Laura. She blushed and shrugged her shoulders.

"Mrs. Taylor mentioned that you helped out with something important right after you arrived at the Inn. She was a bit cagey about what."

"I'm not surprised," Graham told her. "There was a poisoning there."

Laura blinked. "Really? But you caught the person responsible?"

Graham nodded. "It involved a little more drama than I'd have preferred, but yes."

"Congratulations," she said. "And I'm told that wasn't your only success."

The DI shrugged this off. "Our job is to catch criminals, Miss Beecham, Laura. Sometimes it takes longer than we'd like, even a few years," Graham said, remembering the long-delayed conclusion to the Beth Ridley case last November, "but we always try to get there in the end."

Laura looked at him curiously, a slight smile on her face. She wasn't quite sure what to make of him. He seemed accomplished but self-effacing, certainly reserved and something of a local hero by all accounts. There was a worldliness gained through his own undoubted competence that Laura found absorbing, especially on an evening when she was feeling particularly naïve and clueless. And lastly, a hint of melancholy presented itself, the source of which she suspected he kept very close to his chest.

"Ah, Jock," she heard him say. Graham rose to greet the locksmith, a stocky sixty-year old with more wrinkles on his weatherbeaten face than there were hairs on his gleaming head. "I wonder if you're able to take things from here?" he asked Laura. "I gave the desk constable the night off so he could play for the Jersey Police five-a-side, and I don't want to leave the desk unmanned."

"No problem," Laura smiled. "You've been very helpful."

"My pleasure. And thanks, Jock," he said to the locksmith.

"Any time, guv'," the man said, snapping out a salute. "Come on then, m'lady. Let's get you fixed up."

"Please drop into the library if you're passing, Detective Inspector." Laura gave him one of her lovely smiles and followed Jock out to his van.

Graham watched them leave and returned to his seat behind the reception desk. Eventually, he opened his file and started reading again. First, however, he stared out of the window into the Gorey night, deep in thought. He picked up his pen and made a list of all the points of local history he had been meaning to research since he'd arrived on Jersey but hadn't got around to. It was high time he did.

Nobby found that the best method of staying awake was to patrol the museum's rooms in a random pattern, and keep adjusting the lighting.

He ambled from the grand entrance, past the ticket desk, and into the ballroom, ensuring once more that the windows were all locked and that everything was in its place. He shone his flashlight around the dark room, under the piano and along the rows of paintings on the walls. "Right as rain," he said. This was another of his habits. Nobby was fond of chattering away to himself to help pass the time.

The three-room display suite at the back, once a drawing room, library, and smoking lounge, was also in good order. He had long since gotten used to their illustrious bequest. The desk's mother-of-pearl inlay shone, iridescent, in his flashlight's glow. "Ezekiel Satterthwaite," he tried. "Now there's a name to conjure with."

The night guard position was proving the ideal way for Nobby to earn a little extra money to supplement his government pension. It helped him to afford the occasional Saturday afternoon down the pub, preferably one with a big screen that was showing Premiership soccer. He liked to work steadily through three or four pints while enjoying a well-played game.

Nobby returned to the ballroom and sat on the bench of the grand piano for a moment's rest when he heard the unmistakable sound of glass breaking.

"Oi!" he hollered. He rose quickly, a little too quickly. His head swam. He trotted toward the source of the sound. It had come from the museum's rear. "Is someone there?" he called. He turned on the lights and looked left toward the mannequins and then right.

There was a large man dressed all in black, his face masked

by a scarf standing next to the Satterthwaite Desk. The man was frozen in the beam of Nobby's flashlight.

"Alright, just hold it there. Let's not have any trouble," Nobby began, more calmly than he felt. He wasn't armed, but he knew the flashlight could do some damage if it were wielded with force. He also had a radio tuned to the police frequency.

"Don't move," the man said. He had a very deep, gruff voice. "I said, *don't move.*" Nobby saw now that there was a revolver in the intruder's hand, a snub little .38.

The night watchman's hand stopped short of his radio's buttons. "Take it easy, mate," he breathed, his heart thumping loudly in his ears. "No need for anyone to get hurt." He felt a pain in his chest.

"Hands on your head," the man said, his voice low and brusque.

The intruder's demeanor, his clothes, the gun, small but powerful and useful at close range, all told Nobby he was facing a seasoned professional. He knew he should do as he was told, but Nobby hated being pushed around, and the museum at night was *his* responsibility. "What kind of silly bugger breaks into a little, local *museum?*" Nobby asked. "They'll have you for armed robbery, so they will. Ten years, that'll cost you, if not more."

The figure in front of him was not in the least intimidated. The gun rose slightly. "What would *murder* cost me?" he growled.

CHAPTER ELEVEN

THE RED PHONE rang just as Jim Roach was setting his morning coffee down on the desk. "Gorey Police," he said and then listened. He made quick notes on the pad of white forms kept by the phone. "Understood," he said. "Ambulance on its way?" "Good. Ten minutes. Remind the crew to tread carefully," he said.

Graham had heard the phone and was at his office door reaching for his jacket. "Constable?"

"Body discovered at the museum, sir. Curator called it in." Roach began to phone Sergeant Harding, whose shift wasn't due to start for another six hours. He was following the procedure Graham had drummed into them in the event of a major incident. After that, he'd call Barnwell.

"Damn," Graham observed momentarily, but then he straightened up. "Right, I'll be on my way. See you there." He donned his jacket and headed to the museum alone, knowing that Roach would catch up.

On the way, Graham called Tomlinson. "Marcus, body at the museum."

"Just got the call, old chap. I'll be right there as soon as I finish my breakfast." Graham imagined the pathologist sitting at his dining table, boiled egg in its cup, meticulously set aside buttered toast, a glass of freshly squeezed orange juice and equally freshly brewed coffee. He hoped Tomlinson wouldn't be too long about it. "First thing on a Monday morning, eh?" Graham marveled as he steered his marked police car speedily along the lanes which linked Gorey to the rest of the island.

"Death always comes at a bad time," Tomlinson said, dead-pan. "I'll be there soon. Tell the ambulance crew not to..."

"I know, Marcus."

The ambulance was already parked at the entrance to the museum when Graham got there. The Detective Inspector walked around it to find a short, balding man leaning against the outside wall of the building. He was shaking tiny green mints from a small plastic container into the palm of his hand.

"Sorry," he said nervously, tossing a couple of the mints into his mouth and obliterating them immediately with a decisive crunch. "I'm not dealing with this very well."

"Who are you, sir?" Graham asked.

"Sorry," the man said again, wiping his palms on his suit jacket. "Adam Harris-Watts. I'm the curator of the museum."

"Good morning, sir," Graham said with a more sympathetic tone. "You were the one who found the body, I understand?"

"Yes," Harris-Watts said, his jaw twitching for another mint to grind. "It was awful. I mean, I've known Nobby for three years. Such a nice fellow..." The curator sniffed.

"We'll find out what happened here," Graham promised. "There's nothing you could have done." He had said the very same things for over a decade to bereaved spouses, parents, siblings, and other loved ones who were out of their minds with grief. "When my colleague, Constable Roach arrives, he'll take a statement from you. Then you'll be free to spend the rest of the day as you wish."

Harris-Watts coughed. "I have to call the museum's board right now. They'll need to know what's happened."

"Alright, just please don't go anywhere," Graham said. He left the agitated man and walked past the ticket desk and into the ballroom where he spotted the paramedics standing in a room at the back of the house. It was filled with paintings and artifacts, as well as a strikingly beautiful desk. At its feet lay the body of a man in a blue sweater and black pants. His first thought was that there was less blood than he'd expected.

"Morning Sue, Alan," he said to the ambulance crew.

Sue Armitage and Alan Pritchard were dressed in blue coveralls, but were standing away from the body. "Morning, DI Graham. Great way to start a Monday, eh?"

"What have we got?" Graham asked, his hand reflexively bringing out his notepad and pencil.

"Night watchman. No signs of a pulse when we arrived. Seems like he's been dead for a few hours, at least. Thought it best to leave him until you got here," Sue said.

Marcus Tomlinson bustled into the room, carrying his black leather bag and a large travel mug of coffee. "Has he been moved?" the veteran pathologist asked at once.

"No, Marcus. Sue and Alan know your drill, just like I do," Graham reassured him.

"Good," Marcus said. "Good. Well done." Tomlinson visibly relaxed, took a swig of coffee, and handed the mug to Graham. "Hold onto this for me." The pathologist set down his bag and approached the body, immediately beginning to dictate his findings into his cellphone. Graham looked around but, unable to find a suitable place to set Tomlinson's coffee, held onto it. The two paramedics exchanged a glance. They were required to stay until the body could be moved, and so were able to watch the highly experienced – even *famous*, at least in a local sense – Marcus Tomlinson at work.

"The deceased has been preliminarily identified as Charles

Norris, known to everyone as 'Nobby'," the pathologist was saying. "Formal identification will take place before the autopsy. The body is lying face down, at the foot of the Satterthwaite Desk, his head almost touching the right front leg of the desk. His left arm is splayed out under the desk itself." At the pathologist's request, Graham handed him the camera from his black bag, ultimately deciding to set Tomlinson's coffee on the floor next to it. The pathologist began taking close-up photographs. "The head is turned slightly to the right, and there's a quantity of blood underneath it. There's an obvious laceration to the left temple." Tomlinson looked more closely and specified, "A cranial avulsion. There's also damage to the near-right corner of the desk, indicating that he fell and struck his head on it."

Graham peered closely. He winced at the obvious marring of desk's workmanship, especially in such a manner. A smear of Nobby's blood was visible on the cracked wood. "Are you thinking it was an accident?" he asked during a lull in Tomlinson's recording.

"I'm thinking," the pathologist retorted, "that it was a fall. But that's all we can say, as yet."

Graham knew that Tomlinson was, above all, a scientist. He would never jump to a conclusion. For Tomlinson, the evidence was the sole arbiter of events. Nothing beyond it would be considered, especially at such an early stage.

"Alright, I'm going to take some measurements," Tomlinson announced. "DI Graham, this won't be very pleasant, I'm afraid." The examiner lifted Nobby's blue sweater and white shirt a few inches up his back and asked for Graham to bring his bag.

"He has to measure the temperature," Sue whispered knowingly to Alan. Sue had had five years with the States of Jersey Ambulance Service. She was fascinated by forensic pathology and liked to read up on the subject in her spare time, preferably in a sunny room accompanied by a mug of tea and her bulldog, Chester, snoring by her side. "But we can't just use the surface of the skin or inside the mouth because we need to take the *core* temperature," she explained to him. "Dr. Tomlinson will take a reading from within an internal organ. Typically," she added, "the liver." Alan listened patiently. He'd only been with the ambulance service for two years. He was Sue's junior, a fact she repeatedly reminded him of one way or another.

Tomlinson made an incision and gained his reading. "So, you're a budding pathologist, eh?" he said, managing a friendly smile as he stood once more and turned to Sue.

"Thinking about taking some courses, sir, yes." Sue was petite and about twenty-six with dark hair tied back in a short ponytail.

"Then you might be able to tell me how long ago this poor man died. Fancy giving it a try?"

She nodded. "What's his core temperature now, sir?"

"Eighty-nine point eight degrees Fahrenheit," Tomlinson announced. "Or thirty-two point one degrees Celsius, for the metrically minded. What does that tell you?"

Sue did the math in her head. "That the victim has lost just under nine degrees Fahrenheit since death," she said. "Typically, corpses lose one-point-five degrees per hour, so we can say he died around six hours ago." She checked her watch. "Two in the morning."

"Excellent. Now, let's see if the remaining evidence confirms that hypothesis. Let's turn him onto his front." The two paramedics and Tomlinson gingerly tipped Nobby's body to the right and then laid him out flat on his back. They lifted his sweater and unbuttoned his shirt. "You see this, DI Graham?" Tomlinson asked.

Graham was examining the paintings and other objects in the room. He turned quickly and immediately recognized the purple-blue marks on the victim's chest and abdomen. "Lividity," he said.

"The pooling of blood under gravity, after the heart stops

beating," Tomlinson confirmed, turning to Sue and continuing his quiz. "But is it *fixed* or not?"

Graham watched Tomlinson tutor the two much younger medics in the basics of forensic pathology for a moment and then turned back to the paintings. It was so like Marcus to make these opportunities, 'teachable moments," a chance to impart a little knowledge and help the next generation gain some practical experience.

"It's not quite fixed," Sue decided. "Once we turned him onto his side, the purple patches began to move slowly away from his abdomen and toward his ribs."

"A very significant conclusion," Tomlinson said, impressed. "Because fixed lividity begins at around eight to twelve hours after death, and we can therefore state...?" he said.

"That the six-hour estimate of time elapsed since death is still roughly correct," Sue said.

"Or, more specifically, that the poor man expired no more than eight hours ago, and probably between six and eight," Tomlinson told them. "So, what does that tell us about the time of death?"

"Between midnight and two?" Alan dared.

"Spot on. Now, one more thing to examine before we move the body to the lab. Anyone want to guess what it is?" Graham remained silent, perusing the collection and allowing Tomlinson his professorial moment. Neither Alan nor Sue responded. "Rigor mortis," Tomlinson said with a flourish. "Take his fingers... go on," he said to the reluctant Sue. "Can you move them?"

"A little bit," Sue said, taking the pale fingers in her gloved hands with obvious distaste.

"But the grip is not yet *rigid*, you'd say?"

"Not yet," she agreed.

CHAPTER TWELVE

ROACH APPEARED JUST as the three medics were pressing and turning the dead man's joints. He shivered at the sight. "I've been looking around the outside of the building, and I've found something, sir. In the store room on the other side of the house," he whispered to Graham, not wanting to disturb the others.

"Right, good lad," Graham whispered back. "I'll be along in five."

Tomlinson checked Nobby's elbows and knees. "A little more than halfway to complete stiffness, I'd wager," he said. "This tells us *two* things. It's more evidence for our time-of-death hypothesis, because rigor sets in completely within twelve hours. But if we're right, and his death occurred between midnight and two o'clock, his state of rigor mortis should be much more pronounced than it is. Our victim must have had a high level of ATP in his system when he died."

"ATP?" Alan asked. He was younger than Sue, perhaps early twenties, and had bright, curious eyes that darted around, gathering data quickly as they went. The two paramedics were the opposite of the cynical, jaded, older types Graham had experienced in London.

"Adenosine triphosphate," the Inspector told them from the other side of the room, where he was examining a case of military medals. "It's a chemical which is important for muscular energy. ATP is sustained by oxygen from our blood flow, but that obviously ceases at death. This loss of ATP brings about the muscular stiffness we call rigor mortis."

"Excellent, DI Graham. If you weren't such a fine detective, I'd recommend switching careers to medicine," Tomlinson said. "So, we're able to conclude that our victim died somewhere between midnight and two o'clock. He fell onto his front and wasn't moved. He definitely hit his head on this desk, causing a serious wound to his left temple. But was that what *killed* him?" Tomlinson asked.

His younger companions looked at him, wide-eyed. "We'll find out later when we get him back to the morgue," Tomlinson finished disappointingly. He directed the paramedics to wrap the body in plastic. He then watched as they carefully transferred it to a black body bag and onto the waiting gurney. Tomlinson walked out with them to the ambulance. Graham followed.

"What's your gut telling you, Marcus?" he asked. "Natural causes, or...?"

"He fell," the older man repeated. "I'll know more by the end of the day."

Graham frowned. "I've got a funny feeling about this one," he said as the ambulance doors closed. "Let me know as soon as you have anything."

Tomlinson shook the DI's hand. "Depend on it."

Turning away, Graham saw that standing outside the front entrance watching the ambulance trundle off down the street was the museum curator.

"Mr. Harris-Watts?" Graham said as the vehicle disappeared

from view. The man, despite his earlier distress, seemed reluctant to drag his eyes away from the sight to focus on Graham.

"Yes?"

Graham ushered him inside. "We need to have a further word, sir. Would you be so kind as to walk me through your collections?"

It had not taken Constable Roach long to find the broken window at the back of the museum. It opened onto a storeroom for objects that were 'resting.' They were items that were either part of the museum's rotating displays or were awaiting repair or appraisal.

"The intruder," Roach concluded, "broke this window, climbed through into the museum, and then left the same way."

"Damn," Harris-Watts said bitterly. "The blighter did something as *simple* as break in through a window?"

"We'll see." Graham looked around the room. "Tell me more about the method of entry, Roach. What does it show us?"

"He just broke the glass and climbed through, sir," Roach said. "There's no obvious attempt to force the window open, or to saw, or cut around the lock. Guess he wanted to just get in, do his business, and get out. What did Dr. Tomlinson say about our victim?"

"Just that he fell. I think he had a heart attack *before* he fell or died from a head wound *when* he fell."

Harris-Watts shuddered.

Roach lifted his eyebrows as high as they would go. "Dr. Tomlinson wouldn't like us speculating about Mr. Norris' death, sir. Not without any evidence."

"That's true. So, let's not tell him, eh?" Graham quietly ushered Roach between the shelves of stored artifacts and back into the room that housed the Satterthwaite Desk. He turned back. "Please come with us, Mr. Harris-Watts." Turning to Roach once more he said, "There's glass everywhere. See how some of it has been ground into the wood?"

Roach knelt and examined the crushed glass. "It's almost powdered, sir."

"So?" Graham posed. "That tells us something more, doesn't it?"

Roach thought quickly. "That he collected glass on his clothes on his way through the window?" He looked back in the direction of the intruder's entry point. "That the intruder was a big lad?" he surmised,

"A man in all likelihood," Graham agreed. "And not a slight one. What else do we have?"

Roach swiped his iPad. "Well, Mr. Harris-Watts here," Roach looked up to acknowledge the curator, "told me earlier that the CCTV footage is nearly useless, because the victim kept most of the lights off."

"Blast," Graham swore. "They weren't night-vision cameras?"

Harris-Watts shook his head. "Too costly," he explained.

"What about footage of Nobby's death?"

The curator was red-faced now. "The frame rate is so low that... Well, Constable, you've seen it..."

"In one frame, he's standing up," Roach explained, "and in the next, he's on the floor."

Graham's temper frayed. "Bloody hell." He stopped himself from saying more.

"I'm sorry, it's the budget, and..." Harris-Watts appeared to be trembling. He shakily tapped out two more mints into his palm and threw them into his mouth.

Graham had his hands aloft. "I get it. But that doesn't mean it's not frustrating. Corner shops have better security." Thoroughly chastised, Harris-Watts appeared to be approaching tearfulness. Graham calmed himself and gave the curator a conciliatory look. "Alright. I suppose it can't be helped now. But make sure you speak to us later. We'll advise you on appropriate security measures for items of this value in future."

"Mr. Harris-Watts also stated that there's nothing missing from the museum," Roach reported, looking for a way to move on from the camera-related impasse.

"Not a thing, as far as I can see," the curator confirmed. "Perhaps the burglar changed his mind, or ran?"

DI Graham took a close look at Adam Harris-Watts for a moment. "Nothing whatsoever missing?"

The curator wriggled under the investigator's stern gaze. "No," he frowned awkwardly. "Why?"

Graham ignored his question. "I wonder if you'd be good enough to account for your whereabouts last night."

Harris-Watts gulped and took a step back. Roach watched him carefully. "I was... at home," Harris-Watts stammered. "You can't think..."

"Alone?" Graham asked.

"Yes," Harris-Watts said with a shrug.

"Very well. Captain J. R. D. Forsyth of the Royal Jersey Militia."

Harris-Watts stared at Graham again, none the wiser. "What about Captain Forsyth?"

"A recipient of numerous medals during the First World War, or so your display claims. Among them is the Military Medal, quite a high honor."

"Yes," the curator said. "Captain Forsyth is something of a local hero, celebrated for his bravery during the assault at—"

"It's missing."

Harris-Watts stared at him before dashing at once to the cabinet, a horrified expression on his face. "But..."

"Roach? I'll let you ask the obvious question," Graham said.

"Why carry out a risky, dangerous break-in, possibly a murder, enter a room full of valuable, portable objects," Roach wondered, "and then only steal a single medal from a large collection?"

"But these are priceless!" Harris-Watts was saying. "They're irreplaceable historical artifacts!"

Graham took Roach to one side, "Whatever happened here, whether it was a burglary or something else, it's certain that our victim died in the middle of it, and probably *because* of it, one way or another. So, what are our chief questions here, Constable?"

Roach straightened his back. "Who broke in? And, no matter what was taken, why did they take it?"

CHAPTER THIRTEEN

L ILLIAN HART SAT in a deep purple armchair in her living room, watching her most important client very carefully. She took a long drag of her unfiltered cigarette, letting the smoke escape languidly from her mouth for a moment before she sucked it back in. Charlotte Hughes had just come to the end of a long and unexpected call, and she looked worryingly pale. "Is everything okay?"

Charlotte stared at her phone for a moment, and then typed something into it. "Hmm?"

"Was that important?" Lillian reframed, more honestly this time. She meant to keep tabs on her client. As Charlotte's Parliamentary campaign manager, Lillian had a strong aversion to Charlotte acting independently. That was how campaigns got out of control or fell behind in their constant battle to remain ahead of the news cycle and the swirling, unpredictable world of social media. It was imperative that Lillian knew everything. Nothing was to be acted upon unless it was run by her first.

"That was my brother, Eric. Something's happened on Jersey.

A museum's been broken into," Charlotte explained. She didn't look at Lillian as she set aside the phone.

"So?" Lillian asked, crossing her legs. "What's that got to do with the price of beef?"

"Oh, you know, the Channel Islands. My father's estate..." Charlotte trailed off. Her brow had knotted up during the call, and she tried to massage it and herself back into a more relaxed, unruffled state.

Lillian stared at her. "What are you blathering about? Do we need to take any action?" She asked the question in a tone that bluntly conveyed her desire to take exactly none. A plain woman, Lillian attempted to lift her large features by wearing garish make-up, an effort that mostly achieved the opposite of what she intended. Nevertheless, she was respected as an experienced and fearsome campaign manager with connections deep throughout the meandering web of British politics and the wider commerce, media, and national defense interests that supported it. She was not a woman to be trifled with.

Lillian was utterly focused on one thing and one thing only: getting Charlotte Hughes elected as a Member of Parliament. She had donated eighteen hours of her day, every day, for the last three months, as well as the use of her town house that was acting as campaign headquarters. Whatever this call was about, it seemed entirely unconnected to the matter at hand. It was therefore utterly irrelevant in her mind. Lillian expected Charlotte to put whatever this issue was aside and devote her energies to this evening's town hall meeting.

"No, no. Oh, I don't know. My father's desk is on display at a museum and—" Charlotte closed her eyes and shook her head.

Lillian was incredulous. "Desk?" She rolled her eyes. She imagined some cheap, flat-pack affair assembled in half an hour amid much cursing and temper. Charlotte went on to describe the Satterthwaite Desk in great detail, but Lillian was hardly more impressed. "So, it's been stolen?" She was having a hard time following.

"Hardly," Charlotte responded dryly, stung by Lillian's dismissive tone. "It's been damaged."

Lillian sat up in her armchair. It was a measure of the dehumanizing nature of professional politics that her first thought was to wonder whether this event could in any way harm Charlotte's bid for political office. She ran through a number of scenarios in her head, but after a few moments, she relaxed. The links were much too tenuous.

"I'm going to call our family lawyer," Charlotte said. "Give me a few minutes, and then we'll talk about tonight." Charlotte turned away to place the call.

Her campaign manager looked at her in bewilderment. "Go ahead, don't mind me." To Lillian, this was an entirely unwelcome interruption and an even more unnecessary one, but clearly it had to run its course before Charlotte could be free of it. The older woman stood and left just as the call went through, heading upstairs to powder her nose.

"Carl? It's Charlotte Hughes. Have you heard about the incident on Jersey?"

Forty minutes and several phone calls later, Lillian was beginning to lose her temper. This wasn't a surprise to anyone who knew her. Even when she wasn't dedicating herself wholeheartedly to a political campaign, she was known to fly off the handle at the least provocation. Why was Charlotte so bothered about her father's vintage office furniture? This *contretemps* in Jersey was materializing into what Lillian labeled 'a thing.'

"Look, I'm not going off the deep end," Charlotte protested. "Carl Prendergast told me that Don had asked about the desk not three days ago. And now there's been a break-in at the museum where it's on display. You have to admit it's a bit of a coincidence."

"What are you suggesting? That your stepbrother, for a reason we can't even guess, broke into a museum? Because of a *desk*?"

"I don't know. I don't know! It's just—"

"Why, in the name of *all* that is *holy*," Lillian said, struggling to keep her voice even, "might Don English, of all people, do that?"

"I have no idea. Don's a strange old boy," Charlotte admitted.

"I mean, it's just a *desk*, an inanimate object! You're overreacting." Lillian flapped her hand and looked away. Anger had a tendency to sharpen her already angular features, making her look both a few years older and as though she was wearing even more makeup than usual.

Charlotte held up her tablet to show Lillian a full-screen picture of the Satterthwaite Desk in all its considerable glory.

"A very pretty desk, to be sure," Lillian conceded. "But, and I repeat, why would he *care*?" She frowned even harder and sat back in her armchair. "Hang on," she said. "Is this the same Don who had the batty mother?"

Charlotte sighed. "She died just recently."

Lillian groaned. "Your father had her committed to a loony bin!"

"She was very ill," Charlotte said pointedly. "She was a danger to herself. It was for her own good."

"Her own good. Yes. Only now we've got a potentially angry, bereaved, and possibly equally loony son with an axe to grind." Lillian swirled the ice cubes in the glass of gin she'd poured herself even though it was only eleven in the morning. She slugged back the dregs, her long, sharp, purple nails clacking against the glass.

"There's something else," Charlotte said, looking as though she hardly dare tell Lillian her next piece of news, like a child confessing she'd broken a window. "The night security guard hit his head on the desk. He died. They found his body this morning." Charlotte's eyebrows dropped over her darkened eyes.

"Oh, terrific." Lillian said, ever her combative, accusatory self. "So now, we've got a *murderous*, angry, recently bereaved stepson on the case. *Your* case, honey."

Charlotte stood and headed to the kitchen for some much needed water. Finding a glass in the cupboard, she said, "You're right, we're getting way, way ahead of ourselves. We're being neurotic. Don probably didn't have anything to do with this. We don't know whether the guard's death was murder, or an accident, or even natural causes." Lillian didn't seem to hear her. She had gone from thinking Charlotte was completely overdramatizing the situation to making her own leaps of conjecture. Her thoughts about what Charlotte was suggesting and their prospects for her campaign were alarming. "We don't even know," Charlotte said, shouting over the running faucet, "if Don was anywhere near the place. For all we know, he was tucked up in bed in some horrible little flat when it happened, in... where does he live again? Oh yes, Goslingdale." The two women shuddered in unison.

"Only he called Prendergast about the desk completely out of the blue, less than seventy-two hours ago," Lillian pointed out. They had switched roles now. "And he's been furious with your father for decades and, by extension, with you."

Coming back in the room, Charlotte sat and hooked her mousy brown hair behind her ears. She drank most of the glass of water. "No need for the extension," she said thinly. "We always hated each other. He was an annoying little blighter, and his mother... Well, I shouldn't speak ill of the dead," she said.

"Oh, don't stop now, Missy. You have to tell me *everything*," Lillian implored. "It's the only way I can protect you."

"We, Eric and I, always considered Susannah a gold-digger who tricked Dad into marrying her. He bent over backwards,"

Charlotte maintained, "to keep her happy. It wasn't his fault, or mine, that she went off the deep end. But Don seemed to think it was."

Lillian raised an eyebrow. She harbored few charitable illusions as to her client's family. Don's resentment toward the Hughes' was probably both deeply felt and legitimate. If Don was involved in this incident, this was, most definitely, going to be "a thing." "But... why the *desk*? What would he want with it?" she asked.

Charlotte finished her water. She was tapping her glass against her knee.

"Are you sure that's all this is, Charlotte?" Lillian leaned forward, her elbows on her knees. She looked her client directly in the eyes. "Some crazy half-breed relative looking to take out his righteousness on a piece of old furniture?"

The younger woman sighed. Lillian, for once, waited. "There... there were rumors."

"About what?" Lillian pounced. Charlotte looked away. "Charlotte..." Lillian remonstrated. "You need to tell me everything," she repeated.

"Rumors have swirled in my family for years that a letter exists that would shame us, possibly ruin us. We've never found any sign of it, but there was talk that Susannah was privy to the contents." Charlotte's voice was almost a squeak. "That might have been the reason my father put her in a mental institution." She looked away.

"Good grief, are you telling me that your father effectively incarcerated your stepmother for decades, smearing her name in the process, because she knew about some dodgy dealings of his?" Charlotte's head dipped minutely. Lillian stared at the wall, her foot jiggling furiously. "But I still don't see what it has to do with this blasted desk."

"After his death, Eric and I searched and searched. There was a rumor—"

"Rumors, again," Lillian spat, rolling her eyes.

Charlotte ignored her and continued in a small voice, "We thought that the desk might contain a secret compartment and the letter was in there. We looked for days. We even hired an expert. Eventually, we had to conclude that one didn't exist. Now I'm wondering if we were wrong. Maybe Susannah said something on her deathbed. Maybe she knew something I don't. And now maybe Don does."

Lillian threw her head against her chair back. "Whoa, this is bad. *Bad*." Throughout this discussion, Lillian had never stopped calculating. "Okay," she said after a moment's thought. "We need to stop this before it starts. Here's what we're going to do. We need to find Don English. We need to keep the incident out of the national press, and you're not going to comment on it to anyone."

Charlotte squinted at Lillian. "Are you sure?" she asked.

Lillian waved away Charlotte's argument. "I don't want your name anywhere near this," she said. "It's got nothing to do with you. We need to bury the story and do so immediately. What's happening with the desk?"

Charlotte glanced down at her notes. "Carl said Dad's estate will pay for the repairs. They'll cost a small fortune, but the museum will be hard-pressed to afford them otherwise. He's going to ask a local cabinetmaker to take a look at it."

"Good," Lillian said. "The sooner the better. Hopefully, it will all blow over. Keep your distance and stick to your schedule for the week. I don't want the media sniffing around."

But Charlotte already knew that was impossible. "Lilly, look. I know how important it is to keep our eyes on the prize, but you said yourself, we need to find Don."

"Let me deal with Don English," Lillian retorted.

"No, I'll go down there. I'll find out if it was him, if he was involved in this."

The campaign manager stared at her client as though Charlotte was proposing that she star in a Lady Godiva reenactment. "You'll do no such thing."

"Look," Charlotte said again.

"I'm not looking. I refuse to look."

"It'll only be for a few days," Charlotte argued.

"That's not the point! You need to stay here, canvassing, going door-to-door, holding town halls. You need to be seen doing the kinds of things that prospective Members of Parliament do to get elected. And you need to stay out of the tabloids. You do not want," Lillian impressed, "to get mixed up in a possible murder inquiry, with a mutinous stepbrother, or scandalous family revelations. Let me handle him."

"I have—" Charlotte began.

"Charlotte listen, I'm here," Lillian reiterated, "to help get you elected. And to protect you from scandal. This Jersey business has all the makings of a three-ringed circus, and you're going to back away from it with dignity and poise. You know, the kind of characteristics one associates with a professional and successful politician?"

Charlotte stood. "No."

Lillian stood too. This was *her* reputation, *her* time, *her* house. "If you go down there, I can't guarantee anything. If this incident had taken place in your constituency, I'd have you reading the eulogy at the guard's funeral. But no one *cares* about Jersey. It may as well be in the Cambodian jungle. Your place is *here*, winning votes among *these* people," she said, gesticulating wildly at the window.

But Charlotte was resolved. "Cancel tonight's town hall. Make up an excuse." She grabbed her tablet. "I'm booking a flight to Jersey."

CHAPTER FOURTEEN

THE PROUDEST MOMENT of Felipe Barrios' life had been back in 1998 when his friend and mentor erected a new sign above the door of their workshop, *Steadman & Barrios*. For the first time, Felipe saw his name alongside that of the finest craftsman he had ever known, and the two officially became partners in a successful and respected local business. Felipe had, as a newspaper profile expressed it at the time, "come an awfully long way."

The second proudest moment was being asked to carry out repairs to the Satterthwaite Desk. Newly delivered and standing on the hastily cleared floor of his workshop, the desk was as significant to a professional cabinetmaker as Michelangelo's *David* was to a sculptor or as a Mozart concerto was to a musician. It was a model of artistic perfection. Even before beginning the initial assessment, Felipe stood for nearly an hour, freshly prepared coffee in hand, simply admiring the craftsmanship, the proportions, and the original wood tone. Some men fall in love with sports cars or sailboats. Felipe was in love with antique furniture, and none was more deserving of his affection and respect than the work of Ezekiel Satterthwaite.

All that marred the moment was the necessity of the repair. There were traces of blood on the battered front right edge of its surface. These would need to be scrupulously cleaned and disinfected, in case any bacteria might take up residence in the wood and spread their corrosive influence. Then the repairs could take place. Felipe confirmed that the wood hadn't been *ruptured* as much as *compacted* by the impact of the security guard's skull. This meant, thankfully, that he wouldn't need to source appropriate wood to replace any missing fragments. It would have been a near-impossible task. Instead, carefully chosen polish would raise the compressed area, and layer after painstaking layer, he would fill the compaction and return the spoiled corner to its former glory.

Felipe's wife, Rosa, came into the room. "How is it, my dear?" They spoke in Spanish. She knew to announce herself very quietly, lest she disturb her husband during a sensitive moment. "Will it take long?"

He looked at her fondly. Although they had been married for over forty years, his wife, with whom he'd been through so much, was to him still as beautiful as when they'd first met on the beach as teenagers. "Several weeks," he estimated. "These things cannot be rushed." Indeed, patience was a chief virtue in this kind of work, especially when a mistake could prove difficult or impossible to rectify.

Ernest Steadman had taught him that every step had to be carefully planned out. Planning detailed schema was just one of the skills he had learned from his benefactor. The old man had been like a second father to the younger Felipe, and not once since Steadman's death five years before had he been absent from Felipe's nightly prayers.

"God will work through your hands, my love," Rosa said, placing her hand on Felipe's arm. He nodded and she quietly left him to work. He stood before the glorious Satterthwaite Desk, reflecting upon the events that had brought him to this moment. Were it not for the most unlikely of incidents, neither his journey to Jersey, nor any of the memorable experiences he had enjoyed on the island since, would have materialized.

Two hours later, Felipe sat by the desk and examined the damage once more. "Such a shame," he muttered. He started removing the blood from the damaged area, using a non-acidic cotton swab soaked initially only in water. It was slow, painstaking work. He reached down to steady the desk against his gentle swabbing, his fingers finding the underside of the main drawer where it met the front brace of the desk. He felt a tiny depression in the wood.

Felipe stopped and put the swab aside, kneeling and then lying down to peer under the desk. His fingertips hadn't deceived him. There was a slight undulation. When he ran his fingers over it again, it felt manmade, deliberate, not the result of natural warping over the centuries. He pressed his fingertip into the indentation, and the desk resounded with a deep, metallic *thunk*.

Felipe started and stood fretfully, watching for any move-ment, terrified that he had broken a priceless masterpiece. Part of him feared that the desk, absent now some vital structural linchpin might simply fall into pieces on his workshop floor. But the desk was silent, and Felipe carefully approached once more.

His heart beat with excitement as he examined the underside of the desk. He suspected the slight indentation was a catch that opened a lock of some kind within it. He searched using his flash-light but found nothing in the side drawers or under the main body of the desk. When he pulled out the central drawer, however, it slid right to its limit and exposed a raised area at the back.

"Ezekiel, you crafty old..." Felipe had triggered an ingenious, lightweight mechanism unlike any he had ever seen. It had revealed a compartment hardly deeper than a deck of cards and almost as wide as the drawer itself. He stood and marveled at his find. The existence of the compartment was hidden from anyone who was unaware of it. Certainly, the contents inside were not meant to be discovered casually. Felipe donned a new pair of surgical gloves.

Seconds later, he was on his knees, on the floor of his workshop. Stricken and immobile, all he was able to say, again and again, was, *"Madre de Dios...."*

CHAPTER FIFTEEN

AS SOON AS Charlotte turned her phone back on, seconds after her flight landed, it buzzed and beeped with a dozen messages. She ignored all but one. She knew without looking that most of them would be from Lillian, either begging her to return, or demanding an update. The only voicemail to which she listened was from Carl Prendergast.

"Charlotte, hi. Fantastic. I hope the two of you can let bygones be bygones. Here's Don English's number..." Perfect. Prendergast's never was the most incisive of legal minds.

Charlotte had only a cabin bag and was soon in a taxi on her way to a hotel in St. Helier. Her first order of business was to find out if Don really was on Jersey and figure out just what on earth was going on.

She dialed Don's number.

"Don English."

Don sounded as though she'd woken him up, and she wondered at once if he was suffering from another hangover. He always had drunk to excess.

"Don! It's Charlotte Hughes."

"Charlotte?" Don struggled to sit up in bed. Overnight the feathers in his pillow had migrated to opposite ends of the pillow-case, neither of which were now under his head. His camberwick bedspread lay on the floor.

"Charlotte," he repeated. Her features came to mind. She had a thin face with a pointed chin. Years ago, she'd had a long aquiline nose. Surgery had softened that feature, but Don still recalled the Wicked Witch of the West when he thought of her. At least she wasn't green.

"What are you doing calling me?" he asked.

"Carl gave me your number. I hope you don't mind. He told me about your Mother, Don. I'm so sorry. How are you doing?"

"I'm okay," he said warily. He rubbed sleep from his eyes and ran a hand over his rough chin. "How can I help you, Charlotte?" Don was immediately suspicious of this bolt from the blue. Charlotte and he hadn't spoken in years. He was quite sure she didn't give a hoot about his mother.

"I'm on Jersey—"

"You're on Jersey, too?" he said. Don was so surprised, the words slipped out before they'd registered in his brain.

"Why, yes. Are you? That's wonderful! Let's meet. It will be good to see you after all these years."

Don knew patently that this was a lie. The fog of sleep was lifting quickly now. Charlotte no more wanted to see him than he wanted to see her.

"Er, but what are you down here for?"

"There's been a incident at the museum involving the Satterthwaite Desk. Do you remember? Dad's desk. I'm here to arrange for the repairs and show my face. Do the necessaries." Charlotte sounded positively chipper. "I know we haven't always been the best of friends but," she remembered Carl Prendergast's words, "can't we let bygones be bygones?"

She paused. When there was no response from Don, she

pressed on. "Let's just talk. Meet me at the lookout point at Orgueil Castle. Would three o'clock work for you?"

There was a very long silence as Don seemed to weigh up the dangers of meeting his estranged, unpleasant, and potentially very powerful stepsister. "Alright. Three o'clock," he replied.

"Great. See you then. Byeee."

The meeting with Don arranged, Charlotte turned her attention to her other business in Gorey. Hopping once more into a cab, she called and arranged to meet Adam Harris-Watts at the museum. Charlotte kept the meeting deliberately brief.

"I want to confirm that the Hughes estate will fund the repairs to the desk," she told the still-shaken curator. This was no small sum.

"That's so terribly kind of you. The museum would have been hard pressed—" Adam Harris-Watts spoke deferentially. An insurance claim for the full amount would have brought an unsustainable spike in the small museum's monthly premiums.

"Is there anything else?"

"Well, Nobby's – Mr. Norris' family – have set up a foundation in his name. It will provide soccer coaching for talented local youngsters. Nobby, Mr. Norris, was a big soccer fan. Perhaps...?"

'Yes, of course." Charlotte pulled out her checkbook.

"You know," Harris-Watts said as he showed Charlotte out, back through the museum's grand entrance, "things like this aren't supposed to happen in museums. Only in *The Da Vinci Code* or something like that. Did you know your father visited the museum once? And I was the one who suggested to him that... Well, that our museum would be an appropriate display space for the desk. If I hadn't been so insistent, none of this would ever have..." Harris-Watts hung his head.

Charlotte took his arm and gave him her most sympathetic

look. "Mr. Harris-Watts, Adam, this isn't your fault. It's just terribly unfortunate. We've always been tremendously happy to know that the desk is situated here, in a place representative of its history. You've done a fine job with it." The curator nodded his appreciation although he didn't take his eyes off the floor.

Charlotte continued, "I wonder, did you ever find anything in the desk? I heard Satterthwaite was famous for installing secret drawers. It was a childhood game of ours to look for one, but we were never successful." She was fishing. Sir Thomas would no more allow his children to play with his desk than he would sit them on his knee to read them a book.

"You're right about Satterthwaite." Adam Harris-Watts was on surer ground now. He spoke confidently. "But we think he only designed a piece with a compartment for every ten or so he made. At least that we know of. He never let on whether one of his designs contained a hidden drawer or not. It was his little joke. And he only made three desks in his entire career. That's why this one is so valuable. I don't believe either of the others has a compartment. Not one that's been discovered, anyway. Certainly, I examined your father's desk many times but never found one."

"Hmm. So what do the police think about it all?"

Harris-Watts popped a tiny mint into his mouth, orange this time. "They're as baffled as we are but they're working on it," he said as he ground his jaws. "They seem to think it might have been just a plain old break-in. Nothing to do with the desk. They're not even sure if Nobby's death was connected at all. Either way, it's terrible."

"Yes, quite," Charlotte tilted her head sympathetically. "Do they have any idea who it might have been? Nothing on camera?" She looked up at the small grey device mounted discreetly above the entrance to the museum.

The curator shook his head. "Our old camera system is so awful that there are only a couple of blurry frames. The police did say that it must have been a heavyset man who broke in, though."

It was hardly a description that narrowed down the field, but it also fit one person in particular. "Well, I'm sure we both wish them success in their investigations. There's really no need to hold yourself responsible," she told him again. "You're no more to blame than Satterthwaite himself or my father for that matter. What's going to happen now?"

"The desk went for repair as soon as your father's estate so graciously offered to cover the costs. The speed with which the repairs are effected can make a big difference to their success in these cases." Harris-Watts smiled at Charlotte obsequiously. "Fortunately we have the ideal person on the island. Felipe Barrios. Your father's desk is in expert hands. Barrios has been a fine furniture maker for nearly forty years. He will know exactly what to do."

Charlotte gave the downcast curator an awkward hug. She was relieved to leave the company of this fragile, fawning man. Once she'd shrugged him off, she set off with purpose to the Castle for what was her main business of the day.

"Marcus?" Graham said, clicking the button on his desk phone, "What's new?"

"I'm calling about Mr. Norris, the guard at the museum. I've got a cause of death for you."

Graham took a deep, deliberate breath. "Let me have it, Marcus."

"Massive heart attack. Clear as day. Untreated, he wouldn't have been long for this world, even without the shock of the situation he was in."

After blinking several times, Graham began re-visualizing the scene. "Could he have been saved?"

"Anything is possible, but it's doubtful. His arteries were shocking."

"So he just keeled over? The intruder didn't push him or hit him with anything?"

"No signs of struggle, no DNA. Nothing to connect him with an attacker at all," Marcus replied. "For all we know, he could have died before the burglary took place."

"So it might be just a big coincidence?"

"Except I didn't think you believed in coincidences," the pathologist said.

Graham chewed his lip. "Thanks, Marcus. We'll add it to the mix."

"Sorry I can't be of more help."

Graham sighed and put his phone down. He looked at the CCTV footage in front of him. Roach was right. It was practically useless. He'd spent the last thirty minutes scouring the two frames that contained the security guard's last recorded moments. His eyes bored into the images in front of him, willing some clue to make itself apparent.

"Tea, guv?" Janice poked her head around the door. She didn't like to make him tea. It was a bit like offering cheap plonk to a sommelier. She doubted her tea would stand up to his scrutiny, but she didn't feel she could leave him out if she was boiling the kettle.

"Hmm? Oh, no thanks." Graham sat back and blew out his cheeks. "Here, come and take a look at these. Can you see anything useful in them?"

Janice walked over to stand behind him. She leaned over his shoulder, looking intently at the screen in front as Graham flicked back and forth between the two frames.

"There... And there," Janice said.

"What? What is it you're seeing—?" Graham peered at the screen, his chin jutting out as he concentrated.

Janice pointed at the first frame. "That shadow there. You

can just see it, v-e-r-y faintly. Nobby turns toward it. And look, his hand holding the flashlight is raised just a smidge... There was definitely someone there, sir. And Nobby was alive when they were."

Graham squinted, seeing the scene in front of him anew. Now that Janice had pointed it out, he could see what was perfectly obvious. He turned his head slowly to look at his sergeant, who was grinning cheerfully. "Thank you, Harding. You've been very helpful," he said slowly.

"My pleasure, sir. Sure you don't want any tea?"

CHAPTER SIXTEEN

ON WAS SITTING in a small coffee shop finishing his second cup while reading through yet another webpage on his laptop. The call from Charlotte had come as a harsh, unwelcome surprise, but the longer he dwelled on it, the thought of meeting her became less worrying. This would be a strange and probably quite difficult reunion, but it might prove useful if he played his cards right.

Don rubbed his eyes. He'd been doing more research into his "project," as he'd begun to call it. His latest efforts were starting to bear fruit, and his three piles of documents had grown considerably. Using his ancient laptop and the coffee shop's frustratingly slow Internet connection, he had pieced together what he knew and had begun searching for relevant terms.

Don had concluded that there was only one convincing answer as to the identity of Sir Thomas' friend – the man with whom he was pictured in the photo his mother had mentioned but whose friendship he had kept secret. Based on the clues his mother had given him, Don had come to believe that the man was none other than the president of San Marcos, the despised and reviled General Augusto Fuente.

Almost the definition of a "savage dictator," Fuente had been a young and ambitious army officer when he and his cohort of disaffected right-wing militarists overthrew the democratic government in the early 1970s. The results were terrible but predictable. The new *junta* took control of the media, employed heavy-handed secret police tactics, and were responsible for a depressing litany of "disappearances." Some fifteen percent of the population fled, among them anyone with money or an education. All of this left Fuente subject to sanctions and isolated by the UN. In response, Fuente courted black marketers, smugglers, and those with flexible morals. It was just possible, Don thought, that Sir Thomas Hughes had been among the General's new friends.

The idea made Don laugh at first. It sounded like something out of a spy novel. But he double-checked, and it was the only theory that fit all of the available facts. Fuente was an international pariah, and nobody in their right mind would have boasted of their close friendship with him. However, the General was also rich, something of a playboy, and certainly the kind of man to court wealthy foreign guests by inviting them onboard his yacht. The *Gypsy Princess*, Don was amazed to find, was still owned by the "First Family" of San Marcos. It had even been recently photographed in an exclusive marina, only a stone's throw from the presidential palace.

As Don thought this through, he became convinced his theory was correct. He reasoned that, though he could not guess what it might reveal, the content of the letter he was searching for could be a huge embarrassment to his stepsister should it become known. As the time of their meeting approached, Don began to imagine what the letter might say. Perhaps it would reveal humiliating secrets or past indiscretions. Worse still – or *better* still, depending on one's point of view – it might even reveal past crimes. Any of these would be enough to derail Charlotte's bid to become a Member of Parliament.

Don sighed. While she had never bullied him or his mother outright, neither had Charlotte ever stuck up for them against her father who had. The father-daughter bond had been fast. At times, he'd come upon them whispering together, stopping abruptly when he came in the room. He'd always suspected they were plotting against him. Or his mother.

Don found his rain jacket and prepared to set off toward the castle, wondering what the outcome of this rather clandestine meeting might be. Charlotte was now a public figure. Reputation was everything to her. But his, and certainly his mother's honor needed defending.

He looked at his watch. It was 2:50 PM. He was going to be late. He quickly shuffled his papers together, shoved his laptop in his bag, and hurried to the door. He pulled it open and rushed through it, immediately slamming hard into the solid wall of uniform that stood on the other side. Don's papers flew like confetti into the air.

"Careful there, mate," Barnwell said. It was time for his regular afternoon croissant, and he was very much looking forward to it.

"Sorry, sorry," Don said, frantically dropping to the floor to pick up the splayed papers.

"Here, let me help you, sir," Barnwell offered.

"No need, no need," Don replied, shoving the papers haphazardly into the buff folder he was carrying.

"Okay, then," Barnwell said, standing up and squinting curiously at the harried man. He watched bemused as Don scurried up the street to his car. "It's amazing the effect I have on people," he murmured. He looked down at his feet and noticed under one of the outdoor tables, between the legs of two chairs, was propped a loose sheet of paper. Barnwell bent down and picked it from the floor. He cast a glance at the sheet in front of him.

"One decaf almond milk latte and a chocolate croissant!" yelled the woman behind the café counter so loudly that she could be heard through the café's glass door. She held a lidded cup and paper bag aloft.

Barnwell opened the door, rolling the paper up and sticking it in his back pocket. "Ah, thanks Ethel. You're a love. Just what I need."

CHAPTER SEVENTEEN

S IR THOMAS HAD been a National Trust member for fifty years, and Charlotte had run around the gardens and ballrooms of more stately homes and elegant, preserved townhouses than she could count. But this imposing medieval fortress was in a different class entirely. It was a manmade *mountain*, solid and huge and resolutely immobile, commanding the coastline as if defying anyone to trespass on its shores. As she paid her entrance fee and walked through the inner courtyards, Charlotte noted that its massive blocks of worn stone could have been hewed and placed there by giants. It was a place of fairy stories, of roaring ogres and witches on broomsticks, intrigue captured in every crevice.

And yet, standing on its slightly windy battlements up top, dressed in a shabby raincoat and faded jeans, an old, crumpled backpack hanging off his shoulder, was Don English.

"Bracing, isn't it?" she said as she emerged onto the broad walkway that encircled the castle.

He turned to see her approach, his face curiously impassive.

"Looks like we've got the same taste in springtime holiday desti-nations," he said flatly.

As Charlotte had hoped, the battlements were quiet. They'd be able to talk without being disturbed. "It's been a while, Don. How are you?"

He stared out over the sea, which was a shifting, blue-white carpet on this March afternoon. "Mum's gone," he said simply.

"I'm so sorry, Don."

"That's what people say, isn't it?" Don remarked. "They *say* they're sorry."

Charlotte could see the weight of the emotional burden Don carried. It was there in his posture, in the way he dressed, in the tone of his voice. The sadness. The resentment. She searched for an appropriate response. "I hope there wasn't suffering."

Don chuckled humorlessly before drawing a breath, the air hissing between his crooked, yellow teeth, "You know *damn well* that she suffered. Too much, and for too many years." Don turned to look at her.

Charlotte put a hand, very carefully, on the upper arm of Don's jacket. "They're gone. My father, your mother. Now it's just us. Let's at least try to be friends for a little while."

Don gathered himself and wiped his face on the sleeve of his jacket. "Yeah... So, how's the *campaign* going?"

Charlotte blinked for a moment. "It's going well, I suppose. Still two months to go, but my campaign manager thinks we're on the right track."

"You know," Don said, glancing at his feet, "I saw a billboard with your face on it yesterday. Made me wonder what it would look like on TV, in Parliament's chambers."

Charlotte smiled, though she doubted this was the warm endorsement it seemed to be. "I hope we'll find out soon."

"It's a safe seat," Don pointed out. "A great way to get your-self shoehorned into the House of Commons."

Charlotte was as aware of her background as anyone. The

daughter of a rich businessman, carefully selected by the party for her connections as well as her acumen, she would be open to allegations of cronyism and dodgy dealing, almost from the outset. "There's always someone," she told him, rather frostily, "who won't like what I do. But I want to serve the people of my constituency."

Don produced a wry grin. "I hardly think so," he finally managed. "I know you too well. And I know the family you come from."

Charlotte sighed and pushed hair out of her eyes. "Why are you here, Don? On Jersey?"

He regarded her coolly for a second. "I'm taking a break," he said. "Getting away from it all."

"Really? Right when the museum is broken into and Dad's desk is damaged? Something of a coincidence isn't it?" Charlotte waited for his reaction to this verbal grenade.

Don remained silent, his jaw bunching rhythmically.

Charlotte came closer, their shoulders almost touching as they looked out to sea. She angled her face so he had to look at her. She looked deep into his eyes and spoke slowly. "Did you have anything to do with that, Don? The break-in?" she asked.

"Of course not." Don closed his eyes, his shoulders tense, his fists clenched. He pulsed with a burst of fury. "You've misjudged me, my whole life. My *whole* life." he said, his tone laced with accusation.

"Alright, Don, alright," Charlotte said, backing off. She didn't know him as a violent man, but he was strong and powerful, and clearly harbored a grudge. "You're upset. Don, look," she said, moving forward again and placing her hand gently, tentatively, on his forearm, "you'll feel better if you tell *someone* what happened. Why don't you tell me?"

Don turned away again, flexing his arm to dislodge her hand. "What are you talking about?"

"On Sunday night. Tell me. I don't want to believe you could hurt anyone, Don. Certainly not over something like this."

Now he turned to her, blinking, confused. "*Hurt* anyone?"

"The guard. The one who died," she said quietly, careful not to sound accusatory. "It was an accident, wasn't it?"

Don's mouth fell open. "*Died?*" he stuttered. "What?"

"What did you want with the desk, Don?" Charlotte persisted. "Why were you there?"

Don's hands were fixed, vice-like, on the stone wall of the fortress, as if he feared a strong gust of wind might blow him from the battlements and into the Channel.

"I don't know what you're talking about," he repeated. "I didn't hurt anyone. Do you really think I'd risk a criminal record, my life, all over your vile father's lump of old wood?

"Then why are you here? On Jersey?"

"It was something my mother said," he managed to utter through gritted teeth. "The day she died."

"What did your mother say about it?"

"She said your father was always sitting there. At the desk, working. I just wanted to see it for myself. Yes, I went to the museum to see it, but in *daylight*. I never laid a finger on any guard."

"So that's all this is, Don? A trip? A quest to satisfy your curiosity over something you've never professed to be interested in before and one I can't fathom why you'd be interested in now?"

She turned to leave, but Don caught her arm. "Off back to that quaint, oh-so twee constituency of yours? Market Ellestry isn't it?" he said sweetly, drawing breath. "More campaigning to do?"

Charlotte shrugged. "Actually, I thought I'd stay around here for a couple of days," she said, lifting her chin and looking down her nose at him. Then her tone changed and her face became a dark scowl. "Enjoy your little *break*."

Charlotte wrestled her arm from Don's grip and stalked back

to the doorway, the steps down to street level unfurling behind it. She left Don alone with the wind, the bright, sparkling ocean, and his own gnawing worries. It was time to take a different tack.

CHAPTER EIGHTEEN

G RAHAM BEGAN A third page of notes, flipping through another volume on eighteenth-century furniture until he found the section he needed. Amid the peace and quiet of a space intended only for learning and research, he was dedicating an hour to understanding the *context* of the object in this case. It made a pleasant change from interviewing low-rent criminals and calming upset and irate members of the public. His general knowledge was broad. He could usually answer eight out of ten questions on *Mastermind,* even the specialist rounds, and on more than one occasion, he had found himself banned from Jersey pub quizzes after inordinate solo successes. Nevertheless, he was ignorant on the work of Ezekiel Satterthwaite.

The records showed that the desk by which Nobby had been found was one of only three Satterthwaite ever made. The others resided in the private study of Emperor Akihito of Japan and in the opulent Sultan's Palace in Brunei. At auction, a Satterthwaite Desk would, according to one estimate, fetch at least $1 million and perhaps much more.

Graham tutted when he read this. Displaying an asset worth that much without investing in comprehensive security measures or even informing the local police of its value was negligent bordering on the criminal. No wonder Adam Harris-Watts was such a wreck.

"Are you finding everything you need?"

Graham set aside his reading glasses and saw that Laura had returned to his table for the fourth time, seemingly to check on his progress.

"Do you have anything on Captain J. R. D. Forsyth of the Royal Jersey Militia?"

"Let me look," Laura replied.

Graham watched Laura walk away to consult the library's computer. She returned a few minutes later carrying five books, all with bubblegum pink sticky notes poking from between the pages like garish tongues.

"Excellent, thank you," Graham said. "I'm almost finished, in fact. Once again, I must congratulate the library on its collection. For a place so small," he said, glancing around, "it really is well stocked."

Laura beamed at him. "I'm glad," she said. "Do let me know if there's anything else I can do."

"Actually," Graham said as Laura began to turn to head back to the distribution desk, "there is." He had spoken without much thought and now felt committed. A wave of anxiety froze him for a second, but then he saw her smile once more and the words somehow came out. "I wonder if you'd like to have coffee with me sometime." His chest thumped. "If you're free, of course."

Laura's face showed many emotions in a busy split-second. There was surprise, as though this were the last thing she'd expected. She was flattered, he could tell, but there was something else; a kind of worry that seemed out of place. Graham expected that she would have thought such an invitation possible or even likely, but his request left her silent for so long that he began to chastise himself. She was new to Gorey, and he didn't know what kind of romantic situation she might already be involved in.

"Yes," she said finally, and laughed. "Sorry, it's been a while since anyone invited me out. I'd love to."

"Well, splendid," Graham said, finding his words far too formal as soon as he'd said them. "Great," he tried instead. "Let's set a time up tonight."

"I'll be working, but you can always text me."

Laura glanced around for a moment, as if afraid of being seen giving her number to a library patron – a handsome, single one, at that. She quickly jotted it down and delivered one more sunny smile before returning to her work.

Graham quietly finished his research and returned the hard-back books to the correct shelf. He strode out into the afternoon sunshine, feeling as good as he had in a long while. He considered his next step. He'd consult his junior colleagues back at the station. Perhaps one of them might teach him how to send a text.

Lillian paced angrily around the front room of her spacious town house, listening to the repeated tones of Charlotte's phone. There would be the requisite six rings, and then the all-too-familiar invitation to leave a voicemail. She almost screamed at the sound of Charlotte's recorded voice, promising that the call would be answered, "Just as soon as I am able." Deciding against leaving her fourth message of the day, Lillian considered violently pummeling one of the violet pillows that adorned her couch. Instead, she lit a cigarette and headed for the back bedroom where she found it therapeutic to yell at the two young volunteers she had drafted into working for Charlotte's campaign. They had already found that negotiating or debating with Lillian – or worse still, trying to placate her or calm her down – was utterly futile and likely only to result in further outbursts of incandescent rage. They constantly kept an ear open for her footsteps on the stairs in order to brace themselves for an onslaught while feverishly discussing walking out on the job and whether or not they were brave enough to do it.

Back downstairs, Lillian called Charlotte again. "How in the name of Margaret Thatcher am I supposed to *help* you," she growled as the phone rang yet again, "if you won't even *speak* to me?"

Then the miraculous happened. "Lillian?" Charlotte said. "Sorry about that. Busy day. How are you?"

Rather uncharacteristically, the sheer relief of getting hold of her client after hours of radio silence prompted Lillian to take two deep breaths before answering. Her tone was measured and reasonable, which was a long way from how she truly felt. "I do hope," she said through gritted teeth, "that you'll be good enough to pick up the phone when the Prime Minister calls on election night to congratulate you."

Charlotte remained silent. She had anticipated a few moments of acidic fury from her campaign manager.

"I demand that you come back to Market Ellestry right away. Your constituents need you. There's a lot to catch up on. Come home now, and I will deal with Don English. Then we can forget this little jaunt ever happened."

There were five seconds of resulting silence that did nothing to lower Lillian's sky-high blood pressure. "I need a couple more days," Charlotte finally said, "I'm in the middle of something very important."

"Oh, good!" Lillian replied with feigned brightness. "I'm *so* glad it's important. Something about a *desk*, wasn't it? Doing a little *antiquing*, are we? Attending the odd *roadshow*?"

Charlotte ignored Lillian's sarcasm and got to the point. "Lilly, I need you to do something for me..."

When the call ended, Lillian sat on her couch for a while,

feeling the anger coursing through her. Only after a couple minutes did she look down and notice that her unconscious squeezing of the cellphone in her hand had left a sharp indentation in her palm. She stood. She had things to do, but she would do them in a moment. First, she returned upstairs to do the only thing that might help her mood: vent some more of her ceaseless fury upon the utterly petrified, blameless volunteers.

CHAPTER NINETEEN

F ELIPE SAT DOWN slowly. He took off his glasses and
poured himself another cup of thick, strong coffee from
his battered, metal flask. He rubbed his eyes and blinked
a few times, noting again just how tiring this close, exacting work
could be. He had found sleep nearly impossible the night before.
Instead of disturbing Rosa with his tossing and turning, he had
headed down to his workshop to continue examining the
Satterthwaite Desk and plan the layers of varnish which would
salve its unfortunate injuries.

The damage could have been worse. The wood was slightly
bent but not chipped away, and there were no signs of structural
faults to the desk itself. Such a heavy impact could have knocked
the desk's delicate features out of alignment or cracked one of the
internal braces which buttressed the piece. Happily, such severe
damage had been avoided.

Felipe was deeply disturbed by what he had found the day
before. Whenever he stood and took a moment's respite from his
work, he found his thoughts bothering him. A repair that should

have been the pleasure of a lifetime had now become a taxing, debilitating ordeal.

Still, he was making progress. The security guard's blood was all gone from the wood, and the area had been carefully but comprehensively disinfected. On arriving at his workshop just after four o'clock this morning, Felipe had once again checked the workshop's temperature and humidity. They had held steady overnight, and the initial layer of varnish had dried perfectly, just as he had hoped. The second layer was drying now, and he was already preparing the third, a darker tone of polish mixed from three sources. He would need only a tiny amount, but every layer was important. If the underlying work wasn't perfect, the newly varnished corner would reflect light incorrectly and have a different feel under his fingertips.

As he drank his coffee, Felipe's mind wandered yet again. His were painful memories. Eventually, he shrugged them off. There was work to do, and this desk demanded his very best. He knelt by the damaged corner once more and applied a third layer of varnish with the care and attentiveness of a heart surgeon. During those moments, nothing in the world existed but the damaged surface and his brush. He watched every hair, every movement, every millimeter of the application. After fifteen minutes, he stood slowly, rubbing his aching knees, and found himself reminded again of the strange discovery this fine desk had brought.

While the layer dried, he made more coffee and searched on his cellphone for information on the desk's former owner. He learned that Sir Thomas Hughes was a hero to some and a villain to many. One photo of him working at the Satterthwaite Desk survived. Hughes' hair awry, his back to the camera, he was working amid piles of papers strewn all over, while a black spaniel, seated by the chair, looked up imploringly at his frantically busy master. In that single snapshot, Hughes seemed to be a man possessed.

"Was it guilt?" Felipe asked the photograph, in the silence of his workshop. "Is *that* what was driving you?" He pictured Hughes trying desperately to atone for a life of compromises and selfishness, an existence motivated far too much by greed and not nearly enough by compassion. He pulled a piece of paper from his pocket, and as he read what he had found once again, he reminded himself just how complex a man Sir Thomas must have been.

The fourth coat of varnish went on smoothly, raising the damaged layer a little further. Once it dried, it would offer a solid base for the next coat as he built up the marred section of wood. Absentmindedly, Felipe reached for his flask. He needed more coffee. Finding the container empty, he turned toward the tiny kitchenette he'd built in the corner of the workshop and set the flask in the sink before reaching into the cupboard for a bag of coffee beans. He heard a rip as a seam in his workman's jacket came undone.

Rosa knocked on the workshop door.

"*Si, mi amor?*" he said, as he always did.

"Are you busy, Felipe?" she replied through the door.

"Just stitching my jacket, my love."

"There's a phone call for you. It's about the desk, but they would not say more," she told him.

Felipe frowned and opened the door, itself a product of his fine craftsmanship. "The desk?" he asked and took the cordless landline from his wife. She shrugged. She had known Felipe for enough years to know when a project was weighing heavily on him, and she knew this desk was providing a unique challenge even for a man as skilled as he. Felipe smiled at her fondly and closed the door.

"Hello?"

"Mr. Barrios, I'm grateful for a moment of your time." It was a strange voice, slightly metallic and false, with no sense of gender at all. "I understand that you're repairing the Satterthwaite Desk."

"That's correct," Felipe responded guardedly. "Who is speaking, please?"

"I'm an antique collector and a big Satterthwaite fan. Could I possibly arrange a visit so that I could see the desk for a few moments? It would be a huge privilege. Would this afternoon be convenient?"

Felipe's frown deepened. "Ah, no. I'm afraid not. Visitors are not allowed in the workshop. And this is a sensitive matter, I'm sure you understand," he said.

"Quite so," the voice said. Felipe thought it most odd that it contained neither male nor female markers. It was more like speaking with a machine. It was chilling, and it did not dispose him well to this unexpected caller, who hadn't properly introduced themselves. "I wonder, how are the repairs progressing?" the caller asked.

There seemed no harm in answering honestly. "Quite well. The damage was not as severe as it might have been. But, I must ask again, who is this speaking?"

"That's good news. Very good," the voice said. "Did you find anything unusual?"

"What do you mean?"

"Something inside the desk?" the voice asked.

There were perhaps ten seconds of silence. "No. Nothing," Felipe finally said.

"I understand," the voice intoned. "It is not something that is easy to discuss on the phone. Perhaps we could meet this afternoon? Outside your workshop, if you prefer."

Felipe found his courage once more. "I'm afraid that's impossible. I am fully committed to repairing the desk, and I don't know you at all. You have not told me who you are."

"I believe," the voice said, its tone changing slightly, "that you'll find meeting with me worth your while."

"No," Felipe reiterated. "I'm sorry. I'm not able to help you."

"Come now, Mr. Barrios. I have an offer to make you. Shall we say," the voice proposed, "thirty thousand pounds for the letter?"

Felipe's eyes widened. "There is no letter," he said steadily. "I don't know who you are, but there's been a misunderstanding."

"Ah," the voice said. "Well, just so there's no misunderstanding, shall we call it forty thousand?"

Madre de Dios... "There is," Felipe repeated, "no letter."

There was a metallic sigh. "Very well, but please take time to reconsider. It would be in your best interest. I will be in touch. In the meantime, good luck with your repairs." *Click.*

Felipe dropped the phone from his ear and carefully placed it on the workbench. He leaned against the side, the heels of his hands taking his weight. He bent his head as he took in the implications of the call. At length, he returned to polishing the desk, using the focus required to block out his anxieties, but not before re-checking that all his windows were bolted and the door firmly locked.

Felipe worked late again, and by two o'clock in the morning, the fifth layer of polish was drying. A cat mewled loudly outside, and he heard a scratching, scrabbling sound from the back of the workshop. "No mice for you tonight, Leo?" he said.

He paused for a second, trying to calculate just how much coffee he had drunk during this long, complicated day. "Too much," he muttered, but he knew that he had to work. His painstaking restoration of the desk was the only way to occupy his troubled mind.

There was a creak behind him. He started to turn, but too

late he felt a tremendous *thump* on the back of his head. His forehead crashed into the counter, and his knees collapsed beneath him. The weight of his lower body forced his head back, and as gravity exerted its force, his chin again hit the countertop. The floor came up to meet him and there he lay prone, helpless, a small trickle of blood zig-zagging from the corner of his mouth down to the tile of the workshop floor.

CHAPTER TWENTY

JIM ROACH SHIFTED in his swivel chair behind the reception desk so that he could place his aching ankle on the lowest shelf to his left. The ice packs were helping, but he couldn't remember taking a more ferocious whack to the shin than the "defensive tackle" he had endured a few nights before.

"Still in the wars, Jim?" Sergeant Harding asked as she came out from her small office.

"Didn't even get a foul out of it," Roach complained. "If the referee could have seen a replay, he'd have given the guy a yellow card. No doubt about it." The bruising had peaked in the form of an angry, dark purple oval.

Janice sipped her coffee. "Anything interesting happen last night?" she asked.

"Mrs. Hollingsworth, over by the library, called to report a 'suspicious character' again, but I'm not certain she's not seeing things. She is ninety, after all."

"What kind of character?" Janice said.

"She doesn't say exactly. But I can't not go out, can I? Not after the break-in at the museum. She's called two nights last week and three this. I drive out there, only to find the place deserted, and no signs of anyone, suspicious or otherwise. All I see is the new librarian closing up for the night."

Janice shrugged. "Perhaps that's it. She got confused. Old age always comes at a bad time." It wasn't unlike some of Gorey's older residents to become concerned by people they didn't recognize.

"I'm thinking of getting Barnwell to stake out the area and deal with it once and for all."

"You'll really put the wind up her if you do that," She leaned over his shoulder. "So, what's on the menu this morning?"

"I'm going to re-read the pathology report on the night watchman at the museum," Roach said. It was frustrating them all that the evidence relating to the break-in and Nobby Norris' death pointed nowhere in particular.

"The DI's giving you some more forensics practice, is he?"

"I guess," Roach demurred. In truth, he had come close to begging Graham to let him read and digest the report.

"So, what do we finally know about poor old Nobby?"

Roach finished a note he was making on a legal pad. "He had a heart condition, though it seems undiagnosed and untreated," Roach told her. "Tomlinson found signs of hardened arteries, and the levels of ATP in his blood indicated that he was under tremendous stress when he died. But here's the thing, we can't say how or even if anyone else was involved in his death. Nobby could have just happened to keel over on the same night the museum was burgled. A coincidence."

Janice examined the file briefly. "I thought the DI was training us not to believe in coincidences? And we did see someone on the CCTV," she reminded him.

"Yeah, you're right. But we don't even have a suspect. We're nowhere in this case."

"Are there signs of a struggle?" Janice asked.

"There's no bruising to indicate defensive wounds or that Nobby might have hit anyone," Roach said. "Just the one injury to his left temple, where he hit the desk. But that wasn't enough to kill him. It was the heart attack that did for him."

Janice sat on one of the plastic chairs opposite the reception desk. "Alright, let's think about it. Say that we're burgling the museum, and we know there's a guard. What do we do about him?"

Roach closed the file. "Surprise him, tie him up, and gag him."

"Incapacitate him, in other words," Janice said.

"Right. Then burgle the museum's treasures to our hearts' content."

"But say for a moment that Nobby wasn't in the mood to be tied up, and he fought back."

"But there's no evidence. We can't prove that," Roach warned.

"Hmm. Are we sure there was only one intruder?" Janice asked.

Roach was in the middle of answering, "We're really not sure of anything," when the red phone rang. "Oh, hell." He lifted the receiver and grabbed his pen. "Gorey Police." He wrote quickly and flashed Janice a worried look before mouthing, "Get the boss."

DI Graham swore. That reputation he'd been gaining for engineering a big drop in the local crime rate had just been shot to pieces. "I'm not far from the crime scene now. Meet me there, would you? Have Roach hold the fort."

"I should say, sir," Janice told him, "that Constable Roach is very keen to attend."

The DI's reply was delayed by some labored breathing.

Harding asked, "Are you *running* to the crime scene, sir?"

"Yes, if you must know," Graham panted. "And I wish the call had come in a little more than a few minutes after I'd finished one of Mrs. Taylor's quite magnificent breakfasts."

Janice pictured the Detective Inspector dodging morning shoppers on Gorey's high street, having already pelted down the hill from the White House Inn. "I'll be at the victim's workshop in a few minutes, sir. See you there," she said.

"Roger and out." Graham cursed the weight of the bacon, eggs, and black pudding he had consumed not fifteen minutes earlier and pressed on until he saw the sign for Steadman & Barrios. "Of all the places," he muttered, "for a violent incident. Not a pub, or a nightclub, but the workshop of a high-class furniture maker." He puffed and made a mental note to think again about buying a car. Laura hadn't hesitated in that regard, he'd noticed.

When he reached the workshop, Sergeant Harding had already arrived in the marked police vehicle. Graham caught his breath and waved the sergeant inside.

"The ambulance left a few minutes ago, sir," Harding told him.

"Good. Where's the wife?" he asked.

"In the ambulance with Mr. Barrios. I spoke with the dispatcher again and... well, it doesn't sound good, sir."

"Damn," Graham said. "What the *hell* is going on? Send Barnwell over to the hospital to get a witness statement from Mrs. Barrios." The workshop door was open. Graham noted its elegant finish and precise fit as he entered the large, open-plan room.

"The desk, again," he said.

"Here for repairs, sir," Janice pointed out. "Mr. Barrios' wife told the ambulance crew that he was working on it last night. But he never came up to bed. She found him this morning."

The rest of what happened was obvious by the large, darkened pool of blood on the workshop's stone floor. "Head wound?" Graham guessed.

"Yes, sir." Janice was on hold with the emergency dispatcher, who was relaying the initial reports from the ambulance crew. She listened for a moment and frowned. "They suspect a fractured skull. Blunt force trauma. He's gone into cardiac arrest twice already. I have to say they don't sound hopeful."

"Which ambulance crew is it?" Graham asked.

"Same crew as attended the museum."

"Let me speak to them. Can I be patched through?" Janice spoke to the dispatcher and handed Graham the phone. "Alan? What can you tell me?"

"The patient took a severe blow to the back of the head," the paramedic said. Graham heard no siren in the background. Experienced medics knew that it scared their patients, and it was usually only used in heavy traffic. "Seems to have been hit with a large metal or wooden object. He's got a severe skull fracture. Sue thinks he's likely to have intra-cerebral bleeding. He was unconscious for an extended period before being found. At least a couple of hours was Sue's guess. His heart's stopped twice in the ambulance, but we got him back both times. Still, it's touch and go."

Graham ended the call and then walked around the broad, dried circle of blood to examine the desk. "*You* again," he said. "What *is* it about you?"

"Sir?" Janice asked, feeling lost.

"Nobby hit his head," Graham explained, indicating the damaged corner, "right here, and while it wasn't the end of him, it played its part. Now we have Felipe Barrios working on the same desk, and now *he's* in hospital with a cracked skull. *Why?*"

"An attempted robbery?" Janice tried. "I mean, it's clearly very valuable."

Graham stood, hands on hips, and regarded the Satterthwaite Desk. It seemed tiny by modern standards, fit for a more elegant time when the people were a little smaller, and quality was less often confused with quantity. "Hardly. Whoever it was incapacitated the victim and then left without the desk," Graham pointed out. "There's no sign of any attempt to even move it."

Harding's phone rang. "Yes?" she said. "Okay, I'll ask him." She turned to Graham, who was staring, perplexed, at the desk. "Constable Roach requests permission to attend the crime scene, sir. And perhaps I should go to the hospital. Talk to Mrs. Barrios."

"Yes, do that Harding. Tell Roach to direct calls to St. Helier, and have Barnwell get back to the station ASAP."

Janice spoke again into the phone. "Roach says he's already in touch with Adam Harris-Watts and suggests bringing him here to see if he can help us."

"Oh God, alright," Graham grumbled. "But tell him to warn Harris-Watts about the blood would you? That curator is a fragile sort."

CHAPTER TWENTY-ONE

ONSTABLE ROACH WAS examining the desk as though searching for a hidden code within its very construction. "Interesting," he said, more than once. "Very interesting."

Graham indulged him as far as he could, given the circumstances. They had no murder weapon, no suspect, and no reason for Felipe Barrios' attack. He put this to Roach, who seized the moment.

"Well, the attack seems to have taken place in the dead of night, when Felipe was alone in the workshop," Roach pointed out. "The attacker probably knew they wouldn't be disturbed. That constitutes an opportunity."

"Yes obviously, but for whom? We have no idea who, why, or how." From outside, Graham heard the sounds of Adam Harris-Watts' visceral reaction to the large pool of blood. He rolled his eyes. "We'll check on him in a minute," Graham said. "Carry on, Constable."

"We need to find the weapon that was used to attack the victim," Roach said next, looking around the workroom.

"No success there," said Graham, who had spent the previous forty minutes memorizing and minutely examining every tool and object on the walls, in drawers, and on the workbench. "So, what about motive?"

Roach shook his head. "Must be something to do with the desk. That's the connection."

"Certainly. We've now had two incidents relating to it. But what's the significance?"

Roach looked at him and shrugged.

Harris-Watts reappeared, looking gaunt and unsteady. "Sorry," he said, for what seemed like the twentieth time. "I'm rather out of my element with all this crime scene stuff."

"We'd like you to focus on the desk," Graham said. "And tell us if you notice anything unusual."

Doing his best to pull his attention away from the sickening evidence of brutal injury on the workshop floor, Harris-Watts examined the Satterthwaite Desk with an expert eye. "Felipe was obviously making progress on the repairs," he said. "A good portion of the polish is in place." His mind focused now, Harris-Watts stepped around the desk and examined the rear, and then the underside. Roach watched him, envious of the older man's knowledge. "Nothing seems amiss," Harris-Watts said, and then reached for the brass handle to open the main drawer.

"No!" Both Graham and Roach leaped to intervene before the curator placed a naked finger on the desk.

"Sorry, sorry. Of course," Harris-Watts stammered as he put on the latex gloves Graham offered him. He leaned forward, bending over. He ran his fingertips along the drawer at the front of the desk and then reached underneath and did the same.

His response, a pained, stunned gasp, immediately brought Graham to his side. "What? What is it?"

Harris-Watts pressed the mechanism on the underside of the drawer. They all heard the "thunk" from deep inside the desk. Harris-Watts pulled the drawer out. He could barely bring himself to utter the words. *"I've found it.* At last. Of all the... " He looked at Graham, his eyes wide. "There's a secret compartment! It's what Satterthwaite was known for. We always suspected there was one here. But no one could find the mechanism that opened it. Even Charlotte Hughes couldn't find it."

"Who?" Graham asked.

"Charlotte Hughes, the daughter of the original owner. Said the family looked for it many times without success. She was here a few days ago. Paid for the repairs. It was very kind of her. The museum wouldn't have been able to afford them otherwise."

Roach fizzed with excitement. "Is there anything inside?"

The curator showed the two officers the peculiar, but empty little nook at the very back. "No," he said glumly. "Nothing."

But Graham's mind was racing. "Nothing *now*," he cautioned. "But I'm betting there *was*."

Photographing and documenting the crime scene took another hour during which Graham regularly called the hospital for an update. These situations were always deeply frustrating for investigating officers. The victim was perhaps the only person in the world with definitive information on the nature of the attack and its perpetrator, but Graham didn't know if Felipe Barrios would ever speak again.

Roach busied himself chronicling the desk, peppering the pale-faced Harris-Watts all the while with a sequence of questions which made him sound a far more accomplished and thoughtful investigator than his lowly rank might imply. Increasingly, Graham had been bringing him along to crime scenes and never regretted it, although Roach did allow his enthusiasm to boil over now and then. It took the occasional steadying glance from the DI to remind Roach that exciting as all this might well be, detective work was a serious, sometimes deadly business. To emphasize his point, Graham's phone rang with news from the hospital. It was Janice. He knew immediately that the news wasn't good.

"I'm sorry, sir. Mr. Barrios' injuries were too severe. They did everything they could, but the doctors pronounced him dead a few moments ago. Dr. Tomlinson says he'll get to work shortly."

Graham pursed his lips and his knuckles whitened as he gripped his phone. He stomped around in a broad circle for a few moments, wincing at the tragic, pointless *unfairness* of such a death. He punched Tomlinson's number into his phone.

"Can you give me any preliminaries, Marcus?"

"Nothing yet, old boy," Tomlinson told him. "Look, I've got some paperwork to do here, and then I'll begin the autopsy proper."

"Please make a start as soon as you're able," Graham snapped. "And get me everything you can on the likely murder weapon. This place is full of tools but there are no obvious signs that any of them was used. Shape, size, anything. Soon as you can." He hung up.

Roach eyed his boss nervously. It wasn't unlike him to take these cases very personally. He watched Graham staring at the desk, as if willing the masterpiece to explain itself. "He's gone, then, sir?" he finally said to the silent Graham.

"A few minutes ago," Graham scowled. "No CCTV. No witnesses," he continued, mostly to himself. "No nothing."

Lillian awoke and immediately looked at her phone. Blast! It was gone 11 AM, and she'd had no phone calls or texts from Charlotte. Lillian reached for the packet of cigarettes by her bed but groaned and slammed it back down when she realized she'd have to lean out of the window to have a smoke, or worse, get up and go outside. In the mid-morning light, her room was small but bright, her view of the English Channel glorious. The water glistened in the sunshine. She could see a container ship crawling across the horizon.

Lillian had arrived the previous evening. She had checked herself in to the White House Inn, having been assured it was the best guesthouse on the island. Noting the rubber plant and the oak paneling in the reception area, she considered the recommendation to bode poorly for the other accommodations on Jersey. Grousing, she had made her way to her room, determined to waste no time in getting hold of Charlotte. She needed to get her off this godforsaken island as soon as possible, but she'd had zero success in contacting her charge.

Lillian stared at the ceiling for a few moments, before rising. She dressed, winding a purple scarf around her neck in order to guard herself against the chill of the spring morning. She was on a mission to protect her latest and brightest client. On this bucolic March morning, her mission was to save Charlotte Hughes from disaster.

She tapped a message out on her cellphone. It sounded a lot more charitable than she felt. *Charlotte, where are you, child?*

CHAPTER TWENTY-TWO

J ANICE HAD FOUND Rosa Barrios still trembling, surrounded by three of her friends. They were sitting in stunned silence in one of the hospital's quiet waiting rooms. Although Barnwell had taken an initial statement, he had remained aloof from the group and was relieved to see Janice approaching the room.

"Sergeant," Barnwell said simply, stepping out into the hallway to meet her.

"Pretty grim, eh, Constable?" she said consolingly.

"He was well-liked with no known enemies," Barnwell reported. Being around grieving people put him in a distinctly thoughtful frame of mind. He was looking forward to leaving the hospital behind and returning to the station. He handed over a very brief witness statement. "She was upset," was all he said.

"Okay, Constable, thanks. The DI wants you back at the station. Roach is at the crime scene. I'll call if I need you, and you do the same, alright?"

Barnwell nodded and went on his way, happy to be out of the hospital and in the fresh air.

Rosa Barrios made to stand as Janice entered, but the sergeant waved her back down. "Mrs. Barrios, I'm Sergeant Janice Harding," she said. "I'm here to help you if you feel up to speaking to me." She politely requested that Rosa's three friends leave them for the moment.

Rosa was a small woman with big brown eyes and hair pulled back in a bun. "I want to help," she said. "I just don't understand..." Tears welled up but were forced back down again. She would be strong at this moment, and when the time was right, she would allow her grief to wash over her again. "I told the other man everything. The big officer," she clarified.

Janice almost smiled. "Mrs. Barrios, tell me about your husband. You'd been married for, what, forty years?"

"Yes, we were both born and raised in San Marcos. We met on the beach when we were just teenagers." Rosa smiled at the memory. "We came here when we were first married."

Janice held eye contact with Rosa, building an intimacy with her that would encourage her to speak. "San Marcos is where exactly?

"In Central America. We came to Jersey in 1978."

"Why did you leave your home country? Were you not happy there?"

Rosa's face darkened. "San Marcos came upon very difficult times. The forces from the neighboring state of Suriguay assaulted our capital and took control. Eventually, we had to flee." Rosa looked down at her hands in her lap for a long moment. Janice waited for the older woman to resume her story. "We lived through horrible years that followed the 'revolution.' That's what they called it, the *junta*'s propagandists." Rosa's face hardened. She spat out the word, "junta." "It was a military coup. A period of great difficulty. Felipe's parents were professors and were constantly harassed." Rosa's mouth turned down at the corners, paying no attention to Janice as she stared into space, lost in her memories.

"Felipe had dreamed of college, even as the 'education department' closed down almost every institute of higher learning in our country. There was a new government-sponsored curriculum. Dissent wasn't tolerated. Students were encouraged to inform on their classmates and even on their teachers. Many professors were taken away for 'reeducation'! They never came back." Rosa clasped her hands to her chest and rocked gently. "There were rumors of secret political meetings at Felipe's parents' apartment. They were being watched and eventually they were arrested in the dead of night." Tears rolled down Rosa's face.

"Poor Felipe! His parents were idealistic and brave, always defying the authoritarian thugs who had come to dominate our country. I was in awe of them! My family was poor, uneducated, but Felipe's parents taught me that democracy was not a radical, unhinged, sinful experiment, that social mobility was my birthright!" Rosa's lips quivered, and she raised the handkerchief in her hand up to her mouth. Janice leaned in and put her hand on the older woman's forearm, concern etched on Janice's face.

Rosa calmed herself after a few sobs and spoke again. "Felipe said we had to leave, but I didn't want to. I wanted to stay with my family, but he insisted. He said that it would be worse if we stayed. His parents had always warned him it would be so. We used our last money to board a fishing trawler in the middle of the night. There were so many people, little children, babies. We were all crying. I was so scared we would drown. But somehow, the boat carried us to Jamaica. I have never prayed so hard in my life."

"And how did you end up here? From Jamaica to Jersey?"

"An embassy official took pity on us. He allowed us to make one phone call. Felipe called Mr. Steadman. He worked so hard to get us here, paid money, filled in forms, and hired lawyers for us. We made it, and we've been here ever since."

"Mr. Steadman owned the business Felipe now has?"

"Yes, they met when Felipe was a boy. Back then, San Marcos was popular with tourists, and they would come to fish and snorkel. They liked to taste the best rum in Central America. Mr. Steadman, just two days into his holiday, was found on the beach with blood coming from a wound on his leg. Felipe was the first to reach him and understood enough English to realize what had happened." Rosa looked at Janice knowingly. "Sea snake."

"Felipe cared for him as an intense fever took hold of *Señor* Steadman. He was his constant companion through the pain and tremors. He brought Mr. Steadman water and broth, and when Mr. Steadman's fever passed, he fed him meals. He never left his side. Later, Mr. Steadman said he owed his life entirely to Felipe. He promised to help him in any way he could, and he was true to his word. We owe him our lives. But it was a terrible time.

"When we arrived here on the island, exhausted, heartsick, and cold, Felipe was told that his parents had been executed by the regime. For many weeks, Felipe spoke to no one except me and Mr. Steadman. It took a while, but eventually he began to explore Jersey and settle here. He polished his English by taking courses at the local college, and Mr. Steadman taught him wood-working and cabinetmaking. He eventually allowed Felipe to work on his own projects, and just before Mr. Steadman died, Felipe completed a beautiful dining table set, his first major commission. Oh, it was wonderful! So beautiful! Felipe's true passion, though, was repairing old furniture. He was humbled to be working on a piece designed by Ezekiel Satterthwaite."

"Did he tell you anything about the desk? Was there anything unusual about it?" Janice asked, bringing out her notebook.

"He was very excited," Rosa said, brightening before almost immediately clouding again, "but something strange did happen yesterday. There was a phone call. About the desk. That's all I know. The person didn't say who they were and Felipe didn't come up to the house again." She paused for a moment and looked closely at the Sergeant. Her tired, brown eyes were puffy now from crying. "It wasn't just a robbery?"

Janice was making a discreet note. "I'm not sure what you mean, Mrs. Barrios," she said, setting down her iPad.

"The person who came to the workshop last night. The one who attacked him. They were... looking for something, weren't they?" she asked, focusing intently on Janice.

"We don't know at this point, Mrs. Barrios, but I can assure you we will do everything in our power to find out who did this to your husband."

Rosa reached out and took Janice's hand. She had short, broad fingers that were extremely soft, but her grip was surprisingly firm. "God knows," she said slowly, "what happened to my Felipe. I pray that he will guide you and your colleagues to uncover the truth," she added, tears coming again.

Janice never quite knew what to say when burdened by such hopes. "We'll do everything we can," she said in the end. "DI Graham is one of the best investigators in the country." She held onto Rosa's hand for a long, quiet moment, praying that her boss would once again prove himself equal to the task.

Graham met Janice at the hospital. She found him in a dark and brooding mood. She suspected it wasn't due only to the unnecessary and tragic death of Felipe Barrios. Although Graham had never said so, Janice harbored a belief that hospitals held dreadful associations for the DI. She knew better than to quiz such a private person, but more than once, she had found herself speculating at what might lie in Graham's past.

She recounted everything that Rosa had told her, including the mysterious phone call. Graham's face darkened as she spoke. "Poor guy," he said when she'd finished. "To go through all that and then get taken out by some animal." They walked silently along the hospital corridors to the morgue.

"Marcus?" Graham said as the two officers arrived.

"Sorry, old boy," the pathologist said again. "I know you had hopes on this one."

Graham shrugged just slightly. "What can you tell me?"

"It's early days but definitely blunt force trauma, as we thought," Marcus explained. "A long, relatively thin metal object. My guess is a file or maybe a sharpening steel. In any event, he was hit pretty hard from behind by a right-handed assailant."

"What else?" Graham said, memorizing the details and bringing to mind his observations from the workshop.

"He was struck once and then left on the ground. The victim took a well-aimed and ferocious thwack to his head. I can't know if the attacker meant to kill him or simply incapacitate him.

"Could it have been a woman?"

"With a tool like that, yes. It's not heavy, and with sufficient force and precise placement, it could be deadly wielded by a male or a female.

Janice interjected. "So they broke in quietly and attacked him, unawares? Or perhaps," she tried, "Felipe knew the attacker, invited them in, and they hit him when his back was turned?"

"Either of those explanations is possible," Tomlinson said. "Based on our preliminary findings, you understand."

"What about the injury?" Graham said.

Marcus showed him a diagram of a skull, with a star-shaped fracture radiating out from an impact point above the right ear. "The bleeding was very sudden and severe, but because the skull is a rigid container," Tomlinson ringed the diagram with his closed pen, "the blood has nowhere to go except out through the small cut made by the impact, or down the *foramen magnum*."

"The where?" Harding asked.

"The hole in the bottom of the skull," Tomlinson replied, tapping the back of his own neck, "through which the spinal cord passes. Everything gets forced down that way. There's no other escape route. It causes herniation, an increase in pressure. This shuts down breathing and other vital functions. The results aren't usually survivable."

Harding, feeling distinctly queasy, stepped out for a moment while Graham listened to the rest of Tomlinson's findings. "Are there any similarities," Graham asked, his voice grave, "to the death of Mr. Norris at the museum?"

Tomlinson shook his head. "No, other than the obvious proximity of the desk," Marcus summed up.

"There was a hidden compartment in one of the drawers," Graham confessed.

Marcus looked closely at Graham. "Compartment?"

"Yes. Adam Harris-Watts was quite beside himself about it. The maker, Satterthwaite, was known for incorporating hidden drawers in some of his pieces, but no one had been able to find one in this particular desk until now."

"It was empty, wasn't it?" Tomlinson said.

"Yes it was... How did you know it would be?" Graham asked.

Marcus led him from the room. "Come with me, Detective Inspector." They changed out of their surgical scrubs, "I need to introduce you to our new forensics expert."

Tomlinson led him to his own car, parked outside the hospital's front entrance. "It's easier just to show you. Young Mr. Oxley has something that you really need to see."

CHAPTER TWENTY-THREE

TOMLINSON LED GRAHAM through the double doors and into the forensics lab. It was a place the DI had been to many times before, but Tomlinson's eagerness gave the lab an air of expectancy. "A Dr. Simon Oxley. New chap," Tomlinson had told him on the way over, "based at Cambridge University but loaned out to the Metropolitan Police for consulting on cases that need his expertise. Miranda happened to be in a meeting with him when she took my call. He popped straight over."

Dr. Miranda Weiss was the Head of Forensics for the Jersey Police. She resided on the mainland, so Tomlinson sometimes found himself doing double duty as a forensics investigator, or at least overseeing some of the more rarefied tasks that landed on his mortuary table. They were tasks he usually relished – intellectually challenging and generally cutting edge.

"Did you know him while you were at the Met?" Graham shook his head. Tomlinson continued, "Anyhow, he arrived a couple of hours ago. Smartest young man I've met in a while."

Tomlinson tapped his temple. "*Listen* to him, David. Don't let his looks deceive you," he said, ushering Graham into the room.

"Looks?" Graham asked, noticing the faint chemical smell as he walked into the lab. "How do you mean?" He turned to find an extremely tall, fresh-faced young man smiling down at him.

"How do you do, DI Graham?" the youthful-looking giant asked, extending his hand. "I've heard a great deal about you." Simon Oxley was nearly seven feet tall, with an enthusiastic, genuine smile, and glinting, excited eyes that were magnified by thick, steel-rimmed glasses. "I'm hoping I can be of some assistance," he said, as Graham's hand met his own. The young man's grip was surprisingly dainty given his intimidating height.

"I'm hoping so, too," Graham said. "Marcus seems to think highly of you. We've got ourselves a very special and particular case here."

"Felipe Barrios. Yes," Oxley said soberly.

"It was the jacket he was wearing when he was attacked that proved to be of the greatest interest," Tomlinson said. He took Graham's arm and steered the DI to an examination table. On it lay a single piece of clothing. "We're hoping that this jacket is going to teach us *why* Barrios was killed," Tomlinson said.

Oxley showed them two large, glossy photographs. One contained an image of a single piece of paper, the other, a curled-up Polaroid. Graham could see it had originally been black and white but had faded to shades of gray and pink. Oxley placed them next to the jacket on the metal table. "You found these in the pocket?" Graham surmised. It wasn't a staggering feat of detective work. The jacket and the paper pictured in the photograph were almost completely soaked in blood. The Polaroid was relatively unscathed.

"The originals," Oxley explained, "are in cold storage now. We're focusing on the paper that contains the handwriting." Graham looked carefully at the photograph with the handwritten paper. There were only three legible sections that he could see, only a handful of words, he estimated.

"We're going to use a process called lypophilization to freeze dry the document and then sublimate the frozen water present in the blood's plasma by turning it to vapor."

Graham stared at him briefly. "Okay."

"Dr. Oxley is an expert on document retrieval, storage, and reconstruction," Tomlinson told him. "When paper gets wet, as this has with blood, the best method of restoring it is to freeze away the water present, leaving just the original material behind."

"And the remainder of the blood, presumably," Graham said, dubiously.

"Yes, that's true, but blood comprises fifty-five percent plasma, of which ninety-two percent is water, so we should see a great improvement in the legibility of this document.

"It will take at least a day, perhaps two," Oxley said, "even with the new technique we're using. But we've had a very pleasing success rate," he beamed.

"After that, we'll use an X-ray scanner. Hopefully, we'll be able to see what the paper was about," Tomlinson added. Graham could see the pathologist had warmed to this new and interesting project. "Tell him about the papyrus from that Roman villa, Simon."

Oxley was all set to launch into what Graham was certain would be a fascinating tale, but he was far too engrossed in the murder investigation to pay it any mind at this moment. "Tell me about this," he said, standing over Felipe's blood-soaked jacket, his index finger pointing to the metal tabletop.

"This jacket is one of a kind that a carpenter or painter might wear," Tomlinson told him. "Lots of pockets for brushes and tools, and a comfortable fit so his arms aren't constrained. It isn't the kind of thing you'd wear outside the workshop," Marcus said. "And, at first glance, I saw no earthly reason to think that it was anything other than what it appeared to be. But then I noticed this," he said. Slowly, Tomlinson used tweezers to lift some fabric where the stitching at the seam under the armpit had been removed to leave a three-inch opening. "See here? The fabric had been freshly sewn. We found the letter inside the lining of the sleeve, presumably placed there through this gap."

Graham peered at the photo of the document once more. According to the scale placed next to it, the paper was letter-sized, and the few fragments that remained free of blood showed handwriting in a very neat, educated script. Graham's first impression was that it might be a college graduation certificate. "So, what is it?" he asked Oxley.

"My doctoral thesis discussed methods of analyzing docu-ments that were illegible or damaged." Simon told him, peering down at the DI and the document.

"Very high-end stuff," Tomlinson whispered to Graham. "X-rays and such. You wouldn't believe the things they can do."

"Yes, but what is it?" Graham repeated. He wasn't as enam-ored by the scientific brilliance of the process as much as he was by its outcome.

"I'm not sure yet. This is a very difficult case, but I do expect to be able to glean something from the remnants." Dr. Oxley handled the photograph with a soft, measured touch, his long, pale, soft fingers lingering over the image. Graham imagined those hands at the keyboards of a church organ perhaps, or expertly wielding a surgeon's scalpel. "After the water has been extracted, we will have a clearer picture of what we are dealing with. There are other layered tech-niques we can use to recover the contents of the document if neces-sary, including ascertaining the chemical composition of the ink."

"Something in which," Tomlinson explained, "Simon is also a noted expert."

"Gradually," Oxley said, "we should be able to build a picture of what this paper originally communicated."

Graham looked up at the man, once again doubting that someone who couldn't possibly have yet turned thirty had already gained such a reputation, not to mention a doctorate in the sciences. "How long will it take?"

"As I mentioned earlier, a day or so."

Graham sighed. "Is there anything you can tell me now?"

Oxley looked down at the bloodied paper. "We can make a few deductions, yes."

"I'm interested to hear what you have to say," Graham persisted.

Oxley set down the photo and reached for his laptop on the opposite table. "The author was highly educated, probably in the nineteen-forties. We can tell this from aspects of his letter formation. There's also a rigor to the penmanship that spoke of many patient hours of practice, probably under the watchful eye of a strict tutor."

Tomlinson gave Graham a wink. "Told you he was good, didn't I?"

Oxley continued. "The author was a meticulous person, someone for whom the effort of writing a letter by hand was considered a worthwhile investment."

Graham stared at the document again.

"The words we can read suggest that it is a letter of some kind. The formal, rather archaic language supports the idea that the author was educated and disciplined, and I also suggest that this was a letter to an acquaintance, possibly a friend, more than a business or official communication. All of this helps us to date the letter, even before we receive the results of chemical analysis on the ink and the paper."

"So when do you think it was written?"

"My guess is that the paper, and this is only a guess mind, is probably around fifty years old. It is well preserved, and I suspect was only handled fairly infrequently."

"That would fit with what you were saying about the compartment, wouldn't it, David?" Tomlinson suggested.

Graham looked at him, his lips pursed. The pathologist continued. "Once we get the results back, we'll know where the paper came from. Almost down to the individual *forest*."

"Extraordinary," Graham breathed. "But how will that help us?"

"We can home in on the location where the letter was written," Simon Oxley said.

"And how many of us," Tomlinson suggested, "would use an expression like, 'long have endured,' as the author does here?"

"Sophisticated grammatical structure," Oxley explained, "is a hallmark both of high-class education and social standing. This was almost certainly written by someone in a position of power."

"There's something else," Oxley told him. "Do you see these tiny cursive features on the letters 's' and 'p'?" Graham looked more closely. There were curious, almost affected little swirls.

"What do they signify?" Graham said.

"Well, here I'm beginning to speculate," Oxley admitted, "but I would say there's a better-than-even chance that our author was raised in a Spanish-speaking country."

"Could Felipe have written it himself?" Graham asked.

Oxley shrugged his thin shoulders. "I doubt it. Felipe was entirely too young to have been educated using this kind of language and script. Plus, given that he secreted the letter on his person, it's much more likely that it was written by someone who was important to him in some way."

"Tell me about the photograph you found." Graham said.

"I'll go get it from the freezer," Tomlinson offered. "You can take this with you," he said when he came back. "Looks like it's from the seventies to me. It is less compromised and has absorbed less of the blood than the letter." He gave Graham a bag inside which a monochromatic photo clearly showed a beach scene with two men and a woman squinting toward the camera. One man shielded his eyes, his face half in shadow. The woman was fair, her shoulder length hair lying in shiny waves. She was wearing white starfish earrings and a matching necklace.

Graham stared at the photo, staying absolutely still. He was silent for so long that the two scientists exchanged a curious glance. Tomlinson let the silence reign, aware that the longer DI David Graham considered a problem, the better his answer tended to be.

Finally, Graham brought out his phone. "Excuse me a moment." He speed-dialed a number. "Ah, Constable Roach. Would you make your way over to the forensics lab?"

Tomlinson's face cracked into a grin. He was very fond of the obvious bond between Graham and his young protégé, and he shared the DI's high hopes for the keen young constable.

"That's right," Graham was confirming. "I've got a task for you. There's a chap here called Simon Oxley. Tomorrow morning, get over to the lab and do everything he tells you. Right. Good lad." Graham ended the call.

"More manpower?" Tomlinson asked, his smile still in place.

"Something like that. Simon, I'm sending you an assistant. Teach him, put him to work, and get him to help you. You're going to figure out who wrote this and what it says," Graham said, turning to leave. "Most importantly, you're going to discover why we found it on the body of a dead man."

The man reached into his duffel bag and brought out one of the six 'burner' phones he'd brought to Jersey. He had hoped only to use one of them for the purpose of announcing the successful completion of his assignment, but three had already been used, shattered and discarded. Far from the quick, easy solution his employers sought, his time on the island had become unexpectedly complicated. Not to mention increasingly frustrating.

"What the *hell* do you mean?" the voice rasped on the other end.

The man had expected this anger and was relieved to be a couple of hundred miles away, rather than having to face this particular wrath in person. "Things got messed up by that old security guard dying on the job," he said. "There are cops all over the place."

"That was at the *museum*, if I recall," the voice continued, no less furious. "And your business is at the *library*, is it not?"

"Yeah," he admitted. "But there's been another complication. A murder."

"So?" came the exasperated voice.

The man sighed. "People are jumpy. Keeping their eyes open, you know? Some old bag across the road from the library called the cops three nights in a row."

The voice cut him off. "You know what I'm hearing? I'm hearing *excuses*. You have one job and one job only, and I don't want to hear from you again until it's done."

"No problem," the man replied instantly. "I got it covered, boss."

"Twenty-four hours. I want good news in *less* than twenty-four hours. Got it?"

"Leave it with me, boss," the man assured the voice on the end of the line. "I know exactly what to do."

CHAPTER TWENTY-FOUR

"WHERE THERE IS one," Graham noted, "there's the other." He regarded the two of them, Janice and Jack, working side by side behind the reception desk. "Sounds like a law firm, or something, doesn't it? Or maybe," he continued, "a firm of private detectives."

The younger pair looked up. "Huh?"

Graham mimed the sign across their imaginary storefront. "'Harding and Wentworth.' It's got a nice ring to it."

The couple blushed in tandem, a reaction Graham found endearing. "How was the forensics lab yesterday?" Harding asked. "Roach excited to be called down there at short notice?"

"I'm sure he was," Graham smiled, hanging up his jacket on the coat stand behind his office door and re-emerging in the reception area. "He's moving on from furniture analysis to graphology. What are you two finding?"

Jack shrugged. "I know it's my stock-in-trade to remind everyone that criminals can be unbelievably stupid, but this particular criminal has not yet fallen into that trap."

"Blast," Graham groaned. "I was hoping for just that kind of ineptitude. No sign of the medal, then?"

Wentworth shook his head. "Not yet, sir." Despite being an operative who stood outside the police chain of command, the fact that everyone else called DI Graham 'sir' had rubbed off on Jack. "He might be trying to sell it privately, of course. Probably more secure than flogging it online, especially if he has a buyer who doesn't care where it came from. Or he might have passed it on to a fence. But if he's after an anonymous quick return, the Internet auction houses are the place to go. I'm trawling all possible outlets."

"I'll leave you to it, Jack. I need a cup of tea. Let me know if you find anything. Janice, come help me would you? It's making my head spin."

"The tea, sir?"

"This case, Sergeant."

Graham found his teapot and opened a tightly sealed metal container of Chinese jasmine. His ritual was comforting.

Janice sat down in his office, noticing the unusually large pile of documents laid out on his desk. "Research, sir?"

"Yes," Graham replied, sighing at the mess. "That blessed Satterthwaite Desk, among other things. The incidents involving Nobby Norris and Felipe Barrios have to be related, but how? We've got a guard who has a heart attack and dies, damaging a valuable desk on his way down, probably *during* a robbery. And a furniture restorer who is bludgeoned to death a few hours after receiving a phone call from an unidentified caller while working on said desk, and which we later find out had a hidden compartment that no one seemed to know about."

"Was anything in it?" Janice asked. "The compartment, I mean? I can't imagine having a hiding place as perfect as that and then not using it."

"Nothing in there when we opened it. But Tomlinson found a paper secreted in Barrios' jacket that they're attempting to decipher now. I sent Roach to help them. Tomlinson also found this photograph." He showed her the evidence bag with the curled up, faded Polaroid.

"Any idea who this might be, sir? In the photo? Or where it was taken?"

"None. You?"

Janice shook her head.

Graham seemed to drift off, lost in thought, until a loud cheer broke out in the reception area. He was there in three seconds flat. "News?"

Jack was sitting back in his chair, triumphant. "I've got a hit on that medal."

Janice dashed around the side of the reception desk and read the screen. "Silly bugger thought we wouldn't notice. Does that make him brave or stupid?"

"Told you, didn't I?" Wentworth said, printing out the webpage. "Eight times out of ten, we catch them because they're impatient, greedy, or plain idiotic. This guy," he said, pointing to the screen, "takes detailed photos of a medal known to be missing following a burglary, and offers it for a pretty reasonable reserve price. He's looking for a quick sale, aiming at buyers who know what they're looking at and who understand its significance. Got his IP address and everything."

"Well, who is it?" Graham blurted out.

"Adam Harris-Watts," Harding said, looking up from searching the police database on her laptop.

Graham blinked. "Eh? You're *kidding* me."

"And," Wentworth added, "if you can believe this, he goes by the handle, 'Jersey Boy.' Remarkable, isn't it?"

Graham went around the desk to look at Janice' laptop, both relieved to have a suspect, and frustrated that he hadn't seen the connection earlier. "The little blighter burgled his own museum?"

"He's not breaking new ground, sir," Harding pointed out. "It's often staff who turn out to be light-fingered."

Graham growled under his breath. "Alright. Pick him up. Send Barnwell. That should give him a scare."

"Righto, boss," Harding said.

"Should make for an interesting conversation. And for you," Graham said to Wentworth, "dinner for two at the Bangkok Palace, on me."

"Thank you very much, sir," Wentworth smiled.

"Right. There's one little mystery solved. I'm going to check in with noted graphologist Constable Roach and see if he's close to giving us an answer about the rest of this maddening case."

Janice Harding bit into a much-needed egg and cress sandwich and watched Jack Wentworth pacing around the lobby of the police station as though waiting for news of his first born. "Does he usually take this long?" Jack asked.

"Barnwell? It depends. Most people come quietly once they realize the game is up. But there are always those who try to do a runner."

Jack stopped and imagined the scene. "And would he be able to... you know... "

Janice did smile this time. Quite enough jokes had already been made at the expense of her more rotund colleague, and Wentworth was too new to know the extraordinary and creditable journey Barnwell had already undertaken. "I would back him in a foot race against most any common criminal," she replied. "And he's a mean swimmer, if you remember. Brave, too."

Jack gave her an apologetic look. "I'm just impatient."

The Sergeant set down her sandwich and settled further into the swivel chair behind the desk. "Exciting, isn't it?"

Just as Jack was nodding, Barnwell appeared at the door, towering over the diminutive figure of Adam Harris-Watts. "Sergeant Harding, I have some paperwork for you to do."

Janice began typing up the arrest record. "Ah, yes. I have to say, Mr. Harris-Watts, I'm sorry to see you like this."

Harris-Watts had very obviously been crying. He said nothing except to confirm his name and address, and that he understood his rights.

"Turn out your pockets, please," Janice told him. Harris-Watts emptied all the contents on to the desk as Janice catalogued them, noting that in addition to the usual wallet, phone, loose change, and used tissues, there were three plastic containers of green, white, and orange mints. "You need to go easy on those," she said. "Rot your teeth, they will."

Slumped and depressed, Harris-Watts was taken to a cell where he would await what Barnwell, Harding, and Wentworth all knew would be an intense grilling by their Detective Inspector.

Graham came out of his office. A paper on Barnwell's desk caught his eye as he passed. He twisted his head to look at it. "Is he here?" he mumbled.

"Barnwell just took him to the cells, sir. Do you want to interview him right away?"

"No, let's sweat him a bit first. What's this?" Graham waved the sheet of paper that had attracted his attention.

"No idea, sir."

A banging of doors and heavy footsteps indicated Barnwell's arrival back in the office. Graham looked up, "Where did you get this?"

"That? Oh, some bloke dropped it in the coffee shop on the front. In a rush, he was. Thought I might see him as I biked around."

Graham looked down at it, reading. "What did he look like? Did you recognize him?

"No, sir. Tourist, I reckon. Heavyset guy. Late forties, early fifties. Why, sir? Something to do with a case?"

"Maybe, Constable. Keep an eye out for him. Ask around. If you see him again, bring him in."

Charlotte put down her cup of tea. She was watching the local lunchtime news on the television in her hotel room. Felipe Barrios was dead. Murdered. Charlotte's mind cast back to her conversation with Adam Harris-Watts, then to Don. Her eyes narrowed. She picked up her phone and dialed Don's number. "Don? It's me, Charlotte." This time there was no friendly banter. "Meet me at the Castle at 3 PM." She paused. "No, buts. Just be there." *Click*.

CHAPTER TWENTY-FIVE

D ON TOOK THE steps quite slowly, hoping to avoid arriving on the castle's battlements out of breath. It had been another warm day. Once again, he found that he had arrived a few minutes in advance of Charlotte, and he enjoyed the colors cast by the sun over the Channel. He took in cleansing breaths of sea air, and paced along the ramparts to their far end, trying to relax.

"Good afternoon, sir," came a voice. "Beautiful view, isn't it?" Stephen Jeffries, Orgueil Castle's events manager strolled along the battlement's stone walkway toward Don.

"It is," Don said. The sea was taking on a yellow-green hue, the surface sparkling like stars in a spiritual universe. The two men met and stood side by side for a moment, admiring the view over the water.

"I work here almost every day but don't often stop to appreciate the simply *gorgeous* vista on my very doorstep," Jeffries explained. "I do apologize if I've interrupted your solitude," he said formally.

Don gave him a shrug. "I'm waiting for someone."

Jeffries beamed at him. "A romantic liaison? A proposal?" he speculated. "We do the most beautiful weddings, you know."

Don let out a short laugh. "No, most definitely not. Just some family business."

"Well," Jeffries said, straightening his official Castle uniform waistcoat and tidying his hair, "I'll leave you to it. A nice spot for a quiet meeting, of whichever kind." He headed past Don with a nod and made his way down the spiral staircase back into the castle's interior, leaving Don alone in the sunshine. It was glorious, but no ethereal beauty could have calmed Don's nervous, racing pulse.

"I'm starting to like it here," came a familiar, slightly haughty voice. Charlotte joined him on the battlements. "Not too windy, not too cold. A nice place for a picnic, maybe."

Don decided on a gruff, impatient demeanor. "Cut the chit-chat, Charlotte. I'm busy. What did you want me here for?"

She wore a no-nonsense trouser suit and heels that must have made the steps something of a challenge. She walked toward him, her heels clacking on the stones beneath her. "Busy? That's good, Don. Keeping your mind occupied."

Don looked at her sideways. The memories of a whole decade of Charlotte's maddening, high-handed condescension when he was a teen welled up in Don's memory, but he bit down an angry rejoinder and simply waited for her to make her play.

"I asked you here because I think it important that we both know what the other is doing, don't you?" Charlotte said as she drew up close to him. "So, how *is* your investigation into the desk going?" she asked.

"That again! What *are* you on about? I don't *have* an investigation. I'm here for a break. I *told* you," Don answered.

Charlotte shook her head. "Really? No more trips down memory lane, following Mummy's tales of sorrow and strife? Come now, Don. Don't take me for a fool. Are you seriously expecting me to believe you are here merely on some kind of jolly? You're here to look for the letter, aren't you?"

He spotted the tell straight away. "So you *do* know about it."

Undeterred, Charlotte carried on. "And so, clearly, do you. How did you find out about it, hmm? Did mother dearest tell you? I've known about it for years. We used to look for it as kids but never found it. I'd prefer that it stay that way."

Don stared at her. His nostrils flared.

Charlotte continued. "You want to find it so you can humiliate me and my family, don't you? You want your *revenge* for all those years your mother spent in the asylum. You want to destroy my career. Punishment for my father's 'misdeeds.'" Charlotte's eyes alternately flashed and narrowed as she cast out her accusations.

Don was shaking his head. "Perhaps, but I'll bet you want it even more. You're so desperate to make sure that you're the next Member of Parliament for Market Ellestry that you'll do *anything* to remove a potential threat."

"I'm a practical woman, it's true," she countered.

"And you know full well," Don continued, "that your father's reputation is already a bit... *muddy*, shall we say?"

"Nothing was ever proven," Charlotte said.

"Someone who would send away *his own wife* because she cried in despair once too often," Don growled.

"He did *everything* he could think of," Charlotte hissed.

"A penny-pinching tyrant? A tax-dodging tycoon? That's the man whose reputation you're so desperate to protect? Whose reputation could so badly affect your own?"

"Don't say those things! He was my father!" She spoke through gritted teeth. "He *loved* me!"

"Well, I wouldn't know what that felt like," Don shot back. "Tell me, Charlotte, last night you went to the workshop where the desk was being repaired and hit a man over the head didn't you? I heard about it on the news. Felipe Barrios. I knew it was you, straight away."

"I most certainly did not," his stepsister protested, coolly.

"And then," Don said, "you searched for the letter. But you didn't find it, did you? If you had, you'd be in Market Ellestry right now, keeping your head down and hoping the police don't decide to question you as part of their murder investigation."

"You've got a very active imagination."

Don paced in front of her, reveling in this chance to lecture his high-handed stepsister. "*This* is the kind of woman you are. And you're proposing to represent the good people of Market Ellestry? They need someone honest, not a scheming, selfish witch who throws murderous temper tantrums when she can't get her own way."

Charlotte cut across him. "You know what I think? I think it was you who broke in to that workshop and killed the repairer. Giving someone a quick bang on the head would be nothing to you if it meant you could avenge your dear, sweet, old Mummy."

Near the top of the spiral staircase leading to the battlements, Stephen Jeffries listened. He had stepped aside on the stairs earlier to let Charlotte pass him. Now he found himself drawn to the ill-tempered sounds of a heated argument. Only yards away now, but hidden behind the thick castle walls, he listened to this brewing contretemps with genuine concern. "*Murder?*" he whispered to himself, reaching for his cellphone. "God... not again..."

Listening to Charlotte was making Don's blood pressure soar. "Ha! You're so wrong. You thought *I* was the bumbling one. But *you're* the person who broke into a man's workshop and killed him. Which of us is the bumbler now?" he rasped, towering above her, his bulk giving menace to his accusations. "Which one of us," he roared, "is the *murderer*?"

Charlotte shrieked. Her hands lashed out. Fingernails caught the side of his face and raked his skin, leaving bloody scratches. "You're *nothing*!" she yelled, "But a lousy, lumpish loser."

Don recoiled but then seemed to remember the great heft of his own bulk. He came at her, sending her reeling back against the stone walls. "You're not going to push me around anymore," he roared defiantly.

Another harsh swipe of her nails against his forehead drew more blood. She was like a panicked cat, claws protracted, searching for weakness. "You came here for revenge!" she countered. "But you've made everything worse. Just like always!"

Don stood menacingly in front of Charlotte, imprisoning her against the battlements with his sheer size. "What does it say, Charlotte?" he asked, his tone so much milder now. "The letter. The one he hid away in that beautiful old desk so secretly. What does it *say*?" His face was inches from hers.

Charlotte's palms were pressed flat against the stonework behind her. "I haven't," she said, her voice hoarse, "a bloody *clue*."

Don stood, his heart pumping hard, his fists balled, ready for combat. "You *must* know *something*," he insisted.

"I thought," she continued in the same pained tone, "that *you* knew. That's why you're here, isn't it? Because it's something scandalous? Something that would *ruin* me?"

He shook his head and then took her by the shoulders with large, strong hands. "I've got upsetting news for you, Charlotte Hughes," he told her sternly. "You're not the center of every bloody thing that happens in the world. I'm not *here* because of *you*."

Don spun her around, dragging Charlotte along the stonework toward a gap in the castle wall. Her heels scraped on the stones as they struggled, and Don forced her against the crenellations, designed centuries ago to protect Medieval archers, but now the scene of a desperate family struggle.

"Stop, you..." she complained, wriggling from his grip as her heels slipped on the stones. "Don—"

"Thomas Hughes was a *tyrant*," Don growled, "a liar, and a scoundrel. A bully and a crook. A heart attack was too good for him. He deserved a horrible death." He was pressing her against the battlements as though trying to force her body through them.

Charlotte felt the cold of the stone and the harshness of its unpolished surface against the back of her neck. "What about the guard at the museum, Don? Did he deserve to die, too?"

He lifted her now and found her so feather-light in his powerful grip that he could have tossed her up into the air and let the wind carry her out into the English Channel. "Did Felipe Barrios?" Don spat back at her. "Did he deserve to have his skull smashed in? Did—"

"Gorey Police! Stay where you are!" It was an authoritative voice, deep and commanding. "Put her down and step away." Barnwell filled the doorway at the top of the spiral staircase. Behind him cowered Stephen Jeffries.

Don froze. "Or what?" he demanded, reluctant to move.

"Let her go, sir," was the response, more calmly now as the officer inched his way along the battlements, his arm outstretched.

Don English stared at Charlotte. Her hair was askew in the wind, her lipstick smeared, her face ashen. It would have been so easy to maneuver her into the gap between the stone crenellations and simply push her away. But he found there, in Charlotte's face, just that victory he now realized had been his aim all along. The tables were turned, and her life was in his hands.

"Your father wasn't merciful," he told Charlotte in a hoarse whisper. "But I'm not a Hughes. My mother was an English, and

I'm an English too." He let go of her shoulder. "And we don't treat people like this."

He dropped his hands from Charlotte's shoulders and turned to face the police officer, the wind and fury knocked out of him. "I'm sorry about this. I'm not a danger to anyone."

Don looked at Charlotte. "I think we'd better go with him," Don said. "We both have a lot of explaining to do."

DI Graham stood and carried his cup of tea into the lobby. He watched as Barnwell brought in the pair. Charlotte stood defiantly. Don was meek, his shoulders slumped.

The constable left them with Harding and walked over to Graham. "Sir, this is the guy with the paper," he whispered quietly. Barnwell tossed his head over in Don's direction. "The one that dropped all his papers outside the coffee shop."

"Is that so?" Graham eyed the two standing at the custody desk. He thought for a moment.

"Are you going to interview them tonight, sir?" Barnwell asked.

"No, we'll put them in the cells. Let them stew."

"Thing is, sir, we don't have enough."

"Hmm?" Graham was still thinking.

"Cells, sir. We don't have enough for everyone."

Graham walked over to where Harding was registering the prisoners' details. He read over her shoulder. "Put Harris-Watts in the interview room for now, Sergeant. Mr. English can go in his cell. Ms. Hughes can go in the other."

"What about overnight, sir?"

"English and Harris-Watts can share if it comes to that." Graham smiled. "Let's hope it's not a typical Friday night, eh? Closing time could make things interesting in here."

The two old men left the library together, walking through the park near where the man was hiding. After they had passed, he crossed them both off his list of those he knew to be inside. "Empty," he sighed. "Finally."

It had been a long, frustrating day. The library closed late on Friday, but the last patrons had now gone, and Laura was tidying the place up on her own. It was the perfect moment, and one he had been waiting for all week.

He sent one last text on his burner phone: *All good. Target alone. Stand by*. He approached the library, checking his handgun with his fingertips inside his jacket pocket. Silencer on. Safety off. He climbed the few steps to the front entrance.

CHAPTER TWENTY-SIX

I T WASN'T THAT she minded working alone, but Laura found the dimmed, deserted library a little creepy once the sun began to go down. She had noticed the sensation several times during the past few days, that tingle in her skin that told her she was being watched. "Paranoia," she muttered to herself. *Calm down.* And yet, she could have sworn that she saw, or felt, a pair of eyes watching her from among the shelves. "Overactive imagination," she told herself. *Focus on your work.*

Laura had been locking the cabinets behind the large, open tabletop of the distribution desk, and it was when she straightened up that she first saw the looming figure at the library's locked door. With most of the building's interior lights now switched off as part of the evening routine, and with the sun already set behind the row of homes opposite the front door, it was hard to see who this late visitor might be.

Laura smiled as she opened the door slightly. It was a patron she thought, though not one she recognized. "We're finished for the day, I'm afraid," she told the man. He was big, perhaps fifty and dressed in a leather jacket.

"Oh, I won't stay long, I promise," he said.

Laura's immediate sense was that his lilting, sing-song accent, which was hard to place, was not truly his own. "We open tomorrow at nine," she told him and made to close the door.

A large foot jammed itself quickly into the remaining space, and she felt the door shoved powerfully open, sending her tipping back onto the floor of the library's lobby. "Please!" she gasped. "There's no money here."

The man closed the door behind him, and stood over the terrified Laura. One hand was in his jacket pocket, and she knew that it would soon emerge with a weapon. "I'm not here for money," the man told her. "I'm here to shut you up for good."

Laura tried to scramble to her feet, but the man's boot was on her ankle, hard and insistent, painfully pinning her down. "No!" she yelled putting her hand up, the other propping her upper body off the floor. "I promise I won't say another word. I won't testify. I... I won't go back there. Not *ever*."

The man's hidden hand emerged, and Laura watched him bring back the action of a small, silver pistol. He did it steadily, as though relishing the occasion. "No, you won't," he assured her. "There won't be no trial, and there won't be no wit—. *Arggh.*"

A hardback volume of poetry flew through the air, sharp and direct and seemingly out of nowhere. It struck the man hard on the shoulder. He slipped on the tiled floor. Laura's ankle was released, and she bolted for the distribution desk, seeking cover behind its reassuring bulk.

"What the..." Another volume arrived, even before the man could complete the curse. It beat against his chest, and then another sailed over his shoulder. This one narrowly avoided hitting him on the side of the head, causing him to duck. "Who's there?" he bellowed. "Come out here!"

The answer was another airborne book that bounced harm-lessly onto the floor by the man's feet, and then a flurry of quick footsteps. "Damn you!" He leveled the pistol but saw no one, hearing only the sound of running feet as they receded into the space around the shelves in the main part of the library. The man turned. He had no time for flying books. He needed to finish this job. But Laura was gone.

He swore loudly and colorfully at the ceiling of the library. His only clues were the faint footsteps, now two pairs rather than one. They told him that Laura had disappeared into the gloomy depths of the library, and that her erstwhile savior had done like-wise. He unleashed one more powerful oath and stomped toward the rows of eight-foot tall shelves. They lay in chevrons, one behind the other, flanking the central reading space with its tables and magazine racks. As he looked around for a light switch, he heard more shuffling and dashing of footsteps. He swore again as the sounds carried down the corridors between the bookcases.

Laura ducked down behind the shelves. They would shield her from the man's view. She had just caught her breath once more when she heard faint skittering sounds and, before she could even turn, someone appeared beside her, panting as quietly as he could.

"Billy?" Laura whispered. "Oh, Billy for heaven's sake!"

"Are you okay?" he asked. "He didn't hurt you?"

Laura placed her hand on the boy's head. His hair was matted with sweat, but he was unharmed. "No, but he won't stop until he does."

Pistol drawn, the man paced down each row of shelving, stopping to peer over the books or to stoop down and ensure Laura wasn't hiding down low in the neighboring aisle. At the end of the third row of shelves, he turned to check whether she had doubled back toward the distribution desk. Suddenly, from out of nowhere, another heavy volume hit him right in the face. His gun went off, shattering a floor tile. The sounds of the debris skittering across the space were louder than the retort of the silenced shot. In the relative silence that followed, he was certain that he heard the voice of a child.

Roach kept his grip on the phone deliberately strong, as he risked dropping it out of sheer surprise. He was hissing into it as Barnwell told him of the day's events. "You're *kidding* me, right, Barnwell? You're pulling my leg. I get seconded for a day and *this* happens. Three arrests? You're a superstar."

"It was a bit of a madhouse in there for a while, mate." Barnwell puffed and paused as he went down a gear and dug in to pedal his way up the hill away from the front. "What're you doin' in the station, anyway?"

"Dropped in to pick up my soccer cleats. Janice asked me to take the phones while she pops out to get a takeaway for the guv." Roach opened his mouth to ask more about the day's arrests, but stopped himself. "Gotta go. Red phone."

"Okay, Roachie. Call me on the radio if you need anything."

Roach skittered around the corner of his desk and grabbed the red handset. "Gorey Police." He listened for a moment and took notes. Four seconds into the call, his pen paused on his notepad. He abruptly moved over to the radio transmitter.

"Mike Bravo 882, are you receiving? Over."

"Mike Bravo 882 receiving loud and clear. Over," Barnwell responded.

"Report of active shooter situation at Gorey Library."

"Yeah, right, son. Nice one, Roachie."

"No, that's the report, Bazza..."

"Says who?"

"Mrs. Hollingsworth, the little old lady that keeps reporting suspicious strangers in the area."

Barnwell sighed wearily. He braked to a stop and turned his bike around. "Okay, well, roger that, dispatch. ETA three minutes. Don't hold your breath."

"Keep the line open, 882."

CHAPTER TWENTY-SEVEN

"**O**VER HERE!" THE man followed the child's voice but found the whole area behind the shelves empty. It was like chasing smoke, he grumbled to himself as he hauled his generous frame around the spacious building. "Come out, wherever you are!" he called. "You can't escape!"

Another book came flying at him. This time, with a fraction of a second to spare, he caught sight of Billy before the boy ducked down behind one of the desks in the center of the library. "Didn't your mother teach you to treat books nicely?" he muttered, leveling his weapon at the table. His quarry would break either left, toward the Recommended Reading table, or right, toward the New Acquisitions display. Either way, he would be exposed for a moment.

"Over here, you fat gibbon!" Billy's high voice penetrated the murkiness of the library.

The man caught sight of Laura standing in the open, just by the distribution desk. He loosed off a wild round and then another as he steadied the gun, training it on the desk area. But Laura was gone again, apparently as nimble as the kid. He cursed yet again. He turned to see the boy sprinting down one of the rows of shelving to his left. "Not so fat," he shouted back, "that I can't chase you around all night, if that's what it takes!" The boy disappeared around the end of the book shelves.

Then he heard it again, from over his shoulder. It came from the other side, Laura now, drawing out the insult like a boxing announcer, "Fat gibbon!" But still, he couldn't see her. He spun around, tracing the source of the sound, but all he heard were footsteps.

The man fired his pistol at the ceiling twice, and then roared in deafening anger. For a man of his size, he could move pretty fast, but he began to realize that he would never catch Billy, or Laura for that matter, in a footrace. They were constantly wrong footing him, their deeper knowledge of the library outwitting him. He sagged down onto his knees near the distribution desk, catching his breath and taking a moment to check his weapon. Six rounds fired, all needlessly, and only three left. He shrugged off his heavy leather jacket and rose to one knee, still panting hard. "Bloody kid," he muttered.

Billy found Laura on the opposite side of the library, almost as far from the wheezing man as she could be. "We need to escape!" he hissed. "I could—"

Laura ruffled his hair. "No more book-throwing, Billy. Someone will have called the police by now. They'll be here soon, and this will all be over."

"Yes, but—"

"Let's watch him carefully. If, *if* we get a chance, we'll run for the doors." She was being brave for Billy's sake. In truth, her heart was pumping with fear, and there was a strange tingle in her fingertips. She desperately hoped that what she'd told Billy was true, that the police were on their way. She was much too frightened to call them herself.

They both watched the man stumble into the center of the room and begin yet another sweep of the shelves to his left and right. He was too slow, too lumbering, and too unwilling to head down each row to see if they were hiding at the very far corner. He reached the end of the row of shelves, as far from the lobby as he'd ventured.

"Now, Billy!" They ran behind the man and toward the distribution desk and the front door.

The man caught their movements but turned too slowly. He let off a round which exploded through a hardbound volume of the *Encyclopedia Britannica,* throwing up a cloud of paper confetti. Another shot thunked into the wood of the distribution desk. He dashed forward and closed the distance between himself and the pair. Billy opened the library door and ran through it. He ran into the parking lot passing a large, burly police officer coming the other way, baton out and speaking quickly into his lapel radio.

The policeman barged into the library, obstructing Laura's escape. Her assailant grabbed her and pulled her back further inside the library, pressing her body against his and ramming his gun into her neck, his eyes defiant in the face of the bobby's bulk.

Barnwell cursed. He threw himself across the floor, sliding on his hip. He took cover behind the distribution desk. He was armed only with his baton and a canister of CS spray, which would be of no use over distance. "Gorey police!" he shouted from behind the desk. "Let's stay calm now, alright?"

There was a low, cynical chuckle from the gunman. "Oh, dear," he chided, "You've gone and wandered into the middle of somethin', haven't you? You forget, I've got the girl. And the gun."

Barnwell rose to one knee. "Gorey police!" he repeated. "There's no need for anyone to get hurt. Set down your weapon, and show me your hands."

Another chuckle resonated around the library, longer than before. "You think I'll come quietly, eh, copper?" the man shouted. Laura gasped and shuddered against his body.

Barnwell tracked their sounds. The gunman was forcing Laura past the reading desks and toward the library door. The officer drew his CS spray and began shuffling, as quietly as he could, along the length of the distribution desk, and toward the corner. There he would wait. He couldn't risk rounding the edge of it.

"We can work this out," Barnwell shouted back. "How this ends is entirely up to you."

The man laughed.

"Let her go," Barnwell urged.

"Let her go? She's my 'get out of jail free' card," the gunman laughed again. He was still walking forward. Barnwell could hear footsteps, and the man's ragged breath. "I want out of here," the gunman shouted to him. "A car. No funny business, or there'll be more corpses to read about in the papers." As the pair moved forward, Barnwell rounded the corner and slid along the short end of the distribution desk that was now behind them.

In an instant, the man threw Laura sprawling to the floor and bolted for the door. Barnwell set off like a sprinter, CS spray in his left hand, baton in his right. The man began to turn, gun poised, and for a second their eyes locked like bulls in a fight. Barnwell launched himself, grabbing the man around the hips and toppling him with a rugby tackle that would distinguish a professional. The two fell to the floor. Barnwell unleashed the CS spray six times into the man's face. The gunman gurgled and roared and spat at him, but he didn't fire. A moment later, the gunman, his eyes streaming and nausea welling in his gut, found his hands cuffed behind him.

"You're a big, strong lad," Barnwell said, puffing only slightly as he stood up, "to be chasing a woman and a boy around a library, at night, with a gun." Then he spoke into his lapel radio once more. "Mike Bravo 882 to Gorey. Active shooter situation contained. Suspect in custody. One juvenile, one female in need of medical assistance for shock. Firearms team were a little slow, but everything's under control. Over."

The reply was a decidedly non-regulation stream of congratulatory utterances from Constable Roach, followed by, "Hold tight. Transport on its way."

CHAPTER TWENTY-EIGHT

"**N**O LAWYER, MR. Harris-Watts?" Graham asked as he took his seat. "Do you think that's wise, sir?"

Harris-Watts was shattered. He had cried throughout the hours he had spent in his cell, and he periodically broke down again whenever anyone spoke to him, even if it was to ask if he would like a cup of tea. "I was... I was going to plead guilty. I didn't think I'd need... You know... With the cost, and everything."

Graham sat back and folded his arms. "Plead guilty to *what*, exactly?"

Harris-Watts blinked repeatedly. He rubbed his eyes with his knuckles. "The medal. You know. On the morning we found Nobby. I pinched it. I admit it," he sniffed.

"Ah, yes, the medal," Graham said. "I'm glad you've cleared that up for us." Harris-Watts stared at the table in utter hopelessness.

"Tell me all of it," Graham ordered. "Everything about what happened when you went to the museum on Monday morning."

Harris-Watts visibly fought with himself to look at the DI.

"Okay," he said, sniffing. He was rubbing his hands on his thighs, rocking back and forth, visibly trying to bring himself under control. "Okay. I went into work and found Nobby on the floor and glass everywhere. I called nine-nine-nine, and then checked for a pulse, but he was so cold, I knew he was gone." He shivered at the memory. "Then, I checked to see if anything was missing. Nothing appeared to be, so I went to my office and checked the CCTV. With the images being so poor, I knew you wouldn't be able to pin the break-in on anyone." He looked Graham in the eye, more confident now he was confessing, "I've got debts, you see," he admitted. "I've got expensive tastes. Too expensive for my salary. So, I forced open the medal case, instead of smashing it, you know, so it would look professional. I took one that I knew was valuable."

Graham listened, arms folded. "Go on."

"I put it on an underground auction site I sometimes look at, just out of curiosity, and someone bid on it. I thought I'd made thousands, and that no one would ever know. Then your constable came to my house and arrested me."

"And?" Graham pressed.

Harris-Watts shrugged, blinking. "That's it. Now, I'm here. It's the first time I've been in a prison cell in my life. Will I... Will I go to... to *jail* for this?"

Graham closed the door. He took several slow, deep breaths – a practice he called his "Buddha Moments." They were a way for him to bring a greater clarity to the present and help set aside the often fruitless hours of accusations and counter defenses he waded through and was a part of. As he stood there, inhaling deep, slow breaths, he tried to unravel the strange conundrum this case had become.

The DI approached the desk, where Roach and Harding

were listening to the police frequency on the radio. "What's going on?" he asked.

"There's been an active shooter situation at the library, sir," Harding replied.

"WHAT?" Graham stood still, wide-eyed, thoughts careering around his brain like a cascade of shooting stars hurtling around a galaxy.

Harding set down the earphones and smiled. "The situation has been resolved, sir," she said. "All is well. It was very quick. The hostages, the new librarian and Billy Foster, are safe and being checked out by the paramedics. The shooter is in custody. The suspect was apprehended thanks to the heroics of a certain Constable Barnwell. The press'll be here soon, I'll bet. Probably be another glowing article in the paper."

"But... But why didn't you inform me?" Graham was staring at her. He appeared stunned.

"Erm, well sir, we didn't really believe it, see?" Roach said, looking sheepish. "We, Barnwell and I, just thought it was old Mrs. Hollingsworth imagining things again. Seems we got it wrong, sir. Sorry, sir."

"Sorry? An apology is hardly sufficient, Constable! This could have turned into a complete, unmitigated disaster." Graham's voice was hard now, "I can see that we shall have to put some serious effort into more training later in the year." Roach looked at Janice who looked down at her feet.

"Yes, sir," Roach whispered.

Graham glared at them momentarily, then collected himself and thumped the desk, gently. "Barnwell again, eh?" This was the third time the reinvigorated constable had been the hero of the hour in recent months. He was in danger of making it a habit.

"He's bringing the shooter in now, sir," Roach said, talking quickly.

"Where are you going to put him?" Graham asked.

Roach smiled. "We've called St. Helier, and they're sending a firearms unit to meet the prisoner here. They'll handle him. Should be here any minute."

Graham marveled at how far his small, formerly raggle-taggle team had come in a few short months, even if there was still clearly some way to go.

"I'll leave you to it for now, Sergeant, Constable. Do come and find me if there's a terrorist incident on our patch, won't you?" He turned to go back into the interview room, but paused, "I'm all done with Mr. Harris-Watts. Would you be so good as to take him back to his cell?"

"Yes, sir," Harding was looking at him curiously.

"Good," Graham shifted again, "You're quite sure that no one was hurt?"

"Quite sure, sir."

"Well, then. Jolly good... Carry on, Sergeant."

CHAPTER TWENTY-NINE

I T WAS A bright, cold Saturday morning. Don English sat in his cell quietly. He was in whispered consultation with his lawyer as was Charlotte with hers. Unsurprisingly, Charlotte had called Carl Prendergast within moments of arriving at Gorey station. Don was offered, and accepted, the court-appointed duty solicitor on call. When Prendergast finally arrived, direct from the airport, he had exuded the air of someone very reluctant indeed.

"Ready, Sergeant?" Graham asked, setting down his teacup. "I say we start with Charlotte Hughes."

Harding and Graham exchanged a look as they stood at the interview room door. "Is this a case of 'watch and learn,' sir?" Harding asked. "Or do you want me to..."

"Let's see how we get on. You remember the signal?"

Harding nodded, and Graham gave her an encouraging smile as he pushed open the door to the interview room. "Good morning, Ms. Hughes," he said. He took a seat, and Harding sat next to him, opposite Charlotte and Prendergast at the small interview room's table. "It's been quite a few days for you, hasn't it?"

Prendergast laid out the formalities. "My client has decided to exercise her right to silence," he said in his clipped, formal tone. He was short, balding, and somewhere in his mid-sixties. Graham felt he might make a good King Lear or an officious bureaucrat in a period TV drama. There was something about his manner – superior, a bit blustery and bombastic – which made Graham dislike him immediately. Although it was his legal obligation to let the lawyer speak, and for his comments to be entered into the taped record, Graham ignored almost everything Prendergast said.

"As you already know, you've been arrested in connection with the murder of Felipe Barrios," Graham said, scanning Charlotte's face for signs of a reaction. All he saw was a pale, wan visage that signaled exhaustion.

"And when forensic evidence of the crime is presented to us," Prendergast retorted in his testy, nasal tone, "we will understand quite why that is so."

"All in good time," Graham told him.

Prendergast looked at Charlotte, hoping for some kind of sign. She was absolutely white, drained of fight and spark, defeated in a way Graham found almost pitiable. She wore a blue, hooded sweatshirt and pants that Janice had found for her the evening before as they bagged her clothes for forensic examination. Her designer blouse had been torn beyond repair during the bitter exchanges on the battlements.

"You live on the mainland, Ms. Hughes, is that right?"

"Yes, in Market Ellestry. I am, *was*, hoping to become their Member of Parliament at the next election. Doubt that will happen now," Charlotte said, a hint of bitterness creeping into her tone.

"And what are you doing on Jersey? The elections aren't that far away. Shouldn't you be in your constituency? Knocking on doors? Pressing the flesh?" Graham was being droll. He didn't have much time for politicians.

Carl Prendergast leaned forward and opened his mouth to interrupt.

"Shut up, Carl!" Charlotte's mouth curled as she said the words. Her arms were folded. She turned her head away from her legal counsel and stared down at her lap.

"I came here to arrange for repairs to my father's desk."

"I see. Is that all? Couldn't that be done over the phone?"

Charlotte coughed several times to clear her throat. "I was concerned... About the break-in at the museum and the damage to the desk." Graham lifted his chin and waited. Charlotte looked at him, eventually sighing. "And, well if you must know, that Don was missing after speaking to Carl about the desk in the hours before the break-in." Graham stared at Prendergast.

"You spoke to Don English about the desk?"

"Yes," Prendergast said, "Is that a crime?"

"Yes! It makes you a witness! You cannot be representing Ms. Hughes if you're a witness. Get out of here! Harding, take Mr. Prendergast and keep him in reception. If he gives you any trouble, arrest him. Jesus, man."

Prendergast didn't need to be told twice. He scuttled out of the room.

"Ms. Hughes, do you want to call the duty solicitor before we continue?"

Charlotte sighed, wearily. "No, no. Let's get this over with." She leaned her forearms on the table and faced Graham across it. She seemed more at ease now that Prendergast was out of the room. "I thought Don might be here on Jersey looking for something. Something I really didn't want found, something that could damage my bid for election. I wanted to find out what he knew, if he'd found it."

"And what was that 'something' pray?"

"A letter," she croaked, "I've never known what it said. But I knew it would be damaging to my family."

"And does your brother have it?"

"*Step*brother," Charlotte murmured. "No. Yes. Oh, I don't know. I tried to flush him out, but well, you know what happened at the Castle. He just flipped. Crazy. He wants to ruin me, and with a temper like his, who knows what he's capable of?"

"What do you know of the repairs that were being completed on your father's desk?"

"I know the cost of them and the name of the person making the repairs. I also know that he was killed."

"And do you know anything about that? About the killing of Felipe Barrios?"

Charlotte looked Graham squarely in the eyes. She stared into them for a full three seconds before replying. "Absolutely not."

CHAPTER THIRTY

GRAHAM SPIED BARNWELL at the reception desk. "Come with me, Constable. Harding can cover. We've got some investigating to do."

Ten minutes later, they pulled up at Don English's B&B at the same time. Barnwell propped his bike up against the front garden railings. Graham found a parking spot just two doors down. He strolled along the sidewalk to join the constable outside the gate.

"I'm impressed with your commitment, Barnwell. Would never have had you down as a cycling man."

"Does me good, sir. The fresh air and the exercise."

The sun was shining directly on to the small terraced house, the glare from the upstairs window forcing them to shield their eyes. Barnwell pressed the catch of the wrought iron gate with a "ting," and they walked silently up to the front door. Blue and purple hyacinths in pots on either side emitted a delightful aroma as they waited for Don's landlady. They held their police IDs at the ready to reassure her.

"Yes?" Mrs. Lampard said as soon as she opened the door.

She was well into her seventies and tiny. She peered up at the two men through horn-rimmed glasses. Graham reckoned that he towered over her by at least a foot.

"We're from Gorey Constabulary, Ma'am. I rang earlier. About your guest, Mr. English? We'd like to see his room."

"Oh yes, come on in," Mrs. Lampard stood back to let them through. I'm glad to have caught you, I'm just back from the hairdresser's." She gently patted her cotton candy spun hair. There was a faint purple hue to it.

"How is business at this time of year, Mrs. Lampard?"

"It's a bit slow right now, but starting the end of next month, I'll be full until September. It's always like that, like clockwork." Mrs. Lampard held onto the bottom step bannister rail. She looked as though she could barely make a cup of tea, let alone a bed and a full English breakfast on a daily basis.

"When was the last time you had a booking? Before Mr. English."

"Couple of weeks ago. God willing, I'll have another before high season starts. My pension doesn't go very far these days."

"If you'd be so kind as to show us Mr. English's room....?"

"First on the left at the top of the stairs," she said, unnecessarily indicating the flight of stairs that loomed ahead of them. The two men trotted up as she watched.

The room was sunny and decorated brightly. Yellow daffodils sat in a fussy blue vase on a chest of drawers. Next to it, there was a tray with tea-making paraphernalia and a plastic kettle. In the corner was a small, white ceramic sink. Beside the taps sat soap, a face cloth, and shaving equipment.

Graham looked around, mentally cataloging everything he saw. The bed had been made. Don's old-fashioned, striped pajamas were folded and neatly placed on the pillow. A battered paperback sat on the bedside table. In the corner was a wicker laundry basket that had seen better days. Several of the willow twigs had escaped their confines and splayed out waiting to injure the next person who came close. On a table under the window were papers neatly stacked.

"What are we looking for, sir?" Barnwell asked as Graham handed him a pair of latex gloves.

"Anything, Constable, anything that could tie Don English to the break-in at the museum or the Barrios' murder. Here, bag the toothbrush for DNA," Graham held out an evidence bag, "and go take a look in the bathroom." Barnwell picked the toothbrush out of a cloudy glass and dropped it into the bag before disappearing down the hallway to the bathroom Don had shared with his host.

Graham wandered over to the window. After giving the papers that lay on the table underneath it a cursory look, he started opening drawers in the chest next to it. There was nothing in them. Don clearly hadn't settled himself in, and so Graham moved to the open suitcase that lay on the floor. It was a jumble of clothes and belongings.

"Nothing in there, sir," Barnwell said coming back in the room. "Find anything?"

Graham stood up from the suitcase. "Nothing in this case, that's for sure. Take a look at those papers on the table by the window. Do they look like the notes that Don English dropped in the café?"

Barnwell looked them over without touching them. "Yup, I'd say. 'LETTER,' 'DESK,' 'MYSTERY PERSON.' Looks pretty incriminating, sir."

Graham moved over to the tall, imposing oak wardrobe in the corner of the room and turned the key that sat in the lock. The door swung open immediately, creaking. There on the bottom shelf was a gun. Graham picked it up carefully. He knew immediately it was a fake. It wasn't nearly heavy enough to be real. He held it up to the light.

"Cowboys and Indians, sir?" Barnwell asked.

"Cowboys certainly, son." Graham bagged it and set it down next to the piles of paper. "Check under the bed, would you?"

Graham moved over to the bedside table, opening the drawer and flipping through the pages of the dusty Bible that he found inside.

"Sir?"

"Hmm?"

"There's something here, sir," Barnwell was lying on his front, his arm outstretched as he strained to reach under the double bed. Carefully he dragged out an object wrapped in a cloth. Barnwell sniffed.

"It smells of something, sir. Can't place it, though." Graham came over.

"Varnish, Constable. Well, come on. Open it up!"

Barnwell gingerly opened the cloth. His eyes widened. "Got him, sir!" Wrapped inside was a thin round metal file about ten inches long.

"Would you boys like a cup of tea?" The two men turned, surprised by Mrs. Lampard's voice.

"Oh no, thank you. We'll be done shortly," Graham said, disappointing Barnwell who could have murdered a cup.

"Did you find anything? This is my room normally. I can make more money from it than the spare room. Is Mr. English in any trouble? I do hope not.

"Just routine, Ma'am," Graham said.

"Not for me, Inspector. It's quite exciting, isn't it? Are you sure you don't want a cup of tea?"

"Quite sure, thank you. But you can put the kettle on, if you'd like."

"Oh, why's that?"

"Because this room is going to be crawling with a crowd of Scenes of Crimes officers very shortly, and I'm sure they'd like a cuppa when they're done."

CHAPTER THIRTY-ONE

"OH GOOD," DON breathed as the Graham came into the interview room, "I'm so glad you're here."

Graham glared at him as he sat down opposite. "That's not a reaction I get very often," he said. In contrast to Carl Prendergast, Don's solicitor sat quietly, taking notes.

Don shrugged. "I think I'll be the least complicated part of this whole business," he said. He held his hands up, "I confess."

"Really?" Graham opened his notebook in a response conditioned by years of interviews. He began to write.

Don put his elbows on the table and rubbed his face with his hands. When he pulled them away, he sighed and said, "I broke into the museum last Sunday night. I was looking for a hidden compartment inside the Satterthwaite Desk, but I didn't get very far."

"You were interrupted by someone?" Graham asked.

"The guard. We said a few things to each other. Threats and such," Don said. "He was in the middle of backing off when he just went down like a sack of spuds."

Graham kept writing. "He had a name, Mr. English. Nobby

Norris. He'd been working as a security guard at the museum for three years. He enjoyed soccer and having a pint down the pub."

"Yes, sorry. I feel terrible about his death. I'm so sorry."

"And so Mr. Norris collapsed, did he? Right in front of you?"

Don mimed the event with his hands. "*Thump*. I figured he'd just lost his balance, or fainted for a moment."

"You didn't think to come to his aid?"

"I expected him to get right up and chase me out of there! I was so scared that I legged it back out through the window."

"But he didn't get up, did he?" Graham asked.

"I didn't know that!" Don insisted. "It was dark in there, and I couldn't see what had happened to him. Not properly. I'm not an experienced criminal, you know. Never even stolen a pack of gum from the corner shop."

"A man died, Mr. English. He left behind a widow, two sons, and three grandchildren. I doubt they care two hoots about the status of your criminal record at this point. You threatened him with *a gun*! The fact is he may still be alive today if you hadn't broken into the museum and scared him to death."

"Yes, yes, Detective. You're right. I feel terrible, but I didn't *mean* it to happen. If I could turn the clock back, I would. I simply wanted to see inside the desk." Don appealed, his palms up. "I think it better to own up to what I've done and let justice take its course. It was utterly stupid of me, and I won't ever forget it. I'm sorry. I know I need to pay."

Graham sighed and set aside his notebook. "The thing is, Mr. Norris' death notwithstanding, you're in a pile of other trouble, aren't you?" Don looked at him blankly. Graham waited for him to speak, but when nothing was forthcoming, he continued, "That desk you were so keen to check out. The person repairing it, Felipe Barrios, he was murdered." Graham noticed small beads of sweat had appeared on English' brow.

"Yes, I know. I heard about it on the news. Terrible."

"So what do you know about that?"

"Nothing." English shook his head.

Graham looked at him carefully, "Talk to me about your room at the B&B you're staying at."

Don pursed his lips and shook his head slowly from side to side. "It's just a B&B. I checked in on Sunday. The landlady is pleasant enough. Good breakfasts. Why?"

Graham bent to look at the notes in front of him. "What about the object we found under your bed?" He looked up at Don, skeptically.

Don stared at him. "What kind of object?"

"A file."

"A file?" Don asked, at length. "You mean, like papers?"

"A metal file," Graham said.

Don raised his eyebrows and shoulders simultaneously. He gave a sheepish grin. "Oh, I don't know anything about that. I don't do DIY." There was a confused look on his face.

"I don't suppose you do murder, either," Graham said quietly. "Maybe just dabble in it now and again when you're feeling like it, hmm?" He placed both hands on the table. "We have reason to believe the file we found under your bed was used to murder Mr. Barrios."

Don lurched up and to the right, startled into a spasm of panic. "Mur... Murder?" he gasped. "But, I..."

"The file was wrapped in a cloth that we have good reason to believe came from the victim's workshop. Will we find your DNA on it, Don?"

Shaking, muttering, then trying to stand, Don was a miserable sight. "No," he said, over and over. "No, that's wrong, that's wrong, that's wrong. No, no, no, no, noooooo!"

Graham ignored Don's dramatic display. It was just this kind of questioning that brought suspects to those points of extremis and panic where the truth would emerge. "Where were you the night Barrios was killed?"

"In bed, of course. At my B&B."

"Can anyone vouch for you?"

"My landlady doesn't like people coming and going after 11 o'clock, and I've been respecting her wishes. She could confirm it."

"Do you have a key?"

"Yes, but—"

"Hardly a cast iron alibi then, is it Mr. English?"

Don said nothing.

There was a knock on the door. It was Harding. "It's Tomlinson," she said, handing Graham a phone when they were outside the room.

Graham tapped the mute button. "Marcus? Are you going to make my day even more extraordinary?"

"Results on the file, old chap. It was definitely the murder weapon. Plenty of Barrios' DNA on it, but no prints or anything to connect it to Don English. Or anyone else for that matter."

"Damn! What about the cloth? Did that come from the workshop?"

"The chemical composition of the varnish on the cloth matched that found in a can on the workbench next to the desk, so I think we can be pretty sure on that. The strange thing is, there's a hair caught up in the threads of the cloth. Isn't a match for anyone. Not Barrios, his wife, Charlotte Hughes, or English. It's an odd color, a sort of lavender."

"Probably the landlady's. She has a purple tint to her hair. I'll send someone to get a DNA sample from her. Anything else?"

"No, nothing, sorry." Tomlinson rang off. Graham blew out his cheeks and looked up at the ceiling.

CHAPTER THIRTY-TWO

GRAHAM GAVE THE departing van a quick salute. "Farewell, Adam Harris-Watts. Until your trial, anyway." Charged with three different offenses relating to the theft of the medal, he expected Harris-Watts to be bailed and required to wear an electronic tag until his trial.

Graham strode back through the reception area. For Janice and Jack's benefit, Barnwell was re-enacting his rugby tackle of Frank Bertolli, whose arrest was causing quite a flutter at the Metropolitan Police Headquarters in London.

"He's wanted in connection with *six* gang-related murders," Harding told Graham.

"Yes, but what the *hell* was he doing on Jersey?" Graham asked. "And at the *library*, for heaven's sake?" Harding gave him a look that he found hard to interpret.

"...Murder weapon, gun." Barnwell moved on to the find of the morning. "There was all kinds of notes about the desk and such. Even a cloth that smells of varnish. Couldn't be more obvious. A metal file, about ten inches long. We sent forensics down there, pronto."

"Don't count your chickens. The metal file was definitely the murder weapon, but SOCO hasn't turned up anything to connect us to a murderer yet," Graham said, striding through reception on his way to his office. "Barnwell, I need you to get a DNA sample from Mrs. Lampard. We need to rule her out."

Graham's interview with English and his conversation with Tomlinson had left him puzzled. He'd pushed, and Don had wilted. He'd pressed, and Don had looked ready to fold. But the bedeviled man hadn't actually *admitted* anything. Without DNA evidence to connect Don to the crime or a confession, Graham was looking at highly circumstantial evidence at best. That wasn't good enough.

"I'm going to take another run at Charlotte Hughes, Janice. Can you bring her to the interview room?"

"Before you do that, sir," Janice said, trotting alongside him. "Jack has found something interesting." She showed Graham Felipe Barrios' phone records. "Remember he received a call in the evening before he was murdered? We can't trace it. Must have come from a burner."

"Tell him to keep at it, Harding,"

"He also found something else." Janice's tone stopped Graham now. He listened carefully.

"The number comes up again. This time on the records of a completely different phone."

"Whose?"

"Charlotte Hughes. Charlotte Hughes and Felipe Barrios both received a call from the same untraceable number the night he died."

Graham sat opposite Charlotte. He was tired. It had been a long day. "Felipe Barrios received a call on the night of his death. Prior to that call being made, you also received one from the same number. Is there anything you'd like to say about that, Ms. Hughes?"

Charlotte sat back abruptly in her seat. She turned down the corners of her mouth and shook her head. "No. Who is this call supposed to be from? I receive a lot of calls." She shrugged.

"I was hoping you'd tell me."

Charlotte flushed. She looked about her, drawing her breath in one long inhale.

"Is there something you're not telling me, Ms. Hughes?" Charlotte looked up at the ceiling, her hands clasped across her body. Her thumbs were tapping her sides furiously. "Because if there is, and you're not," Graham continued, "I could have you bang to rights on so many charges, your dreams of a future, let alone a parliamentary career, would be but a puff of smoke." He leaned in toward Charlotte, who lowered her head to look at him.

"I don't know anything that's relevant." Charlotte responded.

"Let me decide what's relevant."

Graham waited. He didn't take his eyes off the woman across the table. Charlotte looked away.

"Look, I—" She sighed. "I wanted to flush out if Felipe Barrios had the letter by offering to buy it. But it didn't go anywhere. Barrios wouldn't sell or didn't have it. I don't know which," she added quickly.

"So you called him?"

"No, I couldn't risk it," Charlotte took a deep breath, as she seemed to find some resolve. "No, I wasn't *brave* enough to make the call myself." She looked back at Graham.

"Then who did?"

"I asked my campaign manager, Lillian Hart, to do it for me."

"Where is this Lillian Hart now?"

"At home, I assume. Miles away. In Market Ellestry."

"Are you sure?"

Charlotte stared at him, "Well, no actually. I haven't spoken to her since I asked her to make the call to Barrios."

"And when was that?"

"Tuesday. Tuesday evening."

Graham frowned. "What does she look like?"

"Oh, I don't know. Late fifties, five foot ten, large build. Likes bright loud clothes, lots of makeup. Smokes like a trooper."

"Hair?

"Short. Pixie cut."

"Color?"

"Lavender. Purple is her signature color."

Graham thundered out of the interview room and walked into his office, slamming the door behind him. He dialed a number.

"Mrs. Lampard? It's Detective Inspector Graham from Gorey Constabulary. I came to see you earlier."

He paused, "No nothing's wrong, I just have a couple of extra questions for you. Has anyone inquired about your room in the last few days?"

Mrs. Lampard spoke on the other end.

"I see, did she ask to see the room at all?" He waited as the elderly woman answered his question.

"And did you leave her alone?" Another pause.

"I'm sure it does, Mrs. Lampard. Well, thank you, that is all. You've been very helpful. Goodbye."

CHAPTER THIRTY-THREE

"THEY'VE GOT HER, sir. Boarding a flight to the mainland. They're bringing her in now," Harding said. Two immigration officers had intercepted Lillian and handed her over to St. Helier police.

The doors were pushed open and Lillian, her mascara streaming and her lipstick smeared, jostled her way into the lobby between two bomber-jacketed policemen. Her hands were cuffed in front of her.

"This is outrageous!" she bellowed at Janice, who looked at her without batting an eyelid. Lillian saw Graham standing at the back of the office area, regarding her. "Are you in charge? I demand that I be released *immediately!*"

"Ms. Hart, if you don't calm down, you will be put into the cells until you do," Janice said. Graham hadn't moved, and she knew he had confidence in her to handle the prisoner.

"Don't be ridiculous."

"One more word, Ma'am, and we'll put you in a cell," Janice repeated.

"Well, *really.*" Janice booked Lillian in and took a DNA swab kit from a drawer under the desk. "Would you provide us with a DNA sample?"

"Is it really necessary?" Lillian objected, crossly.

"It is entirely voluntary at this stage, Ma'am, but it will help our investigation." Lillian huffed but submitted, opening her mouth to allow Janice to wipe the swab around her mouth before she took her to the interview room. Graham continued to watch silently.

It took two hours for Ms. Hart's solicitor to arrive. During that time, she sat at the interview table or paced back and forth across the room. Periodically, she'd demand that she be allowed to smoke a cigarette and each time, Sergeant Harding, who'd been given the task of guarding her, refused.

Eventually, everything was in place for the interview to start. Graham entered the room quietly, in marked contrast to the huffing woman. "I am Detective Inspector Graham, Ms. Hart."

"Why am I here?" Lillian almost shrieked. Her voice was shrill.

"You're here in connection with the murder of Felipe Barrios."

"You're being absurd. Do you know who I am?"

"We understand that you flew in from the mainland three days ago? Can you tell me where you were on Wednesday night?"

"In my horrible boarding house, the White House Inn, trying to sleep despite all that clanking. Their heating system is simply appalling!

Graham suppressed a smile. He knew all about the "clanking." "Can anyone vouch for that?"

"I have no idea. You'll have to speak to the staff," Lillian responded.

"So if I spoke to Otto at reception, he'd tell me that he saw you go up to your room and that was all he saw of you until morning."

Lillian's head bobbed furiously. Graham's use of the White House Inn's reception manager's first name appeared to have unnerved her. "Of course," she said, a little uncertainty creeping into her voice.

"You see, Ms. Hart, we understand that your client, Ms. Hughes, asked you to call Mr. Barrios and attempt to buy an old family letter she was trying to locate. And, Ms. Hart, we have phone details that make a connection to Ms. Hughes *and* Mr. Barrios via a third party. Now would that third party be you, by any chance?"

"No."

"So this isn't you, then?" Graham placed Charlotte Hughes' phone on the table and played a voice message. Lillian's voice rang out.

"Charlotte, it's me. Where the hell are you? The fool wouldn't play ball. I'm going to try one more thing. Be in touch soon."

"This was placed shortly after a call from the same number was made to Felipe Barrios." Lillian pursed her lips and shut her eyes briefly. "I'm guessing that wasn't from you, either?"

"So what? All that proves is that I made a call," Lillian practically spat at him.

"Ms. Hughes has already told us that she was looking for an item that might be damaging to her family's reputation. What can you tell us about that?"

"Nothing, nothing at all" Lillian had transformed. Now she was smiling nervously, apparently eager to help but unable to do so. "Charlotte told me she was worried and asked me to help her find it. I did call Mr. Barrios, but he told me he was completely unaware of such a thing."

"And you didn't go to Mr. Barrios' workshop later that evening?" Graham raised his eyebrows.

"No, why would I do that?"

"Perhaps to apply a little more pressure...?"

"Look, I demand you release me. I have done nothing wrong!"

"You see we found the weapon that killed Mr. Barrios in Don English's room—"

"Then why are you questioning me? It is he that should be sitting across the table from you. Not *me*."

"Except that he maintains his innocence."

Lillian scoffed, seizing the opportunity to go on the offensive again. "Well, what does that prove? He would, wouldn't he?"

The door behind Lillian opened and Janice poked her head in. She flashed a thumbs up sign and quickly closed the door again.

"So when we examine your DNA and compare it with the evidence we found alongside the murder weapon, we won't find a match?"

"No." Lillian rubbed her nose. "How could you? I already said. I was in bed being kept awake in that godforsaken guest house."

"You're lying, Ms. Hart."

"No, I am not," Lillian was sitting up in her chair, rigid.

"I put it to you that you knew if this letter were exposed, it would cover your client in scandal, and therefore, you. Charlotte Hughes would risk losing the Parliamentary seat she is campaigning for. And you didn't want that, did you?"

"Are you suggesting I murdered a man all over some letter that may have harmed my *client's* reputation? That's preposterous. Of course it wasn't me. Murder? Me? Why would I do such a thing?"

"Because you thought you could get away with it. To protect your client. To protect yourself."

"Rubbish."

"Ms. Hart, we know you called Mr. Barrios to offer to buy the letter from him. We can also place you at Don English's B&B the day after the attack. I know for a fact that the desk is only manned at the White House Inn until midnight, so we only have your word for it that you were there all night. And we have a match for your DNA on hair found with the murder weapon. It's only a matter of time before we place you at the murder scene. Now tell me, are you sure you had nothing to do with the murder of Felipe Barrios?"

Lillian stared ahead, her mouth turned down, her eyes lidded.

"Ms. Hart?"

Lillian pulled herself to her full height and exhaled. She looked at Graham defiantly. "Yes, yes, I did it. The stupid man wouldn't take my money. I went there to persuade him. He wasn't supposed to *die*. I just wanted to knock him out so I could search for whatever it was I was looking for. And I *still* didn't find it."

"And you planted the murder weapon in Don English's room to frame him?"

Lillian sneered. "Don English is a *moron*. He'll never amount to anything. He'd be no loss to society." Her mouth pursed in an ugly plum streak. She held Graham's gaze, her back ramrod straight. "I did it for my client and her constituents. They are the losers in this."

"It's just marvelous, this," Roach enthused. He had traveled to the mainland to visit Dr. Oxley in his offices. "A few hours ago, this document was completely soaked with blood, but now..."

Oxley held the piece of paper aloft with a pair of tweezers. "Not bad," he conceded. "I've seen better, but this will do nicely. We have the author to thank, though." He set the document down in a plastic tray and slid it under the body of a machine that

was so new that, as Roach observed, it still had that 'new hardware smell.' At first glance, it appeared that a design team had
become confused as to whether it was producing a flatbed scanner, a fax machine, or a high-end cappuccino maker.

"The author?" Roach asked. "How did he help?"

"Well," Oxley said, orienting the tray below a scanning arm
and pressing a sequence of buttons on the machine's LCD
display, "he used a type of ink which was pretty low in iron
content. Blood naturally contains a good deal of iron, and old-
fashioned common iron gall ink would have really confused
matters. As it happens, we should be able to read the whole document, once the X-ray scan is complete."

"Remarkable," Roach breathed again. "How does it work?"

Twenty minutes later, Roach considered himself a minor
expert on the use of X-ray technology to peer inside damaged and
ancient documents. "So, even after its been wet," he summarized,
"the X-ray scan picks up the tiny rises in the contour of the paper
caused by the impression of the pen, and the presence of the
ink?"

"Spot on," Oxley said, relieved that Roach had a quicker and
more agile mind than he had initially expected. "And, drum roll
please..." The printer networked to the X-ray scanner began
producing a high-resolution image, one fraction of an inch at a
time, until the two men were virtually hopping from one foot to
another with impatience.

"So, your boss," Oxley said as the print-out inched glacially
along. "Smart chap, isn't he? Very deductive, I hear."

Roach didn't take his eyes off the emerging printout, as he
replied, "As smart as they come. He's a detective, right down to
his bones. Eats, sleeps, thinks, and breathes crime-solving. He's
been very good to me."

Oxley nodded. "What do *you* think this is all about?" The
letter was almost ready, but Oxley had already warned Roach
against yanking it out of the printer prematurely.

"I think the letter was originally hidden in the desk," he said. "And I think it's going to fill in a lot of gaps in these cases we've been working on."

The printout dropped into the output tray and Oxley promptly picked it up. He turned it, so that they could read together. Three minutes later, as Roach dialed Graham's cell-phone, Oxley said, "What are the chances that the person finding this would have the knowledge to know the significance of it?"

"Pretty tiny, I should imagine," Roach replied.

"Pity Mr. Barrios didn't turn this in right away. He might still be alive," Oxley said.

Graham picked up. Roach spoke seriously into his phone. "He was a traitor, sir. Sir Thomas Hughes. A traitor."

CHAPTER THIRTY-FOUR

The Palace of the People
Antigua de San Marcos
19 May, 1974

My dear Thomas,

What a pleasure it is to write to you amid the peace and quiet of a restful afternoon. You must be concerned about our wellbeing, but let me assure you that the recent unpleasantness is quite at an end. We are relaxing after a lengthy cabinet meeting this morning – Julia sends her kisses, both to you and Susannah, whom we hope is very well. I'm sure she is as beautiful as ever.

Perhaps I should revise my greeting, above – it is Sir Thomas now, is it not? Congratulations on this long overdue honour; finally, your imperialist Queen has seen fit to elevate you as you deserve, some twenty months after San Marcos bestowed her highest award upon our most loyal European friend. It is no less than you deserve.

It is out of friendship that I write today, Sir Thomas. Words *cannot express the great debt that is now owed to you by the free-dom-loving people of San Marcos. I say this only to you, as I am certain of your discretion. We were staring into the abyss, my friend. The rebels were rampaging through the countryside, looting and burning. Even my military commanders were beginning to plan for the worst. There was talk of a massive barricade around the city. Without proper intelligence or air power, the advance would never have been stopped, and we could not long have endured a siege.*

But then, the angels came in the form of you! Long moribund and gathering dust at our three aerodromes, our helicopters, refitted thanks to your kindness, took to the skies and saved the revolution! I begged our neighbors, our friends, even the KGB, for the spare parts to bring our air forces back to life, but only you responded. You recognized the danger, and you took swift and decisive action. And for this timely response, I owe you my presi-dency and the future security and happiness of my country as well as my life and those of my family.

Please be assured of my complete and utter discretion. I am indeed aware of the jeopardy you put yourself in to help us, and the danger to you should your role on our behalf become known. I realize you will be seen as an Enemy of your People. This is not a debt easily repaid, Sir Thomas, but I will find a way. Please know that, should it become necessary, there will always be a home for you here. In the meantime, the people of San Marcos owe you the deepest and most profound thanks. I will forever hold you in the very highest esteem. You have my own deepest and sincerest thanks, as well as my fond and lifelong friendship.

Your loyal and grateful brother,
General Augusto Fuente
President of San Marcos

CHAPTER THIRTY-FIVE

THE RULES WERE firm and clear. Graham knew he couldn't close his office door during this delicate interview with Laura Beecham. Instead, the intensely curious, but assiduously toiling Sergeant Harding and Constable Roach would be able to witness much of the meeting from the open-plan office outside his own. Graham was determined that it appear as professional as possible.

"I know I promised coffee," Graham said, "but in truth, I'm much more of a tea man."

Sitting across from him, in dark jeans and a gray sweater, Laura bit her lip anxiously. Her first scheduled encounter with this attractive, interesting man was taking place, not at a coffee or tea shop as they had planned, but at a police station. In his office, no less. And as part of an investigation that had yielded the arrest of a man wanted for multiple murders.

"Mrs. Taylor did warn me," she said. "What type of tea are you treating me to?"

Graham could tell by the scent of the leaves, without even checking the container. "Jasmine from Taiwan," he said. "Very aromatic, just a little floral. Full of antioxidants too, so they claim. Apparently it can help people recovering from serious illness."

Laura gave him a small smile. "Well, I'm recovering from a bit of a shock, I'll admit, but I have you to thank that it wasn't more serious. That gunman could have killed me."

Graham sipped his tea and began making notes. "I can't take any credit, I'm afraid, much as I'd like to. Constable Barnwell was your savior, not me. I was wrapped up in a murder case. I didn't know anything about it until it was all over.

Laura brushed this off. "You can't be everywhere. And your constable was magnificent."

"I'll make sure he knows that," Graham said. "But I have to ask, Miss Beecham..."

"Laura," she said. "Please."

"I have to ask, Laura, why would a notorious mob figure like Frank Bertolli come down to Jersey to kill you?" Graham had spent a significant part of the last hours developing several theories, but each was less credible than the last. Laura was not the type to have become involved in any criminal activity; at least Graham *hoped* she wasn't. Though he'd have said the same thing about Don English, Adam Harris-Watts and perhaps even Charlotte Hughes. Lillian Hart, on the other hand, was an aberration that couldn't be anticipated.

"Okay, but this must all remain 'off the record,'" Laura said leaning forward and lowering her voice. "That has to be a condition of my explaining it."

Graham closed his notebook and pushed it away. "No problem."

"And," she asked, turning to glance behind her, "could we close the door?"

"It's against the rules," Graham explained, "without another officer present."

"Just for a few moments," Laura requested. "I want to make sure this isn't overheard."

Graham hesitated, then moved to close the door. He thought he caught the tail end of Harding and Roach ducking their heads, but they appeared to be working with an uncommon focus. He sat back down and allowed Laura to tell her story in her own way.

She exhaled and began. "I was working in a pub just by Stratford Station in east London." She gave him a quick smile to hide her embarrassment. "A librarian's pay isn't enough to live on in London, that's for sure. Do you know the area?"

"Vaguely. Where the Olympic Park is?"

"Right. Well, there were a group of men who came in regularly. Over a few weeks we got friendly, you know, them telling me their problems, troubles at home, or at work, just banter, typical stuff," she shrugged.

Graham nodded, "Go on,"

"Well, one Sunday night, they came in quite late and in a good mood. The landlord stayed open after closing time and asked me to stay on to serve them. It was just them and me. I thought they'd come from the Premiership game or maybe the dog track. They were buying champagne and expensive liquor. It was out of character."

Arms folded, Graham leaned back and pictured the scene. "So what were they celebrating? A win on the dogs?"

Laura looked over her shoulder just once to make sure the door was closed. "A diamond heist. One of the biggest. Diamonds worth a hundred million pounds."

Graham couldn't prevent his mouth from falling open. "The Marble-Kilgore heist?" he gasped. "They *admitted* it?"

"Not in so many words," Laura cautioned. "But I overheard enough of what they said. I went to the police and agreed to become a witness, but..."

"You needed protecting. And what better way than to spirit you off to a quiet little island in the English Channel?"

Laura nodded and tucked a strand of blond hair behind her ear. "Exactly. The Met wanted it kept as quiet as possible."

"So quiet," Graham pointed out, his eyebrows raised, "that they didn't even tell the Jersey Police about you."

Laura frowned, "The officer in charge of the witness protection scheme said that..."

"Someone down here might blab," Graham said. "Sensible enough, I suppose, though a little over-cautious. Besides," he added with just a hint of frustration, "if we'd known you were here, *we* could have protected you."

Laura gave a long sigh. "I recognize that now. If I had the time over, I'd do things differently." She looked at him apologetically.

"It wasn't your fault." Graham met her gaze. "Thank you for leveling with me. I have to admit the whole thing had me rather stumped."

Laura feigned surprise. "The legendary DI Graham, *stumped*? Surely not."

He let his professional demeanor drop a little. "Well," he grinned sheepishly, "only for a few hours. But still, if you *hadn't* come down here, we wouldn't have collared Bertolli."

"And we would never have met," Laura pointed out.

There were ten seconds of silence before Graham found the courage to dispense with the rules for the second time in almost as many minutes and say what he most wanted to. "You know, I'm actually due half a day off."

"And the library is closed for repairs." Laura said, smiling.

Graham stood. "I wonder if you would allow me to show you around the island. Maybe take you to some of the sights?" He made a fuss of opening the door and was gratified to find Roach and Harding once more silently intent upon their work. "Any calls come in, Sergeant?" he asked Harding.

"Nothing we can't handle, sir," she replied. "Taking a half-day, sir?"

He shot her a look but only briefly. "I think I will," he said.

"We all deserve a break, I reckon," Constable Roach piped

up. "We've had quite enough excitement for a while. And, I've got my sergeant's exam in ten days.'"

"Ten days?! High time for a quiz then, wouldn't you say?" Harding bustled around, getting down the police duties manual.

There was a bang, and they all turned to see Constable Barnwell burst through the doors.

"Mornin' all. How are we doin?'" Barnwell noticed Graham shrugging into his jacket. "On your way out, sir?"

"Yes, Constable," Graham said in a tone that didn't invite further questioning. "While I'm gone, sort that room out in the back. It's like Piccadilly Circus in there."

Graham and Laura left them to it and headed out into the spring sunshine. "Where first?" Laura asked. "I haven't been to the castle yet."

Graham smiled knowingly. "Let me give Stephen Jeffries a call. The exhibit hasn't opened yet, but there are some displays in the basement that you won't *believe*." He dialed Jeffries number. "Ready?" he asked.

Laura gave him a smile that matched the sunny day. "Ready."

EPILOGUE

T HE FALL FROM grace experienced by Charlotte Hughes and her campaign manager, Lillian Hart, in the days after their arrests was swift and absolute as knowledge of Sir Thomas Hughes' treasonous activities became known.

Charlotte was charged with attempting to pervert the course of justice and was sentenced to 300 hours of community service. She completed it by working on a rundown, drug-riddled estate in Goslingdale. Her tasks included picking up litter, cleaning off graffiti, clearing wasteland, and maintaining community property, all while wearing a distinctive orange vest.

Lillian Hart was sentenced to fifteen years in prison for the voluntary manslaughter of Felipe Barrios. She appealed her sentence and requested a move to an open women's prison, but her appeal was rejected. She has received no visitors during her imprisonment thus far and has no expectation of any in the future. She was offered the chance to learn woodworking during her stay in prison but turned it down.

Don English was found guilty of three crimes, including breaking and entering and perverting the course of justice. A charge of involuntary manslaughter could not be proven. He was given a sentence of six months jail time and two years community service. He served three months in HMP Shrewsbury and later found work as a gardener working in the grounds of a National Trust property. He still lives in Goslingdale.

The Hughes' family solicitor, Carl Prendergast, was a witness in all three cases. In a statement to the press, he claimed that he "would prefer to have nothing more to do with the Hughes family. Spending decades dealing with one dreadful, sociopathic Hughes was quite enough." A week before Charlotte Hughes' trial began, he announced his retirement from practicing law.

Adam Harris-Watts was sacked from his position as curator of the Jersey Heritage Museum. He was sentenced to 75 hours community service and now works as a researcher for a left-wing academic at Manchester University.

Frank Bertolli was sentenced to twelve years for the attempted murder of Laura Beecham and Billy Foster. He also asked for six other murder charges to be taken into consideration. He is likely to die in jail unless he is willing to turn Queen's evidence against those who hired him.

·   ·   ·

Thomas Hughes' estate gave permission for the Fuente letter to be published as part of a full-page London Times advertisement that began an international campaign to seek justice for those mistreated or executed by Fuente's government. The raising of awareness and the important celebrity endorsement led to mounting and eventually intolerable pressure on the crumbling regime. Within a year, a peaceful revolution swept the now elderly general from power. San Marcos recently held its first democratic elections since the early 1970s.

Shortly after the arrests of Don English, Lillian Hart, Adam Harris-Watts, Charlotte Hughes, and Frank Bertolli, Janice Harding and Jack Wentworth took five days' vacation to drive around southern France. On their return, they began looking for an apartment together in Gorey.

Barry Barnwell was once again commended for his valiant and selfless efforts and received a second Queen's Gallantry Medal at Buckingham Palace. He was offered a much higher profile assignment by the Metropolitan Police, one his London-based mother hoped he'd accept, but he turned it down.

Near perfect results in his sergeant's exam and a glowing recommendation from DI David Graham brought a new opportunity for Constable Jim Roach. He will divide his time between Gorey and the forensics lab in St. Helier, where he will study criminology and pathology under the guidance of Dr. Marcus Tomlinson.

. . .

After the case, Simon Oxley resumed his semester of teaching at Cambridge University. He recently published a paper in *X-ray Quarterly* discussing his role in decoding "THE LETTER".

Viv Foster was accepted into Jersey's drug rehabilitation program once again and is doing well. Billy visits her daily. On Sergeant Harding's recommendation, Social Services fostered Billy with Mrs. Lampard for the duration of Viv's stay in the program, giving Billy a stable home base on the island and Mrs. Lampard some company and a regular income. Despite their disparate ages, the two get on famously. As Billy had generally refused to talk about it and was not required to testify at the trial, the incident at the library remains shrouded in mystery among his peers. Harding and Barnwell did, however, refer to Billy as a "hero" during a visit to his school recently, something which has completely transformed his school life.

David Graham and Laura Beecham are often seen together at the Bangkok Palace for their regular Friday "date night." She always has the Pad Thai or Tom Yum soup while he always experiments with whatever's hottest on the menu. The wait staff no longer ask him to confirm his well-being the morning afterward.

USA
Today
Bestselling
Author

Mussels Not Brussels

THE CASE OF THE
PRETTY
LADY

ALISON GOLDEN   Grace Dagnall

THE CASE OF THE PRETTY LADY

BOOK SIX

Published by Mesa Verde Publishing
P.O. Box 1002
San Carlos, CA 94070

Edited by
Marjorie Kramer

CHAPTER ONE

EVEN BEFORE THEY heard him speak, his bulk, the brilliantly white Stetson, and his endearing manner marked him as an American tourist. "You know what I'm wondering?" the man boomed in a Texan drawl. "I'm wondering what on the good Lord's earth a *fo'c'sle* is." He pronounced it "fock-slee," to the amusement of the early lunchtime crowd. "Anyone want to educate a newcomer?" he asked the two-thirds empty bar.

The barman, Lewis Hurd had this covered and not for the first time. "A 'forecastle'," he explained. "It's the front part of the deck of a working ship or a warship."

"You don't say," the American replied. "And how the heck do you pronounce it?"

The regulars at the bar replied in an oft-rehearsed chorus, "Fock-sul."

"Awesome," the American beamed. "But what's a *ferret* doing on a *warship*?"

Hurd leaned in to handle this one while the pub's patrons,

here for the dependable grub or to enjoy the handcrafted ales alongside like-minded souls, returned to their conversations.

Over in the corner, an invective of French rose into the air, followed by a roar of approval. Five men in boots and work pants stood talking over one another as they drank their pints. One man poked a finger at another who gesticulated rapidly as he defended himself against some unknown accusation. The ferocity of their discussion would have seemed threatening were it not for the smiles on the faces of their countrymen. Soon words gave way to back thumps and clinking glasses, gestures that told the other pub-goers that all was well.

Lewis Hurd looked at the group, barely concealed dislike curling his lip. "Keep your voices down, lads, please," he called over, his words more reasonable than the feelings his expression conveyed.

Beyond them, by the big, paned windows with their view of the harbor, Tamsin Porter and Greg Somerville, two thirty-somethings, fit and trim in their high-end outdoor wear, were sitting in sullen silence, refusing to even look at one another. Tamsin stared into her half-finished pint, her hands fiddling with the cord that circled the perimeter of her jacket's hood while Greg let his gaze wander over the masts of the boats in the harbor and the members of a crew who chatted as they sheltered from a sudden downpour beneath a barely sufficient awning.

"So, you're not going to say anything?" Tamsin asked, finally.

Greg sighed, the momentary peace brought to an unwelcome end. "What do you want me to say, Tamsin?"

"I don't know. Something. Anything."

"Shall I stand up, right here," he proposed, "and admit to the whole pub that I'm a poor scientist? Would that do you?"

"Greg, come on..."

"Or that I'm an unreliable partner, that I can't source enough funding for more robust trackers, and therefore my data can't be trusted?" His temper rose quickly, along with his voice. "That I should have found a way to become clairvoyant and *predicted* that our work might be interrupted by a freak storm?"

Tamsin pushed her pint away and folded her arms. "Calm down, all right?"

"I can't stand to hear you complain about my anger when you're the one who does the most to create it. Why don't you stop criticizing and *help* for once?"

Their relationship, once admired by their friends for its stability and endurance, was in a strange, disappointing, some might say vicious spiral. They didn't talk any more. They just argued and nit-picked and called each other terrible names, only to apologize the next day, and begin the acrimony all over again, the day after that.

"We're going to get some good data," Greg promised. "They're coming in, maybe eight or ten of them, and if one comes anywhere near a buoy, we'll pick up the UHF signal, and we'll know *exactly* where our little beauties are traveling to."

"*If* the hurricane doesn't shift their behavior patterns," Tamsin countered.

The rotund American was still wandering around the pub, drink firmly in hand, examining the photos and old examples of fishing gear nailed to the walls. "Tell me, are you guys from out of town, too?" he asked them cheerily, oblivious to the tension simmering between the couple.

Tamsin made no move to even look up, but Greg was glad of the distraction. "We are, but we're working here," he said.

"On what?" the American asked.

Tamsin turned, her eyes tired and still a little swollen from crying earlier. She said simply, "Sharks."

The American's eyes widened, a reaction the couple was used to. "Get outta here," he breathed. "What do you do?"

"We're marine biologists. We're involved in a British government project to track the population of Holden Sharks. This is our third year tracking them."

"Huh!" It was that curious, open-minded sound that meant, "Say more about that."

"They migrate through the English Channel, but no one's proven where they go to breed. We're here to gather that data."

"Neat!" the American exclaimed. "I've never heard of a... what're they called, again?"

Greg folded his arms. "Holden sharks. They're among the rarest in the world," he explained. "Little bit like a basking shark," he added, pointing to a photo on the wall which showed the giant, unlikely animal approaching the camera, its jaw cranked open to reveal not teeth, but rows of fleshy filters, like those of a whale. "And they head through here on their way to the Norwegian Sea, where they mate, feed, and then head back toward the open Atlantic."

"At least," Tamsin interrupted, her fingertip pressing to the table in a sudden rush of frustration. "We *think* that's what they do. Opinions vary." She gave Greg a sideways glance, the now-obvious, strange, electric tension between the pair telling the American visitor that the theory was a major bone of contention between them. "We need the data from our buoys to support any conclusions. It may be that they simply turn around here for some reason and head straight back out."

Greg wouldn't let this go. "That's highly unlikely and you know it," he said, well aware that they were restarting a two-year-old argument in front of a bemused layman. "Sharks don't do one-eighties unless they're lost."

"What about those whale sharks in the Gulf of Thailand?" Tamsin argued. "They swam up there and turned right around."

The American nodded politely to them both and wandered off, unwilling to be neither enabling party, nor participant, in this increasingly bitter confrontation.

"Case in point," Greg retorted. "They were lost and corrected their path."

Before Tamsin could compose a counterpoint, the swing door

next to them burst open and a man walked in, shaking himself dry. The moisture from his waterproofs caught the light in the dim, dingy bar as drips tracked his movements on the floor.

Surprised, Tamsin and Greg looked up, Greg immediately stiffening while Tamsin resumed fingering her hood's drawstring. When he caught sight of them, the man's eyes widened with shock, but he took a step toward them, his hand extended.

"Tamsin, Greg," he acknowledged, looking at them in turn.

"Kev, what're you doing here?" Greg ignored the outstretched hand, but Tamsin filled the uncomfortable void and shook it.

"Just came in out of the rain."

"Not here, *here*. On Jersey. You're not following us again, are you? You know we have a permit, right? And government funding."

"Yeah, I heard." Kev sounded like he'd heard it more than once, too.

Greg half-rose from the bench he was sitting on, his anger along with the volume of his voice increasing again. "Listen, you have no right—"

"Greg..." Tamsin put a warning hand on his arm, and he wavered. He carefully sat down again, catching sight of Lewis Hurd carefully watching the trio as he slowly polished a glass behind the varnished, wooden bar top.

"Be on your way, Kev. We better not see you out on the water, okay?" she said.

"Nice to see you, too. " The man shrugged and sidled off, dragging from his head the woolen beanie that held his bushy hair in check and brushing drops from his beard.

"That's all we need. Another animal rights pain in the bum. If you want to complain about someone, Tamsin, complain about them. Why don't they do their homework and understand that what we do will sustain the herd, not threaten them?"

Greg stood suddenly, forcefully enough to jar the table. The warming remains of Tamsin's pint wobbled dangerously. She moved to steady it.

"The weather's fairing up," he told her, "and I'm due out to collect the in-situ data from the buoys. This might be the last time for a few days given the forecast. You can come with me, or sit here and continue telling the whole pub what a rubbish scientist I am." He grabbed his jacket. "It's entirely up to you." Greg stomped out of the bar and up the stairs to the room they'd been sharing above the pub, leaving Tamsin feeling hollow and strangely abandoned.

Lewis Hurd sidled over to collect Greg's empty mug and returned to the bar silently. Tamsin continued to stare at her drink, but as she pushed it away again, she saw Greg leave the pub and watched him out of the window heading down to his small motor launch, wondering what had happened to the fun, loving relationship they'd once had. And also wondering just how long the strained, combative one that had replaced it could possibly last.

Greg could see the damage from a quarter mile away through his powerful binoculars. "Damn it," he cursed as he applied the left rudder, bringing his small boat gradually alongside the cracked, orange buoy. Sixteen of the buoys, arranged in a pattern between the Portland and Thames sea areas, were intended to give Greg and Tamsin the clearest picture yet of Holden shark movements in the Channel. But this one would never transmit again. The bright orange chassis had split, exposing the buoy's electronic innards to the raging sea. The wind was getting up, and Greg cursed again as he struggled to winch the buoy on board. "How did this happen?"

He sat down in the boat as he examined the buoy. He felt emotionally drained. The constant arguing with Tamsin was wearing on his nerves, and as he'd prepared to leave the harbor earlier, he'd been heckled by a couple of locals. The fishermen resented their presence every year, although there was no evidence to suggest that their methods for collecting data affected the fishermen or their catch at all. The sight of Kev Cummings in the pub had just added to his troubles. Kev was the regional director of the local SeaWatch chapter, a grand title for someone who was, in Greg's opinion, a simple yob. Their annual game of "cat and mouse" was a complication he found tiresome. It was exhausting to be the villain when all you were doing was your best to protect the marine ecosystem, ultimately for everyone's benefit. *If only they could see that.*

Greg frowned at the mess of salt-corroded wires, so bent and misshapen as to be almost unrecognizable. Two wires twisted impotently in the air. The ends were clean cut. Greg stood, feet apart, in the gently swaying boat, the buoy lying easily in his hands as he stared at the horizon. His eyes darkened as his fury built once more. The impending poor weather had driven seafarers ashore early and sidelined the commercial vessels transporting tourists seeking cheap booze from the coastal French hypermarkets. Greg looked around. With the exception of one boat some distance away, he was alone on the water.

He put the buoy aside and set course for the next one. In theory, each time a shark passed by the buoy's receptors, the tiny transponders within the shark's skin would activate, transmitting a long-term record of the animal's depth, speed, and course. Although sharks turned suddenly for all kinds of reasons, Greg's thesis was that they were migrating generally *east*, and that they ultimately emerged in the North Sea where they patrolled off the coast of Norway as they waited for potential mates to arrive. His data would settle long-standing questions about shark behavior and perhaps help to raise money and awareness for shark conservation. *Jaws* had done enduring harm to the reputation and safety of sharks all over the world, and

Greg felt a moral duty to do his part in reversing some worrying trends.

Not everyone saw his research like that, however. Animal activists were a constant irritant to marine biologists. Some felt the moral imperative was to leave the sharks entirely alone, to allow them to continue their natural behavior, honed over centuries, unencumbered by man's efforts to understand them. Others believed that any study was bound to disrupt the animals, provide false data, and even threaten their existence.

Greg found the activists to be largely willful, illogical, and uneducated in the ways of the animals they claimed to be trying to protect. As far as he was concerned, they romanticized the sharks and imagined the threat posed by his research. Thankfully, they usually went no further than making their presence felt on land in low-key ways; they would hang around the launch site or "bump" into him and Tamsin around town. Neither of them felt particularly intimidated, nor did the activists seek to intervene directly in their work. This new possibility that his research was being actively sabotaged represented a significantly increased level of intimidation, one that was concerning, and most definitely dangerous to the sharks. Even perhaps himself.

His next buoy lay a mile away, Day-Glo orange and gratifyingly upright. Like an iceberg, the waves concealed much of its mass. Below the surface, a weighty ballast kept the buoy steady while the orange tower above helped fend off collisions in these busy sea lanes. Greg pulled alongside and reached over to open a panel and slot in a cable. He then waited the requisite ten seconds with his fingers crossed, and checked his phone for the data flow. "Green across the board. Sweet."

Only after he'd returned to the boat's modest pilot house and given the data a cursory examination did he see the good news: *six* Holden sharks had come through over the past three days. Forgetting his earlier concerns, he slapped the boat's wheel and hooted. "Yes!"

Preoccupied with jubilation, he sensed nothing untoward until there was an unexpected noise behind him, sudden and firm, as though something large had collided hard with the stern of his boat. Greg was thrown forward hard onto his hands and knees and shook his head roughly as the sound of feet landing on the deck of his motor launch reached his ears.

CHAPTER TWO

DETECTIVE INSPECTOR DAVID Graham cleared his throat and tapped gingerly on the side of a glass with the end of his fountain pen. "Fellow officers," he began, his glass raised to the man of the hour, "I give you Constable Barry Barnwell, now *twice* presented with the Queen's Gallantry Medal by Her Majesty at Buckingham Palace!" He broke into applause, accompanied by Sergeants Janice Harding and Jim Roach. The four of them were in his office. "It is an honor to serve the community alongside an officer of your caliber, Constable Barnwell."

Blushing, but feeling as proud as he'd been since those two remarkable occasions in London, Barnwell shook his boss's hand and took a polite sip of his lemonade.

"Congratulations again, mate," Jim said next, as Janice found some jazz music on an Internet radio station. Graham closed the office door almost completely, but not quite. The day's investigations were formally over, but they still had to respond to any members of the public who walked or rang in.

Barnwell smiled to himself and focused on enjoying the

moment, glowing with satisfaction. If he were honest, or if Harding prodded him long enough, he'd admit this little gathering meant just as much as a visit to the Palace.

"I mean it," Graham told him as they stood together. "You could have had your pick of assignments after the first QGM, but now... Any thoughts on what you might do?"

Barnwell looked surprised for half a second. "My only plan is to continue on here, sir." He blinked a couple of times, and then added, "That is, of course, if it's all right with you?"

It was Graham's turn to be surprised. "All right?" he repeated. "You're a remarkable officer. I'd like ten more of you." Graham raised his glass again, "To Gorey Constabulary and its officers. A small, but highly effective unit comprised of some of the best officers I've ever had the pleasure to work with."

"Very kind, sir," Janice replied.

"Not at all, Sergeant. It's well-deserved." Graham wandered over to pour himself another drink.

"I couldn't help noticing," Roach said leaning in to Janice, "that you're glancing at your watch a lot. Are we keeping you from something?"

"Nothing escapes your perceptive faculties does it, Roachie?" Harding smirked. "It's Jack. He should be here soon."

"How are things going with him?"

"Good, good. He went with me to Birmingham for that course on Internet analysis a couple of weekends ago," Janice said. "Our first trip away together."

"Birmingham." Roach wiggled his eyebrows. "Romantic."

"It's nicer than you think, these days," Janice said. "Plus my grandparents live there, and Nanna always did insist on meeting my boyfriends before I was allowed to get serious about them. So I killed several birds with one stone."

Roach smirked as he took a sip of his drink.

"And did he pass the Nanna test?" Graham said as he walked up with a bottle to top up their glasses.

"Oh, she *adores* Jack," Harding said. "He fixed her computer, figured out how to lower her gas bill, and then took her shopping."

"Nailed the audition, then," Graham said.

"Never in doubt." She grinned.

Graham imagined the intelligent and articulate Wentworth charming Harding's octogenarian grandmother, a woman she'd described one night at the Bangkok Palace as "Not so much 'pre-internet' as 'pre-electric,' with a short fuse to match."

"Yeah, I can imagine that," Graham smiled. "He's got style, that Jack, the kind of style that nannas appreciate. And how was the course?"

"Oh, pretty good. There's a lot to learn and things are changing faster than anyone can keep up with. But if we get hacked, I should know how to track the hackers down."

"Terrific," Graham said.

Barnwell was regaling Roach once again with the story of how he narrowly averted tragedy on the battlements of Gorey Castle. "He was all set to do it," Barnwell told him. "I could tell. His stance, you know, the way he'd placed his feet. He was getting ready to push her. Right where that young groom died a while back."

"Exact same spot," Graham testified. "That would have been just *too* much. Besides, I'm not sure poor Stephen Jeffries would have made it through another murder investigation at the castle. While he must have nerves of steel and the patience of Job to be an events manager, I think he'd rather face a thousand bridezillas and their mothers than go through that again."

"And he doesn't want his business being the center of attention for all the wrong reasons. I think we can all understand that," Janice said.

"Mrs. Taylor's in the same boat," Graham agreed. "There are still people who visit the White House Inn as part of a 'murder mystery tour' or something. They do all the usual tourist stuff –

the zoo, the castle, the old German tunnels – and then they stand outside the White House Inn, gawking at the window of the room where that murder victim stayed."

"It's the people that set up these tours that I blame. It's nothing but voyeurism," Harding said. "Exploiting tragedy for a quick profit."

Graham shrugged. He'd long since given up trying to understand this aspect of human behavior. "We've always done it, and probably always will."

"Speaking of quick profits, I had to go out to warn off a French boat the other day." Barnwell embarked on another story describing his most recent trip into the unpredictable waters of the English Channel. "So, the Coastguard gets this call from one of the locals, saying there's a French-registered vessel within a few minutes' sailing of the Jersey fishing sector, right?" Groans of unwelcome familiarity met his words. There was a three-mile exclusion zone around the coast of Jersey, jealously protected by the island's fishermen. Attempts by French fishing boats to encroach upon it brought storms of angry protests and occasionally, volleys of rotting fish. "I got hold of them on the radio, but they refused to leave the area," Barnwell was saying. "So the rulebook says I have to head out there with the Coastguard and see what's what."

"You're also entitled to whistle up the Navy if things get really unpleasant," Roach said.

"Well, no one wanted to go that far. I guess the Coastguard thought the uniform and a pair of broad shoulders," Barnwell added with a self-confident grin, "would help me successfully deal with them."

They all nodded. The size of the fish stocks and their impact on the livelihoods of the local fishermen and the broader Channel Islands economies were the common denominators behind these low-level conflicts. Further, the situation was compounded by a strong dash of patriotism or xenophobia, depending on ones' viewpoint. It didn't help that the French fishermen regularly came ashore, an act that appeared to be designed to rile the locals. All the Gorey officers had been called out more than once to calm down some Anglo-French argument that had manifested itself after one too many pints down the pub, a leer in the wrong direction, or a sneaking suspicion that the visitors catch was more sizeable than legally possible.

"How is the new Coastguard commander to work with?" Graham asked. "Ecclestone, right?"

"Yeah, he was brought in to replace Murphy a month or so ago. Prickly customer, I'd say. He was working on the mainland but was reassigned down here. And rather suddenly, so I believe."

"I rather expected him to come to the station to introduce himself. Was he at least helpful?"

"Sure," Barnwell said, "when he wasn't yammering away in French on his phone." Barnwell rolled his eyes. "Something about his brother and a surprise party. His sister-in-law is French, apparently. On and on he went. Then he told us all about what a fantastic life they lead in the South of France and what a great country France is to live in, blah, blah, blah. I got the impression he was showing off. You know, sounding *cosmopolitan* so as to impress us plebs. All it did was put my back up. And he needs to keep his trap shut. He'll have the locals revolting if he's not careful with all that pro-Froggie stuff."

"Sounds a right charmer," Graham said. "Can't wait to meet him. What happened in the end?"

"Oh, the men on the boat threw their hands up and blamed their navigation equipment. Didn't believe them, of course. It beggars belief in this day and age. We're all carrying around GPS devices on our phones. We couldn't get lost if we tried, and yet these guys managed to be *seven miles* off course, and just *happened* to be inside the three-mile zone. Ecclestone wanted to confiscate their equipment, but I wasn't in the mood to ruin someone's livelihood. They didn't look like they were doing too

well as it was. I didn't see a single fish onboard," Barnwell continued. "Anyhow, we ran alongside them for a while, exchanged a
few, ahem, words, and when they got the message, shepherded
them out of the area. I just hope they took the warning seriously.
Next time, I will call the Royal Navy. They're always happy to
enliven a trespasser's afternoon without getting *too* punitive."

"How did the locals react?" Graham hazarded a naval
metaphor. "Did they call for them to be strung up from the
yardarm?" For a man who lived on an island, he was woefully
ignorant about the blue depths that surrounded him.

"Yeah well, I told a few of the guys about the ear bashing I
gave them, and they seemed happy enough. Word will get around
that we're on it."

"Good lad," Graham said. "That three-mile limit is like a
sacred contract. There's nothing more likely to anger them than
encroachments upon it, and the last thing we need is the fishermen up in arms." The list of potential public order issues in
Gorey wasn't a long one, but rioting fishermen – fearing for their
jobs and angry at the French, the European Union, the British
government, and inevitably, eventually as their front line representatives, the Gorey police – was right at the top.

Graham turned to listen as Roach took Harding through the
tricky questions he'd navigated as part of his sergeant's exam. "I
think I had to memorize about a hundred new crimes and every
recent Act of Parliament. I thought my head was going to
explode."

"But you're staying in Gorey," Harding wanted to confirm,
"even though you're an illustrious sergeant, now?"

Roach gave a laugh. "Where else would I go? This is home,
and I couldn't imagine working anywhere else." This was a
departure for Roach. Before Inspector Graham's arrival, Roach
had wanted nothing more than to climb the career ladder on the
mainland, preferably at the Met. Now, it would seem, he had all
the excitement he craved right here on Jersey.

"And what about you, sir?" In the glow of the party to honor him, Barnwell felt confident enough to ask Graham, "Do you think you'll stay, now you've become a local hero, cleaning up the crime rate and everything?"

Graham waved away the characterization. "It's *you* they're impressed with. I just facilitate." He noticed the door of the lobby crack open. A familiar face appeared. "Marcus!" he called, stepping out into reception and waving him in. "Grab a drink, and let's toast the royal success of the good constable." Graham stood back to let the older man pass by into his office.

Marcus Tomlinson, the local pathologist, had a different look about him from the one he normally wore. He seemed vaguely harassed, his appearance just slightly askew. Today, his sky blue necktie looked to be on a journey of its own. "Phew, it's blustery out there. I'll be glad when this weather settles down and all we have to contend with is non-stop rain. Thank you, David." He accepted a glass of port. "And well done, Barry. You're a credit to the force." Barnwell shook his hand.

Graham took Tomlinson aside. He wanted an update on Roach's work in the crime lab in St. Helier where the sergeant was seconded three mornings a week to assist with forensics work. It had been six weeks since he had started. "Have you heard how Jim's doing at the lab?"

"First rate," Tomlinson replied. "They haven't let him do anything too dangerous or sensitive yet, but he's observed some of my post mortems, and he's learning the ropes very quickly. Natural scientific mind, that lad."

Graham felt yet another surge of pride for his diligent, hard-working officers. He had soon formed the opinion that it would be a tremendous waste for Jim Roach to spend decades noting down the details of missing bicycles or booking in the rowdy drunks following Saturday night altercations. His was a mind too fine and sharp for such drudgery, and this arrangement with Tomlinson and the Jersey SOCO team now seemed one of

Graham's better ideas. In truth, he'd have gone to almost any lengths to help further the careers of his three charges, and also to make sure that the increasingly indispensable Jack Wentworth had plenty of opportunities to demonstrate his talents on behalf of the Jersey Police force.

Jack was the last to arrive, and Graham couldn't help noticing the genuine affection between the young computer engineer and Sergeant Harding. "Good to see, isn't it?" he remarked to Tomlinson as the pathologist helped himself to a second glass of port.

"Hmm?"

"Janice and Jack," Graham clarified. "They've really hit it off."

Tomlinson regarded the couple fondly. "Ah, young love," he sighed. "A path that never runs smoothly in my experience, but one well worth taking, wouldn't you say, David?"

The DI gave the older man a skeptical look. "I'd say it's a great thing when someone can see past the uniform, the pepper spray, and the powers of arrest to appreciate the thoughtful, sensitive person within."

"Preach, David."

"I'd also say that I'm proud of my officers, and I sincerely enjoy fêting their achievements, but I've got plans." He looked at his watch.

"Well, enjoy your evening, David. I'll make sure these youngsters don't get into too much trouble."

Graham found his jacket and was in the middle of texting Laura, the local librarian with whom he had a dinner date, when they all heard the reception desk phone ringing. For a few seconds everyone stared, until Jim Roach bowed to the inevitable and left the room to answer it.

CHAPTER THREE

HARDING AND GRAHAM arrived together, noticing at once the strangely subdued atmosphere in the pub. They found Tamsin sitting with one of the bar staff, a college-age girl who had the expression of someone entirely out of their depth. She looked relieved when Harding came over to their table.

"Ms. Porter?" Harding asked. Graham stood behind her, taking in the details.

"It's been seven hours," Tamsin said. Her face was puffy and reddened from an afternoon spent waiting in increasing distress. "He's never been this late before. Never," she ended simply.

Harding sat opposite her and began taking notes on her iPad, while Graham did the same with his trusty notebook.

"We've been in touch with the Coastguard," Janice said, putting her hand over Tamsin's and looking deep into her eyes. "What was his name, love?" The sergeant knew the missing man's name but asking his girlfriend to say it out loud was a gentle way to pull her out of her shock and into the present.

"Greg. Greg Somerville." Tamsin squeezed her eyes tight shut and pressed her hands between her knees. She tightened her shoulders briefly before relaxing them, sniffing, and opening her eyes.

"Why did he go out in his boat?"

Tamsin explained the project they were working on, and how Greg had to manually check the buoys at intervals. "We normally go out together, but he went alone today."

Graham kept a close eye on Tamsin throughout. Right now, this was simply a missing person callout. They were here to gather more information for the Coastguard. Nevertheless, he found himself attempting a rough mental calculation that would tell him how often someone had gone missing precisely because of the very individual who had *reported* them missing. Police work had made him preternaturally suspicious, and while, of course, everyone was innocent until proven guilty, it was also true that everyone carried the *potential* for guilt. His mind wandered to Laura who had graciously accepted his apologies concerning their dinner. She would, he knew, take a different position, her view of the human condition being far more trustful.

"What does the boat that he went out in look like, Ms. Porter?" he asked.

"It's a standard Warrior 175 small motor launch, white with a red stripe. *Albatross*. Basic model. The sea's a bit rough today, but nothing Greg couldn't handle."

"How do you stay in contact when he's out there and you're on land?"

"There's a VHS radio onboard, and sometimes we'll have phone contact. Before calling you, I contacted the Harbormaster and confirmed that Greg had checked in with him as he left. He was always punctilious about that. But we've heard nothing from him since. He left around noon and should have been back hours ago. On a bad day, doing the rounds of the buoys takes no longer than three hours." She reeled off the coordinates of the buoys that had been tracking the sharks' movements. "I've been here ringing and texting and trying to raise him on the radio, but there's been no response at all."

Graham walked outside and made several calls, including one to Barnwell, who was liaising with the Coastguard once more. "It's a Warrior 175 small motor launch, white with a red stripe." Graham described the position of the buoys Greg had been tracking, reading the information that Tamsin had given him verbatim from his notebook because he had no idea what it meant. "Get the word to them, all right? Sharpish, mind. He's been gone since noon. Should have been back four hours ago."

"If we find that the sharks are on their way to a mating location off Norway, as Greg predicted," Tamsin was saying when he went back inside the pub, "we'll be able to pressure the government to restrict fishing activities along their route and help keep them safe." In her shocked state, Tamsin was now sharing information irrelevant to the situation, but the police officers listened to her sympathetically, knowing that it was her way of coping with the fear that was enveloping her.

During the course of the short interview, Graham learned about shark migration, their breeding patterns, the detection of living things underwater, and the technical specifications of the trackers they had been using to monitor the sharks.

"And," Janice hesitated, anticipating the tricky question she had to ask next, "how did he seem in himself? Generally, I mean?"

"He's anxious about the research. We've been doing this for three years now, and we need to start showing some results for our efforts. This is a make-or-break year, really. He was feeling the pressure."

"And how would you say he was responding to the stress?"

"By being irritable and taking it out on everyone, including me. Oh wait, he would never…no, no, that's not Greg at all. Definitely not. He wouldn't harm himself." Tamsin lifted her chin and for the first time during the interview seemed confident and in possession of herself.

"No medical history that might have caused an emergency?"

"No, nothing."

Eventually, Harding escorted Tamsin to her room and arranged for a doctor to visit and prescribe a sleep aid, if necessary.

"She's absolutely wrung out," Harding commented as she returned to the bar. Graham was making notes and occasionally glancing out of the window at the harbor. All the fishermen, including the stragglers, had been back for a while now, their lobster pots and fishing nets mostly full. The bar was filling up as a hard day on the water translated into a lively evening in the pub.

"For sure. She's had a rough afternoon," Graham said.

"What do you think, sir? Man overboard?"

"Probably. The Coastguard's been scrambled, and I've given Barnwell the buoy locations so they can focus their search. There isn't any more we can do." A grisly image formed in Graham's mind. "Wait a second. These… sharks. They're not *dangerous*, are they?"

A few moments' intensive searching on Harding's iPad yielded the reassuring fact that nobody had been attacked by a shark in British waters for many generations. "It's normally a case of mistaken identity," Harding explained. "The shark sees an object silhouetted against the surface, and bites it, just to see what it's made from. But Holden sharks don't feed like that. They filter the water like a whale."

"Okay, I'm with you so far," Graham said. "But these sharks," he continued. "They're big, are they?"

"Up to fifteen feet long," Harding marveled, showing the DI

a picture. "Ugly brute, isn't he?" Although undeniably impressive with its massive, gaping mouth, the Holden shark had a curved, hooked, prehistoric shape born from millions of years of slow change in the silent deep. It was quite unlike the powerful, darting predators of the movies. This was a gentle, slow cruiser, much more like a whale, as Harding said, than the sharks of nightmares.

"Teeth or no teeth, a beast that size could overturn a small boat without even thinking about it." He imagined the scene. "The boat capsizes, and then begins to sink, leaving Greg alone in the water without a radio or even his survival gear."

"Terrifying," Harding agreed. The thought of being lost in that freezing, rolling water as night fell made her shudder. Optimistic by nature, she sought to bolster her spirits by searching for alternative explanations for Somerville's disappearance.

As she and Graham returned to the constabulary in their marked patrol car, she threw out every possibility besides "man overboard" that she could think of. She hoped her boss might latch onto one of them, but in truth, his mental processes remained as mysterious as ever.

"He could have just run out of fuel," Harding tried.

"Anyone who's ever been to sea before would carry extra, and check their tanks before leaving, surely. Besides," Graham argued, "he was only going a few miles from shore."

Harding kept trying. "Then, a mechanical problem?"

"One which wiped out his engine, radio, and satellite gear, all at once? Are we proposing that the vessel was subject to catastrophic, spontaneous combustion?"

Harding felt a little poked at. "Well, how about it?"

"Someone would have seen it," Graham explained. "From the third floor of the White House Inn, you can see most of the way to the South Coast on a good day. A fire would have stuck out like a sore thumb, even a brief one."

"Perhaps he found something fascinating or unexpected and is just chasing it down?"

"Without radioing anyone to relay his plans or his findings?" Graham countered. "And what could so engage his attention that he'd choose to stay out past nightfall?"

Harding shrugged. "Good point."

The DI glanced over at his colleague. "Sorry if I sound negative, Sergeant, but we're eliminating the possibilities and doing so very efficiently. My bet remains man overboard, and the longer he's gone, the more confident I feel I'm going to collect on that bet. Unfortunately," he added quickly before Harding could consider him hard-hearted.

"But," she added, "he could be on his way back, right now, with some story about a balky engine. Or maybe he just felt in need of some quiet time away from his responsibilities."

Harding pulled the vehicle into the small turning circle outside the constabulary. Graham glanced at the clock on the dashboard and stifled a sigh. It was now too late in the evening – yet *again* – for there to be much hope of spending any time with Laura. "If so, Sergeant, I would understand *exactly* how he feels."

They kept an altitude of around three hundred feet above the waves, forming a steady, figure-eight flight pattern in the pitch-black sky. Strong gusts of wind buffeted the sides of the helicopter, but it was holding steady. The search area was large enough to encompass the entire operational range of a seventeen-foot launch. If the *Albatross* was still afloat, they would find it, either from a radar return, or direct observation from searchlights in the helicopter's nose. So far, there was no sign of the scientist or his boat.

Commander Brian Ecclestone liked to sit up front with the pilot. This wasn't strictly necessary, as his responsibilities were chiefly to monitor their radar gear and coordinate with the two vessels below that were also combing the waters. That could be done from further back in the cabin, but being up front made Ecclestone feel "in touch" with events, and it meant he could pester the pilot about his fuel levels, the flying conditions, and other extraneous information not critical to their mission.

"You've been doing this a while, then?" he asked the pilot.

The younger man's eyes were glued to his controls, with the occasional glance outside at the deep, endless black of the sky. With little moonlight, and windy, overcast conditions, there was no real way to tell where the waves ended and sky began, so the pilot relied on his instruments to stay on course. "Since the army, sir," he replied. "Eleven years, altogether."

"Impressive," his boss replied simply. Ecclestone was too new and too incurious to have learned much about the crew he was working alongside. Besides the volunteers who made up a significant part of service, there were a dozen professionals who patrolled this stretch of water between England and France and who had dealt with everything from smugglers and people-traffickers to missing yachts and mysterious floating containers. They oozed competence, which left the comparatively bumbling, traditionally desk-bound Ecclestone feeling decidedly ordinary. So, consciously or not, the new commander felt the need to have his finger on the pulse of the service, placing himself as close to "the action" as possible. He glanced at his watch. "Sorry to keep you boys out so late."

From the mid-deck space behind him, the junior crewman had a standard response. "It's what we do, sir." His tone said the rest: *And we've been doing it perfectly well and for a long while before you came along.*

"Well, this guy owes us an apology, once we find him. A small vessel like that, in this weather? What was he thinking?"

The pilot had this one covered. "We prefer to blame the conditions, sir. Never the seafarer."

These were admonitions Ecclestone had heard before. His ponderously slow rise through the ranks had been punctuated by impolitic gaffes including a deeply unfortunate one the previous year. Ecclestone had been tasked with coordinating the rescue of a family whose motor-sailer had run into difficulties in the Bristol Channel. The rescue was nearly flawless, no thanks to Ecclestone's constant interference, but once the terrified family was safely aboard the rescue boat, he'd given them all a stern dressing down, complete with patronizing reminders about basic sea safety. Traumatized by his experience, and now enraged at having his children lectured on marine safety even as they sat, soaked and shocked in their life vests, the father of the family chose to make a formal complaint.

Memorably written on House of Commons notepaper, the missive came from Jacob Ellis-Dean, the veteran Member of Parliament who just happened to be the stricken boat owner's father. Partly due to this insistence from on-high, Ecclestone was judged "unusually insensitive and lacking in empathy" and reassigned to a less busy Coastguard station where his grating manner and selfish habits would cause less frequent offense. This story of his fall from grace found itself communicated, in humiliatingly rich detail, to every member of the Jersey Coastguard even before he had taken over as their commander and on his arrival at his new post, he found his team willing to do little more than tolerate him.

"Well, blame the weather all you like," Ecclestone was saying, "but people who go out unprepared are just plain stupid. And then we have to come out here and get them, in the middle of the night, when we'd all rather be doing something else. Right, son?" he asked the pilot, wisely deciding against nudging the young man with his elbow to elicit a response.

"Nothing beats flying, sir," the pilot replied. "Even at night," he said. "And for whatever reason," he added pointedly. "The poor guy might have drowned for all we know. His family, at least, deserves our best efforts. And besides, it's our job."

With that, they turned west again to begin another leg of their search pattern. Beneath them, the waves provided only dull, repetitious, unremarkable radar returns, and neither their searchlights nor those of the two vessels below them found any trace of Greg or the *Albatross*.

CHAPTER FOUR

JIM ROACH GRITTED his teeth and pulled hard to open the heavy main door of the Gorey Constabulary building, fighting against the roaring gale that had been building all day. He stumbled in, watched by a bemused Barnwell who was manning the desk while Roach – younger, but now a more senior rank – finished another vehicle patrol.

"Flippin' heck," Roach said as he let the door slam and shook off the first drops of what promised to be an awful lot of cold rain. "It's *fierce* out there."

Barnwell handed his colleague a steaming mug of tea. "Everybody got their hatches battened down?"

Roach took the mug with a grateful smile. "As far as I can tell. I mean, you'd have to be living in a cave to have missed all the warnings. First time in thirty years we've had something like this. No one I've spoken to seems sure just how bad it's going to get, so they're preparing for the worst. Have they called off the search party for that scientist fellow?"

"Yeah, they have." The two men were silent for a moment.

"Well," Barnwell said, stirring and reaching for a portable

long-wave radio, for years his chosen method of listening to the cricket on the BBC, "let's get the latest, eh? I think we're right on time."

It was a phenomenon every bit as British as the changing of the guard at Buckingham Palace or the smearing of toast with Marmite. *"And now the Shipping Forecast, issued by the Met Office on behalf of the Maritime and Coastguard Agency at 1806 hours today. There are warnings of gales in Thames, Dover, Wight, and Portland."* The honeyed, contralto tones of the announcer were a calming contrast to the coming storms.

Roach shrugged. "They aren't kidding around. That's the whole south coast of England."

Barnwell nodded, listening carefully. "And the Channel, too. We're going to be right in the middle of this, Jim."

The BBC announcer continued the formulaic reading of weather predictions for the coming hours, describing each sea area in turn, clockwise around the country. The North Sea was angry, with winds of gale force eight and nine, but the predictions for the Channel areas were far worse.

"Thames, Dover, Wight, Portland. Southwest severe gale nine to hurricane twelve. Heavy, thundery showers. Poor, becoming moderate later."

Roach blinked a couple of times. "All right, that didn't sound good, but what did they actually say?"

Barnwell was already on the phone. "They said we're going to take a big hit tonight. Hurricane force winds, rubbish visibility, lots of rain and thunder."

Jim gulped. A once-in-a-generation storm wasn't something he'd ever prepared for. "What do we do?" he asked, already worried that he'd be out of his depth in this evolving, dangerous crisis.

"Well, the first thing to remember is —" Barnwell advised.

"Don't panic," Roach recited. "Always fantastic advice. I've lost count of how many times that saying has saved my bacon."

"And as for what to do," Barnwell continued, tapping his finger against the phone pressed to his ear, "I'll find out, as soon as the boss is good enough to answer his bloody —"

Click.

"Graham here."

"Evening, sir," Barnwell said, gathering himself quickly. "Bit blustery tonight, isn't it?"

"I'll say, I hope you're doing what I'm doing and staying inside." There was a growl in the DI's tone, a reasonable reaction to a work call during his precious evening hours.

Jim Roach grinned to himself at Barnwell's near *faux pas*. He could hear Graham's distinctive voice even from a few feet away, and he wasn't surprised to find his boss just as reluctant to wade into the middle of a hurricane as he was.

"Right," Barnwell said, making notes. "We'll follow the emergency plan, sir, and I'll call the Coastguard and stay in touch with St. Helier." Jersey's smart, re-built police headquarters would be the operational hub for the coming crisis. "Will you be in attendance, sir, if required?" he asked.

Roach heard Graham grumbling colorfully before assuring Barnwell that he'd be ready if the situation demanded it. His reluctance sounded almost total, but the two men knew that if Gorey needed his leadership and experience, even if it was just to provide an extra pair of hands, he wouldn't let them down.

"Okay, sir. We'll keep you updated." Barnwell replaced the receiver. "I have the sense," he said turning to Roach with a crooked smile, "that this storm may be seriously inconveniencing DI Graham's evening."

"His and everyone else's," Roach replied, "from Bristol to Sevenoaks and beyond."

Barnwell grinned again. "But I think our DI has...shall we say...*plans* for tonight, Jim."

Roach gave his colleague a look of shock. "Wait...You mean..."

"I do," Barnwell confirmed.

"But..." Roach began.

"He might work like a machine, but he's still a regular guy, you know," Barnwell reminded him.

"Wow. I never thought I'd see the day," Roach wondered, his eyes wide.

"We wouldn't be seeing it now, except for the arrival of our new librarian. I think the DI has been," Barnwell looked outside at the weather, "swept off his feet."

Roach continued to marvel at this turn of events, revising his view of DI Graham as a straight-up workaholic and contemplating for the first time the notion that his boss might have a *romantic* life. "Looks like he'll be able to relive that experience tonight, many times over," Roach quipped, following Barnwell's eye. "He can simply go outside. What did they say on the TV news earlier? 'Winds of a hundred miles an hour'?"

"And more," Barnwell told him. "We're going to lose roof tiles, windows, and maybe some boats in the harbor. Lots of flying debris, branches, and such. Flooding, too, I shouldn't wonder. We won't come through completely unscathed, so we all need to be ready to get out there and help, all right? It's an all hands situation."

Roach headed to the small police station's back room, a storage area where they kept uniforms and a small amount of special equipment. He donned waders and zipped up a heavy bright-orange rain jacket, flipping down the hood so that he was left with a letter-box size view of the lobby. He staggered back into reception. "I'll stay dry, that's for sure. Shame I can't see a bloody thing."

Barnwell brought out his phone and took a picture. "I'm going to call this one, 'David Against Goliath,' or perhaps, 'Jim Versus the Hurricane.'"

"What's that for? Posterity?"

"The Constabulary's Twitter feed," Barnwell chuckled.

Jim gave him a dirty look but headed back to find more foul weather gear for his fellow officers.

"Don't forget Janice," Barnwell called through. "She's out on the coast, but she'll be back in a minute." No sooner had he spoken than Janice bustled her way through the door, nearly tumbling into the lobby.

"Whose idea was this?" she demanded, shaking rain from her hair and rubbing her hands together to restore some feeling to her chilled limbs. "I know it's November, but I mean, for heaven's sake!"

"Hurricane force twelve," Barnwell announced from behind the desk. "It's going to get special around here."

"A *hurricane*?" Harding spluttered. "Marvelous. Can't wait to hear what the DI thinks about *that*."

Jim Roach returned from the back room with an armful of more brightly colored gear. "It could be one of Bazza's wind-ups, but according to him, the boss is on a *date*?"

Harding didn't show any surprise. She found tea and blew across its surface while cradling the mug with her freezing hands. "Laura Beecham, right? The librarian? Where've you been, Roachie? They're often in the Bangkok Palace on Friday nights."

Barnwell was shaking his head. "It takes all sorts."

"Why not?" Harding asked. "They're both single, she's attractive and educated, and he's... well..."

"Unique?" Roach tried.

"A strange, workaholic loner?" Barnwell added.

"Very eligible, I was going to say," Harding smirked. "I'm surprised this hasn't happened sooner."

Barnwell began monitoring the BBC's weather website, frowning at the latest radar map. It showed a huge mass of swirling clouds that obscured an area from Somerset, in southwest England, to Brittany, in northern France. He grumbled something and then returned to their discussion. "The DI works like his life depends on it. I'm amazed he's found time for a woman."

"Perhaps he works like a dog precisely because there's nothing else in his life," Roach interjected.

"When the right one comes along..." Harding began, but thought better of it. Their boss' romantic life was a remarkable novelty, but it felt churlish to gossip, not to mention intrusive. Besides, their small island was facing a grave threat, and the Constabulary was about to be dealing with its most serious public safety challenge in years. There were things to do.

The reception desk phone rang. "Gorey Police, how can I help you?" Barnwell said. "Oh, hello Mrs. Taylor, how are things at the White House Inn?" The constable listened for a moment and then began making notes. "Well," he replied, frowning, "I don't know if I can tell him *that*, in all seriousness." Roach approached the desk, curious as to what Mrs. Taylor had to say. "No, ma'am, I'm afraid I can't pass that on...Not tonight," Barnwell twirled a pen between his fingers. "Why? Because we've a hurricane headed our way. Dealing with the serious public safety threat it poses is our priority right now. I don't think DI Graham'll have a lot of time for that kind of thing, not tonight, Mrs. Taylor." He put his hand over the mouthpiece and looked at the other two, raising his eyebrows, "If ever."

Harding mouthed, "What's up?" but Barnwell raised a finger.

"I can pass on your concerns, Mrs. T, but —" He listened as Mrs. Taylor continued for another few moments. "No, ma'am. I really can't ask him to come out for something like that. Not during the worst storm in thirty years."

Undeterred, Mrs. Taylor persisted until Barnwell eventually relented. "Okay, look. I'll tell him that you'd like to speak with him in person, and that it's important, all right?"

This seemed to placate the owner of the guesthouse, and she rang off. Barnwell took a deep breath before making another call to DI Graham.

"Sorry, sir. It's just that Mrs. Taylor has been calling, and she's...No, sir. There's no trouble over there, but she's got some concerns about...Yes... Would you, sir? I'd be very grateful." Then he added, "Er, stay dry, sir."

Barnwell grimaced as he replaced the receiver, ready for the ribbing his two colleagues would inevitably mete out. "Stay *dry?*" Harding queried. "In a *hurricane?*"

Barnwell shrugged. "Hurricane or not, he's headed to the White House Inn," he said, making himself another mug of tea. "And hopefully, he's taking his sense of humor with him."

CHAPTER FIVE

B Y THE TIME DI David Graham arrived at the White
House Inn overlooking Gorey Harbor, the sky had transformed into a dark, brooding maelstrom. The usually
busy streets were empty with shops already shuttered, and the
White House Inn looked as prepared for a hurricane as one
might hope. The ornamental plant pots had been taken in and
every one of the guesthouse's windows was closed and taped. Out
of habit, Graham found himself glancing up at the second-floor
room that had been Laura's during her first weeks on Jersey. He
looked to see if the light was on. It wasn't. Laura had quickly
found a place of her own, a place in which DI Graham had once
again planned to spend this foul, inclement evening until the call
from Mrs. Taylor came in.

The guesthouse proprietor met him at the door and then
securely bolted it again as soon as Graham entered the lobby. She
seemed ill-at-ease, wringing her hands and frowning. "Mrs.
Taylor, I'd wish you a good evening, but I really don't think we're
going to have one."

"Come through, Detective Inspector. Thank you for coming."

She led Graham into the restaurant area and bid him sit down on one of the armchairs by the large picture window that in normal circumstances gave a broad view of the beach and sea beyond. This evening, it was impossible to see anything further than a few feet. The room was perhaps a third full with guests. November, coming as it did between the summer and winter holiday tourist seasons, was one of the quieter times of year. "I'm sorry to call you out in this terrible weather."

"It's going to be one for the record books," Graham reminded her. "Are all your guests aware of what's going on?"

"Yes," she replied confidently. "The staff has been getting everyone ready, and we're as hurricane-proof as I can make us. In fact," she added, "it's the hurricane I wanted to talk to you about."

Graham raised a puzzled eyebrow. "So how can I help you, Mrs. Taylor?"

She sat in the armchair next to him, leaning in as though confiding something sensitive. "I don't really know how to say this, but I need to give you a warning about the storm."

"I think the BBC has that covered, Mrs. Taylor," Graham replied. "The whole south of the country is taking shelter. They've canceled trains, directed people to stay at home, the whole shebang."

"No," Mrs. Taylor said, clasping and unclasping her hands. "No, there's something else."

Very unusually, Graham reached over and placed a hand on Marjorie Taylor's arm. "What's upsetting you, Mrs. Taylor? Are you afraid of damage? Because your insurance will cover all of the —"

"Nineteen eighty-seven," Mrs. Taylor proclaimed, sitting a little straighter in her chair. Graham removed his hand and sat back. "The Great Storm. Do you remember?"

Graham nodded. "Not really, I was too young, but of course,

I've heard of it. Worst gale in living memory, wasn't it? Twenty-odd people killed, houses destroyed by falling trees, and an incredible mess the next morning. Precipitated by the BBC weatherman saying it wouldn't amount to much."

"It's what came *after* the storm that I need to warn you about," Mrs. Taylor said. She looked distinctly uncomfortable in her chair, almost squirming as she tried to get the words out. "Last time, in eighty-seven, there were some very strange goings-on in the days after the storm."

Graham said nothing for a moment. Investigators tended to view stories of "strange goings-on" rather like archaeologists might receive the latest theories about aliens building the pyramids. "What kind of strange things, Mrs. Taylor?" he asked patiently.

If anything, the guesthouse owner became even more agitated. Her hands were a tangle of knotted fingers, and she scowled at the tabletop in front of her as though angry at having to shoulder this burden alone. "Ever heard of Tony White and his son, Tom? They disappeared in eighty-seven, a few days after the storm, while at sea on the *Smart Alec*."

Graham confessed that he hadn't.

"Never found," Mrs. Taylor continued. "No evidence of their boats, no life rafts, no calls for help on the radio. Just *vanished*."

"You believe their disappearance was connected to the storm?"

Mrs. Taylor nodded, her expression dark. "I'm not alone. Plenty of people around here thought there was something funny about it."

"But," Graham pointed out, "they were probably out in rough seas, weren't they? It seems perfectly plausible that the weather, just a few days after a storm of that magnitude or even a simple miscalculation could account for their disappearance. Seafaring is not an innocuous occupation, is it now?"

"No," she admitted, "but something... *unusual* was abroad

during those few days, Detective Inspector. Something *awful*."
She could see Graham wasn't convinced. "Well then, what about
the tiger that disappeared from the zoo?"

Graham blinked at this sudden change of tack. He was
familiar with the story of the missing tiger. It had passed into
island folklore. On his only visit to Jersey Zoo, he'd been told how
a Bengal tiger had gone missing during the 1987 storm.
According to the zookeeper's telling, the striped feline roamed
Jersey for three days, mercifully without harming anyone. "What
about it? The tiger was found, Mrs. Taylor."

"No, no, no," she spluttered. "That's not true!"

Graham had a fondness for Marjorie Taylor. She had helped
him settle into the community during his first few months, and
he'd always respected the professionalism and discretion with
which she ran her establishment. But now, he had the real sense
that he'd been called away from spending what had promised to
be a delightful evening with an intelligent and desirable woman,
braving the opening salvoes of a hurricane in the process, only to
listen to half-baked conspiracy theories. "Mrs. Taylor," he said, "a
tiger has to eat enormous amounts of food to stay alive. We'd have
had complaints from farmers, gamekeepers, and landowners that
their livestock had gone missing. There would be tracks, distinctive paw prints, unmistakable fur left tangled in barbed wire...
This would have happened regularly for years. It wouldn't be
hard to track a full-grown tiger on a place like Jersey."

Mrs. Taylor powered on, apparently undeterred. "Well, how
do you explain the sightings?"

Graham ached for a cup of tea. "Sightings?" he managed
to ask.

"Tony White and his son. People have seen them in the churchyard and on the beach late at night. Two ghostly figures, hovering
above the ground," she described. "And Mr. Croft saw the 'Beast of
Jersey' while walking his dog across farmland just this last summer."

The Detective Inspector found himself on the verge of a withering tirade. How could an experienced businesswoman like Mrs. Taylor possibly lend credence to such claptrap? The sighting of a tiger was in reality most likely an overgrown housecat and ghostly apparitions the result of too much imbibing down at the pub. He was never more grateful to hear the sound of his phone vibrating in his pocket. "Excuse me, Mrs. Taylor," he said. He returned to the quiet of the lobby.

"Sir?" It was Barnwell.

"Constable, you do realize I've battled a storm and wasted a good chunk of my evening in order to hear ghost stories and other such rubbish from Mrs. Taylor?"

"Yes, sir," Barnwell said. "Sorry about that."

"And now, I imagine, you're going to make it up to me by telling me I can relax for the duration of the rest of the evening?" Graham asked, more in hope than expectation.

"I'm afraid not, sir," Barnwell confessed.

"Why am I not surprised?" Graham closed his eyes. "Okay, let me have it."

"We got a call from your old friend and mine, Mr. Hodgson," Barnwell said.

"Ah yes, the seventeen-year-old boy with a penchant for nighttime sailing excursions," Graham remembered at once. "I hope he's hunkered down at home tonight."

"He's fine," Barnwell said, "but he claims his grandparents have refused to comply with the coastal evacuation order."

The problem laid itself out for Graham like a maze seen from above. "Why do I have the feeling I'm about to get involved in this?"

"The fire brigade is swamped and can't get there for another couple of hours. They requested that we attend."

Graham blew out his cheeks and tapped his foot. He looked around, making sure that Mrs. Taylor and her guests were thoroughly out of earshot, before telling Barnwell precisely how he felt about his suggestion.

"Right, sir," Barnwell said, moving quickly past his boss' very negative rejoinder. "Shall I meet you here at the station, then?"

"Very well," he sighed. "I'll see you in ten." He looked outside at the weather. "Maybe fifteen."

After he'd ended the call, Barnwell turned to Roach, who was still dressed from head to foot in luminous foul-weather gear, and said, "I honestly don't know which will prove worse tonight – the hurricane, or the DI's temper."

Laura glanced at the clock yet again. It had been forty minutes since David had left, putting dinner – and the rest of a relaxing evening – abruptly on hold. She was becoming anxious about leaving the lasagna in the warm oven for so long. The pasta would dry out. Inherited from her Italian grandmother, the recipe was completely foolproof, so long as hurricanes and unwelcome police duties didn't interfere. "Hurry up, David," she found herself muttering at the clock. "I'm hungry."

The librarian poured herself another small glass of Cabernet Sauvignon and turned the oven temperature down yet again. There were *antipasti* laid out, so far untouched. She spooned homemade mushroom caviar onto a cracker. Outside, the wind had picked up and now sounded a noisy lament around the tiny cul-de-sac where Laura had been fortunate enough to find a small, affordable place to rent. The larger bedroom had a view of the fields beyond the edge of Gorey, while the diminutive window in the smaller upstairs room showed the very edge of Gorey Castle looming over the village from its imposing cliff-top perch.

As early as 3 PM, Laura had helped to hurriedly close the library, and then retreated to her small cottage where she and

Graham had planned to endure the storm and get to know each other a little better. "Finally," she had smiled to herself. Since her return from a two-week stay in London, where she had been a vital witness for the prosecution in a high-profile, armed robbery trial, thanks to the Detective Inspector's numerous commitments, they'd managed to spend only three evenings together. Their relationship was developing terribly slowly.

"You're an enigma, David Graham," she'd thought during their second date. More than any man she'd ever known, Graham had proved to be endearingly inscrutable. He didn't evince any particularly strong political views, he was dedicated to his work but shy of discussing it outside of the station, he clearly cared about his subordinates beyond their shared profession, but was reserved in his expressions of affection, and more than anything, she was struck by his discretion when it came to his past. Over several hours of conversation, Laura found she'd learned almost nothing about his life before Gorey, except that he'd been in or around London, solving crimes and ascending the promotional ladder faster than he'd expected.

Somewhere along the way, she'd concluded, his wheels must have simply fallen off. The break with London was too sudden and complete to be caused by anything inconsequential. He had left behind his friends and family, his professional contacts and the beats he'd covered for years, all to live in one of Britain's true backwaters. *Why would a seasoned detective abandon the big city and come to live somewhere so very, very quiet?* she had written in her journal after that fascinating, frustrating second date.

"You are a puzzle," she now said to herself, sipping her red wine. "But really a rather good-looking one."

The phone rang. "David?" she asked.

"Hi," he said, rather sheepishly. "I'm the guy who was planning to have dinner at your house a hundred years ago. I wonder if you remember."

She smiled, pleased to hear his voice. "I think I do. Is the lasagna going to be released from the oven any time soon or are there further offenses to be taken into account?" She heard him sigh, and knew the evening was a bust.

"I'm sorry. I'll tell you about it later, but for now I have to go tie a rope around my middle and rescue a couple of pensioners from their own home before they drown."

"Oh, that's a shame! But oh well, I understand. My hero!" she finished, mustering some enthusiasm from somewhere. "Please be careful. It looks *awful* out there."

"It truly is," Graham confirmed, "but the fire brigade can't do it, so I won't be able to relax until I know..."

"I understand." Laura knew this was the time to be supportive, just as he'd stood resolutely by her during the stress of the trial in London. He'd talked with her four or five times a day over the phone, reassuring her and making the whole experience a lot more tolerable. "Take care, okay?"

"Depend on it," he promised her. "I'll phone you as soon as I can."

As Laura ended the call, the strongest gust of wind yet seemed to catch her home with a thunderous broadside. Laura moved over to the kitchen wall where a fireplace had once stood. It was the thickest in the house, and it made her feel a little safer. Through the noise of wild gusts of wind, she heard a tentative knock at her front door and after a moment of hesitation, she moved to answer it.

"Billy! What're you doing here?" Billy Foster was her favorite library visitor. Insatiably curious with a passion for all things related to space and astronomy, the nine-year-old visited the library at least three times a week. His mother was just out of rehab, and he'd gone back home to live with her, but Laura could tell from his increasing visits to the library that things were a little rocky.

She bundled the boy inside. He was drenched from head to foot. "Take off your jacket and your socks and shoes and go and sit in front of the fire in the living room to keep warm. Oh, and ring your mum, tell her you're safe. Tell her you'll stay here until morning."

She grabbed a towel as the boy shuffled off and joined him by the fire, kneeling down next to him. "What were you thinking, Billy? Going out in this weather."

"I didn't think it'd be this bad, miss. I've never seen rain like it," Billy said as Laura roughly toweled his hair.

"No, well, none of us have, Billy."

Billy looked over at the table. "Having someone for dinner?"

"I was, Billy, I was."

Billy, being a nine-year-old boy, didn't ask with whom Laura had been planning to have dinner. Instead, he sat silently, his head buffeted by her ministrations as much as any hurricane.

"There, I think you'll do." Laura sat back and looked into Billy's big, trustful, innocent, hazel eyes that were framed by fair, almost white eyelashes. They'd seen a lot in his troubled, short life. She took his hand. "Billy, would you like some lasagna?"

CHAPTER SIX

S ET APART FROM Gorey by a stretch of sloping
farmland, the tiny coastal community where the elderly
Hodgsons lived was almost lost amid the sheeting, wind-
blown rain. There was a group of six houses, only one of which
had any lights on. "There they are," Barnwell told his boss, as
they pulled up in the patrol car. "Should just be the two of them,
according to young Hodgson."

"Great," Graham told him. "Can we get any closer, do you
think?" An S-shaped gravel driveway led from the country lane
down to the house, and Graham enjoyed not at all the thought of
wading laboriously through floodwater to reach the stubborn
seniors who lived there.

"Sorry, sir," Barnwell said. "If we flood the exhaust system, or
if water gets in the fuel lines..."

"Okay, Constable," Graham said. They were both wearing
rain gear, but Graham knew he'd end this expedition soaked,
freezing, and miserable. Barnwell, on the other hand, seemed
positively enthused to be tackling a rescue attempt in these
dreadful conditions. "Lead the way, lad," Graham said. "Just turn

if you want to say something, so I can hear you, okay?" It was a trick from times long past and half-forgotten, learned in conditions even worse than these.

"Right, boss." Straining, they levered open the car's doors and managed to squeeze themselves out into the ferocious gale. A second later, both doors were slammed closed by windy hammer blows that shook the whole car. Barnwell shouted something his grandmother would have clipped his ear for, and led Graham along the sodden driveway toward the house. The water was past their ankles, cascading down the gradient from the farms that lay inland. Powerful enough almost to knock Graham off his feet, it was an angry, freezing torrent whose only desire was to race headlong into the Channel beyond.

Barnwell turned to his boss. "Get the rope tied on, sir," he shouted over the gale, offering Graham the end of a short line that was already secured around Barnwell's waist.

"We'll be fine," Graham called over.

But the junior officer insisted. "No rope, no rescue," he yelled. "Now please, sir." Barnwell helped Graham get the rope tied, their freezing fingers finding the sodden line hard to handle. They pushed toward the house. Lights were on, both upstairs and downstairs, but in the pouring rain, they shone no brighter than a faltering match.

"What happens," Graham asked as they struggled their way forward, "if they're absolutely adamant they want to stay?"

"It won't matter. They're coming with us, sir, no question. If the water gets worse and takes out a load-bearing wall, they're done for. We'll arrest them if need be." In recent months, Barnwell had built a reputation as something of a daredevil, and given his experience in dangerous situations, was showing he had the confidence to take *de facto* operational control.

"Okay," Graham said simply. He'd have given a month's salary for a Jersey Coastguard helicopter to relieve them of this loathsome responsibility. While they were about it, they could give him a ride back home, preferably to Laura's front door. But it wasn't to be.

Barnwell reached the cottage first, tugging the rope so that Graham joined him. They sheltered under the battered wooden awning that flapped ferociously above the doorway. "Well done, sir," he said. "Now, let's get them out. Holler like you mean it." The two men pounded on the door and yelled, "Police! Mr. and Mrs. Hodgson!" a half-dozen times before they heard the metal clicking sounds of the door being unlocked.

"Oh, hello!" Mrs. Hodgson said brightly, lightly brushing windblown hair from her face. "It's the police, Albert," she called back, rather unnecessarily.

"The police?" an elderly male voice replied, walking along the hallway to be greeted by the sight of two sodden officers at the door. "Whatever is the matter?"

Barnwell barely restrained himself from rolling his eyes at Graham. "Didn't you get the warnings?" he demanded. "There's a bloody hurricane on the way. Evacuation orders are in force for this part of the coast."

"Evacuation?' Mrs. Hodgson marveled. "Surely not."

"No ifs, ands, or buts," Barnwell told them. "You've got ninety seconds to grab some personal belongings, and then we're off."

Albert Hodgson took a couple of steps forward. "Can I get you lads a cup of tea?"

Graham swallowed the urge to arrest him on charges of "sheer lunacy," and "recklessly endangering a spouse." "I don't think you understand, sir. It's hardly the time for tea. We've got to get you to safety, *fast*."

Albert laughed. It boiled Graham's blood in an instant. "Safety?" the old man chuckled, thumping the cottage's substantial, stone walls. "This place is as strong as the Coliseum. I hate to have wasted your time, but we won't be going anywhere."

Graham swore under his breath. "Right. Time to crack the whip," he muttered to Barnwell.

"This isn't a discussion," Barnwell told the Hodgsons sternly. "We're leaving, immediately, all of us. Do you have good boots or wellies? We can't bring the car any closer. We'll have to walk up the hill." Graham glanced back. The car was completely invisible behind icy curtains of rain, blown to an acute angle by the roaring gale.

"You're welcome to spend the rest of the storm here," Albert offered, as though he hadn't heard anything the officers had said. "We've got that baking show on the TV, and there's plenty of tea in the pot."

Graham felt Barnwell's hand on his shoulder. "Action Plan B, sir. Back me up, all right?" Without another word, Barnwell leaned down, threw two huge arms around Mrs. Hodgson's soft, ample waist and hauled her bodily onto his shoulder. "Time to go," he said simply. He turned and began carrying the startled woman through the rain, up the hill.

"Shall we?" Graham asked Albert, who was watching this turn of events open-mouthed. "Constable Barnwell takes public safety very seriously," he explained to the elderly man with a wry smile. "Grab your boots and let's go."

When Graham told the story days later, he compared the sight of Barnwell hauling Mrs. Hodgson to safety to watching King Kong man-handling a woman to his mountain lair. Only, Barnwell managed to do it all while climbing a slope, keeping his footing on loose, flooded gravel, withstanding the outrageous force of the wind that threatened to flatten them all, and ignoring the distressed pleas of the rain-soaked Mrs. Hodgson.

"Left leg, right leg," Graham called back to Albert, now tied to him by the same rope with which Graham had been attached to Barnwell earlier. "Everyone's at the church hall in Fenton," he shouted. "Plenty of tea. And I believe they *also* have the baking show on the telly." Somehow, Graham found, this actually motivated the tiring Albert Hodgson, and within a few minutes of commencing Barnwell's Plan B, they were at the patrol car.

"Never in all my life!" Mrs. Hodgson was still complaining. "Of all the indignities! I never thought I'd ever —"

"You're welcome," Barnwell said, guiding her into the back seat. "Now, if you'd be good enough to pipe down, I'll get on the radio and see how things are." Graham made sure Albert was buckled in next to his outraged wife, and with Barnwell behind the wheel, they made their way slowly through the sheets of rain and roaring wind to Fenton church hall. It was normally only a ten-minute drive, but tonight it took them half an hour. Once the Hodgsons were safely ensconced and unlikely to escape now that they had tea and cake and the ear of other locals who listened with rapt attention to the tale of their rescue, Graham called Laura while Barnwell radioed the station.

"Mission accomplished," Graham said proudly. "I'm sorry it's so late."

Laura tried, and narrowly failed, to stifle a yawn. "Heroics take time. The man of the hour needs... well, a little more than an hour, but I understand," she told him. "It's okay. Hopefully there won't be another hurricane *tomorrow* night, and we can try again."

Graham sighed with disappointment out of Laura's earshot, but managed to keep all of the night's various emotions out of his voice. "It's a date. Let me dry off, and I'll call you tomorrow."

"Please do," Laura said, and bid him goodnight.

CHAPTER SEVEN

THE FOLLOWING MORNING, the skies were grey, the weather squally, but the raging winds of the previous evening had moved on to punish the Atlantic, where the hurricane's force would inevitably peter out as it moved north to colder climes. On the beach, Sergeant Roach surveyed the damage left behind with a furrowed brow. Not in the living memory of Gorey had their seafront come under such a powerful and sustained assault from Mother Nature. The disarray was a stark and unpleasant contrast with the usually neat, traditional feel of the place. Hardly a square foot of sand was absent some form of debris, and a small army of volunteers and Community Support Officers – uniformed, but without the powers of arrest – were laboriously cleaning up the sad mess.

"Now then, James," said Roger Percival, a fifteen-year veteran CSO with whom Roach frequently worked on those busy weekend nights when the locals got a little too drunk and rowdy, "isn't this a thing?" He gazed with Roach over the beach, scattered with branches, plastic trash and old nets long since turned green and slimy from years on the open water. He zipped up his jacket all the way to the top, the better to protect himself from the wind that still swirled, chilled and damp.

"It's not pretty," Roach admitted, "but at least no one died. You know, the hospital at St. Helier went into full emergency mode, but all they had was a couple of lacerations from flying glass, and one elderly man treated for shock."

"We can all be grateful for that," Percival agreed. "The thing now is to make the place shipshape again. Care to join me?"

It was a running joke between them – Roach was as hands-on as any officer on Jersey – and the two grabbed thick, black, plastic trash bags and began scooping up rotten wood and nameless debris with gloved hands and metal pickers normally used to collect litter. To Roach, it appeared their comely, much admired beach had been unsuccessfully stormed by an army of old trees, their casualties now strewn around, broken and forlorn.

"I see your lot got your names in the *Gorey Gossip* again. Have you read it yet?" Percival asked, relishing the chance to rib his senior officer.

Roach grumbled, shoving a weary-looking length of netting into his trash bag. "DI Graham told us to take a professional view of such publications," Roach told him. "And as for what he wrote about last night's operation, Mr. Solomon can take a running jump off the docks, for all I care. Just provided he waits for high tide."

Percival got a good laugh out of this, and he spent the next few minutes revisiting (mostly for Roach's benefit) the excoriating post that local man, Freddie Solomon, had published on his scandalous, salacious, and ceaselessly popular blog. "'Like the Three Stooges caught in a hurricane, except there were four of them," the CSO quoted from the article about the Constabulary's response to the previous night's storm. "'Ineffective disaster management by a bunch of bumbling idiots with all the professionalism of a—'" Percival delighted in the retelling, but he stopped when he saw the look on Roach's face.

It was one so stern and unimpressed that Percival fell silent. For a few minutes, they gathered debris without speaking, finding a severely battered old lobster pot, and to the bemusement of both, a scarlet negligée, now faded to a baby pink by a combination of sun and salt. "I'll guess this made its way over from France," Percival surmised, holding it up between the jaws of his picker. "I'd say plenty of folks enjoyed staying in last night 'n' all," he chuckled.

Roach's thoughts flashed briefly to the Detective Inspector and the speculation around his supposed relationship. Roach liked Laura. She was personable and smart. He couldn't imagine the DI choosing anyone whose mind was not as vibrant as his own. He gave a little smile and hoped the hurricane hadn't ruined the couple's evening entirely.

But then, Solomon's irresponsible and dishonest blog began to truly bother him. How could the Constabulary be accused of being unprepared? Warnings had been issued, no one had been seriously injured. Vulnerable members of the community had been contacted with plenty of time to spare, and if necessary, escorted to safety. Barnwell had pulled off another of his impromptu rescues down at the Hodgson's, right on the coast, for heaven's sake.

"I'd give us an A-minus for last night," Roach said, feeling the need to defend their small team. "We all worked our socks off to keep everyone safe. The DI was out until all hours, helping Barnwell get people to safety, and liaising with the fire brigade about the flooding."

"Commendable," Percival allowed, digging up another length of partially buried old sea rope. "Crikey, this thing's older than I am," he marveled. "Amazing how long things stay intact, what with the sun and the saltwater. You'd think they'd be long gone." He manhandled the rope into his trash bag and moved on, side by side with Roach, along the beach. "I don't think that Solomon fella's fair in the slightest," Percival shrugged. "But he's very *readable*."

"So are comics," Roach retorted.

"The thing is," Percival continued, undeterred by Roach's obvious distaste for Freddie Solomon's sub-tabloid level "journalism," "he always seems to get the scoop before anyone else."

"Hmm," Roach said neutrally.

"Remember 'The Case of the Missing Letter'?" Percival asked. He put up his fingers to make air quotes.

Roach paused. "You're being rhetorical, right?" he asked. Percival, unsure as to what "rhetorical" meant, gathered the word's meaning from Roach's demeanor. He, and much of the island in general, knew that Roach had been a central figure in bringing that complex case to its conclusion.

"Sorry, I forgot. You were heavily involved, weren't you?"

"I am familiar with the case," Roach added, sounding as though he was gritting his teeth.

"Well, young Freddie knew about that all-important letter, long before your lot figured everything out," Percival said. "And before even the great DI Graham."

Roach was tired, his smart uniform boots were covered in wet, dirty, storm-tossed sand, and he could have done without needless allegations of incompetence or unjustified digs at him or his colleagues. It wasn't true that Freddie knew about the letter, but "truth" didn't seem to be an unquestionable underlying principle as far as Mr. Solomon's writings were concerned. Rather than give the usually affable and helpful Percival a piece of his mind, Roach did as he felt the DI might do. "And was the murderer arrested, tried, and convicted?" he asked.

"She was," Percival allowed.

"And has that been the case with every suspicious death on the island since DI Graham arrived?" Roach pressed.

Percival was forced to concede that it had. "A solid record, one would have to say."

"Then," Roach added, letting his temper seep into his voice just a fraction, "what say we ignore Mr. Solomon's half-baked rubbish and concentrate on *this* mess instead?" he said, motioning to the wind-blown beach. As he waved his picker in the air, his eyes caught on something in the distance. Something that he knew was out of place.

"What is it, Jim?" Percival asked, alarmed at how the younger Sergeant had frozen in place.

"I'm not sure, Roger. But I'm going to find out," Roach said, his eyes fixated on the sight far down the beach. He started to walk away from Percival before increasing his pace to a sprint as his legs carried him across the beach seemingly at a rate that rivaled the winds of yesterday's hurricane. Something was most definitely not right.

The boat's engines ceased their noisy rattling as Hugo Fontenelle pulled off his headphones and reduced the throttle to idle. "Ready, *Messieurs*?" he called back to his two colleagues. "At least we have better weather than yesterday, eh?"

Far enough out that they could only barely discern the Jersey coast to their south, the three-man crew of the *Nautilus* were relieved to be at sea again having beaten a hasty retreat to land the previous day on account of the storm.

"Ready," Victor Delormé growled in French. The much older man, a hopeless chain smoker, hunkered over the battered suite of electronics equipment, checking the connections and ensuring that data would show up on his small, green monitors as soon as the dipping sonar became active. "Lower away."

Suspended from a hastily constructed rig, the semicircular, metallic dome of the sonar unit began its long fall. Mechanisms whirred above their heads, letting out strong, metal cable, as the dome splashed into the water and headed down at a rate of a foot each second. Its speed increased as it plunged, leaving the disturbed, surface water behind and passing through the cooler, calmer thermocline and into the depths of the English Channel.

"Below the layer," Victor reported. "Temperatures are low, but nothing we didn't expect." The hurricane had, in Victor's words, "done a number" on the Channel the night before, upturning the careful balance of dense, salty water and lighter, fresh currents. The weather had thrown the two into direct conflict, creating a dynamic, underwater seascape.

"Not too fast," Hugo reminded him as Victor reached for the mechanism's speed lever. Hugo was a slight man, bespectacled, privately educated, barely out of his twenties, and unused to the sea. He had spent his first days out on the water battling seasickness, his moans and lassitude trying the patience of the other two men on this voyage to the point that they questioned the wisdom of their decision to join him. "We don't want the current to catch the cable and whip it around," Hugo said.

"Yeah, we know," Jean-Luc Bisson, a rugged, handsome man in his late thirties said, pushing his thick, black hair off his face. "We've done this before, you know. Relax and let us work."

Their unlikely, three-man partnership was born of necessity. Hugo had the funding to mount such a speculative expedition, while for Victor and Jean-Luc, both experienced deep sea divers, this chance for a few days' well-paid work was as welcome as the start of the Bordeaux wine season, and that was before they considered the "bonuses" their work might bring forth.

Beside the sonar device, Hugo had bought a range of second-hand gear from salvaged fishing boats, and even some old, surplus French navy equipment from the gray market. The *Nautilus* itself was a remarkable salvage and repair story, a trawler given up for scrap, but which, with a cautious initial investment and much hard work, had been resurrected. She was a lumbering, often uncomfortable boat, but there was enough space for their electronics and other gear, and the hull was tough enough for most conditions. Except, of course, those of a full-blown hurricane.

"Want to try the magnetometer?" Hugo called back to Jean-Luc, who was observing the diminutive green screen with Victor. Both stared in hopes of a favorable reading, but beyond typical background scatter from the seabed, they saw nothing.

Jean-Luc rolled his eyes, but casually turned around to focus on his own area of responsibility. According to the scuttlebutt and rumors that abounded around Cherbourg Harbor, Jean-Luc was "curiously gifted" at his task. He used a method that had remained basically unchanged since his grandfather's day; a small, sophisticated, torpedo-shaped device towed slowly behind the boat, poised to indicate concentrations of ferrous metal by their telltale, if absolutely tiny, magnetic fields. "Nothing yet," he called back. It was rather like metal detecting on a scale writ large.

Hugo had the job of piloting the boat, making deliberately slow headway along the figure eight patterns he'd laid out on their charts. It was the classic approach of a team looking for something.

Each of the three found themselves enthused and cautious, by turns. They would have admitted that their main impetus for this unusual expedition was dockside rumors, some of them going back many generations, and most of them spurious. However, Hugo's argument had always been that as the rumors hadn't been disproved, they could be true. To the others, who were older and more seasoned with extensive experience of the sea's capricious nature and the romantic stories that abounded from it, this sounded like fanciful, wishful thinking. If, however, they located their quarry, the payoff would be nearly incalculable. Certainly enough, as Jean-Luc had reflected that morning, to fund a nice villa by the beach on the south coast of France. It was his retirement dream, and to achieve it, all they needed was one strong, incontrovertible signal from their equipment.

"Anything?" Hugo asked, trying to appear authoritative and seaman-like. Both older men shook their heads. "Maybe a school of herring," Jean-Luc told him. "But nothing like what we're looking for."

"*Merde*," Hugo swore. "This was as likely a spot as any," he added, almost to himself. He stepped forward to lean over Victor's shoulder. "*Mon Dieu.*" A pile of damp, discarded cigarette butts surrounded the feet of the chair upon which Victor was sitting. Several were now stuck to Hugo's shoe. Unusually for a Frenchman, he did not share Victor's love of Gauloises and wrinkled his nose in disgust.

"You always tell us this," Victor complained. "That this place is 'likely,' or that over there is 'a good possibility.'" Victor stood, towering at least a foot over the leader of this expedition, whose hold on that position was tenuous at best given his dependence on the two more experienced men.

"The only proof of how likely a spot is, will be the ping of the magnetometer," Jean-Luc explained, in a careful tone, "or a big green mass on the sonar screen. Without those, each place is as fruitless as the ones before." The two men hunched over their equipment again, their point made. Hugo stared at the unresponsive backs of their heads before returning to the boat's pilothouse.

Victor and Jean-Luc would not tolerate optimism for its own sake. They were too tough, too hard-bitten, to take anything for granted, and too knowledgeable to accept encouragement from someone with far less experience, even if he was paying them. Neither would be content nor would their moods improve one iota, until they held their cherished prize in their hands. Only then would they know that enduring the risks this search posed and the potential derision of their fellows back at the docks of Cherbourg had been worth it.

CHAPTER EIGHT

FREDDIE SOLOMON STROLLED along Gorey's main shopping street feeling pretty good about the world. He'd long since learned to ignore the odd glances cast at him, confident in his belief that "no publicity is bad publicity" and was gleefully unselfconscious in his checked, flannel pants and jaunty cravat. He had the air of someone who had just learned an embarrassing secret about a person but had chosen to keep it to himself for the moment. Amid the uniformity and conformity of Gorey locals during this off-season, he was a surprising splash of color, both in attire and personality, and the traditional, conservative community was still divided about whether or not Freddie Solomon was entirely "a good egg."

"Morning, Gracie!" Freddie chirped as he passed an elderly woman in the street. These encounters had become a useful measure of Freddie's impact, and a good barometer of his readership. Initially, he was skeptically ignored or frowned on, but more recently, his online writings had finally begun to garner consistent public attention. Readers of the *Gorey Gossip* considered themselves well informed, and if Freddie chose to spice his reportage with a pinch of hearsay or a soupçon of speculation, then it just made it all the more entertaining.

Gracie gave him a twinkling smile and tapped the side of her nose with a forefinger. It had become the "secret signal" among Freddie's growing cohort of senior informants; people who enjoyed his blog, his colorful character, and the thrill of self-importance he bestowed on them as a result of their association with him. This group of co-conspirators was well-placed to unearth tidbits of gossip from friends, family, and neighbors and was willing to toss what they'd learned on to the pyre of unchecked facts and sensationalism that comprised the writings of Freddie's blog. Freddie had already characterized the myste-rious deaths that had occurred since Graham's arrival as a "spate of murders," a representation that the DI and his fellow officers found to be a gross exaggeration. As a source in Freddie's one-man investigations into the personal aspects behind these deaths, Gorey's retired community was a goldmine.

When the Granny Grapevine went quiet, or had yet to receive news of a particular event, Freddie resorted to his back-up source for hot tips; an expensive police scanner of questionable legality that provided up-to-the-second intelligence and enabled him to ascertain information within seconds of it reaching the hands of the police. Being quick-footed and with loose profes-sional and personal boundaries, he was able to report on this information quickly, on some occasions *before* the police, wrong-footing them and removing their advantage in the process. Need-less to say, he was not looked upon kindly by DI Graham and his officers.

This time, Gracie had nothing for Freddie save a promise to keep her ear to the ground, so he sauntered onward, down to the bottom of the hill where the old post office, two gift shops, and a classy, fine bone china tea room flanked the narrowing street. Steps led down to the boardwalk, which in turn led either to the marina, mostly empty of working boats at this time of day, or to the broad, sandy curve of Gorey's much-loved beach. It was just as he set foot on the sand, hoping to see for himself the fruits of the laborious clean-up operation that had followed the hurricane and to which he had not contributed a single ounce of effort, that he heard a passer-by utter words that thrilled him from head to toe.

"Old Frank at the Harbormaster's office reckoned he washed up last night."

Freddie turned smartly to follow the meandering couple, a woman in her fifties and another who might have been her daughter. He began listening with a single-minded intensity.

"Poor lad," the younger woman was saying. "Have they any idea who it is?"

Freddie crossed his fingers in the hopes of learning more. A real-life *corpse* washed up on Gorey beach would provide at least a thousand words of good, *titillating* copy.

"Remember that young scientist? The one looking for sharks. He didn't come back in the day before yesterday. Word is that it's him."

Freddie almost jumped with excitement. He was, of course, familiar with that missing person case, and he had already been asking questions around the pub and the marina hoping for a juicy story perhaps involving corruption, professional rivalries, or maybe some prurient details about a relationship gone awry. Now, and he barely stopped himself from rubbing his hands with glee, he had confirmation of a tragedy, a circumstance for which he was particularly suited. Freddie felt that he was gifted at expressing the unspeakable in those heartfelt and human moments when people were at their lowest and most likely to talk about a loved one, especially to a sympathetic stranger who showed great compassion while interjecting an expertly timed, incisive question.

Peeling away from the ambling pair, Freddie began accelerating down the beach. He passed the decorative benches that lined the promenade, pulled up the collar of his tweed jacket against the inclement wind that came off the water like it meant business, and was soon faced with a cluster of people, a police car, and an ambulance, but, Freddie was delighted to see, no media people were yet in attendance. He'd have first shot at this story, out-maneuvering the workaday journalist hacks who were unlucky enough, and unenterprising enough in Freddie's opinion, to work for traditional news outlets.

Six people were standing around the body, which did indeed look exactly as though it had washed up during the night. It had come to rest on a small rise about ten feet from the concrete wall of the promenade. Freddie could see that the deceased was still wearing his shoes. He knew from his ceaseless research that this almost certainly ruled out suicide, but little else was visible through the crowd of legs and past the green bags of medical gear brought by the ambulance crew. He moved in closer.

"Do we know his identity?" Freddie asked anyone who was listening. He had the confident, full-throated voice of someone who knew his rights and would vigorously defend his having shown up somewhere he really oughtn't have.

"Step back, please, sir," said Roger Percival, the Community Support Officer. He was looking the part in his hi-visibility vest and neat uniform, grateful for a respite from the coastal cleanup but cold enough to hope that his part in this local emergency wasn't going to take too long. "This isn't a pleasant sight, and we need to give the attending officers room to work."

Such warnings were like catnip to Freddie. He took two or three surreptitious photos, feeling a familiar explosion of adrenaline, moving quickly and discreetly to avoid police censure. He would post them on his blog as soon as he was done here. Depending on whether his photographs went viral, he'd be in danger of being sued by the family of the deceased, but such risks thrilled him, and he was never slow to set aside moral scruples in favor of shooting unforgettable images. It was that *color* he most wanted to capture; that pallid, alabaster skin tone which spoke of a life forever gone and of a story just beginning.

Freddie asked a few more questions before being shooed away by Percival and the ambulance crew who were waiting for Marcus Tomlinson to arrive. Already drafting an article on his phone while he walked away from the scene, Freddie remembered another of his favorite refrains. It was borrowed from the mindset of every irresponsible, rushed, speculative journalist. It was one he was guided by, especially on those rare occasions when he was, just slightly, checked by some doubt as he prepared to hit "send." He didn't need to remind himself of it today, however. The sensation of the moment was enough to carry him through. Freddie Solomon was on his game. The thrill of the hunt, the story, was for Freddie, his life force. Now was the time for a pulsing journalistic thrust forward in the name of ground-breaking news coverage.

Then his would be the glory. *Publish or perish.*

CHAPTER NINE

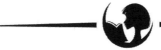

The Gorey Gossip
Wednesday, November 14th

Tragedy struck our community today. It could have happened anywhere, but fate decreed that this misfortune should befall the town of Gorey. The body of thirty-one-year-old Greg Somerville was found at 12:30 PM, washed up on the beach around a half-mile from the base of Gorey Castle, a place with its own recent, blood-spattered history.

For those who knew and respected the young scientist, this is a day for shock and a week for mourning. For the rest of us, naturally upset at this unfortunate loss, Greg's death brings a contemplation of mortality and the infinite, but also important questions about this poor man, and how he met his untimely end.

We know that Greg was working for the UK
Environmental Agency, involved in potentially
dangerous work with large, migrating sharks.
But having seen Greg's body with my own eyes
this morning, I can testify against his demise
having resulted from a shark attack; there were
no bite marks, and Greg's body was pale and
lifeless but entirely intact.

Instead, we must analyze other possibilities. I was shocked to see that Greg had
suffered a devastating wound to the back of his
head. From my own research, this wound appears
consistent with the effects of a large hammer.

How might this unassuming research scientist
have come to harm? Could there have been an
accident at sea? Did someone wish to harm him?
Why have there been no sightings of his small
motor launch, the *Albatross?* Why did he not
return the day before the storm? And what
should we make of the behavior of his partner
and confidant, Tamsin Porter? She was seen
killing time in the Fo'c'sle and Ferret while
her brave man was at sea, the day before the
hurricane. Why did she not accompany him, as
usual?

And if he was attacked, who would have
lurked out in the Channel, ready to accost a
lone, unarmed man? Could Greg have run into
human-traffickers or drug-runners? Found
himself in the wrong place at the wrong time?

I have been roundly critical of Gorey Police
on this blog, but now is the time for the
beleaguered constabulary to take the lead and

show that they can keep the good people of
Gorey safe from harm. The circumstances of this
young man's death must be vigorously investi-
gated and those who perpetrated the crime
brought to justice.

CHAPTER TEN

GRAHAM WAS READY for Harding's mild objection. "I appreciate that she's in a state, and she's had a rough forty-eight hours, but would you get her down here as quick as you can?" He was torn. The Greg Somerville missing person case had become a coroner's investigation, but until Tomlinson confirmed foul play, he could only gather background details. The DI had a firm sense that Tamsin had not yet revealed everything she knew. He hoped a more formal interview here at the station would yield more. "Thanks, Sergeant. See you shortly."

Before interviewing Tamsin, however, Graham felt obliged to spend a few noisy and instructive moments with Freddie Solomon. The DI slid his cellphone back into his jacket pocket and turned to face the blogger.

Freddie was sitting stiffly upright in Graham's office, looking around slowly at Graham's sparse collection of memorabilia and two awards set in small, glass cases. There was a picture of a group of young men, surely only cadets, in blue uniforms, and a framed newspaper front page featuring three mug shots and the headline, "Got 'Em!"

"I don't mind journalists," Graham began, pacing his office and loosening his tie as though this were a convivial chat and not the lecture both knew it would be. "In fact, we rely on the media to get the facts out about a case, descriptions of people we're searching for, and so on. I've had many an occasion to buy a journalist a drink for being mindful of the importance of open communications. We like to work hand in hand with the media. You scratch our back, we'll scratch yours, know what I mean?"

"Prudent behavior, all round," Solomon agreed.

"But you," Graham continued, his tone still level, "are *not* a journalist, Mr. Solomon. I'm not sure if the Internet has yet invented an appropriate term for just what it is that *you* are."

"I'm a *citizen* journalist, Detective. A journalist of the people."

Graham glared at Solomon. The little blighter seemed almost fragile, willfully foppish, but conspicuously unperturbed by Graham's manner. "You could be Citizen Kane and you still wouldn't have the right to drop me two ranks. It's Detective *Inspector*, Mr. Solomon," he rasped. "That's a detail you might find important to include in your *ridiculous* blog."

Solomon remained frustratingly impassive. "I'm not here to interview you, Detective *Inspector*. You called *me* in, remember?" he intoned. "But since you mention it, you'd be an interesting subject for a profile piece." Solomon stood, a half-foot shorter than Graham and side-eyed the inspector for a moment. "Oh, yes. Lots of complexity behind *that* grizzled exterior. A wealth of professional achievement, I'm sure. But controversy, too." He leaned in to whisper, "There always is."

Graham took a step back and allowed his anger to dissipate. "Mr. Solomon," he said almost mildly. "I'll be asking you to remove yourself from my police station shortly, but before I do, I'd like to offer you some advice." Graham looked down to make sure the little squirt was listening. "Interfering with police investigations, by which I mean," Graham clarified, "commenting on a victim's injuries, possible cause of death *and* spurious theories not grounded in any fact about likely suspects, before the police have cleared that information for release, is dangerous and *prejudicial* to our inquiries."

"It's my right, and my responsibility," Solomon reported.

Graham bit back an unprofessionally stern response. "It's 'perverting the course of justice.' Isn't that a marvelous old expression?"

"It's a beauty, but I won't be perverting anything. You can rely on my discretion." It was a bald-faced lie, and they both knew it.

Graham frowned at him like an unimpressed schoolmaster. "I bet I bloody well can," he growled. "Now, if I see details of a suspicious death, or anything else I don't like in your half-baked rant of a blog, we'll meet again. Only this time, you'll be in a jail cell downstairs, and I'll be writing you up for endangering the security of a police investigation. Do you understand?"

"I do," Solomon replied at once. "I apologize if I have overstepped my bounds, Detective Inspector," he said.

There was a hint of flippancy in Freddie's tone that grated on Graham's last nerve and he took the slighter man by the shoulder. For a quarter-second, Freddie wondered if he were about to feel the DI's fist break his nose. "Come again, lad?"

"Nothing, nothing." Solomon held his hands up. "I'll be going."

"Indeed, you will," Graham said, shepherding the blogger out. He watched Solomon find just enough of a strut to effect a graceful exit and then took ten long, deep breaths as he stood in the silent reception area.

Barnwell arrived as Graham was exhaling for the tenth time. "Things that bad, sir? Or are we going for enlightenment?"

"Just bracing myself against the inevitable, Constable. Anything from the harbor?"

Barnwell frowned. "The rumor mill is working overtime, sir. Everyone is talking about the death. The natural assumption would be to assume that Somerville hit his head and then drowned, the vast majority of disappearances at sea do end just like that after all, but some of the fishermen are dreaming up a story that our victim was attacked. Nothing else makes sense, according to them. But you know how it is, they don't have any evidence, just 'a feeling.' None of them noticed anything unusual beforehand or at any time at all, so they reckon."

Shaking his head at this lively creativity, Graham said, "Where do they get this stuff?"

"The prevailing theory is that French fishermen are trying to stake their claim on Jersey's waters and Somerville's death is 'a message.' It's a ridiculous conspiracy theory if you ask me, but they're not happy people down there at the marina. They're unbelievably angry about the new fishing quotas the government has slapped on them, and tensions are running high with the usual anti-French feelings boiling over even more than usual. The Frogs don't help themselves by coming ashore, drinking, and eyeing up the women, of course. You'd think they were deliberately trying to wind the locals up." Barnwell rolled his eyes. "The local boys get territorial, and even if Greg Somerville's death turns out to be a simple drowning, the mood at the harbor is making me worried."

Graham's memory flipped back a few pages and showed him an article that he'd read in the local paper regarding tighter restrictions on the species that could be fished around the island. "Fish stocks need time to recover, but I understand their frustration. If they're not making money from the fish, the entire island economy falters. Everyone suffers," he said with a sigh. "No sign of Somerville's boat, I suppose?"

Barnwell shook his head. "Not a trace."

"Keep an eye on the men, okay? We don't want things getting overheated and some kind of vigilante action occurring." Graham suppressed a shudder. "Hopefully we'll get some information from Tomlinson soon that will take the wind out of their sails and things will calm down of their own accord."

"Will do, sir. I saw that pillock of a journalist on my way in. Did you skewer him without me? It was him who started these ridiculous rumors."

Graham allowed himself a satisfied smile. "All dealt with. I think there'll be a noticeable change in the tone of his blogging," he predicted. "And let's not legitimize what he does. He's not a journalist. He's a rumor-monger and a creepy, lying, little sh—"

"Right-o, sir. It's amazing how he finds these things out. How do you reckon he does it?"

"Probably consorts with other rats down in the sewers," Graham mumbled to himself. Barnwell chuckled at the idea, but turned his attention to work as he followed Graham's gaze to the station door. "We've got the victim's girlfriend coming in. Harding's with her, and I'll join them when they arrive," Graham said.

Barnwell returned to the reception desk just as the phone began to ring. Graham heard him get ready to patch the call through. "Dr. Tomlinson, sir," he called over.

"Excellent." *Click.* "Marcus. What have you got?"

"Well," the pathologist replied, "I've just finished Greg Somerville's autopsy. My estimate for the time of death is sometime on the day he disappeared, in other words, before the storm. The length of time he was in the water and the atrocious conditions confuse matters, but that's my best guess. The cause of death was blunt force trauma. He was hit around the head with something heavy and dull."

Graham sagged in his chair. "Oh, lord. Murder, then, for sure."

"I'm afraid so," Tomlinson confirmed. "We're looking at a deep, non-linear fracture of the skull about two inches in length. I can't be sure what weapon was used," Tomlinson admitted. "The wound had a very distinctive shape, like he was hit twice, or maybe once with a double-ended weapon."

"He didn't drown, then?"

"Definitely not. There was no water in his lungs. He was already dead when he went in the water."

"Well, that's something, I suppose." Graham thought for a moment. "Couldn't he have got stuck out in the storm and injured himself on the boat? Are you sure it wasn't an accident?"

Tomlinson didn't have to mull this over. He'd been as thorough in this autopsy as in any throughout his long career and had considered accidental death as well as homicide. "He has a number of wounds that are consistent with a struggle. The water washed away any evidence though, I'm afraid. Now, could it have been an accident? It's theoretically possible," he admitted, "but that wouldn't explain the scratches and bruises on his arms, and he would have had to have fallen quite specifically on something that caused this odd shaped injury. Was there anything that could match his injuries on board?"

"We don't have the boat. We've got people out looking for it, but nothing yet. And even if we find it, I suspect the effects of the storm will have carried anything loose on board to the bottom of the Channel."

"Yes, you're probably right, there. No, it's my considered opinion that it wasn't an accident, David. His injury was devastating, he would have died instantaneously. I have no doubt we're looking at a murder."

Outside, Graham heard a car engine cut out followed by the sound of doors slamming.

"Tell me, if he was attacked, do you think a woman could have done it?"

Tomlinson looked up at the ceiling of his office and squinted, "With the element of surprise, the instability inherent on a boat? It's possible."

CHAPTER ELEVEN

J ANICE AND TAMSIN bustled their way through the
lobby doors. There were dark circles under Tamsin's
hooded eyes, and she walked slowly to the interview
room, guided by Janice.

"Can I get you a cup of tea, love?"

Tamsin nodded and settled herself at the table, forcing her
hands down into her jean pockets. Janice closed the door and
walked over to the filing cabinet that acted as a tea-making
station. Her heart was heavy. If she were in Tamsin's position,
Janice was quite sure she would barely be able to stand upright,
let alone have pointed questions fired at her in the austere
surroundings of a police station.

"Constable? Sergeant?" Graham called from his office door.
"Join me for a moment, would you?"

The pair came into his office, and he shut the door. "The
Somerville case is now officially a murder investigation. He was
hit on the back of the head and died instantly, dead before he hit
the water." He looked at Janice and pointed in the direction of
the interview room. "Ms. Porter is now a suspect."

"Really, sir?" There was mild objection in Janice's voice. It was true that most murders were committed by people known to the victims, and that close family and friends were often the first people to be interviewed, but she found it hard to believe that the pale, shocked woman she'd just put in the interview room had killed her boyfriend. Still, Janice knew she was identifying too much with Tamsin and needed to put her personal feelings aside. She had a job to do. "Yes, of course. I'll make her tea and get her settled, then I'll run a background check."

"While we're on the subject of computers, could you do something for me, Sergeant?" Graham relayed the concerns Mrs. Taylor had regaled him with the previous evening. "She's certain that the '87 storm caused some mysterious...*vortex*," he said, his face apologizing for the term, "which caused some strange incidents and unfathomable, to her at least, disappearances. She's worried that that's going to happen again this time. Can you track down anything *odd* that happened during the week after the Great Storm but which later proved to have a perfectly reasonable explanation? Don't spend too long on it, just enough to show Mrs. T. that we've followed up and that there's nothing to be concerned about, that there's such things as coincidences, accidents, and mysteries that might appear extraordinary at first blush, but which are ultimately proven to have explanations that don't have their basis in hauntings, beastly threats, or other supernatural phenomena."

"I didn't think you believed in coincidences, sir."

"I'll make an exception in Mrs. Taylor's overly-imaginative case."

"Yes, sir." Janice bustled off to make the tea. Graham turned to Barnwell.

"Sit down, would you, Constable?"

Unsure as to quite what this invitation would lead to, Barnwell took a seat opposite his boss who was absent-mindedly turning in his swivel chair. Barnwell knew that this was another "thinking tactic" Graham had developed, not unlike those crazed scientists who summoned their best ideas when sitting in an odd position, upside down, their limbs awry.

"The woman in the next room," Graham began, clearly following his own train of thought and obliging Barnwell to serve as a sounding board, "is petite, not particularly strong, and apparently of sound mind. Yet, I'm about to question her in relation to an unsolved death. She's our prime suspect at this juncture."

Graham's eyes were glued to a patch on the wall. "Janice and I went through all the scenarios we could think of just after Somerville was reported missing. Listed all the potential reasons for his disappearance, eliminated those that were too wacky, and in the end, we, I, felt that an accident was the most likely explanation. Now Tomlinson says we're looking at murder, one that unusually happened at sea. Who would have gone to that much trouble?"

"Someone who knew how to navigate the water. Perhaps someone who followed him out there or came upon him?" Barnwell suggested. "Someone who might know where his tracking devices were located?"

"Hmm."

The constable picked up a pencil that lay on Graham's desk and twirled it between his fingers, like he'd seen the DI do, warming to his ideas. "In my experience, sir," he said, "people tend to end up dead because of money or love."

"Do you believe there's such a thing as a 'criminal', Barry?" Graham asked as he continued to stare at a blank space on his office wall.

"That'd be someone who commits a crime, would it, sir?" Barnwell asked, as if suddenly concerned that the definition of the word had changed, and no one had told him.

"Normally, yes. But I'm talking about something deeper. A hereditary trait, or a deep-seated psychological characteristic. Something that *makes* someone a criminal, something that they are almost compelled to act out, making them different from the vast majority of law-abiding people."

Barnwell caught on quickly. "You're asking whether someone is capable of murder, sir, like from birth?"

"Hmm. And do you think we can, *should*, spot these people before they commit a crime?"

Following exactly the lessons his boss had passed on during previous months Barnwell answered, "I think it is better to examine the evidence at hand, sir, rather than make...how do you say? Subjective decisions."

His boss' occasional forays into psychology and even philosophy with respect to police investigations were apt to sail right over Barnwell's head. When Graham had arrived on the island, he had started with a policy of smiling and nodding at these musings, but more recently, he found himself turning the DI's gems of wisdom over in his mind at night. Even if he was still bamboozled by most of what Graham put forth, Barnwell thought about the Detective Inspector's ideas more than he would care to admit. And like his fellow officers, he admired Graham's remarkably keen mind.

Graham nodded his head toward the interview room. "You want to step in there and interview Ms. Porter?"

"Sir?" Shaking his head with unmistakable firmness, Barnwell answered, "Well above my pay grade, sir. I'll leave the detecting to the detective, if you don't mind."

Graham looked at Barnwell, reminding himself how much fitter and more *together* the constable looked compared with a while back. "I'm not one to bother people about career progress and such," Graham said, "but I do hope your talents find a broader outlet than Gorey, some day anyway. Don't forget to challenge yourself, son. Move out of your comfort zone."

"For the moment, sir," Barnwell said, rising, "there's plenty to challenge me around here."

Unsurprised at Barnwell's unwillingness to take a professional risk, but not deterred, Graham let the matter drop for now. He picked up his notepad and a big mug of tea, and headed for the interview room where Tamsin Porter was waiting. "Ms. Porter," he began, setting out his notebook and taking a seat opposite her. "We're grateful for your time."

"Yeah, sure," she said. Her voice was weak, and she was pale, clearly badly shaken.

"I hope you'll accept our condolences. I'm very sorry for the way in which you found out the terrible news. That really isn't how we prefer to do things."

Ordinarily, it would have been Janice's job to notify Tamsin of her partner's death, but the *Gorey Gossip* had pre-empted even that courtesy. Tamsin had learned about her loss online, along with everyone else. She'd barely spoken since.

Graham employed his softest tone. "I'd like you to take me back to that morning, in the pub, before Greg left," he said.

Tamsin cleared her throat, dabbed her eyes once more, and began to tell the story of her last conversation with Greg. Graham took notes despite the mandatory video camera in the corner, and simply waited. He felt sure that eventually, if she were guilty of anything, she'd say just a little too much.

But fifteen minutes later, it was clear this interview wouldn't be as straightforward as he hoped. Tamsin was being truculent. After relaying her recollection of the hours before Greg had left to go out to sea, she had only given the briefest responses to Graham's questions. He was frustrated, he wanted to uncover the truth, and this paucity of detail was alerting his suspicions. For her to be numbed by grief and shock was quite understandable. But to be deliberately terse and taciturn while investigators puzzled over her beloved's fate seemed decidedly odd behavior.

"You mentioned earlier that this was a make-or-break year for your project. That Mr. Somerville was feeling the pressure. Was this project going well? Was he getting the data he wanted?"

"Pretty much."

Graham rolled his shoulders. "Could you expand on that, Ms. Porter?"

Tamsin pushed her hands deeper into her pockets. "We play a long game. It's what we do. We stay persistent over years, looking for trends, patterns. And we go where the data leads us, at least we should. A good scientist would never force the data to support a hypothesis, just as you, I presume, would never make facts fit your theories of who was responsible for a crime. And so 'getting the data he wanted' isn't really the point."

Graham opened his mouth to correct her rather defensive interpretation of his question, but Tamsin continued. "Greg wanted to prove his hypothesis correct. I felt he was overinvested in it. That's a lot of what we argued about." She sat up and twisted her body in the chair, her hands to her face. The pain that telegraphed itself in her posture and that which was etched in her expression was impossible to ignore.

The knock at the interview room's door was entirely unwelcome, but Graham knew that the case might develop quickly. "Excuse me for just a moment." He left the room and nudged the door closed, finding Barnwell outside, a troubled expression on his face. "Problem, Constable?"

"Yes, sir. I'm afraid there's something kicking off at the town council meeting."

Graham blinked for a moment and tried to visualize the scene. "The monthly meeting?" He remembered seeing the announcement in the local paper. "Kicking off?" Gorey's council meetings were hardly known for outbreaks of violence, or indeed anything out of the ordinary. They typically took less than an hour, and even public debates were orderly, taking place before an audience of no more than five in his experience. "Who started it?" Graham was immediately keen to know what might have so exercised such a mellow, unspectacular group.

"Des Smith, sir. He's on his feet, right now. Two different

people called the station within moments of each other. They're concerned, he appears inebriated."

"First a hurricane, then a scientist shows up dead, and now I've got an angry, liquored-up salty seadog to contend with. Didn't someone tell me this was the 'quietest backwater in the British Isles?' What a load of...poppycock." Graham paused, looking back at the earnest expression on Barnwell's face. He stood silently waiting for direction.

"Well," Graham said, with a big sigh, "if he's risking a disturbance of the peace or might hurt someone, we need to deal with it. See you in the car, Barnwell." Graham went to conclude his interview with Tamsin.

"I'm, sorry, Ms. Porter, I've been called away. We will need to reconvene at a later time." He turned to Janice who was looking at him wide-eyed, surprised. "Would you please escort Ms. Porter back to her lodgings, Sergeant? We'll talk again soon," he promised Tamsin, "Tomorrow. Please don't leave the island in the meantime." He left the room abruptly, leaving Tamsin staring down at the table, slouching once more in her chair, her hands again shoved in her pockets.

CHAPTER TWELVE

BARNWELL DROVE THEM to the town hall at a brisk pace.

"How did the interview with Ms. Porter go, sir?"

"It would have been a lot easier if a certain someone hadn't published every last detail before we had even notified her of the death," Graham complained. "She wasn't very helpful, but I'm not sure if she was shocked by her loss and the method by which she found out about it, or if she was being obstructive on purpose."

"Annoying little blighter, that Freddie Solomon," Barnwell agreed. "But, 'freedom of the press' and all that. Got to tread carefully."

"But he's stirring things up," Graham sighed. "Getting folks riled up when there's just no information or justification for it. And that's before we get on to his callousness and his prejudicial treatment of the facts."

The converted church hall which served as the town council's venue was unusually busy with people milling around outside. As the two police officers approached, someone in the small crowd recognized Graham. "Evening, Detective Inspector," they said. "Suppose you're here about old Des, then?"

"Just checking things out. How long has he been going?"

The local man screwed up his face as he thought, then looked at his watch and counted quickly under his breath. "About twenty minutes now, I'd say."

"Quite the orator. What's he so angry about?"

"Quotas," six or seven people said together. Then one added, "Bloody unfair, they are."

"The fish probably wouldn't agree with you." From time to time, Laura flirted with vegetarianism and had been prompting Graham to consider it too, but he had found the resulting prohibition of full English breakfasts to be entirely unacceptable. "Well, let's just see how he's getting on," Graham said.

"Good luck in there, sir," someone called.

"Think we should have brought the riot gear?" Graham asked Barnwell, raising an eyebrow. The constable met his boss's glance and thought for a second, "We don't have a complete set, sir. Just bits and pieces. I'm not sure there's even one entire set on all of Jersey. Never been any need for it."

"There's always a first time."

Graham heard the harangue before he saw it. Drinks and snacks were laid out on the table in the small lobby, and through the glass of another pair of doors, they could see the tall, slightly bent figure of Des Smith, one hand aloft, giving someone his thoughts in no indirect manner.

"You've dealt with Des before, haven't you?" Graham asked quietly as they looked on through the doors.

"A few times. There were those break-ins down at the harbor that time. His boat was one of those burgled by the Hodgson boy. And he had a couple too many, maybe three Christmases ago, and had to spend the night at the constabulary bed-and-breakfast."

Graham smirked. "I trust he found our accommodation to his

liking." A jail cell at Christmas sounded like a grim way to spend the holiday.

"He's a bit of a firebrand. Old union leader, as leftie as they come. For years, he's been at the center of protests against quotas, the French, the government, you name it."

"So this isn't just a grievance about fishing quotas then, but the stirrings of a Marxist insurgency, eh? What else will this tiny town conspire to conjure up?" They watched Des' wild gesticulating as he continued his tirade for a few more moments. They could see the members of his audience bobbing their heads in agreement.

"If he sees you here," Graham wondered, "will he get angrier, or accept that his little monologue is over and wrap up?"

A shrug was his answer. "Could go either way, sir."

"We'll just let him know we're here, all right?" Graham pushed the door open and entered quietly before standing against the back wall of the hall. The room was fuller than any previous council meeting Graham had ever seen. Almost a hundred people were there. Every seat was occupied. Graham and Barnwell stepped around the left side of the hall and hovered on Smith's right flank.

A man the size of Barnwell, in full police uniform, was hard to miss, and Smith noticed him at once despite his obvious drunkenness. "Oh, aye. Here's the law!" he announced. "Come to take me away, then, Barry?"

Barnwell stood up tall, arms folded across his chest, feet apart. He felt a hundred pairs of eyes suddenly on him. There were grumblings and a couple of complaints about the police having 'nothing better to do.' In his less conspicuous suit, Graham avoided this level of scrutiny, but nonetheless, they were vastly outnumbered, and theirs was not a comfortable situation.

"Just keeping the peace, Des," Barnwell replied. "Don't let us interrupt you."

Smith most certainly didn't, and revitalized, he continued to reiterate the difficulties facing his friends and fellow mariners in the fishing fleet. "Fish don't just jump out of the sea all by themselves, you know? Someone has to go out and get 'em. People forget that. They don't give a thought to how they come to be on their supermarket shelves or in their fishmonger's cold cases. It's a hard, dangerous way to make a living, fishing is, one that needs investment and protection from the whims of those who don't understand it."

The level of support shown toward Smith was considerable, with jeers and applause greeting his more persuasive statements. "Our boats are getting old," he said. "They need new gear, new paint, and repairs to their hulls. We can't invest in keeping them afloat if we're right up against it all year."

The whole atmosphere of the meeting surprised Graham and put him on edge. "Fancies himself as a bit of a local hero, this one," Barnwell muttered to him.

"It's all all right, provided he doesn't suggest anything violent. Then, we'll have a problem." Graham said, not taking his eyes off the scene in front of him.

"We would," Barnwell agreed. "And I'd not be crazy about having to deal with him in front of this lot." Carrying out an arrest while the suspect had the open support of a hundred people wasn't something Graham relished, either. He quietly hoped the old man would run out of steam, and take it upon himself to sit down.

"But we weren't born yesterday. We understand that fish stocks need time to recover, and that by over-fishing, we're borrowing from tomorrow. Nobody I work with is comfortable with that," Des was loudly proclaiming. The harsh realities of their livelihoods weren't lost on the crowd, who considered the difficulties of an uncertain future as Des pressed on. Graham's mood lifted briefly with this touting of a seemingly moderate position, before Des plunged on again. "But we can't make a living wage with the restrictions they're placing on us, let alone make enough to invest back into our businesses," Des claimed. "The banks aren't interested in helping us out, and the paltry loans and grants the mainland is offering won't even cover the basics. And as for Brexit, pah! What a useless load of buggers those pols are!"

The mention of the European Union brought unpleasant grumbling from the crowd. As everyone knew, Jersey was neither an EU member nor actually part of the UK. Instead, it stood as a third party, with the special status of "overseas territory," and its people hoped that Britain's fraught relationship with Brussels wouldn't damage trade.

"And now the do-gooders have ganged up against us. The green movement tells us we're harvesting the fish unsustainably, pushing them toward extinction, and upsetting the delicate *ecology* of the seas. And the scientists back them up. But you know what? They're busybodies. They'll cook their books and massage their message to make sure we can't make a living. Then, we'll go out of business, our boats will rot in the harbor, and their precious fish can enjoy long and happy lives rollicking about in the sea all while we can't feed our children. It's us against them!" This brought a riot of jeering from the crowd and gained the full focus of Graham's attention. Des sounded angry, skeptical, and put-upon. He was anti-government, anti-EU, anti-conservation, and anti-science. He was proclaiming that the fishermen were being made out to be the bad guys who thought only of the short-term.

"And I haven't even touched on the French!" The mention of their old foe brought cheers and raised fists.

"They're very touched, they are!" someone shouted.

"And they're touching our women!"

There was some scuffling at the back, and Graham pitched onto the balls of his feet like a boxer, alert to the need to intervene. Almost immediately, the fracas subsided away to nothing, and he relaxed again.

"Does that sound something like a motive to you, Constable?" Graham said, in Barnwell's ear.

"Hmm?" Barnwell asked, trying to listen to both Smith and Graham at once.

"He's a bluff old mariner, at the end of his rope, hemmed in on all sides. Tamsin told us that if their research was successful, they could lobby the government to restrict fishing along the migrating sharks pathways. Could that be a reason to want Greg and the Environmental Agency out of the way? That he is a face of 'the enemy?' That his research may disrupt their livelihoods even further?"

Graham watched Barnwell's expression morph from puzzlement to denial, and then to genuine concern. "Des Smith?" Barnwell whispered. "A *murderer*? With respect, sir, pull the other one, it's got bells on."

"Why not? He's angry enough."

"I see what you saying, sir, but...I mean, the idea of it goes beyond 'unlikely,' and well into 'virtually impossible,' if you ask me."

"Hmm, you're probably right." Graham squared his shoulders to lean back against the meeting hall wall. "Still, not bad as theories go. It's worth checking out. If not Des Smith, it could have been someone in this room. All these men want to do is put bread on the table for their families and look forward to retirement in a few years. Right now, they can do neither. Look at them. Any one of them could have followed Somerville out to sea or come across him out on the water. Do they have alibis? We should check."

"What, all of them...?"

"Yes, Constable, all of them."

Barnwell frowned, and looked at Graham out of the corner of his eye. He knew these people. He had lived and worked among them for years. Des Smith was a windbag, no doubt about that, but he was no more a murderer than he, Barnwell, was James

Bond. Still, he couldn't dispute the logic behind the DI's wider approach. They would have to check out everyone who owned a boat or came through the harbor in the last few days.

Smith was going for a rousing finale. "So here's what I'm proposing," he said. "We remind ourselves that we're not beholden to anyone. That we're our own little nation state, down here."

Graham made notes. He knew Smith was wrong about Jersey's status, but a true firebrand like him wouldn't let technicalities get in the way of some useful public agitation. His mind cast back to his confrontation with Freddie Solomon a few hours prior. There were similarities between the two men, however different they appeared at face value.

"And we must assert our rights to fish where we like and how we like. We're seafaring folk and we belong at sea, not tied up in the harbor, waiting for some dodgy bureaucrat who has his fingers in the till, or poncing Greenpeace types to tell us when and how we can do our jobs." The crowd was cheering, some on their feet, while the seven-member council sat at the two top tables. They were outwardly impassive but inwardly very worried. A meeting that should have been filled with decorous discussion was turning into the latest salvoes of a bitter war.

Des sat down, exhausted and pale, while the council members restored order. One of them rapped his gavel on the desk in front of him, "Order! Order!"

Barnwell shifted his feet anxiously. "Should we step in, sir?"

"No, stay where you are for the time being. We don't want to stir them up further."

As Barnwell, who was alert to the heightened emotions of the people around him, observed the room, his lips pressed into a thin line, his arms still crossed across his chest, Graham silently tested out his notion that Des Smith, or perhaps one of the other fishermen, was a cold-blooded killer. As a theory, it wasn't perfect, but he had no leads, and the anger he'd seen tonight appeared emblematic of a larger social unease and a disregard for officialdom and lawfulness.

"Looks as though this will end peacefully after all," Barnwell said after a few minutes. Everyone was shuffling out slowly and mostly quietly. "Want me to stay and keep an eye on things?"

His boss was still lost in thought. He was adding up what he knew, shifting the pieces around, trying out new angles and probing some of the less likely investigatory avenues. It was like a collage in his mind, of pictures and ideas, people and places, objects and patterns, connecting and colliding, being dismissed or considered. More than once, when witnessing this silent cogitation, Marcus Tomlinson had requested that Graham puzzle over a case during an MRI, so that his remarkable brain activity could be charted for science. But Graham could already see the salacious headlines: *Inside the Mind of a Top Investigator*, or some such, and had politely declined.

"Sir?" Barnwell tried again, quietly.

"No, lad," the DI finally said, stirring. "We're done here. Go home and get some rest. I'll do the same."

"I think I'll take myself down the pub. It'll be a good way to keep an eye on things too, and keep my ear to the ground. No plans, sir?" He looked innocently at Graham.

The DI looked at his watch, "Not now, no." Out of Barnwell's line of sight, Graham's fists balled briefly, before he flexed them, trying to relax once more.

CHAPTER THIRTEEN

THE CROWD FELL largely silent as Barnwell walked into the pub, but when they saw he was in his civvies, and ostensibly off-duty, the pub's patrons returned to their pints and conversations, a hum and a bustle returning quickly to the pub atmosphere.

Barnwell took a seat at the bar and fired questions at Lewis Hurd whenever the barman wasn't conveying massive plates of food from the kitchen hatch to diners waiting patiently at their tables. He spent a few moments monitoring three French fishermen who were sitting in the corner, talking low, sipping bottles of beer.

"They often come in here?" Barnwell asked Hurd as he returned back from delivering fish and chips times two to a couple at a table near the fireplace.

"They come and go. There's usually a few around, rarely the same ones. They're not the most popular of customers, but I keep an eye on them and they don't cause any real trouble."

"Were there any in here the day Greg Somerville disappeared?"

"There were five of them. Those three," he nodded over to the men in the corner, "and two more."

"When did the other two leave?"

"Oh, they're still here. They were in earlier. They're all stranded. Their boats were damaged in the hurricane. They're working on repairs, if I understood them correctly." Barnwell looked at Hurd, waiting for him to explain.

"My French isn't the best," the barman said with a shrug.

Barnwell turned round, hunching himself over the bar, dangling his bottle of non-alcoholic beer between his thumb and forefinger.

"Tell me about Somerville and his girlfriend."

"They'd been here about four days," the barman recalled of Tamsin and Greg. "They came here the last couple of years as well, chasing whales, or whatever they do."

"Sharks," Barnwell corrected. "How did they seem, together?"

Hurd pulled down a bar towel that was draped over his shoulder and began polishing the wooden surface in front of him and the already-gleaming metal of the eight beer taps that separated him and Barnwell. "How can I put this?" he said, reflecting carefully on what he'd seen. "It's like I used to say about my ex-wife. Can't live with her..."

"Yeah," Barnwell said. "So, a bit of tension between them?"

The barman guffawed. "Tension? I'd say so! Every other time I turned my back, they'd be at each other's throats about some pointless thing or other."

"About their work?"

The barman nodded. "They had this long-running argument that would crop up every now and again. Something about he was the younger one, or the less experienced one, and how his methods weren't as 'sound' as hers. But he reckoned she was overly cautious, old-fashioned, or something. Most of it was Greek to me," he admitted. "Sharks and sensors and what-not.

Other than that, they kept themselves to themselves, didn't mingle with the crowd. Just as well, one of those animal rights people has been coming in here. They knew one another. I didn't want any trouble."

"So, they're here together, arguing and carrying on, and then the guy leaves to take his boat out, right?"

"Yeah. And she just sits there for a bit, nursing her pint. Then she shoots off, just leaves her drink half-finished, and disappears out the door," the barman told him, his voice rising at the end of his sentences in surprise. His polishing finished, Lewis tossed the towel back over his shoulder. "Just my two cents, of course. I was listening to them, but also the football on the radio, and seeing to the customers, so I was a bit distracted, like."

"But she definitely left, eh?"

"Oh, yeah. Off like a rocket she was."

"Okay," Barnwell said. "That's useful, thanks." The door to the bar opened and once again the murmur in the room dulled as the pub patrons turned to see who was entering. This time, it was Janice. Jack was with her. He looked bashful as he came through the door, not yet used to the attention Janice garnered through her position, but she smiled broadly and patted one man on the shoulder as she greeted him, inching her way through the crowd to the bar where Barnwell was sitting.

"What can I get you, Janice? Jack?" Barnwell said.

"Two pints of best, please," Janice said. Jack nodded in agreement, his ears pink from the cold air outside.

"Evening, Barry," he said.

"While you're getting that in, I'm just going to pop up to check in on Tamsin. Be back in a sec," Janice said.

Jack and Barnwell chatted as they sipped their drinks, Jack regaling Barnwell with stories of Janice's feisty grandmother and his entry into the Harding family fold.

"Baptism of epic proportions, it was," Jack said, "but I

survived." Janice returned from upstairs and joined him at the bar.

"How's she holding up?" Barnwell asked.

Janice made a glum face. "She's not doing so well. I might go back up in a bit, just sit with her so she's not so alone. She's not saying much."

"When she was interviewed, did she say anything about leaving the pub after Somerville?"

"She said she was here all afternoon."

"The boss said she wasn't very helpful."

"No, she didn't say much," Janice agreed.

Barnwell nodded. "Well, even if Tamsin isn't opening up to us yet, the barman was pretty well-informed."

"Oh?" Harding asked.

"Yeah. We've got to speak to the boss. There was an animal activist in here the day Somerville disappeared. He'll want to look into that, and I also have a sneaking feeling he's going to want a more in-depth chat with Ms. Porter after I tell him what I just heard."

CHAPTER FOURTEEN

THE MORNING WIND blew cold off the English Channel, but neither the early hour nor the inclement weather would deter those who had agreed to attend this "extraordinary meeting." They met even before the sun had fully risen, as befit such a rebellious rabble, aboard Des Smith's own fishing boat, the *Queen Sophia*. Des took them a handful of miles out into the Channel and then the six men lit gas camping stoves on the foredeck and produced a large breakfast of eggs, bacon, and richly aromatic smoked fish, the meal protein-laden to prepare them for their tough day ahead.

Des, of course, was the Man of the Moment. His bravura performance at the town hall had spread with remarkable speed, the old mariner's granddaughter already posting an emoji-spattered comment on Smith's Facebook page: *Grandpa! You've gone viral!*

Overnight, recordings of parts of his speech had been shared by campaigners and activists on the mainland, though Des noticed that they avoided those moments where he had slurred his words. He was feeling a little hungover. For a simple man used to a life of reassuring if challenging routine, this new experience was a little much. When he had left home earlier, he had slammed the door of his fisherman's cottage and had broken out coughing and wheezing as he inhaled. He had leaned on the doorframe, hunched over as he waited for it to pass, wondering what he had got himself into. *Fame, for heaven's sake.* It boggled the mind.

At the harbor, Des met up with five other men aged between thirty and seventy, all of them experienced fishermen or captains, and they'd climbed aboard his boat to motor out to sea, away from prying eyes and ears.

"I just want to say," Len Drake began, "that we're all bloody proud of you for standing up for us as you did last night, Des." Drake was one of the stalwart Gorey captains who'd fished Jersey waters for nigh on fifty years.

"Hear, hear," Flip Mukherjee concurred, raising his steaming mug of tea high in the air. Flip was an Australian of questionable parentage and ethnicity who'd settled on Jersey in his twenties some forty years prior. He owned his own boat and worked it with his son and brother-in-law. An upbeat, friendly character, Flip often found himself the cheerleader among a cohort that tended to despondency. Today was no different.

There was warm applause from the men, and Des received hearty slaps on the back until he begged off for fear of precipitating another coughing fit. The cold sea air was irritating his lungs this morning, as it often did these days.

"Someone needed to stand up," Drake countered. "*Someone* needed to tell these fools that we won't take any more." There were murmurs of agreement.

It was the sound of men at the end of their ropes; a note of sullen and downcast agreement, laced with just a hint of vengeance.

"Well, the world and his mother can see you on YouTube now, apparently," Drake told Des.

"Yeah, but watching the box isn't going to bring about ch now is it?" Des replied.

The men again agreed. Des could see they were tired and angry. The unfairness, the burden of these constant disputes, was weighing heavily on them. Simple men, trying to make a living, were encountering only barriers and prohibitions. Archie "Smokes" Mackenzie, a long-time, grizzled warrior of the seas, flicked a cigarette butt angrily out on to the water.

"It's not as though the industry just sprang up out of the ground, yesterday morning," Drake told them. "We've had *generations* to reach an agreement about stocks and fishing areas."

"But they always say that it's our fault," Phil Whitmore said. Phil, a Yorkshireman, had come down to Jersey three years ago. He'd traveled to the island to get work on the boats after the Kellingley Colliery closed, ending centuries of coal mining in Britain. Used to hard, physical labor, he'd soon made a name for himself among the fishing boat owners and was the first on many of their "Contacts" lists when an extra pair of strong hands was needed. His presence on Des' boat that morning was testimony to the regard in which they held him. "We're 'not being flexible enough', or 'we're simply out for ourselves,' they say."

"'Reluctant to take the long-term view,'" Des added, a phrase with which they were all familiar. "What's the point of even *having* a plan for the long-term? Our short-term prognosis is one word: unemployment."

"Well, I'm not standing around for nuthin.' I'm ready to bring in some extra cash," Matt Crouch told them. Barely thirty, Matt was the youngest man on the boat, though fishing was as much a part of his DNA as any of them. His father had fished the world's oceans, from the Barents Sea to the balmy Chagos Islands, while Matt's grandfather had gone down in a gale not twenty miles from where they now lay at anchor.

"Oh, you got yourself a money-spinner then, eh, Matt?" Des

asked him, sheltering his old, darkly polished pipe from the swirling wind as he tried to light it.

"A salvage job, that's the way I see it," he replied. "I've been reading the news, same as you, and nowhere does it say that they've found that bloke's boat."

The other five men thought for a second. "It's gone, though," Drake said. "Hasn't it?"

Matt shrugged, and then, for reasons known only to himself, he adopted the accent of a cowboy from a terrible 1950s Western. "I ain't heard any rumors that it sunk, and I ain't heard no fat lady singin,' so I guess the *Albatross* is still a-bob-bob-bobbin' along around out there somewhere."

Des Smith adjusted to the idea, and the accent, though not without a grimace. "And you're gonna find her, are you?" the old captain asked. Matt looked at him, a little sheepish now. "The boat wasn't found by the Coastguard, even with all their fancy radar, you know?"

"Yeah, but..."

"Neither by a maritime helicopter that has equipment designed *specifically* to find small surface vessels?"

"I know it's a bit of a long shot," Matt admitted, "but I just have a *feeling* about it, you know?"

They knew. Mariners had been learning to trust their guts since boats were first invented. "Follow your hunch, lad," Des told him eventually, "if you believe in it. But I won't be laying any money on you finding anything. It was only a small'un, and whoever killed that boy wouldn't have risked leaving any trace of it. I reckon the French either took it or sunk it."

He removed his woolen hat and scratched at a thin mat of extremely short, thinning grey hair.

"The French? You think they killed him? Aren't you jumping to conclusions a bit?" Matt Crouch said. He hadn't heard the rumors flying around.

"Well, who else are we to suspect?" Des argued. "He's out

there on his own, working to catalog the local wildlife. *We* know that he was counting sharks, but the *French* don't! They're not smart, you know. Have you seen them around town? They're pushing their luck, they are."

"You think they mistook him for a fisheries inspector, or something?"

"They saw him as a *threat*," Des told them. "And they took him out. Or they were sending a *message*."

Matt set aside his empty plate. "That's quite a tall tale, Des," he cautioned. "It's never happened before."

"The French have done everything but *ram* us!" Smith protested. "It's not a big leap from there to a bit of fisticuffs that got out of hand."

"Oh, please," Matt replied. "There's no evidence of any of that. At least," he added, a finger aloft, "not without Greg's boat."

Drake laughed now. "Well, you'd better get out there and track it down, hadn't you?" he said. "Matt Crouch, Marine Detective. You'll make a real name for yourself!"

Des re-started the ship's diesel engine, which gave an unsightly belch of black smoke before catching. As the men, now mostly quiet, finished up their breakfasts, an old idea came up.

"What's wrong with striking for our rights?" Len Drake posited, but the others saw it for the self-defeating strategy it had so often proved to be.

"The public will figure out pretty quickly that fish from else-where is cheaper and more plentiful. They'll buy Spanish mack-erel or Icelandic cod instead," said Phil Whitmore. He had plenty of coal mining strike experience behind him and knew it for the risk it was. "We don't have a monopoly, and many of the whole-salers will go elsewhere or do without altogether. Once they find alternatives to fish, or to our fish in particular, they may never come back, and we'll have contracted our market forever."

There was nodding, and the idea of going on strike was put aside as they discussed other forms of complaint and protest. "No point in writing to our MP, either," Des cautioned. "He's more interested in courting big contributors to his election campaign. He's not interested in his constituents at all."

"Useless bugger," Smokes said. The others murmured their agreement.

"Then, how do we get our point across?" asked Matt. A reasonable man, Matt was at a loss. He was as concerned as the others about their livelihoods, especially with a daughter due to arrive in a few weeks. They needed something fresh and new to catch the attention of the big-wigs in London who made all the decisions.

"We'll get ourselves settled in for a protest at the marina," Smith told them. "We don't stop until we have the promise of fair negotiations on quotas." The others were nodding in agreement.

"And an undertaking," Flip Mukhurjee added, "that the Coastguard and Navy let the bloody French know we're protecting our fishing areas." This was greeted with hearty cheers. There was nothing like the prospect of giving the French a slap to lift the spirits of a Jersey fisherman.

"And in the meantime," Matt Crouch said next, "I'll see if I can't get me a handsome little salvage fee. Can I borrow your radar system, Des?"

"Anything you need, son," Des replied. Although he was among the most elderly of the fishermen in the Gorey fleet, Des had never resisted trying new technologies and had a state-of-the-art radar set that would make Matt's search easier. "You go and find that lad's boat, and we'll kick up a fuss at the marina."

Des Smith gunned the engines and steered them back to the harbor with the carefree ease he'd developed over fifty years as a seaman. Sunlight glinted off the choppy waves, the skies were clear. It was going to be a memorable day.

CHAPTER FIFTEEN

G RAHAM WAS SITTING alone in his office with the morning's second pot of tea steaming quietly on a small table in the corner. Its very aroma was invigorating to him, and just as well, he needed all the sustenance and encouragement in the world this morning.

Before him lay the coroner's report on Greg Somerville, and it made for uncomfortable reading. As Tomlinson had indicated earlier, the formal cause of death was blunt instrument trauma. "Environmental experts don't whack themselves over the head with something sharp and heavy," he surmised. "And especially after they've been in a fight."

Graham again played through a number of scenarios in his head. "Who the hell was out there?" Graham murmured out loud. "And did they happen upon him, or set out deliberately to find him? And why?"

Only when Graham spotted Barnwell lurking at his open office door did his imagination return from the cold tracts of the English Channel and engage once more with the present. "Morning, Barnwell."

"Morning, sir," the burly constable replied. The big man cut quite a different figure to the one that first greeted Graham on his arrival in Gorey. Back then, Barnwell had been the butt of jokes, a corpulent and patently unfit officer, occasionally turning up for duty suffering the consequences of a previous night's hard drinking. His likely prospects amounted to finding himself alternately and reluctantly pounding the beat and manning the front desk throughout an unspectacular career. But now, Barnwell stood tall, the image of a confident and well-prepared investigator. He'd lost weight – perhaps forty pounds altogether – and having taken up swimming and boxing in recent months, looked much more agile on his feet and alert around the eyes. It was a remarkable transformation, one in which Graham felt a small amount of pride, though the achievement was Barnwell's alone.

Barnwell stood in the doorway to Graham's office, looking hesitant and a little apologetic.

"What's up, Constable?" Graham asked.

"Janice and Roach are out interviewing fishermen as you requested, sir."

"Good, good," Graham said. He waited. "And...?"

"It's line one, sir," the constable replied. "I'm afraid it's Mrs. Taylor again."

Graham dropped the pen he'd been twirling between his fingers. "Evil spirits, is it?" he asked.

Barnwell shrugged. "She's adamant, sir." He was often the bearer of unwelcome news, and though Mrs. Taylor presented no more than a minor irritant, it did bother Barnwell that he was so frequently a carrier of such tidings. Just once, he'd like to appear at Graham's office door and announce that Janice had collared someone, or that Roach had picked up a burglar wanted in Paris but who was hiding out on the island. Maybe even a fugitive drug lord or a notorious human trafficker. But mostly, Barnwell's job was seemingly to add more complication to David Graham's professional life.

"Bloody hell," the DI moaned. "All right, put her through. But if I'm not off the phone in four minutes flat, knock on my door with something urgent, all right?"

Barnwell blinked. "Urgent, sir?"

Graham reached for the receiver and sighed again. "Use your imagination, Constable. Anything will do. Just give me the nod, okay?" Then, with a lighter tone that was just this side of forced, he said into the phone, "Good morning, Mrs. Taylor. What can Gorey Constabulary do for you this..."

Barnwell returned to the reception desk and watched Graham through his office doorway as the Detective Inspector listened to Mrs. Taylor's latest story. It was quite an entertaining display. The DI would spark into life at the least sign of something interesting, or plunge into sallow disappointment at the receipt of bad news. Barnwell knew at once when Mrs. Taylor said something interesting, and then moments later, he saw that she'd somehow ruined things and that the DI was in danger of losing his patience. Barnwell kept his eye on the wall clock behind Graham's desk, ready to intervene at the four-minute mark.

"I know how this sounds," Marjorie Taylor admitted to Graham on the other end of the phone, "I know you'll think I've gone loopy, yammering on about spirits and such."

Graham knew that this rare, and to him, unexpected example of Mrs. Taylor's enthusiasm for the paranormal had to be handled with care. "In this job," Graham explained mildly, careful that his tone couldn't be construed as dismissive, "I have to reach for scientific explanations, but I also have to listen to people when they claim to have evidence."

This encouraged Mrs. Taylor sufficiently that Graham couldn't get a word in edgewise for ninety seconds. "It's just like my sister said," she related with gusto. "A huge storm, lots of damage, and then the *strangest* goings-on in the days after. People disappearing. Things moving around in the kitchen.

And you know how proud I am of my kitchen, Detective Inspector."

"I do, indeed, Mrs. Taylor," Graham demurred, "I've used the phrase 'as clean as Mrs. Taylor's kitchen floor' more than once when dismissing suspects."

"Have you?"

There was a pause and Graham imagined Mrs. Taylor puffing with a little self-conscious pride at being mentioned in a positive light with respect to a criminal investigation, however tenuous the connection.

"Well, it's not clean today!" Mrs. Taylor complained. "There are cans of tomatoes rolling around, half my fruit salad is missing, some of my pots and pans are definitely *not* where I left them, and I found my *bain marie* smashed to pieces when I came down this morning."

"So, Mrs. Taylor," he said. "You're there, and you know what you see. Help me understand what *you* think happened."

Her reply was brief. "There are bad spirits abroad," she said. "Think what you like, David." It was the very first time she'd used his name, in all the long months since he'd originally appeared, suitcase in hand, at the reception desk of the White House Inn. "But I know it."

Barnwell knocked loudly on Graham's door, hoping that Mrs. Taylor might hear at the other end of the phone. He glanced up at the clock. "Sorry to disturb, sir."

"No problem, Constable," Graham said. Then, into the receiver, "I'm sorry, Mrs. Taylor, but Constable Barnwell needs me." He then only partly covered the receiver with his hand, and asked Barnwell, "Problem, Constable?"

"The castle's on fire, sir."

"Right, sorry, Mrs. Taylor, we've got to go. Castle's on fire." He looked at Barnwell, pursing his lips. He lifted his free palm upward in a "what the hell?" gesture.

"David?" Mrs. Taylor said before he hung up. "David, please

listen. I know what this is." He'd never heard her sound more deadly serious. "And I know the threat we're all facing. It won't stop, ever. Not until we deal with this other world..." she paused, seeming to search for the right word, "*entity*." She bid him a good day and hung up.

Graham blinked a few times after replacing the receiver. "Well."

"Well?" Barnwell asked. "Has Mrs. Taylor gone to the zoo?"

Graham shook his head. "Not quite yet, lad. But maybe soon. And let's hope she doesn't check the news for the status of some fiery Armageddon at the castle on her way."

Barnwell grinned at his boss. "Sorry, sir. It was the first thing that came to mind." He noted the report on Graham's desk. "I was in the pub last night, and the barman told me that Tamsin Porter didn't remain there all afternoon the day Somerville went missing like she said."

Graham sat back abruptly in his chair. "Did she now? Well, well, well." He looked out of the window, twirling his pen some more.

After a minute of silence, Barnwell ventured, "What do you make of Ms. Porter now, sir?"

"I'm thinking that things are never as simple as they should be," Graham said. "If lying were impossible, I'd be able to retire and hand things over to a trainee constable."

"Perish the thought, sir. None of us would have jobs."

"Hmm, true. I'm wondering what caused her to hide that piece of information from us. What do you think, Barnwell?"

"She's a smart, educated woman, sir, rather stroppy and unhappy, but that's not surprising under the circumstances. She wouldn't be the first to expose a dark side when a relationship is breaking down."

"But what else might we observe about her, Constable? What informed inference can we deduce from her behavior?" Graham pressed.

Barnwell reflected for a moment. Graham's invitations to think more deeply about a question were never his way of simply killing time or even a surefire way of being thorough; there was always *an intent* to these questions. He began to feel a little put on the spot. He looked around and rubbed his palms together. "How's that different from plain, old *guesswork,* sir?" "Informed inference" was becoming one of Graham's go-to expressions, but Barnwell wasn't sure that it wasn't some kind of investigative double-speak.

Graham looked shocked, as though Barnwell had proposed dropping their investigation and was heading out to the pub. "I never *guess,* Constable," Graham reminded him. "You know that. I make informed summations from the information that we gather."

"And what have we gathered?" Barnwell asked, keen to move Graham's focus off of him. For a missing person's case, they had vanishingly little to go on.

"Somerville was a scientist. And, like most people, scientists have enemies," Graham said. "That if he'd been successful in getting additional protection for these sharks, that would have impinged upon fishing areas already allocated to the Jersey fleet. We also know that his relationship was breaking down and that his girlfriend has lied to us about her whereabouts on the afternoon he disappeared."

"And the barman also told me there is an animal activist in town. He knew the couple and not in a friendly kind of way, neither," Barnwell added.

"Is that so? Well, looks like we've gathered that our scientist had rather *a lot* of enemies, wouldn't you say? You should go down the pub more often, Constable. That's some good investigative work you've done there."

"You don't really think the fishermen had anything to do with this, do you?"

Graham shrugged. "My concern there is that someone may

325 THE CASE OF THE PRETTY LADY

have gone out to confront Greg, or perhaps they were already at sea when they saw him, and then when he'd been killed – either by accident or design – someone started a rumor to link his death with the French as a form of cover-up. From what I saw last night at the town hall, the men are so up in arms, they'd blame the French for anything that was even remotely plausible, and perhaps protect their own in the process. We could be heading for an international incident."

Barnwell was shaking his head. "I don't believe it, sir. The men just aren't like that. They are a family, a constantly warring family perhaps, but a family nonetheless. And while Greg Somerville wasn't a fisherman, and you could argue that his research worked against the fishermen's interests, they all care about the marine life in their own way. Really, Somerville had more in common with the fishermen than we do."

"Maybe, maybe. But remember it would only take one rogue fisherman to decide to take someone out. It's not perfect as theories go, certainly. And the idea that it was Des Smith borders on the far-fetched, but it is a workable hypothesis. Hopefully, the interviews that Harding and Roach are doing will clarify things. In the meantime, find this activist and check his alibi. Report back to me when you've done that, okay?" Graham sat forward in his chair and rapped his desk with the end of his pen. "All right, back to work, eh? No rest for the wicked."

"Yes sir!"

Outside, the phone rang, and Barnwell returned to the reception desk, leaving Graham with the strange and unwelcome fallout from Mrs. Taylor's ghost story and a list of unanswered questions relating to the Somerville murder.

"A dead marine biologist. An untruthful girlfriend. A possible saboteur. Angry fishermen. Gorey up in arms," he muttered to himself. "And now some idiot's trashing Mrs. Taylor's kitchen at night, apparently without stealing anything, except for a bit of fruit salad." He made notes as he always did, in a mixture of detailed text and rather more artistic "mind-maps," little sketches that summarized his thoughts pictographically. He drew a dark, brooding storm cloud with forks of lightning stretching out to connect the different elements: *"Fishermen," "The French," "Sharks," "Greg Somerville," "Girlfriend," "Animal Rights,"* and on, until he'd laid out the entire confusing case. Then, he connected the colorful whole with another strand, a broken line: *"Poltergeist at the White House Inn?"*

Outside his office, the doors to the station burst open, and in blew Sergeant Roach encased head to foot in wet weather gear. He stood in reception for a moment, the rain dripping off the end of his jacket, making puddles on the floor as he caught his breath.

"Is it raining, Jim?" Barnwell asked him.

"What do you think, smartarse?" Roach replied. "I'm ready for this weather to be over."

"So how did you get on?" Roach pushed the hood of his jacket off his head. Drops of rain ran down his face.

"I got something. I followed up with the Harbormaster, about what you said about Tamsin Porter," he said, unzipping his jacket and pulling out his notebook from his uniform pocket. He flipped it open and wiped a drop of rain from the end of his nose with the back of his hand.

"Tamsin Porter in the Billy Alley, left the harbor at 12:33 PM; returned 12:57 PM," he read.

Barnwell consulted the Somerville case file. "That's just ten minutes after Somerville went out. She followed him."

"Yep," Roach said, now stepping out of his big, wide water-proofs. "That's what I reckon, too."

"Well, you'd better go tell the guv'nor."

CHAPTER SIXTEEN

FREDDIE SAT NEXT to three piles of books, newspapers, and periodicals, writing with feverish intensity on a yellow legal pad. His work had spread until it dominated one of the main reading tables in the center of the library, but the other patrons didn't seem to mind. Freddie had become a household name in Gorey, and he had far more avid readers than detractors. He filled another page with shorthand, making extensive notes on a storm that had wiped out several of the fishing fleets over a hundred years before.

"Are you finding everything you need?" Laura asked as she passed by his desk on the first of her morning patrols.

Freddie glanced up at her, pleased that the librarian was taking an interest in his work. Enthusiasts of the *Gorey Gossip* were instant friends to Freddie, and all the more quickly if they happened to be gorgeous. "Oh, yes," he said, with a charming smile. "Fascinating story. 'The Christmas Storm of nineteen-eleven.' It's a tale well worth telling again, in our present context."

Laura took a look at the encyclopedias and maritime histories that Freddie had spread across the broad, wooden desk. "Amazing to think," she said quietly, so as not to disturb two elderly readers who were relaxing in armchairs and engrossed in the day's *Racing Post* within earshot of them, "that there isn't a single person left on Jersey who was alive back then."

Freddie's network of sources meant that the island's seniors were very much his bailiwick. "Old Mrs. Parkinson will be a hundred and one in the spring," he said, "but no, I guess she'd need to be at least a hundred and ten to remember that storm."

"So, you're writing about historical events relating to storms off Gorey?" Laura asked. Although she didn't care to read Freddie's blog, like everyone else, perhaps with the exception of the local constabulary, she found him rather charming on the surface. She also knew that some of his methods were unsavory, and that he had come under David's scrutiny for releasing information before the police were ready. On one occasion, he'd mentioned the unfortunate necessity of giving Solomon a "thorough dressing-down." For reasons Laura couldn't quite pin down, this "bad boy" image merely compounded the young writer's appeal, certainly among the locals who were apt to view him as a minor celebrity.

"I'm working to draw parallels between them and the storm we just had," Solomon explained. "I had a local tip about strange happenings in these parts following major storms."

This, too, rang a bell with Laura. Hadn't David mentioned something about Mrs. Taylor losing the plot and seeing ghosts or some such? "Do you think there's anything to it?" she asked, genuinely interested.

Freddie pulled out the chair next to him and motioned for her to sit before showing her a selection of clippings, articles, and yellowed newspapers dating back well over a century. "It seems to be a repeating pattern," Freddie told her. "A gale blows up and causes loss of life and damage, and within the few days immediately after, there's always an *incident* of some sort."

329 THE CASE OF THE PRETTY LADY   329

Laura frowned and skimmed two of the articles, impressing Freddie, who was no slouch at speed reading himself. "Well, it's all very interesting, but you know what they say about *correlation* and *causation*."

"Oh, yes," Freddie replied, "and the Gorey police seem to agree with you. But," he said, suddenly reflective, "when investigating a case, I think it's prudent to examine *all* the angles, don't you?"

"Sounds sensible," Laura said, careful to speak in a neutral tone.

Freddie saw that his subtle dig at the local police had been met with pursed lips, but no impassioned defense. In Freddie's view, that was a very good sign.

Laura was different, he'd already decided. There was a certain calm competence about her, and an unstinting enthusiasm for helping others learn. These were her less obvious traits. Most people, especially men, would be instantly taken with Laura's good looks. In his mind, Freddie compared her to a young Grace Kelly or blond Audrey Hepburn; slender, tall, seemingly unintimidating, but possessed of considerable inner strength. And she was unfailingly polite, he noted too, something he found reassuringly wholesome.

"Let me know if you need help finding anything else," Laura said, standing up. She moved on to check in with a regular who was trying to find something in the health section. Once she had answered his questions and sent him to the right shelf, she returned to the main desk and continued with the day's more mundane work – labeling new items and entering their details into the computer. As she typed, she found her mind, and then eventually her eyes, drawn back to Freddie as he read and wrote in that effervescent way of his.

Laura compared him to David. Freddie was younger, smaller, slighter, and more colorful. He was also morally flexible and opportunistic, two labels that could never be applied to Graham. But Freddie was more "available."

Laura was no more beholden to the Inspector than he was to her, and he'd already made it crystal clear that his responsibilities as a police officer handily trumped his personal life. Laura guessed that went for *her* personal life too, if hers were connected to his. There had been a handful of evenings that one might call dates, but they'd only managed to reach the end of two of them, the others being curtailed for one reason or another. Further arrangements had been canceled or rescheduled, often at the shortest possible notice. But still, she respected him for his professionalism, commitment, steadiness, intelligence, and his moral code.

Was it selfish then, Laura wondered, that she wanted more from him? Was she being childish if a small ripple of resentment toward his work, his colleagues, the countless, endless hours, the dangers he sometimes faced, ran through her? Laura sighed and snapped out of her reverie. She found Freddie Solomon standing on the other side of the issue desk, watching her intently. "Oh, sorry," she said, laughing. "I was miles away. What can I do for you?"

Freddie was feeling bold and decided that he'd strike while the iron was hot. Or, if not actually *hot*, then encouragingly warm. "I did wonder whether you might be a bit of a daydreamer," he said quietly, well out of earshot of the other patrons. "Was it anything good?" There was a conspiratorial glint in his eye, as if encouraging Laura to divulge that which she should not.

"Oh, it was nothing," she said, shutting down Freddie's inquiry as gently as she could. "Just got a bit distracted for a moment. You need anything?"

Freddie summoned all of his courage. Despite his flamboyant persona, he often found himself tongue-tied around beautiful women, and Laura was certainly the most striking he'd seen in Gorey for a long while. "I, er, wondered," he began, "if I could tempt you to join me for coffee one morning. When you're not working, that is." His words sounded confident. Inwardly, he braced himself for what he was certain would be a polite refusal.

But he could see that she was torn. Laura hesitated and when the anticipated immediate refusal didn't occur, Freddie allowed himself to have just a little hope.

"I'm sorry," Laura responded eventually. "I'm seeing someone." *Was that the right phrase?* A noisy mêlée began in her mind, a confused battle between her desire for a relationship with David Graham and the reality of only the modest commitment to her that he seemed able to make.

Freddie's face fell, but he hid the bulk of his disappointment. "I wasn't aware, I'm sorry," he said. "Anyone I know?"

Laura chuckled. "In a manner of speaking. I understand you've already had a cordial chat with Detective Inspector Graham."

Freddie's eyes closed, and he burst out laughing. "Oh, my," was all he said at first. But then he couldn't resist. "A fine detective," he announced. "Wedded to his job and his rule book."

Much was implied in those few words. To her, it was a reminder that a senior police investigator was unsuitable relationship material; that he'd be forever distracted by cases and administrative problems, would lack the time to make a go of it with her, and she'd not receive the attention she deserved. There was also a not-so veiled insult in Freddie's tone, and it sparked a flash of angry defensiveness that Laura quickly tamped down.

"Very fine, indeed," Laura confirmed. "A remarkable mind. Anyway," she said breezily, "let me know if you need help finding anything else."

Freddie returned to his table and began to pack up his research. He felt awkward, but at the same time, he'd learned a new piece of gossip, news that might at some point come in very useful, indeed.

CHAPTER SEVENTEEN

"MS. PORTER," GRAHAM said as he and Harding began another interview with Tamsin. "I hope you don't mind meeting in these more informal surroundings." The section of the pub nearest the back door was almost empty and was as good a place to talk as any.

"It's fine," Tamsin said. Graham could see that she'd barely slept, and that her demeanor and appearance were those of someone who was carrying an immense emotional weight. "I want to help." She seemed a little more cooperative than she had the previous day.

Once more, Graham retraced Greg's steps on the morning of his disappearance, asking for Tamsin's confirmation at each stage. "And there had been a kind of disagreement between you," Graham said. It wasn't really a question, but Tamsin nodded. "Was he angry when he left?"

She thought back, and the pain of recollection showed in her face. "It was bitter, between us, sometimes," she admitted. "I said some things, he said some things. You know how it is."

Graham flipped a page in his notebook. "I think I do," he said.

"But something I also now know is that *you* left Gorey Harbor during the early afternoon. A second Environmental Agency launch was seen heading out in the direction of the buoys with you in it." He waited for Tamsin to signal that she'd forgotten this detail, though he silently hoped she might simply collapse into a full confession even if he did think it unlikely.

Instead, her response was quite strange. She blinked repeatedly as though struggling to come to terms with something, but then blurted out, "I should have told you earlier."

Harding's fingers were alive on her iPad, but Graham studied the young woman very closely as she spoke. "I went out in my launch to catch up with Greg. I wanted to put things right, to help him with the equipment, record the data."

Harding asked the most obvious question before Graham could even prompt her. "Why didn't you mention this earlier?"

Tamsin's reply was a shrug that begged for forgiveness in these days of grief. "Have you ever lost anyone?" she asked Harding. And then she turned to Graham, her eyes inquiring and pleading, but he didn't respond. *Not now, not here, not to you, and certainly not in front of Harding.*

"The bottom fell out of my world. You can't imagine. Maybe I forgot some details, my mind was a mess," Tamsin said.

"Did you find him?" Harding asked next.

"No. I abandoned the idea almost immediately. He wasn't where I expected. Maybe he got a fault signal from a buoy further out and headed for that straight away, I don't know. He could have been anywhere. I quickly gave it up as a bad job and turned back."

"So, you didn't encounter his boat, and you saw no sign of him?"

"That's right. I guess I sat alone on the water for a few minutes looking around, and when I couldn't see him, I headed back to the pub to wait for him to return."

"You didn't radio him to find out where he was?"

Tamsin shrugged. "No, I wasn't sure he would welcome my presence, and I suppose I didn't want confirmation of that. It seemed easier just to turn around. It was another four or five hours before I declared him overdue and all of this began." Tamsin's grip on her emotions was still slender, and she took a moment to collect herself before suddenly sitting bolt upright. "We had problems with the engine on the launch, two days before the storm. Greg thought the wrong type of fuel was in the tank. We'd never make that type of mistake, so we thought that someone was actively sabotaging us. Maybe his death has something to do with that?" Her eyes narrowed. "Have you accounted for all the fishermen?"

"Well," Graham said, "that's difficult. There are many, but we are working through them—"

Tamsin stood. "I'm going down there right now. To the marina." She was fired up, angry, and resolute.

"Wait!" Harding cried, but Tamsin roughly pulled open the bar door and was gone.

Janice turned to Graham who was still sitting in his chair, his elbow on the arm as he calmly watched Tamsin through the window. "Well, we lost control of that one, sir."

"We know where she's going. She won't get far." He pushed himself out of his seat, "But let's get after her."

Tamsin had run down the sloping path to the harbor at speed. She would reach it in no time.

"Are we going to have trouble?" Harding wondered to Graham. "The men are not going to like her throwing accusations around."

"True," Graham said, breathing steadily as they jogged down the slope. "But I'm keen to see their reaction, all the same."

Down at the harbor, Smith, Drake, Mukherjee, and Mackenzie were carrying out their plan to stage a protest. They and a dozen others were holding signs which read, "*Honk if you respect Jersey's fishermen!*" and, "*More Mussels, Less Brussels.*"

Unsurprisingly, Tamsin found them easily enough.

"I want to speak to you," she said bullishly, approaching Des Smith. "I want some answers."

Harding and Graham caught up with her. "Are you suggesting that these men have something to do with Greg's disappearance?" Janice asked.

"Yeah," Tamsin blurted again. "One of you guys interfered with Greg's boat. I know it. You never liked having us around from the start."

Des actually dropped his pipe. "Say that again, young lady." He sounded equal parts of confused and combative.

"You don't want 'government types' around down here," she asserted. "You'd do anything to get us off your backs, to get us out of your fishing lanes. One of you probably killed him!"

Graham and Harding were treated to the noisy spectacle of Des Smith in one of his favorite guises: angry and aggrieved. "What? You come down here, spouting all kinds of nonsense, accusing decent, hard-working men of *murder*, for heaven's sake!" He turned to Graham. "Can't you do something? Isn't this, I don't know, libel or slander, or something?"

Graham took Tamsin gingerly by the arm. "I couldn't say," he admitted, "but I do know Ms. Porter is very upset."

"You're damn right, I'm upset!" she shrieked, wrenching her arm from Graham. "No one is looking in the right place! You're all wasting your time!"

"Come with me, Tamsin," Janice said quietly. She gazed directly at the other woman signaling her concern, and some of the fire in Tamsin's eyes went out.

Harding walked her away from the group. "I know you're upset, and we'll ask them some questions, Tamsin, but you really can't go around accusing people like that." Tamsin very gradually settled down, muttering to herself and to Harding, until the sergeant was able to escort her back to the pub.

Another half-hour of questions achieved nothing.

"As I've already said, we had an argument. I went out to look for him. I returned quickly, having not sighted him, and I waited in our room at the pub until I called him in missing. The end." Tamsin spread her hands, "That's all there is to it. Now, if you don't mind, I would appreciate you leaving me alone to face another day of trying to piece my life together. Greg's parents are arriving from Norfolk later today. They were enjoying a quiet retirement until this happened. Instead, somehow, we'll be putting together funeral arrangements and packing up Greg's belongings."

The incredible strain showed in her every facial expression and movement. As they left, Harding gave her a pitying glance, but she knew there was little to be done.

"Wow," the sergeant noted when Tamsin had left. "I'm not sure what to think. Part of me is incredibly sympathetic, but really? She went out in her boat? And the boat had been sabotaged? And she's only telling us this now?"

Graham wore that intense frown – not joyless, but determined – which betrayed the avid workings of a keen mind. "People under stress do forget things," he allowed, "but those are huge omissions to make at a time like this."

"Is she still a suspect, sir?" Harding asked. Despite her exasperation with Tamsin's lack of transparency, her own quiet hope was that the woman could be eliminated from their inquiries and allowed to grieve in peace.

"I'd say she's our *number one* suspect, Sergeant. She had a form of motive, and the opportunity while they were alone at sea together."

"And the method?" Harding pressed, applying Graham's own rubric. It was fun to extemporize, but she knew all too well that guesswork was unscientific.

"Pretty well any boat afloat in the world today has a tool that could be repurposed as a murder weapon...We need to search her launch, just in case it was her and she was silly enough to leave the evidence behind."

Tamsin's launch was tied up next to other vessels of its type – essentially large dinghies with a single, powerful, outboard motor. It only took seconds of searching to conclude there was absolutely nothing out of the ordinary. "I mean, it's too much to ask for her to put a sign up saying, 'Murder weapon here – please dust for prints,' but there's just no evidence of anything," Janice commented.

There were no obvious footprints, no signs of a struggle, no damage to the vessel. Literally nothing Graham could associate with Greg Somerville's death.

CHAPTER EIGHTEEN

THE SMALL GATHERING at the harbor quickly developed into a major protest, complete with banners and loudhailers. Representatives from the island's tiny media outlets were in attendance, and it was likely that the demonstration would find itself deserving of a slot on the evening TV news. Smith was enthused and passionate, arguing the fishermen's case with passers-by, shouting in response to the five Frenchmen who jeered as they walked along the promenade, delivering vigorous clap backs, and accompanied by appropriate hand gestures. He even gave an interview to that ubiquitous presence in times of trouble, Freddie Solomon.

But by three o'clock, the character of the noisy protest had changed. After arriving back onshore and collecting Des Smith's radar, Matt Crouch had headed straight back out to sea in search of Greg Somerville's boat. Now, six hours later, word was spreading that Crouch could not be reached. "We've tried his radio every five minutes for the last two hours," Drake explained when asked for news of the younger fisherman. "If his radio fails, he's got the satellite back-up, but he's not responding on that, either."

The crowd had began to worry, and by four o'clock, with a half-dozen pairs of binoculars scanning the horizon, and still no sign that Matt was heading back to harbor for the night, Smith put a call in to the Coastguard. When their muted response was unsatisfactory, Smith called the Constabulary. Minutes later, Graham and Barnwell showed up, anxious for news.

"It's Matt Crouch. He went looking for Greg Somerville's boat," Smith explained to them. He was a lot more comfortable talking to the familiar Barnwell than his rather aloof boss, but Graham listened well and asked searching questions.

"Why did he head out alone? How unusual is it for him to be this overdue?" Graham quickly learned that he knew even less about the affairs of the sea than he'd hoped.

"We're often alone," Drake told him. "If we're hauling fish, then there's maybe two or three of us, but Matt just went out for a quick look at a patch of water. No need for other hands. He might have stayed out for a bit, but it's his not returning our calls that's worrying us. First rule of the sea: keep in touch."

"I don't mean to place any blame, I'm simply trying to understand," the DI explained gently. "But what did he hope to find that a thorough Coastguard search had not? They've got all the fanciest electronics equipment."

This opened the floodgates for a veritable torrent of complaint about the Coastguard being under-funded, under-staffed, and unable to retain competent crew. "It's practically a charity. We have to help them out all the time, as do the RNLI," Smith explained. "It's not like the Royal Navy, or the US Coast Guard they have in America. They're part of the military over there. Armed and everything, they are." His point was a little disingenuous. Her Majesty's Coastguard was primarily a search and rescue service, not tasked with the responsibilities of other nation's Coastguard units, and local fishing boats, leisure craft, and lifeboats supplemented the service when time was of the essence, rescue at sea operations nearly always being a race against time. Even civilian spotter planes and French helicopters were called on to help if necessary. "And that new chap, the one in charge at St. Helier..." Des continued to rant.

Barnwell's initial findings, that Brian Ecclestone was prickly and awkward to deal with, had become a general consensus. "He's mean with his resources," Smith complained. "Refuses requests – left, right, and center – and hasn't the foggiest about what our fishing fleet has to deal with. He wouldn't even send the 'Guard out to look for Matt without your say so."

"So when did Matt Crouch leave the harbor?" Graham interjected quickly when Des paused to draw breath.

"It's a miracle we find any bloody fish at all with what we have to deal with," Smith continued, ignoring him. "Ten-ish I'd say," he ended, answering Graham's question so off-handedly that the DI nearly missed it.

Des' anger re-ignited the protest and there were long minutes of slogan-chanting and a chorus of honking motorists.

Graham pulled Smith away from the crowd. He wasn't certain that the old man wasn't discreetly hitting the bottle in between each heartfelt airing of grievances. "We've put a Search-And-Rescue request in," Graham said.

"Hmph, good luck. I bet he cites all kinds of reasons why Matt's fine. He knows that if he delays long enough, we'll go look for him ourselves."

With Des away from the group, Barnwell chatted to the other fishermen, all of whom repeated the same story of Matt's plans and his troubling failure to return to harbor. At his boss' shoulder, and as Des returned to his group, he whispered, "What do you think, sir? Should we be worried? Two men disappearing out at sea in strange circumstances within days of one another is a bit suspect."

"I think it's too soon to say, although I imagine Mrs. Taylor would have a different view on the matter."

"The men here certainly do, sir. They keep mentioning the French, the ones that hang around town?"

"I think, Constable, that those who come ashore are trouble-makers, baiting the locals, stirring things up, but I don't think there's anything more there. They're just a convenient bogeyman for Smith and his ilk. What else have you got?"

"Ecclestone's coming in for some real stick, sir, but he's got a SAR helicopter on the way."

"Excellent, lad," the DI told Barnwell. "Hopefully, we'll get Matt home before dark and this will all be forgotten." The weather forecast for the night was badly unsettled, with squally showers and high winds.

"I'll be heading out with them, sir," Barnwell added. "They like to have someone from the Constabulary join them if there's a sense of anything crime-related."

Graham looked puzzled. "But... they fly off the pad at St. Helier."

"They do, sir," Barnwell confirmed.

"And I can't help noticing that you're not *in* St. Helier, Constable." Graham turned away from the fishermen who continued to blow off steam at any passer-by with enough time to listen.

Barnwell's answer was to glance skyward from where a familiar clattering sound was growing louder. The helicopter, a big, broad, functional design with an immensely powerful main engine rotating its spinning blades, eased over the top of the castle and slowed to a noisy hover over the beach.

"Low tide, sir," Barnwell yelled over the din. "Not a bad spot to land. They said they couldn't resist dropping in and offering me a lift."

The chopper pilot lowered his machine down to the beach while Graham ushered the fishermen to a safer distance. None were unimpressed by the sight of this flying monster descending among them. Des Smith, frustrated at this momentary disturbance to their protests, was simultaneously relieved that the "big guns" were going out in search of Matt. He was uncharacteristically silent. The chopper's wheels touched down softly on the yielding sand, and Barnwell gave his boss a thumbs up before dashing, hand on his head, under the wash of the spinning rotor. A crewman opened the sliding door and ushered Barnwell in. Graham could see him getting strapped in even as the pilot urged the engines above idle. Moments later, the rotors caught the chilly evening air, and the helicopter rose steadily once more into a slate-gray sky.

To Graham, it was like watching a giant bathtub sprout wings, take off, and somehow head out to sea. *Not a bad way to get to work.* Part of him envied Barnwell, but there was much work to do here on shore. Amid the noisy wash of the helicopter's departure, the honking of supportive drivers, and the full-throated chanting of the angered fishermen, Graham entirely failed to notice three new texts from Laura.

CHAPTER NINETEEN

J ANICE KNOCKED ON the door of the neat, modern, terraced house and looked up and down the street. Either side of it was lined with rows of identical homes. A couple of young boys aged around seven were playing on their bikes while close by two young girls were kneeling on the path drawing pink and blue flowers with sticks of chalk. A couple of cones, one with a red flag poking out of it, had been put out to act as a warning to drivers who were apt to travel too fast down this straight, narrow road.

The door opened and Janice turned to face the heavily pregnant young woman who stood in front of her. "Mrs. Crouch? Cheryl? I'm here from the local constab—"

"Is there any word?" The woman's short, brown hair flopped over her eyes. She pushed it behind her ear. She looked at Janice, her pupils bright with fear.

"No, no word, Mrs. Crouch. May I come in?"

"Yes, of course. Please go through to the kitchen. We're in there," the woman said indicating toward a door at the end of the hall. She stood back and flattened herself against the wall, the narrow hallway made even more so by the advanced state of her pregnancy.

"Please, after you," Janice said.

Janice followed Cheryl Crouch into the small, boxy kitchen where, leaning back against the cabinets was a man cradling a mug of tea in his folded arms. He met Janice's eye reluctantly and rubbed his cheekbone. Janice noticed a bruise forming there. Cheryl Crouch came over to him and put her hand on his arm.

"This is Phil. He's a friend of Matt's. He's come over to sit with me until...until..." The woman's voice broke.

"Come on, Cheryl, love," the man said. He put an arm around her.

"Here," Janice pulled out a chair from the kitchen table and Cheryl Crouch allowed herself to be passed between the pair. She levered herself heavily down onto the seat, covered her cheeks with the palms of her hands and closed her eyes.

Janice sat down next to her. "I just wanted to ask you, Cheryl, about Matt's movements. When did you last see him?" Cheryl lowered her hands from her face, and they flittered to a pendant that lay around her neck. She slid it back and forth on its cord.

"He left early this morning, to go on Des Smith's boat. Phil went too."

Phil nodded. "That's right. We all went out for a bit of a chat."

Cheryl continued, "When he came back, he popped in to say he was going out to look for that scientist's boat. I wasn't too keen because it's still a bit rough after the storm, but he didn't pay any attention."

"And how did he seem?"

"Seem?" Cheryl looked up at Janice, frowning.

"Yes, in himself," Janice said, gently. She glanced up at Phil, then back at Cheryl.

"F-fine. Normal." Cheryl's voice got stronger. She sat up a

little straighter and stopped playing with the green pendant. "What do you think, Phil? Did he seem okay to you?"

Phil shrugged. "Seemed so, seemed perfectly normal. He wanted to go looking for the boat. He'd have made a bit of money if he'd have found it."

Janice knew that the boat would have been impounded as evidence the moment it turned up, but said nothing.

"So he came back in after your meeting on Des' boat, popped in here, then straight out again? And you haven't heard from him since?"

"That's right. It's been hours now. I sent him a text asking him to tell me when he was leaving the Harbor. I always like him to do that, but he didn't reply." Cheryl pulled her phone over to her from where it sat on the table, "That was at 10:09 this morning."

"That's 'bout right," Phil said. "We were back here at eight-thirty, nine. He would've popped back here, then gone to the boat, tidied her up a bit, and off he'd have gone."

"Hmm, okay." Janice wrote this all down on her iPad and logged off. "We've got the Coastguard helicopter out looking for him, Cheryl, and some of his mates have gone out in their boats too. We're doing everything we can to find him," she said. The temptation was to share some platitude, to promise Cheryl that her husband would come home very soon, safe and sound, but her words would be meaningless, and she knew that the woman in front of her knew they would be, too.

Instead, Janice patted Cheryl's hand and gave her a sympathetic smile. "We're doing our best for him, okay?" Cheryl, her face crumpling, looked down into her lap as she rubbed her swollen belly. Janice stood and pressed her hand to the pregnant woman's shoulder as she passed. "I'll see myself out," she said to Phil.

As Janice opened the front door to the fading light of the day, she heard Phil Whitmore come up behind her.

"She's very upset," he said.

"That's understandable, of course." Janice looked at the tall, handsome man who she estimated was a few years older than his friend. "Tell me, how long have you known Matt?"

"'Bout two years, I'd say," Whitmore said.

"And the three of you, have you always hung around together?"

Phil nodded. "Often there'd be four of us, but I'm not seeing anyone right now."

"And where were you this afternoon?"

"I were here, looking after Cheryl. As soon as I heard, I came over. Matt 'n me, we're good friends. Work mates, too."

"And what do you think has happened to him?"

"Same as everyone else, he's either out there minding his own business, or..." Phil examined a spot in the corner of the ceiling above where the cornices joined each other.

"Or...?"

He looked down. "He's gone over," he said quietly, ending on a whisper.

"And how would he do that, an experienced fisherman like him?"

"Could be a number of reasons. Boat could have got into trouble, he could have gone over the side to do a repair, he might have had a funny turn and fallen in. But it might be nothing. He could be out there now, just waiting to be rescued." Phil rocked back on his heels and forced a chuckle.

"Be a coincidence for his radio to go on the blink at the very same time, though wouldn't it?" asked Janice.

Phil pressed his lips together, "Yeah. Yeah, it would."

"Well, thank you, Mr. Whitmore. We'll be in touch. Look after Cheryl, here." Janice closed the door behind her and walked the few steps to the gate that bordered the front of the Crouch's property. The children had gone now. They were probably inside having their tea. As she got into the Gorey Constabulary patrol car, Janice glanced back at the house she'd just left. There was no movement that she could see, just a tortoiseshell cat sitting in the upper window, a net curtain draped across its back. Janice paused, meditating on the cat staring back at her. After a few seconds, she stirred and rapped the car roof with her knuckles a couple of times before getting in and driving off.

CHAPTER TWENTY

THE CREW TOOK some serious convincing, but Barnwell wasn't about to be denied this opportunity to experience something he'd often dreamed of. "I did all the dress-rehearsal stuff the other week in St. Helier," he reminded Brian Ecclestone. "I know what to do. And you'll all be there to yell at me if I get it wrong."

"Okay," Ecclestone finally said. "*If* we find Crouch's boat, we'll winch you down."

Only an officer as popular and as respected as Barnwell would have been given this permission. His successful at-sea rescue of two teenage boys had become the stuff of legend, and his recent exploits, tackling a gun-toting professional hit man and dragging pensioners away from rising floodwaters, had sealed his reputation.

"But the light is failing, and there's still nothing on the radar," Ecclestone added.

Satisfied, Barnwell sat alongside the three other crewmembers who were settled in the chopper's spacious mid-deck. The AW-149 was a big, comfortable helicopter that usually sported fifteen seats, but in this version, the mid-deck mostly provided storage space for stretchers and emergency gear. While they searched for the *Cheeky Monkey*, Barnwell received another briefing on the winch system that would lower him toward the sea, but as the wind picked up, blowing green froth formed from the crests of angry waves, small seeds of doubt started to plant themselves in the constable's mind. It was almost dark, the sea was looking treacherous, and there was still no sign of the—

"Radar contact, bearing one-zero-zero!" a crewman called out.

Barnwell was instantly alert, his concerns forgotten. "Is it the *Cheeky Monkey*?" he asked at once.

Ten seconds were needed to gain a visual on the boat amid failing light. "That's affirm," the voice came from the cockpit. All six crew punched the air, and Barnwell very quickly found himself being attached to the helicopter's powerful winch system.

Crouch's boat was modest, and its discovery among these squalls and increasingly tall waves was as unlikely as it was welcome. But the size of his target presented a huge problem to Barnwell. He would have to land feet-first on the small deck while manually allowing out more cable from the winch via a button on his harness. It was a difficult act of coordination that he'd tried on land in ideal conditions back at St. Helier. Barnwell now recalled with a shiver that he'd made a complete mess of the exercise, and his second time around was only slightly better.

"No movement on board," the pilot called back from the cockpit. Barnwell looked out of the window and down at the boat. He had hoped to see Crouch waving pathetically back at him.

Ecclestone looked through his binoculars, and confirmed the finding. "Still want to risk it, Constable?" he asked Barnwell, who was now strapped into his harness.

Barnwell took a deep breath. "Ready when you are, lads," the constable replied, sounding more confident than he felt as he double-checked the straps and connections as he'd been taught. Ecclestone nodded to the two-man crew whose task it was to oversee Barnwell's descent, and if necessary, haul him bodily back up to the safety of the helicopter if things went wrong. Neither man relished the idea of a struggling, inexperienced, still slightly overweight police officer, dangling from a swaying cable, fifty feet above a gnarly, wind-lashed sea, in the dark, but it was always a tough situation, no matter who was at the other end of the rope.

The chopper's big searchlight isolated the *Cheeky Monkey* and the AW-149's side door opened, allowing in a shocking gust of freezing air laced with icicles and sea spume. "Remember," a crewman was yelling to him, "keep your arms crossed, and when you hit, keep your feet together." Barnwell felt hands tugging hard at the harness, ensuring that it wouldn't give when subjected to his weight. "If we hit trouble, you'll hear 'Whiskey Oscar' in your headset."

"Wave off, right?"

"Right," the other crewman told him. "It'll mean we're about to haul you back up. Let go of anything, and just let the winch do its job, all right?"

Barnwell nodded, and without further conversation, found that he was perched on the edge of the chopper. A moment later, with a shot of adrenaline that numbed the thinking part of his brain, he pushed himself out of the door to let the winch take his weight as he crossed his arms across his chest. He looked up; the mechanism that was saving him from an unpleasant death was contained within a black box about the size of a big stereo. He could feel and see the cable extend as his descent toward the waves began.

"Lower away!" he heard, his adrenaline building, sending a thrill through his already jacked body. After that, the noise of the chopper's rotors and the raging sea completely took over. The light from the helicopter dazzled him briefly when he glanced down at the small boat, the beam reflecting off the deck. There were still no signs of any movement.

Above him, the pilot was working as hard as he ever had just to keep Barnwell safe. The wind caught the winch line and sent Barnwell into a slow swing like that of a pendulum beneath a clock. The winch system could do little to check the movement. Instead, the pilot mirrored Barnwell's swing, compensating carefully to produce a central point above the *Cheeky Monkey* around which both the chopper and its dangling passenger would move. The winch gave out more cable, foot after foot, and eventually the aircrew felt Barnwell take temporary control as he maneuvered himself down for a safe landing.

Barnwell considered the possibility of dropping into the sea and swimming to the boat, but one glance down at the furious, green waves told him to pay ferocious attention to landing on deck. He had completed no less than five swims of a thousand meters or more, but a calm, warm swimming pool in St. Helier was very different from the roiling, freezing English Channel in November.

The energy driving the swinging motion was now almost entirely spent, and Barnwell found himself staring down past his own feet and onto the deck of Crouch's boat. Feeling heavy and ungainly, he let out more line, which was now suspending him beneath the chopper like a builder's solid, straight plumb line on a construction site, and the roll of the sea brought the deck of the *Cheeky Monkey* up to meet him.

Clunk.

His feet touched down, and he instantly gave out five more feet of cable and grabbed for the metal rail on the ship's starboard side. Reflexively, he knelt and found himself taking deep breaths, relieved to have something solid under his feet. The boat pitched left, and he had to catch himself against the rail to avoid being thrown clear across the deck. Sea spray flecked his face and a wave broke noisily against the starboard side, soaking him instantly in a welter of freezing, green water.

Once some Olympic-level swearing was out of the way, Barnwell got down to business. *Right, lad. Let's get this done and get ourselves home, eh?*

"Matt Crouch!" he called out. "This is Constable Barnwell of Gorey Constabulary. Are you aboard, sir?" Feeling his way along the handrail, Barnwell was able to pull himself level with the pilothouse.

Bugger.

"It's empty," he called up to the chopper. He looked below deck, shining his flashlight wildly around the small space. "There's no one here." The crew was searching the area around the boat using lights mounted on the helicopter's doors, but they too were finding nothing.

"Not your fault, Constable," the airman told him over the radio.

"Yeah."

Inaudible to Barnwell, the crew was receiving a brief but unpleasant lecture from Ecclestone about the perils of staying too long in a dangerous place where they could do no good. "Let's get out of here. He isn't here, so we shouldn't be, either," their commander was telling them. "Money for these things doesn't grow on trees, you know."

"Whiskey Oscar," Barnwell heard through his earpiece. "Brace yourself." Barnwell crossed his arms once more and felt the cable's slack being taken up. As it went taut, there was a strong pull against his chest and torso, and he experienced the unlikely sensation of being physically hauled off the deck of the storm-tossed fishing vessel and back into the rain-lashed air.

"Bloody hell," he muttered. The deck of the *Cheeky Monkey* receded quickly beneath him, but Barnwell was too distracted by the fresh gusts of icy wind that stung his face to pay any more attention to the boat and its missing owner. Then, to Barnwell's distress, the swinging began again, worse than before. He felt like he had become a lightweight toy being passed between two invisible giants, one either side of the helicopter, their game becoming decidedly more violent as the wind picked up and assaulted Barnwell with its brutal, freezing force anew. "Can we hurry this up just a bit?" he asked over the radio. "It's getting a bit 'brass monkeys' out here."

"Roger that," the airman replied, and Barnwell felt a new urgency in his rise toward the oddly shadowy black shape above him. With clouded darkness beyond and the big searchlight finally out of his eyes, Barnwell saw the chopper as a hole in the sky surrounded by lights into which he was being drawn. Flashes of every alien abduction movie he'd ever seen came to mind. Finally, a stern-faced crewman came into view, and he felt strong hands guide him to the ledge by the door. The hands exerted pressure and Barnwell rolled his body inside so that the helicopter door could be closed.

"Well, that certainly cleared away the cobwebs," Barnwell joked.

Ecclestone failed to see the funny side. "I'm glad you enjoyed your little jaunt, Constable, but we did not find Mr. Crouch."

"What will happen now?" Barnwell asked. His hands were too frozen and shaky even to operate his cellphone and call the boss. He needed help disentangling himself from the harness, which in the final moments had begun to pull too tightly in *just* the wrong spot.

Ecclestone leaned back and put his hands behind his head. "I'll send out a launch to bring the boat in. On second thought, let's get one of his mates to bring it in. Weren't a few of them out here searching for him? He looked out of the window. "Maybe that one." He pointed to a blue fishing boat, tiny against the horizon, barely distinguishable against the grey of the sky. Call it up, and let them know," he said to the co-pilot.

"Roger, that," the crewman responded.

Ecclestone turned to Barnwell and said into his headset, "We've got two hours of flying time left. We'll search the water, but if we don't find him soon, it's probably too late."

"Here," a crewman said to Barnwell mildly, reaching over. "Drink this." A mug of steaming coffee arrived by some cherished miracle, and Barnwell spent the next bumpy minutes carefully sipping its life-giving warmth, Ecclestone's words resonating in his ears. *We did not find Mr. Crouch.*

"Commander, I'm not raising that boat. Want me to send out our lads?" The co-pilot was steadily flicking switches on his instrument panel but clearly wasn't having any luck completing Ecclestone's instruction.

"What do you mean, you can't raise them?"

"They're not responding sir."

Ecclestone let out a big sigh, "Oh, all right. But see if you can identify them. I'll have a word when we get back."

Two hours later, they still hadn't found Matt Crouch, and the helicopter and crew headed back to St. Helier. Barnwell radioed ahead and spoke to Graham, giving him the grim news.

"No luck, sir. No sign of him, just his empty boat."

There was a pause, and Barnwell imagined Graham suppressing an oath.

"What on earth has bloody well happened to him, Barnwell?"

"No idea, sir. He seems to have simply vanished. It was like the *Marie Celeste* down there."

CHAPTER TWENTY-ONE

THE NEXT DAY, Barnwell found himself strolling along the boards of the marina, water sloshing gently beneath him. Over his time patrolling the Gorey beat, he had become accustomed to the unstable sensation as he observed the boats and the people that lived and sailed on them. That hadn't been the case when he'd first arrived on Jersey from his native London's inner city beat. Back then, the only unsteadiness he'd known had been the result of a hard night's drinking. Those days were behind him now.

Up ahead, he saw his target. He watched the man kneeling on the wooden slats of the jetty, leaning over to scrub the hull of his boat. It was a small launch, not unlike the one Greg Somerville had gone out in, and by the way the man was punishing it, it was in need of some serious attention.

"Kevin Cummings?"

The man stopped his scrubbing and glanced back before resuming his back and forth, the muscles in his arm showing, the veins standing out.

Barnwell raised his voice, the tenor becoming harder, lower.

"Kevin Cummings." It wasn't a question this time.

Once more, the scrubbing stopped. "Yeah, who wants to know?"

Barnwell sighed. He was a familiar enough sight that he rarely had to produce his ID, but he slipped his fingers into his pocket and pulled his card out, holding it up so that Cummings could see it if he cared to. He didn't.

"I need to speak to you about Greg Somerville."

Cummings leaned back on his haunches, and with resignation threw down his cloth. It was a sheepskin, wet and matted on one side, rough and rubbery on the other. Cummings pushed on his knees to draw himself up to Barnwell's height and regarded him squarely. Drops of water glittered in his beard, while his eyes, beady and suspicious, squinted in the bright sunlight.

"What about him?" Cummings leaned against his boat, and folded his arms. The boat rocked as it bore his weight but he moved with it until it stilled.

"You were in the pub just before Greg Somerville went out on his boat. His body washed up a couple of days later."

"Yeah, I heard."

"I believe the two of you were acquainted. What kind of relationship did you have with Mr. Somerville?"

There was a pause. Cummings pursed his lips. "We were, what I suppose you would call..." He looked up and over Barnwell's shoulder before returning the constable's gaze, "compatriots."

"How so?" Barnwell asked.

"We both wanted the same thing...in effect."

"But?" Barnwell tried.

"But we differed in the way we went about things." Cummings, looked down at the ground, his arms still folded. He kicked a stone at his feet. It spun into the water.

Barnwell repressed a sigh at Cummings' lack of candor and wearily heaved out a question instead.

"Could you expand on that, sir?"

"I belong to SeaWatch, Officer. We're known as an animal rights group, but really, we're about the environment, the ecology of the sea. We believe in the conservation of sea life in all its forms, but we consider the best way to achieve that is by leaving things alone as much as possible. We intervene only when man corrupts the environment to the extent that the delicate ecosystem is or will be affected if current practices continue."

"So how does that put you at odds with Greg Somerville?"

Again, Cummings paused before he answered. "Greg was a scientist. He was collecting data to understand the migration of the Holden shark. Sounds commendable or at least not controversial until you understand that his constant monitoring was affecting their behavior. He was impeding the very migration patterns he was trying to protect. He was aiming to collect data that would be used to support the sharks in the future, and yet he was distorting how they function. Their displays have evolved over centuries and disrupting them would render his data useless. He was killing his golden goose. His project was a complete waste of time. Worse, it was harmful." More talkative now, Cummings ended his words with a sneer. He leaned his head back, and looked down his nose at Barnwell, waiting for his response.

"So why do you think he continued?"

Cummings lifted his head. "Who knows? Perhaps he didn't see the damage he was doing or recognize the impact it would have on the authenticity of his data. Or more likely, it was a cash cow to him. He didn't want his funding to stop. Research money is difficult to get hold of. Once he'd secured it, he was guaranteed work for years at a time, *and* he got to be a hero. Scientists have big egos, you know? Those egos can get in the way of what's right."

"So you knew him well?"

"We've come into contact over the years. Professionally."

"And what sort of professional activity do you undertake, Mr. Cummings."

"We watch the sea. SeaWatch, get it? As I said, we like to leave things as they are, for the most part."

"But you also said you intervene when necessary. What form might that intervention take, exactly?"

"We lobby local authorities and other governmental agencies over activities we perceive as harmful and which are within their jurisdiction. We sit on the boards of companies whose businesses impact or may impact the surrounding ecosystem. We seek to represent all sea- and ocean-based ecological interests and pledge to go anywhere we feel our voice is needed."

"Do you mount protests?"

"Sometimes."

"And do those protests ever turn violent?"

Cummings pushed himself off the side of the boat and took a step toward Barnwell, his arms by his side now. "Look, I'm not a fool. I can see where you're going with this. We are a peaceful group. I won't deny that tempers haven't frayed in the past, but that's par for the course when you have people as passionate *on both sides* as you have in this game."

"So what was your relationship with Greg Somerville like?"

Kev again looked over Barnwell's shoulder and stared into the distance. He squinted. "It was civil. A little wary, I guess. We were on different sides, remember, but it was cordial. Mostly."

"Nothing physical, then."

Cummings blew air out of his nose in a short, forceful exhale, his head jerking back, a wry smile playing across his lips.

"I wondered how long it was going to take for you to get there." He looked down the gangway briefly before turning back to face Barnwell. "I didn't kill him. That's what you're asking, right? I bumped into him and Tamsin the other morning at the Foc'sle. I was just in the pub for a lunchtime pint. I had no idea they were in there."

"But you knew they were on the island?"

"I had an idea. The Holden sharks are on the move, and Greg and Tamsin have traveled to Jersey for two or three years now to monitor them. It was a reasonable assumption to make."

"So what were your plans?"

"Just to watch, as I said. Their project is legal and above-board. We've been unable to persuade the authorities of our viewpoint, so I was here just as an observer."

"And what sort of intervention might you have taken if things hadn't gone the way you thought they should?"

Cummings sighed. "You really don't know how these things work do you?"

"Enlighten me, Mr. Cummings."

"I would have lobbied the powers that be. The local authorities, the Environmental Agency. I might have pressured a powerful local business or two to grease the wheels."

"Seems a rather...peaceful approach."

"That's how these things go. We're not all rabid saboteurs, you know, no matter how much the media might portray us as such. Our work can be frustratingly slow at times, but we draw the line at anything physical." Cummings eyes were still piercing and hard, but his voice was even, his body still leaning back languorously against the hull of his boat.

"Ms. Porter said that one of their boats was sabotaged the day before Mr. Somerville went missing. Would you know anything about that?"

Cummings laughed. "Have you listened to anything I've said? We don't go in for that kind of thing. Anyone could have switched out his fuel. The locals weren't too keen on his work. It could just have easily been one of them. But please, go and accuse the local animal activist, eh? We're convenient targets."

Who said anything about switching the fuel?

"So tell me about your interaction with Mr. Somerville in the pub."

364 ALISON GOLDEN & GRACE DAGNALL

"There's nothing to tell. Like I said, I went into the pub for a pint and Greg and Tamsin were there. They seemed to be in a bad mood. I would have been happy to chat, but he wanted none of it, I could tell by his face as soon as he noticed me."

"What did you say to one another?"

"I didn't say much at all. Greg immediately took offense to my presence and warned me off. I didn't want any trouble so I just moved on into the bar. Didn't speak to him again."

"Did you see him leave the pub?"

"No. I ate my lunch at the bar, then went for a walk around town. He'd left by that point. They both had."

"Can anyone vouch for you during the period after you left the bar?"

"People might have seen me wandering around although I don't stick out much. Went to buy a paper and some food at the mini-mart on the front. Someone there might remember me. And I definitely didn't take my boat out that afternoon. You can ask the Harbormaster, if you don't believe me. I didn't see or hear of Greg Somerville again until I heard his body washed up on the beach. I'm sorry about that, but I had nothing to do with it. Now, if you don't mind, I have work to do on my boat."

"Going somewhere?" Barnwell persisted.

"Now that the research has ended, at least until they find someone else to carry on Greg's work, I'm heading back to the mainland."

"Wouldn't now be a good time to increase the pressure on getting the project stopped? Seems like you should be talking to a load of people to get your point across."

Cummings shrugged. "I think that would look a bit insensitive, don't you? Oh, that scientist guy died, let's stomp all over his research and wreck his life's work. Yeah, that wouldn't do our cause any good at all. Chances are, the project will die right along with him. Unless Tamsin takes it over." Cummings bent over and picked up the cloth he had been using earlier. He jumped onto the boat and went inside the pilothouse, effectively dismissing Barnwell. The constable stared at him through the window as Cummings appeared to check his instruments, apparently oblivious to his audience. The constable watched for a moment before looking up and down the floating boards between the boats and, turning on his heel, he made to walk back onto solid ground.

CHAPTER TWENTY-TWO

I T WAS A chilly morning, but without too much wind. Jean-Luc found himself with time for reflection as their lumbering boat slowly dragged the magnetometer back and forth along their predetermined search lanes. The device had a distinctive "ping" which alerted him to any unusual metallic reading that emanated from the cold deep beneath them. There had been two false alarms, perhaps wreckage of ships or aircraft that were destroyed during Hitler's bid to control the English Channel in 1940, but nothing that resembled their target.

The dull "thunk" of the cold water against the bow of the *Nautilus* was rhythmic but disconcerting, a constant reminder of how poorly their home-away-from-home was faring in these unpredictable waters. Years of neglect and hasty hull patches had given her unlovely, bulbous lines, and she traveled among the waves as though fighting them. It was one of several frustrations that were threatening to boil to the surface among the three men onboard.

"Why not just say, 'left' or 'right?'" Hugo had complained the day before. "It's as much like driving a car as—"

The Parisian was brusquely cut off by a very different accent, the provincial, nasal tones of a working class man from Cherbourg. "We use 'port' and 'starboard' for turns," Jean-Luc had told him, his patience almost exhausted, "and we use 'green' and 'red' for sightings either side of the bow. So, if I'm turning right to follow a sighting exactly half way off the bow, what would I say?" Jean-Luc pressed as if he were a teacher testing a slow student.

Hugo blinked and looked up, calculating his answer before muttering, "Turn to starboard, sighting at red forty-five," he said quietly.

"Exactly. Works the same under water too. *If* we ever get down there." Jean-Luc cast a baleful glance at the two elaborate scuba diving rigs they'd brought along. Specialist dry suits, which kept a warm layer of air between the diver and the freezing water were hanging up. "Any other questions?" Jean-Luc asked. *You egg-headed dummy,* he didn't add.

It was Hugo's accent, his glasses, his style, his painfully obvious lack of knowledge of the sea that caused this schism. Compared to the two veterans, Hugo was young, incompetent, and slow. He knew all this and hated being judged, but reminded himself that the other two men's experience was essential. This was a treasure hunt, not a stag do.

"I think I've got it," Hugo said genially from the pilothouse, unwilling to test Jean-Luc's patience further. They'd tried him in different roles, but ultimately banned him from surveying the equipment. Steering the boat seemed the best role for him. He was kept occupied, and it prevented him from peering over the older men's shoulders. If they struck gold with their searches, he'd hear about it immediately.

There were long, long stretches of silence on board, with the chugging motor the only soundtrack to this lengthy and frustrating exercise. "Just rumors," his father had insisted of Hugo's idea. "Nothing there but expense and failure," he'd warned. But Hugo wasn't to be put off. He knew a large portion of everything he heard was made up on the spot, of course – mariners love to tell a good story – and much of the rest was hearsay or guesswork, but there was a thread connecting everything he'd heard. Enough people believed the stories that expeditions were planned but later abandoned as enthusiasm and funding to launch them waned. Hugo wasn't letting that happen in his case, nor was he willing for some other team to take all the glory.

He'd traveled to museums to carry out research, sought out translations of books from the time, and studied charts of old wrecks, some discovered only recently. Then, having recruited Victor and Jean-Luc, the three of them had ascertained their search area, and the best timing for their expedition.

Now it was crunch time. There was a narrow window before the winter weather would begin in earnest, and they didn't have much time left. The two older, more experienced men were getting harder to read and ever more grouchy. Neither was interested in getting along beyond the basics, this was purely a mercenary transaction for them.

"Southern leg," he called back, turning to port. The towed magnetometer followed in a broad sweep. He willed for that telltale "ping" to come and tell him that he hadn't spent thousands on this hare-brained venture for nothing. He wanted to be *the one* who found it. He wanted the glory, and most definitely the riches; the fabulous, life-changing, never-have-to-work-again riches. There would be TV interviews and magazine articles, maybe even a visit to the Élysée Palace.

Focus, he told himself. This was no time to falter. They were bounty hunters. The prize *would* be theirs.

Barnwell pushed his bike through the doors of the police station and leaned it up against the wall. He took off his helmet and wiped beads of sweat from his forehead. Even in the cool of

November after a storm, he could still build up a sweat as he rode around Gorey.

"How'd your little chat with that activist chappie go, Bazza?" Roach asked him.

"Eh, denies seeing Somerville after he left the pub. Says he ate lunch there and wandered around town. Didn't go anywhere near the harbor, he says."

"Do you think he's telling the truth?"

"Seems like he is. His story checks out. Chrissie at the mini-mart remembers him, and the Harbormaster has a record of his boat coming in and not going out again. It's just...Oh, I don't know. He seemed a little too wound up to be willing to toe the softly-softly line he maintains his activist group follows. And he knew about the fuel being switched in Somerville's boat. I'm not sure what to make of him."

There was a big sigh behind him, and he turned.

"Everything all right, Janice?" Barnwell asked.

She was slumped over her computer screen, chin propped in her palm, her lips pursed.

"DI wants me to look at local 'happenings' that occurred after the storm in nineteen eighty-seven, things that seemed odd at first, but which after a time, turned out to have a perfectly reasonable explanation. He wants to pacify Mrs. T.'s overactive imagination. Thing is, I'm not sure anything will settle her down. I think we're trying to fight insanity with logic. She'll think what she wants to think and nothing we're going to say is going to persuade her otherwise."

Barnwell went to check the Constabulary email. "Speak of the devil," he said to the others through gritted teeth. "Eyes left, everyone." He rolled his mouse around, and as the front doors swung open, he looked up and said brightly, "Hello, Mrs. Taylor. What can Gorey Constabulary do you for this fine morning?"

"I told Detective Inspector Graham there would be strange events occurring. The dead scientist, and the missing Matt, and now this." She tapped the large envelope she clasped under her arm. Hearing his name, Graham came out of his office, and she leaned in closer over the reception desk, looking around her in order to check that no one was eavesdropping even though there was nobody present except the police officers. "It's happened again," she confided, her voice low. "Last night."

Graham wondered for a second whether anyone on Jersey had a plate quite as full as his. "What happened, Mrs. Taylor?" he asked, half-ready to tune out her response and think about more important matters.

"I've had another...*visitation*," she said. "I know you'll say I'm cracked, that I've finally gone loopy, but I *know* what I *saw*."

Graham sighed. Barnwell sensed his boss' exasperation and took over, bringing out his iPad. "What exactly did you see, ma'am?"

Mrs. Taylor then described the apparition she'd encountered. By turns, the visitor was "ghostly," "elusive," and "intelligent." It refused to be caught by flashlights. Night after night, according to Mrs. Taylor, it was appearing in the kitchen and causing "a god-awful rumpus." She even had a picture of the being.

A few seconds later, five photographs lay side by side on the reception desk. Barnwell had even rustled up the station's old-fashioned magnifying glass. He handed it to Roach and invited him to apply his forensic mind to this latest mystery.

"Take a load of this, I can't make head nor tail of it."

"It's the camera's flash," Roach said. "It reflects off the pans, the perfectly clean floors, the polished windows." He straightened up and set down the glass. "Just combinations of reflections, that's all."

Barnwell looked again. Mrs. Taylor's normally orderly kitchen was a sea of confusion. Bags of produce had been opened and scattered, and a selection of saucepans and baking sheets were strewn around as if by a malignant kitchen elf. "But what the heck has happened here?" he asked.

Mrs. Taylor had arrived at the station with "proof" of her assertions that she held to be incontrovertible. "It's a poltergeist," she announced, confidently. "An evil spirit, released by the storm."

Graham remained aloof from the group. He kept his own view to himself for the moment; that the pictures showed plenty of inexplicable mess, but nothing else. In the name of community relations, he allowed Barnwell, Harding, and Roach the opportunity to try their hand at solving this particular problem, although he wasn't disposed to let them become too involved. He detected a whopping whiff of the absurd in Mrs. Taylor's own findings.

"Are you sure this mess in your undoubtedly fine kitchen wasn't caused by a hungry guest looking for a snack in the small hours, or a sleepwalking child perhaps? A disgruntled kitchen worker causing chaos on purpose? Really, Mrs. Taylor, an unexplained mystical being seems unlikely," he said, gently.

"I've closed the hotel," Marjorie Taylor told them regretfully. "I can't be sure that my guests are safe until this *visitor* has been chased away or caught."

Roach tried, but ultimately could not resist. "It's tricky, Mrs. T. I mean, what kind of organization deals in this kind of thing?" He stifled a giggle and managed to say, "Who we gonna call?"

Mrs. Taylor rose to her full height and addressed the young sergeant as if admonishing a guest for causing damage to their room. "If there are more *Ghostbusters* jokes on the horizon, young man, I advise you to leave them there. I've heard them all."

Roach reddened and apologized. "Sorry, Mrs. T. It's just so —" he caught sight of the stern look on Mrs. Taylor's face and stopped. Graham took over, guiding the guesthouse owner toward the station's double doors. "I'm going to show these pictures to someone I know in London."

"Oh?" Mrs. Taylor replied, instantly animated at this suggestion of being taken seriously.

"He's something of an expert in... well, *these things*. Give me some time, and I'll see what he comes up with."

"Well, please ask him to hurry. I can't stay closed for long, Detective Inspector. It's my livelihood," Grateful and mollified, at least for the moment, Mrs. Taylor reached the door, buttoned up her winter jacket and checked her slender, antique watch. "Oh, good. I'm just in time for my meeting with that nice journalist, Freddie. He wants to hear all about my *visitations*. Goodbye, David." Graham was so tempted to dash after her and prevent her meeting with Freddie Solomon that he actually took three paces forward. He could already imagine Mrs. Taylor's angry rebuttal. *"I'll speak with whomsoever I choose, young man!"* Any pleading on his part would be fruitless.

He groaned briefly and headed back to his office. "Anyone want my job?" he called over his shoulder before closing the door.

But Janice Harding understood Marjorie Taylor's confusion and distress. Closing down the White House Inn even for a few nights was a measure of her anxiety. Quietly, as the others busied themselves with their pending cases, Janice began to form a plan. She would get to the bottom of the "problem of Mrs. T" and put her out of her misery.

CHAPTER TWENTY-THREE

B Y LUNCHTIME, THERE were around ten people in the library, browsing the stacks or reading in the comfortable chairs around the edges of the room. The midday sun shone through the skylight and found its way into almost every corner of the cavernous space. Laura stopped for a second to appreciate the warm glow emanating from the light reflecting off the wood in the room and wished she could take a picture.

"Goodbye, Mrs. Taylor," Laura said as the older woman passed by the library's distribution desk.

Freddie Solomon had been speaking quietly with Marjorie Taylor at the back of the library, but he had now taken over a good portion of one of the large tables, as had become his custom. It was mostly newspapers today, a selection from just after the Great War, all of them covering wrecks or other mysterious incidents at sea. Laura watched him reading with an avid hunger, all the while taking notes in a thick, black, leather-bound volume. She glanced down as she passed behind him, ferrying some returned books to their rightful places, his handwriting giving the impression that a hummingbird had dipped its wings in ink and then breezily flittered across the page.

On the way back from her re-shelving expedition to the science section, she glanced down again as she passed Freddie's table. "Bermondsey Lighthouse," she said curiously. "I've heard of that place. Out on the islets to the east, isn't it?"

Solomon looked up with a smile and nodded. "Been there for a couple of centuries. But it didn't stop ships from getting into serious trouble." He turned the page of a browned, ninety-year-old newspaper toward her. "Look at this one. The *Genoa Star* was a stout, veteran freighter with a crew of just nine, on perhaps her thousandth voyage from the Swedish ore fields to Gibraltar, and then onto Italy. A storm sprang up in the Channel. Her crew became mystified and then disorientated by the apparently conflicting lights ahead. Before they realized their mistake, the keel of the huge ship hammered into submerged rocks, throwing one person overboard and injuring many."

"Seems straightforward to me," Laura observed, leaning over the old newspaper. "They got themselves off course in bad weather and ran aground."

Freddie raised a finger and gave Laura his I-know-something-you-don't grin. "There was a power cut that night on the island," Freddie told her. "There can't have been lights on the mainland, save for the Bermondsey Lighthouse."

Laura shrugged. "So? The lighthouse beacon should have told them where to steer."

Freddie was practically fizzing with the excitement of it now. "But according to sworn statements by *all nine* of the boat's crew," he explained animatedly, "the lighthouse beacon was in the *wrong place!*" His enthusiasm remained undimmed by Laura's skeptical frown.

"They reported," he said, flipping back through pages of notes, "that the Bermondsey beacon was to their port side."

"That's the left, right?" Laura said.

"Right. The left," Freddie said, grinning again. "But they passed by Jersey to the east, of course, so the light should have been on their starboard side, the *right*."

Laura made to move on but couldn't resist a little parting shot. "I wonder," she asked, waving to an elderly couple as they entered the library, "if they were still dishing out lots of free booze aboard working ships in those days?"

Freddie threw up his hands, but he was smiling. The more scientific, clinical part of him knew that the evidence for the mysterious sea events that he was researching was a little thin on the ground. Heck, some of it was downright *hearsay*. And Laura was right, of course. It wasn't unlike mariners to spin a good yarn and further embellish it with rakish abandon until their world was decorated with fantasies of seductive mermaids and fanciful sea creatures and made more dangerous by spurious mumbo-jumbo about immortality and the Elixir of Life.

But something kept Freddie going. Perhaps, among this collection of half-truths and deliberate falsehoods, there might be something genuinely interesting. Those were the tidbits he craved; the curious, never-before-considered "what ifs" that were so tantalizing. And even if the rumors weren't entirely *true*, a gaudy historical mystery would still make for a simply *splendid* article.

At that moment, his phone buzzed. He looked at it and immediately picked up his satchel. He hurried toward the main entrance, leaving books strewn across the tabletop, waving at Laura as he passed her.

"*Enfin, mes amis!*"

The green, circular screen of their magnetometer showed exactly the strange, blotchy shape they'd hoped to see when they first set out on this dangerous and stormy quest.

"It could be a massive school of fish," Jean-Luc warned, his eyes glued to the screen. "But I'd bet my house that it isn't. It's at about a hundred and sixty meters." He scanned the screen again. "It's not a definite shape. More like an irregular blur."

Victor wondered aloud, "Underwater explosion?"

"It's possible," Jean-Luc replied, nodding. "Maybe a U-boat that fell foul of the RAF or the British navy."

"A big metallic lump like that would have been found already by now, wouldn't it?" Hugo argued, trying to keep up with the two men's discussion. "There would be records."

But Victor was alert to the impact of the hurricane. He shook his head and flicked his hand in Hugo's direction. "Shush! If the currents were disturbed, even that far down, they might have shifted something. We won't know until we get down there," he said, snorting.

The boat became a busy, noisy place for the fifty minutes it required to set up a major technical scuba dive. "This isn't like what the tourists do," Jean-Luc said when Hugo asked him what was taking him so long. As the lead diver, he began pulling on a two-layer dry suit. Expensive but indispensable, the suit kept a cushion of air between the freezing water of the Channel and the thin, inner layer which hugged his body. Even so, Jean-Luc knew that he was preparing for a very uncomfortable trip down into the deep.

Victor assisted Jean-Luc in donning the cumbersome dry suit and attaching the inflation hoses while Hugo checked the voice and video feeds that led from Jean-Luc's helmet directly to the apparatus on the boat's deck. Once the suit was on, Victor helped Jean-Luc into the harness that contained two specially marked tanks of modified air. These would keep him alive at depth, while two more tanks, slung under his arms and clipped to the suit, would provide additional oxygen for the most difficult part of the trip. "Computer's ready," Jean-Luc reported. Resembling a large wristwatch, his dive computer would feed him data on depth, pressure, and remaining allowed time. Failing to heed its warnings was the short path to serious trouble. At these depths, he'd have a very limited amount of time to look around – perhaps only ten minutes – but the entire dive would take nearly four hours. "And I'm ready for the helmet," he added.

Victor slid the heavy helmet over his fellow explorer's head and locked it into place. Jean-Luc's view of the world was now through dense glass, but it was the only way to survive in such extreme conditions. A large flashlight hung from his suit, along with a range of safety equipment and a small, yellow spare oxygen tank. Weights that would act as ballast were strapped around his waist. There was even a knife designed for underwater work. Jean-Luc knew that it was the season for Holden sharks to migrate, and though they were mostly docile, he didn't relish the possibility of an encounter with such a massive beast.

Once everything was double-checked, Jean-Luc waddled heavily to the port rail of the ship.

"I really, *really* wish we didn't have to do it like this," Hugo complained. They were on an old fishing boat, not a specially rigged dive vessel. Jean-Luc would simply have to jump over the side and into the Channel. "All set?"

"Wish me *bonne chance!*" Jean-Luc said, and with a tap of all his equipment, a superstitious ritual he went through prior to every dive, he slung a leg over the rail and tipped himself gracelessly into the cold water with an impressive splash.

Below the surface, once the confusion of his entry cleared, all was quiet and calm. He tested his breathing apparatus. At Jean-Luc's insistence, Hugo had splurged on the latest design, a rebreather that funneled spent air into a filter and then to his helmet. It would extend his dive time and eliminate exhalant bubbles. It was working fine. He checked that the line connecting his suit to the boat was secure and then steadily decompressed, allowing a stream of air out from his suit so that he would lose buoyancy and steadily sink into the murk.

380 ALISON GOLDEN & GRACE DAGNALL

Jean-Luc kept both eyes glued to his dive computer. He could descend at any speed he wanted, but once the sunlight that filtered through the upper reaches of the water penetrated no further, the visibility would plummet. There would be no way to see the bottom or his precious target, and he would rely solely on the readings from his dive computer. He flicked on the powerful flashlight. Immediately, it illuminated a tiny shrimp that fled from him; it was the only movement in this still, outlandish place.

Thirty meters. Most recreational divers would go no further, but Jean-Luc dropped past this point, sliding down into the abyss until he passed fifty meters, then sixty. The darkness became complete, save for the cone of rough visibility provided by his flashlight. The water became clogged with silt and mud, a dense soup that yielded nothing. Once his computer read a hundred meters, he called up to the surface.

"Proceeding normally. One hundred. Viz is bad, no surprise there."

"Roger," Victor replied quietly, Hugo listening over his shoulder. Their interactions would be minimal, at Jean-Luc's request. He was a solo explorer now, navigating through a strange and pitiless place. He wanted to focus. A fish approached him, small and silver but retreated in a lightning blur as though the human form were a predator.

"One thirty. No sign of the bottom yet." He continued to descend through the murky gloom.

The stress began at around a hundred and forty meters. The pressure of the water on Jean-Luc's body brought along with it a companion pressure, defensive psychology cleverly designed by eons of evolution to divert him from his purpose. He recognized the feeling, a slight tightness in his chest, the urge to breathe deeper, even to gasp for air. There was a tiny voice, nagging at him: *You shouldn't be here. You're trespassing.* Then it started to undermine him. *Tons of crushing water exists above you. How long will it take to even reach the sweet, fresh air at the surface? How easy would it be to never experience that again?*

But Jean-Luc was a veteran of these depths and mastered his emotions after a few moments. With his breathing under control once more, he felt a new surge of confidence, reminding himself that he was permitted only a brief visit to this underwater world and should make the most of it.

"One hundred fifty," he said into his helmet. "Cold, but doing okay."

Jean-Luc had passed into water that was only a few degrees above freezing. Without his dry suit, he would have succumbed in moments.

His flashlight caught something, and Jean-Luc immediately added air to his suit to kill his downward momentum. Hovering at a hundred and fifty-five meters, he turned slowly in a circle to locate the object that he instinctively knew didn't belong in this eerie other-world. He unhooked his flashlight and began a search pattern. He needed to find it quickly. His dive computer was adamant. He had only twelve minutes left before he would have to head back up again. Ignoring the computer would mean risking a dangerous buildup of compressed nitrogen in his blood. If it later formed bubbles as he ascended, they would expand and cause several days of the most excruciating joint pain.

There you are. He began to make out pieces of debris, odd-shaped and strewn haphazardly along the seabed. "Okay," he told his two colleagues, waiting patiently above him, "I've got wooden pieces of some kind." He knew this would excite his fellow treasure seekers: U-boats weren't made of wood. This, apparently, was something else.

He surveyed the debris field, trying to ascertain where the pieces were more numerous. "More debris to the north," he said. "Larger pieces... And... Wait..."

He swam for the first time now, his long fins taking him steadily northward as he shone the light down onto the seabed, perhaps four meters below him. "More large pieces," he said. Then his colleagues heard Jean-Luc give an unexpected gasp of the most complete surprise.

The experienced diver continued his slow journey over the debris field. His own eyes were now struggling to make out in detail the source of his surprise. It was something that had no earthly business among the sinuous, worn curves of underwater topography: *a straight line.*

His dive computer told him that he had only six minutes before he needed to start his ascent to the surface. Kicking harder, he propelled himself forward until he found the incongruous piece that was bothering his subconscious, a long timber that lay at odds with the other pieces. Then, there was another, by itself to the right, and another to the left.

"Five minutes remaining. I've got wooden debris and timbers," he reported. Thirty seconds later, he was hovering over a large collection of beams, radiating out from a central point. He allowed a tiny sip of air from his suit and descended until he was within a meter or so of it.

"I confirm that I have a shipwreck," he said. "A large, wooden sailing ship. That's my first estimate." He could imagine his colleagues' unadulterated jubilation up above, but they'd achieve nothing if he didn't complete the dive safely and return to tell the tale. "Three minutes only. I'm going to see if I can find the cargo hold."

It didn't take long. The reason for this mighty ship's final journey was laid bare, there amid the wreckage. And as Jean-Luc shone his flashlight into the wrecked, decayed hold of the ship, finding its timbers split and askew but the cargo still within them intact, he hovered, suspended in the dark depths, cocooned in his glassy, insulated world. And then he let out a big whoop of joy.

CHAPTER TWENTY-FOUR

ETECTIVE INSPECTOR GRAHAM allowed himself to worry for just a few moments on whether he was facing the first genuine public order crisis of his career.

Gorey's marina was the scene of an ever-increasing large and noisy protest. It seemed to Graham as though everyone who'd ever called themselves a fisherman was showing up. There were boats from all over the Channel Islands, from the larger Jersey and Guernsey, as well as the smaller Alderney and tiny Sark. Dozens of mainland-based boats were also arriving, showing their solidarity with their fellow fishermen on the island. Their boats crammed the harbor until it looked like the set of a Hollywood movie about the Little Ships of Dunkirk. Neither Graham nor Barnwell would have ever believed such a sight was possible.

As Barnwell drove them over the rise and into town, they began to see the extent of the gathering. "Bloody hell fire," Barnwell exclaimed. He turned to his boss who looked less taken aback than simply exhausted by the thought of the fracas to come. "Are we being invaded by the Germans again, sir?"

Graham took a deep breath and straightened his tie. "Worse, I'm afraid, Constable. By Des Smith and his pals." Graham reached for his phone.

"Stone the crows. Will the Navy be able to cope, or do you think we'll need a special meeting of the UN Security Council?" Barnwell said as he gave a quick blast of the police siren prompting the dawdling pedestrians that were obstructing their path to jump out of the way.

Roach answered Graham's call.

"Close the station if you have to, lad, but I need all of us down at the marina." Graham thought for a second. "You'll have to drive by the Kerry Center and pick up Janice. And Sergeant?"

"Sir?"

"Try to keep a straight face."

"How do you mean, sir?" Roach asked.

"Because," Graham spelled out, "you're going to be hauling Sergeant Harding out of her hatha yoga class."

"Crikey." Roach imagined the scene.

"Just give her a few moments to finish chanting or whatever one does at those things, and get her straight in the car, okay?"

"Righto, sir," Roach said.

Barnwell found a parking place by the baker's. "Shall I call the armed response unit, sir? Helicopters?"

Graham wasn't in the mood. "I hope you're taking this seriously, Barry. There are people in newspaper offices and parliamentary meeting rooms who are going to be discussing in detail what happens here today."

"Sir?" Barnwell asked as they headed through a curious and growing crowd toward the marina itself.

"Anglo-French relations hinge on the amicable resolution of disputes like this one," he explained, leaning into Barnwell so that he could keep his voice low. "Quotas and fishing areas are hot-button issues. Mix them up with a lot of anger and more than a few spoonfuls of grief, and we've got a powder keg ready to blow.

We need to keep a lid on this. And *definitely* avoid any kind of violence." He turned to the constable just as Barnwell raised his voice to the very edge of courtesy in a bid to hurry people along. "So, no antagonism, all right?" he said, sheltering his ears from Barnwell's commands.

"Right, sir," Barnwell replied at a less ear-threatening volume. "I'd feel better if we had some backup, though," he added. "In case things get nasty."

Graham feigned confidence. "These fellas? They're angry, but they're not criminals. Isn't that what you told me earlier? Like family you said."

"I said a 'warring family.' And I think it all very much depends," Barnwell told him, "on how far down the bottle Des Smith has proceeded."

It wasn't a pleasant prospect. Barnwell could still recall the colorful verbal assault Des had inflicted upon him and Roach when they'd locked him up three years ago. "Let's just see what's going on," Graham said, puffing now. "And try to prevent Des Smith and his friends from re-starting the Hundred Years War."

Down at the marina itself, the air was thick with klaxons, shouts, chants, and howls of protest. Perhaps a hundred and fifty fishermen were there, supported by at least as many friends and family. Curious onlookers doubled that number. It was nearing low tide, and the beach that spread off to the right of the marina was crowded as though it were the height of summer. But these visitors were not there to catch some rays, they were there to make a point. They were standing, holding signs, sitting in circles, and milling about as though waiting between acts at a music festival.

"Hands Off Our Fish!" was the second most common sign, behind, "Justice for Matt" and similar pleas. The crowd seemed to comprise three different groups, each led by a speaker who was either whipping them up with call-and-response routines or lecturing them about the situation. From what Graham could hear, only some of this information was valid. Mostly, he heard ill-advised accusations and an upwelling of stormy anger that worried him as much as any hurricane.

"Sir, look," Barnwell said, tugging his boss' arm. Behind them, a TV crew had somehow found a place to park their big blue and white van and was setting up for what appeared to be a live broadcast.

"Oh, cripes," Graham observed. "Things are going to get dangerously busy here, once the word reaches around the whole island."

"The whole *country*," Barnwell warned. "We're going to be on the *Six O'clock News*, boss." He pulled out his phone and ran his finger from the bottom to the top of the screen. "And look, Mr. Solomon has been busy."

The blogger had somehow cobbled together a short piece entitled, "The Gorey Marina Revolution," which encouraged everyone to join the protest and make their voices heard.

Graham said nothing. He continued through the crowd but then stopped and spent a long moment just looking around, taking in the scene. In addition to the fishermen, there were fathers with children on their shoulders, small groups of teenagers with their bicycles, elderly couples curious to see what was going on, and a general surge of people toward the beach and the marina. He guessed that the crowd would reach eight hundred, maybe a thousand in the next half-hour, and with such numbers in close proximity, even if the tide was low, they were facing a serious safety problem. And that was quite aside from the public order issue that Graham feared might suddenly flare.

"We've got to get in there and talk to Smith," he said, pulling Barnwell with him through the crowd. "He's at the center of all this, and he can defuse it."

But reaching Des Smith required a Herculean effort. Members of the press, both professional and amateur photographers, and of course, Freddie Solomon, whom Graham had silently come to refer to as "that odious runt," were crowding around the old fisherman and his cohort, all willingly receiving the Smith's view of the situation. "It's piracy, I'm telling you!" the old man was roaring. "Piracy on the high seas. Unfair restrictions and fish fiddling, ladies and gents, you mark my words!"

Graham swore under his breath but then saw what needed to be done. "Right." He muttered his instructions to Barnwell as they cleared the crowd immediately in front of them and strode more easily toward Smith's group.

"Afternoon, Des," Graham said quietly in his ear. "Might I have a word?" Smith was a practical man, and bore the Detective Inspector no ill will. "Hang on a minute," he said ungraciously to the crowd of protesters, press, and onlookers. He turned his back on them to speak with Graham. He glanced up at the towering Barnwell. "All right, Barry." Then, to the DI, "I see you've brought muscles with you, in case there's trouble."

Graham gave him an affable smile. "Oh, I'm not too worried about that. Bit of a crush on the beach, though, wouldn't you say, Des?"

"Aye," the old man replied.

"Lots of kids here today, too," Barnwell added. "Last thing we'd want is for anyone to get separated, or..."

"You want us to pack up and go home?"

I wouldn't say no. "I'm here to broker an agreement," Graham announced. "I need you to get your men to disperse, Des. This is a public order problem. It's dangerous."

"Oh yeah? Well, we need to be heard."

"Look, why don't I get you some airtime with the TV crew? That way, you can speak in an orderly, coherent manner. You'll get your message across much more effectively that way and to a wider audience too. You'll be on the *Six O'Clock News*, a national platform. And I'll see if I can get the mayor down here."

Smith weighed this up and then turned to his cohort. A few moments' mumbling and one or two objections later, Smith turned back and gave Graham a nod. "All right. You've got a deal. But I want a word in private with you, Mr. Graham. There's something you need to know."

They spoke on board Smith's boat, alone and out of earshot. When Graham returned, he promptly rallied Barnwell, and they headed back up the hill to the car. As they trudged up the slope, they passed a journalist they both recognized from one of the national news shows going in the opposite direction. He was accompanied by a cameraman.

"How did you do it, sir?"

"Oh, I just gave them a call. The media are always desperate for stories to fill up their slots. The public at large think it's a big deal to be on the telly, but it's nothing special, not really. I was on it plenty of times in my old job. The mayor's on his way, too."

Fifteen minutes later, Graham and Barnwell were finally back in the car, taking the gently meandering country road out of town and toward the Constabulary. Smith, for his part, had asked his men to quietly advise the onlookers that the show was over for today, and within ninety minutes, Roach and Harding would report that the marina and beach had returned to some semblance of their usual calm and purpose.

But Barnwell could see that Graham was perplexed. On the drive back, he seemed to be muttering to himself while working something out in his head. "This just got a lot trickier," he said.

"How's that, sir?" Barnwell asked.

"It's these two cases. I just...Well, I just don't know." He lapsed back into a thoughtful silence.

"So, sir, what did he tell you? Des Smith."

"I listened to his daft theories about the French and reassured him we were doing everything we could. He did extract a promise from me to go out searching for Matt Crouch's body again, though. I guess that can't hurt, although I'm anticipating an almighty battle with Ecclestone. But now I have another thing on my mind. Smith told me that if we prove French involvement in either case, he's going to rally the fishing boats and blockade a major French harbor."

"Crikey," Barnwell breathed. "We can't have that kind of thing."

"No, we can't," Graham said. He quite literally shuddered to think of the implications.

As Barnwell drove, Graham made the tricky call to Brian Ecclestone. Despite the Jersey Coastguard's recent liaisons with the Gorey Constabulary, this was the first time the two men had spoken.

"Not a chance," was the commander's first response to Graham's request that he again search the area where Matt's boat was found, but as the Detective Inspector's temper audibly rose, and the commander felt real pressure to be "one of the team," he begrudgingly relented. "I'll dispatch the SAR fixed-wing aircraft for a two-hour search. All the latest electronics gadgets," he promised.

CHAPTER TWENTY-FIVE

Graham was going through his "end of day"
routine, clearing his desk and making a new list of
tasks for the next day, when the phone rang.

"David? Brian Ecclestone." The background noise immediately told Graham that Ecclestone was onboard a helicopter.

"Evening, Brian. What's new?" He grabbed his notepad,
hopeful that this wasn't a call that would lead to a reprimand for
wasting precious Coastguard funds on a wild goose chase.

"We're out here, as you requested, searching the area where
Crouch's boat was found."

"Any luck?"

"Not yet, but I'm sending you the same image that we're
seeing here," he explained. "It's a reading from the seabed. It
makes absolutely no sense."

Graham quickly pulled up the email on his laptop. Ecclestone had sent him a sonar picture. "Looks like a...Well, I'm not
an expert," he admitted, "it could be the Loch Ness Monster for
all I know."

Ecclestone found this pretty funny, and Graham heard him

genuinely laugh – not a sneer or derisive chortle, but a full-throated, humorous laugh. "It's not Nessie," he replied. "But it's dense, solid, *and* fragmented, which is strange, almost like something's broken up. It's large, too. That's all we can say for now. It's in the area north of where Crouch's boat was found and west of where Somerville's body was recovered."

"And you're saying this thing might have had something to do with those cases?" Graham asked. It sounded far-fetched, even as he said it, but he fervently hoped this was the reason for Ecclestone's call.

"We can't know for sure. It's simply an oddity. Something we wouldn't expect to see. And so for that reason, I thought you should know," Brian replied. "My guys are saying it's not a submarine. No sign that it's a conventional wreck either, and there's nothing on the charts to explain what it might be."

Graham waited for some kind of *denouement* to this story. "So...What do we need to do?"

Ecclestone let him down. "Nothing, for now. We need more readings."

Graham said it for him. "Costly."

"Exactly. Now, I've got to go. We're about to buzz a fishing boat that's where it shouldn't be. Looks like it might be the one young Barnwell gave a good talking to the other day."

After he ended the call, Graham closed his office door and spent half an hour in total silence, letting his mind work on the available evidence of the two cases in front of him. He was alone at the station. He had directed Sergeants Roach and Harding to remain down at the marina until the end of their shift. Barnwell was taking some personal time before he started his overnight duty.

The two cases were troubling Graham. He could appreciate just how easily rumors of fantastical beasts and paranormal events could become so popular. The idea that someone had deliberately targeted two unassuming men while they were about their work *at sea* was so problematic that he had trouble seriously contemplating it. The fact that there had been two unexplained misadventures inside a few days, however, forced him to do so. He considered the angles.

Tamsin seemed genuinely grief-stricken. While her romantic troubles with Greg were fraught, even if she had chased after Greg that afternoon, she had returned far sooner than was likely to effect a murder. Graham twirled his pen around his fingers and thought further. It was possible that Tamsin had come across him very quickly, however. They really had no idea at what point in his afternoon or where exactly Greg had met his death and it certainly wouldn't be the first time a grieving girlfriend had ultimately proved a murderer.

Graham's other theory, that a fisherman had confronted Greg for disrupting his livelihood or some other reason, felt weak too, and still left him attempting to explain Matt Crouch's disappearance. They had nearly completed their interviews with all the boat owners who were out the afternoon of Somerville's disappearance, and while several of them didn't have alibis, they all denied seeing him. And who was to say there wasn't, as Des kept asserting, a French or other international boat out on the water that they knew nothing about? He thought back to the boat Barnwell had remonstrated with, the one that was "lost." Boats and ships passed through the Channel all the time. It was like Piccadilly Circus out there at times. They had no way of knowing exactly who traveled on through.

Graham sighed. Even the animal activist checked out. He started to feel hopeless and reflected on the point at which he might decide to "re-prioritize" the active investigation into the two cases. An icy chill ran through him when he considered the impact that news would have on the local people, especially the fishermen.

Graham sat back and stretched his tense back muscles, reaching up toward the office ceiling and letting out a long sigh of frustration. He glanced at his phone. There was a brief yelp of despair when he saw four texts, all from Laura. He called her at once.

"So, how was your 'public order problem?'" she asked, glossing over his graceless habit of remaining *incommunicado*.

"Complete madness," was his description of the situation at the marina. "Dangerous and disorganized. But I think we found a solution. How were things at the library?"

"Quiet. Freddie was poking around again, until someone called him about the protest. He left without even packing up his things."

"Salacious headlines don't write themselves," Graham mumbled. "He's got a lot to answer for."

"Oh, he's harmless. And isn't it good for those in power to be held accountable?"

"He's not even a real *journalist*, for heaven's sake," Graham said, narrowly keeping the frustration out of his voice.

Laura let the topic drop, and focused instead on when she might have the chance to actually lay eyes on the DI, at long last. "Any chance I'll see you for dinner? I'm dipping into my grandmother's cookbook again."

Somehow, Graham mustered the emotional processing power to simultaneously juggle two unyielding cases, three subordinates, and a remarkable woman who simply wanted to cook him a meal. It was a feat almost beyond him, but he was determined not to be defeated. "I promise," he said, knowingly boxing himself in. "Seven o'clock, your place."

Energized by the thought of an evening with Laura, and now constrained by his own commitment, Graham drank a whole pot of tea in twenty minutes. He reveled in the rocket-fuel caffeine boost and very quickly dealt with five separate phone calls.

He spoke first with Sergeant Harding for an update. She assured him that the marina was returning to a relative quiet, and that Smith and his boys had suspended their protest. "They even asked people to take their litter away," Harding told him. "As protests go, that one went. Most of the non-local boats have returned home except for a few whose crews have infused the local economy with purchases down the pub."

The second phone call was one he took from the local newspaper. Graham gave them a quote that struck a balance between his desire for public calm and his understanding of the fishermen's grievances. He finished with a solemn promise to do all in his power to catch those responsible for the murder of Greg Somerville and disappearance of Matt Crouch, whomever they might be. He was, however, mindful to follow the first rule of dealing with women, children, and the press: *Don't make promises you can't keep.*

Then he called Barnwell to confirm their plan to have the constable keep an eye on the marina overnight, just in case Smith and his fellow rebels decided to wake up Cherbourg Harbor at four in the morning with some ill-advised demonstration. "I'll put the station phone on forward to yours when I leave."

He also called his superior to report on events at the marina and his two cases. He assured the Chief Constable that the situations were under control. "No need, sir," Graham assured him, when offered additional assistance, including specialist riot police. "Let us have seventy-two hours, and we'll be in a better position. Might even have a result by then."

The more senior man agreed, but warned Graham against biting off more than he could chew. "Even the very best," he said, intimating that he felt DI Graham was in just this category, "need a little help from time to time."

"Thank you, sir."

His final phone call was to Laura. "See you in ten minutes." He turned out the lights in his office and headed past the deserted reception desk to lock up the main doors and switch on the lighted sign that instructed callers what to do in the case of an emergency. The desk phone rang, but he ignored it. After three rings, it stopped as it switched over to Barnwell's mobile. It rang again as he was setting up the coffee machine, something he always did for the night shift cover. The temptation to pick it up was nearly overwhelming, but some minutes later, as she welcomed him into her small cottage that smelled of Roma tomatoes and sizzling garlic, Laura Beecham discovered that David Graham was as good as his word.

A mile away from Laura's home, Barnwell was cycling to the marina under a moonlit sky when his mobile rang. He braked and put his foot down on the ground to answer it. As he listened, he quickly pulled out his notebook and started writing furiously, cradling the phone under his ear, leaning on his handlebars to write. "Right. Right. Stripe, you say? Three miles north. Got it. We'll check it out, sir. Thank you for phoning in." He ended the call and immediately dialed Roach's number. "Somerville's boat's washed up. Check with the boss, but I think you'd better get yourself up there sharpish."

Barnwell rung off and hooked his foot under his pedal, slotting his phone into his jacket's breast pocket. He made to push off before stopping and pulling his phone out again to send a text.

On second thoughts, don't check with the boss. He's busy.

CHAPTER TWENTY-SIX

L AURA GATHERED UP the two empty dinner plates from the table. "I guess that was okay, then?" she smiled.

"Delicious," Graham replied. "Your grandmother was quite the chef. But you didn't have to go to any trouble on my account. Leftovers would have been fine."

He looked very different in a casual button-down shirt and jeans, and Laura found him a lot more relaxed and seemingly able to set aside the day's investigative travails than he had on previous occasions. "It's no bother, really. I wanted to," she explained. "Well, maybe I was showing off for you," she admitted with a small smile. "Just a little."

Graham checked his phone. There was a text from Roach.

Albatross washed up. Doing prelim forensics. Not much. A bit of damage to the paintwork, maybe a collision. Everything else looks tickety-boo.

Graham sighed and tucked his phone away, determined to enjoy his evening.

Laura motioned for Graham to join her on the couch. There was no TV in her cottage. Instead, virtually every bit of wall space was crammed with shelving containing books of all shapes and sizes. Though Graham hadn't been upstairs yet, Laura had told him that most of her personal library was kept there. "You haven't talked about your cases today," she noted.

"Well, things are at a bit of a standstill," he admitted. "We've got a small crowd of suspects but no way to really eliminate or move forward with any of them."

Laura sat up and folded her legs under her before reaching out to take Graham's hand. "Tell me," she said mildly. "You never know, I might be able to crack the case."

"I wish you would!" Graham replied, laughing. "Someone needs to. And with what I have at the moment, I don't know if it's going to be me."

"Of *course* it will be," Laura told him. "Just like the other times. Tell me the details, and let's see if I can help."

Graham laid out the facts of the case. "Our first victim argued with his girlfriend, went out on his boat, and was struck with an unidentified object. The blow or blows killed him, and he either fell or was pushed overboard. His body washed up a few days later. A couple of days after he was last seen alive, our second victim, a fisherman, goes out to look for our first victim's boat, which hadn't washed up. He doesn't return. The second victim's boat is found empty, there's no evidence, no body, and now the whole fishing community is distraught, up in arms, and developing conspiracy theories."

"And they're blaming the French, thinking it's all to do with quotas and such," Laura summed up. "Is that possible, do you think?" She reached for her glass and took a sip of wine. It was exceptionally robust and fruity.

"Sure," Graham replied. "It's just entirely without precedent, and there's simply no evidence to support such an idea. You have to understand that around here, if there's something awry, the

French are always going to get the blame. Des Smith has got the fishermen so worked up that they're allowing their opinions to run roughshod over the facts."

"So, can we rule them out, the French fishermen, I mean?" Laura asked.

"There's no evidence to rule them in, and there's no evidence to rule them out," Graham told her. "Another idea is that one of the local fishermen killed the two men. We've spoken to them all now. About twenty don't have alibis, but no real motive. Again, there's no evidence pointing the way. There are a couple of other people I can't rule out completely. Tamsin, Somerville's girl-friend, of course. She's still the prime suspect, though we've nothing concrete. The timing doesn't fit."

"And someone else?" Laura asked.

"Yeah. Somerville had a turbulent relationship with a local green who was here 'observing' him. They had history. His alibi checks out, but Barnwell thinks he may have been involved in sabotaging Somerville's boat in the days leading up to his disap-pearance." Graham fell silent before springing back to life. "We still don't know if the Somerville and Crouch cases are connected or even that Crouch is dead. For all we know, he could be living the high life somewhere on the Cote D'Azur." Graham ran a hand through his hair.

"So," Laura said after a pause, "what will you investigate tomorrow?"

Graham looked at her with a kind smile. "We really don't have to talk about this, you know," he said. "It's only work." Both knew this to be a remarkable understatement.

"I think it's fascinating," Laura said. Their hands were still entwined, and his felt warm and powerful within her slender fingers. "But I'm sorry you're frustrated. There just seems to be something missing, doesn't there? A part of the case that you haven't seen or understood yet."

Graham mulled this over. Ordinarily, he'd have bristled at

such an observation, but she was right. "It's all just so strange," he said. "And I haven't even begun to tell you about Mrs. Taylor's ghostly ghoul or today's unusual find on the seabed." He went quiet for a long moment. "Hang on."

Laura watched him thinking. His lips moved slightly, and his eyes flitted from one invisible object to another as if comparing two antique vases to see which one was fake.

"Hang on a minute," he said again, absent-mindedly.

Laura said nothing. Perhaps this was how it was for Mozart in those moments when a new concerto popped into his head, fully realized, transcription-ready. His mental mechanisms were working overtime, and Graham seemed oblivious to the present moment, even when, after four minutes of complete silence, Laura gently squeezed his hand in an attempt to bring him back from wherever he'd gone.

It all clicked into place. "Bloody hell," Graham muttered. He stood suddenly. "Laura Beecham, you're a genius." He leaned down to kiss her, then announced, "Damn. Laura, I'm sorry. I have to go."

"Now?" she asked, largely hiding her disappointment. She stood with him and helped him gather his things.

"Yeah, I'm sorry," he said again. "But you've been truly help-ful." He found his jacket and was heading to the door before he remembered to return and kiss her again, harder this time. "It's just that I hadn't put together the, um... " The idea was yet too hazily formed for words. "Yeah. I've got to go," he said finally.

Laura watched him through the window. A distracted amble became a purposeful stride, and by the time he reached the end of Campbell Street, the Detective Inspector was jogging purpose-fully toward the Constabulary. Laura turned away to survey the detritus of their meal and looked at the clock. It was still early. She went to a drawer and pulled out a roll of aluminum foil. Unfurling a length, she covered the leftovers of their dinner, taping the dish at the sides. She shrugged on her coat and left her cottage, heading in the direction of town. It was dark and the evening was cold, but the smell of the still-warm leftovers energized her. Her grandmother's cannelloni was delicious. Billy and his mum would love it.

CHAPTER TWENTY-SEVEN

S ITTING SIDE BY side, opposite the sliding door of the powerful Royal Navy helicopter, Barnwell and Graham exchanged a glance and each found that the other was smiling.

"You'll be getting used to this," Graham joked. "*Barry Barnwell: Man of Action.* I can imagine the book launch now."

Barry wasn't as confident as he looked, but his recent frozen, harrowing descent onto the *Cheeky Monkey* had at least reassured him that only crew members who knew what they were doing took to the skies. This team was highly experienced with years of service behind them. They had a female pilot and co-pilot, and in the helicopter's cabin, a male loadmaster. These were Royal Navy personnel, not Coastguard or volunteers, and the helicopter they were in certainly wasn't one belonging to the search-and-rescue service.

"Flight time is about seven minutes," the loadmaster told them. Headsets with microphones allowed them to talk without yelling in this noisy space. "Please be advised that this is a no-smoking Lynx helicopter. Just sit back and relax. Can I get anybody a drink? A cocktail, perhaps?" he joked.

"Make mine a stiff double," Barnwell muttered to Graham.

"If I'm right about this, I'm buying. All night," his boss replied. "Just keep your fingers crossed, all right?"

Barnwell comically crossed all his limbs and grinned. "How on earth did you come up with this anyway, sir?"

With a slight shrug, Graham succinctly explained the "light-bulb" moment that had unfortunately interrupted yet another evening with Laura. He ended with, "It just came to me."

The chopper lurched slightly as the pilot adjusted the flight path.

"I'm just trying to picture it, sir," Barnwell said. "You're there, last night, having dinner with someone, and then everything just stops, and you're suddenly dashing down the road to the station?"

Graham grinned sheepishly. "Yeah, that's about right. Laura, my dinner partner, was very understanding, but I'm really trying not to make a habit of it."

Barnwell tried not to smile at the fact that he'd just smoked out a major personal admission from his boss.

"It was those strange readings that Ecclestone called in," Graham explained. "I mean, the Channel is full of wrecks from the last thousand years, and with that French boat hanging around out there, where it shouldn't be, I just put two and two together."

"French boat, sir?"

"Ecclestone told me it was still around, the one you warned off."

"But wouldn't the simplest logic have led us to Tamsin?"

"It would, but we can't link any evidence to her, and her window of opportunity to commit a murder was very tight. No, I don't think Tamsin killed anyone. I believe that her grief was genuine and that she was as honest with us as her mental state allowed."

"And we can strike Des Smith and his friends off the list too?"

Raising his voice slightly, even with the microphone to help, Graham replied, "I think so, don't you?"

"I can't see it, sir. I just can't."

"Everyone else's alibis checked out; Kev Cummings and the French fishermen. I felt we had to look elsewhere, and then it hit me. I spent the rest of the evening double-checking my thinking and then called up one of my oldest friends."

When they left school, David Graham and Paul Connolly had both swapped their school uniform for a different kind. In Connolly's case, he now wore a whole armful of gold braid as a Royal Navy Commander. As such, he was in a position to honor unusual requests at short notice, including ordering the little military operation Graham and Barnwell were now essentially leading.

"She's actually steaming her way south to join three other vessels for a Royal event on the Thames," Connolly had told him the night before. "But I've redirected her to your patch, and she'll dispatch her Lynx to St. Helier and pick you up." Now the two men found themselves aboard the powerful helicopter as it cruised north toward her parent ship, *HMS Northumberland*. Barnwell was the first in the cabin to spot it, a wall of steel and iron atop the water, bristling with threat.

"Bloody hell, boss. What have you gone and done?"

Graham leaned over to observe the aquiline shape of the warship beneath them as they banked for their final landing approach. "Nice, isn't she?" he quipped.

Barnwell was gripped. "I thought you meant some little minesweeper, or a fisheries patrol ship. This is a...Actually, what is it?" he asked the loadmaster.

"Type 23 Frigate," he announced. "One of these could take on a submarine wolf pack and protect the fleet from enemy aircraft, all at the same time."

"Crikey," Barnwell gasped. "That's a lot of firepower, sir."

406 ALISON GOLDEN & GRACE DAGNALL

Graham was grinning as though it were his birthday. "Well, I told Paul I was serious. I can't imagine anyone giving us any trouble once this bloody great thing thunders into view."

"Brilliant," Barnwell smiled.

"Brace, please," the loadmaster told them just as the helicopter was finishing its "flare," shedding some final knots of speed before settling down on the frigate's flight deck. The loadmaster jumped up but motioned for them to stay in their seats while the rotors slowed and stopped.

"Right. If you'll follow me, please?"

Graham and Barnwell jumped down. They were briskly escorted from the gusty flight deck that dominated the rear of the warship, through a metal hatchway, and down a maze of corridors. The loadmaster whisked them along as if late for something, and Graham shortly saw why as they arrived at a small mess hall with dining tables and a serving counter, but no diners.

"This is Major Sheridan and his men," the loadmaster informed them.

Graham gulped slightly. Before him, waiting, were six heavily armed Royal Marines, all in green camouflage uniforms, their faces blackened with painted stripes. They looked tall, powerful, purposeful, and distinctly mean.

"Major," Graham said, extending his hand. "Thanks for bringing your lads out on short notice."

"Morning, boys," Barnwell tried, and the Marines gave him a slight but courteous nod.

"Not a problem," Sheridan told him. "Always glad to help. And it seems you've got yourself some dangerous people sailing around out there."

"I think we do," Graham agreed. "Have you been briefed on the plan?"

He had, of course. "We'll take one of our Zodiacs, but *Northumberland* will provide the major show of force. If anything goes wrong, the Lynx will hit the enemy vessel with gunfire or a guided missile if necessary."

"Crikey," Barnwell exclaimed again. "I don't think we need to—"

"The Navy likes to plan for *all* eventualities," Sheridan told him. "We'll embark on your authority, but the final go has to come from the Commander. He's on the line now," the major said. He handed Graham a cell phone and went to speak with his men.

"Paul, you old sea dog!" Graham said. "You've done me proud here. Can't thank you enough."

"Just so you know," Connolly said, "there's been a minor delay in informing the French Navy of this operation. But only a *minor* one."

"Roger that, Commander," Graham replied. "We'll be as quick as we can."

"Stay safe. And you must come by the house next time you decide to re-join civilization. Anita is dying to see you."

Graham signed off and put Connelly on speaker. "I'm giving you the 'go' order, Major Sheridan," the commander said.

Sheridan nodded. "Right, lads." The six armed men stood up straight and carried out final inspections of each other's gear.

Graham clapped Barnwell on the shoulder. "Ready, Bazza?" his use of Barnwell's nickname an indication of the unusual situation they were in.

His reply was a grin, and they turned to follow the Marines as they jogged out to the windy deck and prepared to board their Zodiac.

Twenty minutes later, the world was a bumpy, confused whirl of sea spray and the most deafening engine noise Graham had ever suffered. Their Zodiac took advantage of the relatively calm waters, despite cool and occasionally blustery weather. It fizzed along the Channel's surface at over twenty knots. The Marines took this all in their stride, of course, but both Barnwell and Graham were left battling seasickness.

"Whose idea was this, again?" Barnwell complained, holding his turbulent stomach.

"You can thank me later," Graham replied, only narrowly hanging on to his breakfast himself. He turned back to see *HMS Northumberland*, dominant on the skyline, steaming steadily toward their target area while they swooped in at speed to surprise their prey.

"Lynx reports only one person on deck," Sheridan told Graham, yelling at almost full volume. "What do you think?"

Graham explained why he wasn't surprised. "Sounds about right. Isn't that good news? I mean, only one adversary is better, right?"

Sheridan smiled thinly. "Depends on the decisions he makes, doesn't it?"

Nodding, Graham turned to Barnwell and found the constable staring resolutely at the gray flooring of the Zodiac, willing his rebellious gut to calm back down.

"Not far now, lad." In fact, Graham could make out the trawler in the far distance. It was coming closer at remarkable speed. "Look," he said. "What do you make of it?"

The boat had obviously been built at least fifty years before, and they were soon able to make out workaday patches on its blue hull. Barnwell looked crestfallen.

"It's not the same boat, sir."

"What? Are you sure?"

"The one I saw was red."

CHAPTER TWENTY-EIGHT

THE DETECTIVE INSPECTOR bit his lip.

"Confirm just one individual in sight," a marine reported, his binoculars glued to the trawler. "No sign that he's seen us."

Graham found this hard to believe. The man on the boat had a military helicopter flying overhead, a launch containing six armed men barreling toward him at high-speed, and a naval warship bringing up the rear. Graham imagined that he was either paralyzed with fear or calling someone for instructions. In any event, the Zodiac quickly closed the distance, and Sheridan began calling over in passable French.

A man appeared at the rail of the boat by the pilothouse, but simply waved at the Zodiac before seeming to reach for the throttle to gun the engines. He appeared to be preparing to move out of the Zodiac's way. "I think we need to make more of an impression," Sheridan told his men. "Firing positions."

The six marines lined up, three kneeling in front, three standing behind. They raised their assault rifles.

Barnwell cast a desperate glance at Graham. "Is this going to get out of hand, boss? I don't want to be on the news tonight for the wrong reasons, know what I mean?"

Graham nodded absentmindedly, but he was focused on the actions of the single man on board the other boat.

Sheridan was listening to his earpiece. "Roger, Henhouse." He roared to his men, "Heads down!"

They abandoned their firing positions and crouched down by the rail of the Zodiac. Graham heard a huge crescendo of sound, and instinctively ducked as the warship's Lynx came roaring over their heads, and directly above the French boat. It was so low they could feel the heat of the engine.

"Christ almighty!" Barnwell bellowed.

On the trawler, Hugo was battling sheer panic. Jean-Luc and Victor were both deep underwater, unaware of the drama that was occurring above their heads. After Jean-Luc had surfaced the previous day, he'd waited a scant twenty-four hours, the minimum safety margin, before returning to the wreck. Victor had gone with him, enlisted to assist with the flotation devices and additional air supplies. Faced with this show of force, Hugo, alone, cold, and terrified, had no plan beyond blustering his way out. He'd never figured on a party of soldiers showing up. As a shell landed in the water to his right with a whine and a splash, he saw that his options were vanishing. He threw up his hands in surrender and shut off the trawler's engine. Then he radioed down to the divers that they were about to be boarded. "I'm sorry, *mon ami*," he said. "Good luck."

"Royal Marines!" someone shouted behind him. "Don't move!" The six marines were on board before Hugo could blink twice. With them were two men. One looked a little familiar and was wearing a high-viz jacket with his name and rank emblazoned on the left breast. The other man was in an unadorned rain jacket.

"Do you speak English?" Graham asked him.

Hugo shrugged at first. "Yes, a little," he admitted, finally.

"What is the problem today?"

"Stand down, marines! Fletcher, Norris, search the boat!" Sheridan ordered.

Barnwell took a long, hard look at Hugo before going with them, ducking to avoid the low ceiling as he descended into the interior.

"How long have you been out here?" Graham asked the Frenchman.

"A few days," Hugo responded, his voice shaking. His eyes darted between the Marines guarding him and Graham. "My colleagues are completing a dive as we speak." His tone was beseeching, as though begging Graham to believe him, but there was a touch of Parisian haughtiness in his tone.

"How many of you are there?"

"Three."

"And where were you headed?"

"We came from Cherbourg." There was a pause as Hugo considered how much he was willing to say. "We would have returned there eventually."

"No one else here, sir," Barnwell reported coming back on deck. The marines took up positions to guard the Frenchman and await the return of his two crewmen from the sea beneath. Barnwell was struck by the soldiers' quiet professionalism and their calm. They seemed to work in silence. They had said nary a word but seemed to work as one cohesive unit and know exactly what to do. He turned to look at Hugo and something clicked in his mind.

"Sir?" Barnwell said quietly in his boss' ear.

"Not now, lad."

"But I *have* seen this fella before, sir," Barnwell hissed in a rapid whisper. "Before the hurricane. You're right, this is the fishing boat that was in the wrong waters. Except it was red then, not blue."

"You sure?"

"Dead certain. It's definitely the same boat, and that's definitely the same guy."

Graham left Hugo with Barnwell and wandered around. He went below deck before returning to the Frenchman.

"Have you encountered either an Environmental Agency launch or a fishing boat named the *Cheeky Monkey?*"

Hugo shook his head resolutely. "I would have remembered."

"And the others?" he asked, pointing at the waves. "Might *they* be able to remember?"

Another shrug. "I can't speak for them."

"And when will they be able to speak for themselves, do you think?" Graham asked. "Is their dive likely to be a long one?"

Hugo checked his screens. "Victor will be coming up in a few minutes. Jean-Luc needs to stay down much longer, for decompression. It takes three or four hours, after a dive to these depths."

"Heroic," Graham noted. "And what have you found that's so important?"

Hugo bristled. "I'm not at liberty to say," he replied. He lifted his chin, "And I am not obliged to."

"So you weren't fishing, then?" Graham sought to confirm.

Hugo, bolder now, saw no reason to lie. "Does it look like it?" He gestured around at his boat. There was absolutely no sign of any fishing equipment, or indeed any fish anywhere on it.

"What exactly are you doing out here, then?" Graham looked around him. This was no ordinary boat. Graham might not know much about the ways of the sea, but he understood that the instruments he'd seen below deck and in the pilothouse were most definitely out of the price range of the likes of Des Smith and his ilk.

Hugo sat. He folded his arms and almost comically, crossed his legs, clasping his hands around his knee. He pursed his lips. He looked out to sea and said nothing.

There was a strange, gassy sound from below and a cluster of objects enclosed in netting and buoyed by flotation devices rose from the deep to bob on the surface. "Victor is here," Hugo said simply.

"And Victor has brought something with him," Graham said. Then, quietly to Barnwell, "Here's where we find out whether I've made a massive fool of myself today."

Hugo deployed a small crane with a winch to grab the recovered objects and haul them up onto deck. He was clearly a novice, and kept sending the arm of the crane the wrong way, almost ditching the net and its contents into the sea. Finally, he set it down on the deck with a resounding *clunk*.

"Sounds important," Graham noted. "Maybe even valuable." Hugo detached the two inflatable buoys from the haul, allowing him access to the net-shrouded secret Victor had brought up from the depths.

At the rail of the ship, three marines were hauling the hapless diver onboard. He complained bitterly in French. The marines shepherded him to a quieter part of the boat where he took off his diving gear, and it was then that Barnwell decided to take a chance. He asked for a marine to give him a hand.

"What's this, Barry? You going swimming?" Graham asked, watching the marine dangling Barnwell precariously over the side of the boat.

The marine hauled the constable back up as he handed Graham a foot-long strip of the beaten-up hull that he'd torn off. "Have a look under the first layer of paint."

Graham took Victor's dive knife and scraped. Everything clicked. "Get Roach on the phone."

It took seconds. "How are you doing, sir?"

Graham ignored the question but fired back one of his own. "Greg Somerville's *Albatross*," he said. "Tell me about the collision."

Roach found the forensic report. "The boat has minor impact damage, some discoloration of the hull just under the…"

"*Which* color, lad?"

"Sorry, sir?"

"The discoloration. Which color?"

"Red, sir. Ferrari red. I saw it myself."

Graham glanced down at the strip of wood in his hands. The new blue paint gave way to a bright patch of its original color; a pleasingly brilliant red.

"Got 'em."

Barnwell was becoming impatient. "Is he communing with the fish down there or what?" he muttered to Graham.

"It's all about decompression," Graham explained. "If he comes up too quickly, he'll harm himself. Only way to do it safely is to go slow."

"Been diving before, have you, sir?" Barnwell asked.

"In Egypt," Graham said. "Long time ago. I also did a day of the police divers' course, just to get their perspective. Fascinating stuff and invaluable, but not a pleasant job, in my opinion."

Major Sheridan joined them. "Hello, sir. Everything all right?"

Graham nodded and shook the man's hand again. "Couldn't be better, under the circumstances. Your men and women have been excellent, major."

Sheridan reacted as though this were a routine response to his regiment's efforts, which it truly was. "Thought you should know that we'll be sailing south rather than taking the Lynx back. Someone felt that a robust display of Royal Navy strength off Gorey Harbor might be just what the doctor ordered."

"I think that's a great idea," Graham agreed. In truth, this had also been part of his initial request to Connolly, aimed at reassuring the fishermen who relished nothing more than demonstrations of British resolve at sea. "She'll be a sight for sore eyes, I'm sure."

"With these three men in your custody, think you'll be able to bring a successful case?" Sheridan asked.

"When we get back on land, we'll really test their mettle," Graham replied. "Then we'll see."

"Of course," Sheridan smiled. "The Commander told me that you were the best investigative mind in the Met."

"He embellishes," Graham said modestly.

"I think not," Sheridan replied with a grin.

Graham changed the subject. "Tell me, was that a live shell you dumped into the water earlier?"

An enigmatic smile played across Sheridan's lips. He merely paused as he peeled off to walk away, before saying "All in a day's work, Detective Inspector, all in a day's work."

Graham regarded Victor and Hugo who were now sitting side by side on the boat's deck. Victor was spitting mad. He refused to speak in English, and swore colorfully at anyone who came close. He resembled an angry cat. Hugo was more composed.

"Barnwell, read them their rights. I'm going to see what all the fuss was about."

Just before Graham opened the net now laying bedraggled on the deck, he heard Hugo say, very quietly, "These are international waters. I am entitled."

"Entitled? To what?"

"To recover the treasure. To undertake reasonable means to retrieve it," Hugo told him.

Graham paid no attention to the trio of heavy, gold bars that were now exposed as he peeled away the nets. He looked up at Hugo. "And you think 'reasonable means' includes murder? Did you really end two lives to make sure no one else found this ancient gold?"

"*Non!*" Hugo replied. He looked horrified. And then, "Not me."

CHAPTER TWENTY-NINE

BARNWELL BREEZED IN through the double doors and strode over to Graham's open office door without stopping. "They bought the blue paint from Foley's. Arthur Foley confirms it, the day before the storm. All checks out. He was able to give me a copy of the receipt and everything."

"Excellent, Constable. This is more like it. We're building our case. Roach is over at the lab doing work on equipment we found on the boat."

"Have they said anything incriminating yet?"

"The two divers are not saying a word. I'm about to go interview the lead again, want to join me?"

"Erm, I think I'd rather stay out here in case Roachie calls in, if it's all the same to you, sir."

"Have it your way, Constable."

When he sat down, Graham surveyed the man across the table from him. Hugo was a slight, weedy-looking man, bespectacled and wide-eyed. He had dark circles under his eyes. His shoulders slumped, but he held Graham's gaze and offered him a weak smile.

"*Monsieur...*" Graham looked down at his notes, "Please confirm for the recording what you were doing out in the fishing lanes. You had been warned off at least once."

Hugo shook his head slowly, they had already been over this. "I would have thought it obvious by now, Inspector, that we were looking for treasure. Quite literally, gold. There have been rumors for decades about a shipwreck in these waters, a valuable one. I wanted to find it. I've been planning for years." He sat up straighter in his chair, and lifted his chin. "I would like to be released so that I can claim it. It is rightfully mine."

"Not so fast," Graham responded.

"Why not, Inspector? I haven't done anything wrong. Finders keepers, isn't that what you British say?"

"Did you ever see this man?" Graham pushed a photograph of Greg Somerville toward him.

Hugo looked at it carefully, fingering his glasses as he did so. "No."

"Not on your boat?"

"Not ever."

"*Monsieur*, this man's boat was in a collision with yours. We know this because traces of paint from your boat were found on its hull. Later, this man," Graham pointed at the photograph again, "turned up dead. Are you saying you know absolutely nothing about that?"

"*Alors*, no. I have never seen him. Are you suggesting we had something to do with his death?" Hugo's eyes were wide like those of a child's.

"I find it hard to believe that you wouldn't know that your boat collided with another."

Hugo shrugged. "If I were below deck..." The bookish man looked to the side. "When you are out at sea, Inspector, there are bumps and jolts all the time. It is nothing. I pay no attention."

"But you would have heard something."

Hugo suppressed a sigh but allowed a small smile to form on

his lips. It felt good to talk to a man who knew less about being at sea than he did. "You don't understand, Inspector. What we were doing requires intense concentration. I am not paying attention to every rock and roll. And I wear headphones. "

"Hmm. I find it hard to believe you had no knowledge of what was happening above you. Your boat is hardly an ocean liner."

"Like I said, Detective Inspector, my attention was elsewhere."

"And you didn't see a body floating in the water? You know, *dead?*"

"*Non.*" Hugo pointed a soft white fingertip at the photograph in front of him. "I had nothing to do with his death, Inspector."

"You had something to do with it. Paint from your boat wouldn't be found on his if that weren't the case."

Hugo's expression was unreadable.

"All right then, where did you shore up when the hurricane hit? I assume you weren't out in that weather?" Graham asked.

"No, no, of course not. We came ashore and moored in a cove until the worst had passed. The hurricane was very frightening."

"What did you do?"

"Played cards, checked our equipment, slept. There was nothing we *could* do."

"So when did you paint the boat? It was red when my officer saw you several days ago out in the fishing channels. Now it is blue."

Hugo shrugged. "Victor and Jean-Luc told me we needed to do repairs. Tidy her up, strengthen her hull. As you saw, she isn't in the greatest of shape. We took the opportunity of a few free hours before the storm arrived to paint her. Then we waited inside."

"Do you always do what your men tell you?"

"Yes."

Graham raised his eyebrows, inviting Hugo to say more.

"They are much more experienced than I. I would be a fool not to. My goal was to find the treasure. Everything else was secondary." Hugo pressed one finger on the bridge of his glasses frames and blinked.

"Secondary, eh?"

"Of course, I do not include death in that. Please do not assume from my words. I am very sorry for the man's passing, but I had nothing to do with it."

Graham sighed. He didn't feel like he was getting anywhere. "Very well. You will wait here. I'll be back to talk to you shortly." He stood and ended the interview for the recorder.

Outside the room, Barnwell came over to him. "Sir, Sergeant Roach's been on the phone. Dr. Tomlinson has a match for the murder weapon. Ballast weights. They match the victim's injuries."

"Yes! Can we link it to any of the men?"

"All evidence washed away, sir. They were using the weights to dive with."

"Damn."

"And, there's something else, sir. Dr. Tomlinson's now determined that the assailant was left-handed."

Graham's eyes lit up. "Constable, I could kiss you."

"I think I'd prefer that drink you promised, sir."

CHAPTER THIRTY

JEAN-LUC LOOKED warily at Graham as he came in the room. He had been sitting for over an hour and was becoming agitated. His heel bobbed up and down at a frenetic pace, turning his whole body into a wobbling mass of anxiety. He picked at the rough skin on his calloused hands.

Graham laid out two photographs. One was of the hull of the *Nautilus* where it had been painted over with blue paint, the other was of a streak of red on Greg Somerville's *Albatross*. Graham tapped the photograph of the *Nautilus'* hull. "Blue paint."

"*Oui.*"

"You painted the hull of your boat the day before the hurricane."

"*Oui,* we needed to do repairs."

"Under that blue paint we found red paint that matched that which was found on *this* boat." Graham tapped the photograph of the *Albatross*. "We can therefore prove a connection between your boat and this one, probably a collision of some kind."

Graham took out another photograph from the manila folder in front of him. This was of a webbed nylon belt. At intervals, metal weights were threaded onto it.

"Ballast weights," Jean-Luc said.

"Yes, what do you use them for?"

Jean-Luc shifted uncomfortably in his seat and eyed Graham from under a lock of his floppy hair. It hung over his eyes. "They help when we are descending in the water. All divers use them."

"We have found that the victim's injuries, the one whose boat had paint from your boat on it, can be shown to have been inflicted by these weights, your weights, the ones you dive with. He was killed with this weighted belt. Wouldn't have been hard, just a well-timed blow or two to the head." Graham leaned forward and looked at Jean-Luc intensely, both hands on the table. "What can you tell me about that?"

In response, Jean-Luc sat back in his chair, away from Graham, and rolled his head to one side. He looked down at the floor and then up at the ceiling. After a moment, he flicked the lock of hair out of his eye and regarded Graham. "He started it."

"Who did?"

"The other guy. He chased us, rammed us. He was mad. He jumped on board and started accusing us. We were sabotaging his research, damaging his equipment so he said. It was ridiculous, but he was angry. If we did damage his equipment, it was because of that fool, Hugo. He had no idea what he was doing half the time." Jean-Luc turned down the corners of his mouth, and spread his arms, palms upwards, as he raised his eyebrows, a typical Gallic shrug. "Maybe we ran over a buoy or two, it wasn't intentional."

"Go on."

"He wouldn't leave, he just kept shouting, and Victor got nervous. There was a fight between the guy and Victor, just some pushing and shoving, and he...he got hit with the weights."

"And then what happened?"

"He was dead. Poof. Victor dropped his body over the side."

"Just like that?"

Jean-Luc nodded. "Victor thought, with the hurricane coming in the next hours, his body would never be found and the boat would sink. I tried to stop him, to call you, the police, but he threatened me. He said he wasn't going to prison for the last years of his life and especially when we were close to crazy riches. He said we should put it out of our minds, that it was an accident, and that no one would know if we just kept our mouths shut." Jean-Luc regarded Graham's skeptical expression. "He'd already killed one man, Inspector. Being on a boat at sea with a murderer and a fool is not comfortable."

"So you're saying that Victor killed Mr. Somerville in a fight?"

"Yes."

"And then he threw his body overboard?"

"Yes."

"And you did not take part in his death or the disposal of his body?"

"No."

"Are you sure?" Graham held the man's gaze for long moment.

"Yes, of course I am sure." Jean-Luc didn't look away, but after a few seconds, there was a flicker in his eyes.

"But you didn't report the murder. And you carried on with your search even after you had come ashore."

"*Oui*, I am guilty of that." Jean-Luc looked down at the table. "And for that I am sorry."

"And *Monsieur* Fontenelle? What was his role in all this?"

"He had nothing to do with it. He was below deck. I doubt he knows anything at all. He isn't very bright about things at sea."

Graham ended the interview, and left, walking immediately into the room where Victor was being held.

The Frenchman was pacing the room. "Sit down." Victor

stopped walking back and forth, but stood motionless. "I said, sit down," Graham growled. He glared, his cheeks flushing. Victor sat and leaned forward on his forearms, meeting Graham's glare with one of his own.

"Your friend, Jean-Luc, denies killing Mr. Somerville." Graham showed Somerville's photograph to Victor.

"I do not know him."

"He was killed on your boat."

Victor frowned. "I have never seen him before."

"Jean-Luc is blaming you for the killing."

Victor shrugged and scratched his grey stubble. "I am not lying. This is the truth. If someone on our boat killed him, it must have been Jean-Luc, not me." He sat back in his chair and folded his arms.

"What's the status, sir?"

"Jean-Luc Bisson and Victor Delormé are both blaming the other like the mercenary rats that they are. Jean-Luc has implicated himself in the cover-up, but he maintains Somerville was the aggressor and claims it was Victor who killed him. Victor, on the other hand, denies any knowledge of Somerville's death, or even Somerville himself, but if he was killed then it must have been Jean-Luc who did it according to him. Fontenelle, meanwhile, is claiming that he heard and saw nothing of Somerville, dead or alive." Graham tossed his pen on his desk. "What a mess."

"There's no honor among thieves, sir."

"So what have we got, Barnwell?" Graham sat back in his chair. He had a cup of steaming hot jasmine tea on his desk. "We can connect the two boats. We can prove our victim was killed with the weights. But we can't prove which one of them did it."

"Is there any evidence to connect them to the missing Mr. Crouch?"

Graham scratched his head. "Nope."

"Perhaps we were wrong. Maybe that case isn't connected at all. The evidence isn't leading us in that direction so perhaps we need to put 'informed inference' to one side this time."

Graham looked at Barnwell carefully. He leaned back even further in his chair and rubbed his eyebrows with the heels of his hands, screwing his eyes up tight as he let out a long exhale. "Yes, you're right, Barnwell. I think we've reached the end of the line with using inference to inform the direction this case is heading. Only hard evidence matters at this point."

There was silence as they both pondered what the evidence told them. There was no getting around the fact that they couldn't prove beyond a doubt who had killed Greg Somerville. Barnwell's face suddenly brightened. "What about the assailant being left-handed, sir. Why don't we set them a test?"

Graham's eyes slowly widened. "Brilliant, Barnwell!"

An hour later, Barnwell brought the men's statements into Graham. He'd typed them up, and together they watched as one by one, the three men read his over and signed it.

All of them gripped the pen with their right hand.

"Damn," Graham said outside the room where Hugo had just added a signature to his statement that claimed no knowledge of Greg Somerville or his death.

Barnwell looked at the DI warily. Graham was tapping the statement with his pen before he came to a sudden decision. "We need more. How many hours do we have left before we have to charge them?"

Barnwell looked at his watch. "Five, sir."

"Get Roach on the phone, get him to go over the victim's belongings, including his boat, again. We need to connect Victor or Jean-Luc to our victim. I'll interview them again and again, if necessary. One of them might break down. Unless we get a confession or more hard evidence, the CPS won't uphold a charge of murder."

"And the leader of the expedition? Mr. Fontenelle?"

"He seems completely out of his depth, if you'll excuse the pun. I think we can get him on a host of maritime infractions," Graham said. "But I think he's in the clear for the murder."

"Are you sure, sir?"

"Yes, yes, Barnwell. Come on, chop, chop. Get Roach on the blower. We don't have much time."

Inside the interview room, Hugo was very still. He couldn't help but overhear what was being said by the two police officers. As he sat, silent and alone, no one saw the smirk that dared his lips to curl before, like a genie in a puff of smoke, it vanished.

CHAPTER THIRTY-ONE

THE MICROWAVE IN the break room pinged for the third time and Barnwell opened the door. He balanced the carton on his fingertips, quickly pulled it out, and tipped the contents onto a paper plate before the scorching heat burned his fingers. Next to it were two more plates similarly laden.

"Mmmm, microwave lasagna. Just what I want for my dinner when I get home," Janice said, sarcastically, bringing in two mugs and setting them in the sink.

"You'll be glad to hear, then, that this isn't for you. In accordance with Home Office regulations, it's time for our prisoner's lunch. This is what's on today's menu; the best microwave lasagna and peas our local police café can offer," Barnwell said, as he placed each plate of food on a plastic tray and added a single paper cup of water and a spoon.

"I hope they appreciate you," Janice said as she ran the tap to wash the mugs. "It's more than I suspect they deserve."

"Well, lucky for them, if we don't turn something up in the next hour, they won't have to appreciate me for much longer."

"No progress?"

"Nah, Roachie says that they can't find anything to connect the victim to either of the two men. We have to let them go or charge them with lesser offenses at two o'clock."

"What about the other guy?"

"The DI has eliminated him." Barnwell leaned back against the counter wiping his hands on a dishtowel. "I think he's being a bit premature, to be honest. I mean, who's to say? The DI seems to think he doesn't have it in him, but that's not evidence is it? And doesn't he tell us to follow where the evidence leads? We don't *have* any evidence, therefore we shouldn't be making judgments one way or another."

"Careful, Bazza, they'll be court-martialing you for insubordination if you're not careful. Or perhaps charging you with thinking too much," Harding said, taking the towel from him and wiping her own hands on it before slapping it back onto his chest with a smile.

Barnwell picked up one of the trays. "Just doesn't seem right to me. But I'm only a lowly constable, what do I know?"

"Grub's up," he announced as he opened the door to Jean-Luc's cell. The Frenchman was sitting on the cell bench with his eyes closed. He stirred and twisted around as Barnwell handed him his food tray and immediately tucked in, taking large, fast mouthfuls.

Victor, however, made no such move when Barnwell opened the door of his cell. Faced with a wall of indifference, Barnwell left the tray on the floor by the door. He checked his watch. "You've got ten minutes, then I take the food away."

Finally, it was Hugo's turn. They were out of cells, and he was still in the interview room. Hugo wrinkled his nose at the sight of the food placed in front of him and looked up at Barnwell.

"Like it or lump it, mate. That's all you're getting."

Hugo sighed and fingered the spoon. "A napkin, Constable?"

"What?"

"A napkin, could I have a napkin?" He gave Barnwell a facetious smile. "Please."

Barnwell muttered something inaudible and left. He went back into the break room and ripped a sheet from the roll of paper towels that stood on the counter. Silently, he returned to the interview room and dangled it in front of Hugo's face. Hugo, who was nibbling at his lasagna, took it from him and dabbed at his lips.

After locking him in, Barnwell stood at the door, tapping his palm with the key. He went back into the break room and ripped off two more sheets of paper towel. He opened up Jean-Luc's cell once more. "Here," he said handing him the sheet.

At Victor's cell door, Barnwell slid open the shutter and peeked inside. He got out his keys again and opened the door. "Changed your mind, eh?"

Victor had picked up his tray and, balancing it on his knees, was chewing slowly and methodically. He ignored the paper towel Barnwell proffered. The constable left it on the seat beside him. Outside, Barnwell allowed this heavy bunch of keys to retract slowly on their key chain as he looked down the hallway to their open plan office at the end. He walked the few steps to DI Graham's office.

"Sir?"

"Yes, Barnwell? What is it?"

"I think I know who did it, sir." Barnwell's body was tense, the expression on his face serious, his forefinger pointed to emphasize the point he was about to make. "It was just now, when I was taking them their food. The killer, I think he's am... ambi... Ugh, what's that word where they use both hands to do things? My brother's like it. Kicks a ball with his left foot, holds a bat in his right hand."

"Do you mean ambidextrous, Constable?"

"That's it, ambi...thingy. Well, I've just seen him eating,"

Barnwell's eyes darted around the room, replaying the scene in his mind. "You know, with his left hand. The leader guy. It was that Hugo who killed Greg Somerville."

Graham sat at his desk, twirling his pen in his fingers. A cup of tea sat cooling in front of him, unusually forgotten such was the depth of his reverie. He was engaging in a spate of deep reflection into his personal prejudices. Barnwell's revelation about Hugo had caused him to examine them closely and not without some shame.

There was a knock at his office door. Roach peeked his head in.

"Sir?'

"Yes, Roach."

The sergeant sheepishly held up a plastic bag. Inside it was a piece of paper.

Graham glared at his sergeant and stood to walk over to take the bag from him. He read the lines of print that was written on the paper inside it. "Where did you get this?"

"It was tucked away in this backpack, sir." Roach held the straps of a battered navy blue pack between his gloved fingertips. "It was left in a locker in the Harbormaster's building. He found it during his weekly cleanup."

Graham let out a big sigh and handed back the bag with Matt Crouch's suicide note in it. "Poor guy. Imagine finding out that your wife was having an affair with your best mate *and* that the baby she's carrying isn't yours. What is it with some humans that they seem bound and determined to annihilate one another?" He shook his head, not for the first time achingly depressed by the potential for cruelty exhibited by a portion of the population.

"And it says here, that the best mate and the wife admitted it to him. D'you think they did that when he came back off Des

Smith's boat that morning? So they were lying to Janice when she interviewed them? She said the friend's face was bruised like he'd been in a fight."

"I shouldn't wonder."

"What should I do, sir?"

"Record the evidence. Then go and arrest Crouch's wife and her boyfriend. Take Janice with you. Interview them and use all that knowledge you gained studying for your Sergeants' exam to come up with as many charges as you can think of. I can name at least two. One starts with "wasting" and ends in "time," the other, "perverting" and "justice." While you're doing that, I'll finish up here. At least now I can stop trying to turn myself into a modern-day Houdini trying to solve a crime that doesn't exist."

Graham went outside into the reception area. "Barnwell! Come with me. No 'ifs or buts,' this time. You're about to attend your first murder investigation interview."

"It wasn't Hugo," Jean-Luc was adamant.

"We have him banged to rights, which means there's no doubt he was the murderer. We have evidence to prove it, and we know you are lying," Graham said. "You might as well tell the truth."

Jean-Luc stood, his teeth bared. His entire body was taut, the whites of his eyes stood out against the black of his pupils. Barnwell watched anxiously and shifted the weight of his body forward on his chair. Graham regarded the Frenchman mildly.

Jean-Luc turned away and took three paces, clenching his fists before tipping his head back, his mouth wide open as he laid bare the frustration, anger, and bitterness that roared from him in a deafening howl.

There was a hurried knock on the door. Roach appeared. "Everything all right, sir?" he asked looking around the room.

"Yes, thank you Roach. Everything is just fine."

Jean-Luc threw himself on the chair and put his head face-down on the table, his arms dangling between his wide spread legs.

"So tell me what happened, Jean-Luc."

There was a mumble from under the table.

"Sit up, and tell me for the recorder, please."

Like a truculent teen, Jean-Luc straightened and began to tell the story, slowly at first. "Hugo rammed the scientist's boat. Only Hugo could be useless enough to hit another lone boat in the middle of a huge stretch of water." Jean-Luc tapped his thumbs against the flat surface of the table. "The guy in the other boat was mad as hell. I was telling the truth when I said he accused us of damaging his equipment. Victor argued with him, and there was a fight, but it was Hugo who hit him with the weights. He died instantly. It was crazy."

Graham imagined all three men yelling in French, gesticulating wildly at one another on a boat in the midst of the English Channel.

"Why didn't you report the death?"

"Hugo didn't want to stop our search. He had planned it for years, made sacrifices, he said. We had all worked so hard and the prize was so great." Jean-Luc looked up at the ceiling and screwed his eyes tight shut. "We tipped his body overboard and left his boat for the storm to deal with. Then we came ashore and painted the *Nautilus*. Over the hours of the storm we discussed what to do if his body washed up. Hugo told us that if we found the shipwreck, as the financier of the expedition only he could claim the bounty. It was a threat. He said if we were questioned, we should keep him out of it, and he would make it worth our while later. Me and Victor decided that we would deny all knowledge of the scientist, and if forced to, take the blame ourselves. We figured we'd go back to Hugo for the money later, when it was all over."

"But that's not what you did, is it? You blamed each other."

Jean-Luc stared at Graham, blinking. *"Bien sûr.* Of course. Victor would never confess, I knew that. It's dog eat dog on the high seas, Inspector."

CHAPTER THIRTY-TWO

"NOT SURE HOW to put this, sir. I think we've got a lead on Mrs. Taylor's recent 'visitations,'" Roach said at Graham's office doorway.

It was mid-morning, and the Gorey police officers were all relaxing, appreciative of the lull in police activity now that their cells were empty. The three Frenchmen had been arraigned in court that morning and were now on their way to Jersey's HM Prison La Moye.

At the sound of Sergeant Roach's words, Graham was up and marching into the reception area in a second. There he found an unkempt little man, older than himself, looking distinctly uncomfortable. "This is Ernie Prescott. Ernie, why don't you tell the Detective Inspector what you told me?" Roach said.

The man spoke in a soft, uncertain mutter that took some deciphering. "Well, you see," he began, "I was down the pub a few weeks ago. I'd had a few, you know. And this fella, a guy I've known for years, says he's got something special that I might want to buy."

Graham nodded, desperately hoping that yet more of his precious time wasn't about to be frittered away on nonsense.

"Plenty of dodgy stuff gets bought and sold in pub car parks, sir," Roach reminded the DI.

"I do know that, Sergeant." Then, Graham asked, "What was it that was 'special?'"

"Well, I'm something of an amateur naturalist," Ernie Prescott told him.

Roach blushed. "I don't think we need to know about your personal habits, thank you very much. Could you just stick to describing the item you bought?"

Graham held back a huge gust of mirth by the narrowest margin. "You're thinking of a 'naturist', Sergeant."

"Oh." Roach blushed again.

Graham nodded at the man in front of them. "This man has an enthusiasm for the natural world. You know, David Attenborough, and what-have-you."

"Roger that," Roach said sheepishly.

"Quite so, quite so," the little man was saying. "And my friend from the pub offered me something I couldn't refuse."

The voice came as a surprise. "A golden tamarin." Sergeant Harding strode in, carrying several eight by five-inch photographs. "Rare, beautiful, exceptionally expensive, and quite difficult to keep," she told them all. "Very nimble little blighters, too. Few cages can keep them for long." She waved the prints she held in her hand.

The little man sighed.

Harding laid the photographs out on a table. "Those camera phone images Mrs. Taylor gave us were next to useless," she said. "So I installed a suite of infra-red cameras. Borrowed them from Special Branch," she told Graham.

"Very resourceful, Sergeant."

Janice continued, "They're movement-activated, so each time the monkey—"

"Tamarin," the little man corrected. "His name's Harvey."

"*Who cares?*" mouthed Roach to Janice over the man's head.

"Each time the *tamarin* went rampaging through Mrs. Taylor's kitchen the camera went off." The pictures were wonderfully clear. They showed the tiny creature galloping up the side of a stack of metal shelves, and then delightedly throwing, pushing to the ground, and nibbling everything he found up there.

"The little blighter!" Graham exclaimed. Then he turned to Ernie Prescott and said gravely, "Selling and owning such a creature is a criminal offense."

"Aye," the man admitted. "That'd be right." His shoulders slumped. "And I wouldn't be here now but for that blogger who wrote all about the goings-on at the White House Inn. Once I realized Harvey had gone, I had no idea where he might be. But when I read about what was happening at the Inn, well, I recognized the behavior, you see. I put two and two together. Then, when I went down there to get him, the bloody woman who owns the hotel called you lot!" he ended indignantly.

Roach found the blog entry in Solomon's *Gorey Gossip*. "Makes a bit more sense than a ghost, doesn't it?"

"Mrs. Taylor had a *fit* when she found out it was an animal causing chaos in her kitchen. I got the keepers from the monkey compound at Jersey Zoo round there sharpish, and they tracked it down to a covered pipe space in the corner of the kitchen, but she was virtually hysterical," Harding said.

"Can't say I blame her, but I'm mostly relieved that another of Gorey's seemingly inexplicable mysteries has been resolved and even more relieved that Mrs. Taylor will now stop badgering us about it. I'll go and see her in the next few days," Graham promised. "Whatever I think about her...beliefs, she's certainly been through it, poor woman. Will the zoo keep the monkey?"

"Yes, sir," Janice said.

Graham turned to Prescott. "Sergeant Roach," he said, "would you favor charging this man, under the circumstances?"

Roach thought for a second. "I'd give him a stern warning, sir, with a commitment that he will not keep any exotic pets henceforth. And I'd invite the health inspectors to visit his home."

Graham escorted the man to the door. "Stay out of trouble, Ernie. And definitely stay out of pub car parks at night, all right?"

The little man left and scuttled home.

"Aaaaand another one bites the dust," Harding observed. "We're getting good at this, aren't we?"

EPILOGUE (PART ONE)

The Gorey Gossip
Wednesday, November 21st

Isn't it amazing the things that can change in a single week?

As I write, three Frenchmen are sitting in jail cells, detained courtesy of Gorey Constabulary, awaiting their fate on charges including murder, accessory to murder, piracy, and criminal trespassing. This reporter has learned that the three men, inspired by tales of sunken treasure, were diving on an uncharted wreck within the Thames sea area, not twenty miles from where you now sit. We have only initial findings, but my background in historical research has enabled me to fill in the blanks.

It was 13th March, 1587 — a Friday, of course. A fleet of three carracks — a very old style of sailing ship that gave rise to the

more famous galleon — were transiting the
English Channel on their way to Holland from
the New World. All three were owned and oper-
ated by Portuguese traders who had made several
risky journeys across the Atlantic, returning
crates of the choicest valuables to a well-
connected merchant based at the port city of
Rotterdam. He paid them top dollar, and this
led to them taking risks.

We don't know if the storm hit quickly, or
if the mariners chose to risk what they knew
would be a difficult transit. But one of the
ships, the *Pretty Lady*, found herself in
trouble and sank in the storm. We can only
imagine that she was lost with all hands.

After that, there were just rumors. No one
knew exactly where the ship had sunk, and the
passage of time dimmed memories and the regret-
tably piecemeal historical record. But from my
research, I've been able to establish that the
wreck discovered last week was the carrack that
went missing on that fateful Friday, well over
four hundred years ago. The *Pretty Lady* must be
one of the most exciting finds in the history
of marine archaeology, and to be at the center
of such a discovery is a tremendous thrill.

But now, the lawyers will descend. Ownership
of the wreck is naturally contested between the
descendants of the Dutch traders who commis-
sioned the journey, the families of the
Portuguese mariners, and the indigenous people
of South America, whose gold and timber was so
ruthlessly exploited. If they are found guilty,
those who discovered the wreck will be forced

to forfeit their rights to the treasure because of their criminal actions. No quick solution can be expected, and my sources have warned of a very protracted legal battle that could take many years.

In the meantime, we grieve for our recent losses, and we pray for the families forever changed by connection to this tragic story. Yet again, greed and selfishness made a bid to triumph over truth and justice but were found wanting. It has been a privilege to help reveal this case to the good people of Gorey and to the world, and I owe this wonderful community my heartfelt thanks for their warmth, and especially for their timely and accurate information. Remember, if you see something...'Say it to Solomon.'

EPILOGUE (PART TWO)

HUGO FONTENELLE CONTINUED to maintain his innocence but was found guilty of the murder of Greg Somerville and jailed for twenty years. It was recommended that he serve at least twelve before being eligible for parole. Jean-Luc Bisson and Victor Delormé were tried for conspiracy and accessory to murder and asked the judge to take into consideration eight other counts relating to maritime offenses. They were jailed for ten years.

At their trials, both divers maintained they had no idea that Fontenelle was as callous and calculating as he proved to be. Had they known, they both claim they would not have embarked on the expedition to recover the lost treasure with him.

Cheryl Crouch confirmed that on the morning of her husband's disappearance, he had confronted her with rumors that she and Phil Whitmore were having an affair. At that time, she admitted the relationship, and there was an altercation between the two men. She and Whitmore were charged with obstruction and were ordered to undertake 100 hours community service each. Once complete, they moved to Whitmore's native Yorkshire where they lived quietly in the countryside until their eventual breakup five years later after a paternity test showed that Mr. Whitmore was not the father of the daughter born to Mrs. Crouch following her husband's death.

The coroner recorded a verdict of death by suicide in the case of the disappearance of Matt Crouch. His body was never found. It is believed that he threw himself overboard and drowned in despair over the revelation of his wife's affair with Phil Whitmore. A small but vocal group continue to suggest that Crouch faked his own death, and at least one person claims to have seen him on a beach in the South of France. Sightings of him around Gorey persist, especially following bad weather. The story of his disappearance has since passed into Gorey folklore joining those of the "Beast of Jersey" and "Marjorie's Monkey."

Kevin Cummings resigned his post as the regional director of the local SeaWatch chapter and was last heard from scaling Sydney Harbor Bridge to protest the sailing of the oil-company-owned ship, *Broadlands*, which was traveling to join an oil drilling fleet in Antarctica. Tamsin Porter returned to the mainland and now teaches a marine biology course at the University of Portsmouth.

Des Smith continues to roam the high seas and never fails to miss an opportunity to regale any audience with his views, regardless of their interest in them. He did not follow through with his threat to blockade a major French harbor on account of DI Graham pointing out that the Frenchmen arrested for Somerville's murder were not fishermen. Quotas have not been raised, suspicion between the fishing fraternity and the government is still deep, and the French fishermen continue to disembark on Jersey and rile up the locals. In fact, nothing appears to have changed since the "Fishermen Frenzy" protests.

Following an incident where he insulted the Lord Lieutenant of Jersey, a representative of the Queen and the *de facto* head of state for the island, Jersey Coastguard Commander, Brian Ecclestone was removed from his post and promptly reassigned to an even quieter Coastguard station in Wales. Two of his new staff resigned almost immediately.

Freddie Solomon's talent for writing salacious, sensational, and popular articles about the events of Gorey continues unabated and is matched only by his ability to earn the Detective Inspector's enduring contempt.

Sergeant Janice Harding has become fast friends with Mrs. Taylor and can often be seen at the White House Inn, exchanging gossip and 'flying the flag,' as the sergeant likes to put it. She's carefully thinking about moving in with Jack Wentworth but is hesitant to tell her grandmother.

Sergeant Jim Roach's forensic career continues apace, and he will now spend two days a week on the mainland to study with Dr. Miranda Weiss, Adjunct Professor in criminology at the University of Southampton and Head of Forensics for the Jersey Police. He will also continue to work with Dr. Tomlinson in Gorey and St. Helier. He claims to never have been happier in his life.

· · ·

Constable Barry Barnwell began a brief lecture tour, re-telling the stories of his maritime exploits at schools and youth clubs. He recently requested a month's special leave in order to climb a challenging Alpine peak. He continues to hone his ability for critical and independent thinking, has developed a new passion for self-help books, recently limited his consumption of the *Daily Mail* newspaper to once a week on Saturdays, and has sworn off reading the *Gorey Gossip* entirely.

Laura Beecham and Detective Inspector David Graham can frequently be seen together, either strolling around town or at the Bangkok Palace. David recently received a "Gold Star for Bravery" for his daring forays into the spicier corners of the Palace's menu awarded by the stunned (and frequently very concerned) Bangkok Palace staff. Graham continues to be "excessively busy," but the couple does find enough time to be together amid the daily challenges of their respective work schedules and Graham recently booked himself some much-needed vacation time, surprising Laura with tickets for a week-long cruise in the Caribbean.

USA Today Bestselling Author

K12 RGF

THE CASE OF THE
FORSAKEN
CHILD

ALISON GOLDEN   Grace Dagnall

THE CASE OF THE FORSAKEN CHILD

BOOK SEVEN

Cover Illustration: Richard Eijkenbroek

Published by Mesa Verde Publishing
P.O. Box 1002
San Carlos, CA 94070

Edited by
Marjorie Kramer

PROLOGUE

BILLY GLANCED NERVOUSLY up and down the alley, his jacket the only protection against the swirling, cold, February winds. He silently prayed that no passerby would notice him. *How long had it been already?* He reluctantly pushed back the sleeve of his sweater to peer at his old, scratched wristwatch, then quickly covered his pale, chilled skin.

They must be inside by now. Billy listened for any sounds of disturbance—a creaking door, a crash of something knocked off a table—but so far, the youths had been the "true professionals" they had boasted they were. Still, they needed a lookout. No amount of "professionalism" would spare them if someone noticed something awry, or those who lived above the shop they were breaking into returned home early. Billy's eyes flicked around. A watchful resident might notice him—a ten-year-old out way past his bedtime. "Hurry up," he muttered. The store had formerly been a stone row-cottage but was now a gift shop that sold items of the expensive, largely useless variety, patronized mostly by tourists. "Get what you want, and let's *go*."

It had only been bad luck that found Billy in this tight spot. His mother was back to her old ways. Earlier, he'd come home from the library to find her slumped against the kitchen wall in a space between two fitted cupboards that had been vacated by their barely serviceable stove the day before. Viv Foster had sold their freestanding oven for a few pounds and next to her on the ground was the result of her transaction, a mostly empty bottle wrapped in a brown paper bag. She'd been careless in her stupor —brown liquid dribbled out of the bottle. It made a pool among the dust, bits of food, and animal hair that had found a home under the cooker before it had been traded for the monetary equivalent of three bottles of whisky. The whisky would be gone by Monday, but now Billy had one more thing to worry about— his ability to prepare hot food.

Billy had known better than to wake his mother. After holding a finger under her nose to check that she was still breathing, he had left her to sleep. He moved to the living room where he emptied his backpack on the floor. Schoolbooks tumbled out, and he had settled down to finish off his homework on the coffee table. It took him only half an hour to complete his math project and read twenty pages of *Treasure Island* when, stomach rumbling, he wandered back into the kitchen. He checked on his mother who was still out for the count. He looked in the fridge. His shoulders sagged. There was a wrinkled tomato, some eggs, three slices of moldy bread, and some cheese that had gone hard.

He slammed the fridge door and looked around. Spying his mother's bag lying like a deflated balloon in the hallway, he rifled through it and found her wallet. It was empty. He ran his hand around the bottom of the suede bag, through the detritus of his mother's life and found a few coins. A total of £1.32.

Billy looked at the money in his hands. He pressed his lips together, rolling them against his teeth as he thought. It was late now, but the shop at the corner would be open. Mr. and Mrs. Bagchi were nice to him. Sometimes, when he went into their shop, they gave him packets of crisps or frozen food that was out of date. They just gave it to him. No charge! Yeah, they were nice, they were.

He slipped on his trainers and shrugged on the warm jacket that Mrs. Lampard had got him from the charity shop in St. Helier. She was nice, too. He'd really liked it when he'd stayed at her B&B while his mum was in rehab. Billy sighed at the memory. He opened the front door. He'd go to the Bagchi's and see what £1.32 would buy him.

It was a freezing, clear, winter night. Billy folded his arms around him as he walked, slipping his gloveless hands inside his sleeves. He heard a peal of laughter come from *Luca and Lizzi's* kebab shop across the way, the meaty smell reaching his nostrils but failing to tempt him. Billy loved animals. He tried not to eat them, but sometimes hunger overwhelmed his principles. Not tonight, though.

As he walked down the dark alleyway behind his house, the silhouettes of two youths walked toward him. They passed under a street lamp. Billy quickly ducked into the shadows. Anthony Middelton and Caspar Freedland were five years above Billy at school. They were bullies, known for their menacing behavior and petty thievery. Janice had told him to stay away from them. She might be police, but Billy liked Janice. Come to think of it, he had some good friends—adult friends. Laura at the library was nice, too. They were nothing like these boys coming toward him, shoving each other and laughing, the ends of their cigarettes glowing red in the dark as they inhaled.

"Oi!" the taller one shouted. It was Anthony with a "th."

Billy cringed and shrank further into the darkness. His heart beat so loudly he was sure the boys would hear it. And they must have because when they came level with him they stopped and peered over.

"'im?" Caspar Freedland asked. There was a rumor at school that Caspar had been named after "the friendly ghost," a point he tried to live down by being as *un*friendly as possible. The two teenagers walked over to where Billy was trying to hide in the shadow of a skip. Caspar grabbed Billy by the arm and peered at him some more. "Nah, 'e's too small and scrawny. Besides, look at 'im, 'e's too young. 'Is teeth are chatterin'."

"'E's got a pair of eyes, and a mouth, ain't 'e? That's all we need. 'Ere, you," Anthony prodded him. "Come wiv us. We've got a job for yer."

"B-but I'm running an errand for my mum. She'll notice if I'm late back."

Anthony bent down, the tip of his nose two inches from the tip of Billy's. He'd been drinking. Billy could smell his beery breath. "You're Viv Foster's boy. My dad drinks wiv your mum down *The Flowerpot*." He shook Billy by the shoulder like it was his fault their parents were drunks. "She wouldn't notice you if you banged 'er on the 'ead with a crate of special brew. She'd notice the swill, though." The two older boys cackled while Billy recoiled, partially because he dreaded what they had in mind for him and also because he knew that what they said about his mother was true.

And so it was that Billy found himself the lookout for the two youths as they broke into *Gorey Gifts & Sweets*. He stood across the road so he had sight of the shop and the street. The older boys had broken in from the back. Caspar had given Billy his phone. He was to alert them if anyone entered the building from the front.

The High Street was deserted. The only sound Billy could hear was the beating of his own heart. His need to pant was over-whelming, but he closed his eyes to control his breathing lest his frozen breath betrayed him. At his feet, a mouse surprised him, winding its way between his feet. Still, he waited, his eyes scanning the street, willing the boys to leave the shop and for his ordeal to be over.

The sound of footsteps, a clopping sound, reached his ears.

Billy shrank further back into the shadows as a woman, her boots sounding clearly against the paved surface, walked steadily down the street. She crossed the end of the alley and after a second or two disappeared from his view, the sound of her steps slowly receding.

Silence descended again. Billy saw a streak of light from a flashlight illuminate the inside of the shop. He looked anxiously around but nothing stirred. There wasn't even a cat exercising its hunting instincts.

The phone in Billy's hand finally beeped, the modern sound strangely incongruous among the old stonework that surrounded him: *2 mins*. "Okay," Billy breathed. The end was nigh. Just as his shoulders relaxed a little, and the cold seemed to release its grip, another sound from his right made his ears prick up. It quickly became clearer, sharper, more distinct, and within seconds he tracked the noise as it bore down the High Street. The sound became extreme, an angry, mechanical roar. Some idiot was streaking a car down the road in a detestable hurry. The noise carried, funneled down the street by the wind, hurting Billy's ears.

He pressed a button. "Anthony?" Billy spoke a fierce, urgent whisper into his phone. "Casper? Come on, we have to *go*! Hurry!"

He turned just in time to see a speeding shape pass the end of the alley. But then, at the limit of his hearing, there was a *thud*. It was almost covered by the howl of an engine in low gear but at maximum revs. Unable to see, Billy's dark-adapted eyes squinted into the well-lit space of the High Street. He heard another *thud*, perhaps three seconds after the first, followed by the sound of the car roaring away.

Billy's attention was immediately distracted from the sounds as one of the boys emerged from the side of the row of shops across the street, the other hard on his heels. "Come *on*!" Billy hissed as they ran toward him.

"You seen someone?" Caspar whispered, worried that some unexpected danger might derail the evening's only objective: the thrill of secret, illicit acquisition. For Caspar, Anthony's quest to lift something for his mother's birthday was inconsequential.

"There's something happening further down the street." It was still hard to define what Billy had heard, and the car was long gone, anyway. The sound of its engine had dissipated as the driver continued away down Gorey's main street, toward the straight stretch that led past the harbor and out of town into the countryside.

"Like what?" Caspar asked. "This place is dead as a doornail."

"I dunno, really I don't. But I reckon the cops will be here soon to investigate."

"Sod that. Let's scarper. Keep yer mouth shut, yeah?" Anthony reached into his pocket and threw a small white box at Billy before running with his friend down the alley, away from the shop. Billy watched them for a second, then raced in the other direction, overcome by the fear of being caught. He was barely into double digits. He had committed a crime.

Billy stopped suddenly, just short of Drovers Lane, another tiny alley that reached off the High Street. Ahead, people were gathering in a concerned cluster. Billy's first theory, that the car had clobbered a poor house cat, gained traction. But then the street flooded with blue light and ear-splitting sirens as two emergency vehicles parked abruptly, just out of view. Billy instinctively retreated a few feet further into the shadows. He counted six or seven people at the corner now, standing or kneeling by a shape on the ground. Another siren started in the middle distance, closing in.

Billy glanced back once more. One of the observers moved away, reaching for support, as though near-toppled by what they were seeing. Only then could Billy see what was unmistakably a human body on the ground. There was no movement at all.

Realization gripped him around the throat like the cold fingers of some terrible ghost. Tremors began in his hands, then his knees, until his whole body shivered. *What should I do...?* He dithered painfully, prepared now to call out in guilt or fear if only he could catch his breath. *The thud... I heard it... I can help... But...*

Overwhelmed, Billy endured long seconds of slack-jawed paralysis as his brain struggled to comprehend the scene. But then, the terror freed him and he was immediately away, darting furiously down alleys, half-blinded by tears.

CHAPTER ONE
FIVE HOURS EARLIER...

"**L**IGHTS, PLEASE." ENJOYING a quiet swell of professional pride, Barry Barnwell clicked the remote to pause the video. As the gloom of the room lifted, and his audience's attention shifted from the display's pixilated, dark-green image to the locally famous police officer out front, heartfelt applause began. The fuzzy, green image on the screen behind him came from a camera position within a helicopter's side-door. It showed a long line dangling into a terrible stormy night. At the far end of the windswept line, the bulky figure of Barnwell stood alone, struggling for his footing on the storm-tossed deck of a fishing vessel.

"I suppose you're wondering," Barnwell began as the appreciation died down, "what riding around in helicopters and Zodiacs might have to do with our topic today. But I assure you, none of this would have happened without our new 'ultra-collaborative' model of information management."

Barnwell had been on his feet for twenty minutes and felt the need for some audience participation. "I wonder if you've had similar experiences in your own police forces."

Agreement came in the form of a hundred nodding heads. "Changed everything," one man claimed.

"Big, *big*, effectiveness multiplier," commented another, an older, senior officer whom Barnwell had yet to meet. "And it couldn't have come along at a better time given the cuts we're facing. We're all having to do *more* with *less*, just now, aren't we?" A disapproving murmur illustrated the audience's shared view.

"True as could be," Barnwell agreed. "Now, I know we all agree that database manipulation isn't as much fun as riding in a speeding boat or dangling from a helicopter..."

Two rows from the back, a clean-shaven Jack Wentworth, dressed smartly in a crisp pale blue shirt and chinos interrupted. "Don't knock it until you've tried it, Barry," he heckled." The audience turned to him curiously.

"We all get our kicks somehow, I suppose," Barnwell retorted.

Jack grinned. "Not all of us are cut out to be superheroes," he added.

"But seriously, 'multiplier' is exactly right. Interrogating the data, and then sharing *everything*, is just as vital as helicopter hijinks," Barnwell said. He tapped the screen with his pointer. "This is another example of the new model of policing that we practice here on Jersey. Cross-disciplinary and cross-hierarchical, all supported by the software's database and communications systems. However, as my esteemed boss often says, 'Hacking, CCTV, and forensics will never entirely supplant the hard-earned investigative acumen of a skilled police officer. We need both. One should not take precedence over the other.'" Quoting Detective Inspector Graham brought applause, such was the respect with which he was held. Barnwell knew it was the ideal finale.

"Loved it, Bazza," Sergeant Jim Roach said, clapping Barnwell on the back as others queued to speak with him. "You got some big words in there."

"And it's only 5:30. Gives us time to celebrate the man of the hour." Sergeant Janice Harding walked up behind him. "What do you say, Barry? An after-hours conference session down the *Foc's'le and Ferret*?" DI Graham, out of respect for the work his team had put into organizing and participating in the annual National Police conference, had arranged that the Gorey station be covered by officers from Jersey Police HQ in St. Helier for the day. Any criminal mastermind who chose to make Gorey the center of his operation between Friday at 12:01 a.m. and midnight would have an alternate set of officers to deal with. It also meant the entire staff of Gorey Constabulary could attend the conference without worrying that crime in the town would explode in their absence.

Behind Harding, his jacket over his arm, Graham, relaxed now that the first day of the conference was over, offered his own congratulations to Barnwell before turning to Janice. "Sounds like a good idea. Let's get out of here and have a change of scenery. I'll put some cash behind the bar. Invite the Met officers —Needham, Trevelyan, Vincenti, and his crew. Oh, and perhaps your liaison. I've asked Tomlinson to join us. Great first day, Sergeant. Well done."

"Thank you, sir," Janice acknowledged.

Collecting his note cards from the lectern, Barnwell gave a bright thumbs-up while Harding spread the word to the invited attendees. Roach provided directions. "Quarter of a mile down the hill, just follow your nose," he said, leading the way.

"Not gonna take your bike?" Barnwell said to Roach when they got outside. He nodded over to where a testosterone-boosting masterpiece of engineering, technology, and design stood. Black, red, and silver paint coated elegantly curved panels that protected valves, camshafts, and a powerful engine all tightly controlled by a computer and topped off with a multi-media system. It was a motorbike that made the sort of noise that turned heads.

"Nah, I'll leave it here. Come back for it later," Roach said.

"Must have cost a pretty penny." Barnwell, while willingly acknowledging his faults, did not consider financial imprudence to be one of them.

"Leased it, mate. Bit of fun, that's all. I'll take you for a spin on it after this conference is over," Roach said before moving off.

"Not on your nelly," Barnwell muttered after him.

CHAPTER TWO

"NICE EVENT SPACE you've got there," one of the conference delegates said. He fell into step alongside Roach as they negotiated the slope to the pub. "Just the right size. Looks recently done-up, too." The man was tall, even compared to the lanky Roach, and equally as skinny. He had a full head of brushed-back hair and long sideburns. He smoked a roll-up as they walked along. Looking careworn, the man wore a black leather jacket over a white T-shirt and jeans. On his feet, he wore scruffy cowboy boots. Roach thought he looked like James Dean if James Dean had lived another couple of decades.

Roach held his hand out. "Sergeant Jim Roach, Gorey Police. It's good, isn't it? They built the building back in 1919, all through public donations. Decided it needed a lick of paint a year ago, so they had another whip-round." In truth, major upgrades to the old community building now offered Gorey a splendid new conference space. Off-peak rates, Jersey's usually clement weather, and the prospect of rubbing shoulders with the famed DI Graham and his team presented the National Police Conferences Committee with an easy choice of location for this annual gathering. They'd even spun the necessity of reaching Jersey by ferry or plane into a positive by emphasizing the "get away from it all" aspect.

"DS Tom Vincenti," the tall man next to Roach said. They passed a row of impeccably neat cottages with winter blooms out front—heathers, jasmine, and cherry blossom. "I'm with the Met. CID."

"Crikey, people really have come from all over," Roach said, breezily. "Some of the forensic computer guys came all the way from Aberdeenshire."

"There's even a chap from Gibraltar," Harding chimed in. "If I've read that list of attendees once, I've read it a thousand times."

Janice was walking slightly behind Roach and Vincenti. She was with DI Mike Trevelyan. Trevelyan was an old mate of Graham's. "We started out together after completing training at Hendon," he'd told her. "He's a good lad, our Graham. Likes bringing on his younger colleagues, mentoring them, and emphasizing the importance of ongoing professional training. We both do. It's a very satisfying part of the job. Balances out the nastier bits."

Janice pounced on this rare piece of intel concerning her senior officer. "So you probably lived it up out of hours, getting rid of the stress of your early years on the beat then?"

"Nah, I was already married with kids by the time I joined the force. Got three girls now. Brought one of them with me. A sort of bring-your-daughter-to-work weekend," Trevelyan said. "She's a bit of a handful and sends my missus round the bend, so I thought a break would do us all good. This evening she's gone off with some gal she met at the hotel."

Roach and Vincenti slowed to allow Janice and Trevelyan to join them. "Janice Harding is our esteemed senior Sergeant. She organized this whole shindig," Roach told Vincenti. "That's got to be worth a Queens Gallantry Medal in its own right, surely?"

"Seems they'll pin one on just about anybody, these days," Barnwell said, catching up with them.

Harding turned to poke Barnwell in the ribs. He had lost so much weight—forty pounds—she could feel bone under her elbow. "Credit where it's due," she said mildly. "'If you're kind to yourself, others will follow'."

Barnwell blinked, surprised at her tone. "Blimey, that's a bit deep for you."

"Eh?" she asked. Then she laughed, "Ah, that little gem came from Jack. He's quite reflective, you know. Reads books that make absolutely no sense to me, but occasionally he'll say something that I understand and even agree with."

"Is he coming to the pub?"

"Yeah, he'll be along in a while."

"Wanted to shake your hand, young man," came a new voice from behind.

Barnwell turned to find that Graham, bringing up the rear of the group, had an introduction to make: the affable, white-haired Superintendent Nigel Needham. Needham was a senior Met police officer with over five decades of service. At 73, he was one of the oldest officers in the UK, but given the rate he was keeping up with Graham, there was little wrong with his physical condition.

Prior to the conference, Graham had talked up his former senior officer. "Don't be fooled by his advanced years, you hear? Even if you haven't heard of him, Superintendent Needham's fame spreads far and wide within the force. He is formidable. In his younger years, he was a street cop who worked on teams that ran the gangs of London's East End into the ground during the 1960's. Later, he led undercover units that infiltrated the unions responsible for the strikes of the Seventies in the North. Intelligent, unrelenting, and canny, he is. So give him the respect he deserves, eh?" Roach, Barnwell, and Harding had all nodded vigorously.

Mindful of Graham's little speech, Barnwell paused, falling away from Janice and the others. He allowed the senior policeman and Graham to catch up before falling into stride beside them. "Pleased to finally meet you, sir."

"Congrats on a very successful talk, Constable," Needham said. "I must admit, you play the role beautifully. A man of swift and decisive action, but also a *thinker*," he said, tapping his temple. "Very important."

"I learned from the best, sir," Barnwell said.

"I remember reading about that helicopter rescue of the two boys," Needham continued, swerving slightly as a young man jogged past him. "And that tricky case with those missing fishermen in the Channel—well done! So good to see young policemen taking ini-initiative and..." There was a pause. Suddenly Needham's face lit up, "Ah, that must be the pub."

"Finally!" someone called out ahead of them.

The *Foc's'le and Ferret* was a proud, white-washed old pub that stood close to Gorey's harbor front. It had withstood Channel storms for nearly three centuries, but its roof was still largely original, pierced by two distinctive double-chimneys. The pub loomed over a small, narrow lane off Gorey High Street where the town's main shopping concourse was located. Its sign, a dark brown and green artistic masterpiece, depicted a ferret standing on the forecastle of a ship looking out to sea through a pair of binoculars. Gold lettering told the prospective pub patrons that they had reached their destination. "Marvelous, marvelous," Needham intoned.

"Sir?" Harding said to Graham. "I'd like to introduce Jason Ashby from the National Police Conference Committee. He's our liaison with the organization."

"Ah, yes," Graham said, leaving the superintendent and Barnwell to chat. He shook Jason Ashby's hand. Jason looked to be in his mid-twenties, his thick fluffy hair an attractive shade that hovered somewhere between blond and ginger. He wore a black shirt and a skinny bright red leather tie that was tucked away between the second and third button. "Thank you for your work. Everything's been first-class." The DI could feel Jason's enthusiasm bubbling over even before he spoke.

"Pleased to meet you, sir. This is simply the *best fun*," Ashby said. "Jersey's perfect, a bit warmer than London, even in February, and everyone here has been great. So professional."

"I'm glad to hear it, although I would expect nothing less. I'm fortunate to have a superb team," Graham said.

Jason carried straight on. "Bringing us together like this on occasion is just *so* important. It's a huge job—I've lost count of how many phone calls I've had to make, or how many emails I've sent, chasing people up..."

"Or how many times we've had to switch the schedule around," Janice added. "But we can't really complain, right, Jason?"

"Absolutely not! A hundred delegates," he said, "in what's basically a brand-new venue..."

"Right down to the wiring and a new coat of paint," Janice said.

"...absorbing data on highly relevant topics pertinent to elevating the quality of modern-day policing. It's magnificent! Even if I fall under a bus tomorrow, I will feel my job here is done," Jason said. A huge grin spread across his boyish, attractive face.

"I sincerely hope there will be higher mountains for you to scale over your lifetime than organizing a conference on Jersey, but it is a credit to you. Very well done to you both," Graham said. "I can't imagine that kind of workload," he added, stretching the truth. It was the *type* of work he had issues with, work he could only too clearly imagine. "Like you say, so much admin. All that chopping and changing, *accommodating*."

"I was wondering if I might ask you," Jason said to Graham, closing in as they walked across the street, "about how you handle social media and other online coverage. Such a vital element of our work these days, don't you think?"

"An entirely new line of potential intelligence," Graham agreed, rather stiffly. "But very open to interpretation and often difficult to decipher."

"Hmm," Jason responded, his face falling a little. "Still, we ignore it at our peril, don't you think?"

"Of course," Graham conceded. "It has its place, and the ability of technology to extract evidence is a welcome development, but we have to be careful. In the wrong hands, problems occur."

There was feeling behind Graham's words. The ill-disciplined spread of local news via the internet was a constant thorn in Graham's side. He'd have loved the latitude to simply ignore his nemesis—the author of *The Gorey Gossip,* a blog written by self-proclaimed local "journalist," and in DI Graham's opinion, all-round muckraker, Freddie Solomon—but the man simply wouldn't give up. Just two days ago, Graham had told his girlfriend Laura that he found Solomon's self-serving blog to be, "painstakingly inaccurate." She'd laughed for the rest of the—

Oh, hell. He cringed inwardly. *Laura...*

CHAPTER THREE

"EXCUSE ME A second, Jason," Graham said.

As Roach led the group inside the *Foc's'le and Ferret*, the sergeant courteously holding open the old, wooden door for the others to file through, Graham found a string of new messages on his phone.

Hello David, how's the conference going? Once you're at liberty, I'd love to cook you some dinner. Let me know your ETA.

"Oh, for heaven's sake, man," Graham mumbled, furious at himself. The self-recrimination only grew as he read the two other messages.

Lamb curry? Can't promise it will be as spicy as the Bangkok Palace, but I'll try ;)

"Sorry, Laura, sorry, sorry, sorry," he muttered. Recently, they had made a habit of taking turns to cook dinner every Friday night. Tonight it would have been Laura's turn. He should have told her he would be unable to make it this week, not with all the officers in town. Graham turned to face the English Channel so that the sea alone noted his snapped-out, heartfelt curse.

Hurry! Still taking reservations but the dining room is filling up fast!

The time-stamp was from nearly an hour ago. Graham knew that Laura was probably using her sense of humor to mask genuine frustration. It wouldn't be the first time. Red-faced and regretful, he labored half-way through an apologetic text before deciding to call her instead. Standing outside the pub, he could hear Barnwell regaling someone with another tale of derring-do whenever the thick, wooden door opened.

"Beecham's House of Curries," Laura spoke into her phone. "May I take your order?"

"Laura, I'm so sorry!" he began.

"Ah, my favorite customer!" she continued. "How may I make your evening more enjoyable?"

"I'm sorry. Bloody phone," he told her. "I had to keep it silenced during the conference. I've only just picked up your texts. Anyway, how was your day?"

There was the sound of a pan being set on a stove, and a gas igniter clicking. "Not bad," she said. "The library was pretty quiet for a Friday. How's the conference going? Have you and the other superheroes solved Britain's policing problems yet?"

Graham smiled. "Car crime has been exterminated. We'll take care of drugs next. Terrorism's on Sunday."

She buttered him up in that way she always enjoyed. "Well, a seasoned professional like you..."

"Speaking of seasoning, was there talk of lamb curry?"

"Well, good food takes time, but it is a possibility. I was expecting you at seven."

There was no way Graham could socialize with the other officers sufficiently and make it to Laura's in half an hour. Thankfully, she didn't hear the brief burst of self-abuse, because it all happened inside his head. Instead, he said, "There's a gathering at the *Foc's'le and Ferret*, but I'll..."

Graham trailed off, only narrowly stopping himself from

banging his head on the pub's whitewashed wall. Once the day's conference sessions were over, the after-hours gathering in the pub, on a Friday night no less, had been as certain as last year's Christmas, but he had managed to double-book himself, all the same. "Look, I need to do my bit here, then I'll come straight over. I'll be a few hours, you know, as the senior hosting officer..."

A major exhalation of air sounded down the phone, but it was exaggerated, and Graham knew he'd gotten away with it. Again. It was more than he deserved.

"Shall I hold you to that?" Laura asked. Graham didn't have the best record of punctuality when it came to dates, sometimes through no fault of his own.

"You can depend on me." The pub door opened again, releasing a gust of laughter like a Jack from his box.

"Okay," she conceded. "But if you're late, and this curry dries up, you and I will have *words*, Detective Inspector Graham." He was relieved to hear there was a smile in her voice.

"I'm setting an alarm on my phone," he assured her.

"Make sure it's not on silent this time!" she reminded him. "Enjoy your schmoozing, and I'll see you later."

"Thanks, Laura. I mean, it." There was genuine remorse in his tone as Graham realized how much her support meant to him. He hadn't realized how much until just now. In that moment, he'd been frightened of losing her. He must do better.

"Och, awae wi' ye," Laura said, in a passable Scottish accent.

"See you later, love."

Graham took some deep breaths before heading into the pub. *How I deserve a woman like her, I have no idea.* He pushed open the door, narrowly avoiding bumping into DS Vincenti who was on his way out. They did a little dance before working out the choreography before Graham gratefully walked into the bar's welcoming warmth.

The February sun had long set, but the moon was bright and to his right, the pub's seaward windows offered a pleasing view of the harbor, the beach, and its wooden boardwalk. In the distance, he could make out the shadow of the forbidding hulk of Gorey Castle. The smokiness of the pub's roaring fire clung to him, making his nose twitch. From another room, he heard a burst of simultaneous laughter. To his left, dominating the wall opposite the bar, his fellow officers had pushed together tables around which several of them now sat.

"Sir, meet Detective Sergeants Kimberley Devine and Patrick O'Hearn, CID, Met," Harding said as Graham sat down next to her. She leaned in and whispered. "Very mysterious people. I'm sure you'll suss them out in twenty seconds flat."

"David Graham," he said, reaching his hand over the table to greet them. "Welcome to Jersey."

Kimberley was a slim, petite woman with pretty features, her dark hair cropped very short. A ring pierced her nose, and Graham noticed a stud through her tongue when she spoke, but they couldn't distract from her large, thick-lashed brown eyes and full lips. She appeared to have taken pains to make herself as plain as possible. She wore dark green camouflage cargo pants with scuffed black boots, and a man's button-down, checked blue shirt. On the bench behind her was a green parka jacket, the hood edged with fur.

As Graham had walked up, Kimberley had looked sullen, but on shaking his hand, her smile lit up her face and revealed two rows of perfect, small teeth. They so closely resembled a set of child's baby teeth that they triggered a memory deep in the recesses of Graham's brain, and he was assailed by a white-hot current of adrenaline that ran through his body into the ground.

The female officer set down her foam-peaked pint carefully. "Heard a lot from Superintendent Needham about you, sir. Has someone got you a drink?"

"I'll do the honors," Janice volunteered. "What's your poison, sir?"

Graham slapped his thighs to bring him back to the present. "Ah, let's have a La Mare," he said.

"Half or a pint?"

"A pint, please."

"Anyone else?" Janice looked around the table.

"Same for me, Sarge," Roach piped up. O'Hearn and Devine shook their heads. Janice stood and pushed her chair back to make her way to the bar.

CHAPTER FOUR

STANDING NEXT TO the shiny, bright wooden bar top, Janice found Superintendent Needham polishing off a half of Guinness. He pushed his lower lip over his upper to wipe off the foam residue that lay there. He smacked his lips. "Thirsty, sir?" Harding asked.

"For a good Guinness? Always," he said, signaling to the barman for another. "Can I stand you one?"

"I'm well taken care of, thank you, sir," Harding said, carefully balancing three brimming pints on a tray. She looked up to see Marcus Tomlinson, his bow tie slightly askew, stalking toward the bar with suspicion in his eyes. "Hello, Dr. Tomlinson!" Janice said, sidling past him, careful to protect her tray. The pub was filling up now with locals and delegates from the conference. "We're just over there in the corner."

"Yes, I saw. You're rather difficult to miss," the local pathologist said, teasing her. He leaned closer. "Especially for a group of detectives and you know, *undercover* people."

Janice laughed. "They throw off their invisibility cloaks," she told him, "when off-duty. Come and join us."

"Be there in a sec. First things first," Tomlinson said. "I'm hoping for a wine that isn't utterly dreadful." As Janice left him, the elderly pathologist began peppering the Friday night bartender with wine-related questions the young man could barely fathom.

Janice returned to the table followed by Needham. En route, they squeezed past Barnwell and Trevelyan who stood in the middle of the pub deep into a discussion about Liverpool's winning goal in the previous May's FA Cup Final.

"Where's Jason got to?" Graham asked. "I was looking forward to discussing social media and 21st century policing with him."

"Very funny, sir," Janice said.

"Saw him headed toward the Gents," Roach added. "P'raps you scared him half to death."

"So apart from both working at the Met, how do you know each other, sir?" Janice asked Graham as Needham plopped himself down rather heavily on the bench opposite. She handed Graham his drink.

"Superintendent Needham was my superior officer when I moved to Serious and Organized Crime. We go back a long way. Been through some things," Graham said.

"Haven't we just?" Needham echoed. "Seen a lot of changes."

"You more than me," Graham said. His decade or so with the police was far outstripped by Needham's length of service but soon their heads were almost touching as they leaned over the table and reminisced about past times.

"So, who's the bloke with the bow tie and facial hair?" DS Devine asked Janice.

"That's Dr. Tomlinson," Harding said, slightly offended at the description. "I might be biased, but he's the best medical examiner in a million miles. He's our forensic pathologist."

"Don't you find it hard to find the skills you need to work on advanced cases on an island this size?" O'Hearn asked. He was a big, beefy guy. Both his ears were thick, bumpy, and swollen. His biceps bulged under his tight, short-sleeved polo shirt, the cuffs of which strained to reach around the circumference of each arm. There was a small St. Christopher medallion around his neck.

"We pull in other specialists as we need them, and get support from forensics units on the mainland. Dr. Tomlinson's been training our Sergeant Roach," Janice said. "Isn't that so, Jim?"

"Spot on," Roach said. "I split my time between working with Dr. T and the constabulary." He glanced around quickly before speaking. "Tomlinson's a bit strange," he confided, "but I've learned a lot."

Harding laughed while O'Hearn commented, "He looks a bit stuffy."

"He's fine socially, but when he's working it's a bit like having a grumpy granddad who thinks he knows everything. Only this one *does* know everything." Roach glanced around again, reassured to see that Tomlinson was still mid-*contretemps* at the bar. "Just promise never to tell him I said that. He's talking about retiring soon, wants to write thrillers, apparently." The thought of such a prospect dimmed Roach's expression. "I might even miss the old boy."

"Are you going to take it further?" O'Hearn asked.

"Hmm?" Roach asked.

"The forensics side of the job, I mean. You could specialize."

"We could do with you in London. There's a *huge* shortage of good detectives with forensic skills. Woefully lacking we are, we miss a lot of collars because of it," Kimberley said.

"I've been thinking about it." Roach looked wistful. It had always been his ambition to spread beyond the shores of Jersey. He'd passed his sergeant's exam and broadened his skills, but now that greater things were within reach, he found himself hesitant. "But I like it here. I was born on Jersey. It would be a wrench, you know?" Jim's words glossed over an internal conflict he had avoided confronting. A little more experience he would tell himself, then he'd push off to the mainland for some real action. Each time he thought of it though, the pit in his stomach would grow. His mother would miss him.

"Nothing ventured, nothing gained," O'Hearn said.

"In a year or so," Roach replied, sipping his pint. "I need a bit more experience under my belt. After that, I guess we'll see."

Tomlinson, frustrated by the barman's lack of wine knowledge, had embarked upon an impromptu wine-tasting session at the bar. Having finally selected a Merlot he considered creditable, he took the seat next to DI Graham at the table. He set down his glass.

"So what's your verdict, Marcus?" Graham asked.

"Australian Merlot," Tomlinson said haughtily. "Far too sweet, but I believe I'll endure it." He turned to see a familiar face. "Wait a minute. You're Nigel Needham, aren't you?" Tomlinson appeared slightly surprised to find the man still alive.

"Yep, that's me. Been stuck with that name from the very start," Needham said, smiling. "We've met before. I never forget a face."

"Southwark Crown Court," Tomlinson said. "Missing young man turned up in the Thames. Angelo? Or was it Angelino?"

"Argento," Needham said, immediately. "Student from Paraguay, washed up near Embankment." Tomlinson squinted as he dug around searching for details of the case. He paused for too long and Needham helpfully added, "Quite literally stabbed in the back. Twice, as I remember."

"Oh, heavens, yes," Tomlinson said. "Kitchen knife wasn't it?"

"Found in the girlfriend's flat," Needham replied.

"That's the one," Tomlinson said, tilting his glass at Needham.

"She got life, served seventeen years. Not heard anything of her since," the senior policeman finished.

"One of my first criminal cases," Tomlinson said, frowning at his wine glass again. The wine was only *barely* tolerable. "Wasn't it '75, something like that?"

"March, '74," Needham said. "Good piece of police work, that was." He winked at Graham with unconcealed pride.

Before Graham could marvel out loud at Needham's ability to remember his past cases, he heard DS O'Hearn in his ear. "DI Graham?"

"Yes. You need me?" he asked, setting down his pint and turning to the younger man standing behind him.

"I've gotta take a call, sir, gonna be a while. Probably won't make it back tonight. Wanted to say thanks before I left. You know, for hosting and all that." O'Hearn had his phone in his hand, apparently mid-call. "This is a great little town," he added sincerely. "Quiet."

"Thanks. Hope you continue to enjoy your time here. See you tomorrow," Graham replied.

"Night, sir." O'Hearn offered his hand to Graham before gently bumping his way through the crowd to the door and the Jersey night.

CHAPTER FIVE

"AH, NICE AND warm," Barnwell said as he sat down.

"Never let it be said I don't do anything for you, Bazza," Jim replied.

Walking over from the middle of the pub, Barnwell and Trevelyan had split up, each taking a seat at either end of the table. Roach scooted over to O'Hearn's now-vacant seat to allow Barnwell to sit down. Trevelyan deposited himself next to Needham.

"Bobbies didn't even carry handcuffs in those days," Needham was saying to Tomlinson. "But it didn't matter so much. I was partnered with a very nice WPC called Brenda Smithson. She would clobber the perp with her regulation handbag. That always did the trick."

DI Graham turned his attention to Kimberley Devine. She sat silently across the table from him.

"So, Kimberley..." DI Graham started. "How long have you been with the Met?"

"Nine years, sir. Joined straight from school."

"So our time must have overlapped."

"Yes, sir. I heard about you, but we never met."

"You work with DS O'Hearn?"

"I do, sir. We work out of the same nick."

"Right. Aren't there supposed to be three of you?" Graham asked, looking around.

"DS Tom Vincenti," Kimberley said. "He came and went. Probably had to make a couple of calls, too."

"Ah yes, that's right. I bumped into him as I came in."

"He'll be back if he can." Then, more quietly, "We're in the middle of something. Lots of moving parts, things to keep track of."

Graham nodded and sipped his pint. He didn't normally drink beer, but after this long day it was the perfect refreshment.

DS Devine continued. "I nearly didn't make it down here myself. I didn't want to miss anything, you know, taking time away like this." She took a sip from her pint and set it down. "But Patrick insisted. Thinks he's my big brother or something." She rolled her eyes and gave a little smile, before leaning over the table. Graham mirrored her, creating an intimate conversational klatch in between the other two that were taking place on either side of them, one of which was emitting a roar of laughter as Barnwell shared a crude anecdote.

"We've got a lot of stuff in place. But not *quite* ready yet," Kimberley said. "Tom's been edgy. I'm hoping the sea air will..." Her eyes lowered to the table for a second before she added, "Let's just say it's good, you know, to get away for a few days."

Having had his own life scarred by the stress of undercover work, Graham nodded sympathetically. "I completely understand."

There was a scraping sound as Jason Ashby pulled a chair over. Graham shifted slightly to let him in. Kimberley leaned back, the sharing of secrets halted for now. She leaned over to listen to Barnwell.

"Now, er, Jason, isn't it?" Graham said.

The police event's organizer swiveled his head at the sound of his name. His blonde mop rose and fell like a dancer's frilly can-can skirt as he spun around. "Yes, sir."

"Jason is from the NPCC. He organized the conference with Sergeant Harding. Does a lot with social media too, I understand," Graham said to Tomlinson and Needham who he knew would be as excited by this information as he was.

"Yes! Social media is *such* an important tool these days," Jason said.

"Ah, so that explains why I've got an inbox full of stuff from you that I don't understand," Needham joked.

"Just trying to grow the reputation of the NPCC," Jason said. "The National Police Conference Committee," he spelled out in response to Needham's frown. "We're still a bit new, so I'm seizing any chance to raise awareness. I was hoping to talk to your computer guy," Jason added, nodding at Graham. "Is he here? Jack isn't it?" Graham pointed to Jack, who had just arrived. He was sitting next to Janice.

To Graham's relief, Jason politely excused himself and walked over to Jack. Hugging his drink to his chest, he offered his hand. "I'm Jason Ashby," he said.

"Jack Wentworth." Jack took Jason's hand. "Sergeant Harding's been talking a lot about you at home."

"It's 'Janice' when I'm in the pub," Harding said.

"Oh!" Jason exclaimed, unaware until now that Janice had a partner. He found another spare chair at a neighboring table and dragged it over. "Jack, I wonder if I can ask what DI Graham has you doing, generally speaking."

"Computer forensics, mostly," Jack said, lighting up. He was a good deal more animated by the process of his work than just about anyone else in the Gorey Constabulary and they were inordinately grateful for that. The results of his work had helped them crack cases. "But I'll stretch to forensic accounting, code-breaking, even basic tech support if I have to." He smiled modestly. "Police work is a side gig for me, really. Most of the time, I go around writing code, designing websites, fixing people's computers, that kind of thing. Anything to do with the guts of an IT system, I'm happy to try my hand at it. Janice is the constabulary's analyst. She works the police databases."

Janice cut in. "We have some pret-ty lively dinner conversations, I can tell you," she said. Her voice was flat, but her eyes shone, and there was amusement behind them. It wouldn't matter to her what she and Jack discussed. She loved having an easy-going, gorgeous man with whom to have dinner every night.

"Fascinating!" Jason gushed. "Wait, were you involved in that missing person's inquiry down here? Cold case, wasn't it? About the teenage girl, some months back?"

As Jack launched into the tale, Janice looked around for a distraction, allowing her boyfriend to lapse into impenetrable jargon about 'block chains' and '32-bit encryption.' No doubt Jason would soon tire of such subjects, but for now, he seemed captivated.

Barnwell and Roach were talking motorbikes so Janice approached the other end of the table where she found Nigel Needham robustly holding forth. "This was before CCTV, mind you," he was saying. "Back then, a detective's training was *intense*. Like a physician or a lawyer. You *had* to pay attention because you often saw the evidence only once. Isn't that right, Dave?"

"What did I miss?" Janice asked as she sat down in the seat Jason had pulled up earlier. "Tales from the trenches?"

"The super," Kimberley said, "is gracing us with an anecdote." She nodded at DI Graham.

"An anecdote? Not about our famously self-effacing DI?" Janice set down her drink and rubbed her hands. "Oooh, goody."

"Ancient history," Graham said, his eyes averted.

Janice turned to Needham. "He's being modest, which means you're singing his praises."

"I was. And I don't do that for just anyone," Needham said. "This was back when David was a DS, on a long stakeout—a council estate in Bromley. Drugs. He was quietly noting the comings and goings, you know, this guy selling to that guy, the time, the place, and so forth. We were building a case."

"You mean our favorite DI here actually came up through the ranks, like everyone else?" Tomlinson asked. "I'd always assumed he was the result of a genetic experiment in the basement of Scotland Yard."

"David Graham as a lowly detective sergeant," Janice marveled. "Imagine."

Graham winced, shaking his head, but he took this gentle ribbing as a good sign. They'd all come a long way since he'd first arrived on Gorey.

Needham barreled onward. "So we were trying to connect David's evidence to another gang from across town," he said. "They were selling the same product, and it was cut in the same way, so we knew if we could find the middle-man..."

"You could nab him for possession with intent to supply," Devine said.

"And then squeeze him until he gave you something on the others higher up the chain," Janice added.

"That's right. We had details of a suspect's vehicle, a Ford Focus that we hoped we could use to make a connection, but the problem," Needham explained, "was that David had no note of it. It was a long-shot, I mean, one in a million, but we showed him a photo of the car. And then... well, it's hard to explain. David went a bit *funny* for a minute."

Silence had fallen around the group as Needham told his tale. From Janice to Tomlinson, Roach, Barnwell, and Wentworth, the whole team was nodding. "Like he's standing there, waiting to be struck by lightning," Barnwell said.

"Or awaiting a signal from his home planet," Roach tried.

"So, what did Detective Sergeant Graham come up with?" Janice asked.

"It was amazing!" Needham said. "There was nothing about it in his notes, but David was able to give us the dates and times of *four* visits the Ford Focus had made to the estate, purely from memory."

"It was the number plate," Graham said. "And some damage to the right-hand passenger door. Just happened to stick in my mind."

Needham flapped his hand at his former protégé. "Psshhtt, he's being modest. I suppose he's still doing that kind of thing?"

"What, pulling up details the rest of us hadn't even noticed?" Janice said.

"Days after the event, sometimes weeks?" Roach added.

"Yeah, that's his favorite pastime," Barnwell concluded. "Making us all look a right bunch of mugs."

CHAPTER SIX

NOT AT ALL interested in mentions of himself, Graham turned to observe the group around the table. Barnwell and Roach had begun to relate to Jack some of the DI's more recent feats of mental gymnastics. Janice was charming Trevelyan with stories of policing Gorey before Graham's arrival. Needham and Marcus Tomlinson chatted quietly, the superintendent drawing a diagram on the tabletop with his finger.

With them all engaged, Graham's eyes wandered again to the officer who sat quietly across the table from him. There was a change in DS Devine's expression. She had been silent for a few minutes, and after glancing at her phone several times, seemed out-of-sorts. Graham caught her eye long enough for her to see him shake his head ever so slightly and raise an eyebrow. "Everything okay?" he asked her.

Devine grimaced slightly. Her eyelids flickered.

Graham made a guess. "Bad news on your investigation?" he asked sympathetically.

Devine leaned forward and invited him to do the same. Under the table, she shuffled her feet, "I think my cover's blown."

Graham frowned. "Oh?" His heart rate ticked up.

"Yeah, this op I'm on, it's starting to unravel. Patrick's been in there for months. Tom too, on and off. I was just gathering intel." Graham knew the scenario well. "I started getting these texts a few hours ago." She hesitated for a second, then showed Graham the screen of her phone.

"Ugly," he said of the messages. They were angry, semi-literate demands to be left alone, all in the foulest of language. "Very ugly. You should talk to Jack. He might be able to help with tracking the source of those texts."

Kimberley put her phone away in her pocket and looked at Graham. "I don't want to get taken off the squad, you know?"

"You need to tell your handler."

Kimberley blew air slowly through her full lips. "I want to make sure there's a pattern."

"Why do you need to do that? Seems pretty solid to me," Graham said, his heart sinking. "This is no time to play the hero. You'll be in danger the moment you arrive back in London." He went to wag his finger at her, before thinking better of it. Instead, he stuck his hand in his pocket. "You need to face up to the fact that you'll have to take a back seat in the investigation or get pulled from it altogether."

"Yeah," Kimberley said morosely. "But this one really got under my skin. Wanted to bring it in, you know?"

"I do," Graham answered, genuinely. "But you've been breached. And these people don't sound like they're mucking around."

"I'll be careful," she promised. "Listen, I think I'll call it a night. Thank you for making us all welcome. Being here is a nice change of pace. A luxury spa weekend compared to what I normally deal with."

"You're very welcome. Do you need someone to walk with?

Barnwell could accompany you. Roach might even offer you a lift on his motorbike if we ask nicely."

"Nah, I can handle myself, and this is hardly a place of high crime, now is it?

Graham raised his hand and waggled it from side to side. "We've had our moments. It's not all white-collar crime and tax evasion here, you know." At DS Devine's blank look, he explained. "Jersey is a tax haven. It attracts wealthy people looking to avoid paying their fair share. Inevitably, the business dealings of a few of them are not always on the up and up."

"Ah, gotcha. I'll be fine, thanks for the offer, though."

Graham's eyes darkened. "Are you sure? It's no trouble."

"Quite sure, thanks," the woman said firmly. She stood and squeezed her way past Roach and Barnwell, smiling broadly and saying her goodbyes. Happy, glowing faces were raised to her, but as she passed by them, Devine dropped her smile. She dipped her head and lifted the fur-edged hood of her parka to shroud her face as she prepared to withstand the wintry air outside.

A knot of disquiet grew in the center of Graham's chest, but as Devine reached out to open the interior door, he felt a rush of air behind him. There was a shout. A second later Graham was violently shoved from behind, roughly pushing him forward, his chest narrowly missing his pint on the table. Next to Graham, Janice quickly looked up. She put a quelling hand on Graham's arm and the flash of anger that had him half out of his seat subsided.

"Sh-orry, matey." Next to Graham, a man with drops of ale in his beard and unfocused rheumy eyes stood unsteadily. "Come on, Fergus. Time to go." Lewis Hurd, the *Fo'c'sle and Ferret's* head barman, stepped in quickly and bundled the drunken man away. The lapsed conversations resumed quickly. Graham took a calming sip of his pint.

"Alright, sir?" Janice said.

"Yeah, I'm fine," he replied.

"You seem a bit on edge."

"No, I'm good. Just took me by surprise, that's all. Instinct took over." He smiled and took another quick sip.

Next to him, Marcus rose from his chair. "Forgive me for rushing off, David. You'd think I'd have been meticulous about it, what with me being a medical man, but my flight's tomorrow morning, and I've not even *begun* to pack."

"Napa Valley, wasn't it? California?"

Marcus painted Graham a picture of a sunlit paradise. "Nice little vineyards with interesting new varietals," he said, his eyes closed as he conjured the scene in his mind. "Long, relaxing afternoons spent learning from expert vintners and sampling the goods. I plan to finally spend some of my retirement savings and build myself an excellent cellar. I'll have it flown back if necessary."

"No one deserves it more, Marcus," Graham said. "Have a great time."

"I'll walk out with you," Needham said. "I'm getting too old for this." He waved his hand around the table at the officers who were at most half his age and clearly energized by the evening. All of them were smiling, laughing, chatting animatedly, listening intently over the hubbub, or drinking.

"Speak for yourself, old boy," Marcus replied.

"Thanks for coming," Graham said. "Say hello to Mrs. Taylor for me, Nigel."

"Mrs. Taylor?" Needham frowned.

"The owner of the *White House Inn*. Where you're staying."

"Oh yes. Will do."

CHAPTER SEVEN

MIKE TREVELYAN MOVED out from behind the table so that Needham could pass him. "'Night all," Needham called out to the group. "Don't do anything I wouldn't do." Tomlinson raised a hand. He draped a red silk paisley scarf around his neck and buttoned his classy camel overcoat. Everyone at the table murmured or waved their farewells to the two senior men, some wishing Tomlinson a good vacation. Janice took advantage of the flurry of action to slip back to Jack's side.

With the junior ranks all now firmly ensconced at the other end of the table, Graham turned to his old friend. "How's the family, Mike?"

"Hectic, you know how things are. Girls." Trevelyan stifled a wince as he realized what he'd said. In addition to training with Graham, they'd been on the same team when news had come that Graham's young daughter, Katie, had been killed in a car accident. "I've brought one of the girls with me, Tiffany."

"Tiffany." Graham cast his mind back. "She must be, what? 12 now?"

"Seventeen, mate. Full of life." Again, Mike Trevelyan realized his faux pas too late. This time he allowed his wince to show.

"Seventeen? Really? Time flies." Graham looked down at his pint and swirled what was left of his drink around the bottom of the glass.

"Yeah, gotta keep them busy. Out of trouble, you know?" Trevelyan cleared his throat. He was sweating. "This is good beer, man," he said looking at his mostly empty pint glass. There was a small amount of pale ale in the bottom.

"Lost Tourist. It's brewed on Guernsey. We're surprisingly well set with local breweries across the islands. Some nice craft ales."

"Huh, who knew?" Mike leaned forward, his elbows on the table, glad to be off the tricky subject of daughters. "So how *are* things in the bustling metropolis of Jersey?"

Graham smiled at the gentle ribbing. "They're good, Mike. Good."

"Like how good? Really good? Or just somewhat good. Come on mate, you can tell me. We were all worried about you when you decided to make your way down here."

"I like it. It's... different. Quieter, certainly. But honest, decent. A good place to get my head straightened out after... everything."

Trevelyan took a deep breath. "And how is that? That everything." They were talking in code, but Graham knew what Trevelyan meant. After his daughter's death, and his marriage breakup.

"It's okay. We move on, don't we? We have to. I have my moments, but mostly things are okay."

"Anyone new on the horizon?"

"There is actually... Oh, good grief." Graham looked at his watch. "And I should have been there half an hour ago. Look, sorry, I have to go." He thought of Laura waiting in her cottage for him, alone. He hadn't taken his phone off silent like she had told him. Would he ever learn?

Mike Trevelyan waved his pint glass at Graham who was standing now, reaching for his coat. "Far be it for me to stand between a mate and his *mate*. I just hope to meet her before my visit is over." He winked and took a final swig of his Lost Tourist.

Graham buttoned his coat and turned to the group. Barnwell was holding court, though Graham couldn't hear enough over the noise of the now-busy Friday night crowd to judge which tale of heroism was being pulled from him this time. "Right, folks, I'm off. Remember, it's nine o'clock *sharp* for the first session tomorrow, so take it easy on the sauce. Alright?"

"Righto, sir," Barnwell said, "I'll make sure no one turns into a pumpkin."

"Enjoy your date, sir," Janice said from behind her pint. To Graham's horror, the table chorused a salacious cheer.

"Settle down, you lot," he said, cringing with embarrassment. "Nothing to see here. 'Night all. Behave yourselves." He left behind a cloud of guesswork and gossip, but DI Graham had a lamb curry waiting for him. At least he hoped he had. He didn't even want to think about the alternative.

A blast of cold air hit his face as he pulled open the pub door. He rubbed his hands against the frigid night's temperature. The streetlight a few yards away illuminated the road that sloped down to the street that curled around the harbor. In the distance, there was the shadow of Gorey Castle again standing silent and proud just as it had since 1204. A tortoiseshell cat sat in the middle of the quiet cobbled street looking at him steadily.

"Off home, are you?" Tom Vincenti asked, panting slightly. He was a few feet away. He began walking toward him up the hill. Light from the streetlamp reflected off his shiny forehead. Vincenti pressed a button on his phone and put it in his pocket. He sniffed.

"Afraid so," Graham said. "There might even be a dinner waiting for me." *Or thrown at me.*

"It's quite a thing you've done, putting on a show like this. Really."

"Thanks. We're happy to host. It feels good to show off our island and modest constabulary like this." Graham nodded down at Vincenti's jean pocket. "Still taking calls at this time of night?"

"Yeah, never stops, does it?"

"No, it never does."

In the distance, Graham heard a familiar noise. A two-tone siren. He knew he would soon see blue lights. As the sound got closer, the siren of another vehicle mingled with it creating a disruptive, staccato cacophony. Watching from their spot higher up, Graham and Vincenti saw and heard the flashing blue and twos of an ambulance that shot along the road below, closely followed by those of a St. Helier police unit. Two seconds later, the local fire department SUV raced after them. Then two more police vehicles.

Bloody hell. Graham roughly pulled the pub door open nearly colliding with a couple of tourists. "Sorry, sorry," he gasped as he ducked around them. "Harding! Barnwell! Roach! Now!"

The three members of Gorey Constabulary looked up at him in alarm. There followed a flurry of activity and noise as chairs were pushed back, jackets were donned, and belongings collected before the three officers chased their Detective Inspector out of the pub into the cold night air.

CHAPTER EIGHT

G RAHAM GOT THERE first. The scene in front of him spread out as he'd seen it so often. Blue lights flickered, lighting up everything intermittently. The police units parked haphazardly, blocking off the road at each end, diverting the occasional car around the incident site. Here and there, small groups of onlookers murmured or stood silently, their arms folded, their silhouettes shrouded by moisture evaporating off their bodies in the cold. Walking toward Graham, a constable from St. Helier unwound police caution tape as she sealed off the scene, ushering the onlookers behind it as she walked along.

But it was in the center of the street that Graham focused his attention. Two paramedics crouched, administering paddles. Their green hi-viz uniforms stood out. Above them, a streetlight lit up their theater aided by headlights and lamps on their foreheads. Graham made out two booted feet. The boots were small. Suddenly, they moved in unison. A fur-edged hood hid the victim's face, but Graham's blood ran cold when he saw it. The body twitched again. The hood fell away. Hell's teeth, it was

Kimberley Devine. She lay on her back, her face to one side, her nose ring twinkling in the half-light.

Graham felt hot even while his skin chilled. He could feel sweat blooming above his upper lip. He looked around. "What's up?" he asked. He didn't recognize this young officer from St. Helier. He flashed his ID. "DI Graham. Gorey. This is my patch. I've just arrived."

"Looks like a hit-and-run, sir. Not looking too good. No sign of the vehicle that hit her." The policewoman turned away, unrolling her tape before tying it off and moving on.

"What have we got, sir?" Roach arrived at his shoulder, Janice and Barnwell not far behind, thankful they were racing downhill.

"Kimberley Devine has been hit."

Vincenti ran up, his eyes wide, "Devine?" He pushed past Roach, but Graham, determined to keep control, put his hand on Vincenti's chest. "You'll go no further. This is my jurisdiction. I'm in charge."

Vincenti dragged his eyes from the sight of DS Devine's body to meet Graham's gaze, his pupils tiny, and his breath freezing in front of him. Seeing in Graham a determination that it was pointless to debate, he nodded and dropped his eyes.

As Graham walked over, the paramedics rocked back on their heels. It was the sign he had been dreading. It was over. "Are you sure?" he asked the backs of their heads.

They turned, and Graham recognized Sue Armitage and Alan Pritchard. Sue was an experienced medic who would know a lost cause when she saw one. She looked up at him, her face pale against the blue of the emergency lights, but her tone matter-of-fact. "She was DOA. No one could survive these injuries." Sue got up and brushed road dirt from her knees while her partner packed away their equipment. "We've paged the doc."

"Right, if you would stand down. This is now a crime scene," Graham said, his voice gruff. Up close, he could see Devine's blue lips, the way her head hung awkwardly to one side, a trail of blood that streamed from her ear. Her mouth was open, her lips pressed back, those small, childlike teeth white against the gray, waxy pallor of her pretty face. Graham's knees gave a little. He thought back to their exchange in the pub. *Nah, I can handle myself.*

"Are you alright, sir?" the young patrol officer from St. Helier interrupted him. "My superior is on his way."

"Thanks for your support, but we'll deal with it," Graham said tersely. He breathed in deeply through his nose.

"But, sir..." Words faded on the young copper's lips as she took in Graham's expression. "Yes, sir," she conceded quietly. She traipsed off, murmuring into her radio about territory concerns way above her pay grade.

Graham shoved his hands in his pockets and stared down at Devine's body. Her face told the story of her death—a look of surprise. "Confirm the scene is sealed, Sergeant, and start interviewing the witnesses," he said to Harding, nodding at the group of onlookers who were still loitering.

They heard a slapping of feet on the street surface and looked up. It was Patrick O'Hearn. "Kimberley! Kimberley!"

Barnwell moved swiftly to intervene. He body checked the burly officer, the only one of them with the size and strength to do so. "Back up, man, back up."

"But..."

"You know the drill. Back *up.*" Barnwell's face went red, his voice tight, as he strained to hold O'Hearn.

Anguish was plain on the big man's face. He panted and stared wild-eyed at Devine's body some feet in the distance until Tom Vincenti quietly spoke in O'Hearn's ear. The younger man tensed, then sagged, and with Vincenti's hand on his shoulder, O'Hearn let himself be slowly walked to a bench next to a bus stop.

"Sir, the scene is sealed. Roach is organizing the St. Helier team," Janice said. Twenty yards away, four uniformed policemen stood around Roach listening and nodding as he pointed with his long arm.

That smile, those childlike teeth. Graham closed his eyes, pinching his eyelids tight as he wrestled with his emotions. He let out a long exhale. "Right, let's get to it. Barnwell, alert the port authority and tell the airport. I don't want any vehicle or person leaving the island until we know more. We'll work through the night to get this scene processed and update them then."

"Yes, sir." Barnwell peeled away as he pulled out his phone.

"Harding, take over from Roach, would you? Send Roach over here, I want him on forensics." Graham gestured at the small crowd that had gathered. "We'll start a formal house-to-house in the morning, but approach any homes or businesses that have their lights on now. We might get something."

"Yes, sir." Janice jogged away.

"Look for CCTV," Graham called out after her as he looked around fruitlessly for cameras mounted on the outside of the surrounding buildings.

"Willing to help, Dave. Where d'you want me?" Mike Trevelyan had run as fast as the rest of them to the scene.

"We'll need to do a fingertip search of the area. If you can muster any of the guys to give us a hand, we'll get it done quicker. Word must be out by now, and it'll give them something to do."

"As good as done." Trevelyan turned at the sound of shouts and saw the truth of Graham's statement as half a dozen young men and women ran toward the scene.

"Sir, you have a job for me?" Roach said, running up.

"Roach, I need you to work with Marcus on the forensics. Start photographing the area and pay particular attention to any evidence that's about. Mike's organizing a fingertip search. Bag anything, *anything*, you hear? We've got to pull out all the stops." Graham made to walk away. "And get ready for a long haul. We won't be getting much sleep tonight."

"Not the kind of long haul I was expecting if I'm honest, David." Graham turned to see Marcus Tomlinson wading toward him, his "bag of tricks" in his left hand. He'd exchanged his classy camel coat and paisley scarf for paper overalls, booties, and a pair of latex gloves. He looked grim as he marched towards Graham. "Long haul *flight* was more what I had in mind." Graham blinked. "Show me," Tomlinson said.

"Take a careful look at this one, Marcus."

Tomlinson took the time to look mildly offended. "I always do, squire."

"Yeah, I know, but really look. It might not be straightforward." Graham was reluctant to voice his suspicions to Tomlinson, to anyone. He didn't want to hear himself saying them. *I think my cover's blown.*

Tomlinson looked down and let out a long sigh. "That flight isn't going to happen, is it?"

Graham acknowledged the truth of the pathologist's statement with a nod. "If I had to guess, probably not."

"Alright, leave me be. I'll let you know when I'm done."

Roach was crouching over the body, the flash from his camera illuminating it momentarily every few seconds. Bright, shattered glass, both clear and yellow, was strewn across the road's surface. It glittered with every explosion of light, contrasting with the dismaying, clearly visible patch of blood, black against the tarmac. "Should we contact the family?" he asked.

"No, a copper from her home nick will visit them. But by the looks of it," Graham looked over at Vincenti and O'Hearn huddled over a phone, "they might already know."

Soon, if not already, a father would hear words that every parent dreaded, words that Graham had heard, once. *Your daughter is dead.* Graham closed his eyes and exhaled. He remembered Kimberley's words in the pub. *This is hardly a place of high crime, now is it?*

She had needed protection. He should have insisted. He had

failed her. Memories, fragmented but sharp, floated across his consciousness, coated with guilt. He had failed Kimberley Devine just like he had failed his daughter.

He should have worked less, been more present in Katie's life. With Kimberley, he could have intervened, informed her handler. But he'd made mistakes. He had allowed his feelings to get in the way. He had gotten distracted. And if he hadn't, if he'd been different, he could have knocked both of them from a path to disaster. And they might both be alive now, too.

CHAPTER NINE

JANICE RUBBED HER hands together. As she walked down Gorey High Street, the pale February sun was just starting to dawn over the tops of the buildings that bordered it. A pedestrian, a newspaper under their arm, walked a dog along the opposite side of the street. Despite the hour and the chill, it was unnaturally quiet and subdued. Short lengths of yellow police tape incompletely removed during the night fluttered pointlessly in the breeze. It was the only sign that a few hours prior this stretch of road had been the scene of a fatal traffic accident.

Despite her years in the force, Janice was always struck by the speed with which normality wiped away tragedy. Those unaffected by the sudden and dramatic turn of events quickly returned to the comfort of the familiar while those impacted were forced to play a mind game that split them in two, their eyes seeing one thing, their memories protesting another. It was as though routine was an unstoppable force, only ever delayed, never halted.

The street had been open to traffic for a couple of hours and the odd car drove steadily by. Graham was standing outside a bakery, looking hard at his notebook. Harding approached him at a brisk trot. At 4 a.m., he'd sent her home for a few hours kip. She doubted he had had any at all.

"Janice. Morning," he said. His face was lined. Dark circles were apparent under his eyes. "I'd ask you how your night was, but I think I know." He smiled weakly.

"What would you like me to do, sir?"

"Help Barnwell finish the house-to-house, then we can get out of here. I'm waiting for Marcus. He worked through the night and has done the autopsy already. He's bringing the results with him."

"Did the fingertip search turn up anything?"

"I don't believe so. Roach took everything they found but didn't appear too hopeful. Glass fragments mostly."

Janice wandered off in search of Barnwell and found him purposefully approaching what she knew was yet *another* door. Gorey High Street was a mixture of shops, service businesses, and residences. Nearly all of them were housed in former fishermen's cottages. Barnwell knocked smartly. "Gorey Police, could you open the door please, love? No trouble, just wanted to ask..."

Janice took the next house, and they alternated down one side of the street, interviewing shoppers, homeowners, and the odd weekend worker. She banged on the door of *Gorey Gifts & Sweets*. After a few seconds, the door opened and a stressed gray-haired woman in her mid-forties opened the door. She was red-faced, panting slightly.

"Ah, at last! You're here." the woman said, eyeing Janice's three stripes. "And a sergeant too. Good, good."

"Erm, sorry ma'am. Can I help you?"

"Yes, you can. Come in. I've been burgled. I called 999 two hours ago."

Janice stepped inside the small shop and as soon as she did so, she could see why the woman was so harried. The place had been ransacked. The floor was littered with gift items. Janice noted china plates, jigsaw puzzles, tea towels, calendars, aprons, oven gloves, little china animals, children's books, books on Jersey's history. They were tossed about the floor. Scattered between them were sticks of rock, bars of posh chocolate, and various types of hard-boiled sweets that Janice remembered from her childhood—pear drops, lemon sherbets, and licorice.

"What's been taken? Can you tell?" Janice was taken aback. Even though the floor of the tiny shop was almost entirely covered with the shop's stock, the shelves, counters, and tables, even the walls—every flat surface—were covered with yet more.

"Of course I can. We're missing a goddess charm bracelet in sterling silver, a pair of amethyst earrings, a scented candle, and a box of *Hotel Chocolat* artisan chocolates. I'm sure there's more, but it will take some time to note it all."

Janice typed this in to a burglary report form. "And your name, ma'am?"

"Jennifer Skinner."

"Where did they get in? Do you know?"

"From around the back. Broke the window in the door and undid the catches."

"Alarm?"

"I don't have one. Have never needed it. My parents managed this shop before me and this is the first time we've been burgled."

"Any CCTV?"

Jennifer Skinner looked at Janice as though she'd asked her to spell   Llanfairpwllgwyngyllgogerychwyrndrobwllllantysilio-gogogoch—the longest place name in Britain.

"Thank you, Ms. Skinner..."

"Mrs. Skinner."

"Right." Janice corrected herself. "Mrs. Skinner. We're very busy with a fatal hit-and-run that happened further down the street overnight, but we'll get to you just as soon as we can."

'Yes, I heard about that. I'm so sorry. What should I do about this, though?" Mrs. Skinner surveyed the floor of her shop.

"You can go ahead and tidy up, take stock, and update the list of items stolen. Please leave the area around the door as it is. I'll get a Scenes of Crimes Officer to you as soon as I can. They'll dust for fingerprints. Is there anything else you can tell me about the incident?"

Mrs. Skinner sighed. "I'm afraid not, Sergeant. I locked up at 8 p.m. I found this mess at six this morning. That's it."

"Well, thank you, Mrs. Skinner. We'll be in touch." Janice forwarded the burglary report to St. Helier police. She added a quick note to request a SOCO attend the premises and closed her tablet screen down.

CHAPTER TEN

T HIRTY FRUITLESS MINUTES later, Barnwell and
Harding were back at the scene of the hit-and-run with
Graham.

"Let me get this straight." The DI turned to face uphill,
toward 'inner Gorey' as he thought of it, and beyond that, the
genuinely rural part of his patch. "The vehicle must have traveled up the High Street from the south," he began. "He or she
had to cross over a set of lights at Egmont Street and then a
pedestrian crossing just over there by the bank," he continued,
pointing. He turned to follow the car's theoretical path down the
hill.

"Someone waiting at the lights might have seen him come
through," Barnwell said. "Doesn't the CCTV show anything?"

Graham pinched the bridge of his nose. "Yeah, I was all
excited about that, too. Control at St. Helier sent me the feed
within minutes. Want to see what we've got?" The DI's new
phone had an adequate screen, and he showed Harding and
Barnwell what he had hoped would be the fateful seconds.

"Oh, you must be having a bloody laugh," Barnwell breathed as the disappointing footage rolled.

"We've got a car coming down the hill, fair enough, but it's in and out of shot and nothing at all of the impact. We can't even be certain that this was the car that hit her. We're going to have to presume based on the time stamp and the erratic driving." Graham paused, inviting his team to name an even more troubling problem.

"And it was pitch dark," Janice said, "and these old cameras are near useless beyond sunset. I can't even make out what type of car it is."

She braced herself for an explosion, but Graham had dealt with his frustration in the early minutes of the morning. Now, he limited himself to a curt summation of the case. "None of us have slept worth a damn. The CCTV footage is so awful we can't even tell for sure what *make or color* the car is. There's nothing from the ports or the airport..."

"Or our inquiries, sir," Barnwell added.

Graham took a deep breath. "I reckon the next person we'll be investigating for murder is going to be me. I could literally strangle someone."

"Morning all!" They turned to see Marcus Tomlinson. Despite his age and lack of sleep, he looked remarkably fresh. "Jim's working on the glass fragments found at the scene," he said. "I've got the post mortem results. Could we talk somewhere quiet?"

"Coffee, anyone?" Two hours of house-to-house inquiries following a sleepless night had left Barnwell in need of a pick-me-up.

"Marcus, do you want anything?" Graham said.

"I'm fine. I drank so much coffee during the night, I'll float across the Channel if I have any more."

"Tea, sir?"

Graham thought of the lukewarm and stewed orange brew

that would undoubtedly be dispensed in a squeaky polystyrene cup. He wrinkled his nose. "No, thanks."

As Barnwell and Harding left to find a café, Graham and Marcus disappeared inside *Bloomers & Baguettes*. It was an independent bakery that serviced the bread and pastry needs of the Gorey locals, and the baker owner had given Graham the use of his large storeroom as soon as he'd arrived in the early hours to find the street full of police activity. It had quickly become their on-site incident command center.

"What have you got, Marcus?" Graham asked once they were alone in the room. They were surrounded by shelves weighted down with flour and the powdery air laced with the fragrance of freshly baked bread tickled his nose and made his mouth water.

Tomlinson cleared his throat and nudged his glasses back up his nose. "At the risk of stating the obvious, DS Devine was hit by a car. The call came in just after 10 p.m., and given the state of her body and the cold night, I'd put her time of death shortly before that. Her injuries were extensive, and I suggest that she was struck at fifty miles per hour, perhaps faster. You've seen enough of these to know the rest, David," Tomlinson said, hopefully.

"Tell me."

It wasn't the first time Tomlinson had had to describe injuries that caused the death of a colleague, but the blind, senseless cruelty of it was enough to bother even a seasoned medical examiner. "Her left femur was shattered. There's a deep, wedge-shaped bone injury we used to call a Messerer fracture of her leg. Entirely consistent with being struck by a regular-sized family car. Not an SUV or anything bigger."

Graham made notes. "Right," he said quietly.

"The speed of the impact can be judged by the manner of her injuries."

"And necessary because," Graham couldn't help grousing, "our CCTV is bloody *useless*."

"Like I said, the impact was fifty or higher. That's the only way she'd have been thrown skyward like that. And we know that she was thrown up because of the initial impact injuries and the secondaries she incurred when she came down."

"What if the car speed had been lower?" Graham asked, framing the arguments in his mind.

"A bit slower, and she'd have bounced off the car into the road, often because those victims are run over by the vehicle before it can stop. High-speed impacts are so rarely survivable because the victim suffers *three* injuries, not one." Tomlinson arranged his hands to mock up the scene. "Leg injuries from the first collision, head and chest wounds from the impact with the vehicle on the way down, and then tertiary injuries from hitting the ground. We see all three in this case."

"Be specific, Marcus," Graham said, his teeth clenched lockjaw tight. "Don't spare me."

CHAPTER ELEVEN

"FRACTURED STERNUM, AS well as heavy bruising to her pelvis and a broken leg, the latter both on the right side." Tomlinson read from his report. "That tells us she was standing or walking at around ninety degrees to the central line of the vehicle."

"Crossing the road? Or half-turned to see what the noise was?" Graham speculated.

"Anyone's guess. But the actual cause of death was a linear skull fracture, suffered when she landed and hit the roadway. That led to major epidural bleeding inside the skull. Her injuries weren't survivable, the skull fracture was too serious, and I found severe *contre-coups* injuries to her brain."

"Slammed back and forth in her skull," Graham said, unhappily visualizing the fatal moment. "Like an extremely severe concussion."

"Yes, indeed. There are also impact injuries to her shoulder, neck, and ear consistent with falling on that same right side, and then rolling several times to a stop."

None of this was unexpected, but Graham's commitment to thoroughness was absolute.

"There were no fresh marks on the road surface, nothing to indicate the driver tried to stop or swerve out of the way. So either the driver didn't see her *at all* and then drove away from the scene once they realized what they'd done. Or it was intentional, and she was murdered. Okay, we're looking for a damaged car possibly with a dented roof, grill, and a cracked or missing windshield. The same vehicle will almost certainly have a smashed indicator light."

"Or a broken headlamp cover," Barnwell said, appearing as he brushed aside the strips of rainbow-colored plastic that acted as a door curtain separating the stock room from the rest of the bakery.

"Or both," Harding added following Barnwell into the room. They both carried extra-large white, takeout cups. "Especially if the impact was offset, and not down the centerline. Like you said, sir, he was in and out of shot like he was doing the slalom down the hill. Could have hit her at any angle."

"Barnwell, I want you down at the ferry terminal," Graham said, bringing out his phone. "Tell them they can get going again, but have them stop any vehicles that have the kind of damage we're looking for." Graham looked at his watch, it was nearly 9 a.m. He'd halted the ferry schedule for three hours and he was not popular with the ferry company. "They're probably backed up right now, so take a look around at the vehicles that are waiting to board while you're at it. We need to find that car."

"Right, boss. The planes are flying. Any change there?"

"They're good. They have flight logs, passenger lists, and CCTV. The vehicle is the priority. If we find the car, we'll find the driver. What about color, make, Marcus? Anything you can tell us?"

"Not yet. The glass fragments at the scene might help us, but we lack the resources to examine them thoroughly. They need to go to the mainland. Do you want us to prioritize that?"

"Yes." Graham turned to Janice. "What time is your presentation?"

"Eleven, sir."

"Right, Barnwell, when you're done with the ferry people, I want you at the pub. Speak with the bar staff, see if they noticed anything. Perhaps someone spoke to Kimberley or followed her. They were some of the last people to see her alive."

"We were, too," Barnwell pointed out.

"Hmm?" Graham was dialing a number.

"The group of us, in the pub. Last to see her..."

"Indeed. I'll interview her team at the station later today." Graham spoke into his phone. "Roach? What's the latest?" He nodded, apparently satisfied. "Roach has found some glass fragments on her clothes. Just a couple of small ones on Devine's jacket," he told the small group around him. "But they look like they match those found in the road so we can presume they are from the car that hit her."

"Well, that's something," Barnwell said.

"Alright, lad. Well done," Graham said into his phone. He looked over at Tomlinson. "I'm asking Marcus to release you into the wild for a bit. Have you head to Portsmouth and show those fragments to the lab." There was a pause as Roach spoke at the other end of the line, "Yes, I'm serious. Their crime lab is ten times more sophisticated than ours. Besides, you might learn something." There was another pause. "That'll take too long, lad! Get yourself on a flight, pronto."

Puzzled at the sight, Graham saw Harding waving him to a halt. "No, sir. Can't. He doesn't fly," she said.

"Eh?"

"Nervous passenger," Janice explained quietly. "Only done it once. Said it was like two hours of dental surgery," she said, tapping a molar through her cheek.

"Well, he wasn't too hot on a ferry last time I traveled with him. either. Look, we can't hold up an investigation for that. He needs to get over it." Janice winced as Graham spoke into his phone again. "There's a flight in an hour, get yourself on it."

CHAPTER TWELVE

"H E CAN'T BE happy about the timing," Barnwell said, as they watched Marcus Tomlinson drive away. "Wasn't he due to fly off on holiday?"

"Yeah," Graham said. "But that's how it goes sometimes. All bets are off when something like this happens. Plans are swiped away quicker than a..." *Plans.* With a blow-like a fist to the solar plexus, a thought occurred to him. Since the devastation of the hit-and-run the night before, he'd had no sleep, an investigation to lead, territory issues to manage, an emotional and concerned Chief Constable to deal with, and a team to rally. All this in full view of some of the top policemen in the country who were now unfocused and listless as they attempted to wrench their minds from the death of one of their own to whatever was top of the agenda at the conference this morning. At least his position that the conference still go ahead had prevailed. But that was no excuse. He'd spoken to Laura nearly *sixteen hours ago* and hadn't contacted her since. She hadn't contacted him, either. Now he'd come to realize his error, her silence was deafening "Oh, hell."

514 ALISON GOLDEN & GRACE DAGNALL

Graham reached for his phone and tapped and swiped the screen.

"We'll be off, sir," Janice said.

"Hmm?"

"Off. Barry's going to the ferry terminal and I'm going to show my face at the conference. I'm only one of the organizers after all. And I've got my presentation, remember?"

"Right, yes."

"And I'll interview the staff at the pub after I've been to the ferries," Barnwell said.

"Yep, sounds good." Graham looked up briefly, "Barry, I'll join you at the pub. We'll tackle the bar staff together."

Barnwell looked relieved. "Thank you, sir." Barnwell was slightly stupefied. He was exhausted but too much so to protest the workload that was causing it.

They headed off and Graham pressed his phone to his ear.

"Laura?"

"Oh, hey," she said. There was a strained affability in her tone.

"Look, I'm really sorry. There's been a..."

"Actually, I was wondering something," she said.

"Yeah?" Graham's chest fluttered with concern. She sounded deadly serious, and he feared that the good-natured barbs of the past might give way to something much worse.

On the other end of the line, there was an intake of breath, but after a pause, all Laura said was, "Oh, never mind."

Relieved that he'd escaped an ear-bashing, Graham launched into an explanation of the previous night's terrible circumstances, hoping it would relieve him of Laura's likely, and justified opinion that he was an unreliable, uncaring moron. "Love, I'm sorry. One of the conference attendees, a cop from the Met, was killed last night. Right on the High Street."

There was a long silence, then a cluster of odd sounds before Laura returned. "David?" she asked, sounding unsure that he'd be there, her tone invigorated from the flat, lifeless one she'd used earlier.

"Yeah?"

"I dropped the phone, I'm sorry. What on earth?"

"Hit-and-run. No witnesses. She died at the scene, instantly."

"My God... Did you know her well?"

"No, but we'd been talking in the pub just before she left to walk back to her digs. She... she was worried. She was working a tough case." Graham rubbed his palm over the right side of his face, pressing the heel into his eye socket. The pressure felt comforting. "I suggested someone accompany her home, but she refused." Anger and heartbreak were etched into Graham's tone. Exhaustion, grief, and a lack of tea threatened to cause his defenses to crumble. His voice wobbled.

"I'm so sorry," Laura said, her voice trembling.

David gave the broad strokes of Kimberley's background, and the dangerous work she'd been doing. He omitted the finer details including knowing that her cover had been blown. "I'll tell you right now, if another violent goon has come down here from London to hurt someone on my turf, I'll make it my mission to get him banged up forever."

"I know you will, darling. It all worked out last time, remember?" Laura had been a witness in a high profile case and was sent to Jersey from London for her protection in the run-up to the trial. A professional hit had been ordered on her and she had been targeted at the library. Her attacker, a Frank Bertolli, was now serving 12 years in HMP Belmarsh. "How's everyone doing?"

Graham cleared his throat. "We're professionals, we're getting the job done. We've done house-to-house. Tomlinson has performed the autopsy. He was supposed to be flying to California today, but he's postponed. Roach is on his way to Portsmouth. Barnwell's not had any sleep but we're interviewing the bar staff at the pub in a bit while Harding is about to present her session at the conference. We're looking for a car with a damaged grill, broken lights. At least, thanks to the conference, we'll have a willing army of helpers to scour every shed, garage, and out of the way place on the island if we need to."

"So, was it an accident?"

"Maybe," Graham admitted. "I mean, a hellish one. Tomlinson said she'd been struck at high speed. It could have been an accident, but her work..."

"Alright," Laura said consolingly. "You know what to do. Work the case. We're all with you, and we love you." The words emerged unplanned but not regretted.

"Thanks, Laura," he said, sighing. "I'll make it up to you, honestly. Once this is done, we'll get away for a few days and just..."

"Go to work."

"Okay...." Graham thought for a second. "Laura?"

"Yes?"

"Do you think...?" Graham's voice shook again. "D'you think that if you make a mistake, a big one, that you can make up for it somehow? Like, totally?"

"You mean, reparations of some sort?"

"Yeah, I guess. Like, tip the scales back the other way. And if not all the way, some at least."

"Yes, yes I do. Isn't that what jail time is, in part? Doing time, paying off a debt to society?"

"Hmm..."

"And... Detective Inspector Graham?"

"Yeah?"

"If this isn't an accident... and someone planned it..." Her voice was tight now. "I want you to *get* him, David, you hear?"

Laura's words penetrated Graham's train of thought. He stood up straight, the urgency of her words translating into determination in his. "Yes, ma'am. *Will do.*"

CHAPTER THIRTEEN

J ANICE'S PRESENTATION WAS about to start. She
was scheduled as the second speaker of the day, the
session before lunch, and she arrived in time to see
Superintendent Nigel Needham finishing up his presentation. The auditorium was half-empty. Janice had been excited
to give her talk, *Policing the Nexus Between Welfare Agencies
and Vulnerable Children,* a subject she felt passionately
about, but after the night's events she had lost much of her enthusiasm. It looked like her audience had too.

She'd thought about backing out. Graham had brought her
around. It was he who had persuaded her, and indeed the conference committee, to continue with the event. "It's what Kimberley
would have wanted," he'd said. "And keeping things normal is the
best way through such a circumstance." He had sounded like he
knew what he was talking about, but he didn't elaborate. She had
hoped he would be there to watch her speak, but now it was out
of the question. She couldn't see Jack either, but there was no
time to worry about it. Still, she would have liked *someone* to be
there, for moral support if nothing else. A bolt of guilt immedi-

ately stung her, shooting across one shoulder to the other. *Kimberley Devine would have been only too happy to give a presentation right about now even if she had had to stand on her head and speak to a hostile crowd jeering their heads off. Stop whinging, Jan.*

On the stage, Needham glanced at his watch, "I suppose," the seasoned officer said, "that this is where I sum things up." The audience seemed attentive, if understandably solemn. Summarizing his main theme, he said, "Seize chances to get involved. Don't hide your ideas. Speak to your senior officers and invite them to consider new points of view. They're not all as old and crusty as I am. You may well get some good results," he said, with a small smile. "Try it. Thank you all," he finished.

The crowd clapped warmly, grateful for the distraction and the effort Needham had put into his presentation, no small feat under the circumstances. As the applause died, Needham gathered his things and headed the wrong way off stage. Jason Ashby put him right and he walked back across, encountering Janice in the wings. "Good luck, Constable," he said, waving to her.

"Well done, sir. You're quite an act to follow."

"Oh, I'd be hopeless without these," he said, flicking through a thick stack of note cards. "But it seemed to go decently. They were polite, at least." He nodded toward the officers sitting in their seats. A few more were arriving, another few milled around.

As Jason Ashby walked up to the microphone to introduce her, Needham said, "How are you feeling after last night?"

"A little wobbly sir, I have to admit." Harding swung her arms by her side. "But the show must go on. I'll be back out there tracking down the person responsible just as soon as I'm done here."

"Such a shame. A highly respected officer. Hit at high speed, I hear?"

"Yes, sir,"

Janice heard her name called. "Good luck, young lady," Needham said. Janice briefly nodded her thanks and made her way up the steps onto the stage.

The next forty minutes went by in a dim haze. Harding found that her words came out, her stories were told, her audience polite and respectful, if rather subdued. It was like they were all speed-skating across the thinnest of ice; if they paused for more than a breath, the fragile base beneath them would crack and they all risked being swallowed by tragedy.

When she was done, her efforts received some pleasing applause and without inviting questions, she left the stage smiling courteously at the audience. As she descended the last step, she didn't linger, but instead, grabbed her things and strode through the lobby of the conference center. She had witnesses to interview, forensics reports to review, and a killer to catch.

David Graham's eyelids flickered. He grimaced and let out a small groan, his head twisting from side to side as though shooing away a persistent fly. Suddenly, Graham's leg shot out as if kicking an imaginary can or possibly something less benign. His fists curled. He emitted another groan, a deep sigh, then his body relaxed, his breathing eased, and all was calm again.

After he and Barnwell had interviewed Lewis Hurd and his Friday night barman at the *Foc's'le and Ferret,* Graham had gone home to freshen-up. He'd sat on his sofa for ten minutes of rest, and inevitably given his sleep-deprived state, had fallen asleep. He'd dreamed of Katie and Kimberley Devine, their faces intermingling, long-lashed eyes, laughter, those perfect white teeth. Katie. Kimberley. Daughters, too.

When he awoke, rubbing his hair and yawning, Graham walked to his kitchen and opened his fridge door, blinking as the brightness of the interior assaulted his eyes. He felt rough. His nightmares had been increasing lately, always when he was alone. He closed the fridge door with a gentle push, the milk carton moist and cold against his skin. As the door drifted shut, the rubber seal catching with a tiny hiss, he caught sight of the calendar that Laura had thoughtfully pinned on the front. She'd bought a "Welcome to Jersey" fridge magnet as a small house-warming gift. The calendar was also her idea. When you were Detective Inspector Graham, it was easy to forget what day it was, and she thought the calendar might help.

But today, the calendar reminded him of something of which she had no idea. As he turned over the page consigning January to the past, he saw it. February 15th. Katie's birthday. A day he had thought would turn Valentine's Day into a two-day celebra-tion was now one that made his whole month feel bleak.

Katie would have been seven this year. She'd have been starting Brownies probably, maybe developing an interest in ponies. There'd have been squeals and laughter and hugs and kisses. But they were long gone now, Graham's grief at her loss and guilt over her death replacing the joy of her existence. For a moment, in the silence of his home, he unlocked the part of his mind in which he kept these feelings. Every day was a form of reparation to Katie, as Graham set about proving to her that her father could be a better man, a motivation he'd shared with no one, a closely guarded secret from those around him, as was her memory. He viewed it as a form of cowardice that he had not spoken of her, but like an oyster under a full moon, he remained resolutely closed.

Too distracted and tired to put any effort in, Graham sloshed milk into his tea, swearing as he spilled some. What was the point of all this malingering? That part of his life was over. He was in a new location, a new relationship, a more senior job. He needed to focus on the case at hand. Graham's tea turned the color of burnt orange and he took the milk carton back to the fridge. As he slammed the door shut again, he glanced at the calendar before placing a fingertip over the date of Katie's birthday. He closed his eyes, and took a sip of his tea.

Graham reversed his car out of his driveway. He was on his way to the conference to tell Needham, O'Hearn, and Vincenti they needed to attend the station for interviews. He was later than planned, his best hope now being to get there before they started the afternoon session. Cross with himself, he called Laura for the second time that day. He was nothing if not inconsistent.

"How is it going? Have you made any progress?" she asked.

"Still gathering evidence and piecing together what happened." Graham laid out their findings while driving up the hill toward the conference center. "What we've got is a bit bloody thin so far."

"I can't believe CCTV didn't catch *anything* useful," Laura said, genuinely amazed. The UK CCTV network was extensive. If viewed from a satellite image, it would look like a shroud of intricate vintage lace.

"Really? I certainly can," he lamented. "Those cameras date back to the early nineties. We'd have had more luck with a Polaroid."

"Well, I keep hearing rumors from my confidential sources about your outstanding investigative acumen so I'm sure you'll overcome."

Grateful for the chance to laugh on a deeply unpleasant day, Graham asked plainly, "You mean Janice, right?" The two women had become friendly over the months Laura had been on Jersey.

Laura tutted down the phone. "A good librarian never reveals her sources."

"Of course."

522   ALISON GOLDEN & GRACE DAGNALL

"But she... I mean, *they* are confident in your ability to pull rabbits out of the evidential hat."

"Right now, the hat's nearly empty, save for a few shards of glass and the worst CCTV I've ever worked with," Graham said. "I'm going to talk with the people DS Devine was working with. See if they can shed any light on what might be lurking."

"Not a bad time to have a hundred experienced officers on the island," Laura pointed out. "Could be a very useful resource."

"Let's see," Graham said. "There are only two things for certain right now: one, a female detective died on a Friday evening in Gorey, and two, *absolutely nobody* saw it happen." His tone carried sadness, but also anger at the raw unfairness of it. "Anyhow," he said wearily. "I'll speak to you later. I hope you have a good rest of your day."

CHAPTER FOURTEEN

GRAHAM WAS ONLY mildly surprised to find that the conference was adhering to its original schedule. It had been organized with military precision, and that same thoroughness had been applied to keeping it on track. "Very successful, given the circumstances," was Jason Ashby's description of the morning's sessions, before he bustled off to prepare the stage for the next speaker. The atmosphere in the lobby was relatively upbeat although Graham suspected that the conference delegates were most likely practicing that most British of responses to an emotionally-charged crisis: retaining a resolutely stiff upper lip.

"Afternoon, DI Graham. Any progress on the investigation?" It was Freddie Solomon, author of the *Gorey Gossip*, literally the last person Graham wanted to see.

"No comment," he said, pulling out his phone and heading off in a random direction. Freddie trotted after him. "That's what you want me to publish? At a time like this? 'The famed DI Graham was unable to formulate a sentence in response to a simple information request'? Doesn't sound like the best way of rebuilding your reputation, does it?" Freddie was provocative as ever.

"Oh, I wouldn't bother him for a story, if I were you," Jason Ashby said, appearing next to Freddie all of a sudden. Jason matched Freddie step for step. "The DI is famously tight-lipped. At least," Jason said with a nod to Graham, "until the great moment of revelation. I've never seen it with my own eyes, but I'm told it's really something. Can *I* offer you a quote? I'm Jason Ashby, organizer of this modest shindig." Jason stuck out his hand, but Freddie ignored him. Lightly lathering oneself with faint praise even if one were being ironic would not work with Freddie. It needed to be troweled on to get his attention.

Rather than stinging the pair with entreaties to leave him alone, Graham found himself thinking of something Laura had said only a few nights before. They had been listening to Radio 3, the BBC's classical music station. "You know," she'd said, "if Mozart had been required to stop after every measure he wrote, and justify every choice of pitch and rhythm and harmony, he'd have lost his temper and written almost nothing."

Graham turned to the pair beside him. "Freddie," he said with a patience summoned from the depths, "I respect your right to publish whatever you desire."

The blogger's face lit up with excitement. "That's so very heartening to hear, because..."

"I'd wait for the rest of it if I were you," Jason murmured.

"However," Graham continued, "your publication has been suspected in the past of having slowed my investigations, contaminated evidence, and compromised the recollections of witnesses. Given that any criminal trial connected with our current case would inevitably take place on Jersey, you also run the risk of polluting the jury pool by making public your *assumptions* about what happened. I do not want to read or hear that you have written anything about this case. I also do not want you following any of the investigators on my team, nor do I want you asking any more questions."

Freddie quickly typed notes into his phone, his thumbs flying.

"Are you listening?" Jason said, keen to back Graham up. He appointed himself Graham's guardian by placing himself between the DI and Freddie. He extended an arm to gently push Freddie away. But the blogger had his quote now, and stepped aside, still thumbing madly at his phone.

"*Listening?*" Graham growled in Jason's ear. "I highly doubt it. I may as well have warned him off in a foreign language. The man's a limpet. I can't get rid of him."

Graham stalked toward a corner of the lobby, where he found Superintendent Needham reading a plaque that commemorated the conference center building's recent renewal. "Marvelous, marvelous," Needham said, apparently to himself.

"Sir?" Graham said, cautiously interrupting the superintendent's thoughts. "Have you got a minute?"

"Oh, hello David," Needham said. "Didn't see you in the morning session. Fascinating stuff."

A faint frown rumpled Graham's forehead. "Well, I've had this incident to deal with. You know." He raised his eyebrows.

"Hmm?" Needham asked.

"The hit-and-run sir. DS Devine."

There was a fraction of a second's hesitation before, "Oh yes, yes. *Terrible* business. But you're on the job. The investigation is in good hands." Needham turned his attention back to the plaque on the wall.

His eyes narrowing, Graham watched Needham in growing discomfort. He leaned close to the man, alert to the signs of alcohol on Needham's breath, but there were none. Needham was hardly likely to sneak out at the coffee break to smoke a joint or pop some pills, but there had to be an explanation for his strange behavior. The first thing, the only thing that Graham expected to be on Needham's mind was the investigation into the death, possibly murder, of one of his officers. And he expected Needham to treat the situation with gravity and deference. Instead, he had been casual and dismissive.

"You alright, sir? You're not finding the conference more tiring than you expected?"

Needham turned to regard Graham, the plaque finally forgotten. "I've the stamina of a bull rhino, man." Needham grinned, his fists clenched as he dismissed Graham's concerns. "Don't you worry about me, David. Now, where's Jacob? He was going to give me a copy of the schedule."

"Jacob, sir?"

"Young fella. Organizer of this tremendous conference." Graham pointed out Jason Ashby, who was speaking with a group of uniformed officers across the lobby. "Ah, there he is. Marvelous, marvelous." Needham stalked off in Jason's direction. After a few paces, he stopped as though he'd forgotten something. He looked around for a while, and then headed back into the auditorium, never getting as far as to connect with Ashby.

"What the hell?" Graham muttered to himself.

CHAPTER FIFTEEN

"I'M SORRY TO press, sir, but now the blogger chap has gone, can I ask if you're closer to settling last night's case?" Spotting that Graham was free, Jason Ashby had returned to his side.

Frowning with surprise, Graham informed him, "Litigators *settle*, Mr. Ashby. Investigators *solve.*"

Jason shrunk a little, then drew himself up tall. "You will pass any statement you plan to make by me first, won't you?"

Graham's pupils dilated as his eyebrows rose a fraction at Ashby's absurd presumption, but before he could conjure a pithy rebuke, Graham found the problem solved for him.

"They need you in the auditorium." Jason Ashby heard Tom Vincenti's voice, then felt his strong hand as he steered the young man away from Graham much like he had Patrick O'Hearn the previous night. "Something about a whistling microphone. Better see about it."

"Right. Right, yes." Jason slunk away into the auditorium, feeling his shoulder where Vincenti's hand had been. Graham found himself at eye level with Vincenti's chin.

"How tall are you, Detective Sergeant?"

"'Bout six-four," he replied. "Whenever I'm home, my mother tells me I'm still growing."

"I'm sorry for your loss, Tom," Graham said. He considered reaching for Vincenti's upper arm with a comforting hand but decided against it. "The medics did their best, but..."

The rims of Vincenti's eyes reddened and the whites became moist, but when he spoke his voice was firm. "I just came from the scene, actually. Wanted to pay my respects quietly after the hubbub of last night. Not a lot to report. Seems fairly straightfor-ward—a car driving too fast plows straight into her as she's crossing the road in the dark. The light distribution from those street lamps is atrocious. You should recommend they're updated before someone else is killed."

"We've got everyone doing their bit, Tom, depend on it."

Vincenti shrugged. "Of course you have. She was really unlucky. Wrong place, wrong time. Probably no one but the driver to blame. Should have stuck around though."

Graham froze in surprise, his eyes locked on Vincenti. "You're thinking it was an accident? Even in the circumstances?"

With a shrug, Vincenti answered, "In our game, there's always a tendency to apply overcooked theories to common, everyday situations. Most murders aren't planned and executed, they're just spontaneous arguments that got out of hand, fueled very often by alcohol. And if it looks like a random, unfortunate traffic accident, that's probably what it was."

"I see." Graham wasn't used to having the rudiments of inves-tigative work repeated to him by a man of lower rank. Still, it had been an upsetting few hours, and in stressful situations, people often did or said things they ordinarily wouldn't.

"You're developing a different theory?" Vincenti asked.

"I'm gathering evidence," Graham said. "The theories come later."

"Happy to help if you need me," Vincenti said. "Anything I can do, anything at all, just shout."

"We'd like to interview you if you don't mind."

"Of course. What do you want to know?"

"Not here. Down the station."

"Oh, okay. Sure. Let me have a fag, then I'll be set."

"No rush, I'll have Barnwell pick you up in an hour."

Vincenti slunk out into the bright afternoon sunshine, speaking to no one and cloaked by his ability to keep a low profile. "Stealthy as a submarine, but sailing in risky waters, methinks," Graham murmured, watching Vincenti before turning to face the crowd in the lobby.

Graham was about to follow Superintendent Needham into the auditorium when he found his path promptly blocked by Jason Ashby *again*. "Look," the young organizer said, his face more apologetic than before, "I'm just worried we'll all look like a bunch of clowns, you know?"

"Clowns, you say?" Graham said, trying to peer over Jason's shoulder and into the auditorium.

Jason spelled it out. "Police officers who are sworn to protect the public, but can't protect one of their own."

Graham took a step back. "You're concerned about *reputational damage*?" he asked, stunned.

"I have to be!" Jason protested. "Ours is quite a new organization, and it's imperative that..."

"Listen, lad," Graham said, exhausted to the point of fury by a police officer's tragic death, the resulting sleep deprivation, and now Ashby's ridiculous priorities. "I don't know how things work in your *organization*," he said, "nor do I understand social media like you do. But I'm a dab hand at figuring things out. Would you mind if I did that? If pressed, all you have to do is make a statement expressing confidence in the investigating officers. Are you up to that?"

Mumbling something that might have been an apology, Jason let Graham pass. In the auditorium, Needham was alone by the stage, apparently lost in thought as Graham approached.

"David! How are you?" Needham said on catching sight of him. He extended a hand. "You know, I don't think I saw you at the morning session. Shame, that. You missed some fascinating stuff."

Graham's mouth opened but nothing came out. Had Needham forgotten that they had been speaking just a few minutes before? "I'd like to interview you about Kimberley Devine down the station. As soon as you're ready. Nothing serious, just routine stuff."

"Yes, yes, of course." Needham stumbled suddenly, and Graham shot out a hand to steady him.

"You alright, sir?"

"Yes, yes. No problem," Needham said.

"I'll drive you. I just have to find O'Hearn. Give me five minutes?"

"DI Graham?" came Jason's plaintive voice from the doorway. "Sorry again, but..."

Striding resolutely, his jaw set, down the aisle that divided the auditorium's seating, Graham conveyed just how frustrated he was becoming and, for half a second, a frisson of fear crossed Jason's face.

"Can't you see I'm busy, boy?"

Twitching and shifting from one foot to the other in a manner that made Graham wonder if Jason needed to disappear to the Gents again, the young organizer said, "Seems I'm not the only one with a passion for social media." He showed Graham his phone. "Freddie Solomon's been busy. Managed to knock out a blog post announcing the terrible news by eight o'clock this morning. This is the second one today," he said. "He must have already posted it when he approached you a few minutes ago."

The DI read Freddie's latest headline. His heart sank. "Oh, for *crying out loud.*"

CHAPTER SIXTEEN

The Gorey Gossip
Saturday, February 1st

Once more, dear readers, it is my unhappy duty
to report a sudden and untimely death in Gorey.
We are united in a sense of shock at a tragedy
which comes all too soon after the recent
deadly events in the Channel—the murder of
scientist, Greg Somerville, and the presumed
suicide of local man, Matt Crouch. Now, either
by accident or design, a twenty-seven-year-old
detective sergeant with the Metropolitan police
has been struck and killed by a speeding car.
Kimberley Devine was a talented and tenacious
investigator, and by all accounts, a charming
and popular young woman. What's more, she was a
visitor to our island, participating in this
week's high-level police conference. Her loss

is as senseless as any on which this author has reported.

Gorey's police have swung into action, but the appointment of Detective Inspector Graham as lead investigator seems ill-considered, however automatic it has become, considering the presence of more senior police officers on the island at this time. Personal ties—DS Devine and Graham both served at the Met simultaneously and likely knew each other—and a conflict of interest—let's not forget she was on Jersey for a conference organized by Graham's team—further underscore the dubious nature of his appointment.

Poor luck—or perhaps, simply poor *judgment* —has attended each new discovery in the case. Behold our woefully outdated CCTV system, a critical underinvestment by those responsible for our safety. Thus far, it has provided few clues and much confusion while ancient lighting down the main thoroughfare of our humble town may have contributed to this tragedy. DS Devine's death occurred at a point on the High Street that has been flagged many times for poor visibility, something our local police have let pass for too long.

DS Devine's demise is a travesty that occurred without witness and—as yet—without responsibility. Would an extra 'bobby on the beat' or two have made a difference? Maybe it is time to review the staffing levels at our diminutive police station. By a stroke of good fortune, Gorey is presently host to nearly one hundred experienced police officers, all delegates to a lavish 'conference,' or some such junket. Why not set these fine officers to work tracking down Kimberley Devine's killer, and discovering their true motive?

And while they're here, usher them into our broom-cupboard of a crime lab to examine the scant evidence. Perhaps then the poor victim's family, already enduring a pain we cannot imagine, might be spared a lengthy wait for answers. Our experienced, if elderly, local pathologist is currently laboring over the most basic questions, assisted only by a temporary and partly-qualified lab assistant, borrowed—yes, you guessed it—from DI Graham's tiny staff of police officers.

My source stated the victim was struck at lethal speed—fifty miles-per-hour, perhaps more. Her body was found in the road between the offices of *G. Paul & Sons Accountants* and the *Lotus Blossom* yoga studio. Other details remain sparse; the assembled officers are tight-lipped, ready to defend DI Graham and his small team. Openness is a powerful investigative tool, and we can only hope that in the future, Gorey's constabulary chooses to reach out more thoroughly to the public and the press, in their search for answers. Many questions need answering!

Was DS Devine deliberately killed or was this an accident caused by a feckless and scurrilous individual? If a deliberate act, who could have borne such ill-will toward the victim? Did a vengeful ex-con callously plan her death, and if so, where are they now? And what about DS Devine's personal life? Could this have been the source of rancor toward her? Undeniably attractive, but rather inscrutable on social media, was the young officer compromised by her romantic life?

Every detail of DS Devine's death suggests a murderous hit-and-run but the lack of transparency more than half a day after her life was snuffed out is appalling. Since DI Graham's arrival, the Gorey public has suffered significant trauma and deserves better. We should now demand answers to these questions and more.

In the meantime, and with precious little to go on, a more experienced leader should be drawn from our fortunate, if temporary, surfeit of talent. With them in place, Ms. Devine's loved ones will have some hope of swift justice which is, after all, only as much as Jersey, Gorey, and DI Graham owe them.

CHAPTER SEVENTEEN

NOT EVEN A frosty gust of February air could dim Freddie Solomon's mood as he bustled into the library. For him, the place had come to represent both an office where he might quietly work and the ideal place to consult local resources for his research. On its best days, the library also acted as the town's 'water cooler,' a place where gossip was whispered and opinions exchanged—sometimes accompanied by the quiet discretion that befit the studious atmosphere of a library, but often not.

As if these attractions weren't enough, Freddie often liked to coordinate his visits so that they coincided with Laura Beecham's shifts. He had long since decided that Laura was the most attractive woman on the island, and definitely among the most interesting, not least due to her close relationship with Jersey's most interesting man.

"Ah, Laura! And how is my favorite librarian today?" Freddie whispered brightly as Laura passed his table. She was wearing a baby-pink V-necked cashmere sweater with a rollover collar and three-quarter length sleeves, a brown tweed pencil skirt, and black kitten heels—a sexy secretary look that draped her lithe figure in an appealing but discreet way. The only thing missing from her outfit was a pair of winged glasses that might act as cover for the passionate, wild, sensual side, that in Freddie's imagination, Laura harbored. For him.

"Not too bad, I suppose," Laura said in a low voice. "Difficult day."

"Tragic, isn't it?" Freddie replied, *sotto voce*. "She was so young, too. Just breaks the heart. I know we're joined in our determination to bring the killer to justice."

Too canny by now to become ensnared in one of Freddie's disingenuously good-natured traps and having already read Freddie's latest blog post, Laura demurred. "It's a long process. Can't be rushed." She headed toward the Romance section to re-shelve twenty or so books that she pushed on a small cart in front of her.

Laura slotted around half of them into their correct spot and was about to meander over to the mass market paperbacks when Freddie surprised her by popping up from behind the end of a shelving unit. "But, I mean, Kimberley's family are *still* waiting for official confirmation," he said, "The police appear intolerably delayed which translates to disrespect and utter heartlessness. And with so many competent officers on the island..."

Laura knew from experience to what Freddie was alluding. She batted aside his assertion like a good cricketer: defensive but confident, steering the game into safe, open spaces. "The reputation of Gorey's police is second to none," she said plainly. "We can have confidence in their professionalism, don't you think?" Hers was a tone that invited only agreement.

"Of course," Freddie allowed. He moved along quickly. "I suppose where I can help most is with accountability. In this day and age, Gorey's public figures have no place to hide, and that's just how it should be. My blog is a tool for this purpose."

"It's exhausting for the police to be harangued by the press," Laura said, wondering if "press" was the correct term for Freddie's line of work. "And mostly by people who don't clearly understand police procedures. It's distracting too. Perhaps you could be more helpful by leaving them alone to do their job?"

To her surprise, Freddie stopped and raised his hands in surrender. "I give DI Graham a tough time," Freddie admitted, "but my readership has its doubts about the investigation. I simply reflect those doubts."

It would have been quite fruitless for Laura to point out the obvious truth: that Freddie *created* those doubts with his ceaseless criticisms of DI Graham and his officers. "I think we should be patient," she explained, "and let the professionals do their jobs." She wrestled the last paperback into its correct place and gave her cart a good push in the direction of the Action and Adventure section.

"That's all I want too," Freddie said, trotting along beside her. "High-quality police work and charges that stick. If providing some commentary helps in that aim," he said, "then my time has been well spent."

"Commentary?" Laura snickered. "What you wrote earlier was a bare-knuckled attack on Detective Inspector Graham *and* his team."

"You've seen it then? My piece?" Freddie's chest expanded and a gleam made his eyes shine. Laura's eyelids dropped fractionally. "I'm sorry if he was upset," Freddie added a little more quietly.

"Oh, he doesn't waste time on things like your blog," Laura said. "Too much to do." She watched with some satisfaction as Freddie's face fell slightly. "I wouldn't hold out much hope of adding the DI to your readership."

"That's alright, provided *you* click on my page," Freddie said. "I hope you do."

"Sure! When I tire of all the fiction in here," Laura said, nodding to shelves packed with novels, "I can always read yours."

Freddie kept his laughter muted and watched as Laura

moved over to the New Acquisitions unit before she returned down the aisle to the table where Freddie assembled his mobile office. He moved quickly down the adjacent row. "How would you feel," he began, slithering around the end of a shelving block just in time to bar her progress, "about contributing a little to my work? Strictly off the record. All unattributable, of course."

Laura brushed past without answering, but Freddie quickly followed her as she headed back to the distribution desk. "I can have you arrested for harassment, you know," she claimed raising her voice a little now that they were out of the reading area. "I've got connections."

"Thirty minutes," Freddie requested, his hands flat on the polished wood of the desk. "Just you, me, some decent coffee, and my notebook. No trouble, I promise."

"A promise," she said skeptically. "Really?"

"Think of it this way," Freddie said, his mind racing. "It would be your chance to put the record straight. You could stand up for your man."

Laura looked at him and raised one eyebrow before picking up a sheet of bright yellow round labels. She began peeling them off the backing, sticking them on the back of her hand before placing them on the spines of several large print books.

"You can be a truth-sayer! Put me right! We'll do as much fact-checking as you want. I'd rather write the truth than a bunch of hearsay, anyway," Freddie said. His words sounded a stretch, even to him.

"The *truth*?" Laura hissed. "You've got to be kidding me."

"Then set me straight! Help me get to know the DI from a new angle."

Sensing the beginnings of an opportunity, Laura found herself considering Freddie's offer. She pressed the final yellow sticker into place. "Just half an hour?"

"Not a moment more if that's what you want. I promise to be

attentive, companionable, and if you don't like the question, we'll move straight on."

"If I don't like the question," she said, "I'll be finishing my coffee and going home."

"It's a deal," Freddie said, excited at the prospect of this unexpected opportunity.

"Thirty minutes, my choice of venue, and no personal stuff," she told him.

"You got it," he promised. "No funny business whatsoever."

"And before we talk, you really should learn the difference between 'unattributable' and 'off the record.' You can't have it both ways," she advised.

More than ready to prove his credentials, Freddie recited the conditions. "If a quote isn't attributed, it comes from a generic or unnamed source."

"Like, 'Senior government officials with knowledge of the meeting,' things like that," Laura said.

"Precisely. And if it's *off the record*, it can't be quoted or published, just used to understand a situation."

"Glad to see you've brushed up," Laura said. "You might even turn into a journalist, one of these days." She grinned. It was fun to give Freddie a hard time, especially considering the criticism DI Graham received in the *Gossip*. Laura wasn't the type to seek revenge, but coffee with Freddie might do some good.

"You're very kind to say so," Freddie nodded, too thrilled at this progress to feel the sting of Laura's back-handed rebuke.

"Our meeting will be off the record. Understood?"

"Understood. How about Monday? 12:30?"

She regarded him for another moment as she weighed his proposal. "You're on."

CHAPTER EIGHTEEN

GRAHAM SIGHED DEEPLY. He'd put the kettle on and was attempting to enjoy a few quiet moments before he moved on to the interviews he was about to conduct. He'd just made a call to police command in St. Helier. They were understandably anxious for a quick collar in this very personal case. The parallel stresses of a murder investigation and the conference had created a tense atmosphere. It was an unusual pressure to perform in front of such an exacting audience. "One of our own," Graham had heard repeatedly. "Killed only a few hundred yards from the likes of Nigel Needham, Tom Vincenti, and dozens of seasoned officers." Graham stared at his whiteboard with its depressingly empty spaces where evidence and theories should be. It summed up exactly how he felt. "You've been put right on the spot here, lad," he said to himself.

There was a knock at the door. "Sir?" It was Barnwell. "Superintendent Needham is ready for you now." Barnwell was sufficiently versed in Graham's idiosyncrasies such that the DI's frequent, barely audible mutterings passed without comment.

"Right, no peace for the wicked, eh?"

"Shall I go pick up DS Vincenti from the conference?"

"Yes, do that. O'Hearn, too. They're expecting you." Graham rose wearily and met Needham, who was sitting in one of the seats that flanked the entrance to the station. "Come on back, I'll show you an office even smaller than your old digs at CID."

"A neat and orderly station, David," the older man said. "Marvelous, just marvelous." Needham took one of the two chairs opposite Graham's desk. "Hah! I see your old teapot is still doing battle after all these years." The teapot with its classic blue willow pattern sat ancient, proud, and a little faded on top of a filing cabinet, flanked by an assortment of tea bags and loose tea leaves in small, glass cylinders.

"What's more surprising? That it's lasted this long, or that you remember it?" Graham asked. Having been moved repeatedly between new homes and offices as it fueled Graham during so many frustrating, late nights 'pouring while poring' over evidence, the teapot's survival was truly a miracle.

"Both. Now, how can I help?"

"Tell me about the op Kimberley Devine was working on."

"Ah. Drugs, as usual. Makes up ninety percent of undercover work these days. She worked with O'Hearn and Vincenti. Vincenti was the senior officer. He's been working the gang for years now. He needed some support. Devine and O'Hearn had been working alongside one another for about a year and a half. She was promoted to DS first, he shortly afterward. There was some talent and motivation there so they were put with Tom. He's been something of a protégé of mine. Not a patch on you, but a bright and dedicated officer. He was doing some excellent undercover work until he hit some trouble."

"Tell me about him."

"Ah." *A delicate topic*, Needham's tone implied.

"Am I wrong to ask about his background?" Graham asked.

"No, no. Routine stuff, as you say," Needham allowed.

"What kind of trouble?" Graham deliberately set aside his notebook.

"He felt he had to fit in, you know. Had to look the part, really *inhabit* his cover role. And for Tom, indulgences which were useful for his cover proved pretty awful for his personal life."

Needham didn't need to spell it out. "White, brown, or green?" Graham asked sympathetically.

"Brown. Lots of it," Needham replied. "Things got dangerous."

"As they often do when one uses heroin. How was he found out?"

"He confessed, told me one night, and I decided to help him. No use throwing a talented officer on the scrap heap because of some poor decisions."

"Risky," Graham pointed out.

"Worth it," Needham retorted. "Tom's one of the good guys, David. Once he straightened himself out, he, O'Hearn, and Devine began sending back incredibly good intel. Actionable stuff on the gang and their suppliers."

"Were they making arrests?" Graham asked. After the risk and expense of prolonged undercover work, he certainly hoped so.

"Nothing big yet. We're waiting for a couple more things to slot into place. You know how it can be. They were biding their time, picking the gang's better-informed underlings until they snitched on their bosses."

"Then why interrupt their work? Why bring them to Jersey?" Graham asked. "Sounds like they were closing in on some good collars."

"They all needed the break," Needham said. "It was their decision, in any event. They were trusted to explain their absence and expected to resume operations next week, once they'd taken in some decent air and mingled with regular folks again."

Graham flipped to a new page in his notebook. "Okay, let's move on to Friday night."

CHAPTER NINETEEN

"I JUST NEED to confirm your movements after you left the pub," Graham said.

"Of course," his former boss replied.

"You were with us from, what, about 6:30?"

"Something like that. I walked with you directly from the conference."

"You left with Dr. Tomlinson shortly after DS Devine. Do you remember seeing her leave?" Graham said, keen to help Needham establish a frame of reference.

The superintendent kept his eyes on Graham but said nothing.

"She was with DS Patrick O'Hearn, but he left earlier, had to make a call," Graham prompted. This didn't seem to help, either. "Mike Trevelyan sat at the end of the table next to you. You told that old codswallop about the Ford Cortina in Bromley."

Needham's eyes lit up, and he sat straighter in his seat, clearly electrified by the memory. "Bloody *marvelous* that was, Dave," he said. "Never seen anything like it. Four different sightings, all from the depths of your memory. It's like you've got a computer up there or something."

"Do you remember seeing Patrick or Kimberley leave the pub?" Graham said.

"I saw..." Needham began, reaching for a memory, but soon there was disappointment in his eyes. "David, I'm sorry. I don't remember, not exactly. It was busy, I do remember that. I'm sure you're correct, though," he finished, brightly.

"It's not a test, sir," Graham smiled.

"I remember telling the Cortina story and then another one. About that case in Scotland you consulted for. What was it, summer of 2009?"

Blinking, David searched his memory to recall the case Needham was referring to. Eventually, he found it—a particularly nasty extortion case involving a wealthy businessman, who when he made his millions, swapped a safe, suburban family life for a much younger woman who turned out to be the daughter of a Russian mobster.

"Sir, I've got to ask," he said, "how it is that you can remember every last thing about that blessed Cortina, and most probably what you had for breakfast twenty years ago, but..."

"Absolutely bugger all about the last few days?" Needham said.

"Well, I just want to establish the facts, sir, and..."

"You think I'm addled." It was a plain statement of fact, absent any show of offense.

"Of course not, sir," Graham said. "One of the best minds in the business, yours. It's just a bit, well..."

"Perplexing?" Needham tried.

"Just a little," Graham admitted.

Needham let out a big exhale. "Details that would have come in half a second, five years ago, they're just *gone*. I know that I know these things, but it's like my brain has forgotten that I do. Can't even find the right shelf, let alone the correct book."

"Sir, I'm sure you're exaggerating," Graham began. He was ready to encourage and defend his mentor, but the whole idea of Needham's formerly sharp, penetrative mind deserting him, especially while on the job, was too overwhelming for him to press the point further.

"That's just the thing, David," Needham told him, candidly. "I might be exaggerating, or I might not. I'm not actually sure."

Graham returned to the events of Friday evening. "Kimberley was a bit put-out that night in the pub. Did you see her glancing at her phone a lot?"

"Can't say I noticed it. Young people do that all the time don't they?"

"They do, sir. Occupational hazard, I'd say. So tell me what happened when you left?"

Needham shrugged, more used than Graham to these frustrating memory gaps. "We could ask the staff what time I pulled up to the hotel."

"You *drove* back to the *White House Inn?*"

"They gave me a hire car when I flew in. Not sure I even asked for it. I offered your chap, what was his name again? Tomkinson?"

"Tomlinson."

"Yes, quite. I offered him a lift, but he said he'd walk. Something about sitting for hours on a plane the next day. Anyhow, I remember going back to the conference center to get the car and must have driven home."

Must have? "Do you remember anything about the drive back to the hotel?"

Again, Needham tried. "Sorry, it's like reaching into a larder only to find it's been ransacked by a starving horde." He shook his head as though to shoo away a buzzing bee. "Bloody *terrible*, this is. I'll forget my own name next."

"No need to apologize, sir," Graham said. "Happens to the best of us." He put down his pen. "Okay, that should do it for

548 ALISON GOLDEN & GRACE DAGNALL

now. Thanks, sir. Can we give you a lift back to the conference center or the *White House Inn?*"

Graham rose from his seat. He had found the interview excruciating. His cheeks were flushed and he felt a drip of moisture scuttle down his back as Needham followed him from his office. *The super should not be in service.*

"Most kind, but I think I'll walk back," Needham said. "A lungful of this brisk sea air is always helpful, especially for an old duffer like me. Might help loosen things up, you know."

"If it does," Graham replied as he shook his old friend's hand before showing him out, "make sure I'm the first to know."

CHAPTER TWENTY

OUTWARDLY, DS TOM Vincenti was friendly enough. He lounged in his chair, his expression open, his wide full mouth curved into a smirk. But he was proving slippery. Twice already, he'd refused to answer questions; Graham's rank and former Met CID status apparently cut little ice. "Making calls," had been his sole response to a request for an alibi during Friday evening.

"Tell me about your operation, Tom. Who, what, where, that kind of thing," Graham tried again.

"I'd rather not, sir. Operation integrity. I'm sure you understand."

Graham unbuttoned his jacket and put his hands on his hips underneath the table. Vincenti was being perfectly polite, but that didn't stop Graham wanting to slap him off his chair and up against the wall of the interview room.

"Sir, I'm not trying to be unhelpful," Vincenti maintained. "It's just that one of my team members is dead, and if there's a leak or a mole or a whatever, we have a..."

"Security issue?" Graham offered.

"I'm being cautious, sir," Vincenti told him. "I don't think it was, but if Kimberley's death does turn out to be murder, then our entire operation is jeopardized. I'm taking a risk even talking to you, and we both know that I could make arrangements to avoid it altogether if I chose to. Got to protect my people."

Graham rose and stood by the window. "If we'd known the degree of risk, we could have arranged cover for her." A silence fell over him. He, too, wasn't speaking plainly. He was hiding behind procedure and displacing responsibility when he knew, *he knew* that Devine had been under threat. He was also unwilling to share what he knew about her cover being blown. What did that say about him? He pushed the thought away. He needed to be careful. Vincenti was right. A carefully placed word in the right ear and he would be ordered to downgrade the investigation or be removed from it altogether. Greater priorities and all that.

"Tell me about her. Did she fear anything?"

"We all fear things when we're undercover. It's the name of the game, you know that. The key is to control that fear, use it to propel yourself forward. She was pretty tight-lipped about her thoughts." Vincenti shrugged. "Probably because she was a woman. Didn't want to appear soft."

"What about O'Hearn? Did she share her fears with him?"

Vincenti shrugged again, pursing his lips. "You'll have to ask him that."

"Were they romantically involved?"

"He didn't say anything, but then he wouldn't, would he? Probably a meaningless fling anyway."

People whose professional lives took them into dark, underground places generally had quiet social calendars. But secrecy and shared dangers bonded people together, even those who in other circumstances would be more reasoned about the wisdom of such entanglements. In the undercover business, an ongoing relationship between co-workers demanded secrecy. Re-assignment and discipline were common tools to deal with them if they occurred. If Devine and O'Hearn had been in a relationship they would have surely kept it to themselves.

"Look, you have your investigation to deal with," Vincenti said. "My responsibility is to the living. To my fellow officers, and to the public."

"But don't you owe it to Devine to find out who did this? To O'Hearn? To the wider undercover community?"

"Our investigation holds real promise, and it needs to continue," Vincenti deflected. He paused, but then let emotions come briefly to the surface. He swallowed and the muscles in his jaw flexed. "Kimberley would have said the same."

There was nothing to do but nod. Graham's hands were tied. "Constable Barnwell will show you out, Tom. Thanks for your time."

"Good luck," Vincenti said. "And keep me in the loop, yeah? My mind has to stay on London stuff, but if I can help in any way, just shout."

As Vincenti shut the door, Graham rolled his eyes at his lack of honesty. Feigned goodwill was worse than obvious hostility. He stood in silence for a moment, before going through his post-interview routine: boil kettle, fill teapot, let Chinese Jasmine steep until its fragrance filled the office. He silenced his phone, sat down with his old-fashioned policeman's notebook, and wrote quickly but deliberately while replaying the interview from memory.

He wrote verbatim. In the margin, he added a note in red pen: *Vincenti—economical.*

Graham stared at his words, wondering about them. *And what does that say about me?*

CHAPTER TWENTY-ONE

DS PATRICK O'HEARN looked like he'd been up all night, probably because he had. His eyes were dull, deep creases furrowed his brow, his eyelids drooped.

"Tea?" Graham said as O'Hearn closed the office door behind him. "Or we have coffee in the main office."

"I think I'll turn into a percolator if I have any more of that stuff," Patrick said, rubbing his sore, dark-rimmed eyes. "Gives me the jitters."

"It's a jittery weekend," Graham said. "How are you holding up?" *Not at all well, it looks like.*

"Alright, I suppose. Just a shock to the system, you know?"

"A very nasty one. You should take time to process all of this," Graham advised. "These things can't be rushed."

"More important stuff going on right now," Patrick argued, curling his fat hands into balls before flexing them. "I'll sit and mope around later, once we've got someone in custody."

"I understand, but take it from me," Graham said sincerely. "You'll do better long term if you deal with it." When this seemed not to affect O'Hearn, Graham pressed on. "You think it was a hit job?"

O'Hearn looked around him and rubbed his hands on his thighs. "I'm not sure. Could go either way." He was tapping his foot. "What do you think?"

"We're going where the evidence takes us. I have an open mind. Tell me about your work with DS Devine. How long had you worked together?"

"About a year and a half," Patrick replied.

"The super said you teamed up just after your promotion to detective sergeant. You two got put with DS Vincenti then. That sound about right?"

Patrick grunted. "Yeah, although I'm amazed the super can remember. Seems to have lost half a yard recently."

"Hmm," Graham said. It pained him to see his mentor laid low, and even more that it was noticeable to others. "Who was running the undercover show?"

Following a reflex honed over his months in the shadows, Patrick glanced around again before replying. "It's daft, I know, in here of all places, but we're trained to believe that walls literally have ears."

"None here," Graham promised. "Our man, Wentworth, regularly sweeps for bugs. He last checked just a few days ago."

"Seriously?" Patrick asked. "In a little station like this?"

"It's somewhere between a profession and a passion for him," Graham explained. "One of a kind. Anyway..."

"Yeah, right. Tom ran the day-to-day side. That is until he needed some time off," Patrick answered.

"And how long was he absent?"

"A few weeks. Didn't make much difference. We kinda made our own decisions," Patrick said with a shrug. "Kimberley and I made a good team. She did the eyes-on work, you know, pretending to hang around alleys, waiting for someone, that kind of thing."

"I get the picture," Graham said. He imagined Kimberley had walked the streets in London's less salubrious districts. That was how things usually worked. That her gender had inevitably funneled her into such a role would have made the task odious, but undercover officers were motivated by loftier goals and did what they had to, to get the job done. "And you were 'on the inside,' so to speak?"

"Yeah. I was doing alright," O'Hearn recalled. "Picked up all kinds of useful stuff about that crew and a few others, but nothing to write home about. I was rolling up the minnows. I was too low-level to gather anything actionable on the big fish. Ever heard of Bob Ketch?"

Just the other day, Laura had called Graham, 'Detective Inspector Google,' and his memory proved unerring yet again. "'Breakout Bob'?" He whistled. Bob Ketch was a London gangster who'd once broken out of jail in an audacious attempt that had involved a helicopter and the blackmail of prison staff. He was later captured, but the nickname had stuck. "Serious stuff. I bet you minded your Ps and Qs around him."

Patrick threw up his hands. "Never even met the geezer. I hang around with lieutenants and couriers, low-level people who don't know one end of the drug operation from the other. Tom had more success, but things are slow. Ketch has been around a long while, and everything is pretty entrenched, not a lot of movement. The system is finely honed, everyone in their place. I suspect the old man's getting ready to retire. He'll choose someone younger to hand things over to pretty soon. Maybe then things will loosen up, but we've been getting frustrated with the situation. We just need a bit of luck, a break. We're sure we can bring the whole thing down if we just catch someone slipping up. They'd have to, eventually."

"Ketch is what? Mid-sixties now?"

"Seventy. Got great-grandkids. Plenty of heirs waiting to take over his empire."

"Generational change," Graham observed. "Always a time of flux in gang leadership. People aren't sure who to trust, and that's how you get rivalries, factions, civil wars. Ripe time for slip-ups."

"Yeah, not sure what will happen now. We may get pulled out."

"So what were you doing on Friday evening after you left the pub?"

"I went back to my B&B. Made a call to my handler, just a check-in, and went to bed. Nice to have a relaxing evening, or so I thought. Then, Vincenti starts calling me about Kimberley. Woke me up."

"Did you get any texts from Kimberley?"

Puzzled, Patrick asked, "How do you mean?"

"She was upset, in the pub, about some texts from her targets. Seems she'd been made." There, he'd said it. Out loud.

O'Hearn blanched, his big, ruddy face losing its color in seconds. "What?"

"She didn't say anything to you?"

"Not a word." O'Hearn put his hands on his head and interlaced his fingers. He screwed his eyes up tight and turned his face to the ceiling. "Seriously? Why didn't she say something?" He growled in anguish and roughly rubbed his face, bringing the color back into it again.

"She should have reported it up the chain immediately, but it was a sensitive time in the investigation, so she said. I get it. Still," Graham argued, "the idea that she was silenced is pretty compelling. We're considering her death a straightforward hit-and-run, but we can't discount murder under the circumstances."

"You think someone came down here and...?"

"Wouldn't be the first time. D'you think this could have been done by one of Bob Ketch's people? Does it feel like one of theirs?"

Patrick considered the question. "They strangled a guy a year or so back, dumped him on a construction site. Someone else was found in the Thames with a knife in his skull. Reckon that was an argument that got out of hand, though, not something planned like this. Both were pretty personal, hand-to-hand. Running someone down in a car is less so, plus she was a woman..."

"Maybe the two features are connected. She was run down *because* she was a woman. Perhaps even Ketch's goon balked at laying hands on her," Graham suggested.

O'Hearn closed his eyes, "Kimberley, Kimberley, Kimberley, why didn't you say something?" he said quietly, before pursing his lips and exhaling forcefully through his nose. Graham's insides coiled up at O'Hearn's words. *She did.*

"Have you located the vehicle yet? Should be easy enough on an island," O'Hearn asked.

"Not yet, must be somewhere, though. Nothing has left without our knowing about it. We'll find it even if we have to search every shed on Jersey."

"The beauty of having a large but completely sealed crime scene, eh?"

"There are certainly some advantages to being on an island." Graham slapped his hands on the table. "Well, thanks for coming in. Are you staying?"

"Yeah, I've got a presentation tomorrow," Patrick announced, rising.

"Really?" Graham said, standing too. "You'd be excused for having your mind elsewhere."

"I got it, don't worry," the officer said, zipping up his jacket. "In and out, tell some stories, no drama." O'Hearn handed Graham a card with his cell number. "Well, anyway, I'm glad you're on the case. Heard lots of good things about you. I know whoever did this to Kimberley will be brought to justice. If you need any help at all, just say the word."

As O'Hearn turned to leave, Graham stuck his hands in his pockets. "Just one more thing, were you and DS Devine in a relationship?"

O'Hearn's eyes widened. "Oh no, Kim was a good mate but that was the long and short of it. I saw her more like a sister." The strong, bulky man paused, his eyes misting. "She was a good cop. I'll miss her."

"Look... you might be at risk. You should have someone assigned to you."

"Me? I'm sure I'll be fine, I'm a big lad if you hadn't noticed." O'Hearn cracked his knuckles.

"Are you sure? I really..."

"I'll surround myself with other cops. I'll be fine."

"Well, report back to your handler. Kimberley didn't do that for some reason. Might have been a fatal mistake."

"I doubt that, but thank you for the advice."

After O'Hearn had left, Graham picked up his phone and placed a call. "Janice? I need you to do something. Get all the passenger manifests from the ferry company and airline for the past week and run them against the database. Look for anyone with a connection to Bob Ketch and his drug operation."

CHAPTER TWENTY-TWO

"**A**SK ME AGAIN." Laura was peering at Graham over the rim of her wine glass.

They were playing Trivial Pursuit. On Laura's suggestion, Graham had demurred. It didn't seem right, considering. "It'll take your mind off things, give you a chance to relax," she'd argued. Then she had dropped the clincher. "And allow your subconscious the chance to noodle. You never know, you might solve the case while you're giving me the answer to..." she pulled a card from the box and peered at it, "...Which Renaissance artist liked to pump iron by lifting weights and was strong enough to bend an iron horseshoe with his bare hands?"

"Okay, just a short one," Graham conceded. He knew he needed to take a break. There came a point when constant ruminating wasn't helpful, and he'd gone way past it.

His phone pinged on the coffee table. It was from Janice.

`Searches pulled up no one of interest. Sorry.`

"Anything interesting?" Laura asked.

"No."

"Well, let's focus on something else. My turn. Entertainment, please!"

Graham reached for a card. "In 1977's number one block-buster, who played the character described in a droid's message from a princess as 'My Only Hope'?"

Laura knotted her forehead. "The guy with the beard. In the robe. In the desert, I think." Then a pleading glance at David. "Can I get his first name?"

"Er..." He took a long moment, thinking about maybe offering to massage her feet, then whether to help her with the question. "Starts with an A."

"Alan Alda!" she exclaimed.

"What, the doctor guy from MASH?" Graham said. "Hawkeye could never have scared off the Sand People."

"Who?" Laura asked.

"Just as likely to offer them a cocktail," Graham reasoned. "Actually, there's your clue. His last name is a kind of beer."

Laura began reciting a semi-encyclopedic list of London breweries. She'd worked in a pub there before landing on Jersey. After she'd listed the major players, she moved on to lesser-known brands. When she started reciting the names of niche microbreweries, Graham flagged her down. "Not from London."

"Boddington!" She frowned. "Wait, wasn't he a mountaineer?"

Graham slid the card back into its' sturdy rectangular box. "Alec Guinness, darling," he said theatrically.

"But Guinness is a stout!"

"Stouts are still beers," Graham reported. "Just made with roasted malt."

Completely unsatisfied, Laura complained. "Guinness is made in Dublin! You said it was an *English* beer!" She made a face like a nine-year-old denied ice cream.

"I said no such thing," Graham protested mildly.

"Did so," she insisted.

"Which of us has the unfailing memory?"

"Show-off." She blew a raspberry at him.

"Do I get more abuse, or do I get my question?" he asked, gesturing whether to refill her glass. She declined.

"Roll the dice, Columbo," she said.

Graham stifled a snort. "Let's get scientific."

"Again?" Laura sagged—Graham was a master at this category. "Right. Which *US Mercury* astronaut had to wait sixteen years for his flight, a 1975 link-up in space with the Soviet Union?"

Graham puffed out his cheeks, reaching for some memory of a childhood museum visit or a clip from a documentary. "I could use some help from young Billy with this one. He'd know the answer in a nanosecond."

"He would," Laura agreed.

"How's he doing, by the way?"

"Very quiet lately," Laura noted. "We're all hoping it's growing pains, or a bit of shyness because of the situation at home. He still comes to the library just as often as he did. I keep an eye on him and Janice checks up on him. Between the two of us, we're hoping to catch any disasters before they happen. I would hate for him to take a wrong path."

"That's good of you."

"What about this astronaut?" Laura said, tapping the question card and hiding a yawn behind her glass. Seeing it was empty, she set it aside; it was nearly midnight, anyway.

"He's got one of those nicknames like 'Stretch' or 'Clipper' or something," Graham dimly remembered.

"Want the answer?" Laura offered. He saw her glance at the wall clock.

There it was. "Deke," Graham paused, "something. The

ALISON GOLDEN & GRACE DAGNALL

NASA doctors found a heart condition and ruled him out, but he was really as fit as a mule."

"Deke Slayton," Laura said. She decided to allow it. "That was ridiculous," she added. "How's anyone normal supposed to know the answer to such an obscure question?"

"Not normal, am I?" Graham grinned at his girlfriend.

She raised her eyebrows and waggled her head. "Were you always like this? Like when you were Billy's age?" she said.

"Pretty much. It's what happens when you're cursed with a combination of a decent education and a near-inability to forget things. I'd call it a gift, and it certainly has its uses, but I did have to practice the heck out of some things."

"You did?" she asked, taking her glass to the kitchen. "Like what?"

"Remembering car number plates."

"I can imagine," she said from the kitchen.

"I made a habit of memorizing them in batches of ten, and then trying to recall them at different times."

"But why would you want to do that? It doesn't sound very useful," she called.

"Not at the time, but years later when I was doing stakeouts, it came in very handy. And it's been useful at odd moments over time."

Laura returned with chamomile tea. Introducing Graham to the benefits of the pale yellow blend had been one of her small victories.

"You know the way to a man's heart," he said appreciatively as she handed him the mug. "I'd recall the numbers after one minute, then five, then twenty, then an hour. You'd be amazed how they stick in one's mind if you do that."

"So, you activated some memory circuit or other," she said, tousling his hair, "which turned you into a wizard for remembering car number plates?"

He laughed. "Guess so." After a glance at the board, he suggested, "Should we call it a tie?"

"You're two pie pieces ahead of me," Laura said. "Sounds like a deal." They shook hands politely.

"Want me to get out of your hair?" Graham offered.

She gave him a look, her fingertips playing in his hair again. "Not particularly."

CHAPTER TWENTY-THREE

CONSTABLE BARRY BARNWELL stood next to Jason Ashby in the well at the side of the stage. They were about to start the conference's late morning session. The earlier presentation had been poorly attended, and it was looking as though this one would suffer a similar fate. Jason was taking it as a personal slight.

"It's a *crucial* topic," Jason complained, hopping from foot to foot. "We *need* an informed debate on body cameras as much as we do about terrorism or undercover work."

"Some are still coming back from coffee break," Barnwell said, hoping to mollify him.

"If they're coming back *at all*," Jason replied. "Everyone's been distracted since the hit-and-run, and it's getting harder and harder to gain their attention."

"Present company included. Look, I dare say I'll get through the introductions in one piece. Why don't you go and have a quiet cup of tea before you give yourself a hernia. Come back when you're ready to roll."

"Sure, that will do my anxiety a load of good," Jason

muttered, still counting the delegates as they trickled into the room in twos and threes. Nigel Needham sat in the front row, next to the center aisle, the same seat he'd sat in the entire conference.

"Mate, if you carry on like this, you'll burst into flames, and then we'll have another emergency to deal with. I haven't tried out my firefighting skills in a long time. I'm a bit rusty."

Barnwell watched Jason Ashby fret. Ashby stepped up on to the stage and flicked imaginary dust from the armchairs placed in the middle. He moved the vase of cut flowers on the table a fraction. Two microphones lay awaiting the next two speakers and Jason spread their cables around so no one would trip.

With nothing left to tidy, Jason tapped his lapel mic to check it was working before flapping his hand in front of his face and blowing out in a whoosh. He looked over to see DS O'Hearn and DI Mike Trevelyan waiting on the other side of the stage. He gave them a thumbs-up sign. When they responded with signs of their own, Jason turned to the sound engineer sitting in the middle of the room in front of his console. To the engineer's right, a video recorder was mounted on a tripod. The engineer nodded and Jason waved Barnwell up onto the stage. He handed one of the mics to the constable. "May as well get the session started. We'll leave the doors open for latecomers. I want you to introduce Trevelyan first and guide him to the left-hand chair, O'Hearn will sit on the right. Debate rules." Jason scuttled off the stage and found the dimmer switch for the auditorium's lights, heralding Barnwell's introduction to the session. As he turned the switch, Jason was hit by the door being opened. Tom Vincenti slipped inside the room and quietly closed the door behind him, standing silently against the wall in the half-light as Barnwell started to speak.

Barnwell had long since gotten used to public speaking. He began with the customary greeting he'd always enjoyed when he watched his favorite heavy metal groups live at Wembley

Stadium, adapted for Jersey of course. "Hello Gorey!" he boomed, drawing out the second vowel sounds. "Who's in the mood for some meaty, consequential debate this fine Sunday morning?"

The sparse crowd might have thrown things at him if they'd had any to hand, but they good-naturedly jeered instead. "Just get on with it, Bazza," someone drawled.

"You're in luck," Barnwell explained, "because I am not presenting this session. Let me introduce those who are." He motioned Mike Trevelyan to the stage and clapped him on the shoulder. There was a ripple of applause. "DI Mike Trevelyan, CID, a former Met comrade of our own famed DI Graham, will speak in favor of the blanket rule on body cameras." Barnwell waved Trevelyan to the chair on the left side of the stage.

"Following him, DS O'Hearn, also Met CID, will make the case for *exceptions* to generalized use of bodycams." There was more applause and even a few cheers for the undercover cop. O'Hearn joined Barnwell and Trevelyan on stage, closely followed by Jason Ashby who stood behind the lectern near the edge. O'Hearn looked nervous. As he sat down in his chair, he rubbed his hands on his trousers. Beads of sweat formed on his upper lip. He fiddled with his mic. A whine of feedback from a speaker made everyone in the room cringe. In contrast, Trevelyan had thrown himself down in his chair and was now leaning back, surveying the room with a grin spread across his face.

"Now, can I have a show of hands? Who's in favor of bodycam use in *all* circumstances?" Barnwell counted 15 hands in the air. 'And who's in favor of exceptions?" Significantly more officers favored some kind of limits. After counting the numbers, Barnwell handed his mic to Trevelyan and exited stage right.

In the debate that followed, it became clear that the majority considered that not every aspect of policing necessitated a comprehensive video record. But others were concerned about the public reaction if there was discretionary usage, something

Jason the moderator, brought up early on. "What right do we have to expect the public," he asked O'Hearn and Trevelyan, "to understand that *this* officer will have their work chronicled on camera, but *this* one will not?"

"It really depends on the nature of the work," O'Hearn said. Someone at the back called for him to speak up as the sound of his voice petered out. "Ah, sorry," he said, glancing at the mic he held in his hand and then at Jason. Ashby beckoned to the sound engineer. "Hold on a sec, everyone. Seems we need to change the mic."

The sound engineer, dressed all in black, wound his way to the front of the stage. Prevented from going further thanks to the length of cable that ran from his headset back to his console, he reached over and gave the mic to Nigel Needham who handed it to Tom Vincenti. Vincenti was still standing, arms folded, by the door. He reached up and gave Jason Ashby the slender, black mic, and he passed it to O'Hearn. "Flick the button upward," Jason advised O'Hearn quietly before returning to his spot behind the lectern.

"Okay..." O'Hearn looked out at the room now decently populated. Half the chairs were occupied. "As I was say..." A light buzzing sound came through the speaker. O'Hearn went rigid. His eyes locked on the audience, but they were filled with terror. A tremor shook his body, his jaw flexed involuntarily.

"He's having a fit!" came the first voice of alarm.

Barnwell strode toward the stricken man from the side of the stage. "Electrocution!" he yelled.

"Don't touch him!" cried another voice.

"Turn off the power!" Jason cried.

"Hand me that broom!" Barnwell shot back, subject now to a sudden rush of memories; last year's emergency training came back to him.

Jason tossed Barnwell a big, long-handled stage broom that was propped up against the wall. It fell short and Barnwell leaned forward to grab it from the floor. Approaching O'Hearn with quick, deliberate steps, Barnwell jabbed the broom at the man's hands trying to slap the microphone from O'Hearn's white-knuckled grasp. He tipped forward in his chair but was still upright, blurting out strange, strangled sounds as his body trembled uncontrollably.

"Get it out of his hand!" someone was yelling. "Yank it away from him!"

Barnwell raised the broom above his head and with a hefty downward strike finally dislodged the mic. It clattered onto the wooden surface of the stage and rolled to its edge. O'Hearn fell back in his seat and slumped to the side.

"Get an ambulance," Barnwell said to Trevelyan. "No one touch anything. Have everyone wait in the lobby. And get DI Graham down here, *now*." Then to the victim, "Patrick? Can you hear me, lad?" O'Hearn started to slip to the floor. Barnwell grabbed him but didn't stop his slide. Instead, the constable gently supported O'Hearn's body so that in seconds, he was lying prostrate on the floor.

O'Hearn's eyes were open, but there was no response. Jason hovered, unbearably uncomfortable amid such drama. "Is he...?"

"I don't know," Barnwell fired back. He was pulling at Patrick's shirt. The hand that had been holding the mic was red and Barnwell knew that where the current had exited O'Hearn's body there would be more burns. "Could just be knocked out, but if the current went straight across his chest, he's in trouble."

Barnwell placed his fingertips on O'Hearn's neck to check for a pulse. *Crikey.* He kneeled immediately placing one hand over the other. He pressed down on O'Hearn's chest. After thirty presses, Barnwell leaned over to breathe into his mouth. He could smell burned flesh. The room had fallen completely silent, the only sound coming from Barnwell's efforts. He sat up and started over with the compressions, his face reddening with exertion, beads of sweat appearing at his brow. Behind him Jason stood, his hands clasped in front of him, his lips pressed against them as he breathed a silent prayer.

A peal of sirens announced the arrival of the ambulance crew. They worked quickly, ferrying Patrick to the vehicle, even defibrillating his heart while transporting him, before setting off purposefully down the hill to St. Helier General. Their quick, efficient, well-established procedure couldn't mask the critical state of the situation for Barnwell, however. He had felt no response from O'Hearn's heart beneath his large, strong hands. As he massaged his palms and silently prayed for a miracle, Barnwell thought about what he was going to tell his boss. He stepped out through the fire exit into the frosty air, savoring the whip of cold against his hot, exposed skin. A few officers stood there having a smoke, and he dodged some expressions of sympathy and other well-meaning inquiries before finding a quiet corner to call DI Graham.

CHAPTER TWENTY-FOUR

O N AN ISLAND as small as Jersey, when a police professional calls for 'all hands on deck,' things move very quickly indeed.

Marcus Tomlinson was at St. Helier General less than twenty minutes after O'Hearn was pronounced dead by the head of the Accident & Emergency team who received him. The sober-looking pathologist had the grim duty of following a nurse back to the cubicle where Patrick had been laid out. "Please move him to the mortuary," Tomlinson said, motioning toward the elevators. "I'll perform a full autopsy." He called DI Graham, who was just getting out of his car at the conference center.

"Damn," Graham breathed. "Barnwell said he just dropped dead on the stage? Never felt a pulse."

"That would be about the size of it."

There was a groan from the other end of the phone. "This isn't the result of some terrible prank, is it?" Graham asked. "I mean, it has to be an accident surely. Who would murder a copper in front of a load of other coppers? That's so brazen, I'd almost admire whoever did it."

"All the signs point to a heart attack, caused by the flow of current across his chest cavity," Tomlinson said, "I'll know more when we've looked for internal burning. Can you tell me a little more about the circumstances?"

"Barnwell said he was on stage, speaking. The mic got switched out because the first one was faulty. As soon as he turned the power on, that was it."

"Do you know how he was? His emotional state?"

"Uh, no. How would it help?"

"Because it looks like," Marcus added, "he had been sweating. Perhaps he was nervous about public speaking?"

"Nervous?" Graham asked.

"Any kind of water, including sweat, helps conduct electricity, David," Marcus reminded him. "But as I say, I'll know more soon. Sit tight." He rang off, leaving Graham feeling bereft in the conference center car park.

Jack Wentworth arrived as the DI was gathering himself. "Thanks for coming. Did Janice fill you in?" Graham asked as they walked together to the glass entry doors of the building.

"Can't believe it," Jack replied. He had the face of a man whose rug had been pulled suddenly from under him. He blew on his hands. "Very uncommon for something like this to happen. I'm talking one-in-a-million. What do you need from me, right now?"

"Take a look around," Graham ordered. "Don't touch or change anything, but give me your gut reaction, alright?"

"What am I looking for?" Jack asked, not unreasonably.

"Anything amiss, not quite right. Or better yet, not right at all, wrong even." His phone against his ear, Graham waved Jack into the conference room, where only Barnwell, Jason Ashby, and a tall, gray-suited man remained.

"Jack! Up here," Barnwell said as he entered, waving him up onto the stage and pointing out the offending microphone, its wire winding desultorily across the stage like a lazy snake in the hot sun. "It's plugged in over there." Barnwell pointed. There was a large, electrical panel full of outlets bolted to the wall on the left-hand side of the stage.

"Has anyone touched it since the accident?" Jack asked.

"No one has dared," Barnwell replied. "I whacked it with a broom."

"Good thinking," Jack said, nodding. "Grabbing the microphone from his hand would have resulted in two casualties, not one. Small mercies, eh?" He shook his head. "Bloody bad luck, though. I'm so sorry this happened, Bazza."

"Hmph, I doubt luck had anything to do with it. He was expendable, more like."

"You think this was deliberate?"

"Two coppers from the same nick dead within a day or so of each other? I'll say. But bloody unfair, I'll give you that. I could have reached him faster."

"I don't see how," Jason said, showing a surprising amount of compassion. "You did everything you could. You can't have known what was wrong for a good few seconds. I know I didn't."

Jack slipped off his black rucksack and brought out a small toolkit and a slender, yellow voltmeter the size of a cellphone. "I don't think we need Sherlock Holmes on this one," Jack said. He glanced down, reconstructing the event in his mind.

"How's that?" Barnwell said.

Jack had still not touched the microphone. He walked over to the sound engineer's board and stared at it for a long moment, then examined the wall outlets. "Where's the fuse box?"

The tall, gray-suited man turned out to be the manager of the conference center. He had been hovering anxiously from the second he heard the sirens and now showed Jack to a box on the wall. The man stammered as he spoke. "O-o-o-over h-h-here." Jack shone his phone's flashlight into it, giving it a cursory once-over.

The door to the room swished open and DI Graham stalked

in, emotionally drained following two difficult phone calls. He'd gotten HQ in St. Helier to back off from getting involved in this second case, assuring them that Gorey Constabulary's efforts would be nothing short of Herculean and, with a call to London, he'd confirmed that, for the moment at least, he was also the Met leadership's first choice to lead both investigations. He knew that much would depend on how things progressed in the next twenty-four hours. He was beginning to feel the white-hot glare of far too many spotlights.

CHAPTER TWENTY-FIVE

"WHAT HAVE YOU got, Jack?" Graham asked, his eyes flitting over the engineer who was stroking his lips between his thumb and forefinger. He was back to looking down at the treacherous microphone. "Anything?"

"The microphone was faulty—tampered with," Jack said, simply. "Or just broken. The wiring's a mess, and the body of the mic is fitted improperly, leaving exposed wires.

"He was sweating apparently."

"Ah, yeah, so if his hands were wet, the sweat could have conducted an electrical charge from the mic to his hand and then, well, curtains."

"Hang on, now," Jason objected immediately. "We can't go leaping to conclusions."

"We can't?" Graham demanded, irritated. "That's a shame. I do so *love* a good leap."

Barnwell took Ashby aside. "Jason, mate, maybe you and the manager here should get together and make some alternative arrangements. We'll be a while. Perhaps wind things up for today, eh? Give people the afternoon off. Can't imagine anyone wanting to listen to a session about..." Barnwell glanced at the wall where the conference agenda was posted, *"Vehicle History Reports and Investigative Tools in High-Speed Investigations* after what just happened, can you? Start over tomorrow?"

Jason nodded, finally defeated. He left the conference room alongside the relieved conference center manager who promised him a cup of tea, or "maybe something stronger."

"He's not a bad lad, but he's a bit of a muppet," Barnwell said to Graham. They walked over to where Wentworth was now examining the electrical boxes in the area off-stage to the left. He was tutting over something.

"So, what do you reckon, sir?" Barnwell said.

Graham ached for a cup of tea. "You're not a DS yet, Barry, but why don't you have a stab?"

Barnwell rocked back and forth on his heels. "Murder by electrocution? Is that really our theory?"

"I'd say so. Tomlinson's working with an open mind, but it's too coincidental to have two deaths inside two days of two coppers who were working the same op."

"On our manor an' all," Barnwell said. "Someone planned this and carefully, I reckon."

Graham nodded, the phone to his ear once again. "A *bona fide* premeditated killing using the mains supply. Unless I've leaped to a conclusion," he said, though his eyebrows confirmed that he believed he *hadn't*, "Jack's findings are going to support that theory. And so should Marcus' autopsy."

"I mean, d'you think the perp or perps have come down from London?" Barnwell mused.

"Probably, although I would have thought it safer to kill them in situ," Graham responded. "Leaving a body or two in a dark London alley would be a lot less risky for a murderer than killing them on an island that they would have to travel to and from in front of hordes of police."

"Perhaps they assumed that Jersey might be an easier place to get away with it." Barnwell was personally offended by this notion; it wouldn't do for others to see Jersey as a sleepy backwater, especially when he knew the island to be a surprisingly dynamic place. Certainly, there'd been no shortage of unexplained deaths and accidental killings recently. "They reckon we're a soft touch, down here, don't they?" he said. "The bloody *nerve* of it."

"I'm going to call Tomlinson," Graham said, waving the phone around as though trying to get a better signal.

"Bit soon, sir. I thought you knew what he was going to say."

"He's had half an hour, and I'm an old-fashioned chap in some ways. I believe in acting on the findings of experts. And I prefer to hear them straight from the horse's mouth. Speaking of which..." Graham heard Marcus grumbling in the background as he answered his phone.

"David? You must understand, dear fellow, that autopsy procedures take as long as they take," Tomlinson tried to explain.

DI Graham put the phone on speaker. "I do understand, Marcus. But was it electrocution?" he asked simply.

"Not content to interrupt my post-mortem, you're trying to pre-empt the results, too, hmm? What would you expect to see, if it were?" he asked.

"Wait, you're *testing* me?" Graham complained.

"Just seeing if this remarkable brain of yours is all it's cracked up to be."

Graham paced in a circle for a few moments, then said, "Let's see, Patrick was right-handed, so it stands to reason the current entered through his right hand, and then shot up his arm and through his chest. You'll see an entry mark, which looks like a damaged, circular patch about an inch across on his hand, and probably an exit mark near his shoulder blades. If he was wearing his medallion, that will have caused burns as the electrical charge heated it to dangerous temperatures."

Barnwell was staring at his boss, rapt as usual. He loved these displays of raw competence and never found them tiresome. Each seemed to rely on a completely different skill set. Plus, Graham was confident in his abilities but never vainglorious or attention-seeking.

"...There will be severe congestion to the organs, and you'll see tiny red spots on the skin above the line followed by the current, from right hand to left shoulder, I'd imagine. They're called petechiae," he said. "You might also see a type of muscular damage called Zenker's degeneration, which looks like a spiral fragmentation of the muscle fibers."

"Top man, sir," Barnwell whispered.

"I'd guess you'll find ventricular fibrillation as the actual cause of death due to the electrical current interfering with the muscular motion in the heart, causing rapid, uncontrolled movement."

Tomlinson cleared his throat. "Anything else?"

"Oh yes, we should probably consider the testimony of forty-some police officers who watched him get electrocuted, and the engineer who believes the microphone may have been tampered with," Graham added pointedly. "Okay, I'm done. Now, please tell me I'm completely wrong, and we're not actually chasing a vicious, conniving double-murderer."

"Sorry, old fruit, but you are absolutely right as to cause," Tomlinson said. "Textbook definition of death by electrocution. Can't say it was murder from my findings, though. I've never seen a murder carried out successfully this way, but you have more context."

"Yeah, rare choice of means but I'm certain. One for the annals," Graham said. "Thanks, Marcus." Graham hung up, pinched the bridge of his nose, and let out a short, angry curse.

Jason walked back into the room. Warmed by a shot of something stronger than tea, he was feeling bullish. "My mother used to threaten to wash my mouth out with soap and water for saying that sort of thing," he chipped in, most inadvisably. "Ow!" he cried as Barnwell's strong hand forcefully grasped Ashby's upper arm as he escorted him out of the room.

"Listen, my fuse is pretty short right now," Barnwell muttered out of the side of his mouth, digging his fingertips into the soft skin of Jason's upper arm. "And that'll go for a lot of folks around here. Just bear that in mind, alright?"

"I only..." Jason began. Barnwell pushed open the exterior doors to the conference center and in unison, they trotted down the steps.

"You're worried about the PR. I get it," Barnwell said as he took Jason further to one side, perhaps twenty feet from the group standing outside the building.

"I mean, there's no need to make it sound like I don't care," Jason sniffed. "It's just that this organization's really new, and it's a big springboard for me. It's important to present the best possible..."

"The dead," Graham reminded them, arriving from behind the looming Barnwell, "are not to be subjected to your spin and posturing."

"I beg to differ," a voice interjected loudly. Graham turned his head and to his dismay found another irritant clinging to him and refusing to let go: Freddie Solomon.

CHAPTER TWENTY-SIX

"HAPPY TO DISCUSS freedom of speech, journalistic ethics, anytime, anywhere, with you, Inspector, but the path to censorship is a very slippery slope, wouldn't you say?" Freddie smirked, delighted to have caught the inspector with a "gotcha". "And a slope it is very easy to find oneself traveling down if one is not careful. I would urge you not to make any attempt to curtail *anyone's* message, lest you find yourself traveling down it."

"Ending up at the bottom on my backside, I suppose," Graham grunted. "Censorship is not what I was talking about as you very well know. I was talking about the accurate presentation of *facts*, something all too lacking in this day and age. And respect, another notion with which you don't seem to be too familiar. But then, given your loose relationship with the truth, living in an upside-down world would appear to be your default position. Reading your blog mirrors the experience of falling down a rabbit hole and ending up in Wonderland. Add a side of condescension and the creativity of a fiction writer, and you've got what amounts to a hairball of disinformation, obfuscation, and propaganda. That it all seems to come so easily to you is a reflection on your character, so I wouldn't charge me with anything if I were you. Pot and kettle come to mind."

"Golly, you seem stressed, Inspector. Under some pressure? Stalled in your investigation and now another death, all in front of..." Freddie spread his arms wide to encompass the crowd outside the conference center, "fellow police officers who must be judging your performance even if they are not saying so. I wouldn't be so down on my blog, you know. It could throw up some useful avenues of inquiry for you to follow."

"I read your last piece," Graham told him, through gritted teeth, "and 'throwing up' was at the forefront of my mind, I can tell you."

"Detective Inspector Graham, the word on the streets is you've got a pair of dead officers who were apparently from the same unit, and perhaps working on the same case." Freddie couldn't possibly know that Devine and O'Hearn had been working together and it was indeed a reach grounded in nothing but Freddie's imagination, but as Graham mused, even a clock is right twice a day.

"There will be an official statement in due course, now if you don't mind, I have work to do," Graham was beginning to regret he'd been goaded into an outburst, despite it being justified. He focused on getting to the safety of his locked car that was still, lamentably, thirty yards away.

"But do you not accept that these officers are to some extent under your protection while on the island?" Freddie persisted, trotting along beside Graham who, several inches taller, was outgunning him in stride and speed.

"Of course," Graham said. "We take that responsibility very seriously, and the full resources of the Gorey Constabulary are now deployed as part of this investigation."

"But doesn't one have to ask oneself if those resources are sufficient?" Freddie argued as Graham bore down, his eyes focused on the handle of his driver's side door. He wanted to get away from this odious little man as fast as he could. "Is it time to review the station's budget, DI Graham? Hand over the responsibility for the investigations to someone more, um, *experienced*?"

"Nothing more, thank you," Graham said, channeling his inner politician.

But Freddie wasn't finished. "If experienced, highly trained officers aren't safe on our streets, DI Graham, then *who is*?" he called out as Ashby, who had been anxiously keeping pace with the two warring men, finally did something useful and put himself between them.

"That's enough now," Jason said, putting his palm on Freddie's chest. Freddie looked down, but not before piercing Jason with a shot of derision. Ashby carefully peeled his hand away.

Graham ignored them. He refused to take any more of Freddie's bait, and he certainly wouldn't dignify his work with an official response. He might be able to summon some neat evasions, but Freddie's questioning would be withering, and Graham was husbanding his energies. He was also cripplingly aware that they had almost no progress in a case that had just gotten exponentially worse. He had very little to feed Freddie, even if he'd wanted to.

"I really think you'd prefer to comment on this before I publish!" Freddie was shouting after him. He was now in grave danger of being manhandled by the exhausted and rapidly short-fused Barnwell who'd seen the trouble and caught up to them. "Alright, I'm going," Freddie told the constable, his palms up. "Harassing members of the press is frowned upon these days, you know. This country is in dire need of the Fourth Estate. We are a valuable and necessary entity."

Barnwell had no idea what he was talking about. "And you

need a boot up your backside, Solomon. Off with you, now. Go scribble in a coloring book or something." Freddie and Jason walked away, Jason eyeing Freddie carefully, keeping his distance.

Ahead of him, Barnwell saw Graham lean against his car and take a call, the message of which was inaudible from so far away, but richly illustrated by Graham's body language. He raised his hand, palm upwards while he bent his head, shaking it as he gently kicked his foot against a curb. He'd promised something but hadn't been able to deliver? Asking forgiveness, perhaps committing to something else? At the end of the call, with the DI looking back up the hill toward him, but a distance away, Barnwell couldn't be sure if he saw him smile, grimace, or sigh. He was seemingly calmer, however, as he walked back to Barnwell.

"Hard to believe this case, isn't it?" Barnwell observed as his boss approached. He knew the inspector would already be working through the possibilities in his mind, interrogating what they already knew and preparing a fresh list of questions.

"Two CID officers," Graham said, laying things out, "assigned to the same case, meeting unpleasant ends less than two days apart." He was pacing, the warmth and seclusion of his locked car forgotten.

"Shall we go inside, sir? Where it's warmer?"

"A bracing chill is good for the brain, Barnwell. Speeds things up, clarifies."

Barnwell nodded and suppressed a shiver. "Do you know what they were working on, sir?"

"Drugs. Now, if I were a gangland veteran, someone who knew when it was worthwhile to take a risk, and I'd already identified those two as moles..."

"Do you think that's what happened, sir?"

Graham took a deep breath. "Devine's cover had been blown. They were warning her off. Telling her to keep her distance."

"Bloody hell. Why didn't she tell someone?"

"She did."

"Who, sir?"

"Me."

"Oh."

"It was while we were in the pub. I urged her to tell her handler, but she refused. She didn't want to stall the op. You nearly got involved."

"Me, sir?"

"I offered you as an escort to accompany her back to her B&B. She refused that, too."

"Wish she'd listened," Barnwell muttered.

"I should have insisted."

"You weren't to know, sir. And it sounds like she didn't want to accept any advice."

"I know, but I didn't do my best, Barnwell. I could have helped her, told someone, saved her even. I was too caught up in the evening. I wasn't sharp enough."

"It was busy, a long day. You were spinning a lot of plates. Don't blame yourself. She wasn't taking responsibility for her own safety. I don't know too much about these things, but they must have protocols."

"They do, and she certainly wasn't following them. But —ugh."

"I wonder if we'll find similar texts on O'Hearns' phone," Barnwell said, seeing that Graham would go round and round this particular mulberry bush if he wasn't dragged away from it.

"Yes, maybe. But surely O'Hearn would have said something given Kimberley's fate? And I warned him, too. He figured he'd be fine. I wonder what they were playing at?" Graham groaned.

Graham steered Barnwell back toward the steps outside the conference center, where some forty officers were still mingling and gossiping. "Reckon you could get statements from them all, then escort them to the nearest pub? Get Janice to help you."

Barnwell surveyed the group. They were standing around in

near-freezing temperatures, waiting for any news, or the chance to help. "forty-odd morose, upset coppers? Shouldn't be a problem, boss."

CHAPTER TWENTY-SEVEN

"THEY PROBABLY CHOSE the conference specifically. Marks out in the open, guards down," Barnwell said in a monotone. He was leaning against the outside wall of the *Flask and Flagon* while Janice called Graham. They'd just dispatched around forty thirsty policemen into the waiting arms of the hostelry's bar staff, having spent several hours taking their statements. "Perfect opportunity for some mobster to decide he doesn't want any more surveillance of his drug operation. Easy and efficient. Killer's best practices."

"But we haven't found a connection with any gangs that we can point to," Janice said.

"Maybe we should put all this lot into searching the island," Barnwell replied. He nodded at the pub, where the volume of activity inside was starting to build to the point he could hear it through the window. "Find the car Kimberley was hit by."

"Bit drastic, but it might come to that." The ringtone Janice was listening to stopped as Graham picked up. "Bazza and I have finished with the delegates," she said. "Nothing. No one saw anything unusual. We've noted names and details, and they're all now drowning their sorrows with help of local brews. Lucky for them that we're so blessed in that regard although even if we weren't, I think they'd have found something to suit their tastes."

"Huh, a whole room full of people, crack oppos at that, with at least theoretical access to the hardware and the microphone, but no one saw or heard anything. Typical," Graham said.

"Is there anything else we can do before we finish up for the day?" Janice was beat. Barnwell looked dead on his feet—his face was pale and the lines on his face were deeper than usual, making him look haggard. He was at this moment yawning with the fulsomeness of a baby hippo.

"What's up with Roach?" Graham asked her, "I'm expecting him back soon with some insights about that glass from the hit-and-run."

"Talked to him earlier, sir, before all the, er, fuss at the conference. He sounded excited."

This was better. "You mean he's got something?" Graham hoped aloud.

"He was learning a lot, so he said," Harding replied. "But I can't speak for any results." She looked at her watch. It was 6:24 p.m.

"Yeah, yeah," Graham sighed. "Patience is a virtue, efficiency is a skill." He went quiet.

"He's due back in about an hour," Janice said to fill the empty void.

"Text me his arrival time, and I'll pick him up from the airport."

"Got it, sir, leave it with me," Janice said crisply.

She pressed her phone's screen again, bringing up Roach's number immediately.

"Evening, lad!" she said cheerily. "The DI's gonna pick you up from the airport, so make sure you look shipshape. And that you have your story straight, preferably a good one.

Roach was a bundle of nerves. "Why would I need to get my

story straight? I haven't done anything other than stare down a microscope for the last thirty-six hours. Is the DI on the warpath? Was I supposed to call before tea or something?"

"Relax, Jim," Harding said.

Roach took a second to glance around the airport's departure gate, where he and fifteen others were moments from boarding. To Roach, the Bombardier twin-prop on the tarmac was a terrifyingly diminutive transport option, one he'd have gladly swum the Channel to avoid. "A big dollop of luck would come in handy right now," he said, his fingers fidgeting. "I thought it would be easier on the way back."

"You'll be as safe as houses," Harding said. "Just breathe in and out steadily. You could try that routine we learned at yoga class."

"Sure." Roach sounded entirely uncertain. "Triangle breathing, right?"

"Square breathing, Roachie, square. In for four, hold for four, out for four, hold for four," she said in the sing-songy voice of someone who had repeated the phrase hundreds of times. "Have you got your lucky charm?" she added.

"Yep." Roach looked down at his great-grandfather's wartime Royal Air Force badge. A wreath of leaves encircled the RAF insignia. It was topped with a crown. Roach was rubbing it between his fingers. "He made it through to Berlin twenty times in the pitch dark," Roach told Janice. "Reckon I can manage fifty minutes from Southampton to Jersey." He looked out of the big glass windows of the provincial airport. Huge spotlights lit up the airplane apron outside, but there was no hiding the darkness of the British winter evening beyond. Roach tried to lighten the mood. "Does Marcus miss me yet?" he asked.

"You'll be flavor of the month if you bring back something useful on those glass fragments. We're getting nowhere fast at this end. There's been a second death."

"What? No!" Roach sat up straight in his seat before glancing around at his fellow travelers. He hunched over. "Who? How?"

"Patrick O'Hearn. Electrocution. He was presenting at the conference and keeled over. Shocked from the mic. Bazza tried to resuscitate him, but he was gone from the get-go. We've just finished interviewing all those in the audience." Janice looked over at Barnwell who was still leaning against the pub wall. He had propped his head against the brick exterior, eyes closed, arms crossed in front of him. She wondered if he was ignoring her. He looked asleep. "Think yourself lucky you missed it all."

"Wow, blimey, that's terrible. He seemed a good bloke," was all Roach could offer. "Do they think Kimberley's death is connected?"

"They sure do," Janice replied. "So we're hoping for big things from you."

"They have all the latest gear here, but..."

"Well, hang on and tell the DI when he meets you at the airport," Harding said. "He's getting a bit desperate." She heard Roach being invited to board over the loudspeaker system.

"Got to go. Everything will be fine," he said, as he prepared to put one foot in front of the other to walk down the short tunnel to the aircraft's door. "Right?"

"Absolutely," Harding said. "Close your eyes, breathe deep, count to four in a square. You'll be here in no time."

"19:20 in fact. Hopefully earlier. The sooner the better."

"See you tomorrow. We're going off duty, but text me when you land, yeah? So I know you're safe." Roach and Barnwell had come a long way since DI Graham had arrived, but Janice still felt maternal toward them, just a little less like a school dinner lady trying to organize them into an orderly line. "You're like a clucky hen over those boys," her mother once told her. It was true.

Janice poked Barnwell who awoke from his doze with a start. "We can go home, Bazza."

Barnwell yawned again and stretched. "Great. Can you give me a lift to the station? Gotta pick up my bike."

"I can drop you home if you like? I'll pick you up in the morning."

"Nah, thanks all the same. I need the exercise."

"You look all in, lad. Let me give you a lift."

'S'okay, fresh air will do me good." Barnwell looked down at his wrist. A digital watch with a rubber strap was wound around it. He tapped it. "Haven't quite done enough miles today yet. A ride home should do it."

"Wonders will never cease," Janice marveled. "Come on, let's go get the car."

As they trudged up the long hill to the conference center, Janice nearly put her arm through Barnwell's before deciding it wouldn't be appropriate. Her dark brown Prius sat alone and forlorn in the car park like an enormous mouse, the windscreen misted up except for two clear semi-circles situated just above the vents. When they got inside, she turned the blowers on full blast, and they waited silently as the screen cleared.

On the mainland, Jim placed his hands on the back of each seat to steady himself as he walked shakily through the plane. When he got to his row, it took him two attempts to get his bag into the overhead locker but when he managed it, he sat down, fastened his seat belt, and drew down the window blind, determined to shield his eyes from the view until the flight was over.

CHAPTER TWENTY-EIGHT

F LANKED BY NEAT farmsteads and the occasional large, sophisticated, white-washed home that exhibited clean lines and odd flourishes Graham was certain would be described as a "triumph of architecture and interior design" by the realtors selling them, the Longueville Road wound its way from St. Helier, the island's main hub, to Gorey. Roach looked around. "Won't be able to live out here until I make Chief of Police," he mused, never more glad to be on the ground. "Foot soldiers like me can only dream."

"Dream away, lad. Dreams are where plans begin. And plans lead to action. If that's," Graham nodded into the dark outside, "what you want, make a plan and go for it."

"Uh-huh," Roach said. He leaned his head against the side glass.

Graham looked over at him. "Well, then," he said, keeping the station's police car at exactly a mile over the speed limit, "tell me I didn't just waste valuable constabulary funds on a flight to Southampton and back."

"I delivered the fragments," Roach said, lifting his head.

"We determined they were from the car's lamps and we spent a lot of time looking at them, but Dr. Weiss needs a few more hours."

"I see," Graham said, biting down his disappointment. "Good science takes time, I suppose."

Roach leaned over to dig in the overnight bag by his feet. He pulled out his iPad. "But I *did* learn all about what happens to headlights when they're smashed open. You see, headlights shine when the car's battery sends current through a thin, metal rod. It gets so hot that it glows, sort of like it's being electrocuted..." He blanched slightly. "Sorry, sir, bad timing."

Graham didn't appear to be paying attention. His eyes were trained not on Roach, or even on the road, but on something on a hill ahead of them, beyond a wooden fence that marked the boundary of a farm. "Incredibly bad, Sergeant, but please go on," he murmured.

"Tungsten." Roach paused. The boss was normally sharp on scientific stuff, but he wasn't saying anything. "Heard of it, sir?"

There was a deep and lengthy inhalation, followed by an equally drawn-out sigh. "Transition metal. Atomic number seventy-four. Very useful in industry, particularly in lighting, and," Graham added, turning meaningfully to Roach, "remarkably *dense* at room temperature."

"Sorry, sir. So, you know that tungsten filaments don't catch fire when they glow, because they're housed in a little chamber of inert gas, right there inside the lamp. Without oxygen, a tungsten filament can't catch fire..."

"... but it emits a surprising amount of light as it heats up. Good for seeing at night."

Roach risked distracting Graham for a half-second by showing him two sheets of laboratory data, shaking them out beside him. "These are metal analyses from the inside of the lamp fragments found at the scene of the hit-and-run, sir. There's no sign of tungsten oxide."

"If the lights were on when the protective chamber was cracked in the collision, oxygen would rush in..." Graham started.

"...displacing the inert gas bubble within the light bulb, and causing the tungsten filament to oxidize..."

"...because, I mean, it's just become *ludicrously* hot..."

"...resulting in a reaction which coats everything with a thin layer of tungsten oxide. It's bright yellow, sir, pretty hard to miss."

"And none whatsoever was found on DS Devine's clothing?" Graham clarified. "Not even a smidgen?"

"No, sir." Roach did a half-tolerable job of hiding his immense pride. "DS Devine was hit by a car which was traveling with its lights off, sir." He waited for some kind of recognition, some words, or even a positive facial expression, but DI Graham drove on toward Gorey, implacable. "That's a... um, a helpful bit of evidence, sir?" Roach asked hopefully after a pause.

"To the extent that it supports the theory that this was a murder and not an accident, yes, it's useful."

"But hardly a case-cracking discovery," Roach said glumly.

"Most of them aren't, lad," Graham said. "Might be important in court, though. And it helps us rule out other vehicles. We know we're looking for a damaged car without any signs of WO_3. It's significant."

Roach gave a small smile. He'd learned a great deal from Dr. Weiss, who offered a kind and patient alternative to Tomlinson's mildly cantankerous ways. Roach's trip to Southampton had been a welcome break from Tomlinson's exasperated grunts, and his steadfast refusal to accommodate his often-queasy assistant.

Graham and Roach fell into silence, Roach rightly predicting that Graham didn't want to be disturbed by something as prosaic as chatter. It was like riding in a driverless car; Graham aware and efficient, but his movements somehow more mechanical than human. Suddenly, Graham pulled into a lay-by and looked behind him. He swung the steering wheel hard to the right and performed a smart U-turn.

"What are you doing, sir?"

Graham didn't answer. After backtracking several hundred yards, the Detective Inspector slowed the car to a halt across from the fenced edge of the long field they'd passed earlier.

"You might blame me later for wasting your time," Graham said. "But I drive down this road pretty often and when I did so the other day, I'm *certain* that that Vauxhall Cavalier on the gravel outside that farmhouse over there was pointing downhill."

"Sir?" Roach asked, searching in the dark. He turned until he spotted the parked vehicle facing away from them on a swirl of gravel outside an old, stone farmhouse at the top of a slight gradient. "But so what, sir?" he said.

"It's moved."

Daring to be flippant, Roach said, "Well, it's a car, sir. Its owners would be miffed if it didn't."

With eyes marked and colored by stress, Graham turned to Roach with a patience necessarily strip-mined from its source. "They're away. Have been for several days. Nothing has moved except that car. And they always park it downhill."

"You know the entire population of Jersey's holiday plans?" Roach was incredulous. There was a pause as he waited for the tenor of Graham's reply. With his words, he knew he'd taken his career in his hands, if not his well-being, but was confident he would be saved by the hint of respect that underpinned them. Still, it had been a long day, perhaps his judgment was off.

Graham appeared to ignore him again. "I could," Graham said firmly, "absolutely *murder* a cup of tea."

"Right, sir," Roach said.

"Perhaps two."

"Back at the station?" Roach asked, keen to move on.

"Let's drop in on Mrs. Morgenstern. She has the property next door. Barnwell tested her burglar alarms last Thursday."

"Erm, did he, sir?" Roach said.

"And, if I recall, Mrs. Morgenstern mentioned that her neighbors would be away for another week or so."

"How in the name of...?"

"I read my officer's reports, Sergeant," Graham said. "I know if you've been naughty or nice, lazy or lackadaisical, thoughtful or thought*less*, because I read about almost everything you do."

"Can't leave much time for a personal life, sir," Roach ventured to say before he could stop himself. He immediately put his right fist between his teeth, biting down.

Graham's flickering eyelids and perhaps the sharp twist he gave the steering wheel were the only signs that he had heard Roach. The car sped through ninety degrees and started up the rutted track.

CHAPTER TWENTY-NINE

THE OLD FARMSTEAD had been parceled off just a few years before into several lots—the original farmhouse on one, and a converted barn on another. The remainder had been left as pasture after the owners—the Naismiths—retired from farming, their potential laying in their suitability for development. Mrs. Morgenstern, widowed these last six years, lived quietly on the western plot occupying a tasteful, converted stone barn of which Graham had occasionally found himself envious. A battered 1980s Land Rover sat outside the barn on the driveway. It had recently been driven. Graham and Roach could hear its engine clicking as it cooled.

"I thought that was you, Jimmy Roach!" Mrs. Morgenstern said as she came out to greet them. The elderly woman had lived in Gorey all her life. "It's not time to check my burglar alarms again, is it? The other bobby came just the other day." She invited them in and made Graham's hour by offering tea. "Rumor has it," she told them, "that the Detective Inspector can barely function without a cuppa."

"I'd say 'barely' constitutes the best-case scenario," Graham responded, smiling.

"I heard about what's been happening this weekend. Just awful," Mrs. Morgenstern said. She was one of Freddie Solomon's most enthusiastic informants. She contemplated the two men from behind tiny reading glasses perched precariously on the end of her nose. "Are Gorey's CCTV cameras really as useless as they say?"

"Not quite," Roach jumped in, tactfully, "but we're hoping for an upgrade soon."

"Here's hoping, though that doesn't help much in these two cases. Instead," Graham told Mrs. Morgenstern, who was quietly relishing this unexpected attention from two good-looking police officers, "we're going to be relying on the public's recollections. That's where you come in."

Mrs. Morgenstern greeted this with a self-effacing simper. "I can hardly recall what I had for breakfast!" she said. "I hope you're not depending on me to help put anyone away. I'd be like a deer in headlights."

"Nothing nearly as stressful as that, Mrs. Morgenstern," Graham assured her. "We just want to ask you a few questions. Do you know how long before your neighbors, the Naismiths are home?"

Mrs. Morgenstern blinked. "Sheila and Crispin? They're in Italy for another week, aren't they?" She rose to check a Grand Canyon wall calendar. "Yes, back in... five, six, *seven* days. Two weeks they're gone in all."

"Italy, Mrs. Morgenstern?" Roach asked, beginning to type on his tablet.

"Fortieth wedding anniversary. Or is it their forty-fifth?" She laid out cups and a teapot on the kitchen table. "Sugar?"

When both men declined, Mrs. Morgenstern reached into the fridge, pulling out milk for their tea. "There's an old Roman villa, up in the hills above Sorrento. Sheila had a watercolor of the place on their living room wall, said she'd always wanted to see it with her own eyes. Those marvelous tile mosaics, you know. Just beautiful." Then, with a glint in her eye, she added, "They enjoy their wine too. Some good vintages from that part of the world, I shouldn't wonder."

As Roach typed fluently, Graham pressed on. "So, no one has been at the farmhouse in the last week?"

Mrs. Morgenstern glanced east, through the bay window and over the field toward the Naismith's home, before answering. "Well, no," she said, logically. "If anyone had come, I'm sure I'd have seen them. And if I hadn't seen them, I'd have heard them."

"What time do you go to bed, Mrs. Morgenstern, if you don't mind me asking?"

"Around midnight. I get up at six."

"That's not too many hours."

"No, I doze off in the afternoon quite often, especially if I'm watching TV. I do love *Flog It!* What they get sometimes for old tat!"

"Do you nap at any other time, like in the evenings?"

Mrs. Morgenstern sighed. "Yes sometimes, if I've had a long day. I am 79, you know."

"And you're still driving your old Landy, I see."

"Of course, for trips into town. Got to keep up with my friends. We're all old biddies now, but we're full of life." She frowned. "What are you getting at young man?"

"Just trying to understand your movements, Mrs. Morgenstern." *And your reliability as a witness.*

"The DI is certain," Roach explained, "that the Naismith's old Vauxhall has been moved during the time they've been away."

"Moved?" Mrs. Morgenstern asked, curious.

"It was facing downhill a few days ago," Graham said. "It's turned around. It's facing uphill now."

Mrs. Morgenstern pondered the problem as though tasked with solving it. "Well, hmm."

"Perhaps the Naismith's have children or friends who might have used the car?" Roach speculated.

"They have a son," Mrs. Morgenstern recalled.

"Any chance he borrowed the Vauxhall?" Roach asked.

"Probably not. He lives in Dubai."

"Ah. Is there anyone else who might have borrowed it?" Graham said.

"That old thing?" Mrs. Morgenstern said, surprised. "I mean, it gets Sheila down to the shops, but I think the wheels would fall off if it went above thirty. My Landy, on the other hand," she began, but Graham pulled her onto the hard shoulder with a patient smile.

"Thank you, Mrs. Morgenstern," he said. "Would you keep an eye on the Naismith place for us? Call us if you see, or hear, anyone?"

"What, little old me, spying for Scotland Yard?" she tittered.

"We rely on members of the public to remain vigilant and report anything out of the ordinary," Graham reminded her. He eyed Mrs. Morgenstern carefully. He was unaware of her relationship with Freddie Solomon, but there was something about her that gave him cause for concern with respect to her judgment. "Just be sure to inform those most in a position to respond to your information effectively."

"That would be us, Mrs. Morgenstern," Roach added to make it plain.

Mrs. Morgenstern, chuckling at the very idea that she would do otherwise, rose to pour the officers more tea. Graham put his hand over the top of his mug to stop her. "Nothing much out of the ordinary ever happens here," she said.

Roach gave his boss a patient look. "That's not always how it feels to me," he commented quietly.

CHAPTER THIRTY

"**N**OR TO ME, lad." Graham stood and tipped his head back, draining the last of his tea. "Good cuppa that, just what the doctor ordered. Thank you." He put away his notebook and shrugged on his jacket. "So, Mrs. Morgenstern, you'll be in touch if the car moves again, or if you see anyone nosing about?"

"Depend on me, Inspector. Consider it as good as done. I say, what do we have to call Constable Barnwell now?" she asked as she showed them to the door. "After all his medals from the Queen? I wasn't sure how to address him when he came last week."

"PC Barnwell is perfectly fine, Mrs. Morgenstern," Roach said, kindly.

"He's not a 'Sir' yet then?" the elderly lady asked, half-seriously. "People who show up to the Palace in their finery normally come out with a knighthood, don't they?"

"Not yet, he isn't. But you never know what he might get up to next." Graham politely thanked Mrs. Morgenstern for her time, handed her his card, and headed back to the car with Roach.

"Imagine it," Jim said. "'Arise, Sir Bazza'."

"I can see him now, swinging into a garden party under a Sea King chopper," Graham added. "The Dangling White Knight of Gorey."

Both men managed to close their doors before being overcome with laughter, a welcome respite from the strain of the past few days.

Graham pulled out of Mrs. Morgenstern's driveway and onto the long track to the Naismith's farmhouse. While he carefully navigated the muddy, pitted dirt, Roach recovered from the giggles. "They'd make a fortune selling all this off," he said, looking around. "The housing developers will be queuing up to grab a piece when the Naismiths are ready to sell."

The battered Vauxhall they were seeking was parked despondently a few yards from the front door to the farmhouse. Its' original forest green color had faded, the chassis leached and rusted by the elements. Dents were evident in places, patches of sanded down filler in others. It was an unglamorous presentation, even for a thirty-year-old clunker. It sat at a twenty-degree angle to the farmhouse like it had landed there after being tossed and abandoned.

The farmhouse was a large, symmetrical, boxy construction. It had good-sized windows and a sturdy wooden front door that was adorned with only a small diamond beveled glass window and an old iron knocker. The scruffy front garden was bordered by a picket fence badly in need of a coat of creosote, the grass a little too long to be neat. It was divided into two by a paved path and surrounded by borders of hardy, green shrubs and bare earth.

"The car seems out of place," Graham said.

Roach looked around. "It looks totally *in* place, if you ask me," Roach said.

"I mean, it's shoddily parked."

"Yeah... and?" Roach was genuinely confused.

"As if whoever drove it arrived in a hurry, threw it down, and left it there before rushing off."

"Maybe they're just poor at parking. It's not like they have any white lines to guide them."

"I pass along here all the time. The car is always parked neatly, precisely."

"Maybe they were being sloppy for once, coming home straight after closing time at the pub after one too many on a rainy night," Roach offered.

"You spend too much time dealing with people who do that, Sergeant. Do you really think Mr. and Mrs. Naismith, married for forty-odd years, completely unknown to the local constabulary, off in Italy to sample the cultural delights, would drive while under the influence?"

Roach shrugged. He knew it unlikely.

Graham left the light of the car on dipped beam to illuminate the area and approached the Cavalier, taking careful note of the tracks in the dirt. "Hmm, the plates are missing. I wonder where they've got to? That tablet of yours has a camera, right?" he called over to Roach.

"Yeah, a pretty good one, too." Roach leaned into the car and pulled out his tablet. He began recording the scene, careful to follow in Graham's footsteps. "What are we looking for?"

"Signs that the car was recently moved," Graham said. "Although I think we're about to see something more interesting."

As they came around the side of the car, Graham came to a halt. "Here we go. This old tank," he said, "has suffered some battle damage."

"What is it, sir?" Roach asked him as he came in close to Graham, still filming.

"Broken indicator cover, dents to the radiator and the front edge, top of the car. Recent, too." The inspector, his heart beating quickly, knelt down to get a closer view, before making way for

Roach who leaned in to film the front end of the car. "There's a faint smell of engine oil or another lubricant."

"So, it's been driven more recently than a week ago?" Roach guessed.

"I can't be certain, but I reckon it was driven away, and then brought back, in the last few days," Graham surmised. He lifted the handle to the driver's side door. There was a click and the door popped open. "The careless parking, at this funny angle, it just doesn't *fit*, Roach. And this *damage*."

"Perhaps some kids took it on a joy-ride. I mean, they wouldn't give a monkey's what happened to the car."

"Sure, but think about the usual pattern. They drive around like lunatics, then leave the car in a ditch and run off," Graham told him.

"Might not have been thinking about that," Roach said. "They're hardly the sharpest knives in the drawer, most of them."

"And long may they stay so," Graham said. "For all the technology at our disposal, the smarts so many of them don't possess is often the most important thing going in our favor. Now who else would take a car back to the place it was stolen from?" Graham tapped his chin with his forefinger. "I suspect we're dealing with a slightly more clinical type of criminal, than the young, dumb, and feckless. I also think a certain someone had better begin sweeping for hair and fibers."

"That would be me, I suppose?" Roach said. Any progress was energizing, but he'd already had a very tiring weekend. And the less he thought about the flight back to Jersey, the better. His stomach had still not settled. He'd been looking forward to a nice, relaxing evening, perhaps a snack, maybe a beer. But they were investigating the murder of two police officers and it couldn't get more serious than that.

"Well volunteered, lad!" Graham said. He opened his mouth to say more but was interrupted by his phone. "Graham." He listened for a few seconds. "I'll be right over." Turning to Roach,

"The super sounds like he's in a spot of bother. I need to go talk to him. You make a start here. Have you talked to Marcus recently? Is he on a plane to California, yet?"

"Oh, no, he pushed all that back," Roach said. "I spoke to him when I landed. I don't think he felt comfortable disappearing off to drink wine in the Californian sun with two murder cases still open."

"Good," Graham said genuinely. "Right, let me know what you find. Call Janice or Barnwell for a ride home. Or get them out here to help you, if you want."

Roach knew that with Janice and Barnwell off duty, that idea would go down like a crook weighted with bricks in the Thames. "Ten-four," Roach said. "Let me get my kit out of the car. Do we have floodlights in the back?"

Graham waited while Roach positioned lamps so that as much of the car was illuminated as possible. When he was happy, Graham waved and set off toward St. Helier while Roach carefully regarded the battered, once-green Cavalier. He pulled his coat around him against the chill and blew into his cold, bare hands. "Right then, my beauty. Let's see what you can tell me."

CHAPTER THIRTY-ONE

GRAHAM FOUND THE Goldstar Rent-A-Car office just a few minutes' walk away from St. Helier's police headquarters. Needham was sitting alone in the waiting area opposite the main desk, looking resigned to an unpleasant fate.

"Sir? Everything alright?" Graham asked with a brief nod to the two employees who were standing behind the reception desk. They were a study in opposites. One was reed-thin with long legs and what struck Graham as an almost equally long bright orange tie. The other man reminded Graham of Barnwell before his weight-loss. It was clear from the way they were standing who was the senior of the two. The bigger employee had his arms folded. He pressed a clipboard against his chest. The skinny lad had his hands in his pockets.

"David!" Needham said, as though he hadn't seen Graham in months. "Fancy seeing you here."

"Returning your hire car, sir?" Graham asked, taking a red, plastic seat next to Needham.

"I'm trying to, but they say I'm in all kinds of trouble. Five hundred quid, they want. Daylight robbery. Only came in here to drop the thing off and cadge a lift back to my digs. Had visions of a good night's sleep, a pleasant couple more days at the conference, a taxi to the airport, and a flight home to Veronica." Veronica was Nigel Needham's wife, his second. She was a glamorous, confident woman who knew what she was doing when she married a middle-ranking policeman with ambition. That he was married to someone else only two months prior hadn't seemed to bother her in the slightest, and she had relished her position and the respect being the wife of one of the most powerful policemen in the country afforded her. At least it always seemed that way to Graham.

"Well, robberies are our forte!" Graham joked. "Mind if I have a word with the staff? I'm sure we can iron things out." Graham walked over to discreetly speak with the two employees who were standing watching them. He drew them to the far corner of the room. "What's the story, fellas?"

"He brought it back with dents," the younger employee said, brusquely. "Didn't sign the collision damage waiver so he has to pay for the repairs."

The other man flapped his hand in front of his colleague's chest, summoning his silence. He kept his eyes on Graham. "I'm Mark Jones, sir, the manager of this office, and this is my colleague, Lennox Broughton. We don't mean to be unhelpful, but Goldstar has a clear policy concerning damage to our vehicles." He showed Graham a leaflet. Graham ignored it, his mind whirring.

"Actually, if it's not too much trouble, I'd like to see the car in question, please Mr. Jones."

"You would? Why?" the junior employee cut in defensively. His boss sighed and rolled his eyes.

Graham brought out his ID. "I could ask again," he said, "but then you'd be wasting even more of my time." He raised an eyebrow and noted with a certain pleasure that the twiglet in front of him withered to a height two inches shorter than a moment ago.

Leaving Needham sitting in reception and his belligerent junior employee manning the desk, Mark Jones escorted Graham through the messy, cramped office and into a three-car bay. "This used to be a repair workshop," Mr. Jones explained. "But we don't do work on the premises anymore. Going to have to farm this out."

Needham's rental was a smart, silver Mercedes. "Looks brand new," Graham said, taking out his notebook.

"It is, almost. Only got three thousand miles on it. But look at the state of this," Jones said.

They walked around to the front of the car. Graham stared at the grill. *Holy hell.*

"The front's all smashed in," Jones said unnecessarily. "Dinged the radiator something proper. And look at this." There was a long depression across the front of the car. "Going to need to fix that and get a new indicator light, too. Not gonna come cheap."

Graham scribbled in his notebook and glanced at the damage. "Has anyone else touched the car apart from you two and the customer?"

"Not since he brought it in.'

"And was there any damage before it was rented to Superintendent Needham?"

"None. This is our swishest vehicle. Police HQ ordered it, and we always reserve our best for our best, sir. Besides," he explained hurriedly, "we would never send a vehicle out like this. Head office would have our guts for garters."

Graham looked back at the damage. Much would depend on forensic analysis, but there were some deeply troubling signs. An impact had dented the radiator and the front part of the car—an almost exact replica of the damage to the Vauxhall up at the farm —and the yellow housing of the indicator light was shattered.

Graham took a deep breath. "One more time," Graham said, "has anyone, *anyone* touched the front of the vehicle?"

"I suppose I did when I inspected the damage. No one else," Mark Jones said.

"What about your colleague?"

"Lennox? He might have. He was the one receiving the car back into inventory. I was off today but Len gave me a call. He's new and a bit highly strung. He got a little het up when he found the customer a little, ah, unwilling, shall we say? I don't live far so I hopped on over. Cool things down, you know?"

"Okay. A few things are going to happen now," Graham warned. "Let me tell you about them."

CHAPTER THIRTY-TWO

"I'M IMPOUNDING THIS vehicle. It is not to be touched by anyone until my officers come to take it away. You'll have formal paperwork before the end of the evening. And we'll need to fingerprint you, your employee, and everyone else who works here. But look, I want to show you something. Come over here." Graham beckoned with his forefinger. Mark Jones approached Graham with the wariness of one not entirely sure whether the request was benign. "What did the customer tell you? About the damage, I mean."

Jones' face was blank for a second or two, but then he looked at the clipboard he was carrying. "Er... 'Collided with a bollard while parking,'" he read.

"Where?" Graham said hopefully, imagining the chaos of Mrs. Taylor's too-small, jammed, and jumbled parking lot. There was a bollard at the end of it.

Jones looked at his clipboard again. "Doesn't say."

"Does this look like a bollard collision, to you?" Graham asked.

Jones paced around the vehicle. "You know, I worked in

Australia for a year. Helped run a car body shop with a mate of mine. One day, a Toyota pickup gets towed in, guy says he hit a kangaroo going sixty-five." He modeled the shape with his hands. "There was a wedge slammed out of the vehicle like it had hit a bridge pillar."

Graham waited with vanishing patience for the punch line. "And this is instructive how?"

"The next week, another pickup comes in, guy hit a telephone pole at forty after nine pints of Tooeys. You know what?"

"Enlighten me," Graham said. *Or shoot me in the head. Either way.*

"It looked exactly the same!" he observed. "You can never tell *what* someone hit, just how much it's going to cost to fix the damage."

"So, there's no way of knowing what caused this kind of impact, that's what you're saying? This car could have hit a deer, or another car, or a mailbox. Who knows, right?"

"Right," Mark Jones said.

"Wrong," Graham stated, unable to resist educating the man. "Impact damage is a historical record of an event, often encoded, but always available to the right expert with the right tools." Graham didn't wait for the car rental manager's response as he immediately set about taking photographs. He dialed Roach's number.

"Roach?"

"Yes, sir?"

"Where are you?"

"I'm in a taxi on my way home. I've got the samples, sir."

"Change of plan. I want you to go to Goldstar Rent-A-Car in St. Helier and make arrangements to impound one of their cars. It's been turned in damaged."

"Yes, sir."

"Take it in and examine it first thing. Bring the Cavalier in too. No delay. We don't have time to fanny about." Graham abruptly cut the line and immediately dialed Marcus Tomlinson's number.

In the back of the taxi, Roach blew out his cheeks, leaned forward, and tapped his cab driver on the shoulder. "Change of plan, mate."

As Graham hung on the line waiting for Marcus to answer, he reflected on how Tomlinson's professionalism had made his own forensic assessments much more crisp and pertinent.

"So, you're gonna try reading the damage like they're tea leaves or something?" the befuddled manager of Goldstar piped up. He was trying to follow along, but was lagging far behind the detective inspector.

"I'll be looking for patterns, and evidence on the surface of the metal. That's why it's vital no one interfered with the car."

"Well, she's all yours now," Lennox Broughton said, walking into the garage area. "Do we charge you guys per day, or what?"

"N-no, no, no, no, no," Mark Jones said to his colleague walking briskly toward him, his palms face out. Graham gave Broughton a look so withering as to be scarcely survivable, just as Marcus' voice finally came down the phone. "I will not, repeat, *not* be rushed in my work, David. I won't have all the results on the O'Hearn death until the morning." Tomlinson sounded sincerely ticked off.

"No, Marcus, this is something quite different," Graham assured him. "You know that adage about waiting ages for a bus..."

"Only to have two come along at once," Tomlinson growled. "Of course. Does this mean Sergeant Roach's continued adventures in automotive forensics have yielded news?"

As Mark Jones led his younger colleague away, Graham retold finding the Vauxhall Cavalier at the Naismith's farm, and that Roach was carrying out the initial analysis. "And now this rental exhibits almost the same pattern of damage."

"A rental car? Who hired it?"

"Jersey HQ. On behalf of Nigel Needham," Graham replied quietly.

Once he'd unlocked his jaw, Marcus managed, "The *superintendent?*"

"I don't make this stuff up, Marcus. He's here now, and I'm going to take him back to the station for a serious chat. I want Roach to start work on the cars first thing. They need to be a priority. When he was in Southampton, he found that the vehicle that hit DS Devine was driving with its lights off. There was no sign of tungsten oxide on the lamp glass found at the scene, so we need to see if either of these cars show any traces of it. If they do, we can eliminate them."

"Right-o. I'll assist him as necessary. Is that what you rang to say?"

"Not entirely, I wondered if there was a phone with O'Hearn's effects."

"There wasn't. But there was something else... something *unusual.*"

"Oh?"

"I found a small, high-capacity USB drive."

Graham looked around. Both car rental employees were out of earshot, and through an internal window, he could see Needham staring at the tiled floor of the office's waiting area, apparently lost to the world. "What's on it?" Graham asked.

"That's just the thing. It's encrypted in some way. I can't get into it, but I'm no expert. We need Jack."

"I'll send him over in the morning. Where did you find it?"

"That's the thing, David... I found it in O'Hearn's stomach. He'd swallowed it."

CHAPTER THIRTY-THREE

"SORRY ABOUT THAT," Graham said to Nigel
Needham as he returned to the waiting area. He slid his
notebook back into his inside jacket pocket.

"I'm sure I'm the one who should be apologizing," Needham
said, rising from his unhappy vigil by the reception desk.

"Not at all, sir," Graham said. "I'd never let a couple of local
youngsters boss you about. And rental car employees are
always *exceptionally* glib, have you noticed?"

Needham grinned. "Gave them what-for, did you?"

"Everything's in hand," the DI replied.

Taken aback, Needham began, "Really? Well, good heavens."

"Not at all, sir. We'll just go have a quick chat at the station.
I'm sure that'll sort everything out."

On the drive, Needham sat quietly, staring out into the pitch
black of the countryside. Graham made idle chatter before
lapsing into silence as his mind churned.

He pulled up outside the police station. "We're here, sir."

Needham jumped. "Oh, right. So we are."

Inside the building, it was quiet. Janice was sitting at her desk. She was frowning and peering intensely at her computer screen.

"Janice! I thought you were off duty," Graham said.

"I was, but I wanted to run some more searches through our database, follow up on something from this afternoon. What are you doing here?" Janice eyed Needham who stood behind Graham, his eyes on the ground.

"Just brought the super in for a chat." He gave her a big smile.

Janice nodded. 'Would you like me to bring you some tea, sir?"

Graham closed his eyes and exhaled, his shoulders dropping two inches. "I'll do it, Sergeant, but I wouldn't mind a biscuit or two. I can feel my blood sugar sinking by the second." He nodded at Needham who was now staring at the notices stuck on the wall of the reception area. "And it might help with shock."

Janice's eyes flashed in alarm, but Graham turned away from her. "Come on in," he said, waving Needham into his office.

"That teapot will have pride of place in the Met museum one day," Needham joked as he sat down in the chair opposite Graham's desk while Graham boiled water and selected a robust Chinese blend. "Mind," the superintendent added, "I probably belong in a museum myself."

There was a knock on the door. Janice brought in a plate of shortbread. She left it on Graham's desk and swiftly made her exit.

"Come, now, sir," Graham said. "You don't see Mick Jagger or Roger Daltrey slowing down as they get older. That's how I'd rather see you," Graham said. "A legend."

This got a laugh. "*The Who*, and *The Rolling Stones*... You've finally broadened your listening, then?" Needham knew Graham as a man of passionate enthusiasm but very narrow tastes, music-wise anyway. "'Most pop songs written after 1971 were mistakes their creators should regret.' Wasn't that what you once said?

And, 'Every last vestige of *ABBA* should be consigned to the purifying flames'?"

Graham colored. "I was younger and brasher, then. Insufferable as well, I'm sure."

"David," Needham said next, gravely. "I know why I'm here."

"Yes, sir," DI Graham said. He handed Needham a cup of tea and moved to sit behind his desk. "All you need to do..."

"Is to account for my movements, between the time I left the pub on Friday and when I arrived back at my digs," Needham said, crisp and businesslike. "I knew you'd come back to talk to me eventually. I've written down what I can recall." The notebook he brought out wasn't a formal police issue, but a school exercise book bought, probably, in a local stationery shop or given to him by a grandchild. "I've done my best," he said, bending back the notebook cover and turning a half-filled page toward the DI. Needham pushed it across the desk with a forefinger. As he sat back, he reached over to take a shortbread.

Graham looked down at the page. There were enormous gaps. Needham recollected arriving at the pub with the others, telling some stories, and leaving, but then things got patchy. "I found where I'd parked the car," he said. "That Tomlinson fella helped me with directions—and I drove back to the White Horse."

Horse? Graham let it go.

"Seemed to take longer than I remembered but I got there in the end," Needham added.

"So Friday evening was when you got in that scrape? The one with the bollard?" Graham asked. Following a decade-old impulse, Graham's right hand went for the pen on his desk, and his left for the notebook permanently lodged in his inside jacket pocket.

"I believe so," Needham said, memories slipping through his fingers like a handful of frogspawn. "Banged into one of those stone bollards at the end of the car park. Not sure the time.

Eleven-ish? The hotel staff will confirm, I'm sure. The collision caused quite a noise, I'm afraid. People came out to see what was going on."

Stone is the ruin of metal. But a speedy impact with a human, that'll bend a fender just as effectively. "How fast were you going?" Graham asked. "And didn't you see the bollard? Did you have your lights on?"

Blinking, Needham grasped again and again but found the memory jar to be empty. "God's truth, David, I just can't tell you. I remember the look the barman gave me. He was standing there, hands on hips, like I was some seventeen-year-old who'd borrowed his dad's car and brought it back scratched. He had a good sense of humor about it eventually, but I decided not to use the car again. There was no need for it really, I could walk to the conference center, so it stayed parked until I took it back to car rental people this evening."

"Okay, it's easy for me to check," Graham said. "So when you returned the car, the rental company guys noticed the damage."

"Yes, they most certainly did," Needham frowned. "Very upset about it, they were. I mean, I did my best. Restoring my old E-type Jaguar, that's one thing, but these modern cars are made from God-knows-what, some hi-tech metal, and it's just the *devil* to bend back into shape."

"You tried to repair the damage?" Graham asked, his heart falling. His respect for professional convention failed him for a moment. "Please tell me you're joking, Nigel."

"Well, I couldn't take it back in that condition! Those two kids would have had me over a barrel. Could have billed me thousands!"

Whereas now, you're only in danger of being charged with evidence tampering, perverting the course of justice, and just maybe, causing death by dangerous driving and leaving the scene of a fatal accident. Graham turned back to Needham's fragmented Friday evening schedule. "Let's say you drove back to the *White House Inn* and parked—after a fashion. What did you do then?"

"I suppose I might have watched some TV in my room. I like to catch the news."

"What was the news that night, sir?" Graham asked.

For a second, Needham had the face of a man in full flood about to disgorge a catalog of details. But then his face fell.

CHAPTER THIRTY-FOUR

NEEDHAM'S FACE CRUMPLED. Graham saw that the superintendent was balling both fists. "I can't express," Needham said, "what this is like. I just hope you never have to experience it yourself."

Graham nodded. There was acceptance and sympathy in his features, but he simply couldn't let this pass. He quickly tapped out a text to Mrs. Taylor.

"You need for me to tell you, right now, in black and white, whether I did it or not, don't you?" Needham said. He was merely summing up the realities, but each thought required a trek across the uncertain ground of his memory. "Whether I might have taken my car, driven down the hill onto the High Street, and killed DS Devine." Needham looked at Graham unflinchingly. "I looked on a map. I can see how it was done. I could easily have bashed the bollard to cover up other, earlier damage. That's what I'd be thinking if I were you."

The silence was truly awful. That was exactly what Graham was thinking. Needham was now both Graham's best *and* worst suspect. Even imagining him behind the wheel at that fateful moment made Graham feel physically ill, but Needham lacked an alibi, and his version of events was erratic, to say the least. "I'm trying to eliminate you from my inquiries, boss," Graham said. "That's all."

Needham stood. He lifted his chin and squared his shoulders. "I cannot be ruled out," he said. "You're interviewing a potential suspect who is emotionally distressed, and who cannot adequately account for their movements. I don't appear to have a motive, but I can't explain where I was when DS Devine was killed, nor do I have a complete memory of what happened that night. You need to speak to people. You need to investigate. I know the drill. I understand you have a job to do."

Such candor was unexpected enough to knock Graham off his stride. "Sir, there's no way I'd consider you a..."

"David?" Needham said, loud and clear, like a parent demanding a child's attention. "I may be a little addled, but I remember teaching you this stuff. You're a professional. Your success is due to you leaving no stone unturned. Am I right?"

With no other option, Graham nodded.

"So get on and do your thing. You do me no favors by treating me differently from anyone else. DS Devine deserves nothing less than a complete and thorough investigation into her death. Please do your duty. I shall make myself available to you at any time."

"Very well, sir. We'll be in touch. We know where to find you. Please stay on the island until we have completed our inquiries."

"Of course. Thank you. I'll walk back to the White Horse. Fresh air will do me good."

Graham followed Needham as he walked through the station. "Sure you'll be able to find your way?" he said to his former boss.

With nothing but a heaving sigh, Needham stepped through the double doors. "I feel I've walked all over Jersey in the past twenty-four hours *trying* to clear the cobwebs," he said, disappointment and frustration not far from the surface. "I think I know my way now, and if I think of anything, David, you'll be the first to know." Needham headed off toward the road that traversed along the cliff edge high above Gorey and which led to the *White House Inn*.

As Needham strode away, an almost heartbreaking dignity showing in the set of his shoulders, the Detective Inspector stood watching him under a dark sky until he heard his phone beep. He looked down. It was Mrs. Taylor replying to his text. The hotel proprietor, normally very sharp, had no recollection whatsoever of a car colliding with a bollard in her parking lot on Friday night or any night, she told him, but he could be assured that she would make inquiries among her staff.

Graham sighed. He couldn't fathom that Needham might have killed Kimberley Devine, and the idea blew the possibility of a gangland-related double murder to smithereens, but he had to follow where the evidence took him. He turned to Janice who was still pulling faces in front of her computer screen.

"I'm off for the night, Janice."

"Roger that, sir. I'm nearly done too. You get off home, now. I'll switch the phones over to HQ for the night. Barnwell's opening up at eight."

"I imagine I'll be in long before then," Graham said. "I can't sleep when an investigation is in high gear." Janice chewed her lip, her teeth turning the pink flesh white. "What are you working on so har...?"

"Got it!" Janice's face lit up. "You know you asked me to look for any visitors who had links to London gangs?"

"Yes, you didn't find any."

"Well, I've done some more digging around the database, sir. I looked for *residents* with links. And I've found someone. Wasn't recent, but it is significant. Eight years for drug couriering, served five. Nasty stuff. He only got out three months ago."

Graham came around the end of her desk to look at her screen. "Who, Janice, who?"

"Johnny Philbin, the sound engineer at the conference."

"Well, I guess I know what you're going to be doing tomorrow, eh?" He rapped a forefinger on the surface of the desk. "One more thing: Needham damaged his car. I don't know how, exactly. He said he'd hit a bollard at the *White House Inn*. Mrs. Taylor says she doesn't know anything about it. She's going to check with her staff, but I think you should call George. He's the barman. Apparently, he came out when he heard the collision. Get him to confirm what happened and what time, would you? You can do it in the morning."

Thirty minutes later, as he walked into the cold night air, Graham dialed Laura's number. She was at home in her cottage at the end of a *Clos*. It was cold and quiet outside except for the calling of seagulls.

"Detective Inspector, how are things going?" Laura answered. There was a formal tone to her voice, but he could tell she was smiling into the phone.

"Uh, you know, they're going."

"Any progress?"

"Not much to be honest. Lots of things to check up on. No conclusions as of yet. Look, love, I'm not going to make it over tonight. I need an early night and well, frankly, I'm not the best company at the moment."

"Okay, I understand. Tomorrow, maybe?"

"Let's hope so. Speak to you then." He rang off.

Laura sat back in the fat, floral chintz-covered armchair she was sitting in. "Well, I guess I'll have to make my own fun this evening," she told the walls of her living room. She flipped through a folder of DVDs, then perused the shelves Graham had helpfully installed above the living room couch, running her finger along the spines of the novels, before remembering she'd brought a new release by one of her favorite authors home from the library—one of the benefits of her job.

"Solving murders would be more fun," she said quietly. "But I guess reading about them will have to do." She made a cup of chamomile tea and got tucked into the book, but soon found herself distracted. "What am I to make of you, David Graham?" she asked the four walls. "After all the investigating and managing, what do you think we will actually *be* to each other?"

CHAPTER THIRTY-FIVE

The Gorey Gossip
Sunday Late Night Edition

More than anywhere I've lived, Gorey has had its ups and downs in the last few years. You've felt it too, I'm sure—the journey of our failures and successes, good catches and bad, fair weather and foul.

But recent events in Gorey have asked more of us, something we frequently avoid considering—that we reflect upon our mortality. We will all, sooner or later, be whisked off to whatever comes next, but yet again this weekend, we had cause to feel sympathy for yet another soul gathered up long before their time.

And in the most extraordinary of circumstances.

If I told you that you'd meet your maker

while battling for gold in a sailing race, or while scuba diving an unexplored cave, you might be contented enough. But if I said your death would come during a debate, and in front of a significant crowd of onlookers, that might dampen your spirits somewhat. Unfortunately, DS Patrick O'Hearn discovered that the bumbling of Gorey's scatter-brained constabulary is not limited to scanning woeful CCTV footage or wasted hours of intrusive interviews. These supposedly highly trained professionals can't even flick a switch without inviting disaster.

Facing the tragic loss of another of their own—the second in as many days—the hundred or so officers currently on Jersey have circled the wagons. Public involvement in such investigations is critical, but DI Graham and his fellow detectives have adopted a siege mentality. They deny access to the press, dodge difficult questions, and keep on trying the same old, failed methods.

As of this writing, the officer in charge of both investigations, Detective Inspector David Graham, hasn't even formally confirmed that DS O'Hearn's death was malicious.

I managed to speak briefly with several attending delegates, and they reported seeing a bright, blue flash before DS O'Hearn fell convulsing into his seat, his hand locked around the defective microphone that killed him. This grisly spectacle was apparently insufficient to convince DI Graham that DS O'Hearn's death was the result of malice aforethought.

We must also consider the "operational" connections in the victim's lives that may have contributed to their deaths: both DS Devine and O'Hearn were with the Metropolitan Police Criminal Investigations Division, and despite DI Graham's deflections, my sources indicate that both dead officers were working on the same case. These inquiries were likely "undercover" in nature, and we must now assume that the officers were identified as spies, and summarily punished. But the next question is the most terrifying one imaginable: *Is an experienced gangland murderer operating on Jersey?* We are left with no option but to surmise that this is a dangerous case and dangerous actors are in our midst.

I hardly need remind you of the dangers to our security posed by imported thugs. Only months ago, our new librarian, Miss Laura Beecham, was herself threatened by an East-End hoodlum. All who know her are proud that she testified bravely in court, but her presence on the island was not without threat—to her and by extension—to us all.

In that instance, the wider public was not harmed. But who is to say that this will remain the case? These gangs do not discriminate; if they see a threat, they act. Our remarkable island is fast becoming an easy place for Britain's worst villains to do their dirty work, a useful annex for the violent battles that occur as part of London's ongoing drug war. Here, Gorey's finest are proving little match for London's worst—hardened criminals who operate here with impunity it seems.

This is a new challenge, and to respond to it seriously, we must admit what has been obvious for many months: neither our surveillance system, nor our investigators, are up to the task.

CHAPTER THIRTY-SIX

THE KETTLE WAS already boiling by the time Janice walked through the double doors of the station. "Morning, sir!"

Graham emerged to stand in the doorway of his office, leaning against its frame. "Glad you're here, Sergeant. You can help me decide how to handle this little conundrum I've got," he began. "For some reason, I signed up for updates from the *Gorey Gossip*."

"Ah." Janice set down her discreet, black purse. "Freddie Solomon."

"Our very own crack investigative journalist has a new article out. I'm sure a major award for keeping the public informed is on its way to him, but I'm reluctant to read it," Graham said, phone in hand.

"Concerned it will derail your morning?" Janice asked, reaching to flick on the coffee pot, her preference.

"Actually," Graham only half-joked, scrolling to find the article on his cellphone, "I'm concerned it might turn me into a homicidal maniac. But one must keep an ear to the ground, no?"

Harding had read the piece over breakfast and knew that Graham's undoubted reaction to it threatened to be the most difficult part of her morning. "I think you should forget about it, sir," Harding said. "Other things, more important things, are going on this week."

"Right you are." Graham turned and closed the door. The station went deathly quiet. Janice felt her heart sink.

She set about quickly tidying the reception area, calling Jack as she did so. "Hey, love," she said, turning away from Graham's office door lest she was overheard. "How are you getting on?" Jack had driven over to Tomlinson's lab the night before to retrieve the USB drive Tomlinson had found during the post-mortem. He'd been working on it for most of the night.

But before Jack could answer, the quiet was wrecked by a loud, desperate plea to the Almighty. It came from Graham's office. Janice put her hand over her free ear. For the moment, that was her boss's only comment.

"Uh-huh," Janice said into the phone. "And what does 'sixty-four bit' mean?" She half-listened as she paced the office to find a mug and fresh coffee grounds. "So if O'Hearn's USB drive is encrypted like that, can we still read it?"

Another curse, angrier and more colorful, fractured the air. Janice winced.

"Hmm? Oh, that's just the DI," she explained. "He's reading the *Gorey Gossip*. Go on, love, I'm listening."

The door to Graham's office burst open and the inspector stood, red-faced, phone in hand, his eyes squeezed shut. Janice wondered if he were willing the article away. Or wishing he were on a deserted, Tahitian beach. "I'm beginning to think," Graham said, unaware or unconcerned that Harding was on the phone, "that our laws protecting the freedom of the press are a mistake."

"Hang on a second, love," Harding said into the phone again. "As bad as you expected?" she asked Graham, "or worse?"

"Perfidy," he railed, furious. "Calumny, mischief, and hearsay."

"If I become a cat lady in my later years, those will make four fantastic names," Harding said. "In the meantime, sir, do you mind if I catch up with our engineering expert? Jack's on the phone. He's working on the USB drive. He's confident he'll get past the encryption. He just needs some time."

"Thank God someone's honest and reliable," Graham fumed.

He left Janice to finish up with Jack, walking back to his office and sitting heavily behind the desk. He knew the importance of de-stressing during these moments. Laura had been teaching him meditation and simple breathing exercises. They had been somewhat helpful. Today, though, his decision-making was driven by whatever part of him delighted in raging self-sabotage. And so he read the article again, one hand tightly clasping his phone, his teeth firmly clenched.

Thirty minutes later, when Graham refused even a cup of tea, Harding knew something was terribly wrong. There was only one thing to be done.

"I'm so sorry to call, but I just didn't know what to do," she said quietly into the receiver. Graham's office door was closed, but she knew the DI had the hearing range of a bat.

Laura was not exactly overwhelmed with surprise. "This case is turmoil for him," she explained. "He's taken both of these killings personally. His feelings have been, well, a mix of the tragic and the humiliating, you know? Not to mention an audience of a hundred of his peers."

"Freddie Solomon is putting the boot in," Janice told her. "I've never seen the DI so angry."

"Freddie knows what his audience wants and doesn't hesitate to give it to them."

"And a hit-piece always gets more clicks than a glowing portrait," Harding said. "Grossly unfair. But what am I going to do with him, Laura? He's there now, in his office, with the door closed, steaming like a hot kettle."

"Hold tight," Laura said. "I'll be right there."

After an hour of searching, Roach was adamant. "There's not even a speck of it, sir."

"Oh, for heaven's sake, Jim, you've earned the privilege of calling me 'Marcus' by now, 'Dr. Tomlinson' even," the pathologist told him over the phone. "Now, are you certain there isn't even a hint of the stuff?"

With the knowledge that the car that killed Kimberley Devine had had its lights off, Roach had been examining the Naismith's old Vauxhall and Needham's rental for signs of tungsten oxide. If he found even a trace, it would prove that the car's lights were on and therefore not the car involved in the hit-and-run. "I mean, it's bright yellow," Roach reminded Tomlinson. "Stands out pretty well on a metal filament, or plastic housing, or any kind of dark background, or..."

"We have to be *certain*, Jim. This is a crucial piece of evidence for eliminating or pursuing either line of inquiry. If Needham hit that poor DS, I'll drown him in the ruddy Channel myself. But we can't arrest a decorated superintendent for nothing."

"You've changed your tune, Marcus," Roach said. He straightened up with a groan. He'd spent the last seven minutes squatting as he stared at the smashed front-end of the rusted, green-ish Cavalier. "You've threatened my life multiple times before now over what I'd call 'nothing'. Rank makes a difference, does it?"

"I am merely," Tomlinson maintained, "striving to ensure excellence in your work, young man. Besides, you're not a decorated superintendent—yet. Anyway, you're sure? If you've found some tungsten oxide on his lights, he didn't do it."

"Nope, not a sausage. Not on either vehicle. Both had their lights off when they made contact with whatever they collided with."

Now it was Tomlinson's turn to groan. "Did you get the other stuff off, like I said?"

"Yes, sir."

"What about the hair samples?"

Roach put Tomlinson on speaker and arranged the hairs he'd collected from the front seat of the Cavalier on a table in front of him. "Everything would be easier without these gloves on," he complained. "Feel like I'm getting ready to dig up moon rock, not check for fibers." He finished laying out the thirty small sample bags, organizing them from darkest to lightest.

"Mrs. Morgenstern told me that the Naismiths have a chocolate Labrador," he began, pushing sixteen conspicuously canine samples to the side. He had called the Naismiths neighbor earlier, just as she'd been making her morning cup of tea. "Mr. Naismith is completely white on top, and his wife has graying blond hair so, that probably takes care of most of them," he said, sidelining a dozen more samples.

Only two remained. "Marcus?" Roach said over the still-open line.

The sound of shuffling paperwork preceded Tomlinson's response, "Hmmm?"

"How fast can we do a DNA test?"

"Pretty fast, some hours, maybe."

"And how fast," Roach asked, "for two hair samples that we can't identify as the owners or someone related to them?"

The shuffling stopped. "Mitochondrial DNA? Faster than a British Airways Boeing 787 heading to California."

"Where's the patient?" Laura asked, striding into the station to find a relieved Sergeant Harding standing at the reception desk.

"He finally consented to a pot of tea," Harding said. "Was that wise?"

Laura waggled her head ambivalently. "Depends on what type. I've been encouraging him to expand his range." Graham's office door was open, but from the station's doorway, Laura couldn't tell if Graham was at his desk. "So, it's safe now?" she ventured.

"Depends if I picked the right tea, I suppose."

"Ginger and chamomile are calming," Laura said, taking off her long, blue coat. "But he probably wouldn't drink it in the middle of the day. I've managed to get it down him late at night. He finds it helps him sleep, even if he does think that it tastes disgusting."

Janice raised her eyebrows slightly at this reveal of personal intelligence about the DI's nightly habits. "Well, I did consult Google on which tea was best for a nuclear reactor approaching meltdown, but in the end, I chose one that came in a nice, orange tin." She took Laura's coat. "What are you planning to do?" she whispered.

"Trade secret," Laura said. "We've been practicing something."

A low, worried "okay," summed up Harding's views on whatever Laura and Graham had been "practicing."

"All completely above board. You'll see." Laura walked over to the doorway of Graham's office and stood there, her arms folded. "Right, you," she began. "What's the problem?"

Laura closed the door. All Harding could hear from the

reception desk was Laura's muffled, but forceful voice, followed by four minutes of apparent silence. Eventually, the office door opened, and DI Graham appeared, looking a little more put-together than he had earlier.

"Janice," he said, "this is a bit weird, but we're going to need your help."

CHAPTER THIRTY-SEVEN

ARDING BROUGHT THE removable cushions from the chairs in the lobby and dropped them on the floor of Graham's office. "Here you go."

The DI lay down on top of them and wriggled around until he got comfortable. "What are the others doing?"

"Roach is with Dr. Tomlinson working on the cars," Harding said as she manually rolled down the blinds. "Jack's working on the USB. Bazza's running interference at the conference for me. It's proceeding nicely thanks to Ashby." The shutter mechanism reached its end with a satisfying click. Janice turned to survey the room.

"Relax now, remember?" Laura was saying to Graham. "Close your eyes, breathe, and empty your mind."

Graham took in a deep breath and exhaled long and slow. Janice looked at him curiously. He seemed quite unlike his normal self. Pliant.

"We need to turn down the lights," Laura whispered.

"See that panel in the corner?" Harding whispered back,

pointing. "Flip up all the switches, except the last two on the left."

The office took on a muted hue without the wintry light of Gorey coming in. With the shutters down and the station quiet, Graham's office felt shut off from the world. Laura took a chair behind Graham's head. Janice pulled over another and sat next to her.

"Is this the sort of thing you were going for?" Janice whispered, twirling her forefinger.

"Perfect," Laura whispered back. "Good thing this office is roomy."

"Why's that?" Harding wanted to know. The two women's heads were almost touching.

"Sometimes, when we do this, he needs certain things laid out exactly as they were during the time he's trying to remember. It helps prompt more information," Laura said. "We've only done it for small scenarios before, like finding lost keys. Once, he mislaid his passport. This process calms him down and helps with recall that lies deep in the subconscious. I'm hoping for both in relation to the case. It's easier than it sounds, once we get going."

"Where *are* we going?" Janice asked.

"His 'mind palace'. You're coming along, too."

"Eh?"

"Relax, Janice."

"I'm not going to regret this, am I? This isn't some religious mumbo-jumbo nonsense that's going to get me sucked into a cult, is it?"

"The DI Graham Personality Cult?" Laura posited. "D'you think he'd get legions of adoring followers?"

Janice pursed her lips and waggled her head. "Maybe. He has a certain charm."

As Laura and Janice dissolved into giggles, they heard a voice beneath them.

"Closing my eyes doesn't render me deaf, you know."

Laura tutted. "Doesn't appear to keep you quiet, either."

"Hard to get in the groove with you two yammering on."

"Sorry," Harding said. "Just not sure what to do."

"We're going to travel back in time to Friday night. I want to review what happened before Devine got killed. I feel certain that somewhere there is the key to her death. I want to go back there. I want to see if my memory throws up any clues. Laura will help. Take a seat, listen carefully, and write notes. If anyone comes through the doors, it's your job to deal with them.

"Right-o, sir."

They spent a few minutes in the strangely calm police station, sitting in peaceful silence. Laura would have preferred longer, but Janice started fidgeting.

"You are outside the conference center." Laura spoke in a low voice, one Janice hadn't heard her use before. "You're feeling good about the successful day, proud of your team, happy to meet up with old friends. It's Friday evening and you're walking from the conference center to the pub. Who walked down the hill with you?"

Graham was already there, reconstructing the scene in his mind. "I was walking with Needham. Ahead of us were Janice, Barnwell, and Mike Trevelyan." Graham spoke slowly in a monotone, as though he were drowsy. "In front of them, Roach and Vincenti. As we passed Santorini's, the Italian restaurant, Barnwell joined me and Needham, and Janice and Trevelyan walked ahead with Roach and Vincenti. Jason Ashby came out from somewhere, and I finished the walk talking to him and Janice."

"And what happened when you got to the pub?" Laura asked.

"I called you, and after that, joined the others inside."

"And then?"

"The pub was fairly quiet. The lights behind the bar were on

—the glasses and bottles of spirits looked bright, colorful. The subdued lighting in the rest of the pub gave it its warm, homey feel. I looked through the window and saw the silhouette of the castle against the black sky. Two fishermen stood at the bar talking to Lewis Hurd, and there were a couple of tourists. They were sitting at one of the tables, tucking into the fish and chip special. From the back, the restaurant area, I heard laughter so the pub must have had a party booking. The fireplace had a good fire going, and in front of it, they had the wrought iron fireguard with the anchor on it—I prefer that to the overly-fussy Victorian one they have. Reminds me of a peacock's tail. Ferocious birds when threatened, they are." Graham's hand came to life as he emphasized his point with his forefinger.

"Okay, what else did you notice?" Laura redirected Graham gently, keen to avoid going down a rabbit hole full of exotic birds. "I noticed O'Hearn first. Rugby player, prop or second row would be my guess judging by those ears. He and Devine sat next to each other on the bench against the wall. They already had their drinks. They must have just got there because their glasses were almost full. There was space on either side of the bench next to them. Roach sat on their right. Janice sat across from them on the other side of the table."

Laura looked up and with her eyebrows asked Janice for confirmation. Janice nodded.

"I joined them," Graham continued. "Barnwell and Trevelyan were standing in the middle of the pub. They got lost in a crowd of folks who came in shortly after we did. Needham was at the bar ordering a pint of Guinness. Janice introduced me to Devine and O'Hearn. She offered to get the drinks in. I let her because she'd think I was being sexist if I didn't." Janice turned down the corners of her mouth in a half-smile and nodded in agreement at Graham's assessment. "I'd put money behind the bar earlier."

Seeming to have exhausted himself, Graham lapsed into

silence. Janice opened her mouth to say something but closed it when Laura put a finger to her lips. Outside the room, they could hear seagulls, their territorial long calls piercing the quiet.

"Janice," Graham said, starting up again after a long pause, "you shared a joke with the super at the bar, then spoke to Marcus Tomlinson when he arrived. You came back to the table followed by Needham. The super sat across from me and next to Devine and O'Hearn on the bench against the wall. Tomlinson joined us. He sat next to me. O'Hearn left and Roach budged up so that Barnwell could sit next to him. Mike Trevelyan joined us at the other end of the table, next to Needham. I was chatting to Devine until Jason Ashby appeared out of nowhere, and plonked himself down next to me. He quickly decided talking to Jack was more exciting and moved to the end of the table where they started talking digital nuts and bolts. Janice moved to sit next to me. It was like flipping musical chairs."

There was another pause.

"Needham retold some silly tale about a case we worked on eons ago," Graham began again.

Janice rolled her eyes.

"I had a discussion with DS Devine about her cover being blown, and then she left. I suggested someone accompany her home, but she refused." Graham stopped. "I should have pressed." He inhaled deeply and let out a long sigh.

"What happened after she left, David?" Laura prompted, her eyes deep pools of concern.

"That idiot fisherman bumped me, and I got distracted. If only..."

"After that? What happened after that, David?" Laura pressed again.

Graham squeezed his eyelids tight. "Tomlinson left citing a requirement to pack for the holiday-that-never-was. Needham went with him. Mike Trevelyan and I had a quick chat until,"

Graham winced, his shoulders twitching as he wrinkled his nose, "I realized I was late for dinner, and I left the scene."

"Where was Tom Vincenti throughout this?" Harding said.

Graham's mouth fell open, but the answer refused to come out. In his mind, he reached for details drawn together through an interlocking network, uniting senses and impressions until a representation of reality presented itself in his mind. Then, "He was outside the pub. Devine said he'd gone off to make some calls. I got the impression he was ending one when I saw him. We saw all the commotion down below on the High Street, and I came and got you lot."

"Okay, now you know what to do. Go deeper," Laura said. "Get back in there and tell me what you see. We'll be quiet until you're ready," she promised with a quick scowl at Janice, then a smile. "Thanks for doing this," she mouthed.

Harding gave her a thumbs-up, and then they were still again.

CHAPTER THIRTY-EIGHT

THERE WERE NO signs of mental struggle now;
Graham appeared to do nothing at all. He simply lay
with his eyes closed, his hands clasped across his stomach. His breathing was calm and steady. Now and again, he
would raise his hand to outline a shape in the air.

Beneath Graham's eyelids, the table of the pub formed into a
surface as hard and real as the station's floor. He could feel its
polished texture, the chips and imperfections caused by decades
of use by clumsy patrons. To his right, he sensed Marcus Tomlinson's aftershave, mingling with the musky notes of Irish brew that
came from Needham across the table. Opposite, the bulky,
round-shouldered figure of Patrick O'Hearn leaned forward over
his drink. Next to him, Kimberley Devine was listening, her
bright, curious eyes alighting upon each speaker. Janice appeared
as a jovial cloud, hardly defined at all.

The scene quickly gained detail. Graham spotted Barnwell's
dark jacket hanging from a hook on the pub's wall. Next to Barnwell, Roach gestured, his hands typically a little uncertain mid-air, as though seeking validation and praise. For Jack Wentworth,

the others were all but invisible; his focus was on Janice. Even when invited by Jason Ashby to discuss his favorite subject, Jack's eyes followed his girlfriend to the other end of the table as if to apologize for the geeky interruption. Trevelyan, Graham's old mate, whose lined face and widening girth were the only changes Graham could discern in the years since they'd first met, listened respectfully to the two older men either side of him.

Graham's attention swept the bar like a high-powered beam. Nothing escaped his notice; the scene, the people, the objects, the sounds, all had been recorded in his memory.

"Needham was favoring his left side. I saw his right hand shake a little." Graham had discarded the finding as circumstantial at the time, but the more he learned about Needham's problems, the more sense it made. "And Devine was very nervous. She put a brave face on things, but..." The memory of the dead officer began to vibrate, to take on colors of a spectrum invisible to anyone else. "She was scared for her safety," Graham told Laura and Janice. "Elevated pulse, darting eyes. Fidgety under the table."

The DI winced, his mouth curled in pain. "Ah..." His hands were aloft again, but there was no searching or shaping. Instead, they were protecting him from a danger unseen by the others. He shivered visibly, one hand balled in a fist, even as the other tried to ward off the threat. "She was only minutes away. Just down the High Street. I could easily have..."

Laura was quickly by his shoulder, her hands under his neck and at the back of his head. "Breathe with me, David," she said, taking in a long lungful with him, and waiting so that they could exhale together. The invisible threat receded and Graham's hands became still, hanging in mid-air.

"So, DS Devine left, O'Hearn went earlier, Superintendent Needham and Marcus have gone. Who's in the pub now?" Janice asked, checking her notes.

"Yourself and Jack. Barnwell and Roach. Trevelyan." There

was a brief mental struggle. Graham frowned, and his eyes opened for a second. "Jason Ashby, I think."

"Nuh-uh," Janice said. "Ashby wasn't with us. He went to the Gents as Tomlinson and Needham left. I remember seeing him go. I moved back to sit with Jack. Didn't see Jason again until the next morning. Must have had a dicky tummy he was in the toilets so much."

"But did anyone see him in there?" Graham pondered. "He seemed alright to me. He could have slipped out the back."

Janice frowned and pursed her lips. She cast her mind back. "Hmm, you're right."

"So have we managed to establish that Jason wasn't actually in the pub after the victim left?" Laura asked.

"I suspect not, and he was definitely missing at the time of her death," Graham murmured.

"Wait, really?" Concerned, Janice began flicking through her notes, checking both her notebook and her tablet. "That's not what he said when he was interviewed," she said. "He told Barnwell that when he came out of the toilets, we'd all gone, and he simply went back to his room at the conference center. Didn't know anything about the hit-and-run until the morning when he woke up." She leaned forward, her elbows on her knees, now intensely curious as to what would result from this unorthodox interview technique.

Graham wanted to confirm another detail. "So we can't place him after Needham and Tomlinson leave. What *time* was that? It wasn't long after Devine left."

For Janice, this is where her memory fractured. "I... I really couldn't say," Janice confessed.

"Shhh, let me see..." Graham went quiet. The two women sat as still and as silent as birdwatchers. "Tomlinson was going home to pack. Said he had the first flight out of Gorey the next morning."

"I can look it up, s—"

"7:30 a.m. He'd be at the airport 45 minutes before... Got it! The bells. From the church. The half-hour chimes."

"Wow, you have good hearing, sir. That church is a mile away, at least."

"Like a dog's, Sergeant, like a dog's."

"We think David was probably a Golden Retriever in a former life," Laura said.

"Hey, don't take this stuff too far, okay? No reincarnation nonsense. Tomlinson and Needham left at 9:30. Ashby could easily have reached the High Street from the pub in time. Let's get him in. That over-excitable social media saucepot needs a good talking to."

CHAPTER THIRTY-NINE

"I'M GOING TO call it Harding's First Law of Policing," Janice decided. "Apparent innocence is inversely proportional to the amount of time spent in our interview room."

Barnwell attempted to navigate this statement, "You mean, that the longer they sit there, the more guilty they seem?" Ten minutes earlier, Barnwell had brought a reluctant, sullen Jason Ashby into the station.

Janice called him to the window. "I mean, just look at him." Ashby was sitting at a very odd angle, curled up in the chair, facing away from the window. He presented a crumpled, depressed figure. "Keep an eye on him, would you? I've got a call to make."

Janice stepped down the hallway that led to the office area, speaking quietly into her cellphone. She made a note, then dialed another number.

Her call was connected. "Hello? May I speak to George, please? I'm so sorry to disturb you during your time off... Oh, you're in Greece? How nice... Look, I won't keep you long. Just

652   ALISON GOLDEN & GRACE DAGNALL

need to ask about a little incident in the *White House Inn* parking lot, Friday night."

Janice promptly derived the necessary details from George, making a page of notes. She returned to where Barnwell was watching Ashby.

"This room tars everyone with the same brush—'You're in here, so you must have done *something* wrong,'" Barnwell summed up. "A great equalizer, isn't that what they call it?"

DI Graham appeared behind him, returning from freshening up in the station's tiny bathroom. He pulled at his cuffs as he said, "What happened to 'innocent before proven guilty,' Barry?"

"Sorry, sir, but you know what I mean, right? It's like he's been hauled into the headmaster's office. If he has any brains, he'll start singing straight away. And really, how can it be him? Where would he get a car?" Barnwell wondered.

"He has a car rented for him in his capacity as organizer. He had a lot of stuff to move around," Janice said. "Besides, he could have hotwired one."

"Does he seem like the kind of person who even *knows* how to hotwire a car?" Barnwell was incredulous.

"No, but he's lying. We need to find out why." Graham made a quick decision. "Want to join me in there with him? If the surroundings don't loosen his tongue, a burly copper in uniform ought to." He smiled.

"Before you go in there, sir. I called George," Janice said. Seeing Graham's blank look, she added, "The *White House Inn* barman? About the super?"

"Oh yes, what did he say?"

"He remembers it all clearly. It was his last shift before going off to Greece. He confirms that a silver Merc hit a bollard while parking. Quite the kerfuffle. Happened around 10:15."

"That's a relief," Graham said.

"But he also says, he thought the resulting damage was a bit much considering the driver only tapped it."

A long groan came from Graham's mouth.

"You think he could have been trying to cover up something bigger?" she asked.

"It's possible, Sergeant. And even if he's not, he's still in the frame." He turned to look at the morose young man in the interview room. Jason's shock of light orange hair looked flat and lifeless in the gray light.

"Well, I'll leave you two to it. I'm going to interview Johnny Philbin, the sound engineer," Janice said.

"Ah yes, I'll be very interested to hear what you find out, Sergeant. Please report back as soon as you can." Graham patted Barnwell's shoulder and opened the door to the interview room, holding it for him. "After you."

As he entered the room, with its three plain chairs and simple table, Graham noticed Jason was ashen. He was trembling slightly. He clutched himself like he was chilled to the bone.

"Please," Ashby murmured desperately, "you have to let me out of here..."

Graham sat. "Jason, take it easy. You're just here for a chat."

"But I'm *innocent!*" he pleaded.

"We're just firming up our timeline, Jason," Graham said calmly. "No one's escorting you to the gallows at Spithead."

"Where?" Jason asked at once.

"Royal Navy history," Graham explained. Jason stared at him blankly. "Never mind. Constable Barnwell, over to you."

"Right, sir."

Graham had increasingly been encouraging Barnwell into the interview room with him. Initially, the constable had been reluctant, but over time had gained confidence and gone from being a silent brooding presence in the room to an active participant. Recently he had even started to enjoy these "interrogations" as he preferred to coin them. As a kid, Barry had loved playing "CIA and KGB", chasing his "superspy" of a brother around the streets of the East End of London, or evading the

"HQ's resident sniffer dog"—a curious-looking grey-hound/pointer mix named Mopsy. Barnwell recorded the time and date for the digital recorder.

"We're sure you'll be as helpful as possible, and there'll be no need to detain you at length," Graham said.

"Length?" was all Jason could manage.

Barnwell gave a disappointed sigh. "Your earlier interview was... shall we say *inaccurate*, wasn't it Jason?"

"In what way?" he snapped.

"You told us you left the pub on Friday night after we left, which was around 10:15, but you actually left at least forty-five minutes earlier than that."

Jason stared at them, and then said, *"That's* the issue?" He laughed, sounding relieved. "You've brought me in for questioning because of *that.* I'm sorry if my recollection was a few minutes out, but it was a very busy evening and had been a very busy day."

"While you were missing," Graham said, deciding to spell things out for Jason, whom he considered affable and earnest but not exceptionally bright, "DS Devine was killed. What can you tell us about that?"

"Nothing!" Jason insisted. "Absolutely nothing."

"Then where did you go, after you left the pub?

"I didn't!"

"Didn't what?"

"I didn't leave the pub. I went to the bathroom and when I came out, you'd all disappeared. I thought you'd gone on somewhere without me, so I drunk up my drink and left."

"We can't place you in the pub after 9:30," Barnwell told him. "If you were in the bathroom that long, you'd have been in no fit state to do much of anything, let alone drink up and walk back to your room. I repeat, there are no reports of you being seen after you went to the bathroom. We interviewed the bar staff and they make no mention of you."

Jason's mouth opened in response, but the flow of information was obstructed somehow.

CHAPTER FORTY

"CONSTABLE BARNWELL," DI Graham said quietly, "I want you to observe this very closely."

"Sir?"

"Our suspect's demeanor has changed, do you see that?" Graham said.

"Suspect?" Ashby wailed.

"Yes, sir," Barnwell replied. "He's looking rather guilty. Tight-lipped, even."

"Unable to account for his whereabouts," Graham said. "Very suspicious, wouldn't you agree, Constable?"

"*Very*, sir," Barnwell said. "Everyone else can explain these small gaps in their chronology," he added, relishing the chance to employ the word he had heard Graham use more than once, "but for some reason, Mr. Ashby here is struggling."

"Seems to me," Graham said, "that Mr. *Ashby* might have had reasons to want Kimberley and Patrick out of the picture."

"You what?" Jason shrieked, his loudest objection yet.

"You mean," Barry asked, "you think he was involved with a criminal gang in London?"

"What criminal gang?" Jason demanded.

"Might be," Graham said, leaning back to think about this. "What if they sent Mr. Ashby to Jersey to undertake some *business*?"

"Indeed, *nasty* business. Very nasty." Barnwell fixed the younger man with a stare Jason found unbearable. "As in *murderous*."

"Wha...?"

"Perhaps you'd like to tell us what you know, Mr. Ashby."

Jason blinked, then let the air out of his body in a noisy exhale. He started to jiggle his foot from side to side, simultaneously rapping his knuckles on the tabletop. He closed his eyes. "Tiffany Trevelyan," he said. "I don't get the chance to see her often and..."

It was Barnwell's turn to blink. "Wait, you mean Mike Trevelyan's daughter?"

"Yeah, Tiffany," Jason said with the beginnings of a sheepish smile. "She's one-in-a-million."

"She's also only seventeen," Graham pointed out. "Much too young for you. And her father's probably the dictionary definition of a 'protective dad'."

"Not to mention he's a former Metropolitan Police heavyweight boxing champion," Barnwell pointed out. "That's true, isn't it, sir?"

"It is, Constable. Got to admire your courage, Jason. I'm impressed by such willing self-sacrifice. You must be very fond of her."

Jason stared wide-eyed, first at Graham and then Barnwell. He saw Barnwell roll his eyes.

"Come now, Constable. You were young once," Graham mused. But then in a swift movement that shocked Jason, Graham shot out his arm and knocked the table in front of Ashby with his fist. "Spill the beans, lad. You lied about your whereabouts, you were missing during the time a police officer was murdered, and you're involved with the teenage daughter of an experienced detective. You're not looking too smart right about now, so I suggest you gather the few brain cells you possess and lay it all out on the table."

"I—I met Tiff—Tiffany in Manchester. She came with DI Trevelyan to the technology course and conference we ran there."

"Yeah, Sergeant Harding went up for that," Graham remembered.

"Tiffany was there, taking photos and such—she wants to be a photographer—and she didn't know anyone, but we hit it off." Jason looked down at his lap, where he was nursing his hands between his thighs. "I arranged for an invitation for DI Trevelyan to speak at the conference in the hopes that he'd bring her along."

"Charming," Barnwell said. "I'm sure Mike's gonna love hearing that the invitation wasn't down to his brave, storied career, talents, and intelligence but that you wanted to enjoy the delightful company of his creative, vivacious, and exceptionally beautiful *seventeen-year-old* daughter." Barnwell's eyes never left Jason's face. He was enjoying skewering the unfortunate young man.

Jason whimpered before turning to stare out of the window.

"So what did happen on Friday night?" Graham asked him. The young man's eyes were wild with fear as he looked pleadingly from one policeman to the other.

"I made arrangements to meet Tiffany at 9:45. Her Dad didn't know, obviously. I made as though I was going to the bathroom when those two old guys left, and I slipped out the back of the pub."

"Where did you go?"

"I met her back at the conference center. We just walked around for a bit, got a takeaway. We ate it on a bench in a playground."

"You sure know how to give a girl a good time, don't cha?" Barnwell said. "Why didn't you tell us this first time around?"

"What, and have DI Trevelyan after me?" Graham and Barnwell stared at Ashby for a moment as they considered this, eventually silently acknowledging the truth of his statement. "We nearly got caught as it was! Superintendent Needham passed us as we walked from the takeaway. I didn't know anything about DS Devine's death until I turned up for the conference the next morning, I swear!"

"What time did you see the superintendent?" Graham asked.

"Oh, I don't know, bit before ten? We'd just got our food."

"And it was definitely him? Needham?"

"Definitely. I saw light bounce off his uniform gold. He was driving a silver car. It was weird though, he was driving without his lights on."

"And you were walking from *Luca and Lizzi's?* The kebab shop?"

"No, we got a Chinese. I dunno what it was called."

"The *Flower Drum.*"

"That was it. It was more out of the way. We didn't want to bump into anyone we knew."

"It's certainly that." The *Flower Drum* Chinese takeaway was on the very edge of Gorey, almost outside its limits. Nowhere near the conference center, the *White House Inn,* or Gorey High Street.

Three more minutes' of questions and Barnwell's very professional but cringe-making call to Tiffany Trevelyan confirmed that Jason was telling the truth.

"I don't know, lad. I should be hanging you from a lamppost but I've got more important things to do than hound pipsqueaks like you," Graham said, privately relieved that the young man hadn't succumbed to any dark intent. "But I suggest you call it off with young Tiffany. If you don't," Graham cracked his knuckles, "well, her father is an old mate of mine. I'm sure you wouldn't want him to hear about any shenanigans involving his *creative, vivacious, and exceptionally beautiful* daughter now, would you?"

"No, no, thank you, sir, no. I'll be off then."

"Yep, off you go." Graham shooed Ashby out of the interview room. Jason gathered his things and hurriedly left.

With his hands in his pockets, Graham watched the young man retreat. He sagged against the doorframe at the lack of progress in the investigation and his concern over Needham. "What's next?" he asked the room.

CHAPTER FORTY-ONE

FREDDIE ARRIVED EARLY for his "chat" with Laura and found the elegant, century-old teashop she had suggested brimming with customers. Only by making extended eye contact with one of his long-time informants, Mrs. Morgenstern, did he secure a table for himself, sliding into her seat only moments after she'd finished her lunch. "Can't thank you enough," he said flashing his most beguiling smile, one he hoped would make Mrs. Morgenstern's day thereby storing up goodwill for future payback.

The *Gorey Granary* tearoom was housed, unsurprisingly, in a former granary. The wooden beam and stone structure provided a rustic charm that was offset by a Victorian interior. Unchanged through the years, Gorey's five-star rated teashop offered its own interpretation of Victorian taste, complete with a black and white-uniformed staff, impeccably arranged plates of cucumber sandwiches, white starched linen and lace, and a range of brews to thrill even the most discerning tea drinker. Unbeknownst to Freddie, Laura had taken Graham there several times. He'd enjoyed the teas but she knew he'd overlooked the finicky nature of the environment to humor her, and she loved him all the more for it. It was one of her favorite places on the island.

For his part, Freddie didn't care two hoots about the tea or the Granary. He found it stuffy and overdone, but his informants loved the tearoom, and so, despite his preference for a pretentious coffee from the café on the High Street, it paid dividends for him to embrace the Granary's formal, privileged atmosphere and eye-watering prices.

As he waited for Laura to arrive, Freddy set out his notebook and began prioritizing his questions. Laura would be a wary interviewee, and his promise to respect her valuable time was sincere.

"It's like stepping out of a time machine coming into this place." Laura had materialized across the table from Freddie, catching him unawares. "Always feels like the set of a costume drama, but I love it!" she said with relish.

Freddie quickly regained his footing. "Well, a little drama—especially the overwrought kind—is grist for my mill. How are you this chilly lunchtime?" he asked, smiling up at her.

"Chilly," Laura replied. "I thought Jersey was supposed to have the mildest winter in the whole of the UK."

Freddie couldn't resist. "It's also *supposed* to be a quiet and peaceful little island paradise..."

Laura ignored his meaning. "Do you have a preference?" she said looking at the menu that described teas in flowery terms so rarefied and obscure they sounded priceless.

"Hmm?"

"Tea. Do you have a preference? Inspector Graham is always very exacting when we come here."

"Me? No. You go ahead. Choose for me. I'm sure whatever you decide will be delightful."

Perusing the menu, Laura overlooked both a Prince Vladimir black tea that promised a "seductive" experience that was likely to "induce swoons," and a Silver Needle white infusion that declared itself the "champagne of teas." Neither was suitable for the conversation she had in mind. Eventually, she chose a straightforward Assam, one that the menu described as "sensible," "sensational," and "brisk." While she was sure Freddie was no connoisseur of teas, she wanted to run no risk at all of sending the wrong message. The Assam would do perfectly.

A few minutes later, as Laura let the tea brew in its elegant white and gray-striped teapot, she said, "I'm happy for you to interrogate me, but before you do, I've got a question for you." From her plain brown leather cross-body purse, Laura brought out an article. She laid it on the table next to the teapot. "Would you tell me about this?"

It took Freddie only half a second to recognize the piece. It was from a local newspaper serving the Southampton area. The shock of seeing it caused the words on the page to swim before him momentarily. Blood rushed to his cheeks. "Has DI Graham been training you in the art of sleuthing?" he asked, his smile faltering, his tone a little sharper than usual.

"All I needed was Google." Laura knew Freddie favored direct questioning and took the same approach herself. "Is it true?"

With a heavy sigh at this unexpected tangent, Freddie came clean—somewhat. His instinct to muddy the waters when challenged remained. "Yes, I'm afraid so. I was detained by Southampton police while I was a student at the university. Not unusual."

"Arrested and *charged*, it says here," Laura pointed out, tapping the paper. She was unwilling to let him dodge responsibility. She'd even highlighted the relevant sentence. "Burglary and handling stolen goods."

"Look, there's a..."

"'Perfectly reasonable explanation for all this'?" Laura said, her eyebrows shooting up. "I can't wait. Because if I'm not wrong, it would really help clear up some things." She sat back and folded her arms.

Freddie threw up his hands, his palms facing Laura. He pressed his lips together, his head sinking into his neck, his eyebrows raised slightly. "I am unmasked," Freddie said. He dropped his hands and leaned forward, looking at Laura with apparent regret. "Stupid business, to be honest. Two of my housemates got themselves into a spot of bother. Card game with some local lads, rough neighborhood, you know. Rules were bent, and my friends owed money they couldn't repay. So," he sighed, "they did something unbelievably dumb."

"According to this, the haul comprised a laptop, a DVD player, and a state-of-the-art sound system," Laura said. "Crikey. They must have been *awful* at cards."

"That wasn't their worst mistake. The person they burgled was our *next-door neighbor*," Freddie explained. "When he got back from holiday and found out, the police descended. Honestly, you'd think they didn't have anything better to do."

Laura raised an eyebrow. She suspected that if Freddie had been the one burgled and Inspector Graham the investigating officer, he would take a very different tack. "Really?"

"Anyway, when the fuzz came a-knocking, my two idiot housemates lost their nerve. Decided to blame me, didn't they?"

"Uh-oh," Laura murmured. She dropped her eyebrows and lowered her eyelids to half-mast. She was enjoying this. She regarded Freddie across the table. He shifted in his seat, making the delicate wooden chair beneath him creak.

"I was away visiting my parents at the time and the plonkers stashed the loot in my room."

Laura nodded. "Wow, nice friends you've got. Wouldn't your parents give you an alibi?"

"Sure, for the time I was with them. The prevailing story was that I must have stolen the goods while my neighbor was away, stashed them in my room, *then* gone to my parents. When the police searched our flat, they found the items under my bed. As if I would be so stupid!"

"Ah, details, huh? Vexing. Tell me though, the police should have believed you, protected you, and collared your housemates, right?" Laura leaned forward, her eyes narrowing. "But somehow," she reasoned, watching Freddie's reactions, "I don't think that's what happened."

CHAPTER FORTY-TWO

FREDDIE SPREAD HIS hands out, nearly hitting a waitress who was carrying a multi-tiered tea stand laden with finger sandwiches, scones, jam, cream, and petit fours. "It was a *travesty of justice*," he continued after apologizing to the waitress. "There was no fingerprinting, no forensic analysis, just a pair of handcuffs and a humiliating perp-walk to a marked police car outside our digs. Never lived it down, not even when the charges were dropped due to 'procedural irregularities.' My uncle's law practice put the boot in, but the damage was done. I have a police record, my name in the paper, my reputation stained."

"Did you have to abandon your degree?" Laura asked, a little sympathetic to his plight now, despite herself.

"Transferred to Aberdeen," Freddie explained. "Fresh start. Never spoke to any of the Southampton mob again. Scarred me for life, you might say."

"And," Laura asked, even surer now of her footing than when she'd first discovered the article, "gave you a life-long sensitivity to poorly-executed police work." She suspected that, in truth,

Freddie's sensitivity extended to *all* police work, no matter how it was executed, hence his line of work and its bias.

"You'd better believe it," Freddie said ruefully. "No one should have to go through that. Certainly not at the tender age of nineteen, with a new relationship blossoming, good things on the horizon, a bright future ahead."

"A very bitter pill to swallow. And at such a young age, too." Laura picked up the teapot and leaned over to pour Freddie a cup of tea. She spilled a little in his saucer.

"Bitter as poison," Freddie said. He barely noticed Laura now as he slumped forward and stared at the clear brown liquid in his cup, slowly stirring it with a small silver spoon. He inhaled deeply through his nose and sat up, looking directly at his companion. "But I pulled through in the end."

"I'm sorry to bring it up," Laura said. "But it explains why you have a personal vendetta against David. I mean, Detective Inspector Graham."

"Nope," Freddie said simply. "He's a decent gent and a professional. I just want to hold him to account and keep him that way. That's how we maintain standards."

"I get it," Laura said. "You believe that people only stay honest if you haul them over the coals. If you don't, they will stray sooner or later, if they haven't already. So you attack them, humiliate them, are skeptical of them, whether they deserve it or not. You don't trust them to police themselves, to hold themselves to honest, high standards. Am I right?"

If Freddie intended to persuade Laura that his methods were justified, he still had much work to do. "I give *everyone* a hard time. It elicits discussion. Remember that piece I did about thoughtless yacht owners, clogging up the marina's north exit?"

"No," she said honestly.

"Well, the Harbormaster read it and changed the marina's policies as a result. I'd call that a win for public safety."

Laura wasn't even slightly convinced. "How is that the

same? DI Graham's entire being, his complete existence is predicated on catching those who do criminal harm. Crime is at an all-time low on the island. Do you really think he'll thank you for the scurrilous treatment he receives from you? Call you for advice?"

"I'm not expecting him to phone anytime soon, I admit."

As Laura sipped her tea, Freddie, his interview utterly derailed, searched for a way to get back on track. Laura was compassionate and level-headed, uncommon traits in his experience. He wanted to recruit her to his side and hadn't yet accepted that that was not going to happen. "If I tell you something, can I be sure it goes no further?"

Narrowly suppressing a sputtering, incredulous laugh, Laura said, "You mean, the writer of an online gossip column is asking *me* to be *discreet?*" But then, after a thought, "Alright, I'll bite."

"A lot of the stuff I write is just theater," Freddie explained. "A little drama concocted for the page. Harmless entertainment, for the most part. It brings in clicks, gets people fired up—distracts them from their miserable little lives in the process."

"Harmless, *except* when you risk interfering with a police investigation or lowering morale," Laura objected. "I don't find that entertaining, and neither do Gorey's law enforcement professionals. And you're actively undermining the public's confidence in them. That isn't good for our community."

Freddie conceded her points, but explained, "I'm pushing them to do better. To be sharper, more aware of possibilities. To leave no stone unturned."

"And how do you think they're doing with this most recent case?" Laura asked.

Freddie flipped open his notebook, but then set it to one side, next to his plate upon which a fondant fancy sat. "They were brutal hits. Despite what you think, it bothers me that two police officers died right here in Gorey. A knife fight between some hoodlums, that wouldn't be quite as awful. But these deaths were just so, so... cold-blooded and unjust."

"This is exactly what I mean!" Laura said, her voice raised slightly. She paused from cutting her fondant fancy in half and waggled her butter knife at him. "Long before all the facts are in, you—of all people, a total layman, without access to any array of evidence—have decided it was murder!"

"*What* facts? *What* evidence?" Freddie objected. "There *is* no evidence, precious little anyway. We've got a shamefully out-of-date CCTV system and a medical examiner of similar vintage who's got half his mind deep in the cellars of California's wine country."

"You be nice to Marcus," Laura warned sternly. She resumed cutting her fondant fancy into quarters. "He's a treasure."

"A *fossil*, more like," Freddie retorted. "We should bring in someone from the mainland. Someone more current with the latest technology."

"Nonsense. And if you publish something like that, I'll never talk to you again."

Hands raised in surrender, Freddie tried to bring the discussion under control. "I promise I won't write anything unreasonable about him."

"Or DI Graham," Laura prompted, pouring herself another cup of the nearly-forgotten tea. After almost nine minutes—David had taught her well—it was likely to be too strong. She added a little extra milk.

Freddie sat back, contemplating this unusual state of affairs. "More than anything," he explained, "I value my editorial independence. That's why I don't write for a conventional newspaper." Laura dipped her chin and looked at him skeptically. "I could, you know. I've had offers," Freddie continued. "But with the *Gossip*, I have the freedom to express what I think is important."

"And it's *important* to denigrate a highly respected officer, is it?" Laura said, her tone increasingly challenging.

"Tell me why I shouldn't. He's a public servant. We pay his wages. He is accountable to us."

"Because..." Laura stopped. This was decidedly not the venue for any admission of her true feelings for David Graham. Instead, she stuck to the facts. "He's some kind of genius, Freddie. I know," she said as Freddie rolled his eyes theatrically, "that's an overused word, but I saw him working recently. His ability to recall details is amazing."

"I've heard a bit about that," Freddie said. "But I've never been completely convinced."

"Good investigators bring more to the table than an unerring memory, I know, but he brings all of those other things, too, as well as years of hard-won experience. Just give him some *time*, alright? Stay off his back, and let him do his thing," she pleaded.

After draining his teacup, Freddie said, "You sound awfully confident. As a layperson yourself, I mean. Unless the investigation has made sudden progress, overnight." Freddie raised his eyebrows comically high. "Has it?"

"Haven't a clue," Laura said truthfully. "I simply trust David and his team. If capturing the person behind these murders, or accidents, or whatever they are, is possible, they'll do it."

CHAPTER FORTY-THREE

JOHNNY PHILBIN WAS checking his sound equipment. He was a slight, reedy, unobtrusive man dressed entirely in black—black roll neck sweater, black jeans, black socks. On his head, he wore a flat black cap. His wire-framed glasses steamed up as he gulped his early morning tea. As Janice watched him, he let out a cable that ran from the stage to his console in the middle of the room before getting on his hands and knees to tape it securely to the hardwood floor of the conference room.

"Morning, Johnny," Janice said.

He looked up at her. He sat back on his heels. "Morning, Janice." He spoke quickly, his Estuary English accent shortening his vowels.

"How are you doing after yesterday?"

Johnny pulled off his cap and rubbed his brown hair. He flicked his wrist to hook the cap over the back of his head, pulling it on again. Janice had known Johnny to be a quiet, efficient man. He'd been polite, but not overly friendly, pleasant, but not forthcoming with small talk of any kind. He had come with the package she'd booked for the conference and she had no complaints about his work. But she hadn't gotten to know him either. So she was surprised when, by his standards, he was positively effusive. He immediately pivoted from her question to a defense of his equipment.

"Look, I've gone over and over what happened. It makes no sense to me. All the mics were working fine. There were no exposed wires or damaged housing, no problem of any kind that I could see. I test them before every session."

"What about your spare?"

"I always have at least one back-up and that's tested just as much. It's me who looks the fool and has to fix things with an antsy audience looking on if things don't work, so you bet I make sure that doesn't happen. It's a basic part of my job."

"The mic DS O'Hearn held, the one that killed him, you're sure it was one of yours?"

"Of course. I had it laid out on the table next to me. I handed it over."

"Did you ever leave it alone, the mic I mean?"

Johnny looked at her. "Of course I did. I wasn't expecting anyone to turn it into a deadly weapon was I now? I'm in and out of here all the time."

"Was there anyone around?"

"I'm sure there was. I didn't pay too much attention. Look, I wasn't expecting anything weird to go on during a police conference! Normally I lock my gear up, but I thought this was the safest place on earth. Wouldn't anyone? Made a nice change not to have to worry about thousands of pounds worth of equipment being nicked." Johnny threw his hands up. "And then this happens. Unbelievable."

"How did you get this gig, Johnny?" Janice walked around the stage and sat on one of the chairs in the front row. She leaned her elbows on her knees, bringing her face level with his.

Johnny's expression immediately became guarded. His eyes

narrowed and tension appeared along his jawline. His lips thinned.

"Why d'you want to know that?"

"Just curious. You don't sound like you're from around here."

"My brother-in-law's the manager. He recommended me." Johnny picked up a dust bunny from the floor and rubbed it between his thumb and forefinger.

"That's nice." Janice looked around. "Where did you learn all this stuff? Looks complicated."

"Ah, you know, here and there. Picked it up at school originally, plays, and that. When I left school, I worked as a roadie. Just small bands, small venues. Went all over Europe I d-did." He eyed Janice nervously, still rubbing dust between his fingers.

"Did you go to Germany by any chance?"

"Er, yeah."

"You stayed there for some time, didn't you?"

Johnny slumped, his shoulders dropping. "Yeah, so?" He pushed himself up from the floor and sat on one of the conference chairs, two down from Janice. She sat up and leaned back to regard him more closely.

"Three years, according to my records," she said. "After that, you were transferred courtesy of Her Majesty's Prison Service to Sheerness where you stayed for two more years."

A trace of defiance appeared on Johnny's face. He lifted his chin, a steely glint appearing in his eyes. "Seems you know all about me."

"Drug running's a serious crime, Johnny."

"That's all behind me, all of it. This is my home now. Don't even go to the mainland if I can help it. 'S better that way. Besides, I like it here." Johnny looked around the room, at the spotlights that were mounted near the ceiling behind the stage. "Quiet," he said.

"But you understand why I'm talking to you? Two officers who were working a drug case are now dead." Johnny opened his mouth to interrupt her, but Janice pressed on, "And you had intimate links with London's underworld, links that involved couriering large amounts of drugs throughout Europe. You received an eight-year sentence after being arrested in Celle, serving three of those years in a German prison before being deported to finish the remainder of your sentence here. You were released early, three months ago. It's only natural we look at you."

Johnny had started to rock. "I had nothing, *nothing* to do with the deaths." He clenched the skin on the back of his hand between his front teeth. He bit down hard. "Yeah, I was stupid. Yeah, I was a drug mule. I can't change what happened. But I've admitted everything, *everything*. I've done my time. I have *no* connections with anyone from back then. I just want to be left alone to get on with my life, away from the smoke, away from everything back there. I never want to return."

"So you don't keep in contact with anyone from those days?"

"No one. And I never would. Police wanted me to grass, but I didn't know anything, and if I did, the gang would have killed me the moment I got out! I want to stay right out of it."

"So how did it work? The operation."

"It was all done anonymously. Dead drops, pick-ups. I was traveling with the bands and there was always drugs everywhere. Provided the perfect cover. I'd hide the gear with the band equipment, and if we were ever busted, the fuzz would find the stuff we had lying around for personal use. They'd turn a blind eye to it or give us a telling off and just wave us on. It was so easy. They never looked any further." Johnny sighed. "Until they did." Now he was fidgeting with a loose thread in his jeans. "Put a cop in the crew, didn't they? Eventually, I got caught. I was arrested leaving 20 lbs of cocaine in a mailbox where we were playing a gig. Got me for that and five other drops. They'd been watching me for months."

"Hmm." Janice nodded. "Tell me what you were doing Friday night."

"I was at home."

"Alone?"

"Yeah." Philbin shrugged. "But listen, I had nothing to do with those deaths. You can ask anyone around here. I wouldn't do such a thing. I'm my own worst enemy, not anyone else's."

"But you could have done them. You have no alibi for Friday night. And you could have tampered with the equipment."

"Yeah, sure. I guess. But I'd be pretty stupid to, especially like that and in front of all the fuzz. Be obvious. And why? I have no reason to. Besides, I don't drive."

"This cop, the one embedded in your crew. Did you ever find out who it was?"

"Not at the time. People constantly came and went so it weren't obvious. Roadies aren't exactly known for their long employment records."

"But you found out later?"

"Yeah, just a few days ago. Gave me the fright of my life. Recognized him immediately."

"Someone here? On Jersey? At the conference?"

"Yeah. He recognized me, too, I saw it in his eyes. The tall geezer. Never smiles. The one that looks like James Dean."

CHAPTER FORTY-FOUR

AMID THE PALE winter late afternoon light coming through the big windows, Laura stood at the new bank of six computers opposite the circulation desk. She was assisting Ernest Hetherington, one of her regulars, and enjoying the elderly man's frequent gasps of amazement. "It's something, isn't it?" she said to him. "Researchers have relied on the International Genealogical Index for decades. Helped all kinds of people to find relatives and answer questions like yours."

A widower for twenty years, Hetherington was dedicating his retirement to unearthing what he felt sure would be a colorful family history. "Oh, yes, it's just marvelous," he agreed. "All these *people*." With a crooked finger, he traced the names and dates brought up by his latest search. "So many lives lived."

They'd already found the splendidly named Clement Emmanuel Asketh, the first of Hetherington's clan to emigrate to New York, back in 1870. "It's a long time ago," Hetherington noted, "but then again, it's a blink of an eye." He seemed to mist over and become distracted for a second. "My wife used to say, 'Countless are the turnings of the good Earth.' Such a *poet,*

Angela was," he remembered fondly. "She'd be knocked off her feet by all this," he said, nudging at the mouse with stiff, balky fingers until the cursor hovered over the 'Search' button. Mr. Hetherington was a bird-like man—thin, small, unassuming. A former town clerk, he had been born and bred on Jersey and had seen many changes in his eighty-odd years. Also thin, small, and unassuming was his wife's memory which would have been destined to be limited to an entry on Jersey's electoral roll for the years of the latter half of the last century and a gravestone in the Gorey churchyard if it hadn't been for the fact that her husband mentioned her at every opportunity. He'd miss her except for the fact that she was always with him. Laura found it endearing.

"Go ahead and click," Laura said. "Who knows what we'll find this time?"

As Hetherington painstakingly searched the list for more Askeths, Laura checked on the other patrons. Mondays were usually slow, and just a few people were browsing the shelves, searching online, or in the case of her two most dependable patrons, reading the *Racing Post* for the week's runners and riders.

Sitting alone, almost completely surrounded by a stack of books, was Billy Foster. In the past few months, the boy's sweet, curious nature had changed dramatically. More than once, Laura had witnessed his terrible losses of temper, and two weeks before, Janice had passed on some news that was too embarrassing for Billy to relate: he'd found himself in the head teacher's office, receiving a "weapons-grade telling-off" after some playground fisticuffs. Bullied, worried, vulnerable ten-year-old or not, neither Janice nor Laura condoned violence, but when it came to helping Billy, they had learned to move slowly and carefully. "His mother's already been in rehab. We avoided Social Services that time, but I'm not sure we'll be so lucky again. We need to tread carefully," Janice had told Laura.

"Planetary geology?" Laura marveled, finding a reason to

walk past Billy's book-crowded desk. His answer—a brief, silent, noncommittal shrug—was oddly heartbreaking. She saw he'd been poring over a brightly colorful map of a place Laura didn't recognize. "Wow, where's that, Billy?"

"Venus," he muttered. When Laura waited for a longer answer, he added, "It's a heat map. Venus is super, super hot, all year round."

She tried to engage him further, but he gave the impression of resembling an unexploded landmine, or a curious artifact ringed by an electric fence: there was no safe way to approach.

"Hi, Laura! And good afternoon, Billy!" Sergeant Harding breezed past them.

"Hey." Billy hardly lifted his eyes from the map.

Janice looked at the boy curiously but decided to leave him be.

"Returning a book?" Laura asked her.

"And taking out another, I hope."

Laura walked with Janice to her destination—three shelves at the back of the library, far from areas of scholarship and research, which held nothing but over-ripe romantic fiction. "What did you think?" Laura asked, slipping Janice's return—a slender, lurid volume entitled *The Jade Nightgown*—into its rightful place.

Harding puffed out her cheeks. "Soppy and a bit much, I'd say. Chock full of ridiculous romance blossoming in the most unbelievable situations."

"In other words," Laura grinned, "you *loved* it."

"Got any more by the same author?" Janice asked sheepishly.

Laura displayed the set of seven sequels, all with enticingly stylized "bodice-ripper" covers. "Enough to keep you happy for weeks."

"Perfect," Janice said. She tapped the cover of *The Vermillion Scarf*, and sighed, looking wistfully at the picture on the front.

"Are you alright Janice? Things okay with you and Jack?"

"Yes, everything is lovely, just lovely." Janice turned the book over to read the blurb on the back cover. "My Nan would prefer we got married, but we're fine, fine."

Laura leaned back to catch Janice's downcast eye, a small smile on her face. "Fine, huh?"

"Oh, you know. It's just a piece of paper, it won't change anything. We're great, really."

"But...?"

"Well, I would feel happier with a commitment. I'm not getting any younger, and... it would just be so nice. I've always dreamed of a romantic proposal and a big white wedding. I know it's old-fashioned, but, oh I don't know, Jack's the one and everything's good. I'm just being silly."

"I'm sure it'll all work out. A few hints, the odd nudge, a bottle of wine should do the trick." Laura smiled.

"Maybe." Janice pressed her lips together. "I'll let you get on," she said, her hand on Laura's arm. "I'm needed back at the station."

"Let me check you out."

The two women walked over to the distribution desk. Laura picked up the barcode scanner.

"What's that lovely smell?" Janice said.

"Hmmm?"

"I can smell jasmine."

"Oh, it's my candle." Laura pointed to a brilliant white box next to her computer screen. "Billy gave it to me earlier. Sweet of him, huh? It'll make my cottage smell heavenly."

Janice picked up the box and brought it to her nose. "Mmmm." She casually turned the box over. *Gorey Gifts & Sweets, 13 High Street, Gorey, Jersey, JE1 1GO* was printed on a label on the underside. "I wonder where he got it."

CHAPTER FORTY-FIVE

"**B**ILLY?" JANICE SPOKE softly.

"Hmm?" the boy murmured, not lifting his eyes from his map.

"Billy, I need to speak to you."

"About what?" he said. He put his forefinger on the map and turned to a book that was open next to it.

"The candle you gave Laura."

Billy gave no indication he had heard Janice and turned the page of his book. Harding gently reached over and closed it.

"Hey!" Billy cried, throwing himself back in his chair, finally looking at her. Janice put her finger to her lips and shushed him.

"I want to talk to you about where you got it. Come on, let's go outside." She straightened up and held out her hand. Reluctantly, Billy took it. As they passed the distribution desk, Laura smiled at them and raised her hands, her fingers crossed. Billy kept his eyes firmly on the floor.

Outside, Janice led Billy to a wooden bench. A plaque on the back announced it was dedicated to a Rodney Mainwaring for whom the library had been "a second home."

"I remember him," Billy said. "He only came in to read the newspapers, and he smelled of cigarettes. Fell asleep sometimes. He..."

"Billy," Janice interrupted carefully. "Where did you get the candle you gave Laura?"

He looked at her directly. "She's nice, Laura is. Always helping me with my research."

"Billy, how did you come by it?"

"Eh?"

"The candle. How did you get it?"

Billy held Janice's gaze, but his voice faltered. "I-I bought it." He shifted in his seat and sat up a little straighter. "Like anyone would," he said, more confidently.

"With what, Billy? This is an expensive, luxury gift. It probably cost more than twenty pounds."

"I saved up!"

Janice's heart began to break. The young boy kept looking at her, desperately trying to hold on to his dignity, but his eyes filled with tears. His chin was wobbling. He blinked, and a tear ran down his cheek. He roughly chased it away with his sleeve.

Janice hadn't let go of Billy's hand and now she squeezed it. "Billy, I think this candle was stolen from the gift shop on the High Street on Friday night. Did you have anything to do with that?"

Billy tore his eyes away from Janice's face. "N-No."

Janice hooked her finger under Billy's chin. "Look at me, Billy. Did you have anything to do with the burglary at *Gorey Gifts* on Friday night?"

"Th-They made me, Janice!" he wailed.

Harding pulled a tissue from her bag and wiped his face. "Shhhh, it'll be alright, lad. Just tell me what happened. Who made you?"

"Anthony Middelton and Caspar Freedland. They made me be their lookout. I was hungry and on my way to the Bagchi's shop. I-I stood in an alleyway. It was my job to tell them if anyone came, but no one did, except a woman, and she was hit by a car, and I think she died and..." Billy crumpled as the reality of his wretched existence finally overwhelmed him. He fell sobbing into Janice's arms. She rubbed his back as she waited for him to cry himself out. His hair smelled of "eau de boy."

When he had exhausted himself, she lifted him upright and with her arm around his shoulder asked him, "Did you see the car hit the woman?"

"No, but I heard it. I saw it go by, then a thump, then another thump."

"What kind of car was it?"

"I dunno, cars aren't really my thing."

"What can you tell me about it? How big was it?

"Medium."

"What color?"

"Hmmm." Billy squeezed his eyes shut. "It was the same color as Mercury."

"Did you see who was driving it?"

"No, not really."

"Man? Woman?"

"Man, I think."

"Okay, thanks, Billy. Listen, when was the last time you ate?"

"Lunchtime."

"At school?"

"Yeah."

"And before that?"

"Um..." Billy mumbled something.

"When, Billy?"

Billy took a deep breath. "Yesterday," he said. "Lunchtime."

Janice rubbed Billy's cheek with her thumb. "Okay, let's go get you something to eat. I'm going to make a few calls."

"Are you going to put me in care?"

"I'm trying not to, but you can't go on as you are. Come on, everything will seem better after you've had your tea. Let's go."

Janice stood and Billy pushed himself off the bench.

"What would you like – fish and chips, kebab, or Chinese?"

"Can we go to the café on the front for an ice cream?"

Janice looked down at the boy. White eyelashes that surrounded his hazel eyes stood out against their red rims. He gave her a hopeful, watery smile.

"Okay, but only if you have something decent to eat first."

"You're on!"

As they walked to the seafront, Janice pulled out her phone and found a number. "Mrs. Lampard? It's about Billy Foster... Yes, that's right... He is, yes... Could you? That would be awesome. Thank you."

CHAPTER FORTY-SIX

BARNWELL PUT DOWN the phone. "Sir? Jim's on his way with Marcus."

Graham's face lit up. "Terrific!" He rubbed his hands together. "Perhaps they have something for us."

The whiteboard in Graham's office was filling up quickly. Having dropped Billy at Mrs. Lampard's, Harding had joined the Detective Inspector and Barnwell for a brainstorming session, the goal of which was to review what they knew for sure. Tea was steeping, ignored, in the corner as they stared hopefully at the board.

Graham took a black marker and made a short column on the right-hand side. He proceeded to fill in the timeline of the hit-and-run. "Kimberley Devine left the pub at 9:15 and is killed at 10 p.m."

"She must have been walking awfully slowly to take that long to go such a short distance," Barnwell said.

"Jack told me she was sending texts," Janice said. "He said they seemed pretty innocuous, but they'd have taken time to send. She probably stopped for a bit."

"Nigel Needham was telling stories with us until he left with Marcus at 9:30. Jason Ashby disappears at the same time, but we've an alibi for him. Needham, however, has a damaged car and Ashby gave us a sighting that he was driving with his lights off shortly before DS Devine's death," Graham continued. "Although not in the vicinity of the High Street."

"Sir..." Janice said. Graham didn't seem to notice.

"Why would Superintendent Needham kill anyone?" Barnwell said.

"Maybe Devine's death was an accident, and O'Hearn's was... done by someone else?" Graham said.

"Two killers? Oh boy..."

"But, sir..." Janice tried again.

Barnwell was thinking. He tapped his chin with his forefinger. "Wait, Needham was in the room when O'Hearn was killed. He handled the replacement mic before it got to O'Hearn. The sound engineer handed it to him. Needham handed it to Vincenti who handed it to Ashby who handed it to O'Hearn. Perhaps he fiddled with it in those few moments?" Barnwell said. "Or during the break. But why? What would have been his motive?"

"Sir! We have one other suspect, sir."

Graham and Barnwell swiveled their heads in unison to look at Janice. She finally had their attention.

"We do? Who, Sergeant?"

"Johnny Philbin, sir. The sound engineer at the conference."

"That's right. You were going to talk to him. What did he say?"

"Well, of course he said he had nothing to do with either killing. He's been trying to start a new life for himself on Jersey. But get this, he recognized DS Vincenti. He was embedded in the crowd Philbin was running with. It was probably his evidence that put Philbin away."

"Whoa, whoa, whoa." Graham leaned back against his filing cabinets, tapping his lips with his whiteboard marker. He started writing names and drawing lines connecting them all on the board.

"This Philbin? Does he have an alibi for Friday night?"

"No, sir. He went home alone. Stayed in all night. Says he doesn't drive, but who knows?"

"He could have fiddled with the mic, no problem," Barnwell added.

"Okay, so we have two people in the frame, Needham for Devine, maybe O'Hearn, Philbin for both. Alright," Graham drew a big line under everything he'd written. "Let's look at the evidence."

From outside the room, they heard the sound of voices and a door banging.

"Yoo-hoo!" Roach's voice called out.

"We're in here!" Janice called back. Tomlinson followed by Roach appeared in the office doorway.

"Evening fellas," Graham said. "Just in the nick of time. We're looking at the evidence."

"Right, sir," Roach said.

"Now, we know that Devine was killed by a car with its lights off, right?" Graham said.

"Right," Roach confirmed. "No tungsten oxide residue on either Needham's rental car or the Vauxhall Cavalier. I scoured both cars, but there wasn't a trace of any yellow powdery stuff meaning neither of them can be eliminated from the inquiry for that reason."

"But..." It was Janice again.

"So both cars are still possibilities. What else have you got for us? Hair? Fibers?" Graham asked.

"Sorry, sir," Roach said, "I took thirty samples, but none of the hairs found in the Vauxhall produced a match for anyone on the database."

"You're kidding," Graham said, genuinely stunned.

"The samples didn't belong to anyone in the family based on

DNA analysis," Marcus explained, "but they don't belong to anyone on the database, either. We got quite excited at first, but it was a false alarm. They could just be from friends, anyone who rode in the car recently or ever, really."

"So we're back to Superintendent Needham in his rental car?" Barnwell concluded. "Philbin would be on the database and would have shown up."

"Not necessarily, Constable. The absence of a match doesn't mean an absence of person. It just means we didn't find *evidence* of a person that was a match," Graham countered.

"And there's seven million entries in the national DNA database," Marcus pointed out. "It's a lot, but it's not *everyone*. Not by a long shot."

"And a careful criminal isn't going to spread his DNA around. If the murderer was a clever sausage, they'd know how to avoid contamination," Roach added.

"Sir..." Janice interrupted, her forefinger raised like she wanted permission from the teacher to answer a question. None of the four men in the room gave any recognition that they had heard her.

"You're *sure* it was moved, sir?" Barnwell asked. "I mean, it's so hard to say, passing by at forty-five like that..."

Roach brought Barnwell to a halt. "If he says it was moved, then it was *moved*, Bazza," he said. "Whether it was a gangland murderer or a joy-riding kid, or simply a friend of the owners taking it, we have to take the Cavalier seriously."

"But there's no evidence of it being involved in DS Devine's death," Barnwell persisted.

"Barnwell's right to an extent. Besides the damage, we need something to move it into the frame or move it out," Graham conceded.

"Sir!" Harding insisted. All the men turned to look at her. "I had a conversation with Billy Foster earlier. Remember him?"

CHAPTER FORTY-SEVEN

"YES, OF COURSE," Graham said.

"He saw the hit-and-run, well, he heard it. But he *saw* the car that hit DS Devine."

"But, that's what we need, isn't it?" Barnwell exclaimed. "Why didn't you say so?" Janice rolled her eyes.

"Finally, a break!" Roach cried. "What did he say?"

"That someone approached at speed. He said the car was medium-sized."

"Well, that only narrows it down to around 50% of the total number of cars in circulation," Roach said.

"38.3 million, to be precise," Graham added. "What else did he say?"

Janice closed her eyes for a second and breathed in through her mouth. "He said that the car was like Mercury."

"Eh?" Barnwell frowned.

"Mercury, Billy's really into planets. Anyway, I looked it up, and Mercury is..."

"Gray," Graham finished for her.

"What color is Needham's rental?" Janice asked.

"Silver," Roach said.

"What color is the Vauxhall?" Barnwell asked.

"Green," Roach said. "Faded, but green nonetheless."

Graham, Tomlinson, Janice, Roach, and Barnwell paused as they considered this.

"But that pushes Needham *into* the center of the frame," Roach said, giving voice to what the others were thinking.

"Thanks, Captain-bleedin'-Obvious," Barnwell said.

The only sound in the room was the tinkle of Graham's teaspoon as he stirred his tea. It had gone cold, but he found the action comforting. He still couldn't comprehend that his former mentor had killed a woman even if it was the result of fading mental faculties.

Barnwell jumped up. He began pacing around the room like the DS he deserved to become, but for which he lacked the ambition. "But wait! Under street lights, all colors are muted. They're bleached out by the light, like an overexposed photo." He looked at the others, his eyes alight. "Faded green would look gray!"

Graham stopped his stirring. "You're right, Barnwell! Both cars are back in play."

Roach's phone started to buzz. "Dr. Weiss from Southampton is on the line. Hold on a sec, yeah?" He walked out of the room to take the call.

Graham blew out his cheeks. "Right, let's take a short break until Roach gets back," he said. "Keep your thinking caps on."

Outside, Roach pressed the button on his phone to accept the incoming call. "Dr. Weiss?" Roach listened as the Head of Forensics for Jersey Police identified herself and asked after him. "Yeah, I'm fine. You?" There was a pause as the likable criminology professor recited details of her robust hike across Hordle Cliffs the day before. "Good, good. Got anything for me?" Roach was tapping his foot now. "Really...? Uh-huh... Really... Wow... *Really?*"

Five minutes later, Roach sprinted back into Graham's office, his eyes shining, his cheeks pink. "I've got it, sir."

"Well, have at it, lad."

Roach surveyed the whiteboard once more, trying to synthesize what they knew. "Everyone ready?" he began. "Remember the glass we found on the street?" The other four nodded. "Well, we also found some glass fragments on Kimberley's clothes. So Dr. Weiss and I did a density analysis of the pieces using a bromine solution to see whether they were all from the same vehicle."

"And were they?" Graham asked.

"The fragments consisted of two types of glass. The glass found on the victim's clothes matched some of those in the street. So, we got into the weeds with spectrographic analysis."

"Is there any other place to be," Graham asked, "when it comes to spectrographic analysis?"

"See, every manufacturer adds impurities to the glass," Roach explained. "The added metal compounds give it a unique color. We quickly identified that one of the types of glass wasn't from a car at all but probably from a bottle. But the other fragments *were* from a car. I couriered glass fragments from both the rental and the Vauxhall over to Dr. Weiss this morning, and she's been able to match the glass we found at the scene with one of them!"

Graham was champing at the bit. "Don't make me wait, lad."

"Vauxhall, nineteen ninety-seven vintage, or Dr. Weiss said, maybe the first half of ninety-eight."

"Woo-hoo!" Harding cried. "So we can remove the super from the frame! And with that, and Billy's evidence, and the lack of tungsten oxide, we can move the Cavalier *into* the frame."

Graham took a half-second to enjoy a swell of pride; these were *his* officers, and their undoubted professionalism always refreshed his zeal and confidence, especially when he was flagging.

"Now we just have to find who was driving it!" Roach said.

Standing at the whiteboard as she absorbed their findings, Harding began to feel more confident than earlier. "We can pursue our other suspect, Johnny Philbin. He could easily have tampered with the mic. He doesn't have an alibi for Friday night. He could have done both killings. As to the motive, I don't know. Perhaps the drug gang threatened him. Or he's still part of their active network and carried out their direction."

"He doesn't drive, though," Barnwell said.

"He could be lying," Roach countered.

"Roach, are you sure there is nothing in the car that we can tie to Philbin?" Graham asked.

"No, sir. There was nothing, no fingerprints, no hairs, no fibers. He would have turned up on the database. Whoever they were did a good job."

"Did the license plates ever turn up?"

"No sir."

"Hmmm. What about the mic?"

"Loads of fingerprints there. Philbin's obviously."

"Several people handled it before O'Hearn, sir," Barnwell said. "I don't think fingerprints will help us there."

"And no one saw anything suspicious? None of the delegates?"

"No, sir."

Graham leaned back in his chair. He interlaced his fingers and placed them on his head, staring at the ceiling. "We need to tie someone to the Vauxhall. Sergeant Harding, go check Philbin's driving record, would you? See if he's telling us the truth."

"Yes, sir."

"And if you don't mind, the rest of you, I'd like a few moments to myself."

Everyone left the room. As she turned to close the door behind her, Janice saw Graham sitting at his desk with his eyes closed. He breathed in deeply.

"What's going on?" Roach asked her.

"I think he's going to his 'mind palace,' Roachie."

"Eh?"

Harding opened her mouth to explain, "Oh, never mind."

CHAPTER FORTY-EIGHT

"TONIC WATER," GRAHAM said quietly, his right hand circling his left knee slowly, "half a Lost Tourist, pint of Rocquette, pint of Session IPA, Guinness, pint of Wonky Donkey, Merlot, Prosecco, pint of La Mare, half of Shipwrecked, mojito. Our drink orders, clockwise around the table, beginning with Barnwell."

With his eyes closed, Graham continued his survey of the table. "Uniform shirt—open-necked times three; crimson polo shirt and jeans; blue checked shirt, green jacket, and cargo pants; uniform shirt and tie; white shirt and khakis; pink shirt with white collar and cuffs, bowtie; t-shirt—black, lettering; black shirt, thin red leather tie," he recited shivering in disgust at the degree of sartorial offense present in the final outfit.

Eyes still screwed shut, he carried on. "Two North Face jackets in teal. He liked vinegar, she preferred ketchup. People at the bar, or sitting at other tables. Noise from the back room."

Graham spent another three minutes in an intense, pensive silence, his eyes shut, fists occasionally balled. He sat upright but winced as though his posture caused him pain. Gradually, he relaxed. The DI was journeying back from the pained, intractable territory he'd been exploring. "It starts like a forest," he murmured. "Dense and tangled, everything dark. But with effort, it becomes clearer, more defined."

Janice was clacking away on her keyboard. She got up to make a call. She spoke quietly into her phone and then sat, tapping her pen on the tabletop, silently agitated, before starting to type again. From the inspector's office, there had been no word. Twenty minutes had gone by since they'd been sent from his room. Marcus Tomlinson had gone back to his office.

"Tea, Bazza?"

"Yeah, please." Roach and Barnwell were in the break room.

"Do you ever get the sense there's not enough for you here?" Roach said.

"Here at the station? On Jersey? Or are you noodling about the meaning of life?"

"In the constabulary. On Jersey. I mean, both Janice and I are sergeants, but there isn't enough action to sustain the two of us. I know the DI has given me additional duties, but still..."

"It's not exactly Hawaii Five-o?"

"Yeah." Roach looked out the window. A woman was leading a child on a pony down the street.

"Well, if there's not enough for you here, you need to move on. I mean, what's keeping you?"

"Oh, you know, too comfortable, I suppose. I like it here, it's all I've ever known. And my mum would miss me."

"Well, listen, lad. Your mum wouldn't be too happy to hear she'd stopped you from broadening your horizons, now would she? And for all you know, she might be glad to get shot of you."

Roach smiled at Barnwell's blunt assessment. "But I'm all she's got."

"Then it might be good for both of you to have a break. And it's not like it has to be forever. You can come back. We'd survive, and you'd get more experience."

"Mum could come visit me, I suppose. Might give her a new lease of life, a bit of travel."

"There you go."

"Alright, I'll think about it some more. Thanks, Bazza."

"Anytime, mate."

A shout went up. It was Janice. The printer in the main office began to whir. "Sounds like some action's going down. Jersey One-o, that's us," Barnwell said.

The two men emerged from the break room to see Harding dashing over to the printer. She hovered as it spat out sheets of paper that she eagerly gathered up and quickly read.

"What is it, Janice?" Roach said.

"It can't be Johnny Philbin."

"Why not?"

"He was telling the truth, he can't drive." Janice looked at the printout in her hand. "He has no license, never owned a car, never passed a test. I've just had his case report translated from German—Philbin was caught because he was easy to monitor. He always used public transport. The German police literally followed him around using CCTV. That's how they caught him."

A door banged behind them. Graham stood there, his hair askew. A crease from a cushion ran down his cheek at a thirty-degree angle. He blinked rapidly several times. His team looked at him startled.

"Congratulations, Sergeant. You are absolutely correct. Johnny Philbin is not our murderer."

"Did you remember anything, sir?" Janice asked him.

"When I saw the Vauxhall outside the Naismith's, the license plates had been removed. Sergeant Roach, I presume you dug up the license plate number assigned to the vehicle under the ownership of the Naismiths at that address?"

Roach pulled out his tablet. "I did, sir. I contacted the DVLC with the name and address of the owners. They were able to trace the number."

"Good, you see when I left the *Fo'c'sle and Ferret* on Friday night, parked five cars down was a faded green Vauxhall Cavalier that I had forgotten about thanks to the fracas that happened shortly afterward. At that time the car had its plates on. The number was K12 RGF. Tell me, Sergeant Roach, what number was the car registered under?

"K12 RGF, sir!"

"But who...?" Barnwell started.

"DS Tom Vincenti. He was standing next to it."

Harding, Barnwell, and Roach stared at their boss. Ignoring them, Graham explained. "I think after he'd mown down Devine, Vincenti drove up to the pub to establish a sighting, then took the car back to the farm later. I suspect we'll find the plates in or around Mr. Philbin's address, planted there by Vincenti. I also suspect that Vincenti killed DS O'Hearn by tampering with the electrics at the conference. What I'm not sure about is why."

"Wow, sir. You're like a magician." Roach said. "Now I think about it, I had to push the Cavalier's seat forward when I got into it. If Vincenti had pushed it back in order to drive, that makes sense. He's taller than me. Do you want us to go pick Vincenti up?"

"No, I have another idea."

CHAPTER FORTY-NINE

"THANKS FOR COMING in Tom," Graham said. The two men shook hands. "Reckon you're the one officer who can help us."

"No problem, but please, Detective Inspector, tell me you were kidding on the phone. You're not really going to arrest Nigel Needham for the Devine hit-and-run, are you?"

"I know how it sounds, but there are big gaps in his story."

"There are big gaps in *all* his stories. The man has Alzheimer's."

Graham bristled. "I think it's unwise for us to speculate."

"He told me," Vincenti said. "Straight out, one evening a few weeks ago. Called me into his office and let it all out. Said he couldn't deal with the rumors, the way people would have to watch him gradually decline. He's off on retirement next month. Just wanted to come down to Jersey and see you, though he'd never make a fuss about it. He thinks the *world* of you. And in his mind, what's left of it, the conference was a chance to pass on some wisdom to the young 'uns."

"Before he forgets it all," Graham added morosely.

"I think he's having a hard time letting go of the job, myself. The uppers were glad to send him off here, to a place where he could do no harm for a few days. I don't know why they don't let him go early, but they seem to have decided to protect his pride and keep him on, if out of the way of anything useful."

"That may not have been wise. Awkward that it should end like this. Hauling the man over the coals, I mean."

"Yeah," Vincenti said. "It kills me, too. The super we know will be gone very soon. It's a sad situation."

"Very sad," Graham said.

"But what about O'Hearn's death? Surely you're not tying that to him too."

"Not sure. That's why we're interviewing him again."

"Well, he'd want you to follow the evidence," Vincenti said. "No matter where it led you."

Superintendent Nigel Needham looked perplexed and uncertain as he entered the lobby of the police station, but seeing two familiar faces seemed to help a little. "David," he nodded, "and Tom, how are you both?" He took off his quilted winter jacket. It was made for skiing in Austria but was very useful on a gray February day on Jersey.

"Just one more brief chat, sir," Graham promised his old boss. "Tom's going to sit in, maybe help out if he can."

"Perfect," the elderly police officer said.

"So, if you'd both leave your effects with Constable Barnwell here, we'll make a start."

The two Met police officers emptied their pockets. Needham laid his jacket on the back of a chair.

"Your cellphones too."

"My phone?" Vincenti queried, surprised.

"Yeah, sorry, no technology except for our digital recorder in the interview room. Thanks, Barnwell," Graham said.

"No problem." Needham handed his phone over.

"Sure," Vincenti added. He, too, gave his phone to Barnwell.

Graham ushered Superintendent Needham into the interview room. Vincenti followed. "I believe I've told you everything I can dredge up," Needham said as he sat at the table "but if you..."

"Just a moment, sir. Let me get set up," Graham said.

Vincenti sat next to Graham across the table from Needham. He folded his arms and sat back. Graham spoke for the recorder and then looked Needham in the eye.

"You hit something with your hire car, sir." Graham pointed to an image of the damaged rental car printed on photographic paper in front of him. He twisted it around for Needham to see. "It happened on Friday night, between 9:30 and 10:30 p.m. That's the time you were seen arriving back at the *White House Inn*. What can you tell us about that?"

"I've already told you. I'd have thought it was old news by now," Needham said dismissively. "I hit a bollard in that damned geometry puzzle of a car park. I can't have been the first, but it was an idiotic thing to do. Hasn't the staff confirmed what I said?"

"Not exactly. They said you hit a bollard while parking. But we believe that most of the damage happened *before* you arrived there."

It took a second, but Needham cottoned on. His face dropped as Graham's meaning dawned upon him. "Ah, I get it, David."

"Sorry, sir?"

"I know what you're doing." Needham wagged a finger. "Don't think that I don't see it. If it were anyone else," he said, his voice rising as he looked at Vincenti, "I might have expected a tactic like this, but..." He shook his head pityingly. "Well, from you, I'm shocked. This is *disgusting*."

Taken aback, Graham tried to interject. "Sir, I'm just trying to..."

"Let's take the addled old man, the forgetful one who can't explain every minute of his day, and pin a killing or two on him," Needham said, his voice full of contempt for his former protégé. He shook his head again. "That it should come to this, really. I guided you from the time you were just an ordinary copper on the beat. I don't know which is worse, the anger, or the disappointment."

"Sir, please..."

"Nothing more important than a quick collar, eh, Dave? Is that what I am? Something to help you look good in the papers again? Other coppers breathing down your neck, eh?"

"Now, just hang on..." Vincenti began, but Graham waved him down.

"I submit," Graham said, "that you hit DS Devine with your car around 10 p.m. on Friday. You then returned to the *White House Inn* and deliberately hit a bollard to mask the damage."

Lips pursed, Needham scowled defiantly, staring Graham down. But before long, the old man's eyes misted over, his gaze wavering. He blinked quickly and asked, simply, "How?"

Graham shivered. "I am indebted to Sergeant Roach for some excellent forensic work on the car."

Needham heaved a huge sigh. Eyes closed, arms folded, he seemed to will the world away. But then he said simply, "Alright," and let out a long sigh.

"Sir?"

"I got lost."

Excited, the DI started filling a page of his notebook. "Go on, sir."

"I missed the cliff road to the *White House Inn*. Stupidly, I ended up going down the hill to the High Street. Those bloody streets are like a maze. I went through a poorly lit area, and it was only then that I realized my lights were off. I was fiddling around trying to turn them on, but I couldn't find the bloody switch, lever, or whatever. They've changed things all around in these new-fangled cars. They're nothing but computers on wheels these days. Anyway," Needham cleared his throat, "I must have hit her." The memory of it seemed to amaze him, as though it couldn't possibly be his.

Staring at him, DS Vincenti growled, "*You* killed Kimberley Devine?"

CHAPTER FIFTY

"SIR, FOR HEAVEN'S sake," Graham said. "If it were an accident, why didn't you..."

"Because," Needham said, standing suddenly, proclaiming from his full height, "I'm already a bloody laughing stock! The *only* thing I'll have, in a couple of years, is my name, my reputation, and my service history. The rest will all be gone. Gone!" He looked imploringly at them both. "I wanted my name to *mean* something, David. I wanted the service to think of Nigel Needham as a good investigator, a skilled interviewer, a decent boss. But now, all they'll say is that I killed a woman, a police officer at that, on Gorey bloody High Street." Fighting back tears, he sat slowly. "I don't even remember it..." He stopped, his face in his hands.

One of them had to ask, and it fell to Vincenti. "And Patrick? Was that you too?"

Needham blew his nose. "I don't know," he wailed. "I wanted to be in the first row for the debate so I went into the auditorium early. Tripped over the mic cable, didn't I? Pulled the plug out of the outlet. I pushed it back in, but maybe I damaged the mic somehow, exposed the wiring. You must believe me. If it was me, it was a complete accident. Oh, how will I tell Veronica?" he said, looking up to the ceiling of the small room. There was a pause. "So, what will it be?" Needham asked pointedly, pulling some pride from somewhere. "Aren't you going to arrest me?" He wasn't daring Graham to detain him so much as obliging the DI to follow his own rules.

"You want me to arrest you? One of my oldest friends, the person who taught me how to process evidence when I was a brand new copper on the streets. You want *me*," Graham clarified, "to put *you* in handcuffs and bring you in?"

Upper lip as stiff as ever, Needham said, "If you feel that's what the evidence demands."

Graham pictured the distinguished Superintendent Needham sitting in one of their small cells, holding it together and looking defiant as he reminded Graham, yet again, of the importance of proper procedure. Graham could also imagine that as soon as his back was turned, Needham would likely dissolve into confusion, unable even to understand where he was.

Graham and Vincenti shared a look. "Sir," Graham said after a respectful silence, "we'll need to take new fingerprints, and we'll ask you to give us a DNA sample."

"Yes, yes, of course. I know the drill." Needham caught Graham's eye briefly before looking away. He began to shake his head slowly.

With a glance at Vincenti that mixed confusion with apology, Graham stepped around the table and brought out handcuffs from his belt-clip. "Sir, I'm placing you under arrest on suspicion," he said, "of causing the death of Detective Sergeant Kimberley Devine by dangerous driving. We'll place the death of Detective Sergeant Patrick O'Hearn on file for now. You do not have to say anything," he said, pressing the quick-cuffs down over Needham's wrists until they clicked into place, "but it may harm your defense if you do not mention when questioned something which you later rely on in court. Anything you say may be given in evidence." He patted Needham's shoulder gently and opened the door of the interview room.

"Harding, Barnwell!" The pair came to the interview room. "Would you take Superintendent Needham to the hold?" he said, preferring to use the euphemism for "cell" in this instance. Silently, the pair escorted the compliant Needham to the reception desk and began the formal paperwork.

"We'll both need to make reports," Graham said to Vincenti.

"Yeah, I'll write mine out right now," Vincenti said. "That was nuts. I mean, *Nigel?*"

The knowledge that Nigel Needham, his old mentor, had possibly killed two people seemed to puzzle Graham just as completely. "I guess all we can say is that a man's name is all he has in the end. And to some men, that's worth everything." Graham sighed. "Quite a few days, eh?"

Barnwell appeared with Vincenti's phone and courteously returned it. The Met officer sat down at one of the Constabulary's desk computers and spent a dutiful fifteen minutes pecking out a formal report of the events inside the interview room. After he'd hit "Send," he stood and grabbed his phone and wallet off the table beside him, stuffing his wallet into a back pocket.

"Do you need a ride somewhere, Tom?" Graham asked him.

"Nah, you've got enough going on and besides," Vincenti waved his phone, "I'll have a cab here in a minute. You know, I might stay for a day or two more. It's even colder back home, and this is a pretty nice island. I can see why you've made it your home."

Graham shook Vincenti's hand. "Enjoy the rest of your visit with us. Give us a bell before you finally leave."

Vincenti thanked the team and left, heading through the double doors to his waiting cab. Graham, Barnwell, and Roach watched the vehicle pull out. Janice missed his departure; she was busy texting Jack.

A moment later, Jack appeared from the break room. "Has he gone?"

"Jack," Harding said. "What were you doing in there? Setting off a nuclear reactor or a tracking device?"

"Neither. Just helping out a bit," Jack said cryptically. He smiled.

"He was working on something for me," Graham explained. "As for the rest of you, don't just stand there!"

Jack looked at the phone in his hand. "Looks like he's on his way to the Elizabeth Terminal."

"Just as I suspected," Graham said. "Get after him!"

"And do what?" Barnwell said. "Did I miss something?"

"Tom Vincenti told me he'd be staying on the island for a few more days, but I'm pretty sure he isn't going to be pottering around Jersey's shops for the next day or two," Graham told them. "Unless I'm mistaken, he's fleeing safe in the belief we've got the wrong man. Probably already got a flight booked to a non-extradition country. Qatar and Bahrain are popular spots for wanted outlaws. Be nice, this time of year. But he's got to get off the island first and that's where you and Roach come in. I want you to tail him, at a distance. Don't let him know you're there if you can help it. Wait for my word, but be prepared for trouble."

Barnwell and Roach looked at each other.

"Better get ourselves tooled up," said Barnwell, reaching for the car keys on the reception desk.

"It'll take too long in the car," Roach said. He went to the break room and came back with two motorbike helmets and two stab vests. "Here you go."

"You'll need a Taser. I'll sign it off," Graham said. The atmosphere in the room sank a couple of degrees as the severity of what they were dealing with punctured them.

Barnwell went to the locked weapons safe and pulled out one of the chunky yellow Taser guns. After noting the serial number, he locked in the cartridge and set the gun in a holster mounted on his protective vest. He put the bike helmet over his head. No one but him heard the curse he emitted as he anticipated his immediate future.

"Jack?" Graham said, ushering the young engineer into the middle of the reception area. "While those two race heroically to the ferry terminal, you get on with what we agreed."

"Will do, sir, but while I do that, could you keep an eye on this cellphone?" Wentworth gave Graham the phone he carried.

"Of course. What are we waiting for?"

"I'm not sure," Jack confessed, "but we'll know it when we see it."

CHAPTER FIFTY-ONE

THE SAFETY BRIEFING lasted less than thirty seconds. "Just hang on to my waist, and don't lean left or right, got it?" Roach said.

"Don't lean where?" Barnwell said. Getting no response from Roach, he cleared his throat. "*DON'T LEAN WHERE?*" he repeated, louder this time.

"Anywhere," Roach responded. Barnwell had slimmed down considerably, but his large frame, especially relative to Roach's light one, certainly could destabilize the bike. "Hold tight. And grip with your knees." Denied the satisfaction of an old-fashioned kick-start, Roach pressed a button and his 1200CC Ducati chugged into life. "My pride and joy," he yelled over the sound. Roach quickly finished what he called his "pre-launch checks." "All set?"

"Erm..."

"I'm going to floor it. Alright?"

"Nope," Barnwell said, just as Roach fizzed the bike out of its parking space and onto the St. Helier road. "Hell's teeth!" Barnwell cried. Roach ignored him. Without a siren, he had to overtake several cars, swerving into the right lane and speeding past drivers who would spend the evening complaining about whippersnappers with more horsepower than brains.

Suddenly and to Barnwell's shock, Graham's voice came through on a Bluetooth earpiece tucked behind his ear. "Right, listen up, you two."

"You'll have to speak up, sir!" Barnwell shouted into his microphone. At the other end of the line, Graham frantically pressed the volume down button on his phone. "Jim's driving like a..." There was a loud, whining noise as the bike passed a car whose driver was honking his horn at them.

"Jim's driving perfectly, sir. Just tell us," Roach said, dropping a gear to pass a delivery van, "what to do. But don't take long about it. The range of these helmets is less than a mile."

"Okay," Graham said, much louder. He surveyed his whiteboard once more trying to synthesize what they knew. "I'm expecting Vincenti to be on the ferry to the mainland."

Somehow, Roach managed to talk while pushing the bike past seventy on a two-lane road. "Should we arrest him, sir?"

"Just tell me when you find him," Graham replied.

Roach slowed to ease the bike neatly into a line of traffic. Once an oncoming tractor had passed them, he accelerated to overtake the tail of slower vehicles.

"You just want us to watch him? *Jesus, Roachie.*" Barnwell squeezed his eyes shut, as Roach made only the most cursory genuflection at a stop sign.

"Until I say the word, yes." Graham's voice stuttered as the reception broke up and Barnwell and Roach continued their journey in silence save for the roar of the bike.

"Argghh!" Barnwell yelled, as Roach shot through a red light, crossing Victoria Road in the center of St. Helier. He joined the A4, a broad avenue that took them directly to the ferry terminal. Shortly afterward, Roach brought the bike to a stop.

"Jim's got us to the terminal." Barnwell switched to his police radio. He was panting. "Alive—just."

"And in record time," Roach said.

"Give me my police regulation pushbike any day," Barnwell grumbled, breathing fast, his heart still several moments from slowing down.

Roach pulled off his helmet and shook his hair out. "Stop complaining, let's get in there."

As they ran across the forecourt to the terminal, the pair attracted the concerned stares that customarily followed uniformed police officers in a hurry. They came to a halt in front of a startled gate agent. "Gorey Police," Barnwell said flashing his ID. "We need to speak with one of your passengers."

The young woman stared, frozen, but handed him an iPad with a long list of names. "Right," Barnwell said, scrolling through, "Vincenti's already on board. Which way?" He handed the tablet back to the woman, and she pointed to a walkway thirty feet ahead. The sleek, white mainland ferry was completing preparations for the two-hour cross-channel trip to Portsmouth. "Leaves in ten minutes," she said as the two uniformed men jogged over to the broad walkway leading to the ferry's first passenger deck.

"Sergeant Roach? Constable Barnwell?" Graham barked. "Can you hear me?"

"Loud and clear sir," Roach confirmed. "Onboard, starting our search."

Barnwell pulled him up short with a hand on his shoulder. "There," he whispered, looking over to the other side of the deck. Tom Vincenti was sitting in one of the lounge areas at the end of a row by one of the boat's tall windows.

"Don't let yourselves be seen," Graham told them, regretting now that they were in uniform. Pacing around the station's reception, he was agitated not to be a part of the action. "Jack," he called over to where the IT engineer was feverishly setting up a five laptop network, "Remind me what's going to happen?"

"When Vincenti uses his phone, we will see everything replicated on this one," Jack said, pointing to the expensive model Graham was keeping his eye on. "He may have a pay-as-you-go, but unless he switches the chip out, we'll see it. I installed some remote-access software while you were interviewing Superintendent Needham."

"The marvels of technology," Graham said, punching Jack's shoulder in gratitude.

There was a ding from the phone. Jack looked at the screen. "And there we have it. A text message."

Exhibit A:

Text from cellphone 020-8914-xxxx to cellphone 020-1515-xxxx

Sent 1321h, Tuesday, February 4th

Party A: Leaving now for location two. Is the caviar on ice?

Party B: Yes.

Party A: And the champagne?

Party B: Yes, nicely chilled. Any heat following you?

Party A: No way. I've got them all chasing shadows.

Party B: Well, good luck. Pick up as planned.

Party A: Sure. It's been emotional. Bye now.

CHAPTER FIFTY-TWO

"T HAT'S IT," GRAHAM said. Into the radio, "Make the arrest."

"Roger that, sir. What are we arresting him for?" Barnwell asked.

"Suspicion of the murders of Detective Sergeants Kimberley Devine and Patrick O'Hearn," Graham replied.

"Any advice for us, sir?" Roach asked, his voice quivering.

"Put him down as fast as you can. Don't let him run around, get off the boat, or do anything colorful. But don't take any chances with this bloke, you two. If you say the word, I'll call in the Armed Response Unit. They'll be there in no time. We're on our way. Harding is ordering the Harbormaster to delay the sailing."

"Copy that."

"He hasn't seen us yet," Barnwell noted quietly to Roach. "Let's just play it cool until we're close, then be ready with everything." Outside, against the ship's enormous windows, rain had begun, a debilitating drizzle well-known to British February afternoons.

Roach grabbed Barnwell's shoulder. "You really don't think we should wait for the firearms team? I mean, they're the professionals. And this guy, he's real hard..."

"And what were you on that bike? Or were you just playing at being a jack-the-racer? Besides, people running around with guns on a cross-channel ferry? On Jersey? What the bleedin' heck would Freddie Solomon make of *that*? And what was that you were saying about not enough action?"

Roach puffed out his cheeks. "Okay, I'm ready if you are." He held a black can of pepper spray in his left hand and a police baton in his right.

"Make yourself big, loud, and confident. Knock him off balance. Right?" Barnwell said. Roach nodded. "*Go.*"

"Tom Vincenti, this is Gorey Police!" Fifty passengers whirled around in surprise. "Stay where you are and don't move," Roach yelled.

Roach advanced on Vincenti down a row of seats holding his pepper spray out in front of him. Barnwell went left, his arms out, palms up. "That's it, just stay still. We don't want any trouble."

"Listen, fellas," Vincenti said, keeping his seat, his hands up. He smiled at them.

Barnwell hooked a hand under Vincenti's armpit and lifted him to standing. He grasped the man's wrist and twisted it behind his back, not quite believing how compliant Vincenti was. "We are arresting you on suspicion of the murders of..."

Barnwell didn't get any further. In one swift movement, Vincenti lifted his other arm and elbowed Barnwell in the face. It was a weak blow, but Barnwell, caught off-balance, staggered back. Vincenti dodged Roach and leaped over the seat in front of him, bolting for the fire exit. He struggled to fling the door open as Barnwell, furious and adrenaline-fueled, chased after him, the ferry's high-pitched fire alarm now pealing loudly forcing stunned passengers to cower and cover their ears.

As Roach stumbled trying to vault a row of seats, Barnwell

got to Vincenti first, charging at him and landing heavily on Vincenti's back. Another elbow connected hard with Barnwell's nose, pitching backward, his arms flailing, the metallic tang of blood reaching his taste buds. With Barnwell's weight falling away from him, Vincenti levered the larger man off with a loud grunt, then burst through the fire door and out into the dim, gray afternoon light.

Roach chased after him. "You alright, Bazza?" he shouted as he passed.

"Keep moving!" Barnwell was nearly back on his feet, his fingers feeling fat and cumbersome as he replaced his tiny earpiece and lapel mic. He panted, his face red, a trickle of blood descending from a nostril. "He turned right!"

Roach flew through the door and past a cluster of people standing by the ship's rail, despite the squally rain. He caught sight of Vincenti climbing the stairs to the next deck. Roach took the stairs three at a time, grateful for the speed that made him a regular for the Jersey Police five-a-side team. "He's headed back inside," Roach gasped into his radio. "We're on the upper deck."

"I'll go up the middle," Barnwell said as he ran toward the center of the vessel where there were flights of stairs that would take him up or down. His face and sleeve were smeared with red and sweat seeped into a cut on his nose, making it sting. "Be careful!" he shouted over the fire alarm.

"Police! Stand aside!" Roach yelled. A static-y, patchy announcement intermittently urged passengers to stay calm. It mingled with the fire alarm, making a cacophony of sounds that was almost painful to bear. "Vincenti!" Roach yelled, yanking at a door to see the man racing away from him across the lightly populated bar. Roach pushed aside cheap, plastic armchairs and jumped over low plywood tables, some covered in used, fingerprint-stained glasses. "Stop! Police! Give yourself up before someone gets hurt!"

There were screams ahead. A passageway divided the bar

from the café and lounge. "Where?" Roach yelled to a terrified group of holidaymakers. They pointed outside, to the front of the ship. Roach, scrambling, found another door and headed back out into the rain, slipping as he turned right toward the bow. He saw no sign of Vincenti among the tourists taking photos of the open sea, oblivious to the sights and sounds around them.

"Bazza, you hearing me? He's coming back your way." Roach passed a row of lifeboats and piles of orange vests. The rain was morbidly cold.

"Roger," Barnwell said. "Got my eyes open."

From somewhere out of sight, Roach heard a clatter, and then another, followed by shouting. He found the source of the noise down a stairway near one of the games centers. "Bloody lunatic in there!" a man in chef's whites shouted.

"In the kitchen!" Roach yelled into his radio. There was a rush of air at his shoulder and he turned to see a familiar face as he felt a hard punch to his side. There was a stab of pain, a cloud of lightheadedness, and a roar in his ears that drowned out the siren before he fell like a plumb line to the deck.

CHAPTER FIFTY-THREE

WITH THE URGENT whine of the police siren efficiently parting traffic, Graham and Harding sped across Jersey only slightly slower than Roach and his catalog of misdemeanors on the Ducati. They had left Jack working on cracking the encryption that was still locking in the data held on the memory stick that O'Hearn had left them. "Another piece of the puzzle," Graham had told Jack, before leaving the station. "Let's hope it's a huge one." Graham drove with half his attention on Jack's progress, relayed piecemeal to him via Harding. "I know this is high-end stuff," he said impatiently, "but is he any closer?"

Harding watched the road and listened as Jack typed in noisy spurts, chattering to himself all the while. "Doing my best!" he called out over the line.

With the phone to her ear, Harding frowned at Graham from the passenger seat. "No need to stress, Jack. You just take your time. I'll put you on speaker."

"It's encrypted with a polyalphabetic cipher," Jack explained. "He must have known cybersecurity, no doubt about it." Between each utterance, Harding could hear code—or something, at least —being typed at a blistering pace. "I've been struggling on my own, but I've written some code and got half the police computers on the island slaved to my system," he said. "Just a second..."

"Darling?" she asked sweetly, "how many seconds are we talking?"

"Some," Jack answered. The sound of typing reached a furious peak. "But not many." With a sound like an octopus berating a keyboard, Jack ran three "cracker" executables simultaneously. One of them was making real progress. "Thousands of times a second, my software bombards the security module on the USB drive with possible PIN combinations until it finds the right one. It's called a 'brute force' attack. Unlocking this data is a matter of how much processing power we can bring to it. See, our new architecture can..."

"Hey, Jack?" Graham called out as he spotted the ferry ahead. "I'm hoping to prove that Tom Vincenti was in league with Ketch's gang and that he was on the fiddle."

"Right, sir," Jack said. "We're almost... there..."

Graham parked, after a fashion, inside the pedestrian area of the terminal, getting as close to the walkway as he could. To his right, he could see Roach's abandoned Ducati. "Let's get in there," he said, relieved not to hear screaming or gunshots. Graham took the phone from Harding, "Jack? Keep talking to me, lad."

Three seconds. "I think we're nearly there... hang on... hang on... yes!" Jack yelled. "Cracked it!"

"You're looking for any mention of..."

It took no time at all. "Got it, got it," Jack said. As Graham and Harding jogged up the walkway to the ferry, Jack started to read out loud.

"'Tom Vincenti isn't clean, but he's irreplaceable'," Jack read at random from the first file to mention Vincenti's name. "'I don't know how long he'll keep going, or if he'll even make it to the trial, but there's no way we're getting Bob Ketch without him.'"

"Give me some context, Jack," Graham demanded. "Who's it from?"

"Nigel Needham," Jack said. "Three and a half years ago. Seems to be establishing Vincenti as essential to the operation."

"What else?"

"More recent messages," Jack said, scanning the list. "Emails from one officer to another about Vincenti, people claiming some pretty bad things, sir. That he might have intimidated witnesses, and, well... There's a *lot* more."

"Good, but not good enough. What's the most recent thing?"

"An email from two days ago, records of time the team spent working together, notes about the subjects of their surveillance," Jack said, reading from a long list. "There's several gigabytes of data, sir. Everything they were working on."

"Photos?"

A burst of typing right in Graham's ear played counterpoint to the sound of his footsteps on the ferry's hallway floors. "Lots. Surveillance photos of Vincenti, some with an older guy. Money, or something, being exchanged between Vincenti and other types. Sending through to you now."

Graham's phone pinged, and he slowed to a walk to scroll through the sample of photos Jack had sent him. "That's Ketch. Looks like he knew him, and well by the looks of it." In the photo, the two men were leaning in, clasping hands, and patting each other on the back. "Good chap, O'Hearn," he breathed. "I think this might be enough, Harding." Graham showed her the photo of Vincenti and Ketch.

"Sounds like a mish-mash, sir. The super supporting him, but then this incriminating evidence."

"Hmm, it could be he duped Needham, but that those on the ground were more suspicious. This material shows us other people were onto him. Needham could have been an unwitting foil, keeping him on a team when he was dirty. Perhaps O'Hearn was holding evidence against Vincenti in case of trouble," Graham said.

"But why didn't he say something after Devine was killed? If he knew he was at risk, and he obviously did, why didn't he grass up Vincenti?"

"Pride, maybe. A sense of infallibility. Being undercover does a number on your judgment. It's easy to get a God complex. When you're dealing with the types of danger Devine and O'Hearn were dealing with, it's necessary to compartmentalize. They may have seen themselves as heroes or they may have been paranoid especially if they had been dealing with a dirty cop. O'Hearn may have had a plan to bring home the evidence *and* a murderer, avenging his partner's death in the process. But he was killed before he..." Before Graham could say more, he heard a muffled shout in his earpiece. He urgently pressed his finger to it, the better to hear. "Barnwell? You alright?"

CHAPTER FIFTY-FOUR

HARDING AND GRAHAM raced up a flight of
stairs and rounded a corner to find Barnwell
breathing heavily as he leaned on a row of blue seats.
His eyes darted around the vast cavernous space of the passenger
lounge. "He's a slippery blighter," Barnwell panted, "We might
need some help here, sir. I don't know whether..." There was a
curse on their shared line, then a scream, and more muffled
shouting. "Jim's in trouble!"

A long groan of pain traveled through their earpieces.

"Jim?" Graham said. "Where are you?"

"Upper... deck," Roach ground out. "Suspect armed. Knife.
I've been... stabbed."

"Harding—take the port corridor, make your way up to the
top deck. Barnwell—go up the stairs. Find Roach. I'll take the
starboard side. Taser Vincenti if you have to, but be careful of the
public."

The team dashed down the hallways and stairs, spreading
out, shouting for passengers to stay together and keep low.

It was Barnwell who reached Roach first. "Christ, lad... He's here! Out by the rail, right side. Er, *starboard* side." He approached quickly, brushing aside two bystanders to find Roach half-kneeling on the deck.

One hand clutched the railing while the other was pressed to his ribs. Blood seeped through Roach's fingers. "This *bloody* hurts!"

"Shh... shh... shh," Barnwell said. Laboriously, careful not to hurt Roach more than he had to, Barnwell helped him into a sitting position and examined his wound.

"Crikey, he caught you good and proper." Barnwell winced at the sight of the injury between Roach's first and second ribs. "I think you should lie down. That's it, careful," he said as Roach grimaced and groaned but allowed himself to be supported onto the deck.

"Maybe I'll get my own medal," Jim said hazily. He was slurring. His hand was now completely covered in blood. His uniform was soaked. "'Bout time someone else got one."

"When you get through this, sonny, you can have mine, you stupid idiot." Barnwell pulled out a handkerchief and pressed it against Roach's wound. Roach started to shiver. Barnwell unbuttoned his jacket and one-handedly draped it across Roach's prone body, his starched white shirt immediately becoming sodden with spray from both the sky and the sea. "Stay with me, lad. Ambulance'll be here soon."

A French doctor bustled through the small crowd that had gathered, summoned from his seat by the screams of passengers. He quickly set to work on Roach, taking over from Barnwell.

Roach waved for Barnwell to leave. "Help the others," the stricken sergeant said, sounding breathless and weak.

"No, no, the others can manage it.

"Go, man. Finish the job."

"Can you keep him stable?" Barnwell said to the doctor. He could hear sirens in the distance. "I need to go."

"*Oui*," the Frenchman replied. Barnwell ran off.

"But your nose! It is broken!" the doctor cried after him.

"No sign of him here!" Harding shouted into her radio. "I'll check the cafeteria." Graham searched the kitchen. They met up by the Bureau de Change.

Strapped into their stab vests and with Janice holstering the constabulary's only other Taser, they passed clusters of frightened passengers, and others who were pacing around. Harding ushered them into spots with clear sightlines. "Six foot four, black hair. He's wearing a white t-shirt, jeans, and a black leather jacket. Do not, I repeat, *do not* try to apprehend him."

Graham knew Vincenti had no choice but to come out of hiding eventually. One way or the other, he would try to leave the boat. "Where would I be...?" Graham muttered, striding down the side of the ferry, his eyes searching. "If I wanted to hide and make a dash for it." He passed a lifeboat. He stopped. A barely noticeable change in color in the keel of one of the lifeboats alerted him to the fact that the cover had been moved and not put back quite square.

With one remarkably hurried movement, Graham flipped back the weathered gray tarpaulin covering the lifeboat. Tom Vincenti leaped up, knife in his hand. He advanced on Graham, shouting at him. He took but two steps before Harding, coming upon the two men from the bow, shouted at the top of her voice, "Stop, Police!"

Vincenti took his third step, and Janice fired two charged Taser darts at his back. The man froze, juddering like a stuck record, unable to finish his angry condemnation. With the five seconds that it bought him, Graham jumped on board.

Harding dashed toward the lifeboat, wires streaming from her Taser. "Sir! Have you got him?"

Graham ran straight at Vincenti, barging into him, his arms

locked around Vincenti's waist. They fell together into the well between the lifeboat seats. Graham's weight held Vincenti down, but Vincenti, still shivering from the electric shock, flipped Graham over onto his back. His eyes burning, his mouth twisted into an ugly grimace, Vincenti raised the knife ready to plunge it into yet another colleague.

Graham's senses took in everything around him—the weight of Vincenti's body, the vibration of the ferry's engine, the high-pitched alarm that still pealed around him. As Vincenti bore down on him, snarling, an image of Katie surfaced in Graham's mind. It was floating, swimming. She was twirling. He heard her giggling and saw those teeth, those small, perfectly neat, white baby teeth.

Graham hurled himself upward. He head-butted Vincenti between the eyes, smashing his nose. Vincenti howled like a wounded animal. He fell back onto the floor of the boat.

The force of Graham's strike pitched him forward. Graham pinned Vincenti to the floor with his body, gripping the wrist holding the knife with one hand, punching him in the kidneys, and then the throat with the other. He didn't let up until he heard Harding's voice.

"Sir, *Sir!*" Janice sounded as if she were at the end of a very long tunnel. "It's alright sir, you've got him. I'll cover you." Harding had climbed into the boat and was next to him, holding out her reloaded Taser, trembling. She didn't need it. Vincenti was done. Graham wrestled Vincenti onto his face and cuffed him with one hand as his other hand gripped Vincenti's head, his knee firmly in the small of Vincenti's back.

CHAPTER FIFTY-FIVE

WITH VINCENTI SUBDUED, Harding stood over him as Graham crawled to the end of the boat and sat panting against its side. Standing a discreet distance away, passengers who had held their phones aloft to record the arrest, began to chatter among themselves.

"Well done, Sergeant," Graham said to Harding, but before he could say more, the throng of curious onlookers crowded around until it seemed every passenger on the ferry was gawking at them.

Graham groaned. "Well, there's no need for the whole world to see this. Let's get him down to the station."

"You got him?" Barnwell appeared from among the horde.

"Yup, give us a hand, Constable."

Together, the painfully swollen, red-nosed Constable Barnwell and the bruised and bloodied Detective Inspector Graham manhandled Vincenti off the lifeboat, and grasping him under the shoulders, guided him briskly through the ship, past amazed onlookers and staff.

As they walked through the ferry, the sagging Vincenti stumbled unsteadily between them, the passengers watching them silently, until one person broke the silence with a clap. It was cautious and quiet but catching. Gradually, the passengers' appreciation for the officers' heroics followed them along the ship's long halls, across the passenger lounge to the walkway. There, Graham, Barnwell, Harding, and Vincenti paused, allowing the paramedics carrying a stretchered Roach to walk ahead of them to the waiting ambulance, the French doctor fussing behind.

"Alright, Jim?" Graham said as the stretcher passed them.

"Alright, sir," was Roach's response. He offered them a pale, weak smile. His thumbs-up sign was strong, though.

By the time Tom Vincenti was finally pushed, his head protected by Barnwell's hand, into the Gorey Constabulary's marked car and Roach had been lifted into the ambulance, the last thing they heard before the doors of their respective vehicles slammed shut, from one end of the harbor to the other, was wild, enthusiastic cheers, and applause.

As the ambulance drove off, its blue lights flashing, Graham, Barnwell, and Harding stood staring at Roach's Ducati, propped up on its stand in the middle of the forecourt. It looked powerful but forlorn standing there on its own.

"What on earth are we going to do with it?" Harding asked.

"Either of you want to ride it back?" Graham said.

"No idea how, sir," Janice replied.

"Not on your nelly," Barnwell added. "We'll get someone from the garage to come and get it. That's the best thing, I reckon."

There was a sound behind them. They turned to see Jack Wentworth speeding in Janice's dark brown Prius toward them. He threw the car into "Park" and, shock and concern spread across his face, he rushed to envelop Janice in a bear hug.

"Jack. *Jack!*" Janice cried, embarrassed.

"Are you alright? I heard everything." Jack held Janice's face between his hands before crushing her to him again.

"Yes, yes, I'm fine."

"Thank God for that. I couldn't bear..."

"Right then, let's get back to the station," Graham said, keen to be spared this scene of romantic terror and yearning.

"I'll drive. You look done in," Barnwell said.

"You don't exactly look in peak condition, yourself."

Graham walked around to the passenger door and looked over the roof of the car at Barnwell. "Tell me, which part of that ultra-collaborative, cross-disciplinary, cross-hierarchical investigative model did we just employ for this arrest, Constable?"

Barnwell thought for a few seconds. He looked at Vincenti sitting in the back seat of the police car, angry and flushed. Then, he looked over at Graham. His senior officer was bleeding from a graze on his forearm, and there was a scratch running down his cheek. The skin between his eyes was red and beginning to bruise. Dark circles were forming under each eye. Barnwell knew that by tomorrow, the DI would be sporting two black eyes that would be matched in discomfort only by his own already bulbous red nose. They were in for a rough few days.

"Which part of that ultra-collaborative, cross-disciplinary, cross-hierarchical investigative model did we just use?" Barnwell repeated. He paused as he thought. "The bollocks part, I reckon, sir. The bollocks part."

Graham smiled. It was a big, broad smile, the like of which Barnwell had never seen from him. "I think you're right, Constable. Let's go, shall we?"

CHAPTER FIFTY-SIX

"WHAT DID YOU think, eh? That you could come to our town and do whatever you liked? That you could target your fellow team members, right under our noses? And for what?" Graham demanded. He, Harding, and Tom Vincenti were ensconced in the station's interview room.

Vincenti looked daggers at him, then turned away. "You'd have done the same if you had lived my life."

Hands flat on the desk, not impressed in the slightest, Graham said, "I highly doubt it. And what kind of sick universe do you live in exactly? Tell us."

"The kind where the most dangerous people in London have a knife to your throat, day in, day out," Vincenti explained, through gritted teeth. "The kind where if there's one wrong word, one wrong move, you're *done for*. Do you know what that's like? Having to play both sides until you can't tell the good from the bad?"

"Goes with the job," Harding told him, her arms folded. "The others were keeping things straight. They carried out a clean investigation... until you murdered them."

Vincenti looked at the officers on the other side of the table, neither of them having an ounce of sympathy for him. "I didn't have any choice! It wasn't just me. He threatened my daughter!" Vincenti yelled, slamming his fist on the table. The vein in his temple throbbed.

Vincenti's words quietened Graham. He leaned forward. In a low, soft voice he said, "I think you need to tell us exactly what was going on."

Vincenti ran his cuffed hands through his hair. "I'm not saying any more. Not until she's safe."

Graham looked at Harding and nodded.

"What's her name?"

"Amy. Amy Vincenti."

Quietly, Janice pushed back her chair and padded out of the room.

"Harding will take care of it, now tell us what was happening."

Vincenti leaned his elbows on the table and covered his eyes with his hands. He rubbed his face and then, seeming to come to a decision, dropped his hands to the table. He growled. "Ketch gave me a deadline. Emphasis on the '*dead*,' you know?" He stood reflexively, but immediately crumpled back down again.

"I persuaded Ketch I was more useful alive than dead. I promised to help him, and in exchange, my daughter would remain safe, and I would be allowed to leave the gang. I was going to grab Amy and head off into Europe, maybe North Africa. I've got some mates there."

"And by helping him," Graham noted heavily, "You had to murder fellow officers."

Vincenti slumped in his chair. "I made it quick."

"Were you the one that gave them up?" It was an educated guess.

"I didn't rat on anyone. They sussed Patrick on their own. Ketch knew weeks ago. From there, they quickly cottoned on to Devine. They'd known about me for ages, but they increased my supply, and like a fool, I fell for it, hooked me deep. Again." Vincenti's fingers danced as though itching for a cigarette. "If you ever want to see a puppet on a string, watch the relationship between a junky and his dealer. Ketch had me dancing to his tune. I was debasing myself daily. I repeatedly compromised the work the others were doing. I was the reason the investigation was faltering.

"Then when the others were made, Ketch turned the screws. They followed Amy, took photos of her leaving school and such, then hauled me in. Told me to take Devine out. She was expendable. Plus, she was a woman. Ketch didn't like being fooled, and he *definitely* didn't like being fooled by a female. I gave Devine plenty of warning... texts I sent her. She could have gone to ground. But she didn't. And I have no idea why. She should have seen the writing on the wall."

"She wanted to see the op through."

"Then she was a fool. She forgot—they *both* forgot—who they were dealing with."

"A murderous colleague?" Graham said.

"A mobster capable of terrible things," Vincenti clarified.

"And O'Hearn?" Graham said. "Ketch ordered his execution too?"

"Not at first. He wanted me to recruit him," Vincenti answered. "He wanted to flip Patrick and use him, just like he was using me. The Met, Needham especially, never understood Ketch could turn an undercover cop like he was casting a spell. He could blackmail and threaten and intimidate whomever he targeted until they couldn't tell up from down. Then when they were broken, Ketch would get his target hooked. They'd have done anything they were told then. I'm serious: Ketch can turn undercover cops working *inside* the Met *and* the gang, all in a few days."

"Charming skill set," Graham said.

"For Ketch, it's all about finding the right pressure points. But I never got a chance to bring O'Hearn to him like I planned. Silly bugger. He confronted me, told me he knew what I was doing, that he suspected me of killing Kimberley. That he had evidence of my involvement with Ketch. He gave me a chance to come clean. That was his big mistake. He underestimated who he was dealing with."

"You're that hard, eh?"

"Not hard, hooked. I'm pathetic. Ketch, though, he's brutal. I had to do what I was told. When it was clear O'Hearn wouldn't be intimidated, Ketch gave me the order to kill him."

"So how did you do the killings exactly?"

"I think I've said enough." Vincenti folded his arms. He swallowed. His foot jiggled, and he looked out of the frosted window nervously.

Graham went to the door. "Janice?" he called.

"Yes, sir."

Graham raised his eyebrows.

"All taken care of, sir. She's being collected from school now."

"Hear that, Tom?"

Vincenti rolled his eyes. He tipped his chair onto its back legs and stared at the ceiling. Suddenly, with a bang, he dropped the chair to the floor. "Okay, okay."

CHAPTER FIFTY-SEVEN

"I PICKED OUT the car on my way from the airport. On Friday night, I ran out to that God-forsaken farm, it's not far, less than a mile. Drove the car back into town. Waited up the street from the pub and followed Devine when she left. Afterward, I drove the car back to the pub so I'd be seen by you lot. I put the car back in the early hours after I'd helped with the fingertip search of the scene. It was a stroke of luck Johnny Philbin was working the conference. I never accounted for the super, though. You set me up well there."

"You took the plates off to frame Philbin, I suppose."

"Yeah," Vincenti sighed, ready to let it all out now. "You'll find the plates in a skip at the back of his house."

"And O'Hearn?"

"That Ashby kid had them following debate rules so I knew where Patrick would be sitting. I loosened a wire in his mic over the break. Then, I made a quick adjustment to the backup mic, made sure it was turned off until it reached O'Hearn. He turned it on and, poof, Bob's your uncle.

"Did you know he'd swallowed a memory stick encrypted with evidence of your double-dealing?"

Vincenti's expression opened. "Did he?" He leaned back on his chair again. "Hah! What a gent!" He shook his head, a wide grin splitting his face. "That's cracker, that. Smart move."

Graham let out a welcoming sigh as he saw a steaming pot of tea sitting on one of the main office desks. He looked over into reception to see Nigel Needham sitting there with his legs crossed. He was chatting quietly with Laura.

"Hi, love," Graham said, "didn't know you were coming in." He bent down to kiss her cheek. "And very well done, sir!" Graham said, taking a seat beside his old friend. "I had no idea you had a flare for the dramatic."

"You know," Needham said, eyebrows raised, "I haven't had so much fun since I did Shakespeare at the West End."

"You were in the West End?" Laura exclaimed. "Of *London*?"

"West End Theater, Doncaster, actually, but they're a much more sophisticated audience than you'd expect."

"Well, I'd have given you an Oscar," Graham told him.

"Too kind. Just don't ask me to do it again," Needham said. "I fear I may only have one of those masterpieces in me."

Graham glanced at the interview room, then back at Needham. "You want to talk to Tom before we charge him?" Once formally accused of the two murders, Vincenti could not be interviewed by any of them without a lawyer present. "It'll be your last chance to hear from him. Next stop, Crown court."

"What, in six months or so?" Needham said, standing. "I'm afraid there won't be much left of me by then, David. Nah, I don't want to spend any more time in the company of abhorrent human beings. But I'll try never to forget what you all managed to pull off this weekend. Marvelous, just marvelous! And thank you, young lady, for your company." Needham smiled at Laura.

"Oh, my pleasure. I've got enough David Graham stories now to fill the first volume of his biography," she said.

"Great," the DI said sarcastically before plastering a grin across his face.

"But tell me, did you ever get to the bottom of my little, er, indiscretion with the car?"

"Yes, sir. We found recent damage to a tree on the cliff road, just at the edge of town. There were signs a car had hit it, paint scrapes and some glass found. There was a broken branch on the side of the road. No sign of tungsten oxide. Earlier you were seen driving without your lights on—easily done on well-lit surface streets—and so, well, I suspect that if we were to do some analysis, we'd find a match between your car and the debris found by the tree. All rather inconvenient but innocent enough."

"Well, that's a relief. And no one got hurt, that's the main thing." Needham checked his watch; he had two hours until his flight. His cab was due. Needham clapped Graham's shoulders proudly as they reached the station's doors. "I've no nuggets of wisdom left to impart. Except one," he said, a finger aloft. "*Make great memories*. Make as many good ones as you can. You never know which ones you'll be left with."

Graham took Needham's hand. "Thank you for everything, sir," Graham said.

"Thank *you*, David. My best to Barnsley and Rhodes. And that lovely sergeant," he added. "Do give my love to Katie, won't you? She must be all grown up now."

CHAPTER FIFTY-EIGHT

The Gorey Gossip
Tuesday, February 4th

Detective Sergeant Tom Vincenti, a decorated undercover operative with the Metropolitan Police, was today sensationally arrested in connection with the deaths of two fellow officers as he sought to return to the mainland aboard the ferry, the Eagle Rapide Jersey Expedition.

Vincenti was chased to the ferry by crack police outriders as he sought to flee Jersey jurisdiction and was ultimately cornered hiding inside a lifeboat.

The drama unfolded Tuesday afternoon after officers followed Vincenti to the Elizabeth Terminal. Despite the ferry being full of passengers, police confronted the fugitive and armed with Tasers, sparked a frightening chase throughout the boat.

Vincenti was eventually found cowering like a rat underneath the tarpaulin of a lifeboat. Following a struggle, he was detained at Her Majesty's Pleasure and later charged with double murder. More charges are pending.

One police officer from Gorey Constabulary was stabbed in the fight. His condition is described as "serious but stable." No members of the public were harmed.

The population of Gorey, and indeed, the whole of Jersey can now rest easy in their homes. Our collective resources have been put under great strain these past few days, but thanks to public vigilance and the alleged killer's fatal errors, the risk to the populace of Jersey has been snuffed out.

The entire Gorey Constabulary was involved in the capture of the murderer and all were in attendance when he was detained, an arrest so dramatic that it would have deserved an Oscar had it originated in Hollywood instead of real life on our beloved island. Our boys and girl in blue are to be congratulated. Indeed, may we see them walking the red carpet very soon.

CHAPTER FIFTY-NINE

"**N**OW THEN, YOU 'orrible lot," Barnwell said to the scrum of TV news people, bloggers, and more traditional journalistic types. "Let's try to keep things down to a dim roar, alright? There's nothing to see here. The hospital administration has given you a statement, so you can all go home." Barnwell felt the beginnings of a headache. DI Graham had offered him a few days sick leave while he recovered from the worst of the pain from his broken nose, but Barnwell had preferred the distraction of work.

Marcus Tomlinson's umbrella burrowed a channel through the center of the throng. "Constable," he said, "may I be permitted entrance?"

"Evening, sir. Hardly California weather is it, now?" Barnwell fell into step beside the septuagenarian pathologist, his job with the crowd now complete as everyone dispersed quickly. His shift was finally over, and he would join Marcus and the others inside.

Shaking the freezing rain from his umbrella as the glass doors slid open, Marcus said, "Ah well, not long now." Under his arm, he carried a wicker picnic basket. "Let's go and enjoy ourselves, finally."

In room 3C, the patient looked a little wan, but he was smiling and happy to see his friends. A small, dignified celebration was deserved, and they'd chosen to come to him in the hospital to have it. Marcus Tomlinson grinned for the photo he'd persuaded a nurse to take. Barnwell attempted one also, a challenge as most of his face felt numb. His nose was bandaged and still obviously sore. Jack clutched Janice around the waist while Laura had persuaded DI Graham to loosen his tie. No one seemed to notice that he and Laura were holding hands, although Graham was acutely aware of it. Public displays of affection did not sit comfortably with him, but he was determined to suffer through the strangeness of it until it became familiar and not awkward. In the middle of them all, sat Jim Roach, propped up by three pillows, an IV taped to the back of his hand.

When the nurse had left, Marcus smartly pulled the curtains around Roach's bed. The small crowd was effectively enclosed within a fabric cell. He pulled out the picnic basket from under the bed and made a show of unbuckling the straps while the others watched him in amusement. With a flourish, he removed a picnic blanket to reveal four bottles of wine, a bottle of Talisker, two tumblers, and five crystal wine glasses. There was also a bottle of cordial.

"Are we allowed alcohol in a hospital, Marcus?" Janice whispered pulling a face.

"They won't say anything, not with me here." Marcus winked. "But none for you, young man," he said to Roach. "You'll have to stick with lemon barley water for now, but I brought you some crystal to drink it from and some wine for when you are off your antibiotics."

"Congratulations everyone," Graham said, holding his drink aloft. "I'd like to raise a glass to the end of a successful conference organized most admirably by our own Sergeant Harding."

"Hear, hear," Barnwell said, the others murmuring their assent as they took a sip of their drinks.

"And to the successful conclusion of a distressing case..."

"Well done, everyone," Roach said, raising his glass of cloudy, pale, yellow cordial, the color coming back into his cheeks.

"And to absent friends, two officers who didn't get to see their investigation through and for which they paid the ultimate price. May their contributions be honored in the future."

"Absent friends," they choroused.

"How's the wine, Marcus?" Roach asked. "Up to your standards?"

"An ambitious attempt, young man," Tomlinson said, "but quite pitiable. But, no matter, for tomorrow I will be whisked away to a land of sunshine, fine wines, and a pleasingly favorable exchange rate."

"Napa Valley, at last?" Graham said.

"Back in three weeks," Marcus replied. "Unless I find something there to persuade me to stay. Or some*one*."

"A fellow wine connoisseur with a massive cellar?" Roach suggested.

"I was thinking more of an attractive Californian heiress," Marcus said, a devilish look in his eyes.

"Thought any more about what I was saying?" Barnwell said to Roach. "You know, while you've been lying here relaxing. You nearly copped it for your job. You won't get any more action than that anywhere."

"Still thinking about it, Bazza, still thinking about it. Gave my mum a shock though. She's decided Jersey is a dangerous place. Thinks I might be better off elsewhere. Imagine."

"What about you, sir? Got any travel plans?" Barnwell asked Graham.

"I was thinking of taking a few days, actually. Go to the mainland. I haven't been to visit since I arrived."

"You going too, Laura?" Janice asked.

"Ah, no. Not this time." Truth was, this was the first Laura had heard of it.

Jack Wentworth caught Graham's arm. "We're going to head out, sir. Just wanted to thank you for the chance to help."

"Couldn't have done it without you, Jack. Thank *you*."

The young engineer took Harding's hand and led her through the double doors. "At least the rain's stopped," she said. "But it's only nine. Why did you want to head out?" she asked.

"Oh, well, no reason as such." Jack held the car door open for her.

"Very chivalrous, sir," Janice said.

Once he'd taken his seat and started the Prius, Jack gave her a broad grin. "All set?"

"That's it, you're officially acting weird."

"I'm probably nervous," Jack said as he began to drive.

"Nervous? About what?"

"You'll see," Jack said, grinning again, "when we get to the castle. I'm glad it's stopped raining."

Graham pulled up next to the curb outside the church. It was exactly as he remembered it. The fourteenth-century stone building stood silent, and he wondered at the great and terrible memories it harbored within its four walls. He preferred not to dwell upon his own memories of the place. He had visited the churchyard only a few times since Katie's death, but he remembered exactly where she was buried. He gathered the things he'd brought with him and got out of the car into the bright cold winter morning.

He hadn't told Laura what he planned, just that he needed to get away for a few days. He'd missed her on Valentine's Day, but he'd called her twice and arranged for a huge bouquet to be sent to the library. She'd accepted things peaceably enough, intuiting his need to be alone and possibly his sense of purpose. He was glad for that. There was no threat to their relationship, quite the opposite. He needed to confront the past so he could move on to the future. He needed to lay Katie to rest.

He slipped through the kissing gate and virtually tiptoed to Katie's resting place. It was tidy and well-cared for. Fresh flowers had been recently left, the grass neatly cut, the headstone clean, and well-polished. Graham lay the red, pink, and white flowers he'd brought with him on the still-bumpy ground and leaned a blue teddy bear against the words of Katie's epitaph. He clutched a balloon in his hand. The bear, the balloon, the flowers had come as a florist's package. They were the kind of thing he usually refused to buy, considering them extortionate and tasteless, but Katie would have loved them, so he had.

A few yards away there was a bench. He went over and sat on it, still clutching the balloon. He tied it to the arm of the bench, and it floated incongruously above him, its bright, shiny, garish colors contrasting with the bleakness of late winter. A tiny robin sat in a tree, its red breast startling against the greys and browns of winter. It stared at him for a moment, its bright eyes shining before it effortlessly flew away across the graveyard to alight on Katie's headstone.

Graham thought about daughters: Katie, Tiffany Trevelyan, Amy Vincenti, Kimberley Devine, even Janice, and Laura. He thought about the emotions they elicited, the pleasure they provided, the pain, the joy, the sorrows, the protection they demanded. He couldn't change the past but he could make a better future. And if he didn't do that, what was there for him? And Laura, she deserved his full presence, too.

The robin jumped onto the damp sod, hopping over to the flowers Graham had left there. It was nest-building season and the robin pulled at a petal, determined to take a prize home to his mate. Graham watched, as with a shiver of its feathers, the robin tugged and tugged until finally, the petal came away. Graham smiled wryly and the bird blinked. Then, with an audible flutter of its wings, it streaked away.

It started to drizzle. Graham turned his face to the sky. The fine mist felt like an angel's fingertips on his face. He sat silently, letting the rain caress him, grateful that no one could see his tears. He would move on. He owed it to Laura. Katie would approve. It was time.

EPILOGUE

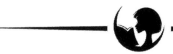

THE TRIAL OF DS Tom Vincenti was a three-week media sensation. To prove Vincenti's guilt, prosecutors used forensic evidence from the conference center's electrical system and the stolen Vauxhall Cavalier, Vincenti's phone, and a cache of files found on the body of DS Patrick O'Hearn. The jury agreed that Vincenti had carried out the killings of DS Kimberley Devine and O'Hearn, and had been routinely feeding sensitive information to Bob Ketch and his gang while giving false intelligence to the police operation. Vincenti was sentenced to fifteen years for six offenses related to conspiracy, perverting the course of justice, vehicle theft, and perjury, and thirty-year terms for each of the two murders, all to be served consecutively. Vincenti is held in solitary confinement in a prison on the Isle of Dogs and will be eligible for release at the age of eighty-one.

On his return to London, Superintendent Nigel Needham quietly retired. He lives with his wife in Cambridgeshire, near his daughter and her family. He enjoys walking and reruns of old TV shows.

Sergeant Jim Roach was treated for three days in the hospital before being discharged, with no permanent ill effects. DI Graham formally recommended him for the Queen's Gallantry Medal. Sergeant Roach relinquished his Ducati at the end of his lease and now rents the flat above Barry Barnwell.

Jack Wentworth proposed to Sergeant Janice Harding on the ramparts of Orgueil Castle. He went down on one knee and gave her a diamond solitaire ring of nearly a carat. Janice accepted immediately, and the two will be married next spring.

Jason Ashby and Tiffany Trevelyan drifted apart but still exchange the odd email. Jason continues to run the NPCC office and is planning the next police conference in Harrogate, Yorkshire.

Constable Barnwell took three weeks' leave after the incident on the ferry. He traveled to Europe with his brother. It was his first time out of the country.

A month in the wine valleys of northern California proved the ideal mix of relaxation and stimulation for Dr. Marcus Tomlinson. He returned bronzed and chirpy with enough wine to fill his cellar and keep him satisfactorily imbibed for several years.

Anthony Middelton and Caspar Freedland received a late-night visit from Sergeant Harding and Constable Barnwell in connection with the burglary at *Gorey Gifts & Sweets*. As a result, the youths are completing community service hours by helping out the owner of the shop after school. While they do not enjoy selling candles, linens, jewelry, and the like, nor the ribbing they get for doing so, they understand it is better than the alternative.

Billy Foster soon got used to eating three or more meals a day at Mrs. Lampard's. Although nothing formal has been set in place, no one has discussed ending their arrangement. They are discussing adopting a rescue dog. Social Services have not been informed.

Detective Inspector Graham received plaudits for his handling of the Vincenti case, and following its resolution, he vanished on leave, together with Laura. Thus far, Laura has given no indication that she is aware of DI Graham's daughter, Katie, but Graham accepts the need to tell her, and he is working up the courage to do so. He is a work in progress.

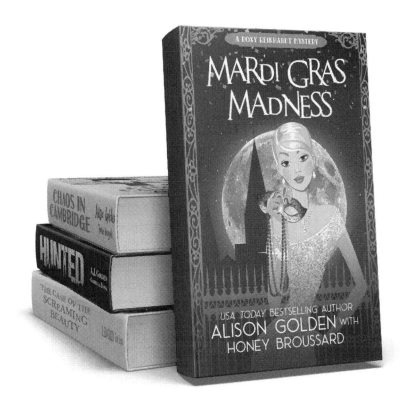

To get free books, updates about new releases, promotions, and other Insider exclusives, please sign up for Alison's mailing list at:

https://www.alisongolden.com/graham

BOOKS BY ALISON GOLDEN

FEATURING REVEREND ANNABELLE DIXON

Death at the Café

Murder at the Mansion

Body in the Woods

Grave in the Garage

Horror in the Highlands

Killer at the Cult

FEATURING ROXY REINHARDT

Mardi Gras Madness

New Orleans Nightmare

Louisiana Lies

As A. J. Golden

FEATURING DIANA HUNTER

Hunted (Prequel)

Snatched

Stolen

Chopped

Exposed

ABOUT THE AUTHOR

Alison Golden is the *USA Today* bestselling author of the Inspector David Graham mysteries, a traditional British detective series, and two cozy mystery series featuring main characters Reverend Annabelle Dixon and Roxy Reinhardt. As A. J. Golden, she writes the Diana Hunter thriller series.

Alison was raised in Bedfordshire, England. Her aim is to write stories that are designed to entertain, amuse, and calm. Her approach is to combine creative ideas with excellent writing and edit, edit, edit. Alison's mission is simple: To write excellent books that have readers clamoring for more.

Alison is based in the San Francisco Bay Area with her husband and twin sons. She splits her time between London and San Francisco.

For up-to-date promotions and release dates of upcoming books, sign up for the latest news here: https://www.alisongolden.com/graham.

For more information:
www.alisongolden.com
alison@alisongolden.com

facebook.com/alisongolden.books
twitter.com/alisonjgolden
instagram.com/alisonjgolden

THANK YOU

Thank you for taking the time to read books 5 through 7 in the Inspector Graham series. If you enjoyed them, please consider telling your friends or posting a short review. Word of mouth is an author's best friend and very much appreciated.
Thank you,

Printed in Great Britain
by Amazon

54466491R00441